Granada

Lyn Miller

DEDICATION

To God be the glory.
To Jake- Thanks for listening in the dark. You give unselfishly, and I am not me without you. Crazy schemes never do surprise you.
To Taryn- You believed in me even when I didn't. Multiple times a day. Thank you for your unfailing support.
To my children- Remember God makes all things possible, even when you can't see how.
For my Marie. Who is still very much alive and well. Even if she doesn't sing anymore.

Lyn Miller

The Beginning

Her lips were turning blue. They were a dusky hue much like the sky beyond the windshield. The engine of her 1955 Lincoln purred quietly after the race it had run from deep in the heart of the city to where it sat now high above the ocean on a rock cliff. She fancied it was tired, too. These thoughts flashed in her mind disjointedly, not like the continual flow she normally had.

Her gown was completely saturated with blood. There was no way for her to staunch the flow herself. It had been a true work of art the way the dress fit her, revealed one last time what had once been a great work of art by God's hand. Now both pieces of artistry were gone.

She knew this was it. The end of the line. Although she had anticipated this outcome, she realized she really had no way to prepare herself for this very moment. The very moment she would look death in the face and transition to whatever came next for her. She knew, too, that what she had done may not be forgiven. The wrong thing done for the right reasons doesn't abolish the blame.

Whatever came next. At one time she wanted no more next. She had rallied and transitioned to this moment throughout her life. Now all the nexts she was ever going to have were spent.

She longed for the strength to cry.

She thought of him.

Had he survived? That had been all she wanted. For him to walk away with his life intact. It hurt so to think of him. She wanted desperately his face, his arms, his lips. Foolish longing only made her predicament more painful.

Would he come? Would he make it to her in time? He had before. But this time, was he already waiting on the other side?

*****

September 1949

It began as each day had before. The sun rose in the east, its rays threading their fingers through the streets and windows, parks and warehouses, never delaying nor hesitating in its ascent. Waiting for no one, not even those who chose to rise late. But for those who had chosen not to sleep at all, it was just a continuation of the day before. Which really wasn't a day at all, but rather the portion of time that required no light bulbs or bourbon. No holiday, no depression, no joy, and no milestone held those rays ascent. It was a cycle that stretched on into oblivion.

It was in this attitude that he sat stoically listening to Mickey Delano as he edged on the accelerator of his new black '49 Cadillac Fastback. It neither gave Valant pause nor rush to feel the car moving smoothly along, parked cars on the street whipping by. Mickey liked to drive, and truth be told he was a more capable driver than Valant. Everybody is good at something, even if it does them no good.

Mickey sat with his elbow on the window, his black suit jacket lending to the color of the car. His left forefinger was pressed firmly along his top lip. His breathing was low and slow, which meant he was no longer in the car, but somewhere else entirely. Valant knew where he was. He also knew better than to call him back. It was something he knew from the passage of time, memories made and lost, happy laughter and desperate drinking in the hours of hell. Valant knew also that where Mickey was, his body could never go again. Nor could his own. They were memories tainted with a soft golden light, the feelings of nostalgia so strong they could pull a barge upriver without a rope.

"What about the club?" Mickey had straightened and casually draped his left hand over the steering wheel. He didn't look at Valant.

"Your call," came the deep and gravel reply.

Mickey's mouth tugged at one corner as he tipped his head and looked out the window. "I want it."

Valant said nothing, just looked straight ahead. He was known within the city of Los Angeles as The Dark Horse. His reputation had far exceeded what Mickey had hoped it would. He was a violent man with no pity or remorse. The Dark Horse was coming into his prime despite his graying hair and sharp features.

Mickey looked at him then. "You think it will be hard?"

"Does it matter?"

"No," was Mickey's reply.

"You coming?" Valant asked in a low voice.

"No." There was a long pause. "If he's there, kill him."

Valant scoffed quietly. "Yeah, like the last twenty-five years didn't happen."

Mickey looked at him sharply. "The day is coming and it's been coming for a damn long time. Just cause dear ol' dad never had the balls to do it, doesn't mean it ain't going to happen." Mickey jabbed his finger at Valant. "Don't act like Julian wasn't preparing you for it. I know he was because I told him to."

Valant didn't move or change his expression. He had walked this road before. He also knew well this day was coming. Julian had wanted it as badly as himself. "Ok. If you want the fight I'll go get it for you."

Mickey ground his teeth together. It was the way things were. The club was perched precariously on the edge of his territory, which of late he had been diligently working to expand. Mickey's father had passed away fifteen years previous leaving Mickey with an inheritance sixty years in the making. His father had never suffered from burning ambition like his son. He had done well to keep things running status quo from what his father, Mickey's grandfather, had given to him.

Grandpa Aldo had been like Mickey. He was a gritty man who had come from Milan and a life of poverty as a young man in 1868. He had survived New York and the trip west. He was the true entrepreneur, gaining his ground by way of crook. Violence had never caused him balk. It didn't Mickey either, which was why he readily gave Valant the go ahead. Mickey knew that the club was a dive, small and nothing compared to what he had envisioned for himself one day. It was the purpose of gaining ground that meant the most.

He had sent some boys to investigate. The proprietor didn't seem to have any ties and he was so blatant that he hadn't bothered to get into the good graces of Mickey before opening anything on his turf. He felt certain that the man would soon regret that choice, because the tax he would incur from not gaining permission first would be high. Mickey now controlled most of the east and south side of Los Angeles, but he wanted more. He wanted to be on top.

Valant was able to acquire anything that Mickey had even cast his eyes at. All that stood in Mickey Delano's way was Vinny Vinnetti. Bigger than Mickey by far, Vinnetti controlled the west and north side and grasped more holdings in the business than Mickey had the opportunity to grab. Vinnetti and Georgio Delano, Mickey's father, had garnered a very tenuous truce between them in the years Mickey's father was alive. But, Vinnetti was intelligent. He knew that Mickey's ambitions stretched far beyond what his father could have ever imagined. He had no regard for peace, no desire to keep status quo. Mickey would do whatever he had to do to push Vinnetti out, including start a turf war.

That was why Mickey was sitting with his lips pursed together, the left hand that had been so casually draped over the wheel was now balled into a fist. Vinnetti had matched his strategy, blocked Mickey's gains whenever possible without starting an all-out war. Each time new ground had become available, they had quarreled over it like school boys and a Cracker Jack toy. While no serious blood had yet been shed, it was a matter of time before something of too great a value was laid on the line.

Everyone has something they can't afford to lose. Mickey thrilled each time he thought of finally besting the old man. But, he thought with a rueful grin, Vinnetti had never been blessed with any offspring, legitimate or otherwise. Perhaps it was just a matter of out-living the old bastard.

Mickey had yet another card up his sleeve. Valant, even more ruthless than himself, had in the name of Delano committed unpardonable atrocities to get Mickey what he wanted. Val had been trained by Mickey's father's own right hand man, Julian. It was Julian who was the only reason Mickey's father hadn't lost everything. Julian had done a job on Valant that could only be equated to a creation of masterpiece. Valant was Julian's masterpiece. He had no fear, no love, no mercy, and no forgiveness. He had, if Mickey were willing to admit it, which he wasn't, built Mickey's empire. It gave Mickey great elation to have such a dog on his leash.

"Get your guys in there early. Don't give an inch."

Mickey pulled the car into the alley behind his restaurant that also served as his headquarters. He hesitated when Valant made no move to exit the car. He cast Valant a quizzical glance. Valant calmly opened his door and stood, buttoning his suit jacket. He swept his eyes up and down the alley, their empty depths coming to rest on Mickey who leaned on one arm against the cab of the car.

"Thy will be done."

*****

As was his custom, Valant arrived at the club alone. He didn't like to travel with an entourage that just made him more obvious. It was in this that he differed from Julian. He parked on a dark side street, careful to keep his eyes moving as he made his way to the entrance. He was late. He had sent guys in early to scout and get the lay out.

The place was a dive.

It was located in an old rundown cargo warehouse not far from the docks far to the south of Mickey's territory. Valant could smell the littered sea water of the harbor that was still a ways off. He wondered what the hell either Mickey or Vinnetti wanted with such a shithole. But, he knew better than anyone. It was a matter of property rights.

He came up to a side entrance and pulled the handle. It opened easily and he cautiously looked through a small crack. The door opened into an area behind the stage where no one seemed to be about at the moment. He slipped in silently, and unconsciously checked his jacket button. It was an old habit. The band was already playing. He caught a glimpse through a slit in the curtain the back of the lead singer's green dress. It fit a bit too snug. The cello player danced jerkily to the beat he played. The floor was littered with boxes and various things Valant couldn't identify.

He made his way to a small set of stairs to the left and gave a slow look. The main room that set before him was small and very cramped, the temperature already causing faces to glisten. The band was loud. The sound reverberated around the room mercilessly. Valant moved forward into the crowd, pushing impatiently as he went, shoving when necessary. He earned several looks of irritation from both men and women. He wove his way between the great pillars holding up the ceiling, wondering if such a structure could stand up to the strain.

Ahead of him he recognized his own right hand making his way to him as inconspicuously as possible. Cobby strode with his right hand leisurely resting in his pants pocket, occasionally resting his eyes on the face of a smiling young woman. In such circumstances he bestowed a lavish smile as he continued on. Cobby was young, not as tall as Valant, and more handsome by far. Although his father had been Italian, his mother's brown hair had prevailed. His eyes were a light brown as well, set in a smooth but apprehensive face. He was as serious a young man as ever came along. He met Valant's eyes and withdrew his hand from his pocket, resting it against his navel. He stretched his hand and five fingers.

A full house. Vinnetti had stacked his deck.

Cobby and Valant neared each other. They both avoided eye contact. As Cobby passed he spoke lowly to Valant. "Lower right."

Immediately Valant headed to a set of stairs that lead to the next landing and found himself a lookout next to a pillar by the wall. His eyes scanned the room taking note of everything. Everyone who was dancing, who was not, and most importantly, the men not engaged in anything. The bar was busy with patrons shouting in an attempt to be heard over the din. A woman in an abundant white fur clung heavily to a portly man as she threw her head back and laughed, nearly falling over backward. The ash from her cigarette fell down the front of her coat and singed the fur.

The couples out on the floor looked agitated. There was little room for movement and doing so without bumping into someone was impossible. All tables surrounding the floor were taken. The few that weren't had spilled drinks atop. On one table a man lay face down, passed out, his drink still in hand. The shrill laugh of an unseen woman pierced through the sound of the band, and Valant watched as a group of young men groped the women who happened by. The whole place screamed of a vulgarity Valant hadn't seen since his last trip to Mexico. The coarseness made him desire to set fire to it in its entirety. It would be easily done and no one would escape alive.

His eyes moved to the place that Cobby indicated. The deck was indeed stacked, for at the table closest to the stage sat Vinnetti himself. He was unmoving, unspeaking, his arms folded across the broad expanse of his chest. Valant also recognized Vinnetti's right hand, Robert "The Heart" Vantino. He took into account various other nameless men that could only belong to Vinnetti within close proximity. He wondered where his own guys were, but he knew them well enough to know that they would be dispersed as not to draw any attention to themselves.

"What do you make of this?" Cobby had come to stand next to Valant, bathed in shadow as well. Valant only shook his head slightly.

"How long?"

"Since before any of us got here. He has guys so thick in here you can't move without bumping one." Cobby stood looking right where Valant also looked, his hands in his pockets.

It meant something. To Valant's way of thinking, it was more than just acquiring more territory. Vinnetti never showed anywhere, let alone show up to a land fight. That was beneath him. His presence was an indication of something, especially to show up to a back alley dive like this one.

"Where's the boys?"

Cobby leaned closer to reply. "Deano's at the bar, Martin's by the entrance, and Alfred's outside. I didn't put anyone on the stage since Vinnetti has made a wall across it. I didn't want to be spotted."

"Doesn't matter, he already knows you're here." Valant said in a low voice. It was the voice he used when he was ready for a fight. He looked at Cobby who stood with his mouth screwed up in a look of anxiety. His eyes moved to the exits taking each possibility. Valant looked back to Vinnetti.

It meant something.

Vinnetti was making a clear statement. This ground was his, no questions, no exceptions. With another sweep of the room Valant concluded that Vinnetti must have had about every man he could muster there. To Valant though, it was suicide to show himself no matter how many men he brought.

Jackpot, you old bastard. You've finally exposed yourself.

Valant was calculating the possibility of getting to Vinnetti. He sensed a shift in the room as the band began to play softly. The crowd dimmed some, leaning toward the stage.

Valant leaned closer to Cobby, the shoulders of their identical suits brushing. "Get out."

"Val," Cobby began, at a loss for words. He knew this was coming, that this was what Mickey had been intending. Valant shot him a piercing look. Cobby had learned better than to push Valant past that look.

"I'm staying," Cobby pointedly assured. The room had become quieter. Valant put his right hand inside his jacket, gripping the gun that rested in its holster under his left arm. He did not draw it out, yet.

"Make for the entrance. Shoot to make way if you have to." The two men met eyes and an unspoken understanding of directives passed between them. Cobby nodded imperceptibly.

"Ladies and gentlemen, please welcome the flower of the Lamplight Lounge to the stage!" The voice of the presenter boomed as he shouted into the microphone.

Valant moved to the stairs placing his left hand on the railing. Cobby was right behind him. Valant again locked eyes on Vinnetti. The crush of the constantly moving crowd began to still and time did as well. Cobby was the only one who noticed.

Her voice started out faint and uncertain, but by the time she hit her stride Hoagy Carmichael's *The Nearness of You* flowed from her in a rich and deep sound that cut the audacity of the room down to a standstill. Nothing moved and no one spoke.

Cobby stopped just short of Valant whose focus was on something toward the stage.

She wasn't very big, and so obviously young. Her coal black hair hung down past her shoulders and curled ever so slightly at the tips. Her red dress was meant for a more mature woman. One more endowed in all the right places, but her body shone with potential. Her eyes closed after each glance into the crowd, as if she were too scared to keep them open. Her frame belied the voice that resided within and she kept her audience enraptured. Her small hands trembled slightly as she clasped the microphone stand.

Cobby again looked to Valant who stood focused, unwavering. Valant moved back into the shadows once more just to watch. He made no comment, and Cobby wondered if something were wrong with his gun.

Valant had a strange look on his face, almost as if contemplating some possibility. Cobby looked down to see several men watching them, talking with one another.

"Val," he seemed to snap back to Cobby, looking at him sharply. "Ten o'clock."

Val looked and his face turned to granite. His moment had passed.

Val glanced to Cobby who stood watching the crowd, his body rigid, his lips mashed into a very thin line. Nothing seemed to make any sense standing on this precipice as they were, men from Vinnetti's gang making their way to them in a fan shape. The kid Cobby was about to meet his Waterloo. He stood grounded next to Valant like he was made of steel, his resolve to see the end shoulder to shoulder with the man who had rarely shown him any kindness or amiability.

Valant glanced back at the stage to see the young woman smile faintly, then turn to leave. She swayed with an inborn natural grace she wasn't aware she possessed. His eyes then went to Vinnetti who now stood, his hands in his pockets with a look of finality on his face. He didn't blink nor waver as Valant tipped his head back slightly to look down at him. Valant eventually bowed his head to him as he held now empty hands palms up.

I'll give to you, but not without blood.

Vinnetti spoke to "The Heart" Vantino who was beside him without looking away from Valant.

"Move." Valant pushed Cobby who took residence at his side as they moved to the stairs. Valant kept his hands up, his eyes burning with fire as they passed each one of the men at the bottom of the stairs.

He was waiting for the fight, the one movement that would start a conflagration of hate so deep it would disintegrate every piece of Valant's soul with violence. What was left of it, anyway. They made for the main entrance with little choice. Now was the time for Vinnetti to either keep the truce struck so long ago with another man, or wage the war Valant was literally built to fight. It was Vinnetti's choice to either kill the only man dark and evil enough to slowly destroy him, or let the peace stand another day knowing the inevitability of it all.

A woman stepped into Valant's path unwittingly. He grabbed her by the arm and flung her to the floor. The crowd gathered near all focused on him when the woman let out a cry. The beast in Valant's soul roared and tore at its cage in the desire to be set free, to savage anything within reach, quenching the thirst for violence the only concern. He was ugly inside, scarred and marred of his own making and doing, until nothing human remained of him. The crowd struggled to let him by, some aware of his identity, others merely afraid of being thrown as well.

Killing Valant "The Dark Horse" would end a lot of Vinnetti's problems. It would take Mickey Delano a lifetime to replace him, if he were ever able to. But, he clung to a promise made twenty-five years before, a promise he was bound to keep for reasons of his own. If it had been twenty years before, Valant would have drawn his last breath. But not now. Not with everything at stake.

Killing The Dark Horse would never be as easy as it was that night, but it would have to wait.

*****

Mickey Delano drew up the corner of his mouth as he looked at the cards in his hand. He counted out seven one-hundred dollar bills, then laid them in the center of the table. He reached to his ash tray to take hold of the cigar that lay there, a thin layer of smoke rising above it. Mickey had come to one of his own card houses to play a few hands and see what other endeavors he might find to pursue later that night. Right now that endeavor was sitting at the bar smoking, watching with large brown eyes, her long legs crossed temptingly for him to see.

Valant walked from across the room and unbuttoned his suit jacket before he sat. He withdrew a wad of bills from his jacket pocket and nodded to the dealer to be dealt in. Immediately Mickey's attention left the endeavor and settled scorchingly on Valant.

"Well?"

Valant slouched in his chair as his eyes raised to meet Mickey's. He shook his head slightly.

Mickey scoffed. "I know that asshole. What happened?"

Valant merely shook his head again. Mickey sat back.

"At all?"

Valant's penetrating gaze cut into Mickey.

"Protecting something perhaps?"

Valant nodded his agreement.

"Well, then find it, crush the blood out of it, and shovel it onto his front steps."

*****

Vinnetti settled back into the seat with a deep sigh. The lights of the street lamps illuminated his face intermittently to reveal the deep lines around his droll mouth. Robert looked ahead, slouched to one side as he leaned against the door of the car he drove. He didn't look into the mirror to see Vinny, just kept going, wondering if they would make it home with Vinny alive. Never had anyone who so successfully trapped The Dark Horse lived much past the hour in which they did. Vinny was weary, and wary, but that didn't change what had to be done.

"I can't lose this, Vantino." Vantino sensed rather than heard the break in Vinny Vinnetti's voice.

"I know." A long silence ensued. Robert "The Heart" Vantino deliberately looked ahead to avoid the older man's eyes.

Vantino had spent a lifetime watching out for Vinnetti, mirroring his moves and carrying out his decisions. The Heart was a man of great loyalty and sense of duty. Nothing about his stocky frame and smooth black hair spoke of anything beyond common. But, he was a force that ruled firmly long before The Dark Horse was out of grammar school.

"I will give that bastard everything, and everyone else first." There was again a pause and Vantino understood that Vinny meant him as well. "Do you understand what I'm telling you to do?"

"I understand."

Vinny rubbed the grayed hair away from his creased forehead. "For this, I will lay down my life."

*****

June 1936

"Get your damn hand off the dash!" Mickey yelled at Valant between spasms of laughter. "You are nothing but a coward!"

Valant, who sat stoically next to him in the passenger seat of the little coupe sent him a seething glare. "I was wiping dust off your old jalopy."

"Do you always get white knuckles when you dust my father's house?" Mickey hugged the rock ledge while pressing the accelerator as they passed the apex of the curve. Mickey's wavy black hair flew wildly against the smooth olive skin of his forehead. The wind rushed in from the open windows. His muscles flexed under the rolled up sleeves of his white shirt, and air fluttered his collar where he had unbuttoned the top three buttons. Coarse black hair resided there.

"My mother drove better than you." This dry comment made Mickey laugh harder.

"Didn't your dumb ol' ma kill herself and your dad in a car wreck?" Mickey asked sarcastically.

"Shut your damn mouth before I shut it for you," Valant stated.

"Come on, you know I loved your mother." Mickey looked apologetically at Val.

The tires on Mickey's car squealed as he took another corner, only to be met with a truck carrying a load of rock. He didn't blink as he swerved, narrowly missing a jagged rock that reached out beyond the face of the wall. Several thousand feet below them the ocean rolled and rose in great walls of white mist as it collided with the granite cliff. Mickey now drove along at a brisk seventy-five miles an hour as the road clung to the wall.

"The only thing that would have made this better was if you had stolen Julian's coupe and raced me to the top." Mickey pushed the accelerator to the floor in the few open stretches between sharp corners.

"That would still only prove you a supercilious prick." Valant spat.

Mickey burst out again. "You're a lucky man, Valant. I need you. Forget about what I said about your ma. If I didn't need you, I'd push you out into the ocean."

"Mickey, you don't need me. You just haven't figured it out, yet."

"Oh, but I do. We are going to build an empire, Val. An empire like the world has never seen. I need you, and you need me. Blood brothers, remember? Shoulder to shoulder right to the end."

*****

1949

Damn shoes.

Her ankle twisted for the fifth time that evening as she stood behind the curtain waiting to go on. She was certain her ankle was swelling, it was sore to be sure. What a night. But of

course, she reasoned with herself, it would help if the clothes
she wore weren't three sizes too big. The band began to slow
and she knew that momentarily it would be her time to go on.
She prayed again.

Let me do well. Please.

Within a moment she was moving through the curtain,
smiling a pasted smile as she tried to maneuver the minefield
that was the stage. One false step and down she would go. Her
features were fine, her legs still thin and her knees knobby. Her
skin was smooth and olive in the Italian tradition, her frame
under developed. She was beautiful in the way of a young girl,
not yet bold like a woman.

The biggest thing on her was her smile, beaming across
the room to capture even the darkest of hearts. She was Marie
Barelli. A nothing really, known only for the voice her wisp of
a body housed protected beneath bone and tissue. Rarely did
anyone speak to this young woman long enough to discern
what her thoughts and emotions were, how deep they ran, how
fixed they were.

She kept herself to herself, a trait that had been so deeply
ingrained even the dearest of her heart knew little about her.
But she did love her talent. That much was evident to everyone.
She was allowed to perform only a few songs a night, and in
reality, she was what packed the house. Patrons drifted in a
while before she went on, then drifted out again when she was
done. Only the hard core trash that frequented the
establishment ever lasted the whole night, and they weren't
there for the entertainment anyway.

Jerry Barelli kept a tight hold on his daughter, not because
he felt it his duty to protect his own, but rather a duty to protect
his property. He knew, just as anyone who listened to Marie
sing knew, he was sitting pretty on a diamond that was yet to
be polished. He instructed his four sons to guard her and never
leave her for a minute. They often argued who would be in
constant attendance since each of them had a tendency for the
card tables Jerry ran in the back rooms of the club. But, out of
fear for their father and his reprimand, they kept Marie close.

This proved a detriment to her personal life and ambition
to be anything but Jerry Barelli's daughter. She had been raised
disposable, and that desolation had followed her into young
womanhood. But now Jerry was beginning to see return on all
the years he had kept his daughter fed and clothed despite his

desire to do otherwise. It was an old family tragedy that spurred this on. Far be it for Jerry to blame himself when blame was due.

The lights of the stage shown down a thick yellow ambiance that cast everything in a sickly color. The lead singer winked at Marie as she passed, exiting the stage. The band started up again, picking up a fast tempo, the cello player plucking his strings in a lively jive, bouncing back and forth. The small trumpet section that consisted of two players raised their instruments to their lips, sweat beading on their faces. Marie didn't know the band very well, something she would have liked to change. She reached the microphone and gripped it tightly as she gazed out into the sea of darkness where few faces were visible in the dim light of the club.

She closed her eyes and began to sing, fearful that looking out into the crowd would cause her to lose her pace, or forget the words. She didn't want to know who was watching, didn't want to see their thoughts written on their faces. She wanted to be alone with her voice.

*****

"Hey Tom." Marie laid her sweater on the bar as she greeted the bartender. It was very late, or very early, depending on how she chose to look at it. The club was empty. Everyone who was left was in the back rooms playing cards. Her brothers were there too, she figured. It would be a long wait for a ride home.

"What can I get you, Marie?"

"Oh, anything you've got left. Coffee, whatever." Tom well knew she had a long wait coming.

"I'll heat some water. You can make a cup of tea." She smiled at him shyly. "Thanks, Tom." He moved away from the shelf he had been stacking clean shot glasses on and went to get the water.

"That was really good tonight, Marie." She turned in surprise to see Ada, the lead singer, approach the bar.

"Thanks. What are you still doing here?"

Ada's cheeks reddened slightly as she looked down to pull her barstool out. Marie knew that her oldest brother David had been seeing Ada. Not really in any kind of respectable way, and she suspected from the buttons undone on Ada's blouse they had spent time together after the show.

"Can I get a gin and tonic, Tom?" Ada slid onto the bar stool and looked at Marie without acknowledging her previous question. "You are gathering quite a following, it seems." Ada looked steadily at Marie. It was Marie's turn to flush slightly.

"Well, at least they don't boo me off the stage." Ada chuckled softly at Marie's comment.

"I have it from a very reliable source that a certain gentleman has made a habit of coming to hear you sing." Ada spoke as she lit a cigarette.

"Who?" Marie looked confused.

Ada turned and looked down into her drink as Tom set it before her.

"Well, maybe gentleman isn't the right word. I can't say I've ever heard anything very gentlemanly about his behavior."

Marie tried to look disinterested as she steeped her tea bag.

"Aren't you curious?" Ada looked at her again, her faded blue eyes contrasting with her red hair. Marie looked back to her and shrugged her shoulders. Ada took a breath before she continued.

"I guess maybe I shouldn't tell you. It might mess up your performance, thinking he was out there." Ada took a long drag on her cigarette.

"Is it Vinnetti?" Marie asked cautiously. This was a subject she never liked to broach. Ada laughed.

"No, opposite I'm afraid. He's Mickey Delano's guy." Marie looked up sharply.

"Delano's? Which one?"

"The one." Marie's stomach began to turn. "Which?"

"Oh, what do they call him, Dark something or other." Ada took another drink.

"Dark Horse," Marie whispered.

Ada looked at her almost sadly. "Yeah, that's the one."

"That can't be true."

"David assures me it is. He slips in somehow, just before you go on, then slips out again when you go off. He comes every so often. He stands behind the pillar at the top of the stairs, in the dark."

Marie looked down into her cup, then raised it to her mouth.

"Hey, it doesn't mean anything. You do have a beautiful voice." Ada sounded reassuring. Silence followed, Marie certain that Ada regretted her confession.

"Well, I better go. Night, Marie, Tom." Ada walked quietly away, leaving Marie to the bitterness of her tea.

Marie well understood what obsession could bring, how easily she could be traded, or taken. Either way, the result was the same for her. She knew The Dark Horse well, having closely followed him through stories about his deeds, things Vinny told her, things her brothers spoke of. His violence was something of legend. She shivered. God help her if she had indeed caught his eye.

*****

Marie never knew, thankfully, when he was there. Someone would casually mention later that he had been, or that they had seen him leaving. Although, oddly, no one ever saw him coming in. Several times she had glanced to his hiding place behind the pillar but the darkness made it impossible to see him if he were there. She said nothing of it to Vinny.

Then she heard he had beaten a man to death in an alley not ten blocks from the club and she wondered perhaps if she should, but something kept her from doing so. It was rumored he set fire to a car with a man still in the backseat. She resolved to tell Vinny, but he had gone down to Mexico on business. Before he returned Jerry told her that she was allowed to sing two more songs in the line-up. He had also allowed that she could practice with the band and that had caused her great excitement. In the end, she decided to deny his presence on any night but opening night. Ignorance was bliss.

It was raining on a late October night, and David, drunk and angry, had taken Marie with him to a poker game among friends. Between the rain and his inebriation, it had taken longer than anticipated to get Marie to the club. Ada had already remained to perform several extra songs as both the band and audience waited anxiously for Marie's arrival.

When Marie did finally climb out of the car into a heavy downpour, what little her hair offered for possibility was completely washed away into oblivion. The fearful ride her brother had given her left her face ashen and drawn. He stopped at the front door instead of the rear near the dressing room, but she knew better than to challenge him in his current frame of mind. He would not let it go on account of her gender or relation to him.

She blew through the front doors to be hit with the stale aroma of cigarettes and mildew. The dampness in the air mixed with body heat created a sort of putrid humidity. It was like a wave, completely unstoppable. She hurried along when she noticed her father whose face was red. He immediately moved toward her but she put her head down and veered away. He had been waiting, obviously, ready to seize the opportunity to strike out at her. She cut to the right, into a row of tables lit only with small candles. She heard her name called and she turned slightly to look back at her father who hadn't advanced any further, but was clearly wanting her to return.

She struck something large, as it turned out, a man, who gripped her arm to steady her as they hit. Marie looked quickly forward to be met with a white shirt front narrowly gleaming through a black suit jacket. The impact was great from her speed and his steadying hand kept her from going down. She looked up briefly into his face to offer an apology, but nothing came out.

His face was granite, his eyes showed no concern nor emotion of any kind as they lowered to hers. He was tall, taller than she had expected, and she felt trapped by his eyes. His lips were drawn and he said nothing in the eternity it seemed that he held her arm. Marie found she couldn't say anything, move or even think beyond the gaze that told her she had erred greatly in running into him. She was indeed senseless. In running from one dangerous man, she had collided with another.

Visibly shaking she tore away from him and dashed away, looking back only for a moment to see his dark gaze following her, burning her insides with fear. It was a fear that only The Dark Horse could arouse.

Her performance that night was less than stellar. She wondered which would get her first, her father who neither loved nor respected her life, or the man she had mistakenly insulted. Her small frame shook and several times tears burned so hot that she had to shut her eyes to stop them. The band exchanged looks among themselves many times, wondering what was happening. She concluded to run, as soon as possible, but one look to the right revealed a drunken David already waiting near the stage. Her voice broke. She left at the end of the song, smiling in an attempt at bravery, giving a small wave to the audience as she went. She made the dressing room somehow, locking the flimsy door behind her. There she sat for the remainder of the evening.

When Ada knocked at the end of the show, Marie eventually stood up from her hiding place crouched behind one of the dressing tables. Ada assured her that David was nowhere to be seen, and neither was Jerry, who had been called away on some type of business. David had gone with him. Marie doubted she was that lucky. She changed slowly after Ada had gone. She moved cautiously up to the bar, clutching her sweater and music magazine. But, just as Ada had assured, no one was around except Tom. He was moving crates of booze in from the alley, but he greeted her as she sat down on a stool.

"Just coffee, Tom." Her tired voice cracked as she spoke. He offered a reassuring smile as well as the coffee, then again moved to the alley to uncrate more bottles. The door shut behind him leaving Marie to the vast silence around her.

Marie began to thumb through her magazine, trying to forget her troubles, looking twice at the chart toppers for the previous week. She briefly wondered what it would be like to see her name in bold black letters there. She smiled softly at the thought of it.

"You have a true talent in your voice."

Marie's head jerked in the direction of the deep voice located just three stools down the bar. The sharp dagger of fear that ripped through her stomach left an acid trail. Her breath caught. When had he come? She had been alone only moments before.

He sat in a lazy posture, his right leg hitched up on the rail of his stool, his left leg stretched out before him. He leaned on the bar with his right elbow, but his muscles were rigid, his black suit blending perfectly with the darkness behind him. He looked at her without any hint of the previous compliment in his flat eyes. He waited for her to respond, cocking his head slightly to one side. Marie cast a glance towards the door Tom had departed from, then swept a look behind her to confirm she was alone with this man.

At length she whispered, "Thank you."

He just continued to watch her, unblinking.

"I appreciate you listening." She tried to speak louder, but her volume didn't increase much.

He wasn't handsome. Far from it. It shook her to see the legend up close and in the flesh. His hair was short and mostly gray, only a few flecks of black remained. He was so very tall, as she had discovered, but in her mind the stories she had heard of him conjured up a much thicker man. While his shoulders were broad, they certainly weren't that of a giant. But, indeed, he possessed something powerful, dark, suppressive. She looked down and away. He was quiet for a time.

"Do you know who I am?" His voice cut like a knife in the vast emptiness. She met his eyes.

"Yes, sir," she whispered, again looking down and away. "I'm sorry I ran..."

"Doesn't matter." He cut her off sharply. "Do you enjoy singing?"

It took all her effort to cast another glance at him, noticing that nothing about him had changed. She nodded her head as she began to speak.

"Yes, I do." She looked into her coffee cup. "It's one of the few things I enjoy." Unsure of what to do, she rested her chin in her hand. "Do you come and listen often?"

"When I can." He was to the point and he revealed nothing more than was necessary. "Why do you close your eyes when you sing?"

Marie looked up at his direct observation. She smiled slightly and laughed at herself.

"Because I..." She shook her head dismissing her own answer. She examined her coffee cup again for a moment before leveling an honest gaze to his firm one. Her brown eyes were soft and their depths reflected a part of herself she didn't like to reveal.

"The truth is, I like to sing alone." She looked down and away. She took another sip of coffee to find it was growing cold. The silent stillness of the man beside her made her heart hammer. She had never encountered a man of no action or intent, so she knew this one would soon make his move. The cup rattled as she returned it to the saucer with a shaking hand.

"Another truth is," her small voice continued, "I'm a klutz. I can't walk well in heels."

"Neither can I." She looked up to see the seriousness in his stone features. Without restraint she let out a small laugh at the image of him wobbling around in heels and his black suit. She quickly looked away from him. After a moment she looked back at him and smiled softly. Something made her want to grasp the lifeline he was offering.

His look was calculating as he tipped his head to the side and studied her. The corner of Marie's mouth twitched and she asked, "Is it still raining?"

"You disrespectful idiot!" David's voice disrupted the ease of the past moment between the young singer and the violent killer. "Don't you know who that is?" He grasped her arm and ripped her off her stool. She stumbled but he pulled her up, her face burning crimson.

The Dark Horse's jaw clenched as he slowly stood. He said nothing, but his hand reached slowly behind his lapel, and Marie knew that she had reached her end. David seemed not to notice.

"David!" Tom's voice rang out in the stillness. He stood behind the bar, but he held a small wooden bat cradled in his hands. His gaze was steady on David.

David smiled and let go of Marie. "Ok, ok. Just helping her out to the car." He took hold of her elbow. Marie cast a cautious glance at The Dark Horse who had lowered his hand, but Tom hadn't moved.

"Gentlemen." David nodded respectfully, then moved Marie away.

With her heart pounding and the humiliation a fresh sting, she chanced a look back. Her dark eyes were almost pleading an apology as she met his eyes. The Dark Horse stood with his eyes locked on her until she was gone.

*****

Robert "The Heart" Vantino watched the dark clad figure leave the club and disappear around the side of the building into the alley. He remained as still as possible, not wanting The Dark Horse to notice him. He knew that Vinny would be livid about The Dark Horse speaking to Marie. Vinny knew about the comings and goings of The Dark Horse at the club, and that they were obviously centered on Marie. He contemplated just killing him now, but he knew that would launch an epic war and now was not the time for that. The time for war would come, just not then.

Vantino had also waited in a dark booth, just as The Dark Horse had done, just to see what his intentions were. They had spoken only briefly before her brother had taken her away, but in that time The Dark Horse could have easily taken her with no one the wiser. Neither Vinny nor "The Heart" Vantino trusted her father and brothers to watch out for her.

Vantino had been Vinny Vinnetti's right hand most of his life, and in that time he had watched Marie grow up. He felt just as Vinny did, that singing at her father's club was a good idea, but only if they could control the situation. They had claimed the club as part of their territory, which they knew wouldn't sell well with Mickey. Especially since they had done it rather undiplomatically.

Vantino knew it might start a gang war, but he was ready for it.

He waited until the black car left the alley and was out of sight before he sat up in the driver's seat. He started the engine and drove off down the street. This would be another problem on a long list of many concerning The Dark Horse, who had since the club incident been making a real nuisance of himself. He had been picking off some of Vinny's smaller contacts. He caught one of Vinny's bookies and cut off his right hand just for crossing through Mickey Delano's territory. Then two nights ago he caught up with a business associate who had been heard saying derogatory things about Mickey. The Dark Horse relieved him of his tongue. They were simple reminders that Mickey was now enforcing his border. He might have backed down from the club, but nothing else.

Vantino pulled up to the gates that secured Vinny's home and was greeted by several guards. They chatted a moment about goings on and Vantino made a few remarks about general things. As he pulled through, Vinny Vinnetti's house loomed before him. He dreaded the conversation he was about to have with his long-time friend.

*****

The rain ran down the window as Vinny looked past his own reflection. His hands were resting in his pockets and his face was drawn smooth with his flat lip line. His thin moustache didn't quirk as it usually did as he clenched and unclenched his jaw while in thought. He just kept looking beyond the wet glass into the black night.

Vinnetti wasn't as formidable a man as The Heart. His build was not that of Vantino's, but he carried with him an air of authority, some type of quiet respect that could be felt. His graying hair and aging face told of his experience. Those were offset by his large nose and firm chin.

Robert sat equally motionless, staring at Vinny's back, his forefinger pressed along the grim line of his mouth. The news he had just spoken didn't surprise Vinny. They had both spent the better part of nine years discussing what would happen when this day came, but they certainly had never envisioned this.

The door to the study abruptly opened and a frail looking older woman entered the semi-darkness. Her blonde hair was immaculately kept, her make-up flawless. Her radiant smile found Vinny immediately, but her eyes held an obvious emptiness behind them. A heavier dark haired woman entered the room behind her, but did not advance further.

Vinny took his hands out of his pockets and moved to the blonde woman and placed a hand on the small of her back. She stood in a soft white cotton night dress and sheer robe, holding both in one hand as she slowly turned before Vinny.

"Do you like it?" The high voice asked as she searched his features. Vinny's smile was genuine, but his brown eyes reflected sadness.

"Have Robert bring the car around. We haven't gone dancing in ages." She placed her hand on Vinny's chest as he dropped his gaze from her face.

"Not tonight, my love. Ana has just gotten you ready for bed."

"Ana?" She looked questioningly at him. He took her hand in his.

"It's a beautiful night gown." Vinny whispered in her ear, hoping his words would bring realization.

"Night gown?" She glanced down at herself, a look of bewilderment crossing her fine features.

"I..." She shook her head as she glanced down again.

Ana, her nurse, stepped forward when Vinny looked at her. "Come, Mrs. Vinnetti. We will get you some warm milk, eh?" Ana spoke kindly in a thick Italian accent as she reached for her.

"But we were going dancing?"

"Some other time." Vinny gently kissed her cheek. He smiled down at her again. Her face changed suddenly from confusion to radiance.

"Oh, I was on my way to bed, Vinny love. Can I get you anything before I go?" Her voice full of concern.

"No, thank you, sweetheart."

"Alright then, I'm off to market." She smiled
determinedly as she moved quickly out the door her head high,
shoulders back, a woman bent on accomplishing a chore. Ana
quietly followed her out and softly closed the door. Vinny
stared at the door for a long moment before he spoke quietly.

"Send Marie to New York."

*****

It was like the world revolved for her. It was the last thing
she thought of before she drifted to sleep, the first thing to
dawn with the sun. She smiled to herself throughout the day,
and was amiable in hopes her father wouldn't jerk the rug out
from under her dream.

New York.

Was it true or would she wake? She had worked so hard
hoping one day an opportunity like this would come. Never,
though, had she actually thought it would happen. Again and
again she packed her suitcase in her mind preparing for the
moment when she would actually go.

Vinny had brought the news to her himself, staying late to
visit after a show. She had come to sit at his candle lit table,
across from him, laughing at Vantino who visibly brightened at
her sudden appearance. The Heart never could keep a straight
face when she was around. Vinny sat watching her while one
corner of his mouth tugged.

Marie didn't hug Vinny, it was rare when she did. He
understood she didn't like to be touched, and he figured that
was normal. When she was young, he would often hold her
hand, or rest his large hand on her shoulder. Vantino, on the
other hand, had been less respectful of her personal preference
and had constantly swung her around with their hands clasped
tightly together, her feet flying out and her hair streaming, or
carried her on his shoulder. He was reduced to a big mischief
making kid when Marie was around. Neither man said they
loved her, they really didn't need to, but still, she hadn't
guessed at it yet.

"That was lovely, Marie. Each time I hear you, you have
improved." Vinny paid her his mature compliment, saying
something his patient countenance portrayed.

"Thanks." She darted a glance at Vantino who looked at
her out of the corner of his eye. He said nothing.

It seemed odd to see them both so late in the evening and
looking so formal, so professional. "Thank you for coming to

28

see me. It's good to see you. I haven't seen you in a while."
Marie smiled a soft seeking smile, the same one she always
gave Vinny. It was like the nod a dog gives when it asks to be
accepted.

"I love to listen to you, but that's not the only reason I
came to see you tonight." He leaned forward onto the table
toward her. "How would you like to go to New York, Marie?"

Her brows knit together for a split second in confusion,
but her eyes stayed on Vinny. He reached up and traced his
dark moustache with his thumb.

"I have secured a spot for you at The Diamond." He sat
still waiting for her to absorb this. A look of utter disbelief
crossed her features.

"For how long?"

Vinny raised his shoulders. "Until you have the
experience you need to headline."

She opened her mouth but no sound came out as she
looked from one man to the other.

"And this is Marie dumbfounded." Vantino grinned.

Marie's eyes twinkled as she replied, "Maybe we could
use Vinny's Sunday car to travel in."

Vantino brought his index finger to his lips then shook it
at her. Having stopped his treacherous teasing she looked back
to Vinny who knew this routine well. Vantino was the only
man Marie would openly challenge. Vinny had fostered this in
both of them, knowing the time would come when she needed
to be bold without the certainty of winning. The fact struck
Vinny with the same uncertainty that he knew Marie felt. She
had to learn to be alone on her own merit. She was reflecting
that uncertainty as she looked at him.

"Headline? Am I going to headline?"

"No." She looked disappointed at Vinny's response.

"You'll enter the ensemble as a back-up singer. You'll
work your way up."

She looked down at the table while shaking her head.
"The Diamond…"

Marie knew well of The Diamond, one of the most
prestigious clubs in New York and beyond. Any entertainer
that had ever sucked air and become successful had graced the
stage of New York's Diamond. She was stunned, yet thrilled
deeply.

"When?"

"They expect you at rehearsals in two weeks."

Marie let out a happy laugh. "Vinny, I..." Her eyes fairly danced. She grasped his hand, but missed the touch of pink that stained his cheeks. "Thank you, Vinny. Thank you."

Vantino's cheek began to twitch just below his left eye. Marie looked at him with a soft smile as if willing him to be the first to know her precious news. His stoic features broke with a wink.

Since that night Marie had been living as if her life were a dream. She had feared her father would deny her this opportunity, but he had relented rather easily. That had cost Vinny a fair amount of money, but Marie was free.

Word had gotten around to all her followers that she would soon be gone. Each evening the house packed and nobody pretended it was for Ada. Vinny didn't come again, but Vantino did, frequently. He even waited until after the show was over to take her home. Marie loved it, spending time with him again, laughing at his outrageous stories, and in her youth it never occurred to her to ask why he came, or why she was going. She believed that opportunities like this came to all young people.

Ada gave her as much advice as she could, but so much depended on her maturity, which Ada felt was adequate for the life of a show performer. Ada spent plenty of years growing a tough shell to survive show business. She knew Marie was naturally wary of everyone which would help her in the long run. Marie kept to the shadows until she was confident of her position. Ada also knew that Marie needed to mature physically before she would be thrust into the forefront. While Marie was beautiful, she was clearly still a girl.

On her final night, the band hung around after the show to give her a grand farewell, which consisted of too much whiskey and cigarettes. Jerry called a halt to the whole affair before two a.m., unwilling to pay the bartenders to serve such a small crowd. Glances of mockery bounced from one face to another as pay checks were already two weeks late. But, the poker in the ante rooms never ceased, so it was hard to believe he hadn't the money.

Marie accepted well wishes from everyone, then thanked them. Each spoke of how lucky she was to be singing without any audition. It was some luck. Her talent would serve her well. Marie gathered her coat and walked from the dressing room out onto the faintly lit stage. She looked out beyond it and envisioned the crowd that had just hours before stood enraptured as she sang for them for the last time.

Her glance stole to the blackened pillar where the infamous Dark Horse had once watched her from the silent depths. She closed her eyes and felt the band behind her, the spotlight on her face. This had been the place where her dream had begun, from this stage her wings had opened. In her heart she knew this Marie Barelli would not return.

She took hold of the microphone that was now off and her mind recalled her most precious memory. As a young girl Vinny had taken her to a theater to hear a group of Italian performers. She had always loved to sing to herself, but when the small Italian woman took to the stage and then released a voice bigger than the sea, something within Marie broke free. It soared heaven high with the sound that filled that theater. She sat transfixed, the hair on the back of her neck raising. Her memory burned each note into its recesses. It was the memory she played now.

Vinny bought her a record of Alfredo Clerici singing the same song in Italian. Marie listened to it until she could recite it word for word. But now, Alfredo poured out of Marie's mind as her own voice poured out from deep within.

Tu, Solamente Tu

She didn't need the microphone, her sound reached and stretched out into the empty room, strong and beautiful, confident and unique. She felt no nervousness here alone, but still she kept her eyes closed. At last the song ended, and after a few moments she opened her eyes to look out beyond into the darkness. She whispered goodnight then slowly descended the stage steps. She passed the small tables, their candles now unlit, chairs resting upside down on the surfaces. Her long hair fell across her face as she walked. She brushed it aside without thought.

New York.

She climbed the stairs to the bar area and turned toward the front doors. Vantino would surely be waiting for her, or perhaps Patrick. One thing was for sure, she was done here.

A small red ember caught her eye to the left. It seemed to be suspended in the darkness, but as she stopped to look it moved. It took her a moment to realize it was a cigarette. A dark shape moved as she stared, fear jolting her insides. The shape slowly moved to the light and he stood before her again as if forming from the particles of blackness behind him. He stopped a few feet from her and as he looked down at her he once again raised the cigarette to his mouth. Marie looked slowly from his chest to his eyes, her mouth drying as they met.

New York...

The sharp features of his face looked gray in the soft light. She would have liked to flee but he blocked her path. Her feet felt rooted. They considered each other a few moments.

"Miss Barelli." He hadn't been addressing her, more like contemplating the sound of it. He was now looking at her shrewdly. "New York is it?"

It took time for sound to come. "Yes."

He took a step closer and she had to bend her neck to see his indecipherable eyes. Even the height lent to her by her heels did little good. He took another drag on his cigarette then blew a smoke stream out his nose. His left hand was in his trouser pocket, his jacket buttoned. Everything about him was deliberate.

"And the angels wept."

She looked down and away. When she looked up again his head was cocked and a new expression laid across his features. When again she spoke it took several tries to get her voice steady.

"Thank you again for listening."

"Tu, Solamente Tu." It was said in a very low voice, but the sound cut into Marie. It had been something special, kept so deep within her no one had ever heard it. "I will hear it in the darkness."

She looked at him squarely, then whispered, "It was the only gift I had to give."

"Then I accept it with gratitude."

In her heart, she felt sure she would never see New York, but as the moments passed he finally said, "Good luck in New York."

He faded away into the dark behind her as if dissolving again into particles of air. He made no sound as he moved, nor could she tell which way he went. She stood silently looking after him when Vantino's voice cut in.

"Marie?" She faced him with a smile, her anxiety melting her rationality. She hurried to him. "Everything ok?"

"Course." She looked at him briefly. She took his arm and he led her away from the club. As Vantino closed the car door behind her, she thanked God she was leaving this place for good.

*****

New York

New York wasn't just an eye opener, it was earth shattering. From the moment Marie arrived with Vantino she was repeatedly hit with the realization that nothing would ever, could ever be the same. The pure speed in which the city moved was beyond what her up-to-now existence had ever encountered. She was very aware of the darker side of mortality, but New York opened up the door to wonder and possibility. In LA power and success was measured by wealth and violence, but for the life Marie was thrust into, talent and hard work won the day in New York.

She was completely smitten.

Vantino stayed only a few days. She auditioned for Pete Monroe at The Diamond. Although Vantino knew it couldn't possibly go any other way, Marie didn't relax until she got the OK a day later. They set her up in a small studio apartment not far from the club, within walking distance. Vantino also gave her a small .32 snub nose to keep with her always, satisfied she could use it as he had taught her how himself many years before.

The morning he left was the morning of her first rehearsal. He stood with his hands in his pockets looking for all the world like a lost man. Finally he cracked a lopsided half grin and gave her an embrace.

"My Marie. May God keep His eye on you."

That was it. He was gone.

It was soon evident that she had much to learn. She wasn't even started as a back-up singer, instead she debuted as one of the company dancers, singing only in big performances and then as one voice of many. Her dancing lacked, her social skills lacked, her worldliness lacked. She rehearsed each morning from nine to three, then took a short break until six when she was due in to dress for the performance. If it wasn't necessary for her to rehearse, she helped move props, sort and hang costumes when they came in from the cleaners, clean dressing rooms and backstage areas.

And for a time, she felt lost, alone, like she didn't belong.

That first Christmas she called home to Vinny. She wanted to be grateful, so she spoke only of the grand performances she was only a small part of. When later she spoke to Vantino, she cried and told him she was having a great time. He knew better but said nothing. She thought about his wild stories and the way he clasped her hand. She missed him deeply. The rest of her first year went about the same.

Eventually, she began to get to know some of the other dancers. She was at last beginning to feel at home with the other performers, spending Sunday afternoons at the picture show with the other young women without a boyfriend. They would eat dinner down the street from the theater at a boxcar diner and laugh about the stuff that went on at the club, who was sleeping with whom, and share their dreams.

Finally Marie moved out of her lonely studio and into a large top floor apartment with four other girls. It had no rooms, just open space. The toilet and a bath tub were in the center of the room. They put up partitions for privacy. That year she went home with one of her roommates, Ruby, for Christmas. That year she forgot to call Vinny.

Marie quickly made up for the lost ground she had suffered and climbed the ranks of the dance company by the end of her second year. Her style was that of charisma mixed with pure elegance and sex appeal. Her singing was a secondary thought to her. She did sing some with friends, but that was more in a fun way than in any type of entertainment setting.

Of her roommates and fellow dance company, Ruby, a small blonde, had become her closest friend. She was the first girlfriend of Marie's life, and they spent much of their time together. Marie, however, kept most of her past in LA a deeply buried secret. She never told anyone who she came from, or that she knew the iconic men who had such a great influence over her life.

Vinny came to see her at the beginning of her third year. She had auditioned against 30 other girls for a back-up position. She won out by a very slim margin, but it greatly changed her life. Vinny didn't say much as he sat next to Vantino for the performance, but the three of them had gone out to an extravagant dinner after the show. Both men had been quietly surprised at the Marie who sat before them. Gone was the young girl who refused to meet their eyes. In her place was a beautiful woman who spoke confidently on the subject matter. She had also cut her long black hair. It was now in the very short fashion made so popular by Jean Simmons, who like Marie, had coal black hair.

She laughed quickly and often, but she never once asked about or mentioned LA.

She spent a year watching and learning from various talented stars. Doris Day made repeat appearances as well as the charming Jo Stafford. Both women had been free with advice. She earned herself cameo solos that year and at the urging of Pete Monroe auditioned for a late night spot at one of the lesser clubs in the area. She continued her performances at The Diamond and had the opportunity to meet a young man named Frank Sinatra and dance to the sounds of Harry James.

Just as she had at her father's club in LA, she soon had a late night following. She climbed the rungs of popularity and was billed by two other concert houses at the beginning of her fourth year. Gone were the Sundays at the movies and lunch at the boxcar diner. They were replaced by matinees where she sang in a traveling troupe with three other artists.

It was soon evident she had out grown her back-up singing position. When a two week headliner opening became available, Pete Monroe decided to gamble on a late night chance. Marie hadn't seen Vinny in almost two years, but he flew to New York for her opening performance.

Marie Barelli was gone. The woman who stood in the soft glow of the spotlight stepped straight out of some kind of dream. She was neither shy nor terrified, and when she sang, some kind of new sound came from her soul. She had always sung beautifully, but it was different now, almost as if the sound she possessed was unearthly. She had also chosen to grow her hair long again, opting instead for the variety of styles available rather than the one the cut specified.

She stood on stage that night as the spotlight cast down on her and was reborn into a headlining performer.

She was too busy with rehearsals and photography to spend much time with Vinny. He came to watch the performance for two nights then would be going home. He asked when she might have time to come to LA for a visit, but she smiled softly and confided that she had no intentions of ever returning. Vinny stood with his hands in his pockets and looked away, saying nothing. Marie kissed his cheek and thanked him for everything he had ever done for her, which was everything. She was nothing except for him, this she knew, but she wanted nothing more to do with LA or her past.

That was the last she saw of Vinny.

Her two week spotlight was her key to success. She was billed at the beginning of her fifth year as a permanent headliner. She had the chance to sing next to a variety of stars. In January of that year a young and talented singer/composer joined forces with Pete Monroe to keep the performances at The Diamond new each week. His name was Alex Rogers.

He was a handsome and charismatic young man, catching and keeping the eye of every woman in the company. He was always funny and he had a warmth that drew everyone to him; he was never awkward or shy, but obviously confident in his good looks. He had black hair and his brown eyes sparkled with amusement, but his manners and generosity out shown even these. Marie was taken from the moment she met him.

They worked closely together during rehearsals and spent time together going over music and dance sequences. He played the trumpet and performed many duets with Marie on stage. The talk among the company involved the blossoming romance evolving for anyone to see. It wasn't long before they were dining together whenever possible, and spent every free moment listening to record albums. Marie would sing whatever his latest compositions were. They strolled hand in hand in the park. Within six months they were engaged.

Marie never saw the change coming on the horizon.

The Return

It had been a long time since she had thought about the way of life she had left behind over six years before. She hadn't played by any rules except those that she had made up for herself. So, one afternoon in August of 1955 she opened the apartment door expecting to see Alex. She was shocked to see her brothers David and Gabe standing there looking old and haggard. Her brothers made it apparent that she didn't have much choice in returning about the time they put a gun to Ruby's head and stared at her while the realization of the situation began to sink in. She had no doubt they would pull the trigger. So, she relented.

She took the time to pen a note on the toilet seat in lipstick that had her Los Angeles address when she was supposed to be gathering her make-up. Ruby stood by all ashen and tearful as she watched Gabe and David push and strike Marie in their effort to get her to hurry along. When it came down to it, Marie realized she wasn't prepared to use the gun Vantino gave her on her own brothers.

When she hugged Ruby goodbye, she whispered, "Toilet." As she was drug away, she told Ruby to tell Alex. Then she was gone. They took her straight to an airport, forced her on a plane, flying her back to LA and a nightmare she thought she left far behind her with all her success.

Success.

She had fought for it, spending endless energy working and learning, watching and accommodating, changing the very fabric of her nature to ensure she would never see LA again. Everything she had ever dreamed of was hers of her own making, a name and success she didn't owe to anybody but Marie Barelli.

Barelli.

Another piece of her past she was about to change. Now that was intangible as well. She knew Ruby would give her message to Alex. That she knew with certainty. So how long would it take for him to come?

Marie came home to a prison. The windows of her childhood home were barred, although she couldn't see that the neighborhood around it had changed much. Whoever Jerry Barelli was trying to keep out didn't live next door. The utter devastation settled into her stomach like a lump of rock hard and bitter bile, sending burning shock waves of anger and fear to the farthest reaches of her body. It was far worse than anything she had imagined on the long plane ride home.

Marie waited for Alex to come, to show up and demand that his woman not be treated like a simple rag to be applied where Jerry Barelli chose. But, she had been home for several days and he had neither called nor shown up. Marie knew he hadn't been there and then been turned away by her brothers, because she had waited by the door the entire time. She prayed urgent and frenzied prayers that came back to her in flat feelings, as if the answer was simply no. That led to begging which yielded similar results.

Her mother had avoided her, saying nothing but only looking down upon her from the moment she arrived. Her brothers would not tell her the reason why she had been forced from her comfortable life of happiness and brought back into hell. But, she listened carefully and heard bits and pieces of desperate telephone calls that revealed Jerry was in deep debt. To whom she was unable to ascertain.

Then her father spoke to her. He made it clear her purpose for returning. Jerry Barelli felt the key to Marie's success had been him, and now it was time to repay the family. Marie openly scoffed at him and called him the son of a pig. Jerry had come at her as if to strike her, but she stood tall and straight and looked down at him with all she had. His red rimmed eyes and gray skin shown with sweat and tears, revealing his desperation. He took hold of her hair and drug her down the hall to the coat closet, and with the help of her brothers locked her in just as he had done when she was a little girl. Marie kicked and flung herself against the door screaming and tried to break it down. But, to no avail.

When Jerry returned six hours later, he explained that she was now the lead singer of the Lamplight Lounge. Thanks to the advertising he had been doing for the past two weeks, she was expected to sell out the house.

"What makes you think I'll do it?" She had screamed at him.

He looked at her and calmly replied, "You'll do it."

She was taken to the Lamplight the following night where she was greeted by the sight of a long line that ran from the front door around the corner of the building. Her breath caught at the thought her reputation had reached that far, and for a moment her troubles were forgotten. No wonder they brought her back.

Gabe pulled the car to the back entrance and took her into the club and to her dressing room. It was little more than several canvas tarps hung together.

"What about the old dressing room I used to use?"

"This is good enough for who it's for." Gabe then pushed her through the opening. He pointed to some peach colored atrocity hanging from a spike in the wall. "You've got ten minutes."

What a wreck. This was a dismal failure just waiting to happen. Not to mention the irreparable damage that this would do to her career. She couldn't imagine performing in such a horrible pit to a bunch of low lifes. Nobody but bookies and hookers.

Then she looked at her dress.

What there was of it was hideous. The color was an off peach shade that dipped low in the front and rose high at the hem, leaving very little fabric between. It was sheer and so obviously meant to be transparent. It had thin strips over the shoulders and was meant for someone slightly smaller than she. She was pushed up and out, her skin prickling in the damp cold of the old brick warehouse.

David came for her this time, not bothering to warn her he was about to enter her dressing room, just shoving the tarp aside and taking hold of her arm. Marie's mind drifted back to the .32 snub nose and she could almost feel the movement it made as the bullet left the chamber. She wished she hadn't been scared to use it back in New York.

She stood there looking out into the semi-darkness, noting the flames on the candles that sat on the table tops, and the old fear returned. She wasn't in New York any longer. And frankly, it hit her hard that she wouldn't ever be again. Her father and brother sat and watched her from the front row of tables, Jerry's face a hard mask of bitterness. His cold hate for her shone through his eyes, and she cringed inwardly knowing that nothing was any different from when she was seven years old. He would still beat her senseless and lock her in the hall closet the first chance he got.

She hated him and wished he would just die.

She looked back at the three man band standing behind her and whispered low that she was ready. They began off time collectively, each trying to speed up to catch the others only to have Marie cut them off angrily and start them again. She glared at her father with all the hate she could muster just to have him look down his nose at her.

Damn old fool! I'll be damned before I'll save your hide.

Her chest heaved in the restrictive dress as she tried to sing along with the band, but none of them were able to match each other. She could feel the cold air rushing up under the short hem of the dress to caress her buttocks. She braced her legs and slowed again to meet the band. The sax was on the wrong note. So was the trumpet, but sadly neither were on the same wrong note. She cut them off again and covered the microphone with her hand and turned to them.

"Do you know G?" She waited for their reply as she looked back at them, but they didn't speak or nod, just stood there watching her. She glanced at her father who had risen from his table and was coming toward the stage.

"Go again!" She shouted at the band as her father reached the stage steps. She looked down and mouthed *get lost*. He gripped the rail and his knuckles went white. She knew this was everything to the old bastard. They started again and it was worse than before.

Her jaw clenched as she stopped them with a chopping motion of her hand. "Just listen awhile and see if you can pick it up!"

"Marie!" Her father hissed.

She looked at him and her eyes blazed. *Be damned old man!*

She stood at center stage with her head bent and her eyes closed listening briefly to the murmurings of the crowd. Several bouts of laughter burst out in the vast expanse of the darkened room. She remained still. She breathed deeply and slowly exhaled. She shook her head and tried to swallow the anger and temptation to tell her father and the crowd to go to hell. How could she have ended up back here?

She raised her head and started to sing with her eyes still closed.

Picture The Diamond. Hear Alex playing next to you. If you listen he is there again.

She carried through the first song completely alone, no accompaniment except those in her head. She finished the song and started into the next after only a brief pause, all the while

41

singing to a crowd several thousand miles away. She just kept going. Finally well into the sixth song she heard the trumpeter slowly pick up behind her. It still wasn't good, but he had obviously attempted to pick up her speed and style as he listened.

Marie opened her eyes to study the group who had assembled to hear her perform that night. No one was moving or speaking, just sitting transfixed on the lone sound coming from the stage. Her heart fell a great distance at remembering where she was and why. She was alone again. Not even Vinny had come to hear this debut. She couldn't identify one person who might be one of his guys. Not one, and no face in the crowd was familiar or friendly. She felt certain that more than half the crowd was staring at her gaping cleavage.

As her eyes again scanned the crowd, she saw him. He leaned against his usual pillar, his hands in his trouser pockets. His face didn't show any emotion, he just stood there against that pillar. Her eyes met his and she looked at him. Tears began to burn at seeing him there.

The Dark Horse.

It was as if she were caught in some horrible time warp. Everything that had been six years ago was still alive and waiting for her. The table had turned on her and she was again nineteen, gangly and inexperienced. The good that had come to her in New York was once again a fairy tale that she hadn't yet lived.

She stared at him. He stared back.

He hasn't forgotten me. God help me he hasn't forgotten.

He looked exactly like he had, no older, no more handsome, not that he had been before. He still made the blood in her veins turn into ice with that cold stare. As the song ended she just kept looking at him, and in the stillness of the room she whispered to him through the microphone.

"I guess some things never change."

He mouthed something to her, and it took her a moment to realize what it was across the distance.

Tu, Solamente tu.

She clenched her jaw tight. Her breathing stopped. He wasn't hiding in the shadows this time. He didn't sneak in, then keep to the dark. He was standing in plain sight. Maybe that was his way of telling Vinny to go to hell. Marie's gut clenched hard at the realization.

He isn't bothering to hide because this isn't Vinny's turf anymore.

*****

Marie stood shaking uncontrollably while bracing herself against her bedroom wall. She looked across the room to her mother who stood blocking the doorway. The woman was Marie's own height, but she stood just an inch or so higher because of the heels she wore. She didn't move, just glared at Marie waiting for her words to sink in.

Marie had been brought home from a trip to the salon that was suggested by her father. She thought that was odd, but went along out of lack of better options. Gabe brought her home a few minutes before to find her yellow traveling case sitting beside the barred front door with her jacket laid across the top. Her heart had leapt at the possibility that Alex had finally come for her, and that he laid down the law telling her family she wouldn't be staying. A smile touched her lips.

It quickly vanished as her mother stepped around the corner from the hallway. She held a cigarette between her two fingers near her mouth. Her long thin nose only accentuated the disdainful look in her eye. She tipped her reedy neck back to look down at Marie.

"Sit down on the sofa." She indicated which one with a flick of her wrist on her cigarette hand. Marie didn't move. "I said for you to sit."

"What's going on here?" Marie asked cautiously.

"You're going." She took another drag off her cigarette.

"Going where?" Marie demanded. She wasn't about to let her mother push her off so easily.

"Doesn't matter. I've packed all your clothes. What I felt necessary." Marie cast a glance at the small case next to the door. She strode across the room to the stairs and quickly climbed them, her mother not far behind.

"Get down here! You ain't gonna make him wait."

Marie kept going without looking behind her. "Marie!"

She went straight to the bedside table and jerked the small top drawer open. Alex's picture still lay there where she had left it that morning. She had slept with it the past nights that she'd been home, and although it had been only three, it felt like one hundred. She kept it in her heart the night previous when she sang in her father's slum. Before she could stow it her mother tore it out of her hand and ripped it down the middle. She dropped the pieces then pointed a long boney finger at Marie.

"Won't be any of that! You hear! He's gone, like he never was! You mention his name and I'll kill you myself." Marie crouched low to grab the biggest portion of Alex's face. Her mother stepped on her fingers. Marie cried out in pain and shoved the fragment of the picture down next to her breast.

"You're gonna do this. You're gonna do it cause your father needs it. You're gonna go to him and do just whatever it is he asks. You're gonna smile and like it the whole time. Your father made these arrangements for you and this will finally be your payment to this family. You've never done one thing to make me proud. Never not one. Well, now it's time to make it up to me." The older woman hissed in Marie's face. The words stung like acid in a wound.

"What haven't I done that would have made you proud? What? I walked out of this family and made something of myself! I'm not addicted to cards or booze......."

"You listen!" Her mother cut her off with yelling. "You ain't nothing! You ain't nothing except for me and your father! The life in your veins is yours because of me and I am regretful of that! You owe this debt to your father. Pay it and be done!"

"What debt?" Marie yelled back. "What debt! All I ever did was suck air. If anybody owes anyone it's you who owes me! For all the times he beat me till I couldn't stand then locked me away in that closet! Where were you? Out turning tricks to save his ass! That's where!" Marie was now shouting in the face of her mother whose eyes flashed fire.

"You go on and do what Vinnetti has been teaching you to do for years. You think we don't know how you got to New York? On your knees, that's how!"

Marie burned with a rage that surged from her heart through her veins and down the lengths of her arms to the tips of her fingers. She held her fists back not wanting to cross the lines of barbarism and strike her own mother, or the woman not deserving of the name.

"Maybe you're right." Marie spoke quieter now, but she spoke through clenched jaws. "Maybe forgiveness will never be mine. But it won't be denied me because I have committed any of the crimes you have accused me of." Her mother looked her over with a triumphant glare. She backed to the doorway, as if the next words she spoke would make Marie want to run.

"You are so self-righteous." Her mother spit out the words. "But soon, no more. He will break you the first time he sees that pious look in your eye."

"He sold me didn't he? That's why I'm here. That's why the house is all locked up tight. So dear old papa wouldn't finally have to pay the price for all his shady deals with men bigger and more powerful than he could ever dream of. And where is he? Huh? Where is the dirty bastard who sold his own daughter!" Marie was screaming again. "Where? Hiding from all the guilt he'll never feel? Too big a coward to watch his own flesh and blood pay for his sins with her body?" Marie took a book from the night stand and hurled it at her mother.

The rage of twenty five years spilled forth and took away all restraint. Her mother raised her hands to defend herself and was struck in the wrist with the sharp edge of the binding. At the cry she let out Marie's brothers appeared. Marie quieted and pointed at her mother.

"You tell me. You tell me who it is."

A vicious grin spread across the old woman's mouth. "Mickey Delano."

Anguish rose in Marie's throat like rushing water. She covered her face with her hands and turned away. She let out a sob of fear.

"That's right. Not so brave now. We don't want to keep them waiting." With that her mother left the room. Panic hit Marie.

They're already here.....

Both Gabe and David started towards her and she backed away to the wall. She began to slide down when they both grasped an arm and pulled her up. She jerked back violently only to be yanked forward off her feet. They didn't stop to help her up, just drug her along.

A wail rose from within her. "Please. Please no!"

Time slowed, the pictures and events that took place before her eyes seemed to be happening to someone else. The noises began to distort in her ears, and the yelling from her own mouth came from somewhere else. She was aware that her mother was following as her brothers pulled her body down the stairs, yelling insults that Marie's mind refused to acknowledge. She was aware her knees and shins were being bruised from the blunt trauma they were receiving. The front door loomed ahead, and she fought and struggled against the two men violently. But it only hurt her worse.

Dignity, Marie. Dignity is the only thing that separates us from them.

She had a clear picture of Vinny when he had said it. It was the first time he took her back to her father's house after a long stay. He had carefully explained that dignity was all that stood between respect and being a victim in one's own mind. To respect one's self is far greater than the respect anyone else can give.

She knew he was right. If she went to Mickey Delano like this, it would make everything harder for her. He would still do what he would do, but at least she wouldn't disgrace herself. She quit fighting. She pulled her legs up underneath herself and struggled to stand. She made it to her feet just as David opened the door. She stepped through quietly, too afraid to look up and meet her doom, too scared to look up and see who was waiting for her. But in her heart she already knew. They took her down the steps and to the sidewalk. It was then she looked up. She had been right.

He was by far the tallest of the four men. He looked like granite in his white shirt and black suit, watching her with hard eyes. It had been many years since she had seen him up this close, and she shuddered at the fear he evoked. His face was neither piteous nor welcoming. A tear slid down Marie's cheek unchecked. Two men stepped forward to take hold of her, but The Dark Horse didn't move.

"Good riddance to trash." Her mother's last words stung, although Marie had expected nothing less from her own mother. She stopped walking and turned towards her one last time despite the bruising grips on her arms. The Dark Horse nodded and the two men stopped pulling her.

"No matter what happens to me, Mother, no matter how painful, how awful, this is the last time you will see my face on this earth. You will never again have the opportunity to ask my forgiveness. But I give it to you, free and clear. I go with a clean conscience." With that she turned and gave herself over to the men who waited to put her into the black Lincoln. Her mother screamed things at her as she bent to look through the car door, but Marie could no longer hear her as she had given herself over to the fear as well. Her mother was thrown violently away and she fell to the grass.

Marie slid across the backseat looking back out the open door when she hit someone. One of the four men had already climbed into the car and sat blocking the opposite door. As she sat upright, she tried to move away from him. She was shoved hard and she toppled into him again. Someone sat on Marie's leg and she struggled to pull it free only to hit the man on her right again. She glanced up to the man on her left only to be met with the cold stare of The Dark Horse.

Panic erupted at the mere thought of touching him. She jerked violently to the right, and was hit squarely in the ribs by an elbow. She looked fearfully at the man to her right who was much younger than The Dark Horse, but about as welcoming. He shoved roughly against her to make more room for himself pushing her again into The Dark Horse. However, The Dark Horse didn't push back. He looked down at her, and she moved towards the younger man she felt less fear for. The younger man elbowed her in the middle of the back. She winced at the pain of it. Marie's thigh rubbed against The Dark Horse's leg whose only response was to raise an eyebrow at her. She took another elbow to the spine. She pulled her arms and legs tightly to her focusing her energy into not crying or moving; men like these despised crying women.

The young man to her right shifted restlessly. The Dark Horse remained still.

Marie's fearful eyes moved around the car that was rapidly accelerating down the street. What did they have planned that would take four men to carry out? She squeezed her eyes shut tight while The Heart Vantino's face came to her. A tear slipped between her eyelids, and she brushed it swiftly away. Did they even know she had returned from New York? If only she had kept in contact with them. Maybe they would have known about this and somehow helped her. She thought back to the last time she saw Vinny in New York. It had been so long ago.

A sharp turn made Marie lean into The Dark Horse. She clasped her hand over her mouth to staunch the flow of chaos about to flow free from her. A small sob escaped.

"Uh uh." The Dark Horse shook his head at her, his cold eyes piercing her soft brown ones making her feel smaller than a cock roach. Marie wanted to climb onto the young man's lap to get some distance.

She again focused on what might be their plan. In panic her eyes darted around the vehicle to the four men posted at the doors. Jumping wasn't an option, even if she were able to get the door open in the first place. Then she would have to somehow get over a lap. That thought made her shudder. At any rate, attempting to kill or maim herself wouldn't really serve in the end since they would just stop the car and pick her up. But, at least she would feel as if she had fought. That she had a small say in what happened to her. She wondered how she would act in her final moments. Would she cry and beg? Or would everything Vinny taught her come through and she would die with dignity and courage?

Dignity again.

It suddenly occurred to her why she was sandwiched between the two men. Surely if they had intended to kill her they wouldn't have taken precautions to insure she didn't jump from the car. Why would Mickey Delano send The Dark Horse for her? Who was she that she warranted an escort of such dark esteem? She closed her eyes again, her breathing became very rapid making her feel light headed.

You've got to calm down, Marie.

She forced her breathing to slow down, to remove her mind to somewhere else. She clenched her eyes closed as her mind drifted back to her favorite memory.

Italian Opera.

The woman was so beautiful with the soft light radiating around her. Her voice flew up to the rafters with its magnificence and grace, as if the woman merely stood while the living soul that was her voice simply poured out her open mouth. Marie didn't remember her name, just that in those short moments she had brought Marie's dream to life.

It was a voice that awakened some part of Marie's soul.

In all the years since that night, Marie could hear her just as clearly as if she were still sitting in that opera theater. It was a wonderful memory to pull out and listen to, and look at......

The car's right front tire jammed into a pothole cruelly yanking Marie back to her reality. Her breathing was normal again. She had that sleepy feeling she always got when she retreated deep into her mind to listen to song. The consuming feeling she got while there made the world go. It relieved the intolerable cruelty of her life as well as forget the

disappointment, regret, longing and depression. She had
forgotten to be fearful.

The young man to her right shifted restlessly while he
looked at her out of the corner of his eye. She glanced down at
her legs to see what he was looking at. In the struggle for space
she had forgotten to keep her skirt pulled down. It was now
bunched in her lap, the hem line pulled well past her mid-thigh.
She grabbed it and yanked it down then clamped her hands
tightly around her knees to keep it there. The young man sat
smirking while a dark crimson stained Marie's cheeks. Her
heart hammered in her ears as she turned slightly to look at The
Dark Horse out of the corner of her eye. He wasn't looking at
her legs, but rather at her face. He sat still, just looking down at
her. She slid to the young man, who immediately pushed her
back, pasting the length of her leg against The Dark Horse's.
Her arm touched his, but he didn't thrust her away.

Her mind drifted back to Alex. She sat with her eyes
closed watching and listening to him play his trumpet, the dark
auditorium behind him. The soft glow of the stage lights lifting
up to meet him, and reflect off the intricate curves of the
trumpet itself. He always played with his eyes closed, but she
never asked if like she, he preferred to be alone with his music.
Would she ever see that sight again?

She was lost to the world now. She freed herself from this
horrible way of living, of being surrounded by violent men who
used people solely to the betterment of their own lives. Even
Vinny did so, Vantino, too. Now the slab of granite that sat
beside her owned her life, subjecting that life to death on the
whims of yet another power greater than she. She fought to
keep her head up, for this was the end.

The car took them deep into the city past the territorial
lines between Vinnetti and Delano. She was now traveling on
unfamiliar streets as they drove on for what seemed like a day.
She did not know their destination, but she could only assume
it was wherever Mickey Delano was. Eventually the car slowed
and pulled over to a curb. All four men exited the car
simultaneously.

The young man on her right offered his hand down to her,
but she quickly realized after taking it the gesture wasn't
gentlemanly. He drug her rapidly from the car, then stood
buttoning his suit jacket. The door slammed behind her while
the young man and the stocky one led her to the front door of

the building. Looking through the window she recognized it as a restaurant.

She moved along with them at a quick pace as she was pulled through the opening. There was nowhere to run. It was pointless to try. The interior of the restaurant was empty, the tables sat ready with wine glasses turned upside down atop pure white table cloths, the flatware and fine china plates shining. This wasn't some corner diner, but a gown and tuxedo affair. There were several different levels of booths with small tables scattered throughout. The carefully placed draperies afforded privacy and seclusion. Marie had never been to such an experience. Not even in New York.

They led her past all the tables, the different candlelit lover's nooks, to the big double doors that the empty kitchen lay beyond. Once through they turned sharply to the right and down a dark hall lined with pictures of people Marie didn't know. The hall contained several closed doors, but at the end of the hall a door stood open, a light coming from within. Beside it a man, a very large built man, rose from the chair he'd been sitting in and watched their approach. Another man came out of the room and stood in the hall to watch as well.

They watched Marie with a carnal curiosity that flared panic into her veins, the sharp grip of her stomach contracting painfully. She passed by them without making eye contact, moving into a large wood paneled office that smelled of leather and cigar smoke with just a hint of bourbon.

There was several leather chairs and sofas surrounded by mahogany tables around the room, most of which were occupied by black suited men who all turned to look as Marie entered the room with her escorts. All of the quiet talk subsided, and she felt rather than saw their gazes. She made no move to closely survey her surroundings, but locked eyes on the man who sat behind a huge oak desk. He was the man who she knew must be Mickey Delano.

She had never seen him before, not even a picture, but she knew by the way he sat in a relaxed manner while his body was taut that he was the man who ruled supreme here. Above his head were several portraits, one of a beautiful black haired woman, and the other of two young boys. Numerous photographs lined the walls around them, but only the portraits hung behind the desk.

They roughly stopped her in front of the desk, but the man made no move. He sat quietly and still as he assessed her from top to bottom with his dark eyes. He didn't bother to look at her face. The silence of the room was so thick it felt like a woolen cloak about her shoulders. She clenched her fists in an effort to stop her hands from trembling. The anticipation of the moments ahead made her palms sweat and her underarms sting; this would not go easy. She was new property and would be treated as such.

Mickey brought his finger to his chin as he asked no one in particular, "Fight much?"

"No," the sound of the deep voice directly behind her made Marie flinch involuntarily. She could feel The Dark Horse's body heat searing her backside.

Mickey nodded his head and her escorts moved away to take up empty chairs around the room. The Dark Horse claimed one immediately to her left. Marie felt naked as Mickey slowly rose and moved around the desk to stand before her, then leaned back onto the desk. He folded his arms across his chest as he continued to look at Marie. His eyes were neither kind nor welcoming, and Marie knew her presence was not a wanted one. She was the less than equal trade in the place of money. Nothing she did could give Mickey what he wanted, his money.

She tried to keep from wrapping her arms around her breasts, knowing he'd then restrain her. She looked into his face hoping to read at least some intent there, but could not. Mickey looked to be around forty, his black hair combed back with a slight wave to it, his skin fairer than her own but no less Italian. His shoulders were broad, and it occurred to Marie that had he not been who he was, she would have found him a very attractive man.

"Well," Mickey finally spoke causing Marie's palms to sweat even more. She bunched her skirt in her hands to soak it up. Mickey stood and came forward to look down at her while putting his hands in his pants pockets.

"You don't look like much trouble. You gonna give me trouble?" His voice was nearly soft.

"No, sir." Marie replied with a small voice that echoed in the silence. He stood for a moment watching her, so she bowed her head and looked at the floor.

"Do you know why you are here?" His voice belied the violence she knew was coming.

"Yes. Yes, I think so."

Mickey stepped forward, again closing the precious distance that was all that stood between her and the memories of hell she barely kept repressed inside her mind. Her eyes drifted up as far as his lapel, but the fear stopped her from meeting his eyes. Her own eyes burned and her breathing stopped.

"Well, let me clarify it for you. Your papa owes me a lotta money." He withdrew one hand from its pocket as he clicked his tongue. "A lotta money. And I kept my end of the agreement by waiting a specific amount of time before I came for it. But your papa, he didn't keep up his end." He slowly reached up and took hold of a lock of her hair from where it laid down her arm. Marie kept her head down and her shaky breath in. She pursed her trembling lips, as he fingered the softness of her hair.

God help me.

"When I told him I'd slit his throat, he told me he thought that we could make a little trade." He dropped the hair to move around behind Marie and look at her backside.

"I told him I wasn't interested, but he assured me this trade was worth it." Again he paused as he gathered up the thick mass of her hair in his hand and held it to the side. A tear pushed out from between Marie's eyelids and fell to the floor by her shoe.

"What do you think it was I needed so badly?" His breath blew stinging needles along her neck as he spoke softly into her ear. He let out a low chuckle. "Granted, we took plenty of his blood while your brothers fetched you from New York. It was a risk I decided to take, waiting for you like I did." He ran his hand down the smoothness of her arm.

"Your papa repeatedly assured me you were worth the risk. Seeing you now, I'm not so sure." He stepped around to face her and gently raised her face to his, tilting her head as he examined her face, then traced the contours of her jaw and neck with the tips of his fingers. Marie could feel the tenseness of his touch, the force he used to control himself.

"If you don't work out, I kill you. Your papa still owes me the money, but you give your life for his. I agree not to kill him. I'd like to say that pains him greatly, you dying for him, but lying won't change anything." He reached down and took hold of her skirt and raised it so he could see her leg.

Marie balled her hands into fists as she stared at the red spot behind her eyes caused by the intensity of her eyelids being squeezed shut. She greatly feared his intent here in this room full of men. Men who would watch with vile interest just as they already were. She thought of The Dark Horse, but heard no movement in his direction.

Mickey stood less than a foot away from her looking at her bowed head. She knew his scrutiny was over. He'd made his assessment and he would now act. It was the way men in his position did business. Harsh was an understatement to what came next. She braced for it, unable to listen through the pounding in her ears.

Without hesitation as he stood there looking down at her, Mickey grasped a handful of her hair at the top of her neck and jerked her head back. Marie grimaced but was able to stifle a cry as he did so.

"Now, what do you suppose you have that I need?" His eyes reflected the mockery evident in his voice. With his free hand he cupped her neck, then rubbed his thumb across her esophagus. Marie stood still, frozen by the look of hate in his eyes.

"You might think you know," he shook his head. "But you'd be wrong." He pressed his cheek to hers, his mouth against her ear. "Your voice," he whispered.

He took hold of the muscle in the base of her neck and he gripped it tight. The pain made tears spring into her eyes.

"You mean nothing to me." He stated flatly. "You are but an insignificant payment on a debt that can't be paid. But, you belong to me. All that you are belongs to me. I own every inch of you and each day you live you earn the privilege of getting up the next day to earn it again. Your freedom is gone. Your life before is gone. And so help me, if you act like the Barelli trash you sprang from, I'll kill you with my bare hands. Do you understand me?"

Marie nodded her head.

"I can't hear you!" He yelled in her face.

"Yes, sir!" He released his hold on her, but didn't step back.

"You are disposable, but you have a single redemption. To please me. And right now you will please me with your voice."

She felt confused. What type of lunatic enslaved someone just to hear them sing? He stepped back and leaned on the desk once more. He looked for all the world to be relaxed. It seemed an hour passed as he examined her.

"It has long been a dream of mine to open my own club. Long been my desire to possess the type of place that drowns even the likes of New York and all its slums. And now, within a few weeks my dream will be real. Which leads me to you. You come very highly recommended, but I've never heard of you. Never heard you sing. For all I know you open your mouth and shit dribbles out. You being Jerry Barelli's daughter inclines me to believe that." He pressed his index finger to his lip as he crossed his chest with his other arm. "What else do you do besides sing?"

She was required to speak for the first time and found she wasn't sure she could. "I…I..I play piano…" Mickey cut her off sarcastically.

"Yeah, and you have one hell of a stutter, too. Where did you sing in New York?"

Marie swallowed hard, "I headlined at The Diamond for almost two years. By headlined I mean I was the house act, and I performed in conjunction with acts brought in to perform weekly. I sang at a small club called Cabrito's as part of a four piece ensemble. Also various auditoriums with a traveling concerto."

"What was the ensemble at Cabrito's?" He asked as if he knew the other information, but Cabrito's was new.

"The ensemble was a cellist, sax, myself, and my fiancé played the trumpet."

Mickey lunged from his place at the desk, and with his back hand sent Marie crashing to the floor. She hit without realizing, unable to see through the stars or hear past the loud ringing in her ear where his hand had struck. He grabbed a handful of her hair, pulling her to her feet. A small squeak escaped her throat.

"No, no, no, no." He put his face close to hers. "No fiancé. No lover, no sweetheart. Nothing." He pointed to his chest with his whole hand. "Only me. What he gave you now comes from me. If he comes for you, he dies. If I hear about anyone looking for Marie Barelli, I cut 'em into little pieces while you watch. You get that?" He pulled harder on her hair.

"Yes, sir."

"Yes, Mickey," He emphasized.

"Yes, Mickey."

What a fool. She knew better than to give herself away; small pieces he would use later, to hurt, to twist, to burn, to destroy. Mickey obviously hadn't known about Alex, or Carbrito's wouldn't have been unfamiliar. He would have checked on her long before she ever left New York. She was beginning to remember the rules of the game Vinny taught her.

Never expose yourself.

Vulnerability was a bitch to live down. Mickey had found a vulnerable spot. Now he'd twist.

"I'll kill him Marie, I'll do it. I'll go to New York and burn him alive if I have to. Will I have to?"

"No, Mickey," she said it firmly.

He clicked his tongue several times. "I'm gonna have to. You're gonna do something stupid. I can feel it. You're gonna try to get word to him, try to go to him. That dumb bastard'll come riding in and think he'll be the hero." He paused a moment. "Uh uh." He shook his head as he spoke.

"Maybe I send Valant over there." He pointed with a jerk of his head. "He could bring you back a souvenir." He said this with excitement. "Yeah, a souvenir of your time in New York. Your lover's heart on a string." He chuckled at his own ironic joke. "Valant loves souvenirs. What do you think? Wanna souvenir?"

"No, Mickey," Marie's voice trembled.

"So what about that ensemble at Cabrito's?" He pulled her hair again with as much force as he could.

"A, a sax, a cello, and some asshole on the trumpet." Marie forced out the words in a rush.

He released her hair. "Very good."

Marie lowered her head and closed her eyes. Alex's image as he played the trumpet on stage drifted into her mind. Another of her father did as well. She was lost, so far lost she doubted God's ability to see her. She drew in a ragged breath. If Alex came, he would die, and she would be the cause. Another tear slid past her eyelid.

"Nope, no, no," Mickey angrily ground out.

He grabbed her by the waist lifting her off the floor. He took a step toward the desk, then threw her backside down on top of it. The force drove all the air from her lungs, but as she gasped she saw him coming. She rolled onto her stomach and grabbed the edge of the desk and tried to pull away from him. Pictures were flung in her struggle, a wooden case fell to the floor and cigars rolled everywhere. A decanter and tray of glasses shattered on impact sending brown liquid seeping across the floor.

Marie let out a cry. Mickey grabbed the tender skin just below her armpits and pulled her back to him, rolling her as she came. He settled his weight on top of her, pinning her right arm, then circled his hands around her throat and shut off her air. He then shook her violently.

"You're gonna do this. You're gonna do it, or I'll put you on the street and sell you for a dime to every man that passes. You'll pay papa's debt one dime at a time. One way or another, I get something out of you."

Marie could no longer see his face through the stars as she began to choke out. Just before she lost consciousness Mickey flung her with great force to the floor. Her vision blackened a moment before air came rushing back into her body. She raised herself up on one elbow while holding her throat, then shook her head in an attempt to clear her vision. Mickey stood over her straightening his jacket.

"Get up." She immediately moved to do as he ordered.

"I'm always pleased how well a choke out changes perspective." The dry comment evoked laughter from around the room. The deep burn of humiliation stung Marie sharply.

"Now this is about the time you make up your mind to run. Well, that won't happen either, cause I'm keeping all eyes on you. You'll never be alone. You'll never get the chance." Mickey pointed a finger at her. "But if you do, if you do try to run, you'll get special treatment." Mickey took hold of Marie's face and roughly turned it towards The Dark Horse.

He whispered in her ear, "That's Mr. Valant. You might know him as The Dark Horse, maybe you don't know him at all. But you will. If you run, he'll be the one to come for you. When he finds you, and he will find you, you'll be his. He'll amuse himself with you, then kill you in whatever horrible way he feels like. But, you can bet it will be slow, painful."

Valant sat in his leather armchair, looking disinterested, his eyes moving up Marie's body. He locked eyes with hers as if to confirm what Mickey spoke.

"Treat him with the utmost respect." He turned her to face the rest of the room. "As for the rest of my boys, they are an extension of me. To disrespect them is to disrespect me. You do as they say. Since they will be taking you to and from the club as well as anywhere else you may need to go, you will always be in their sight. You eat when I say eat, sleep when I say sleep. I'll be providing an apartment down town for the moment, but I don't want to know you are there." Again he pointed at her.

"Keep your shit picked up, keep it clean, or you'll sleep in the alley behind the club. I don't want one damn thing to remind me you are there. Opening night is in two weeks, you meet with the band tomorrow. As far as I am concerned we are done here." With that he walked around his desk, avoiding the debris as he went. The young man as well as the heavy one stepped forward to take her arms, leading her out. She kept her eyes down.

"Do we understand each other?" His voice called after her. They stopped and turned her to Mickey once again. He stood beside his desk, his eyes on fire.

"Yes, Mickey. Completely."

*****

The car left the restaurant and headed up the street, the opposite way they had come. Marie kept her face hidden as it burned crimson while her mind played over the scene she just left. Only the two men were with her now, one in the driver's seat, the young man planted firmly next to her. Already her neck muscles were sore, in the morning they would be unbearable.

She had heard that Mickey was building a club. It was supposed to be the biggest in LA, and, she supposed, maybe even New York. In order to build his masterpiece, they had knocked down a full block of old buildings. He either bought out or ran out everyone else. Now she would be a part of it. Not the type of career move she had hoped for.

The car parked in the street below a high-rise apartment building in the heart of town. She was taken from the backseat and moved inside. No one spoke to them as they walked across the marble flooring to the elevators, the doorman watching silently. The lobby contained very nice sofas and armchairs as well as coffee tables that didn't look used.

The trio moved inside the elevator as the door slid open. Marie pressed against the back wall, staring at the backs of the two men in front of her. She kept her arms wrapped around her body in an attempt to ward off the chill that had crept over her.

The doors simultaneously opened to the tenth floor, and as Marie stepped out she was surprised to see that Mickey's apartment was the tenth floor. Straight ahead were two double doors that lead to the living area, but to her right was a comfortable sitting area equipped with a television set. The doors ahead were heavy but elegant with their carved ornate flowers. The young man opened the door on the right then stood aside for her to pass through.

"You ok, Cob?" The heavier man asked.

"Yeah, I'm good, Dean." The younger man replied. The heavier man made his way to the television set as the young man closed the door.

"Welcome to housekeeping's nightmare." He extended his right arm in suggestion for her to look around. Marie did so.

Marie had never seen anything like it. It was huge, and completely open. The floor was covered in plush white carpet, and all the furniture was trimmed in gold. Two beige sofas sat opposite each other in the center of the room and a glass coffee table sat between. Two beige armchairs sat on the end of the couches to square off an entertaining area. On the far side of the open area sat a baby grand, black and shiny on a raised dais. Beside that an enormous grandfather clock stood stoically ticking away the seconds of Marie's life. Along another wall was a large fireplace hemmed in by two enormous portraits, one of Mickey, the other a black haired woman Marie could only assume was his wife. Immediately to her right, a bar ran the length of the wall with a mirror and cabinets. To her left a kitchen was framed in with oak cabinets.

"Mickey doesn't want you here. Let's make that clear now." They stood awkwardly facing one another. The young man obviously older than Marie, but his brown hair showed no gray. He was very handsome in respect to his symmetry and height with build. He ran an impatient hand through his short hair while his brown eyes reflected irritation from their height above Marie. His mouth was serious, and although his lips were sensual, he clearly didn't use them that way.

"You'll be here until Mickey says otherwise, so enjoy the luxury while it lasts. Keep it clean, which as you can see is next to impossible," His voice turning sarcastic. "Don't just throw shit anywhere."

Marie blinked at this. She had nothing but the light yellow day dress she wore. She felt very much the dandelion among the roses.

He turned and walked to the bar and reaching below the counter brought up a crystal decanter of amber liquid with a tumbler. He set them on the bar and pulled the stopper on the decanter. He spoke as he poured.

"My name is Cobby. I don't want to see you. I don't want to hear you. "I really don't want to know you are here. Keep your mouth shut, keep your clothes on, and if you need something, learn to do without." He pointed across the apartment to another set of double doors. "That's your room. Get in it." He took a long gulp then stared at her.

She bent silently and removed her shoes, then padded across the carpet to the double doors. She felt the sting of the young man Cobby's stare on her shoulders. She cast a glance at the baby grand out of the corner of her eye. What a beauty. How much an instrument like that must have cost. The handle opened easily under her hand as she opened the door.

The bed stood directly in front of her, and it too was draped in a white comforter with gold pillows atop. A large bureau stood to her left, as well as a desk and a chair. Opposite that were two French doors that led to a tiled bathroom with a large tub, but beyond she couldn't see what else it held from her vantage point. She closed the door behind her.

She stood there for a long while, taking in the gold vases filled with silk roses on the table tops, the photos of Mickey and his wife on the nightstands. There was a giant painting of the seashore above the headboard of the bed, very intricate in its detail. This was no place for Marie Barelli.

So, she picked the corner between the bureau and the wall. She sat and pulled her knees to her chest. She looked out the window into the purpling sky. Night was coming. So would they. All that was left to do was wait.

*****

Vinny stood by the large bay window in his office watching the last streaks of orange give way to the black behind it. A few stars began to twinkle, but he didn't bother to look at them. It was the vanishing orange that held his attention.

The Heart Vantino stepped quietly through the door behind Vinny, but he didn't bother to close it. "It's done."

Vinny sighed as his shoulders sagged. "God forgive me."
He whispered.
Vantino spoke nothing, just waited.
"God keep her." Vinny again whispered.
Vantino slipped silently from the room. He had his own
wounds to soothe.

*****

October 1936
"Did you get the bread, Marie? It's hard to feed geese without
any bread." He reached out and smoothed her black hair then
gently squeezed her shoulder.
"Yes, Nan sent a whole big bag!" She held up a large
brown paper bag filled with bread. She smiled her half smile,
then turned her small face back towards the window. Her hair
was down, just a red ribbon to keep it out of her face. Vinny's
own dark eyes rested on her just a moment before replying.
"Good. Vantino and I have to make one stop first, then
we'll see if we can get those geese to eat straight from our
hands, ok?"
"Ok, Vinny." She was such a small built child. So frail
looking, but so beautiful. So very beautiful. It hurt Vinny so to
look into her young face. Although she did the best a seven-
year-old girl could at keeping her pain hidden, it sometimes
dulled her shining dark eyes. She never asked his business,
somehow she knew not to. Vinny said they would feed the
geese, so they would. Even if they made a stop first.
Vinny sighed deeply, the sound causing Marie to look up
at him. She studied him a moment before he smiled at her
reassuringly, the apprehension melting as she smiled in return.
"You sure he'll be there?" Vinny asked in a low voice.
"Yeah, they meet every morning at headquarters."
Vantino replied from the driver's seat in front of them. He
slowed the car and pulled into a space next to the sidewalk.
"Maybe one of those geese will fly you around the park,
Marie." Vantino said as he glanced back at her in the rearview
mirror.
"They can't do that. I'm too big." She said disappointedly.
"That's good. What if they thought you were so pretty that
they didn't bring you back?"
"Nobody would think that." She quickly replied.

"Well, I tell you what," Vantino said as he reached into his jacket pocket. "I only travel with beautiful women. I only speak to beautiful women, I only like beautiful women, and most importantly, I only share my Wrigley's with beautiful women." He reached back and handed her a stick of chewing gum as he finished speaking. She grinned shyly as she put the gum in her mouth. She looked up at Vinny as he chuckled, again smoothing her hair with his hand. She looked out the window at the people passing by. Several shops sat with their doors propped open in the warm morning.

"That's him." Vantino's low voice stated. Marie and Vinny both looked down the opposite side of the street where he pointed. A group of five or six men emerged from the restaurant, all wearing identical black suits.

"Which one?" Vinny asked. Marie's eyes were drawn to the tallest. His action was deliberate as he stood with his hands in his pockets looking down at another man who spoke. He was not handsome, and his face was chiseled from granite. He and an older man scanned the street, but didn't notice the two men and little girl who sat watching them from a car way up the street.

"Him. There." Vantino pointed again. The men were talking and eventually the tall one opened a car door for an older man.

"Who is he?"

Vantino shook his head. "No one seems to know anything about him. Where he came from, name, anything." Vinny sighed again. Marie knew better than to ask what significance the "man" had, nor ask which one they were speaking of.

A pause came before Vinny asked, "What do they call him?"

"The Dark Horse." Silence filled the car as they watched for several more seconds.

"Well, no matter how ominous, I wanted to see and so I saw. Now I believe Marie has a date with some fowl characters." Vinny said the last in a mock tone. Marie let out a small laugh as Vantino started the car and turned quickly in the opposite direction of the stranger that Vinny needed to see.

*****

1955

Valant sat across from Mickey in his office at the restaurant. He pushed his empty plate away from him, then drank down the last swallow of his black coffee. It had been a late dinner as it was nearly eleven o'clock. Mickey tossed the dice he'd been toying with onto the table as Valant stood and put his jacket on.

"Where you off to?"

"Thought I'd check in at Dixie's card house, then maybe get a little sleep," Valant said, but he knew better. He'd felt it when he'd left his car and walked through the dark into the restaurant. The night was alive. It moved in its inky blackness, the vibration of anticipation pulsed like a living thing. There'd be no sleep tonight.

"Go home to Eva." At the suggestion Mickey pressed his hand to his chin and stretched and popped his neck. Valant stared down at him.

"Come with me and we'll play some cards." Mickey stated. Valant didn't answer.

The telephone on Mickey's desk began to ring and Valant didn't take his eyes off Mickey as he moved to answer it. "What?"

Mickey watched in silence as Val listened to the telephone. "Alright," he then hung up.

"Tony down at the pier," Valant spoke as he buttoned his jacket. "Guess that leaves Eva." Mickey stretched back in his chair as if he had no intentions of leaving.

Valant drove down to the pier alone, Cobby having been charged with watching the girl. It didn't take long to get there, the hour late and the streets empty. Valant didn't pay much attention to stop lights anyway.

He pulled into the fenced parking lot behind the warehouse slowly, looking for any clues as to an ambush; it was a way of life for him, expecting death at every moment. Valant had lived a long time with what seemed to be the luck of the devil. But he knew it for what it was. God was too disappointed to trifle with him, yet.

A door opened and Tony stepped out into the small flood of light that came from behind him. Val drove up to the door and stepped out of the car not taking anything with him. He already had everything he needed. He kept two revolvers tucked safely in their harness under his elbows covered by his jacket. He carried a switchblade in his trouser pocket, brass knuckles traveled opposite the knife.

"Hey Val. Gotta guy here. Some kinda messenger. Claims he don't know anything." Tony spoke as he held the door for Val.

The warehouse was filled with wooden cases that were stacked to the ceiling. A small office had been constructed from these cases, all of which contained booze smuggled in from Mexico for a quarter of the cost of booze obtained in the States. Most of it was tagged for the opening night at the club, but the rest fueled Mickey's well-hidden gambling joints.

Within the office area three men stood looking down at a man tied to a chair. His chest heaved and sweat rolled down his face at the sight of Val. Valant was very tall and formidable as his shape emerged from the dark outside. Two of the men stepped back to make room for him. Valant put his hands in his pockets as he glared down at the man.

"Who are you?" Valant's voice was as dark as the night.

"H-h-arold Portneuss." He panted out. Blood trickled down his chin as he spoke from a split lip. The name meant nothing to Val.

"What are you doing here?"

"I..I..I was sent to deliver a message." He began to sob some. He was a large man, and that coupled with the crying was very unbecoming to Val. Play with fire, take your burning.

"What message?"

"I don't know!" Val looked down at the man with disdain. "It was on a piece of paper. I don't know what it meant!" Harold cried out. Valant held up an open hand for the paper. Tony gave it to him.

Val unfolded it and read what was there. It was nothing but a few lines of continuous letters and numbers with a few symbols all jumbled together.

"Who wrote this?"

"I..I..I did."

"What does it mean?"

"I don't know!" Harold wailed out.

Valant's patience was gone. He swung his fist, hitting the man in the temple hard. Harold made a grunting noise on impact, then lolled his head.

"What does it mean?" Valant spoke slower this time.

"I don't know! I don't know!" Harold became frantic. Valant took out his brass knuckles and put them on. He then drove his fist into Harold's gut. He tried to bend forward, but being tied to the chair made that impossible. He just sat moaning.

"Maybe you should tell me what you do know."

Harold sat panting, trying to speak. "A..a man ….. called my courier service... asked me to…… asked me to deliver a mess….a message. Didn't leave a name…. j-just said to….. to..to bring it here. Said there'd be….an…. an envelope with a.. a hundred dollars in it….. where…. where I was to leave the paper. Then…… spouted off that…. that rubbish on the paper." He was quiet a moment, then said, "My wife and I were going to Morocco." Then he bowed his head and closed his eyes.

"No Morocco." Val replied. "Where were you to put this?"

"Under a rock by the fence. Big one by the gate."

"Why in the dark?"

"The man said….. said don't get caught."

"Wise advice." Valant said ironically.

Valant looked to Tony. "We caught him sneaking around about ten o'clock, brought him in here. Couldn't get more out of him than you just did." Val folded the paper and slipped it into his jacket pocket.

"How many times have you done this?" Valant asked Harold.

"T-twice before." He sobbed out.

"Where? Here?"

"N-no. Both times up by the cemetery on Lowell."

Valant tipped his head back and looked down at him. Lowell was Vinnetti's turf. Val drove his fist hard into the crying man's gut one more. He lowered his face down close to his.

"Anything else you care to impart?"

"I know nothin' else! I swear!" Harold emphasized.

"Then die with it in you." Valant pulled out his pistol.

*****

Marie kept to her corner that night. She had rolled herself into a tight ball pressing her back against the wall facing the door. It was a long and sleepless one. The grandfather clock mercilessly ticking away the endless march of seconds, the onslaught of time becoming so heavy the thought of another set of chiming might break her fragile hold on sanity.

She was terrified to sleep. She had nearly wrought herself deaf listening for the click or scrape indicating the door opening. But that wasn't what held her captive in fear. It was the nightmares she knew would come, images that would parade continuously in her mind as they always did at times like these. So, she warded off sleep.

She drifted off once, but she had been able to struggle to the surface again. She had seen Vantino standing calmly, his hands in his pockets, while The Dark Horse mercilessly blew a hole in his chest at close range. She couldn't staunch the flow of tears. They ran down the bridge of her nose and dripped silently onto her sleeve. Her arm had served as her pillow and it had long since gone numb. She made no sound.

Her neck was stiff from the hits she'd taken from Mickey the day before, and experience told her it'd be days before she would move right again. Finally the grandfather clock chimed five times. Her belly ached and growled. Her memories of her last meal consisted of toast and tea the morning previous.

She wondered who waited beyond the door.

If she weren't in so much pain, she'd swear she was having a nightmare. But the pain was too acute, too definite, to wake from. She recalled each moment from the day before. This was real. From the moment her mother had told her she was going, to the moment Mickey choked her out while pressed down on top of her. Even the feel of her leg pressed against The Dark Horse's. How deeply her mother's hatred ran.

She was here. Alex was not.

That stung the deepest. Just yesterday she prayed he'd come for her, now she prayed that he wouldn't. She'd never know if they killed him, and she never got to say goodbye. She recalled the tender press of his lips on hers the last time that they had been together, the heat of his palm on the small of her back. The feel of his breath on her neck. The brush of his fingers on her hip. She remembered these well. Too well. She shed more silent tears.

When the clock chimed six times, she knew the time for regret was over. She knew Vinny wasn't coming. If he were he would have gotten her as soon as she hit LA. It was no secret that she was there. Neither he nor Vantino had made any kind of appearance, so she knew she was on her own. She was still struggling to accept that she had been so cruelly taken from her life with this as the intent.

Survival.

The game had changed. New players, new rules. It was a balancing act of obeying rules she didn't know whilst learning them, all the while doing a job she didn't want.

Marie also knew how deep the danger would be if any of them learned she knew Vinny. Hell and torture would ensue. Mickey would assume that she was of some importance if he knew how much time she had spent with Vinny. Whether she was of importance to Vinny or not didn't really matter, if Mickey could use her to twist, he would. Since he made it clear she was of no value and been very cruel, what was he capable of if she were of value?

God help me.

The hunger pangs were becoming unbearable, the tingling and aching finally driving her to her feet, slowly, quietly, popping and cracking as she straightened. A soft pale light streaked across the clear morning sky, and she took a moment to look out the window at the deserted street below. She would never taste freedom again. She felt that with certainty. The carefree days of girlhood were gone, the few she had.

She walked to the bathroom and stood before the sink. The vanity mirror was large and framed with lights. It was a huge counter with double sinks, the embroidered towels with the initials ED+MD in gold thread. She turned the faucet on a trickle. She drank some water to ease the ache in her belly. She looked in the mirror taking in the red sunken eyes, tangled hair that lay limp, and the wrinkled yellow day dress. She used her fingers to comb her hair, then smoothed the wrinkles with a shaking hand. She didn't look any better.

She retreated to the armchair in the sitting area to wait. No more crying. No more waiting for rescue. There was no one to come. She mentally made a list of all the songs she had performed in New York, then silently sang them to herself. She also sang, in Italian, *Tu, Solamente Tu* that was written by Frustaci Galdieri. It was the song she heard at the Italian Opera so many years before. It had awakened her soul. She sang to herself while the bright color of dawn splashed across the walls.

*****

Cobby was a bit surprised when he opened the door and found the girl sitting in the armchair waiting. One glance told him she had not used the bed. He wondered if she had spent the long night just sitting like that in the armchair. Even tousled as she was, she was still pretty, but Cobby knew from his experience at her home that this girl came from trash.

Cobby himself hailed from the south pier where his dad worked on the docks as a labor man. They had been poor. Poor as they were they had been a respectable family, far above the all-out indignity he witnessed when they had collected Mickey's new proposition. Truth was, Cobby really couldn't remember her name at that moment, nor did he care to.

There was a bet going around among Mickey's guys as to how soon the singer would crawl to Mickey to use her body to get what she wanted from him. Women like her were all the same. They could be bought with trinkets and clothes thinking they had the upper hand, but, when Mickey had used to his own contentment, they were gone. There was no long goodbye or fond memories. Many a woman learned this the hard way.

"Let's go."

Her eyes were focused on him in an unusual way. She was not eying him to ascertain his vulnerability, but rather like a dog waiting to be commanded. She rose silently and walked to him, her eyes cast down as he took hold of her elbow. He had expected her to beg, to lure, even cry the night before, but she had made no sound.

Cobby hated that she was his responsibility. He figured with her demeanor she wouldn't last long. He knew Mickey would soon put her to the fire, and nothing about the beautiful young woman spoke of any kind of strength.

*****

They went down by the restaurant again, but instead of going there, they pulled up to the curb up the street. The young Cobby sat next to her as they drove, braced and unwelcoming, saying nothing as they went. The large homely man said nothing either, and the three occupants of the car worked at not looking at each other. It occurred to Marie a long night had been passed by all.

Cobby took hold of her arm and pulled her roughly from the car, then moved quickly to the building. Marie saw mannequins dressed in brightly colored dresses as she glanced up. A bell tinkled when Cobby opened the door to what was obviously a dress shop. Light perfume hung softly in the air. Marie took in the colors and fabrics of all sorts and sizes of dresses; some for coffee meetings amongst housewives, others for evening affairs. Marie could easily picture the women who wore such attire, laughing and talking in a sophisticated manner. The trio stopped at the counter. Cobby sighed impatiently behind her.

To the left a set of swinging doors hung and through them a tall, dark haired woman came. She was very graceful as well as very beautiful. Marie judged her to be in her early fifties. When she spoke she had an Italian accent.

She smiled. "Ah, Cobby. Mickey isn't here yet, but I'll take the young lady back and get her ready." Cobby looked as though he'd protest, but instead he shrugged and stepped back.

"Come." She reached out toward an apprehensive Marie. "Yes, come." She smiled as she looked down into Marie's face, then placed a hand behind her shoulder as they passed through the swinging doors.

"My name is Imelda. You must be Marie? It is Marie, right?"

"Yes," Marie replied in a small voice.

"We will get you dressed while we wait for Mickey, eh?"

They were in a larger room with several daises with dress mannequins, and two sofas sat back to back in the center of the room, each facing a dais. It was an elegant room. Vases with flowers sat on the coffee tables. Around the room hung framed sketches of dress designs. The light perfume scent that had been the official greeter as Marie came in the door emanated from Imelda herself.

They passed between the daises and through a door into a smaller dressing room. A hanger stood beside a row of mirrors and a folding privacy screen split the room.

"Sit, Marie." Her words were kind and Marie sat in the armchair indicated next to the hanger. Imelda sat next to her and turned a tea service tray at an angle where she could best use it. Imelda began to pour.

"Mickey wants to see you in the line-up of show gowns I currently have." Marie's stomach began to burn at the prospect of seeing Mickey again. "Sugar?"

"No, thank you," Marie spoke softly. Imelda handed her the cup. Marie took a sip knowing it would rouse her hunger to an unbearable height. Imelda studied her a moment.

"You are very beautiful, Marie. Do you think so?"

It took a moment for Marie to answer. "I suppose so."

Imelda smiled at her. "The reason I ask is because a woman can possess a beauty that surpasses that of those around her. If she does not believe this she will wear simpler clothing that does not accentuate what God has given her. Put her in something powerful, and she will neither move confidently nor do the gown justice. A confident woman can be less beautiful, but her radiance will be the way she defines the dress, not the other way around. A dress is meant only to highlight what you have that makes you beautiful, not the gown itself."

Marie thought a moment. She had heard of Imelda, but when anyone spoke of her they referred to her shop's name, not hers. She was by far the best, making gowns for many of LA's elite, as well as a few in the working class who could afford to buy their daughters that once-in-a-lifetime dress. Marie sat in silence. Mickey did intend to go big time.

"Mickey chose just a few, maybe three, show gowns I had made for a woman in Hollywood. But, those won't be enough. So, my hands will be busy in the next two weeks!" She again smiled warmly.

Marie sipped her tea, feeling her stomach bunch and stretch, waiting for something solid. She hoped the tea would keep it from growling. Imelda sat back and speculated.

"I judge you to be a size eight, but the dresses are sixes. I can let them out some, the rest I'll make eights." She rose to her feet and reached down for Marie's hand. "Come, let's get you measured."

She stood Marie up in front of a full length mirror. "Raise your arms, please." She wrapped the measuring tape that hung around her neck around Marie's back and breasts. She looked at the number.

"Hmmm, you're a bit more blessed than the woman I made the gowns for. Thirty-six D." She lowered the tape to Marie's waist. "My daughters work here with me, but, one just had a baby and the other is on her honeymoon." Imelda's face was lit as she spoke, as though picturing them in her mind.

"How wonderful," Marie replied.

"Yes, but that leaves me here alone, trying to get everything done to Mickey's specifications!" She laughed as she measured Marie's hips. She stood back to again contemplate Marie as she hung the tape around her neck. "Let's get you dressed."

Marie was feeling self-conscious what with her puffy eyes, tangled hair, and wrinkled dress. At that point she didn't feel she would flatter sack cloth, let alone a show gown. Imelda brought another privacy screen and set it up in the corner.

"Let me get the appropriate underthings." Marie moved behind the screen and began to unbutton her yellow sun dress. She listened for the sounds that would indicate Mickey's arrival.

"Here, Marie, let's be quick." Marie took the clothes from Imelda. She quickly put on the underthings that felt like silk against her skin. Holding the hair from her face, Marie looked down to examine her legs for any tears in her hose. She found plenty. She rolled them down her legs and off, tossing them into the corner. She was looking at her legs when Imelda stepped in with a gown.

"Step into this." Imelda held it open and Marie stepped in.

It was a dark blue satin, it plunged into a deep v and followed the rounded curves of her breasts. It was tight against her form and her cleavage was quite pronounced. Imelda assured that when she let it out it would be the correct fit. Marie didn't think she could possibly have enough to let out. Marie stood studying herself when Imelda moved around the screen. When she came back, she held a brush and hair pins. Marie's heart leapt with gratitude.

"Sit, and let's put your hair up."

Imelda brushed out her long waves of hair, then deftly gathered it up in her hands and rolled it up into a chignon, pinning it as she went.

"This gown is meant to accentuate the shoulders and neck. Can't do that if you can't see them! Your hair is so lovely. Let's have a look in the mirror." She spoke as she smoothed the short strays in Marie's hair.

Marie stood transformed. She had never owned anything so accentuating, so catching, so elegant. Even at The Diamond her costumes had been simpler. Marie felt a little confidence return. She could do this, for it was her voice that he wanted. Imelda would clearly take care of the rest. The woman smiled behind Marie in the reflection.

"Oh, very fine. Shoes!" Imelda went to a box by the hanger and produced a pair of dark blue satin heels. She bent down and put them on Marie. Voices came from the outer room.

Imelda looked into Marie's eyes. "It's going to be alright." She then squeezed Marie's hand.

As they moved into the viewing room, Marie felt the pinch of the small shoes and the confinement of the gown. All voices quieted as she entered.

Mickey occupied one end of the floral print sofa, The Dark Horse the other. Cobby stood with his hands in his trouser pockets a step or two behind The Dark Horse.

So you're The Dark Horse's dog.

Marie then kept her eyes down. She and Imelda stepped ono the dais together then turned to face the men. Imelda fussed over the way the gown was hanging for a moment.

"Good morning, boys." Imelda spoke without much respect, but rather with deep familiarity. "She's very beautiful, Mickey." Mickey had stretched out and draped an arm across the top of the sofa. He said nothing, just stared at Marie.

Marie stood quietly through the scrutiny, betraying nothing in her expression. Imelda stood patiently by on one foot, arms folded across her chest.

"She's fat." Imelda raised a brow at Mickey's statement. Mickey got to his feet. "She's fat." He stated more emphatically.

He came to stand before Marie and she tensed at his nearness, remembering how quickly he went from standing to hitting. He stepped up onto to the dais and circled her as he had the afternoon before.

"Fat, sloppy, inelegant."

"Mickey, you're crazy. This dress is a size six, our Marie is an eight. I'll let this out....."

"An eight? A damn eight? I need a four!" Imelda shook her head.

"A four won't offer you such beautiful curves." Imelda argued.

"Bullshit! Neither does an elephant!" He spat.

"Mickey, a four will have sharp points and sharp shoulders, sharp knees, no bum." Imelda spoke in a convincing tone. Mickey looked at her incredulously.

"Four won't make an impossible dance partner!"

"Mickey, she is only an eight because of the generosity of her breasts and hips, which gives her an hourglass figure."

"Hourglass? She's old school Italian breeding stock. One bambino and she'll have tube sock breasts and an ass like a Mercury. Hourglass." Mickey scoffed as he stepped down off the dais to return to the sofa.

"Well, then don't impregnate her, Mickey." Mickey stopped and slowly turned to Imelda, his shoulders bracing. Marie visibly flinched as he did so.

"What the hell did you just say to me?" Mickey ground out.

"I said don't impregnate her, Mickey." Imelda took a step forward and pushed the words out at him. "If you can keep your hands off this beautiful young woman, then you are a much stronger man than I would make."

Marie's chest heaved against the tight garment, she cast a glance to Cobby who stood with a raised brow, looking from Imelda to Mickey. When Marie looked to The Dark Horse he sat staring a hole in her panicked face. He seemed more intent on her reaction than Mickey's. Mickey stepped back onto the dais.

"Are you accusing me of something, Imelda? If I were gonna rape somebody, it sure as hell wouldn't be this." Mickey jammed his finger at Marie. "She ain't worth it."

"If she's so bad Mickey, then why is she here?"

Now he pointed a shaking finger at Imelda. "That's none of your business." His voice was filled with deadly calm.

Marie watched his fist clench and relax. The muscles in his arm were taut. Mickey wasn't just violent; he was explosive.

Marie took a step back as Mickey came closer to Imelda who was still standing next to her. Although his eyes were on Imelda, Mickey saw Marie move and took hold of her arm in an iron grip. He yanked her forward to stand between them. Marie was trying to hold back the fear that shot through her, choking back the tears. Her soft brown eyes were brilliant from the oncoming moisture. His grip bruised her arm.

"Valant," Imelda requested. Marie knew Valant would do nothing to stop Mickey.

"If you think she's so fetching, I'll put her on the street where she'll fetch what price she can." Mickey shook Marie hard as he yelled. "Don't you stand up for something you don't know shit about!"

Mickey took Marie and flung her toward the edge of the dais as hard as he could, her body like a limp ragdoll, flying with no control. But, instead of hitting the floor, she was caught by The Dark Horse who had come to stand at the edge of the dais. He set her away from him roughly, but she was at least on her feet. He kept his eyes on Mickey.

"She's not a four, Mickey. Please don't make her one. She'll lose so much appeal in the process." Imelda spoke confidently.

"Gowns will be a size four." Mickey straightened his jacket then turned and moved with ease to the swinging doors. He cast a glance at The Dark Horse as he left. The Dark Horse in turn cast a long look at Imelda before going as well.

Cobby still stood with his hands in his pockets. Marie stood with her arms wrapped around herself. Imelda sighed. "That man is impossible."

"It would help if you didn't bait him." Cobby stated flatly.

"Somebody's got to slow him up." She looked at Marie. "I knew it when he looked at you. He's gonna make a hard road for you, Marie. Are you alright?"

Marie merely nodded.

"We gotta go, Imelda. She's due at the club in twenty minutes." Cobby said. Imelda only looked at him.

She took Marie back into the dressing area and helped her get out of her show gown. Marie was still trembling. As Imelda lifted the yellow day dress Marie had worn in, something fell to the floor. Imelda bent to pick it up and looked at it. It was all that was left of Alex's torn picture. Imelda studied it a moment, then looked to Marie who had a tear on her cheek.

"Oh, child," Imelda said with great sympathy. "Don't let them catch you with this." She handed it to Marie. She folded it and put it back down her bra next to her breast.

"Wait a moment." Imelda disappeared, then returned with a green dress. It had short sleeves and a narrow skirt with a split in the back. The large round buttons down the front were black.

"Wear this. If you can't make good with the band, you'll really have nothing."

They quickly finished dressing her, her hair still neatly rolled into the chignon despite being shaken and thrown. Only a few wisps fell about her face lending to her soft look. Marie looked as a professional singer should, trim, fashionable, not the wrinkled mess she had been.

"Imelda, let's go!" Cobby yelled from the viewing area. Imelda squeezed Marie's hand and offered her a confident smile.

"Thank you, Imelda." Then Marie was gone.

*****

Marie kept her head down and her eyes closed during the short ride to the new club on 46th Street. Cobby glanced back several times to see if she were crying, but he saw no obvious signs of tears. She was nothing if not quiet. He was alright with that. It made his job easier.

Indeed Marie was not crying. She kept her head low as she pictured her next moves down to the spacing of breaths she would be taking. She visualized every move, word, body position. Confidence was a well-practiced game. Somewhere in the wee hours of the morning, after the last waves of desolation had receded, she had made up her mind. She had one option to survival. Succeed. She had spent six years in New York, and while that wasn't long by most standards, it had been enough to give her the foundation she needed to succeed. Imelda was right. If she couldn't make good with the band, she had nothing.

So, in the length of the short drive, Marie became someone else. The person she had been in New York. The woman who had become a rising star out of a group of hopefuls. She had what she needed, if she could carry it out long enough to convince even the most skeptical, which not having gone through the try out process like everyone else, would be just about the entire ensemble. She carefully tucked away the Barelli portion of herself, and only left visible the actress portion. The portion that would appeal to Mickey. He wanted a performer, that's what he would get.

When the car came to a halt, Marie opened her eyes. It was huge. The building was at least twice the size of The Diamond in New York. It was made of brick, and great steps lead to the row of glass doors forming the entrance. The Ruby was written above the doors in bold red lettering. A billboard protruded below that. "Grand Opening August 31st" was spelled out on both sides.

Cobby opened her door but didn't bother to help her out, just waited on one foot with his hand on the black Mercury's door.

Marie stood slowly feeling the overwhelming rush of adrenaline she always felt just before a great performance. This was going to be a defining moment in her life. All that had come before was merely preparation for this.

Cobby took hold of her arm and led her in, the larger man following behind. Her heart pounded in her ears at the approach of the door, but she kept breathing deeply and kept hold of her anxiety. She also kept the clear feeling of her voice in her throat, the notes in her mind, and the feeling of success in her heart.

The interior of the club was massive. Just inside the main entrance was a lobby that ran the width of the building. Velvet ropes marked the maze to gain entry into the bar and main floor. It would be a long wait at the back of this line. Cobby unhooked several of these ropes for them to pass through making the walk direct. Huge pictures of musicians were spaced evenly along the walls. They passed through another doorway into the main part of the club. Marie's breath caught at the sight of it, the capacity of this room must have been near 800.

The bar area was to her left, running the length of the wall, lights hanging low above it and rows upon rows of glass shelves lined the mirrored wall behind it. Men were working putting bottles away on some of the shelves, while another stood polishing glasses. It was an open area filled with small tables and chairs on the printed carpet. It was a long walk across the bar area, and a wooden balcony with stairs led to the lower seating area, dance floor and show stage.

To her left another elevated floor rose high above the dance floor and looked out directly onto the show stage. It was surrounded by heavy drapes pulled back with red ropes that hung close together making it difficult to see much beyond a few tables. She couldn't see where the steps to it were, but assumed they were around the front where she could not see. It was a very private seating area.

At the top of the steps Marie paused before descending down to the main tables surrounding the dance floor area. Cobby put his hands in his pockets and pointed to the private seating area with his head.

"Mickey's up there, watching. Everything you do, he'll see. Everything you say, he'll hear." Marie said nothing to this, just nodded her head and smiled up at him.

"Let's go." She began the walk down with her head up, a dazzled look in her eye, a swing to her hips. She swung her arms in perfect time with her hips, and crossed her steps so that one foot fell just slightly in front of the other. Cobby fell behind her, allowing her to make her entrance alone. As her heels made their first clicking on the enormous dance floor, all voices coming from the group of people on the stage fell silent. One by one each head turned to her, some even standing from the chairs which they sat in. She expertly took the first of the carpeted stairs to the stage area and walked the five strides to the next. By then some of the men had lined the top step to watch.

"Ain't it just like the lead woman to be late?" She said with a small laugh. She walked the four strides to the last step and several men moved aside to clear an opening for her. Behind them stood the band stand and rows of velvet chairs, black music stands, and an ornate half wall boxing it all in. Microphones hung from somewhere in the rigging above the stage.

A tall man dressed in a tan suit stepped forward, his dark brown hair combed back away from his oval face. "Miss Barelli. I'm Roland Howard. But everybody just calls me Rolly. I'm your opposite in this lyrical nightmare." He stuck out his hand and Marie knew with this he was the leader, but she didn't know if he was also conductor. She took his hand and smiled warmly. His lips softened into a smile.

"Mr. Howard, uh, Rolly. Please, call me Marie."

"I won't lie to you Marie, you've caused quite a stir. We've been practicing for over a month, then we get the news we are to have a leading lady. Most unexpected." She smiled and looked down a moment before answering.

"Uh, yes, it has been quite a shock to me as well."

"Well, I think we're all a little curious about you." He gestured to the crowd that stood around him, comprised of mostly men, but women as well, no doubt those who made up the in house dance company. "Maybe you could tell us about yourself."

"Well, my name is Marie, which is what I prefer to be called, I haven't been Miss Barelli since Catholic school." Marie paused to let out a soft laugh. "I am currently on loan from The Diamond in New York. I don't know how long I will be here," she looked to the stage behind her and gestured gracefully with her hand. "That depends on how long I can impress our mastermind Mr. Delano." She laughed politely. "Whom by the way, has artfully created one of the most magnificent entertainment palaces I have ever even heard of. I stand in awe of all he has accomplished." She looked about with a dazzled smile on her face. "And I suspect that if he has gone to such great lengths to do this than he has no doubt meticulously chosen each of you for your own individual talents. I only hope that I have enough qualifications to be presentable in such company." A few low chuckles sounded with her own.

"I started out in New York with The Diamond, as a member of the dance company." She spoke as she walked looking each person in the eye. "I did not possess enough talent to range successful there at the start," she said with amusement at herself, "But, I was taken under the wings of several accomplished dancers who helped me come along. However, dancing was not my main intent, and I continued to work on my vocal talent. I spent many a night in back alley dives singing to drunks and hookers." She laughed openly at this. "I'm sure many of you know what an experience that is." Many agreed to this with laughs or head bobbing.

"Eventually, I was able to gain enough recognition that when I auditioned for a two week headliner position at The Diamond, I won out by a narrow margin. After these two weeks, I went on a concert tour with seven other performers which opened my eyes to the realities of life on the road with five men. Knowledge sometimes I wish I didn't have," the ladies of the group laughed in agreement. "I returned to The Diamond and less than a year later was offered the permanent headliner position. Like any sane person I took it. But, I was again offered a once in a lifetime opportunity to come here and be part of the foundation of The Ruby, and honestly, who would pass up the chance to be part of history?" She stopped again in front of the group.

"I would be honored to know everyone's names, although it may take a while to remember. Please tell me what instrument you play as well." She moved to Rolly in an acknowledgement that he was leader, and he began to take her down the row of fellow performers introducing them. They came to a young black man who stood smiling broadly as he looked at Marie. She stopped short and studied him.

"Stephen, right?" she said after a moment.

"Yes, ma'am." He politely responded.

"The Diamond, two years ago. Trumpet?"

He laughed softly. "Yes, ma'am. I didn't think you'd remember."

"I never forget talent. As I recall, you had just married? How is your wife?"

"Real well, ma'am. Gonna have our first baby."

"Well! A successful marriage!" she said as she shook his hand. "At least once?" She asked teasingly.

He laughed softly again and looked down as he replied, "Yes ma'am."

"How did you end up out here?"

He shrugged. "Little woman wanted to see the world. So here we am."

"I am glad to be performing with you again. And please call me Marie. I've never been ma'am, not even in Catholic school." She winked at him.

She came to a tall young blonde headed man. He stood up from his slouched position along the half wall. "Nice to meet you," Marie said.

"My name is David, and you are the most beautiful woman I have ever seen." Laughter and whistles came from around the group as he stood boldly looking down into her eyes. She smiled and blushed according to cue, breaking eye contact. It was a well-practiced talent of hers, acceptance of male flattery.

As the group quieted, she replied, "Well, after the morning I've had, that's a welcome compliment." She cast a sarcastic glance at the private stage. She looked up at Rolly.

"What's the numbers in the band?"

"Well, we've got a full band, strings included, obviously. All told we have a thirty piece orchestra."

"Impressive. Full rehearsal today?"

"Yep."

"Can I get a line up sheet?" A young blonde who had introduced herself as Helen handed her one. Marie perused the song list, which was nothing she hadn't heard before, but some she hadn't performed before.

"Well, since we all know a little about each other, I guess we're down to audition time. When I auditioned for Mickey, it was at a performance of mine and I didn't know about it.

Which is better. But, I think, he as well as all of you, would like to hear me and know what you're working with. So, without further ado," Marie moved along the line of performers until she came back to Stephen, and another young black man named Hugh beside him. "Would you humor me a moment gentlemen?" They looked at her then picked up their instruments.

Marie moved to the lower stage and stood just below the step. Both Stephen and Hugh had followed her as she went, now they stood waiting to hear her request.

"I assume you both know George Gershwin's *Summer Time?*" Both trumpeters nodded. "Just play boys, I'll follow you."

She turned to face the microphone. She inhaled deeply, letting out the anxiety that tensed her neck muscles. She turned her head slightly to feel the stiffness and sharp pain that radiated down her spine, a reminder of all she had waiting for her. She felt the bruised flesh of her arm, remembered the spike of pain in her ear as his hand met the side of her face. All she had waiting.

The players started behind her, the notes low and deep. She closed her eyes and saw only the notes before her eyes, felt the voice come deep from within her chest, flow free from her mouth. She was alone again. She took all she had and felt and blended it in to her sound, rising and falling as the notes did before her eyes.

On the three performers went, matched in perfect time, perfect rhythm, as if the song had been practiced many times, over and over. They drew out each note, and lingered over each pause, staying true to the origin of the song.

As they came to a close, Marie stood at the microphone with her eyes closed a moment, then looked directly at Mickey, who had come to sit along the balcony to listen. She stood straight, and kept her gaze steady.

This is it. This is what I am good for.

"I could sing anything. If I chose, I could be downtown recording Doo- Whop right now, catering to teenagers parked in the bushes necking in the moonlight." She shook her head. "But I am a grown woman. I have lived and lost, loved and hated. Been burned in my own desire, and scorned for less. I sing what lives inside of me and I don't apologize when it comes out truthful and sad. I refuse to sing something that will embarrass my listeners ten years from now who will not admit to listening to my music. I am what you want, hold on to me and I'll get you to the top." She paused a moment to read his reaction. With a great sweeping gesture of his arm, he nodded his head. With that she turned to the band.

"I am not a lone performer. Without you, there isn't much me. If I sound like shit, I want to know. If I look like shit, I want to know. Me being the forefront only reflects on you, so it's best for us all if you keep me where I need to be. I ask for your patience in the next two weeks. I realize I am behind. But I will accomplish what needs to be done before opening night. Let's begin with choreography." With that she moved to Rolly who stood looking approving, and asked the dance company to join her.

With the stiffness in her neck, it was going to be a long day.

*****

Mickey looked at Valant who also stood listening to the girl sing. Valant had no expression on his face, but he turned to Mickey and shrugged his shoulder. Mickey looked back at the girl. Cobby stood behind Valant, his arms folded across his chest.

She was good. Very good.

She had walked into the club like she owned it, head up, chest out. She shocked the band without running them out, then blew them all away. It was a smooth move picking two jazz players then following it up with a jazz sound. She revealed her talent without picking an overwhelming song.

Was it possible Jerry Barelli had been right?

Jerry Barelli had balls to trade off his own daughter, but, that might play to his advantage. Mickey had been incredulous when Barelli had made the offer, expecting some little piece of trash in a tight skirt to come sashaying in, then reveal her frog's croak of a voice. This girl was a surprise.

But something was amiss. He knew it and Valant knew it. With three failing clubs, why the hell had Barelli not put her up in one of those? She would have no doubt saved his ass. Why send her to New York for six years? And then to top that, have to drag her home? She had been brought at gun point, Mickey knew that.

Mickey also wondered about Vinnetti. He had braced around Barelli's club and held on with his teeth, then, let it drop like a bag of shit. No, something didn't add up here. Mickey was also leery that it was obvious, and not just to him.

*****

It had been a very long day. The stiffness in her neck had screamed out throbbingly minute after minute. The entire ensemble painstakingly covered each song, each move, and while Marie hadn't actually done much dancing yet, she had gotten the grasp of the show. What normally took a week, they had done in nine hours.

There had been no break, and those with a lunch ate it when they could. Obviously Marie wasn't among the fortunate. At the end of the day she found she could no longer concentrate no matter how hard she tried. When rehearsals finally broke, Cobby materialized by her side, then quietly waited as she finished discussing the line-up with Rolly. During the course of the day she had forgotten this was anything more than another production.

To her immense relief, Cobby took Marie back down by Imelda's to Mickey's elegant restaurant. She prayed silently they would let her eat. She was so weak and shaky that she forgot to worry that Mickey might be in there. Being an early dinner hour, there were people dining this time. The smell of food nearly made her go down, but, she weakly kept up with Cobby as he walked through the restaurant. He deposited her in a lone booth in the far back of the establishment next to the doors of the kitchen.

"Wait here." Cobby then walked through the double doors into the kitchen.

It struck Marie as odd that he would do so, leaving her alone. There were no diners in her area of the restaurant. No one sat in the booths nearby nor chatted as they ate. As Marie widened the area where she looked, she found she was *not* alone.

Across from her sat an enclosed dining area. He sat at a back table, alone in the shadows. The Dark Horse watched her intently, one arm stretched out on the table as he wrote in a small leather bound book. His other arm was under the table, hidden from Marie's view. He kept his expressionless glare on her. A chill ran down her aching neck and spine, so she looked down at her table and kept her eyes away from him.

Cobby came back out the doors but said nothing to her as he went past and sat with The Dark Horse. Marie's head began to ache along with her neck, so she put her head in her hands and closed her eyes. She dreaded what the long night would bring.

"Pardon me, miss." The waiter set before her a small bowl of soup and a single, although huge, slice of crusty bread. "You may have tea."

She looked from her repast to the waiter who stood holding his tray under his arm. *You may have tea.*

"Yes, please."

Knowing she was being watched she said a blessing over her meal. She did it almost thinking prayer of any kind in this place would be like an exorcism, but, nothing happened. Neither The Dark Horse nor his counterpart fell writhing to the floor smoking and wailing. She chuckled at the sight she envisioned.

Just as she dipped her spoon into the broth, the waiter brought her tea. Marie remembered herself and thanked him generously. He smiled at her as a touch of rose reached his cheeks. She finished her meal only slightly better off than before. If this were Mickey's tactic, she'd certainly be a size four by opening night.

*****

Valant had gone out of the city with Mickey to his home out in the Hills. They took Valant's black '55 Ford Thunderbird and had spent some time at a short stop at one of Mickey's smaller card houses. They went on to Eva, who greeted them at the bar in her bath robe. Her black hair hung loose down her back and she had pink slippers on to match. Eva's face was very hawk like in both her features and in the way she watched everything. She wasn't the most beautiful woman, but she had the ability to read into things and bend the circumstance in her favor. She used what she had to her advantage.

She poured them a drink and sat curled up to Mickey on the white sofa while they talked. She played with his ear, which under normal circumstances would have led Mickey to other interests, but he just looked annoyed as he spoke with Valant.

After an hour or so, the phone rang, and, Valant wasn't surprised when Eva held the phone out to him. He rose and walked to the bar, taking the phone from her without acknowledging her, then answered with his usual "What."

Valant had not yet told Mickey about the courier and the unreadable message. He knew that Mickey wasn't really ready to handle much else but the club. So, he kept quiet about it, figuring it wouldn't amount to much anyway. But now as he left the house he knew there was more to it. The phone call had been Tony again. He said they caught the man who was picking up the couriers message.

He went back to the card house they had visited a few hours before to get Deano, who was there watching the door. Then they both went downtown to Mickey's apartment were Cobby was again staying with the girl. Cobby hadn't been happy about that, but, Valant trusted him the most to do as he was told and not "enjoy" the girl. Cobby was a gentleman, although his career spoke otherwise.

Cobby had been sleeping on the sofa with his head facing the door to the bedroom when they arrived. He woke instantly to stand and greet them.

"Everything ok?" Cobby asked knowing something was amiss if Valant had come for him.

"No. I need you to come with me, Deano'll watch the girl." Cobby nodded and turned to grab his jacket.

"Give you trouble?" Cobby turned to Valant as he pulled his jacket free where it had hung up on the guns holstered beneath his arms and shook his head.

"Nah. Don't move, don't talk."

"Tony called from the pier."

"Note?" Cobby asked and Valant nodded.

Both men were silent on the drive, but as they drew near Cobby reached into the glove box and pulled out a small canvas bag with tools in it. This he kept in his lap, while he pulled out his revolver and checked for bullets. It was a familiar action, one he did so often he no longer even registered he had done it. It also kept his mind away from the events that were coming, kept his hands from getting shaky. Valant had taught him long ago he would not tolerate weakness of any kind. Those lessons had hurt greatly.

Tony had been watching for them from the door of the warehouse, the same door that he'd been watching from the night before. To Valant that seemed like an eternity ago, although he hadn't actually slept to mark the separation the days. As they approached, Tony walked out to meet them, shaking his head.

"I don't know what to make of this, Val. We haven't questioned him any, figured it'd be best to leave that to you."

"Why is that?"

"Well, I think he'll be a hard case, but the main reason you'll see in a moment." Valant raised an eyebrow at him as they passed through the door.

The man in a plaid suit sat on the floor with his head bowed, his hands and feet tied together with rope. He raised his head and looked at The Dark Horse with hate filled eyes, but behind that Val saw the twinges of fear. This was a man who knew what came next. He was hideous, a puckered scar took up the space of his forehead in the shape of an X. It had obviously festered and that caused the scarring to get so thick and raised. He was marked for a traitor.

It was an old custom, one Valant hadn't really used much himself, but he knew it was done. This man had been caught at something against his boss. Although whatever it was wasn't serious enough to kill him over, he still warranted a punishment. And with that, a way to keep the rest of the world informed about his untrustworthiness. So, they marked him. There was a series to the marking, depending on the crime, but the main point was to shame the wearer. There could never be any doubt to anyone what this man was when they looked at his face. Whoever did this to him had done a great job.

Whoever had done it. Valant knew that this man wasn't a traitor of his own ranks, for Valant hadn't done this to him. He came from somewhere else. Valant stood and looked down at him, Cobby beside him doing the same.

"Traitor." Was all Valant spoke.

"Go to hell."

"Where'd you get it?" The man clamped his mouth shut. Valant lowered himself and crouched before him.

"Vinnetti?" The man fixed his gleaming eyes on Valant.

"Go to hell."

Cobby moved now to a barrel close by and unrolled his canvas bag.

"Last chance." Valant's voice was like rock on rock.

When the man didn't speak, Valant reached back with his hand open and Cobby placed something in it. Valant looked at a pair of pliers. He held them for the man to see, but he spoke nothing.

"Where'd you get it?"

Nothing.

Valant reached forward and grabbed the man's hand and using the pliers, started pulling fingernails. Tony had taken hold of the tied man but despite his thrashing, he couldn't get free and away from the pliers. The nails came free with a snap and after about three of these, he yelled.

"The Heart, Vantino!"

Valant stopped and waited for him to continue. "What for?"

"I stole. That's it. I took money from a cash box in a poker joint I was supposed to be running for Vinnetti. That's it."

"Do you still work for Vinnetti?" Valant waited a moment. When the man didn't speak he continued to pull out fingernails. He had completed the man's left hand before he spoke again.

"No!"

"Not surprising. Who do you work for now?"

"It doesn't matter what you do, I have little I can tell you."

"Then tell me what you can."

"No."

Valant reached back again and this time Cobby handed him a small ball peen hammer. This he held up for the man to see. He gave him a second, then nodded to Tony who pulled the man's legs out straight. Tony sat on his feet so as he writhed he couldn't get his legs back. Valant raised the hammer up and swung with great force, hitting the man in the knee. The man yelled loudly. He raised the hammer above his other knee but before he swung, the man again spoke.

"He told me you'd do this! He told me! He said don't get caught. Don't get caught!" Valant knew this was the streak of cowardice he'd seen in the man's eye.

"Who?"

"I don't know his name!" Valant raised the hammer and swung again hitting the other knee. It took a minute for the man's screaming to subside. When it did, Valant raised the hammer over the first knee he had struck.

"No! No! Pacheko! He calls himself Pacheko!"

"Boss?" The man shook his head as he sobbed.

"No. No. Gets orders from above him. But, but, he doesn't say from who. I don't think he knows who it is." He sat gasping for air, trying to control his shaking.

"Where can I find Pacheko?"

"I don't know. We always meet at the old pier down on Vinnetti's side. He calls, I go."

"What does this mean?" Valant held up the message with the random lettering and numbers on it he'd acquired the night before.

"Don't know." Quick as lightening Valant struck the man again in the knee.

"Don't know! Don't know! Pacheko just sent me for it!" he wailed out. He sat yelling, his head rolled back.

"When were you to meet again?"

"Tonight! Now! He'll know I was caught when I don't show!"

Valant looked at Tony. "Send a couple of guys to the old pier. Look for this Pacheko." Tony nodded and left.

"Are we done here?" Valant asked the man. The man nodded weakly.

Valant pulled out his gun and fired.

"Get me a clean shirt." Cobby moved to do his bidding.

*****

Marie laid still in the darkness, her only light was what filtered through the window from the street lights below. However, those were so far below they did little good. She could just make out the backs of the sitting area sofa and chair, barely see the outline of the portrait on the wall. Her eyes had stars in them from straining so hard to see.

She was again balled up in her corner, using her arm for her pillow, as she lay listening for sound. Cobby had poured himself a drink then sat at the bar. The sound was low and far, but she knew what he was doing. They had come straight from the restaurant to the apartment. Cobby immediately sent her into her room. She was grateful she hadn't seen Mickey again. Her stomach burned and growled in the dark. It was now late into the night and everything had gone silent.

When she came into her room she saw that Imelda had sent her yellow dress to be laundered then brought here. She was so thankful that she would have at least two dresses to alternate between. She also found on the bed a dress box full of necessities. Hose, several changes of underwear, cotton night gown, robe, hair brush and pins, soap, make-up, feminine monthly requirements, and a few other things Marie had no way of getting herself. She smiled as tears came to her eyes as she looked at the items. It was a very kind gesture. Imelda obviously knew what Marie was up against.

A noise snapped Marie back to attention. It was what she thought was the apartment door opening. When it closed, she raised her head to better hear. She heard Cobby's voice come low from somewhere near the kitchen. Her heart thundered in her chest when she heard the returning voice of The Dark Horse. He came further into the apartment as he spoke, but she couldn't make out the words. She sat up and pressed her back against the bureau. She drew her knees up to her chest and sat still.

Marie waited, heart pounding so loud in her ears it made them ring, for him to open her door. She jammed her face into her knees and her breath came in short gasps. Why was he here? And so late, too? Had she displeased Mickey today? Had she disappointed him with her performance? She made a few digs at him, but they weren't much. Her mind reeled with the possibilities and she pulled herself into a tighter ball.

It was just like when she was a child.

Those memories were so vivid that when she thought about them they became reality. The stiffness in her neck was unbearable as she bent her head forward. She could even smell the wood paneling in the closet she was locked in as a child. Her heart pounded just as it did now while she listened and waited.

But this man was different. He was dark, and what her father had done out of spite, this man did out of evil. The voices drifted away and she heard the door of the apartment softly close. This brought no relief. It may have been that he had sent Cobby away. She didn't know.

Her body was shaking with fatigue and hunger, the toll of the high stress she endured the last thirty odd hours was taking a devastating toll on her body. While she knew she should sleep, she refused. It was not the nightmares only that she feared this time, but also that The Dark Horse would catch her unaware. She had no idea what she would do to fight back.

As the hours slowly ticked by on the grandfather clock, the silence remained. Nothing moved or sighed. She began to wonder if she were alone. The thought took shape, and after a long gap of listening intently, she thought of the possibility it was true. That led naturally to the next thought. If she were alone, then would it be possible to escape? Surely she could ride the elevator to another floor, wait there, or find stairs and make her way down to the darkened street. This again made her heart race. They'd kill her if they caught her.

She sat awhile longer and contemplated, then decided she'd better move before they returned. She tried to stand silently, but her joints popped and cracked after sitting bent in that position for so long. She waited and listened still hidden behind the bureau. When she still didn't hear a sound, she took a step toward the door. A thin beam of light filtered through the crack between the two French doors. It bathed a line on Marie's face. She crept closer so she could peer out into the apartment. Her field of vision was very narrow, but she could see one of the sofas, which was empty, and part of the bar.

The thin beam of light was cut off by a large shape that moved in front of the door. Marie looked up to see the face of The Dark Horse, his eye peering back at her through the crack. She let out a small gasp and stumbled backward into the bed. The handle on the door jerked violently as the door was flung open. He stood there, with a grotesque grin etched across his features. Marie fell onto the bed as she let out a scream.

He leered down at her for a moment, an evil laugh sounding from deep in his chest. He lunged for her then, with one quick movement he took hold of her shoulders, pushing her down on the bed. Marie screamed and struggled, but his weight pushed her down and suffocated her. She let out another muffled, terrified scream.

It was her own muffled scream that woke her. She was still drawn up in a tight ball, her head resting on her knees. She tried to lift her head, but the stiffness and pain were so sharp she gave up. She was able to turn her head to look over her small portion of the room. The heavy purple light of the coming dawn filtered into the room. It seemed more hopeful than the blackness of the night before.

Her heart slowed and she focused on Alfredo Clerici, rather than review the horrid scenes from the nightmare she just endured. There was stillness and silence, but she no longer felt the urge to investigate. Her eyes burned from being so tired, her muscles were atrophied. She had no idea how to get her neck moving again. She felt like crying, but there was no moisture in her eyes to produce tears. So, she closed her eyes and kept Alfredo playing; eventually, a softer, more welcome version of sleep came with the sun.

*****

"You know, that thing, over there, with the flat top, cushy pillows, that's what we call a bed. Modern society sleeps on those. They're comfortable. You should try it." He shrugged his shoulders. "I think they even have them in New York."

Cobby crouched next to Marie, and when she woke at his voice she snorted a little. She couldn't lift her head, so she just watched him out of vulnerable brown eyes. He folded his hands as he looked over at her, completely unwrinkled in his black suit and white shirt. His brown hair neatly combed and a light teasing look in his green eyes.

"Rehearsal is at nine. I thought maybe you could take a bath, fix your hair, I dunno," he paused, "change your clothes." He emphasized the last part. "Get the stink washed off you." He stood and noted that she didn't move or raise her head to look at him. He slid his hands into his pockets and cocked his head as he looked down at her dark hair still rolled into a bun. She was beautiful, that he wouldn't deny.

"I thought after you're changed and ready we could sit at the dining room table and eat imaginary pancakes. Heck, why not go all out and have an omelet, too. Whatever your mind will allow." Her shoulders sagged some at his mockery. He resisted the urge to laugh.

After some contemplation he extended his hand down to her. It took a moment for her to take it, and when she did she didn't raise her head. Without decorum or delicacy he hauled her to her feet only to find she still wouldn't straighten her head.

"You know, it doesn't matter where you sleep. If he wants you, there's no corner he can't find you in." He stood looking over at her honestly, his hand back in his trouser pocket. She looked back out of the corner of her eye. She looked innocent and disparaged.

"You want me to fix that?"

"No. It will go right in a minute," She replied softly, with certainty.

"Get dressed."

*****

June 1933

The two horses were locked in a dual to be the first across the line. The gray stretched out his gleaming neck as he pounded harder down the track, dirt spraying out behind him. His legs reached further and he broke over with a barely visible movement. His challenger pushed him down the railing at a greater speed, flecks of sweat flying in the air like rain drops. The gray's eyes searched for his opponent, trying to see around his blinders. He could hear the bay, he could feel the heat coming from his body, but he could not see him.

In the last 50 yards the bay moved up neck and neck with the gray. The bay kept his eye on the straining contender, hovering there a moment before the jockey touched him with the quirt. The bay fired again, surging a stride ahead, then two. The crowd was now on their feet roaring and shouting, sending another shot of adrenaline through the bay's blood. He had the heart of a champion. He well knew his purpose, and that he would win. And so he did. The cheers from the crowd deafened ears for a moment before the jockey was able to get the bay to slow. He moved on, his neck arched, his ears forward. The bay didn't have to be told who won.

Val frowned deeply and set his drink down on the glass table with a thud. Julian stood and applauded with everyone else, a satisfied smile on his face. He cast a glance at Val, his smile turning to mockery.

"It was a fine race. The gray put up one hell of a fight."

Julian sat back down and took a long drink of his bourbon. His dark hair had flecks of gray in it, and his widows peaks were sharp. He wasn't a very tall man, but he had the strength of men twice his size. Julian wasn't one for quitting, and he never gave up on something once he had a bite on it. Which was one of the many reasons Val stood looking down at him at that very moment.

"Sit, Val. It was a good race." Julian looked up at him and spoke solemnly. "A fine horse under any circumstances."

Val clenched his jaw and sat. He leaned back languidly in his chair and looked over to Mickey who sat grinning at him. Val gave him a look of malice. Mickey laughed out loud.

Mickey's father Georgio sat next to Mickey and he said nothing as he looked from Mickey to Val. He well knew the antics that passed between the two since they had been around each other for many years. In many ways Val was more a brother to Mickey than his own blood brother Samuel had been. But he pushed that aside. Samuel was gone, and this was not the time for the memories to render him immobile. He looked to Julian who sat watching him, almost as if he could read Georgio's mind.

Julian was Georgio's first cousin and they had been raised together. It was a family tradition, even back in Italy before the family immigrated to America. The heir to the family business was raised with his right hand man. It was difficult to choose a life-long companion when a boy was very small and his characteristics were not yet developed. Who knew how a boy might turn out? But it was thought that a loyal companion from childhood, one who spent all the development years, the learning years, the years spent struggling for independence, would build a bond of friendship that would last and keep them loyal to one another. More often than not the logic worked, as it had in Julian and Georgio's case. They were loyal to each other, loyal to the family business.

Mickey's brother Samuel was older, by seven years, and he was in line to inherit. Georgio had not improved on things much, mostly maintained what his father had given him. But, Samuel died nearly ten years before taking all the years of training and patient teaching on Georgio's part with him. It was natural now, looking from Mickey to Val, they had been together their whole childhood, witnessed each other's formative years, grew close with the passing of time and experience.

But Mickey wasn't Samuel. He was filled with passion that ran hot and cold in the blink of an eye. Justification was not a necessary ingredient in his makeup. He was much like his mother. Although he was far more intelligent then Samuel, even Georgio had to admit that, he did not always choose the more intelligent path. He had an ambition that Georgio couldn't identify with, and the only one who could talk Mickey down from an angry explosion was Val. Or Maryanne, but that was another matter altogether. Mickey was soon to be a father, and that concerned Georgio as well. He just wasn't steady enough to pursue anything without selfish intent. A lesson Georgio knew God would provide with harshness.

He looked again to Val. Valant was different in entirety. He was quiet. Steady. And, he possessed an inner ability to understand Mickey. Val could identify his mood changes and react accordingly. It shamed Georgio greatly to realize he had cast his younger son aside to focus his energy on Samuel. A realization that came long after Mickey grew to be a man and no longer wanted his guidance. Some mistakes a man made without realizing.

"Old son of a bitch," Val muttered. Julian turned to him.

"What was that?" he asked challengingly. Val looked at him steadily.

"I said you're an old son of a bitch." Julian stared hard at him a moment. Then he laughed loudly.

"Val, you are a sore loser. You can't have everything you set your mind on."

Val shook his head and looked again to Mickey who just shrugged his shoulders, grinning. Julian knew that once Val set his mind to obtaining something, he didn't turn loose of it.

It started as an argument between them, about horse color and some absurd notion that specific colors ran faster than others. Val argued that gray horses were the fastest, that something in their color made them crazy. Which was true, even Julian had witnessed incredible feats made by gray horses; horses that had nearly torn apart their bodies in a quest to win with a palatable vengeance. But, Julian admirably argued that intelligence can win over aggression if used correctly. A point that was proven that day by the bay. He had stalked and pushed the gray, running him harder into the rail, staying just out of sight but making his presence known. He had indeed driven the gray mad, who pushed himself to greater speeds too early, and when it came down to it, he had nothing left to challenge with when the bay made his move.

Julian leaned forward and put his elbows on the table and leveled his gaze at Val. "I think we all know and appreciate the point you attempted to make today. And, I agree with you. I've seen gray horses that can do anything it takes physically to win. They are hard to handle and unpleasant to be around, but they succeed at what they do. But, take the bay. He was plain to look at, quiet in the stall, he made no movements beyond what was required of him. He came from nowhere, he didn't show the pedigree the gray did on the dossier. He showed nothing spectacular what-so-ever in his physical appearance. He made no move to convince anyone he was a champion, not until the appropriate time came. He didn't strut around blowing and tossing his head, prancing. He knew he was a champion, and he was the only one he had to convince." Julian looked to Georgio then back to Val.

"You might ask how I know the bay will handle the pressure. I watch him. See how he handles his environment. Then I put a little pressure on him, if he takes that, I put a little more. Can he take the speed when they breeze him? Does he blow up? I look for old wounds and injuries, poke them, twist them. Is there inflammation and scarring? If not, then I put him in the race. Throw it all at him. If he is wise, he watches his opponent, learns his mistakes. Seeks out where he is weak. The gray was arrogant. That was his weakness. The bay knew that each time he put a little pressure on the gray, gray would respond with arrogance. That's how he beat him. Pushed him beyond his own limits. The bay didn't have to be faster. He was slower than the gray by far, all he had to do was be fast enough to push him, and then, intelligence wins the race.

"It isn't wise to bet only on the grays of this world. Consider the heart and intelligence of the bays. What they have inside is what makes them the challenger. Aggression won't get everything in this world. Not the important things, anyway."

Julian looked to Mickey and held his gaze a long moment. Without looking away he pointed to Valant.

"Always bet on that dark horse. It will come through for you every time." It was spoken with finality. Both Mickey and Val knew this was the blessing. Mickey looked at Val and tried to read the look in his eyes, but could not. For Mickey could not read Valant the way Valant could read him. He exhaled slowly.

The Dark Horse.

*****

1955

Marie's second day at rehearsal was far more demanding than the first. By now the constant gnawing hunger had shifted into a weariness that settled all the way into her bones. It took a great amount of will to force her hands not to shake and keep her knees from just dumping their load. As Cobby brought her in through the main glass door of the club that morning and walked her along the carpet in the bar seating area, Mickey had come up the steps. He stood waiting for them at the top of the stairs with a smirk on his face. Marie kept her head up all the while her heart beat faster. It was the only time that day she didn't feel sluggish.

"Good morning." He called out in his kind and gentle voice that belied the tension she knew would be visible in his hands.

"How was your dinner last night? Was it satisfactory?" It took all she had not to reflect her thoughts in her expression.

"Yes. It was wonderful. Thank you very much."

"Was breakfast ok? Can't let you waste away on us, now." He leaned forward to look into her face, the tension in his now was from suppressing his laughter.

Sarcastic bastard.

"No fear of that, Mickey." She smiled at him and looked into his eyes and he held her gaze a moment. Something passing in his look she couldn't read. Then he stepped aside and gestured for her to pass. She bowed her head respectfully at him as she did so. She continued down the stairs alone when Cobby stayed beside Mickey, both men watching her make her way to the stage where the band was gathering.

They finished out the last five numbers with choreography, thankfully two of the songs she didn't have to do anything for. She sat those out as Rolly had practiced solo. But the final two it had been decided after much debate that Marie would perform alone. One, *I'm Beginning to See the Light,* written by Duke Ellington, would be the opening song. Marie couldn't think of anything but lying down.

Eventually the day passed. She felt like she'd able to keep up with the pace even if her usual enthusiasm was gone. She had determined to rise to Mickey's challenge and not let him beat her. She couldn't match him with her fists, but she could match him will for will.

She was taken to the restaurant and given the same meal as the night before. She took it gratefully. She ate alone and in silence, Mickey and several of his guys sat at the private table across from her. As she left with Cobby she had boldly gone to him and thanked him for the meal. He looked annoyed at her but said nothing. She bowed her head and left behind Cobby.

When she retreated to her corner that night her body was thankful when she lay down on the soft carpet. Although it was very early, she fell asleep almost immediately. Her dreams that night far kinder than those of the previous two nights. They were mostly of Alex, whose picture was still tucked safely beside her breast. She dared not take it out and look at it for fear she'd be caught with it.

But one dream was of her when she was a small child. It came just before the dawn, and it kept her through the next day. Her mind no doubt seeking comfort.

"Come on Marie. Just do it." Vantino had bent low to whisper in her ear. "You know you want to know." He stood straight again and peered down at her.

"I can't." Marie shrugged her thin little shoulders.

"You won't know if you keep standing there like that." She shook her head. Her long black hair hung down, curling slightly at the tips. She wrapped her little arms around her narrow body and looked down. Vantino looked incredulous.

"Ha! That's what you said about dropping Vin's bowling ball off the second floor balcony. You became the biggest bad ass I know when that ball went through Nancy's glass table."

Marie remembered the moment well. That ball fell through the air for what seemed like an eternity before finally crashing into that table. The sound it made caused Marie to clamp her hands over her ears and tears to squeeze out the corner of her eyes. But Vantino, as well as the three men standing below, had cheered and clapped for her.

Vantino put a big hand on her shoulder that swallowed her up with its size. His knuckles were bruised and raw. "I'll be right here. You won't be alone."

When she looked up at him he smiled a soft, gentle smile that held her attention. Nobody ever smiled at her like that. She felt she could trust him, but had felt those feelings before only to be wrong. Her fine features and olive skin were marred by the bruising on her face; bruising that was close to being healed. She looked back to the situation at hand.

"But it's Vinny's Sunday car." Vantino gave a shrug that said, so what? He looked over to the gray LeBaron Roadster.

Although Vantino's shenanigans always caused some form of mayhem or another, he made sure she never took any of the blame. He had told Nancy that he and the boys had been arm wrestling and knocked over the glass table. Not that the excuse explained the crushed tile. Rules were bent for Marie.

Patrick and a few of the boys standing around gave encouragement. The small form stood quiet a moment then said, "Alright."

Vantino laughed and clapped his hands together. "Yeah!"

He reached down and took hold of her small hand in his large one and gave her a confident smile. "This is gonna be fun." He put her behind the wheel then ran around the front of the car to get in on the passenger side. He slid in and looked over to her. She couldn't see over the wheel and reach the pedals at the same time. She looked searchingly at him. He softly tucked her hair behind her ear.

"Turn the key."

Marie woke from her dream as the sound of the engine roared. She lay a moment smiling at the memory. She had hit a lawn sculpture and dented the car. When Vinny got home nothing was said. But she saw Vantino polishing the car later, something she never saw him do.

She felt some of the stiffness in her neck had gone, so she sat up and stretched. It would be another long day. A hungry day. She pushed that aside. Thinking about it only made it worse. She put her green dress on then waited for Cobby to come for her. To her surprise it wasn't Cobby, but the large homely man. They called him Deano. He didn't say much, just grunted for her to follow.

Mickey was present for rehearsals that day. He sat at a table near the stage watching the proceedings. Rolly had deferred to him when there was any question. But Mickey did prove to have bold ideas and an eye for the entertainment business. He was also merciless.

Any number Marie performed, he commanded that she do four or five times in a row. Soon it was just accepted that after the performance was over, the band would look to Mickey for permission to quit or continue. Soon whispers ran along the band stand about what the relationship between the two might be. None of the speculation was good. Marie knew nothing about this because all she did was try to keep upright.

She wanted to quit, but didn't have the strength to face what Mickey would do to her. So, she kept going for lack of better options. When the day did end, no one in the band would look at her or respond when she said good night to them. She was low. She didn't know what to do. It continued this way for several days. She kept still to conserve energy when she wasn't rehearsing. She slept for 13 hours straight. Her nightmares returned, but she was too exhausted to rouse herself from them.

Things went on that way for a week, by that time Marie was hardly able to stand. But she didn't quit. She put her soul into it, prayed desperately for the strength while the bones in her shoulders became sharp. So did her hips. It became increasingly difficult to wake in the morning, but she did. Each time she saw Mickey she graciously thanked him for the meals. Eventually the sarcasm left him, and although he wasn't polite or generous, his eye took on a different gleam.

The band also changed. It became obvious that Marie wasn't eating. It was also obvious that it took all she had to just stand up, let alone rehearse for eight or nine hours at a time. Mickey made no attempt to hide that he was singling her out. Rolly was as helpful as he could be, when he saw that she could take no more, he would insist on going through his numbers a few times while she sat. On a few occasions Helen gave Marie whatever she could to eat, usually Cracker Jacks or saltines. Helen didn't have much herself. Stephen always came by with an encouraging word and gentle smile.

As Marie sat resting at one of the tables near the stage, Rolly grabbed a few song sheets and came to sit down next to her. He spread them out and gestured to them while the band took a five minute break. He didn't make any reference to them when he looked at her.

"You know, I thought it might help you to know, that there's more than a few of us that are here 'cause we owe him something. And while you suffer greatly, you've earned a great amount of respect here, too." With that he stood and left, leaving Marie to think over what he said. It helped immensely.

Marie had not seen Cobby since the morning he woke her and teased her about the bed. She'd been kept by Deano, who wasn't exactly friendly, but he didn't turn out to be as awful as he looked either. She ate alone every meal. She took her time and savored her one cup of tea as long as possible. She still slept in her corner, the nightmares coming and going.

Two days before opening night she was taken back to Imelda's dress shop for a final fitting. Imelda was deeply displeased when she saw Marie and how thin she had grown. She clucked and sighed, shrugged and muttered. At last she stood back and looked into Marie's eyes and tried to smile but couldn't.

"By the looks of you he picked unusual ways to be unkind." Her voice was low and her accent thick.

"It's alright. I'll go as long as I can." Marie knew she wasn't being reassuring, but it was truthful. Imelda shook her head.

"Well, what does he expect? He'll have to find another girl before opening night. And I can't believe he would do this what with all the coverage he's getting in the papers! Nobody in this town is talking about anything but the opening of The Ruby! Here he is starving the lead singer to death." She turned sharply then, walking angrily to the dress rack.

Instead of being tight, her dresses had room to spare. Imelda said nothing more as they tried on the costumes, but Marie could see the anger burning in the woman's eyes.

That evening when Marie went to eat at the restaurant, she was greatly surprised to see The Dark Horse again sitting alone writing in his book. She cast him a glance but said nothing. She kept herself to herself. When her food was brought to her it held a surprise as well. She was given a breast of chicken, roasted vegetables, a slice of melon, and bread. The waiter looked pleased. He tucked his tray beneath his arm.

"Would you like your tea?" He said with a broad smile.

Marie laughed softly. "Yes, please." He bowed slightly and left.

Marie stared at her plate a moment before reaching for her silverware. The waiter returned with her tea. She wondered if it were possible Imelda had something to do with this.

"Enjoy, my lady." He blushed a deep crimson when she winked at him. She enjoyed the meal with relish. Part way through Mickey came to sit at his table. He spoke with The Dark Horse, but Marie didn't bother to listen to what he was saying. When Deano came for her, she walked across to him, and he cut off what he was saying to The Dark Horse to look at her. She gave him a brilliant smile and thanked him, bowing her head low.

A laugh woke her from her sleep the next morning. Cobby crouched next to her when she opened her eyes in surprise.

"Why don't you use a pillow at least? That looks terrible." He looked tired, but his green eyes sparkled with mischief. He stood and reached down for her.

Her body was stiff and her elbow popped when she took his hand. "Your neck looks better."

She nodded as she rubbed it.

"You're a strange one Marie."

*****

The day of the grand opening the entire company went through the show in a dress rehearsal. Everyone could feel the hum of excitement coursing along like electricity in a wire. Costumes were ready for the dancers, tuxedos for the band, and Marie wore the gown Imelda had worked so hard on. Thanks to Mickey's obsessive desire to see Marie perform numbers four or five times in a row, she felt more confident about knowing her moves as well as her lyrics than she had at any other performance she'd made in her life.

She tried not to think about the consequences that would come if that night weren't to go well. Everyone had been working hard, but it was a different story when you filled the room with people. And the room would be full. Imelda had been right about that. Outside Mickey's restaurant was a small newspaper stand and Marie had read the headlines each time she passed it. The Ruby was a well-documented happening, and so was she. She saw her name on the front page many times.

It took five hours to run through the entire show, then everyone was encouraged to get some rest while the club was put through final preparations. They had been wheeling in cases of alcohol by the dozens, filling the stockroom behind the stage. Table tops were wiped down and white table clothes spread over them. The dance floor was waxed and polished when the company was done with it. The billboard out front read: GRAND OPENING TONIGHT- ROLLY HOWARD AND THE HOWARD ORCHESTRA- MARIE BARELLI FEMALE LEAD.

Marie had to admit, it took her breath away to see her name on the billboard like that. She was a part of history now, no matter what happened that night.

Cobby had taken her back to the apartment for just a few hours. She went into the master bedroom and sat on one of the fine chairs and prayed. So much depended on her ability to perform an incredible feat that night. She sat and recalled the times she had headlined at The Diamond. She had loved it so. The people, the music, the lifestyle, the camaraderie, and being in the spotlight. She hoped the experience she had gained there would be enough.

When Cobby came to get her to take her to dinner, he found her sitting there, her hands fisted together, her head resting on them as she leaned forward. She had her eyes closed, concentrating on something.

"Let's go, Marie."

She was wearing the green dress Imelda had given her, her hair down. She looked at him as if confused as to where he came from, then nodded ok. She stood and moved quietly, looking apprehensive. Cobby had no doubt she was. Her dinner was the same as the night before, and she was grateful for the strength it would provide. The restaurant was empty but for her and Cobby, who sat at the private table across from her.

They left the restaurant and headed to the club after she had finished eating. There were cars lined up and down two blocks on each side of the street. A ball of people stood in the street and up the great steps leading to the club. Marie knew instantly this wasn't a waiting line to get in as tonight was an invitation only event. As the car neared the front, Cobby had to push through the throng of people who surrounded the car, knocking on the window. A camera flashed and Marie knew them for what they were. The press.

"Cobby," she looked but couldn't see past the faces and cameras that now enveloped the car she sat in. It would be near impossible to get to the door. Cobby stopped the car.

"Ah shit. Just stay right behind me, we'll push through. My advice is say nothing to them." With that he pushed his door open with a strong arm. As he did so Marie's door was opened and cameras were put in her face.

"Miss Barelli! Miss Barelli! Can you tell us about opening night? Are you nervous?"

"Miss Barelli! Can you tell us why you left New York? Is it true you're having an affair with Mickey Delano?"

An affair with Mickey?

"How many people do you expect tonight?"

"Marie, get out!" She recognized Cobby's voice from somewhere, but couldn't see him, then she saw him push through to her only to get brushed aside again.

"Please tell us where you came from." A flash went off in front of her.

"Are the rumors true that Mickey fell in love with you in New York when he heard you sing, then opened this club to bring you here to LA?" A man clamored to get a face in the car. Another flash.

"Does Mickey Delano own you?" Shouted another. She ground her teeth in frustration.

"No comment! No comment!" Marie tried to push her way out of the car, but couldn't budge them. She caught a glimpse of Cobby roughly pushing them aside. They'd never get her inside.

Suddenly several men fell backward, another was pushed into the car next to her, and shouts broke out around her. Then the men started shouting questions at her more fervently. One by one they were pushed down or tossed aside. She caught sight of one man being pulled by his ear.

"Let the lady out." She recognized the gravelly voice of the Dark Horse. Finally he stood next to her open door and reached down for her. She forgot about being scared, just took his hand as a lifeline in the sea shouting and pushing. He pulled her out of the car and put his arm around her waist, using his free arm to shove and make room. Cobby made his way to them, then they fell in behind him. The Dark Horse kept a tight hold on her as they made their way up the stairs. Cameras flashed in her face and questions were thrown at her as the throng slowly moved along. She reached across herself with her left hand and took hold of his lapel. The questions they asked were personal, devastating, and should have been private knowledge. She began to realize the scandal she had become.

As bright flash went off that temporarily blinded her, she turned her face into the Dark Horse's shoulder. He covered her face with his hand as they moved up the last few steps to the entrance. Cobby was literally throwing anyone who got in the way. At the door several men came out to help them in, and as they passed through, the shouting stopped. The Dark Horse kept hold of her until they reached the bar area. She stood with her arms folded across her chest. She felt as if she had been violated in some way.

"What the hell was that?" Cobby exasperatedly asked.

Marie just softly chuckled without much changing in her look. "Show business, I think."

She looked up into the cold eyes of the Dark Horse who stood watching her, expressionless.

"Thank you," she whispered softly. "I wasn't expecting that."

"Bring her in the alley entrance from now on." With that he buttoned his suit jacket as he walked toward the private stage.

"Come on. I'll take you back to the dressing room." Cobby moved off without waiting to see if she'd follow.

The backstage area resembled the street. Men and women alike were rushing around, some already in full costume, others still tying bowties, or searching for tuxedo jackets. The dance company was crammed in the women's dressing room preparing. A few of the girls still wandered in bathrobes. The rest of the crew was busy moving costume racks while the lighting and sound crew ran checks.

Marie inhaled deeply and her heart stopped racing and fell into a steady beat. Her lips formed her usual show stopping smile. It was here that she was in her element, where she could leave the realities of her life and become someone else. She thrived in this environment.

"Ah, you made it. That was the most awful mess of people I ever had to wade through." Rolly came up to her grinning. "You know, they asked me if we are lovers. Kinda made my day." He winked at her and sauntered on.

Cobby took her up to a door on the right and stood next to the single step leading in. "This is it. Break a leg, or whatever you crazy assholes say to each other."

"Thanks," she replied flatly.

The dressing room was large. There were girls in various state of dress moving about or sitting at vanity tables that ran along the left wall. On the brick wall to the right were rows of clothes hangers that held covered costumes. She could see she had her own dress rack as her name was above it. She would have more gowns than everyone else. It was a perk of being lead. Straight to the back was a row of individual dressing stalls, one of these also had her name above it.

"Evening girls!" she called.

"Hey, Marie!"

"Evening!"

She went to her dress rack. Twelve dresses hung there waiting, and she knew this would only be the beginning. It was customary in a large production like this to change gowns several times in a show. Depending on the song there may be a particular outfit to be worn. But she knew which gown was first. She took it to her private dressing room. She hung it then closed the door.

She had avoided bathing that morning simply for the fact that it would be easier to get her hair to do what she wanted. Her private vanity was well stocked. Imelda saw to that after Marie gave her a list of things she'd need. It helped she didn't ever have to ask Mickey for these things.

She quickly took off her clothes and put on the corset, then the slip over that. It was a low cut slip in front. She unrolled her hose up her legs and then grabbed a thin pink robe that hung on the back of the dressing room door next to her gown. She left to go to her vanity. She didn't worry that the door hung open to the backstage area. She had learned long ago that there wasn't much modesty in places like these.

"I'm about done Marie. You want help?" Helen asked.

"Yeah. Let me get my make-up done while you finish. Thanks, Helen."

Marie opened the drawer on the left to find brushes, combs, and hair pins. In the drawer below that she found lovely decorative hair pieces. In the top drawer on her right she found her make-up. She set to putting on her foundation.

When she had finished her make-up, she took a brush to her long black hair. "You want an iron?" Paula, a small blonde girl asked.

"Yes. I need to smooth it down." This took some time as Marie had such long hair. When she finished, she combed a wave in front by her face and pinned it securely.

"Are you gonna roll it up?"

"Uhm. Will you help me pin it?"

"Sure. You have such beautiful hair, Marie." Marie smiled in return. Then Marie rolled it tightly while Helen pinned it in places as she went. When they had finished, Helen brought Marie a large white rose from the vase on the table in the center of the room.

"This will contrast beautifully." Helen carefully tucked it into the roll just behind Marie's left ear. Then it too was pinned. Helen smiled down at her.

"Ten minutes!" A loud bellow came from the doorway. Marie turned to see a short middle aged man she recognized as the stage master. He controlled show time, lighting, and anything else to do with behind the scenes.

Marie went back to her dressing room and slipped out of her robe. She could hear the girls outside doing the same as some became frantic to complete their dressing. She took the gown from its cover. She unzipped the back and carefully stepped in. The silk was smooth on her skin.

"Shoes and gloves?" Paula asked as she zipped Marie's gown. She nodded. She put the open toed dark green heels on, then slipped her hands into the elbow length white gloves. She moved to the full length mirror.

"Helen, will you see what jewelry I've got?"

Marie looked at herself admitting she'd never worn a gown like it back in New York. It was a dark green floor length number, a deep cut v in front that flowed down to accentuate her hips with a tight skirt. It remained tight down her legs until it reached mid-calf when it flared out into a flower that covered her feet and brushed the floor. The shoulder straps were wide, but when Helen put a diamond necklace at Marie's throat, it touched off well. She also had small diamond earrings.

"Four minutes, let's go ladies!" The voice was getting more belligerent. The band began filing past to take places, as did the three back-up singers. Soon Marie was alone. She waited till the crowd had passed then stepped out.

"Good luck, Miss Marie." Stephen smiled his shy smile as he looked back at her appreciatively.

"You too, Stephen."

Rolly came to stand next to her looking impossibly tall in his black tuxedo.

"Well, this is it. May I escort you?" Marie smiled through deep red lips and placed her hand through his elbow.

"Would it make you too nervous if I told you that I think you are exquisite?" He looked down at her as he spoke.

"No. I would appreciate the complement from such a dashing gentleman." He smiled.

Rolly squeezed her hand with his as they passed through the door and onto the dark stage. She could hear the muffled shuffling as the orchestra was still getting seated. Rolly guided her carefully to the left side of the stage where her microphone stood. He softly kissed her cheek then whispered good luck. He left her to stand behind his microphone in front of the band. His job was two-fold. While the band played mostly without a conductor, Rolly at times filled that position too. They were his band. All the long hours of practice was what made it possible for them to carry on without his actual conducting.

Marie took a deep breath while listening to the sound of the crowd behind the huge red curtain. It seemed odd to hear voices where before there was only the echo of musicians. This was it. It was real. She focused on the task at hand and said a prayer once again that this night would go well. They were ready, that she felt sure, but that didn't change circumstance.

The curtain made a soft swishing sound as it moved past just a few feet in front of her. The cavernous room was dark except for the lighting on the stairs and the candles on the table tops. The room was full and then some. She could see people lining the balcony as they watched in anticipation. Against her better judgement she cast a glance to Mickey's private seating area. There too, people lined the balcony and steps that reached down to the dance floor. She swallowed hard.

Once the music started she would be able to lose herself in it forgetting about the private stage and its occupants. For the moment, it loomed in the blackness like a ghost ship sailing straight for her.

"Ladies and gentlemen, welcome to the grand opening of the entertainment spectacular of Mr. Mickey Delano, The Ruby!" The loud voice boomed over the speaker system throughout the building. Excited voices quieted as a hush came over the room. Movement stopped. Marie could see the minute reflections of light off the instruments as the band moved them to position and held them there, waiting to begin.

"And now, we would like to introduce Mr. Rolly Howard and The Howard Orchestra!" A sudden blinding light flashed as the spotlight burst onto Rolly. He stood smiling and never flinched despite the feeling of temporary blindness Marie knew he was going through. Her turn was coming.

"Good evening ladies and gentlemen and welcome to The Ruby!" Rolly hollered into the microphone. The crowd clapped and cheered. He paused only a moment waiting for them to subside. "I am pleased to introduce to you the delightful Miss Marie Barelli!" He extended his arm her way. Her heart had only begun to hammer as she too was immediately bathed in white light. On her face she was already wearing an enchanting smile as she leaned slightly forward and spoke into the microphone.

"Good evening, Mr. Howard." He exaggerated a wink in her direction and turned to the band and with a single flick of his finger had the sax section playing. Rolly turned to Marie and spoke again.

"My, aren't you enchanting." He drawled out. Her face exploded into a mischievous grin.

"Why, thank you, Mr. Howard." She replied in a deep and sultry voice. A few whistles sounded to her left.

Rolly began the song. It was Duke Ellington's *I'm Beginning to See the Light.* His voice was strong and deep as the words to the playful song rolled off his tongue like a man who had lived the lyrics. The rest of the band joined in with the saxes as Marie took over the second verse. When she had completed her verse, Marie looked to Rolly, and again his strong voice rang out steady and true.

Another spotlight lit on the band as they played behind Rolly and Marie. They met in the middle of the stage, the beams of their spotlights blending together as they danced a few steps. Rolly danced her back to her position then had to run to make it to his microphone in time. This round he put more emphasis in his singing as he placed a hand over his heart. Marie also put more emotion in to it, lingering on the words. Her mind drifted and she was lost in the music.

Marie couldn't help but grin at Rolly who gave her a broad smile in return as the band slowed to the end of the tune. But, Rolly wasted no time between songs, and after a brief pause he again motioned them to begin the next song.

"Ahh, New York, eat your heart out!" Rolly yelled just before his voice rang out again in Charles Trenet and Jack Lawrence's *Somewhere Beyond the Sea.*

Marie stood swaying in time to the music behind her microphone. To her, it was just herself, Rolly, and the band. A smaller spotlight had come on and bathed the three back-up singers in a soft blue light. Little blue beams reflected off the sequins that covered the black dresses they wore. For this number, Marie joined them. She walked to them and they happily made room for her. Marie put her arm around Helen. Marie was supposed to stay at her microphone, but she didn't work that way. She went wherever the fun was.

As the band moved into an instrumental version of the song, Marie left the back-up singers moving across the stage then down the steps to the dance floor. It was hard to see much with the brilliant light around her and the dark beyond, but she moved elegantly with confidence. She moved across the dance floor, headed to a small table. A young man sat watching her approach. When she held out her hand to him he readily stood and took it, taking her into his arms for a waltz. She was lucky he was good. He was handsome, just a little bit taller than she, but he smiled at her as they moved. Rolly came down and did the same, however, he wasn't so lucky in his pick. She was a heavy set woman and she took hold of him like he was real estate to be jumped. But, he played it off well. Marie paired her partner off with someone else then chose another. The band went through the song several times while Marie and Rolly filled the floor. They met in the middle and danced a moment, then headed back to the stage.

As the band ended *Beyond the Sea* and moved into Sy Oliver's *Opus One*, Rolly looked at Marie and spoke into his microphone.

"Oh, sweet Marie, will you marry me?"

"I'd love to Mr. Howard, but I'm already marrying a man from over there later on tonight." She pointed to the left.

"Ah yeah? What's his name?"

She pressed an index finger to her chin. "I don't know." Her voice turned devilish as she continued. "But he's got a fat wallet. It gave him a limp the whole time we danced!"

"Ha ha ha!" Rolly laughed into the microphone. "You know, I gotta big fat wallet." He looked slyly at her.

"Yeah, but yours is full of cocktail napkins!" Marie sarcastically replied.

Rolly looked out to the audience. "Uh oh. She's on to me." He paused a moment for the crowds response of laughter and cheering. "Well anyway, I think that lady over there is gonna abduct me later tonight!" He pointed with his head in the direction of his robust dance partner. Marie winked at him.

"Have fun big guy." The spot light went out on them and reappeared on the dance floor over the dance company. Rolly took Marie's hand and they moved down to wait their turn on the floor. The dance company was to go first, then Rolly and Marie would do a solo dance amidst them. After they had done so, Rolly would perform a solo number, then Marie would as well.

When Rolly sang his solo, Marie hurried back stage to her dressing room. She changed out of her dark green dress in to a silver sequined strapless. It followed the contours of her body and the right side had a slit clear up to her upper thigh. It was striking in contrast to her dark hair. She kept her white gloves and changed to backless open toed silver heels. She also left the rose in her hair.

She moved down to the lower stage and waited for Rolly to finish, happy that her costume change hadn't taken long. She had stopped to look in the mirror, just to make sure all was well. Something she learned never to forget to do.

The band finished and fell silent. This was Marie's cue to allow them a short break before continuing. As the spotlight flooded her and the light refracted off her sequins, she looked out beyond her beam to find faces among the crowd.

"I would like to sing a little something for all the lovers out there. You might recognize this as one of the great Jo Stafford's songs, and I know I won't do her justice, but I hope she'll allow my try. Can we get lights on the floor?" The soft golden glow of the dance floor lights lit a romantic ambiance. "You're a wonderful crowd. You put New York to shame." She smiled softly as the first notes of Stephan's muted trumpet began. She closed her eyes listening as the sounds of Hugh's unmuted trumpet joined Stephan. Marie's velvet sound started low and climbed in volume as she flowed with the verses of *I Never Loved Anyone*. Marie deeply loved this song, and in particular Jo Stafford's version.

Couples began filling the dance floor and Marie looked out among them. It was a soft and sensual song that brought out the feeling among lovers that can only be known between two people who feel the same.

Marie's eyes fell on the tall lean form of the Dark Horse as he moved out onto the floor with a woman on his arm. He was dressed in a well-tailored tuxedo, the white of his shirt gleaming in the soft light. The woman he escorted was breath taking. She was tall and well matched to his size, her golden blonde hair pulled back from her face of fine features. Her breasts brushed against the planes of his chest as they moved together to dance.

Her golden colored gown accented her hair and Marie recognized Imelda's work. The woman's hand slid up onto his broad shoulders while her fingers played with the back of his neck. Her lips brushed against his ear. They moved together as one, and as his back turned to Marie, the lights caught and reflected off the huge diamond on her left hand. His hand slid lower to just above her hip as she caressed his neck again with her fingers. The closeness and raw desire was evident between the two lovers. The Dark Horse was a married man. Somehow this shocked Marie.

As they again spun, he was facing Marie. He looked up to meet her gaze and she smiled softly. She looked away to the rest of the crowd. She found Imelda among the crowd, dancing with a handsome gentleman.

Mickey was there as well. He was dancing with who Marie could only assume was his wife. She was a tall thin woman, but she wasn't the most beautiful on the floor. Her nose was long and pointed; nothing in her look spoke of any kindness. Her jet black hair was pulled severely from her face into a bun, and she wore a long black sequined strapless. A matching wrap hung loosely from her elbows. They danced stiff and awkward. Mickey looking tense as he glanced about the room. He would smile and nod when he was spoken to, but he never seemed to lighten.

Marie kept her eye out for anyone who could be one of Vinny's guys, but the crowd was so thick, she knew they would blend if they were there. She felt sure they weren't. It was just something in her heart that knew. He was gone from her life, as surely she was gone from his. She was completely alone in the world.

The night went on. When the dance floor wasn't being used for a dance number it was packed with couples. Time seemed to stop while the music played making Marie forget where and who she was. She was no longer concerned with Mickey and what would happen when the curtain closed. Her aching heart lost focus on Alex's face. In his place she kept her mind on Rolly, who was her guide through the evening.

The band was incredible, playing nearly non-stop for almost five hours. They kept up in great time and perfect rhythm. Marie performed far beyond what she ever had in New York, and if she had to admit it, the club was better than anything she had sung in New York as well. It was easy to sing for her life. It was natural to her to go out in front of the crowd and give everything she had.

For their final number, Rolly and Marie sang *Mambo Italiano,* written by Bob Merrill. They stood together before the microphone wishing everyone a good night and thanked them for coming.

"You know Marie, I think LA is gonna like you." He moved away from the microphone to look at Marie.

"Well, what can I say, Mickey Delano sure knows how to make a dream come true."

"I know mine came true tonight when I got to sing with you." Rolly smiled.

"Then I guess Mickey knows more than we give him credit for."

"Ladies and gentlemen thank you and good night!" Rolly shouted into the microphone just before the deafening roar of praise began. They waved to the crowd then the spotlights went out and the curtain closed.

Marie's legs ached.

Rolly offered his arm and she gladly took it. She was exhausted, something she hadn't realized until the stage went black. But she was happy. He took her back to the dressing room where they could still hear the audience talking and laughing as they made their way out.

"That was incredible tonight. Way to go, Marie."

"You weren't so bad yourself." Marie replied as she smiled at him. Rolly winked at her before he walked away to his own dressing room.

Excited voices filled the dressing room as the girls congratulated each other. Emotions ran high with adrenaline and excitement.

"That crowd was absolutely intoxicating." Paula stated.

"I'll tell you who is intoxicating. Rolly!" another named Jean interjected. Marie laughed with the others.

"I couldn't control myself when that fat broad got a hold of him and nearly pinched his bum off." Helen chuckled.

"He was nearly a goner wasn't he?" Marie laughed. "I thought to myself- how am I gonna help him without starting a fight?"

"She was so much bigger than you. "

"She woulda ate you." Kate said through the cigarette in her lips. Kate was a tall brunette that danced with the company. This comment caused an eruption of laughter.

Marie laughed as well while Helen unzipped her dress. "You girls looked marvelous tonight. All of you."

"Is Rolly married?" Jean asked. Several of the girls looked at each other, not sure of the answer.

"Uh, yeah, I think he is." Helen replied uncertainly.

"He doesn't wear a ring." Jean said.

The stage masters voice shouted through the door. "Mr. Delano wants the entire company up front in the bar as soon as possible!"

The girls all looked at each other.

"One of the waiters said Mr. Delano wanted to throw an after party for us if the night went well." A shy little blonde named Mindy stated.

"I'll drink free booze." Everyone giggled at Kate.

In groups of three and fours the girls left the dressing room, eager to see what Mickey had in mind. It took Marie awhile to get her costume off and put away. Truth be told she enjoyed a moment to collect her thoughts. She didn't want to face him yet.

Music started up over the sound system and Marie could hear the excited laughter of the company. She could also hear applause. Marie sat before her vanity to look at herself. Except for her make-up and hair, she looked ordinary again. She took a deep breath.

She walked quietly out of the dressing room to an empty backstage area, then crossed through the stage door. The stage lights were on, but it was also empty. The curtain had been opened and she could see the company up near the bar celebrating. Music played loudly and the two separate sounds competed with each other. It took Marie some time to walk across the vast space, but as she walked up the steps to the bar area, Rolly, who had been waiting, yelled, "Ah, here she is!"

Everyone turned and began to cheer for her, many of the boys whistling. A blush came to her cheeks as she stood listening to their applause. She smiled and bowed her head. She then moved forward to stand by Rolly, placing her hands over her heart. She kept repeating, "Thank you," but they kept up the applause.

She raised her hands to stop everyone. "Thank you. Thanks." She reached out to Rolly taking his hand. She smiled up at him and his eyes twinkled. She bowed her head to him, then moved to the man next to Rolly doing the same. She made her way through the company, congratulating and thanking. When she reached David, the trumpeter, he swiftly took her in his arms, kissing her firmly on the lips. This caused a riot among the company as whistling and shouting broke out. He held her trapped a long moment before letting her go.

"You're still the most beautiful woman I've ever seen." Struck speechless, Marie raised an eyebrow and shook her head. Laughter followed this. David leaned back on the bar staring triumphantly down at her. She moved on to Stephan who couldn't stop laughing at her astonished look.

"Where did we get that guy?" She asked to no one in particular.

"Ah, I bet he ain't so cocky without his pants on." Rolly yelled over the crowd. Marie burst out laughing at this. David looked a little red in the face.

"How's the little mama, Stephen?" Marie asked softly.

"Good. She's here tonight, Miss Marie." Marie became excited.

"Where?"

"Over there. She don't like for people to see her right now. But she's prettier than she's ever been to me." He pointed to a booth along the wall. A pretty little woman sat in a bulky maternity dress out of sight. Marie waved to her. She shyly waved back. "That's my Mae." He spoke with pride. "Mr. Delano let spouses come for the after party."

"I'd like to meet her." He nodded his head. Applause interrupted them and they both turned to see what was causing the fuss.

They came up the steps from the private stage area like a dark mass moving together as one. It made Marie's heart stop to see them. She knew the gig was up. It was the whole of Mickey's entourage, their women included. Such elegance accompanied them in their finery it was something to watch. Mickey had pasted on his kind smile, and in truth, Marie could see excitement behind it tonight. His hands were steady.

Marie stood at the back of the group near the bar. She cast an uneasy glance at Rolly who stood looking at her. He offered a weak smile, but he knew, too. As Mickey came to stand in front of the crowd everyone fell silent. He put his hands in his pockets while looking around the room. His wife stood triumphantly next to him, her chin up, clearly declaring territory.

No one had to be told that this was a defining moment for Marie. The rumors had run like water over rocks since she had come so unexpectedly. After she had been treated rather harshly throughout the weeks of rehearsal, everyone knew that Marie and Mickey were not lovers. At least not any longer if they had been. Slowly the group parted, leaving a clear path to Marie, who stood single in the midst of her peers.

Mickey's dark eyes found her, and she waited expectantly for what he would do, or say. She could see Cobby behind him, The Dark Horse with his wife, and countless others staring at her while she waited for the outcome. Mickey looked down his nose at her. She bowed her head slightly in response. His face cracked a firm half grin. He tossed his wife's hand off his arm then started towards Marie. Her heart pounded. Harry James' *You Made Me Love You* began to play over the sound system. He came to stand before her and did so for a moment without speaking. Her palms began to sweat. No one made a sound as they watched him progress.

Slowly he reached out and took hold of her hand. With gentleness he brought it to his lips. He bowed slightly as he kissed her fingers. He kept his eyes on hers, but she could not decipher the look in them. It ranged between amusement and violence. He then bowed to her graciously smiling a wicked smile. She sucked in air.

"That was spectacular tonight! I want to thank everyone for a great performance! Please, stay and enjoy yourselves. The drinks are on me!" The company all cheered as he turned and walked back to his wife. Mickey and his entourage took up the tables surrounding the bar area. Drinks were served. Laughter rang out as the night was rehashed.

Rolly came to stand beside Marie and he squeezed her arm. He gave her a reassuring wink.

"Dance with me."

"If you think that's prudent." She smiled at him challengingly.

The sound system quieted for a moment, then Billy Holliday's *Don't Get Around Much Anymore* came over loud and clear. Marie laughed as she began to sing out loud with the record. Rolly joined her singing as they danced a few lazy steps together before Marie turned to include several girls at the bar. Before long the whole ensemble was singing, as well as a few in Mickey's crowd. Marie stepped off to dance with David, who was singing obnoxiously.

Marie moved on from David to lay her back against the cellist's for a moment as they danced, back to back. She closed her eyes not seeing anything but the color of the music in her mind. Marie felt lost in the crowd, but yet without realizing it, was the center. Mack, one of the trombone players took Marie for a deep dip, then picked her up and spun her around. It was an exaggeration at work, the end of a well-strategized game.

*****

Mickey sat turning his tumbler on the bar top slowly, watching the ring of moisture move with the glass. The club was finally quiet. Everyone had gone home to get some rest before rehearsal in just a few short hours. He wore a satisfied half-smile on his face. He turned and looked out across the expanse to the stage area feeling like the world was his. At least the material part, anyway.

"She was good."

Val answered by raising his tumbler to his lips. He sat leaning against the bar, his jacket off, his bow tie loose about his neck.

"Do you think.." Mickey stopped himself before he said anymore. "No. No, that's not possible." Mickey took a long swallow.

Val sighed before taking another drink himself.

"People don't live again."

"Maybe not the way we'd like them to," Val replied. He rested his drink on his leg.

"Well, anyway, she was good. Now you don't have to kill her," Mickey stated.

A shadow crossed Valant's face. "Not yet anyway."

*****

"Six egg omelet with diced ham and onions, chopped peppers and a side of bacon. Sausage links, too."

The voice cut into Marie's mind and brought her out of a rewarding sleep. Cobby crouched next to her, the scent of aftershave and bourbon clung to him like a vine.

"And coffee. Lots of it. Maybe a Danish or three. You know, since I've had to cart your skinny ass around I don't get to eat breakfast?" He paused a moment. "I don't miss breakfast. If I eat nothing else all day, I eat breakfast. I don't even get lunch when you're around." He reached over and smacked her on the butt hard.

"Get up sugar tits. Delano cleared you for breakfast. Who knows, you keep it up and you might even get lunch one of these days." Marie glared up at him as she rubbed her bum.

"You know, you should at least use a pillow." He stood. "I think you were sleeping so hard even Deano coulda snuck up on you. And for shitsakes you can smell that kinda ugly three blocks away. Sleeping in the corner ain't gonna help you if you sleep that hard."

Marie rubbed the exhaustion out of her eyes.

"Hurry up. Mickey wants to see you after you eat."

*****

Mickey sat behind his massive desk alone. Cobby closed the door leaving the two of them in silence. Mickey didn't stand when she approached, just watched her with a still expression on his face. She walked warily to him then stopped in front of his desk. She did not sit without being invited.

"Good morning, Mickey, thank you for the wonderful breakfast," Marie spoke softly as to not disturb the solitude he was obviously enjoying.

"Sit, Marie." She did so, but remained on the edge of her chair. She noticed a stack of newspapers on his desk.

"That was very good last night. Very good. I feel compelled to tell you that I am impressed." He kept his hands from view, almost as if he knew she could read his mood by them.

"Yes, it was." For some reason her father's face flashed in her mind. He was contorted with anger. She licked her lips.

Mickey reached forward and handed her a newspaper. She took it and unfolded it to look at the picture on the front page of the society news. It was her picture, but it was difficult to tell since The Dark Horse's hand covered her face. Her lips stretched into a thin line.

"Not impressive," she whispered.

"Not really. One, you look like you were being escorted to a courtroom, and two, because Valant made the papers." He leaned forward to rest his elbows on his desk. He suddenly looked bigger.

"Anonymity is difficult to maintain in the papers. But, after that picture and the adjoining headline, I'm guessing curiosity will no doubt get the best of everyone. It will work if it packs the house." Marie looked above the picture to read the headline.

Delano's Lover? Or His Prisoner?

Marie exhaled slowly.

"Don't worry. The rest of the papers chose to print pictures of you singing. And even the reviews in that paper were raving."

"I'm sorry your wife had to see this."

He shrugged. "She likes to take advantage of the dramatic." He settled his hands below the desk again. He studied her for a long time.

"You aren't what I expected. All this time I've waited for the Jerry Barelli to burst forth from you, but you keep me waiting." Marie again licked her lips while entwining her hands.

"It amazes me that you have such incredible talent, and the charm to go with it. Someone had to teach you that." He finally stretched his hand along the desk and she watched it tremble.

"How do you know Vinny Vinnetti?" It wasn't a question of if she did, he knew already that she did. He wanted to know the depth.

"He owned the club my father ran over six years ago."

"The club you sang at?"

"Yes. I was nineteen."

"Did you meet him?"

Marie nodded her head. "Yes, he came a few times and listened. Not just to me but the whole band. I suppose he felt that as an investment he would like to see it in action."

"Did you speak to him?"

"Yes. Never more than polite conversation, but, he did take time to acknowledge me." She looked him in the eye, but tried not to act too bold or he would know she was leaving drastic information out of it.

"So how'd you get to New York?" It was time for the truth, for she felt he probably already knew how she got to New York.

"Vinnetti sent me," she whispered. His hand balled into a fist. He nodded.

"Why?"

She shrugged her shoulders. "Maybe he felt sorry for me, maybe he thought I had talent worth conditioning. Or maybe he had something like what is splashed on the cover of that newspaper in mind. I don't know. He offered the opportunity, and being nineteen I took it, not thinking there could be more to it." She again shrugged. "In all the time I was in New York, I never heard from him or anyone else, including my own family. To me, I had made my break, I never intended to come back here."

She waited a moment before continuing. She looked down at her hands. "When I got back here, no one told me anything. I was very surprised to learn that the club no longer belonged to Vinnetti." She was careful not to refer to him as Vinny. Mickey's eyes bore into her.

"Does he have children?" She looked up in surprise.

"Well, none with his wife. But, that doesn't mean he doesn't have some somewhere else."

"Are there rumors?"

"I heard once that a young man that was always with Vantino was actually Vinnetti's. But, I never heard if that rumor was true or not. They certainly don't look alike. But, that really doesn't mean anything."

"What was his name?"

"Patrick, I believe. I don't know his last name." She looked at him steady on. He brought the fist to his mouth and sat with his index finger along his lower lip.

She felt shame for having sold Patrick away, but she felt sure that Mickey would no doubt quickly discover that Patrick was Vinny's nephew. His sister's boy. Patrick was old enough to look out for himself. Plus, he was not in Delano's possession. She was.

"Well, you better be on your way. Can't miss rehearsal." She stood slowly and bid him farewell.

As she reached the door Cobby opened it.

"I hope you can keep this up, Marie. The performances, I mean." Marie turned to look at him.

"Oh, Mickey. We've only just begun." With that she left.
*****

Valant looked up and down the darkened street, but nothing caught his eye. He stood in a circle with Cobby on his right, Deano on his left and three others surrounding the car. The snores that drifted from inside were faint, but the dead silence around him made them audible.

"Wake him up."

Deano opened the back door and grabbed the man by the collar then drug him out. He threw him down on the pavement before kicking him in the stomach. The man named Pacheko coughed and sputtered to life. He rolled around smashing his face into the hard, cold pavement.

"You Pacheko?" Valant asked.

"Who asks?"

"Me." Valant tipped his head and looked down at the man who was now trying to stand. Recognition dawned and a look of horror came across his features.

"What do you want?" He slurred his words from obvious drunkenness. His breath reeked of booze.

"I want to know who you work for." The circle came in to tighten around the man.

It had taken serious inquiries to locate this man. They had spent the evening tracking him from dive to dive till they saw his car parked on the street. It was down by the docks amidst the chain linked yards of an industrial division.

"I can't tell you that. I don't know who he is."

"How can you not know who he is?" Valant asked caustically.

"He uses couriers to do all his work. Uses 'em once, then they're done. I get messages in an envelope with cash. I do what they say and I keep getting' paid. That's all I know."

"How'd you get mixed up with them?"

"My cousin is a courier, he got me on to it." Valant slowly lit a cigarette.

"That doesn't tell me anymore than I already know."

The man shook his head. "What do you need to know?"

"Who was the man with the x on his head? What was his purpose?"

"They had him getting' some information about Vinnetti. Rumor has it he was training a replacement. Ya know, somebody to take over for him. Mr. X still had a few connections in Vinnetti's network. That was what he was gettin'." Pacheko held his hands palms up in front of his chest.

"Did he get it?"

Pacheko shrugged his shoulders.

"Why is that so important?"

"They're coming for him. Vinnetti."

"Who?"

"Can't say." Pacheko said firmly.

Valant shook his head. "Put him in his car."

It took three of them to get him back into his car, Pacheko kicking and yelling the entire time. A police patrol car came down the street about that time. Pacheko started calling out for them. As the car approached, Valant looked at the man in the passenger seat and waved them on. They did so without returning.

"Gas." Martin moved along to the back of the car they had arrived in and opened the trunk. He pulled out a gas can then brought it back. He dumped it all on the ground around and on the car. Valant came to stand next to the window where Pacheko sat struggling.

He was breathing heavy with sweat running down his face.

"Who wants to know?" Valant again asked.

"They call themselves The Underground. That's all I know about them. They don't talk to me directly," he panted out. "They aren't from here. They don't base here. I've never talked to them. They use couriers!" His voice was becoming high pitched and frantic.

"What couriers?"

"Random guys off the street! Guys they can silence when they need to!" Again Valant tilted his head.

"Like you?" The man said nothing just nodded his head as the realization hit him. He wasn't above it.

"Give me a name."

"I haven't got any!"

Valant took a drag off his cigarette then held it between his thumb and index finger where Pacheko could see it. "A name."

"I haven't got any!" Pacheko emphasized each word.

"Give me a place."

"Docks down in Vinnetti's turf!"

This took Val where he had already been. He wanted something new. "Which building?"

Pacheko shook his head. "No building. No building! Just an old fishing boat. But it's gone now. Disappeared last week."

"Give me a name."

"I got no names!" He screamed.

"Then we're done here." Valant dropped his cigarette.

*****

August 1939

He saw her long before she ever noticed him. He had watched her, his eyes drifting up and down the length of her as she moved about the party. He'd been loath to come, but now that he was here he was not so put out. Mickey and Maryanne were always dragging him someplace, attempting to bring him out into society.

He knew little about her. When he'd seen her standing by the refreshment table he asked Mickey who she was. Mickey replied that she was the daughter of their host. Their host happened to be none other than Edgar Muller, who owned the majority of the Los Angeles Bank and Trust as well as various other holdings that put him at the front of the pack. He was willing to work with Mickey's father, Georgio, to further his position within the city. To Val's way of thinking, this didn't bolster his intelligence level, just his position.

When he finally got up the nerve to go and meet her, he drifted out into the yard and under the shade tent close to where she was standing visiting with a group of girls. She was by far the most beautiful girl he had ever seen, with her honey blonde hair rolled neatly at the base of her slender neck. Her white dress had purple flowers on it, and while not beyond the limits of what was considered proper, it gave the right amount of accentuation to her lovely figure. She was sensual in her behavior, the way she finally caught her eye. She only took long stolen glances at him from the corner of her dark lashes. Her skin was creamy and smooth, her soft bell-like laughter floated softly on the breeze to him. He was smitten.

Once she knew she'd captured him, she made him work for it. She carried on a gay conversation with her friends all the while he looked over the refreshment table, waiting for a polite opening with which to make his move. When a young man approached the group, she laughed even deeper while making a habit of repeatedly putting her hand at various places on his arm and shoulder. Val wasn't one to be hopelessly reeled in by a woman, so at length he turned and left. He went back to the table where Mickey and Maryanne sat only to be scoffed at.

"Go for someone else. She's a horrible tease." Was Maryanne's advice. But, having seen her, Val felt helpless to even register his own name, let alone meet someone besides her.

He had not gone unnoticed though, and the young blonde kept her eye on him for the remainder of the afternoon. She kept drifting ever closer to where he sat, tempting him, not allowing him to forget about her. Finally, as guests began to leave the garden party, she made her way to Maryanne. She tried to appear like an old friend, but in truth neither of them had ever really cared for the other.

"Hello, Maryanne. How have you been?" They spoke politely for a moment before Maryanne turned to introduce her to the rest of the small table.

"Mickey, I'd like you to meet a friend of mine. This is Margo Muller. Margo this is my fiancé, Mickey Delano."

"Fiancé! Well congratulations! How wonderful!"

"Thank you. And this young man over here is Mickey's best friend, Val." Maryanne shot him a sly smile. He ignored her and stood to gently take hold of Margo's hand.

"Pleased to meet you, Margo." He held her look for several moments before Mickey cut in.

"Would you like to sit down?"

"Oh, I wouldn't want to intrude." She smiled uncertainly.

"It's no intrusion." Val was quick to pull out a chair for her.

"Alright, thank you." She gave him a blinding smile and he wondered what happened to the ground he had been standing on. It seemed to have fallen away. He sat down beside her. Mickey chortled.

"This is such a lovely party." Maryanne tried to open up a conversation since Val seemed at a loss for words.

"Yes. Mother is so good at planning these events. Of course it helps that we have such a large lawn." With that she gazed into Val's eyes and her words seemed to drift off.

Mickey grinned and tried not to laugh. Maryanne cast a warning glance at Val who didn't notice. He didn't have enough experience with society girls to realize each move they made was with calculated intent. Margo was neither innocent nor sweet. Maryanne shook her head at Mickey who just shrugged his shoulders.

"How long have you and Mickey been friends? I mean, I haven't ever seen you around before." Margo smiled at Val.

"That's because he hates to be anywhere people might see him, and his manners follow that of a dog at the dinner table."

Mickey interjected. Val shot him a look of painful death. Maryanne jabbed him in the ribs.

"Oh, I doubt that." Margo eyed Val innocently. "You might be rough around the edges, but you are quite the gentleman." The corner of Val's mouth twitched.

She turned to Maryanne. "Have you enjoyed the summer?"

"Yes. It's been busy, what with wedding plans and all. But, yes, we have enjoyed it."

"I just got back from a trip to Virginia. Went to see some of Papa's family. It was nice to get home. What do you do, Val?" At the moment he couldn't remember.

"I work for Mickey's father. Help out with errands and things." He spoke low and quiet.

"Don't be so modest," Mickey cut in. "He is a very important man that seconds to Julian Delano."

Val shot him a warning glance.

"Oh, I see. Do you like what you do?" Margo slowly licked her lips.

Val's mouth stretched into a grim line. "Yes." He took a long sip of party punch. It tasted sour.

An awkward silence followed. Maryanne caught Val's eye and she tried to reassure him with a smile. She knew more about him than Mickey did only because she was far more observant.

"I don't suppose any of you would be interested in going for a swim? I know of a real nice beach we could enjoy alone." Margo had thrown Val a line and he wasn't sure he should take it. Maryanne chose for him.

"That sounds lovely. The guys can wear their under shorts, but I don't suppose I could borrow a suit?" Margo's face lit up.

"Oh, certainly. Between my things and my sister's, we should have something!" The girls stood and began to talk excitedly as they walked toward the three story brick house. Maryanne looked to Val and winked at him.

Maryanne hated spontaneity. She like things to flow in order. Which was what grounded Mickey who chose to fly by the seat of his pants. Val knew the price she was paying internally to give him this chance. Mickey did as well. He just sat grinning at Val.

"Quite a girl."

"That she is. That she is." Neither of them were referring to Margo.

*****

1955

Things began to roll along for Marie. After opening night the rehearsals and evening performances accelerated the passage of time to a point where memories became blurred some. She still kept her picture of Alex, but had found a place to hide it behind the bureau in the bedroom. She took it out and looked at it in the soft light of the night. She remembered his touch, his laugh, the way it sounded when he played his trumpet. She missed him dearly. A feeling of near panic would overwhelm her if she thought about him for very long. Thankfully for her, exhaustion took over most nights, and she was lost before too many memories flooded her mind. She wondered if he had ever come for her.

She spent time thinking of Vinny as well. She hoped that the answers she had given to Mickey were enough. He never questioned her again. She felt that she must have satisfied him somewhat. The question about Vinny's possible children had thrown her. What difference did that make? But, after consideration she realized it made all the difference. If Vinny actually had someone to replace him, his legacy lived on. If not, Mickey was in line to rule with no one to stop him. He was just volatile enough to make it happen. She prayed for Patrick.

She began to wonder who was in line to take over for Vinny. The Heart Vantino? No. He was only a few years younger than Vinny. He must've had some plan; she knew he would never give up an empire. But, she hadn't really been around the business side of things much, so he could have had a nephew he was quietly working on, it was none of her business anyway. He certainly wouldn't have told her about it.

The club was booming. Every night opened to a packed house. Mickey insisted that each week they open a new show. He had been pleased with her, that she knew. She went from two dresses to four, and she was allowed any meal she chose to eat, anytime she chose to eat it. But, she was still watched constantly. She was never alone.

Cobby came and went. Sometimes he reappeared in the early hours of the morning after a week long absence, only to disappear again a few days later. She never asked his business.

She really didn't want to know. He looked like he rarely slept, and often times he carried with him the scent of bourbon. He took great delight in teasing her at every opportunity. She sensed that it was his way of forgetting about whatever was on his mind. So, she took it good naturedly.

The club was open every night but Sunday. Those slow days passed painfully. If Cobby was around, he'd let her sit at the bar, maybe visit with her some, but the rest of the guys refused to allow her any luxuries. Not out of dislike for her, but respect for Mickey. On one occasion Mickey stopped by the apartment to meet up with a few of the guys. She had poured drinks, but for the most part her solitude away from the club was complete.

She ate her meals alone, never being a part of what was going on around her. Mickey kept a tight hold on her after the press incident. She entered the club through the back stage entrance and the one time they saw photographers in the alley, Cobby took a billy club to them. They had not returned. They were still allowed into the shows, so they must have decided that was enough. After the first several weeks, the rumors died down anyway. The scandal was replaced with her talents.

One Sunday morning Cobby took Marie to breakfast. He became engaged in conversation with The Dark Horse as well as Mickey, Deano, and another man they just called Frankie. They spoke low, but they visited for quite some time. It seemed they had forgotten her, but eventually Mickey stood up to go. Marie wished for a newspaper or magazine with which to pass the time, but, not having money of her own to purchase one, she went without.

Cobby came to her table to retrieve her, buttoning his suit jacket, looking troubled. "Come on." He had developed an unconscious habit of holding his hand above the small of her back as they walked together anywhere. She wasn't even sure if he was aware he was doing it, but for some reason it made him less formidable. Like he cared enough to treat her like a man treats a woman he respects.

As they passed through the door and out onto the street, Cobby turned to her. "Wait here a minute."

He turned and walked to The Dark Horse who was talking to Deano beside the building. Marie turned and went to the newspaper stand. She perused the headlines with her arms folded across her chest.

"Good morning."

"Good morning." Marie smiled at the man inside the stand.

She took several slow steps as she read each cover until she came to an entertainment magazine. She reached out and took hold of it, turning to the first page reading what was written. It featured various articles based on current singers and song writers. The writing held her entranced.

"Marie! Let's go," Cobby called somewhat impatiently. She looked up at him from her magazine and frowned. She glanced regretfully down at the wonderful distraction that would pass her long afternoon.

"Marie!" This time he shouted gruffly and yanked the car door open. He stood staring at her.

She pursed her lips and looked at him. He mouthed, *now,* at her. She put the magazine back on the rack.

"Thank you." The man behind the counter smiled at her.

She walked with her head down to the car and didn't look at Cobby as she slid into the back seat. He slammed the door hard in her face while she stared ahead looking disgruntled. He walked around the front of the car unbuttoning his suit jacket. He got in, slamming the door. As he did so, Marie's door was jerked open. Instantly her heart burst into rhythm as the thought of her slight insubordination shot through her mind. It was the first time she displayed any kind of desire to disobey. Her fear was further deepened to see The Dark Horse standing there glaring down at her.

She was too afraid to move. She just sat there staring wide eyed up at him waiting for him to jerk her from the car. He looked like a giant from her angle. He glowered down at her for a moment before thrusting something at her. She flinched slightly then looked down at what was in his hand.

The magazine.

She looked back up at him and the corner of his mouth was twitching, but the look in his cold eyes had not changed. She was unaware of what to do. He made no move, just waited for her to take it. Finally, unsure of what to say to him, she took it from his hand. As she looked up at him, he slammed the door and walked away. She sat frozen a moment before looking up at Cobby. He gazed at her in the mirror.

The look on Cobby's face was strange. He said nothing just shifted his eyes down as he cranked the engine and drove away.

Marie looked down at her treasure. She ran her hand over the smooth paper of the cover. A smile spread across her face as she pressed it to her heart. She opened it and began to read the first few pages. It didn't take long to reach the apartment. As soon as she could reach her corner, she spent time reading and rereading.

As time passed, she felt like she actually left her life and ventured out into the world for a moment. She relaxed a little, forgetting about the picture tucked away between the wood and the wall. She read the Weekly Top 10 Chart, singing to herself the ones that she knew, and wondered about the ones she didn't. She found familiar faces she performed with at The Diamond. She smiled to think she actually knew these talented performers. Rosemary Clooney. Bing Crosby. The fast growing talent, Bobby Darin. How she longed to sing with them again.

When the bedroom door opened it surprised her a bit. Cobby walked in holding a cigarette in his right hand, and reached down to her with his left hand.

"Escape with me." She arched a brow at him.

"Where?"

"Who cares? Just come with me for a while."

She thought a moment, then slowly reached up and took his hand. He pulled her up to him and grinned.

"I have long sensed a troublemaker in you." He held on to her hand as they passed through the apartment. It was hazy with smoke. Marie began to wonder what was on his mind. Something he intended to forget for a while. When they reached the street, he opened the front passenger door for her. She looked at him only a moment before sliding in. Cobby laughed as he shut the door, then winked at her as he slid in. He turned the engine and left black marks on the street next to the curb when he pulled away.

He took her down a street she had never been down before, to a building lit up with dim yellow lights and music. When he opened her door he didn't bother to button his jacket, but took hold of her hand like he needed the encouragement. They entered into a smoky haze not unlike the one Cobby had left at the apartment.

"Hey, Mack." Cobby gave a salute to the man behind the bar.

"Good to see you Cob."

It was a billiard hall. Lights hung above the tables, but beyond that there was semi darkness for the evening hour.

"Any trouble?" Cobby asked.

"No. Ain't seen no cops today." It was Sunday, and although this man ran a legitimate business, alcoholic establishments were not to be open that particular day of the week.

"Just gonna shoot some pool, have a few drinks."

"Yeah, ok, Cob. No problem." Mack watched Marie as he continued to wipe down a glass. He wasn't menacing, just curious.

Cobby chose a table way in the back, one away from everyone else. He told the waitress two bourbons without really looking at her. Marie noticed the way she looked at him longingly. Cobby didn't. He walked to the wall and retrieved two pool sticks handing one to Marie.

"How much do you know?"

She shrugged her shoulders. "Enough to play. You go first."

He nodded and removed the rack off the balls. He removed his jacket laying it on a stool. Marie took a seat on a stool next to his jacket. The waitress returned left their drinks on a high table next to Marie.

Cobby split the bunch and sank two on the break. "Five in the corner pocket." He sunk it without trouble. "Four in the side pocket." That shot was stopped by the bank.

Marie stood and looked at the table. Her red dress had a narrow skirt with a short split in the back. She wore open toed black heels that made it hard to make a shot. Cobby stood next to the drink table his pool cue in one hand, his drink in the other, watching her pick her shot.

"Eleven in the side pocket." She sunk it without trouble. "Fourteen in the side pocket." Again, it went down.

"Nine and thirteen in the corner pockets." Cobby raised a brow at her proposed shot. She hit the nine ball first, then sunk the thirteen as her ball flew across the table to hit it into the opposite corner pocket.

"Were'd you learn to play?"

"My brothers." She stated a lie. It was The Heart and Vinny who had spent long evening hours teaching her to play. Although she never could beat either of them, she was still good. Cobby said nothing, just downed his drink, waving for another.

Marie missed a shot and went to sit back on her bar stool then took another sip. Cobby stretched across the table to make a shot. He had undone the top two buttons on his white shirt and he looked like the bourbon was having the desired effect.

"You know, you look almost human when you're relaxed." He glanced up at her before making a shot. He missed.

"Should I take that as a compliment? Or understand that I look like shit as a regular basis?" Marie didn't look up at him as she eyed her possibilities. He downed half his glass in one swallow.

Marie gave a sigh then removed her shoes. With that restriction gone, she felt surer. "Ten and twelve in the corner pockets."

Cobby was watching her play with interest.

"You don't look like shit as a regular basis. You just look relaxed." She moved to the opposite side of the table. "There's something about a black suit that makes a man appealing."

Cobby stopped his arm as he raised his glass to his lips. "Marie, are you coming on to me?" He asked in a husky voice.

She smiled through red lips. "No. Simply stating a fact that any woman would agree to if she looked at you."

Cobby grinned and shook his head. "For some reason that means more coming from you."

Marie continued to run the table. Cobby waved for yet another as Marie racked them up again.

"Where do you come from?" Marie asked as she finished her task and picked up her cue again. Cobby didn't look at her as he spoke, just planned his shot.

"Docks on the south side. My Dad was a boat welder. Worked on those big iron beasts that float the ocean."

"I see. I thought I smelled fish." Cobby looked up at her sharply only to see her soft smile. He pressed his mouth into a thin line. She laughed. "Oh, Cobby. Why would I insult you? My father is Jerry Barelli."

He gave a slight nod to indicate he agreed with her point. They were quiet a moment as Marie took a drink.

"How long have you worked for Mickey?" Marie asked. Cobby shrugged as if he didn't remember.

"I guess it's been about thirteen years now. Since my Dad died." He said it in a low voice and she knew he would go no further. She sat quiet as he ordered another drink.

"What the hell is your story? How do you come from Jerry and end up Marie?" It was Marie's turn to shrug.

"Did your dad ever knock you around?" she asked in a small voice. When he looked at her surprised, her face was drawn, nothing like she had been just a moment before. He looked away and made a shot.

"No. But, Val was never afraid to set me right. Obviously, he doesn't have to do that anymore." Cobby's voice was bitter as he stretched out to make another shot. "That doesn't explain anything about you, you know. Alotta kids get knocked around and they don't turn out like you." He cast her a doubtful glance.

She laughed softly. "My dad used to knock me around until I couldn't stand. Luckily, a relative stepped in and helped me along."

"Who was you're relative, Bing Crosby?" She laughed out loud at this.

"No. Just a second cousin of my father's." This also wasn't true, but there was no possibility of explaining to Cobby she had spent a great deal of her childhood with the hated Vinny Vinnetti. They grew silent for a time.

"You know, the guys all had bets going; about how long it would take you to come slithering to Mickey's bed. Even Mickey." Marie didn't change as he said this. Cobby started into his fourth bourbon, and his game was starting to falter.

"Well, I don't blame them. I might've too, if I were one of you." She made a shot and stood to look at him. He was leaning on his pool cue watching her, a soft look in his eyes. She looked away.

"I'm glad you didn't. Slither to Mickey, that is." She looked back at him. "Something told me you weren't that kind the day you met the band."

She again looked away from him to make another shot.

"You don't show your real self very often. I see you every now and then at the club when you and Rolly get to laughing about something. When you really feel emotion over something said. Or like when Mickey tried to starve you down and you kept going anyway. Right now, when you don't have to perform to someone. I like Marie the singer, but I like who you are best when nobody's watching." He kept looking at her squarely as he spoke.

She took a long drink. "You've had too much to drink. It's loosened your tongue."

"If I didn't feel that way before the bourbon, you'd still be sitting in the corner of the bedroom." Something passed through her eyes, something close to fear, but yet not directed at him.

"Why do you sleep in the corner, Marie?" It was spoken quietly.

She looked down and away from him. "Just an old habit." She took a shot and missed entirely.

A song came on over the radio, Billie Holiday's *I'll Be Seeing You*. Marie moved over to Cobby who still stood leaning on his pool cue.

"Come on. Dance with me. Good music should never be wasted." He gave her a lazy half smile and took her hand. They moved out away from the table and she moved into his arms. She gave him a sly grin.

"Well, let's see what you've got." Marie was enlightened to the fact that although he never did so, Cobby could dance quite well. "Who taught you to dance?"

"Valant, when I was nineteen. He took me to a brothel. He paid one of the girls to partner with me till I got it right."

She raised an eyebrow. "Got what right?" Then she laughed at his scowl.

"Dancing you moron! Took me back four times. That poor girl had to work harder teaching me to dance than she did doing her regular job. But, Valant paid her well." He spun her, and after a while, they were joined on the floor by other patrons and the waitress, as she was the only other girl besides Marie.

It seemed they fit together naturally, the way they made each other smile with such ease. Cobby's eyes were full of a light that rarely showed itself. Marie was able to quit pretending and laugh whole heartedly at foolish jokes. Cobby never made those either. Despite the restraints of the situation, Cobby felt himself soften towards an illusion.

*****

1942

Valant sat at the table eating dinner. He'd been out all
evening making rounds to the card houses. He was glad just to
sit for a moment and eat, time would tell what his next
destination would be. Julian sat next to him drinking a glass of
water. He didn't look too good. Val had taken most of
everything over, Julian not really having the strength to do it
anymore.

"I'll take you home. It's late." Val said as he cut his meat.

"No. Won't do any good. I'll just sit there staring at the
wall."

"Well, I'll take you to Georgio's. You can stay there
tonight." Julian shook his head. Valant couldn't look at him
anymore. It was like watching Mount Everest fall away into the
ocean. It seemed it could never happen. Yet as the last of the
crags and rock slipped beneath the water incomprehension at
the reality of it took the place of disbelief. Valant couldn't
comprehend this.

Val began to cut into his steak when Mickey sat down
across from him. If Julian looked bad, Mickey looked worse.

"How's things?" Mickey wasn't anymore present these
days than Julian.

"Fine. I'll take you both to Georgio's. Just let me finish
eating." Mickey shot him a look of hatred. Val wasn't looking
at him, but he felt it just the same.

"Or, I could take you both into the alley and put a bullet in
each of your heads. You're a couple of melancholy assholes."
Both Mickey and Julian stared at him. The idea may not have
gone totally against their feelings.

Mickey lit a cigarette. He sat blowing smoke rings into the
darkness above the table while Val ate. The restaurant was
closed. Only a few lights were on. It gave quite an atmosphere
to the way the mood felt. As they sat in silence, the man
watching the front door stood and opened it. A young man
passed through with a nod. He continued on into the restaurant
towards the table were the three men sat.

Valant sat back and watched him approach, taking note of
everything about him. His worn out brown suit, the scuff marks
on that worn out suit, and the way the young man walked
boldly to him.

"Good evening, sirs." He came to stand next to Valant,
respectfully nodding his head towards him. He spoke clearly.

"House take on number five, sir." He held out a brown leather
money bag with a triumphant look.

Valant reached out and took it, weighing the contents.
"They send a receipt?"

"Yeah, it's in the bag."

Valant had been keeping an eye on this particular young
man for the past week. He was a new courier, having only been
working for the past three weeks. He was an honest kid of
about seventeen. He did his job, but something was amiss.

"What happened to your face?" Valant asked.

The young man had turned to go, but stopped to reply.
"Nothing. Just fell." With that he walked away.

After he had left the restaurant, Julian looked at Valant.
"Young. Those streets are hard."

"Yeah."

Mickey had risen and gone over to the bar to retrieve a
bottle of scotch. He had uncorked it and returned to the table
taking a long swig straight from the bottle. Julian's eyes met
Valant's. Neither man spoke. Mickey was living in a hell far
too deep for Valant to help him out of.

The next evening Valant took a drive over to card house
number five. He parked way down the alley and killed the
engine as well as all the lights. He sat alone in the dark waiting.
There was a light above the rear entrance to the card house, and
Valant had a good view of everything going on there.

He had waited nearly an hour when he saw a shadow
moving up the alley. The slim form gradually took shape. He
recognized the young man from the night before. He moved
cautiously into the light then went directly to the door and
knocked. Valant could see him exchange words with the man
through the portal in the door, then it was opened. He
disappeared inside.

He was inside for several minutes, and as Valant sat
waiting, three more shadows moved up the alley settling
against the wall just beyond the beam of light surrounding the
doorway. They pressed back and were unnoticeable. At length
the young man came back out the door, holding a brown
leather bag. This time he was far more cautious. He looked
around taking several deep breaths, then he began to walk away
from the door. He had just about reached the darkness when the
three shadows reappeared. With that the young man stuffed the

brown leather bag down the back of his trousers. He stood his ground.

Valant silently got out of his car. The three shadows moved into the light. Valant recognized one of his own couriers. The young man backed up a few steps.

"Gimme that bag." The tallest of the group ordered. The young man shook his head.

"Then get ready for another beating."

The young man inhaled deeply before exploding into speed. He ran at the tallest who had spoken driving his shoulder into his stomach. But the man was ready. He got a hold on the young man's neck and began driving his fist into the kid's side. But, the kid took hold of the man's flesh with his teeth and clamped down as hard as he could onto the tender skin. This loosened the choke hold he had on him a moment, which was long enough for the kid to stand up again. He drove his fist into the man's face as hard as he could. The man staggered, but it didn't matter. Another from the group came up and hit the kid in the lower back with a club. He arched his back in pain. With that the last of the group came at him and hit him in the stomach. Once he had the kid doubled over he kept driving it in. Into his side, into his kidneys, in his face.

But the kid stood.

Valant had seen all he needed to. Even if he survived this beating, he'd only get the same the next night. Assuming he didn't lose the money. If he did, then Valant would have to kill him.

The shot hit the first man in the head. He buckled immediately and the kid fell with him. The other two turned to run down the alley, but Valant got those two before they made it very far.

The kid sat with wide fearful eyes as Valant approached. Blood ran out of his nose and mouth. He looked like he couldn't see straight for he kept rubbing his eyes. Valant stepped into the light and came to stand above him. As he looked down at the kid he put his gun back into the holster next to his left arm.

They remained like that for several seconds, just looking at each other. Finally the kid raised a hand to the blood that was flowing freely from his nose. Then he reached back and pulled the brown leather money bag out of his trousers.

"House take from number five, sir." He said as he handed the bag to Valant. Valant gave him a short nod.

"Come on. We'll get you something to eat." He reached down and hauled him to his feet. It took a moment for him to straighten his back. Valant handed him a handkerchief.

Valant walked to the door of the card house and spoke to the man who was now looking through the open portal to see what had happened. They exchanged a few low spoken words, then Valant turned and started towards his car.

"What about them?" The kid asked in a shaky voice.

"What about them?" Valant asked as he looked back at the kid. Eager to be away from such an easy killing, Cobby stumbled toward the car and got in. He kept the handkerchief pressed to his nose.

Valant took him back into the city to a small diner that stayed open twenty-four hours catering to the factory crowd. The kid vanished into the bathroom immediately. It took several minutes to get the dried blood washed off his face. He kept trying to wipe away the fear he'd felt when the first bullet hit the man who had been holding on to him.

When he returned to the table, the man they called The Dark Horse was holding a cup of black coffee. There was one where the kid was supposed to sit. He looked out of place in his black suit. His granite face and unforgiving manner went against the dirty men who sat at the lunch counter. He watched the kid for several seconds before he spoke.

"What's your name?"

"Martin Cobbinelli, sir. But, everybody just calls me Marty." He replied in a quiet voice.

"Where do you live?" He raised the coffee to his lips.

"I live over by the ship yards, on Hammond Street." The kid took a tentative swallow of his own coffee. It was strong and bitter.

"How'd you end up with this job?" His look bored into the kid, and his voice was deep and unkind. The kid studied his coffee cup.

"I work over at the ship yard during the day. I load and unload boats. It don't pay much. My dad died." Here he took a pause before going on." My dad died almost a year ago. There's six of us counting my ma. Guess I figured sixteen was old enough to be the man of the family. My ma worked at a laundry place, but that meant nobody was home to watch my kid brothers. I told her to quit and I'd make up the difference. So she did."

He looked down again and took a swallow of coffee. "A kid at the ship yard told me about bein' a courier. Said he did it at night. That it was easy money. You just pick up the money, take it to the boss man. That's it. So, I asked if he'd take me to see somebody 'bout it."

Valant leaned back in his chair and pressed a thumb to his lip.

"If I done somethin' wrong, I'm sorry. You just set me straight. As to how you want it done. I'll do it like you say." He stopped short and looked down again. It wasn't fear that Valant would hurt him, but the fear Valant would fire him. Valant knew this.

"You have done no wrong. Do you understand those men intended to kill you? If not tonight then tomorrow?"

"Yes, sir." His voice was barely audible.

"How long they been thumping you?" The kid shrugged.

"All was well for the first couple weeks. They caught me about a week ago. First couple times it was just the one. I out ran him. Then he started bringing friends. I had to stand and fight."

"Why didn't you tell somebody?"

"Didn't wanna make a fuss. A man who can't do his job gets cut loose."

"Neither can a dead body rotting in an alley."

The waitress set before the kid a plate of chicken fried steak, mashed potatoes and gravy, green beans with a biscuit. His eyes grew wide. He looked to Valant. He made no move to touch it, although it was obvious he was hungry.

"Go on," Valant told him.

The boy looked at him appreciatively. "Thank you, sir." It might be his last meal, but he was going to enjoy it.

Valant remained silent while the kid ate, watching him closely. If the kid noticed, it didn't slow him down any. The waitress refilled his coffee and offered to get him something to eat. Valant declined but ordered apple pie for the boy. Watching the grateful kid eat somehow helped him forget his own troubles of late. Life was simple and so was happiness. At least when you're starving, anyway.

When he finished his pie, the kid sat back and looked at Valant. He said nothing, just waited.

"You can't courier anymore. Your mama lost a husband, she doesn't need to lose her son to alley thugs." Disappointment etched deep into his young face. Valant tilted his head to look at him.

"You'd go missing a long time before they ever connected you to your family. Do you know the kind of hell that would put your mama through? Not to mention the fact she'd be broke and completely on her own? All for some easy money? From what I saw tonight that money was far from easy." He spoke firmly.

The kid nodded slowly. Valant hooked his arm on the back of his chair.

"You come down to the restaurant where you drop your money bags in the morning at nine. I'll find you something else." The kid looked up sharply in surprise. "Don't worry about the ship yard anymore, either."

*****

1955

Marie looked into the mirror and smiled. Imelda was an artist. It was a light yellow floor length. The satin was cool against her finger tips. It was a strapless, which was Mickey's favorite style, and it softly followed the curves of her body. Imelda's fingers could work magic, Marie was sure.

"You like it." Marie turned to see a satisfied smile on the older woman's face.

"Yes, I do. You are the master of your artistry, Imelda."

"As you are of yours! I have heard nothing but good things! It seems that the time has gone so quickly to think the club has been going for a month already." Imelda fluffed the skirt. "Mickey waited so long for it, and now here it is. So successful too! He owes that to you."

Marie said nothing to this. Maybe that was true, maybe not. But one thing was certain, she wasn't about to go flaunting it to Mickey. He had been very easy going of late. No sense changing the mood that would so quickly change itself anyway.

The club was marvelous. Rolly and she were able to keep up with Mickey's ideas and schemes as they rolled along. He decided that the routine would be changed weekly. The ensemble had to work like hell to get the next week's routine rehearsed while still keep on top of the current week's show. She was grateful that he had allowed her to eat.

Marie kept to herself and focused on her work. That seemed to keep Mickey pleased.

"Come, we'll get you out of this. I'm happy with the fit." Imelda said.

Things at the apartment had changed some. Rarely had anyone stopped in, except for one occasion Mickey had met up with a few of the guys there. The Dark Horse had come to get Cobby a few times, but beyond that it was always quiet. That was different now. On any given night after a show, Cobby and Marie often arrived to find a card game in full swing at the dining room table. It was the closest of Mickey's guys: Deano, Frankie, Martin, Paulie, and Shorty. They were always polite, and unlike Mickey didn't expect Marie to wait on them.

Sunday's were the same. Martin and Shorty had wives and children, but those who didn't came to the apartment and either played cards or just sat at the bar and drank. Marie became accustomed to their banter. Although she was never directly invited, she was allowed to sit and listen to them. Eventually, she was drawn into conversations. It seemed natural for her to be there. Only Cobby noticed this. The fact was he enjoyed her humor and she brought a diversity to the conversation that had never been there before. She wasn't afraid to laugh at herself. Marie also did not assume that the tolerance of her presence meant she was an equal.

They would do anything for her. But she did not abuse this fact.

The club was packed each night. It was not uncommon for the waiting line to be down the street. Mickey had also been asking Marie to come up to the private stage during her breaks to mingle with his personal guests. She did not particularly care for this, for it meant sitting on the lap of a friend of Mickey's while pretending to either not notice, or like it when they put their hands all over her. It was degrading. Many a night ran late while she sat in on a private card game after the show.

If she had been getting paid, the money wouldn't have been enough.

"You look good. I am pleased to see he is no longer starving you." Imelda's voice cut through her thoughts.

Marie smiled self-consciously. "Yeah. Things are going better."

Imelda hung the dress on a hanger. "He's very volatile. But, when he appreciates someone, there is no greater ally. You must be very good at reading him." Marie said nothing to this statement.

"Very few people in his life mastered that art."

Marie didn't bother to tell Imelda that she had a life's worth of experience dealing with volatile men. It was not an art; it was merely a survival tool. Once she knew the signs to look for, she found most violent men reacted the same way. She was used to that. It was the ones whose intent wasn't obvious that she struggled with.

After the fitting Marie went on to rehearsal. The day flowed easily and evening came. After she ate dinner at the restaurant Cobby dropped her at the backstage entrance in the alley. Marie went to the dressing room. Already the backstage area was in chaos, but it looked like that every night.

"Evening," she said to everyone she met along the way. She was greeted kindly in return.

Marie danced with the company for several of Rolly's solos. Rolly spent time out on the floor with guests or taking a break while Marie performed. It gave Marie great excitement to look out among the crowd and identify faces. It became normal to see celebrities looking back at her. A few she had even performed with in New York. Marie nor Rolly made a point to single them out, they were there to be entertained, not photographed. Marie recognized a few that night.

"Ah, Marie we got us a good crowd goin' here tonight. I can see 'em lined up along the balcony up there." Rolly spoke with the intent to give the band a moments rest before going into a fast paced song.

"I see that. I am impressed. But, honestly, do you think tonight's crowd beats out last night's crowd?" Marie said in an unsure voice.

"Hmm. I see your point. Last night they were dancing by the tables 'cause the floor was so full. We haven't had that happen yet have we?"

"No." Marie shook her head regretfully.

"What do you think we ought to do about that?" Rolly asked looking at her.

"Well, maybe if we could get some lights on the floor." She pressed a white gloved hand to her chin. "Hmm. And you know, Rolly," she turned to look at him.

"What?"

"You know, I don't think we've really challenged them yet. We've been goin' easy on them all evening. Maybe we should kick it up a notch."

"You think that'll make 'em better than last night's crowd?"

"I do." Marie nodded her head.

"Alright, darlin'. Let's see if we can't get them a swingin' beat." Rolly turned to the band and nodded. The song started out mellow and slow. Rolly began the first words to Hoagy Carmichael and Sidney Arodin's *Up a Lazy River.*

The tempo started slowly, and Rolly's voice was strong above the sounds of the instruments that started in after him. Marie waited for him to finish his first round of lyrics. Rolly's voice rose slightly as the tempo picked up. When Marie joined him in song, Rolly's voice was forefront, hers merely accompaniment. They blended together perfectly. They were one sound.

As the song again increased tempo, the floor filled. As did any space large enough for dancing. The band took a round as Marie and Rolly danced together center stage. The gown that Imelda had fitted that morning was beautiful in the bright light and reflected the personality that radiated from Marie. Rolly laughed as he dipped her.

Towards the end of the show, Mickey sent for Marie. It meant some of his associates wanted to meet her, or would like the chance to dance with her. This wasn't unusual. She wasn't sure how much he was paid for these privileges, but she guessed he made a fine cut. The more contact with her, the higher the price.

She took the hall entrance to the private stage that ran along the side of the building. This was the door that Mickey and his group used as to not be visible to the crowd. As she walked onto the private stage, the band began Hoagy Carmichael's *Stardust.* The private stage was full of women dressed in the latest fashion from New York. They sparkled in the soft light. Men in tuxedos laughed and watched the women with intense interest. White fur was a favorite wrap in pairing with dark evening gowns. Gloved hands raised champagne glasses to deep red lips.

"Good evening, Mickey." Marie said in a gracious voice.

"Ahh, the star of the show." He extended his arm to her drawing her near. He kept his hand on her lower back. Marie couldn't help notice the look on Eva's face from where she sat at the table next to them. Cobby and The Dark Horse stood along the balcony watching. Marie noticed how loud the band sounded that evening. The crowd laughed and talked as they enjoyed themselves.

"Marie Barelli, this is Mr. Peter Casanov." He held out a hand to her. Marie took it and noticed his palms were slimy with sweat. Mr. Casanov had combed his thinning hair over in an attempt to hide the fact that he was balding. The sparse graying hair was matted to his scalp from perspiration. He wore a scruffy overgrown moustache that nearly covered his mouth. The dull brown of it was also etched with gray.

"Nice to meet you, Mr. Casanov." He winked at her. His eyes glittered as he did so. The pressure in his hand and the feel of the sweat in his palm gave way his tension. The corner of his moustache twitched.

"Oh, the pleasure is mine, Miss Barelli. All mine." Marie had no way of knowing this man, nor did she feel that Mickey really did either. Mickey hadn't moved from her and she could feel the rigidity of his presence.

"Mr. Casanov was a high stakes winner down town tonight. As an added bonus, we brought him in here to enjoy himself." Mickey's hand was shaking ever so slightly as he gently took hold of her elbow possessively. Marie made her notations quickly, as to not appear to see these things. Mr. Casanov was not a welcome guest despite what Mickey said.

"I have a bill from my winnings for you to sign. If you will indulge me, Miss Barelli." Something in his eyes was calculating. Sweat was visibly beading on Casanov's forehead.

"Certainly." Marie glanced indiscernibly towards The Dark Horse before lowering her gaze. Her smile brief and forced.

The man reached into his trouser pocket. "A little memento from the night lady luck was so generous as to sit with me. When I think of her, I'll see your face." His eyes became opaque.

Marie said nothing in return, just gave a slight smile. From the corner of her eye she saw The Dark Horse move up to the table behind the man. He had been frisked, but there was something in his deliberate movement that had even Marie wondering.

He pulled out a roll of hundred dollar bills. As he did so, a white piece of paper came with it. It drifted slowly down to the floor by Casanov's abraded wing tip oxfords. His thin lipped smile faded as he noticed it there. Marie caught his downward glance and looked down, too. It was a note. It was hand written, but the letters and symbols on it made no sense. She looked back up at him. A crazed look came into his eye as he looked at Mickey.

"Same place!" Was all Casanov said before The Dark Horse stepped between them, driving his fist into the man's stomach. He drew his arm back quickly and hit him again. Casanov let out a cry. Cobby took hold of him from behind clamping a hand over his mouth, smothering whatever sounds he was about to make. Gasps and cries came from the tables around them.

The band became deafening as time stopped. The Dark Horse kept hitting the man in the stomach, red circles forming after each hit. It took a moment for Marie to register that The Dark Horse held a knife in his hand. He plunged it repeatedly into Casanov's mid-section. A fine spray of blood flew from the knife and settled across Marie's face. Casanov began to crumple yet The Dark Horse did not weaken. Blood covered both men now.

Marie let out a small cry and Mickey flung her towards Deano who had come to assist. "Get her outta here!"

Deano grabbed hold of her arm and pulled her to the hallway and closed the door. He stood looking at her, smacking his gum. "Get on back where you belong. Change your clothes."

Marie hurried on shaking legs. The blood on her face had dried and was therefore hard to wash off without removing her make-up. Her face had gone pale. She changed into another gown and quickly tried to compose herself. Imelda's work of art was now nothing but scrap. As she walked back on stage she put on a smile that she knew didn't reach her eyes.

Block it out.

Rolly knew immediately something was amiss, but he didn't draw attention to her. Just quickly got the band rolling into the final number. She hoped she was composed on the outside, for she was a mess on the inside. The words to the song came out automatically without much emphasis. Before her eyes all she could see was the writing on the note.

V/8@#3-M

*****

Marie sat silently in her corner that night, her knees drawn up to her chest, her face buried in her arms. The image of The Dark Horse was burned into her mind. Each time she closed her eyes the scene again played out. It was a haunting nightmare, but then, after a while, she began to examine more than just the emotion of it.

V/8@#3-M

The note. Casanov had been acting strangely, but then, not knowing the man who was to judge what was normal for him. In Marie's experience, he was definitely at odds with a powerful faction within himself. Who was he and why had Mickey let him come to the private stage?

The Dark Horse. He had wasted no time in killing Casanov. Why? The note? It was the note that seemed to change the man's demeanor. That made no sense. Valant had already come to stand behind the man before the note fell. However, it was his job to look out for Mickey. Casanov was acting as though he intended to do something drastic.

Marie did eventually drift into an uneasy sleep, where dreams haunted her. She would see The Dark Horse with a knife. He would be using the knife on someone, usually Casanov, but then the person would change into someone she knew. Alex made his usual appearance. She found no comfort in seeing his face. She would try to run and warn him he was in danger, but The Dark Horse always got to him first.

Just as the pale light of dawn began to hint in the eastern sky, Marie dreamed her last dream. Casanov was standing before her holding the note. His lips were pressed into a thin smile. That same wild look he gave Mickey was now upon her.

"Same place."

*****

"Who the hell was he?" Mickey yelled.

Valant stood next to Mickey's desk and popped his neck. His shirt still had blood all over it and that aggravated him. He hated wearing bloodied clothing. After the stabbing Valant had taken everything out of the man's pockets then ordered the body to be removed. Everything was cleaned up and normal within five minutes. They left immediately for Mickey's office in the restaurant.

"That asshole comes into my club, pulls out a roll of hundreds, and you stab him to death. What the hell is wrong with you! Every high class private guest in that club is gonna think twice before comin' back! Damn you, Val! Damn you to hell!" Mickey's voice rose with each word. He came to stand before Valant. The two men were comparable in height.

"Trust me, Mickey. Have I ever done something unnecessary?" Valant's low voice was collected.

Mickey folded his hands together and pressed his index fingers to his lips. "What happened?" Mickey's voice was tightly controlled.

"We've found a lot of these notes. It is some kind of messaging system. I don't know what they mean, all I know is that we have a group working underground." Valant slid his hands into his pockets as he finished speaking.

"Were you going to tell me this?" Mickey asked.

"Eventually."

"He didn't have anything on him. Money, a pen, that note. What was he gonna do?" Mickey gestured with his hands to emphasize the words.

Valant said nothing, just stood looking at Mickey with his hands in his pockets. Mickey shook his head. He walked around the corner of his desk to flop down disgustedly into his chair. He pressed a finger to his lips.

"Cobby, where's the roll of hundreds?" Valant looked to where Cobby had been sitting silently across the room. He rose and went to the card table where the roll lay next to the note. He picked it up and tossed it to Valant.

Valant slipped the rubber band off then flattened them out. It was a roll of twenty one-hundred dollar bills. He began to look through the bills. He stopped when he came to one with writing on it. It was nothing but symbols. Valant handed it to Mickey. He frowned as he looked at it.

"Val." Cobby said from the card table. Both men turned to look at Cobby who was holding up the pen. Only it wasn't a pen. Cobby had taken it apart and was now holding nothing but a blade. A small one, but capable of cutting a throat.

Mickey looked at Valant. "I feel like we're behind in the game."

*****

A week passed after the stabbing incident. In that time Marie had rarely seen Cobby. She was kept mostly by Deano and Frankie. She was accustomed to these two, but, she by far got along better with Cobby. Drinking coffee together before leaving the apartment in the morning was habit. Sometimes they would talk, but usually Cobby read the funny pages while Marie read the entertainment section.

Contemplating more on of the night of the stabbing, Marie wasn't sure what she thought. Often she wondered if The Dark Horse had not stepped in what would have happened. Did the man actually have intentions of harming Mickey? And even more disturbing, was Mickey the intended target or was she? Pushing those thoughts aside, she shuttered at The Dark Horse's unpredictability. It did not take much to set him off.

She had thought back many times to the night before she left for New York. He had appeared out of the darkness to speak to her. He'd waited until after everyone was gone and she was alone. It made her gut clench and her palms sweat to think how easily he could have done something to her.

She should have told Vinny. Maybe, just maybe, she wouldn't be back in LA . She'd still be in New York with Alex. But on the bright side, The Dark Horse had shown no interest in her since that night.

Frankie took her down to breakfast Sunday morning. An intense conversation took place at Mickey's private table between Valant, Cobby and several subordinates. Marie had enjoyed several cups of tea while they talked seriously on a subject she couldn't hear enough of to define. It was a relaxing opportunity. Her magazine from The Dark Horse was behind the bureau with Alex's picture. She wished she had the magazine. The chance to thank The Dark Horse for the magazine had arose, but it was easier to avoid him than to look in his face.

Leave him to himself.

When their conversation did conclude, Frankie asked her to wait at the magazine stand while he got the car. The Dark Horse leaned against the open door of his car. His watchful eyes drifted to Marie intermittently as she looked over the headlines. Cobby lit a cigarette. They both turned to observe a passing car.

Something caught Marie's eye on the cover of *American Band Stand*. Her heart leapt. Snatching it up tears burned her eyes. She looked at his handsome face. Alex. His trumpet was resting on his lap. His hand was underneath his chin and he wore a brown suit. The same suit he'd worn the first time he'd kissed her. Seeing that breath taking smile of his made her heart freeze where it had been leaping out of her chest.

Hastily flipping through the magazine to the article written about him, Marie found he was posed in a picture close to that on the cover. Frankie was coming down the street. She scanned the article about what he was doing. Alex was releasing an album with a singer in New York, and playing full time at The Diamond. She turned the page to see what was next.

Something like a freight train hit her. Nothing around her moved, but she felt the impact. Alex was pictured again, only this time not alone. He was sitting next to Ruby. The picture was identical to the one she and Alex had taken together that now rested safely behind the bureau. Below the picture the caption read:

Roger's announced his engagement to Ruby Friedly earlier this week.

"Yo, are you deaf! Get your ass in the car!" Frankie yelled at her from the street.

Marie started and closed the magazine. She carefully put it back where it belonged and thanked the man. He nodded. He was accustomed to Marie looking over his goods by now. Hurrying to the car she slid in. The air seemed to drop in temperature. It was odd that no one on the street noticed as they rushed up the sidewalk. The ringing in Marie's ears spiked to an unbearable pitch so she put her hands over her ears. Squeezing her eyes shut and bracing tightly against the door, she felt the car lurch forward.

Cobby and Valant watched them go. Cobby flicked his cigarette away then retrieved the magazine Marie had been reading and brought it to The Dark Horse. Being a man who remembered small details, Valant recognized the name Alex. He flipped to the article. Scanning through it as Marie had done, he saw nothing that would disturb her. Then he turned the page.

He showed the picture to Cobby who slid his hands into his pockets.

"Well, that's one less asshole floating in the bay," Valant said as he tossed the magazine back to Cobby.

*****

It was Sunday. A good day to fall apart and silently cry in a ball in the corner. It cut her so deep. Ruby, of all people. Her dear friend. At least Marie now knew The Dark Horse hadn't done to Alex what he'd done to Casanov. Alex's heart still beat, he still made music, but now he would make love to someone else. The cut burned.

Now she was truly alone. She'd kept hope that she would eventually see Alex again. The dreams of him, the good ones, fueled her to survive. Now they weren't necessary. Bitter tears flowed until her body ran dry. Then she sobbed in dry, silent fits. Her face was swollen and her body ached, but she stayed where she was. She had no reason to rise.

She thought of Vinny. If she had stayed in contact with him, he wouldn't have let this happen. She would have been there with Alex. He wouldn't have moved on to someone else. That struck her as odd. She had only been gone a few months. Had she really been so easy to forget? She collapsed again.

She remembered as a child how Vinny would comfort her when she cried. He held her on his lap while the tears flowed freely, smoothing her hair and shushing her. Knowing now how truly kind he had been, she buried her face. With deep sadness she realized that there was no love on earth for Marie Barelli.

*****

Several weeks went by and the shock of that afternoon gazing upon Alex an engaged and happy man started to dull a little. She still dreamed about him relentlessly. She often woke with tears on her cheeks, but Marie began to wonder just what it was she was grieving over. Was it Alex? Or was it the life he had represented? He was the final link she had connecting her to New York. A link to a time that had now passed forever.

She was left with only the short stretch of uncertain future ahead of her. She could not shake the feeling her own Revelation had begun with the trumpets sound.

Life went on. It was now just past the first of November. The club had not slowed any since the opening. Each week saw great crowds of people swarming the club with Mickey making money hand over fist. Marie had heard a rumor that he was bootlegging illegal half price alcohol so fast that he got a shipment from Mexico every night. That was impressive. Buy it at half price, sell it at double.

But that wasn't his main money maker. No, it was the deals he struck each night during the performances up on his private stage. It made Marie's head go dizzy thinking about how difficult it must be to keep track of it all. From what she could tell this kept The Dark Horse and Cobby very busy. It seemed a rare occurrence that she saw them idle anymore.

Marie was sitting at the bar on the private stage drinking a martini, waiting for a card game to end so she could get a ride back to the apartment. It was a Saturday night of a long, hard week. Her feet and legs ached. Her body longed for the relaxation of sleep. It was nearing four when Cobby took his turn to shuffle the cards. He glanced up as Deano stood from his spot at the table.

"You out Dean? If you are, run Marie to the apartment." Deano looked uncertain and frankly a little agitated.

"I got it, Cob." The Dark Horse tossed the cards that Cobby just dealt back to him. He stood and put his jacket on.

Marie looked desperately at Cobby who reshuffled not looking her way. She turned to the bar downing her drink in one swallow. Turning she found he had already walked to her and stood waiting for her to rise. Her heart thundered. She did not want to be alone with this man. He held his hand out politely as she slid off her bar stool. She didn't look at his face as she did so, just began to walk. The tightness in the bodice of her dress irritated her where it cut low in the front. It was stark white against the darkness of the atmosphere around her. The bun she wore relaxed hours before and wisps of hair fell beside her face.

He followed her closely as they walked across the private stage. He cut in front of her to open the door to the hallway for her. His jacket brushed against her shoulder as he did so and she was aware of nothing else. She couldn't breathe. They turned right down the hall walking to Mickey's private entrance. He stopped at the door and unbuttoned his jacket, then without saying anything put it around her shoulders. She jerked only slightly as his arms and the jacket temporarily held her trapped.

She raised her eyes to his face only for a second to whisper, "Thank you."

His face was disapproving as he looked down at her, his arm extended and holding the door open. Looking down and away she moved through the door. She heard it close behind her as something made a desperate leap in her chest. The darkness of the parking lot engulfed them. Marie felt his hand at her elbow as they walked to the car. He was silent, blending in with the dark as if he weren't there. The only sound was her heels clicking with each step.

He pulled her to a stop before he opened the car door and looked around inside a moment. He then held out his hand to her. She wasn't accustomed to this as none of her other escorts bothered about it. She took it lightly and slid into the car. He closed the door on her hammering heart. She shrunk inside his jacket pulling it around her, but it smelled like him, a mixture of aftershave, bourbon and cigar smoke. Her earring caught along the collar and she tilted her head to free it. He started the car and moved through the parking lot to the street accelerating rapidly.

The awkwardness of the situation was to Marie very palpable, but The Dark Horse sat comfortably with one arm on the steering wheel, the other on his leg. It occurred to Marie that he never felt awkward. It just didn't happen. When that high up and dangerous, you had no reason to trifle with such a petty emotion. She envied him for it.

She lay her head back against the seat and closed her eyes. The Dark Horse glanced at her. The light coming from the street lamps reflected off the diamond earrings that lay against her neck. Her skin was smooth and softly illuminated in the weak light. Her legs crossed away from him. It was then she mumbled something.

"Hmm?" the sound was low and deep.

"She's very beautiful." Marie whispered from her state of half sleep.

"Who?" After a moment she spoke again.

"Your wife."

He was silent a moment. The car had passed into the dark and away from the street lamps.

"Margo's somebody's wife. But she isn't mine." It was said flatly.

He turned to watch her slowly open her eyes and sit up straight to look at him. Her eyes were wide with fear. For a moment he thought she would jump from the car. The artery in her neck pulsed and her chest stopped fighting the constraints of the gown for breath.

"I'm sorry. I saw her ring..... I'm sorry." She spoke firmly this time but her eyes glistened as they looked at him straight on, almost willing him to believe her. Valant sighed deeply as he looked again down the dark street ahead, the hand on the wheel gripping into a tight fist.

Marie turned from him staring blindly out the window, her entire body beginning to shake. She didn't want to know how painful this mistake would be. How deep the bruises would run, how much strength he had in his hands. The swiftness he used to redouble a fist. She leaned against the door, shrinking into his jacket. He kept taking angry glances at her.

Don't cry. Don't you dare cry. That will enrage him. It always enrages them.

She had called him out as an adulterer.

He pulled the car against the curb, then cut the engine. He glanced at her before getting out. She was so frozen with fear she couldn't even make a run for it. And she hated herself. She wanted to fight, but the fear settled on her like a suffocating blanket. He opened the door and reached for her.

She sprang from the car without taking his hand. The sound of her heels on the concrete was no longer weary. Marie could feel his body moving without him touching her he was so close. Valant nodded to the doorman when he moved her to the elevator. It opened immediately, but Valant had to crowd her inside. Once in she took the opposite corner he did. She kept her face down, but he could still see her lips trembling.

The elevator opened with a hum. She slipped quickly past him and made for the door. Marie realized she was trapped, that she had nowhere to hide. Grasping desperately for the handle, she opened her own door this time. He came through after her slowly, watching each move she made. Stopping suddenly, she slid his jacket off her shoulders and walked back to him. Marie held the jacket up without meeting his eyes.

"Thank you," she whispered in a trembling voice. Before she could continue on his voice stopped her.

"He must have been very cruel." It was spoken with directness. She froze, the artery in her neck was throbbing again.

"Who?" She was barely audible.

"Whoever taught you to respect men the way you do."

With this she looked at him from the corner of her eyes, then turned her head slightly. She looked down at the floor again. Something inside must have broken because her shoulders fell. Her lips stopped trembling and instead a tear fell silently. She sniffed softly then looked at him again, her head still bent forward.

"Yes, he was." her voice was barely perceptible.

He slid his hands into his pockets and waited, just looked at her. "It's better to face it head on, then to let it control you."

He stepped forward and reached up slowly. She fought the wild urge to jerk away. He softly took hold of a hair pin that had come loose and pulled it free. He slid it into his pocket. She seemed to visibly steel herself. She accepted whatever she thought he was going to do to her.

"Good night, Marie."

She looked at him in surprise. He remained still but his look was hard. She smiled a soft uneasy smile and was gone.

As her door closed softly, he turned to the bar and reached into his jacket pocket pulling out a small leather bound book Marie hadn't noticed. He removed the string that held it closed and took up the pencil that was held tightly in the pages. He had work to do.

*****

September 1940

They spent that summer together in the sun on the beach. At first they went as a group, Mickey and Maryanne, Val and Margo. It was the last burst of youth before adulthood took over. They swam in the ocean and picnicked in the sand under the rock overhang by the cliffs. They laughed and talked, dreamed and plotted. Life wasn't going to end up taking them where their elders had been. No, it was going to be far kinder to them.

As a little time passed, Val and Margo began to forgo the rules of propriety. They went to the beach alone. Nature took its course, and before long they spent lazy days below the rock overhang making love. Testing the limits of pleasure in yearning to know more. For Val there could be no other. Margo felt the same, or at least she said she did. Val saw no reason not to believe her. The evidence was in the passion they shared, and fulfillment of it each time.

Julian never said much about Margo. When talk turned to her, he would stand off to the side and light a cigarette. He had concerns, but hadn't yet taken them to Georgio. When he finally did, Georgio shrugged his shoulders.

"Her papa is an important man, yes. But I have a feeling this experience will only bring him along."

So, Julian said nothing. He stood by and waited, hating the fact that what was coming wasn't going to be a very pleasant experience for the young Val. But it was necessary.

Val proposed to Margo for the first time in October of 1939. Margo had smiled a happy school girl smile saying, "No, let's wait. Until you can get set up. Maybe we could buy a little house." She had burrowed into his chest as she spoke. "Get a yard with a fence for the babies."

She looked up at him with passion in her eyes. Val succumbed to her reasoning and body without thinking beyond what she said. He waited. He found a little three bedroom house with a fenced yard and bought it against Julian's better judgment. Even Mickey had to step in and say he felt that perhaps Val was moving a little fast. But Val felt no need to slow it down. In fact, he felt the opposite.

He surprised her with the house Christmas 1939. He took her to it blind folded, relishing every minute of teasing her along the way. When she saw it, she didn't speak for a full two minutes, just stood there staring with tears in her eyes. He became concerned and took her into his arms and kissed her gently.

"You don't like it?"

She smiled reservedly and said, "No. It is the most wonderful house I've ever seen. I just, I didn't realize how serious you are."

"Of course I'm serious. I love you."

"But just now, it isn't the right time." She looked away. "You have just begun making a name for yourself. And, I.." She looked back at him to see him frowning. "I think we shouldn't rush you into anything. You have a lot to keep up with just now."

His arms slacked around her. She took hold of him, kissing him passionately, tightening her arms around his neck. He responded with desperation. She pulled away and whispered, "I wanna see the inside of the house." So, he swept her up and took her inside.

Val began to change after that. He became quieter, more thoughtful, angrier. The months passed and Julian watched him carefully, conferring with Mickey frequently about the state of affairs with Margo. Mickey would shrug sadly. He kept close to Val. It seemed everyone knew what was coming but Val.

Then one day in April of 1940, Margo asked to picnic down on the beach. So, Val drove them down on a Sunday afternoon, expecting that she would finally yes. They ate their lunch in the sun below the overhang, listening as the waves rolled onto the shore. Val felt a contentment he hadn't felt in many months of waiting.

"Val, I'm getting married." He stopped gazing at the ocean and looked to her surprised. It was an odd way of saying yes. She wouldn't look at him straight on.

"I don't love him, but I'm going to marry him. Next week." The hurt confusion in his eyes seared into her.

"What?"

"It is an arrangement I can't break. I won't break. It means too much to Daddy."

"But the house...." He realized it was a pathetic argument. He understood what a fool he had been, buying a tiny house for a girl raised in a mansion.

"How long have you known?" He asked, the anger in his voice becoming evident.

"Since February."

"But you knew before that, didn't you? You told me no back in October." He was no longer curbing the anger.

She put a hand on his arm. "Val, my love, this doesn't change anything between us."

He threw her hand away. "This changes everything."

She slid her hand up his thigh. "It changes nothing. We are still us. Always will be. Nothing will change that."

Valant visibly melted with her touch. The anger did not soar high enough to ignite the fight in him. He watched helplessly as she took his body in her hands and put words in his mouth. A small part of his heart turned black at the manipulation, but her naked flesh moving beneath his buried it deep so it could fester alone and unchecked.

Mickey took Val across the border into Mexico for the full two weeks of her honeymoon. Val spent that time in a drunken oblivion playing cards and fighting. Something within him came apart and the beast they trained finally exploded into rage. Fighting like hell didn't make Val feel any better, but it was a side Mickey had never seen before. He was not so much concerned as it had struck a spark to a wicked dream. Valant was far more than he appeared. Far more. Any mercy he had before was gone now.

They returned home to find Margo anxiously waiting for Val. She called many times trying to reach him, but Julian blew her off. When she got news he was back, she was right over to him. She now lived in a fine house with many rooms, but she asked Val to take her to the small house he had bought just for them. He did so, and the love she made to him soothed his heart only for a moment. Without wasting any time, she rose and told him to take her home. Her husband would be home at six.

*****

1955

Marie woke the next morning in a tight ball in the corner. She sat there for a long while listening to the silence, thinking over what he had said to her.

It's better to face it head on than let it control you.

Maybe he was right. But, she felt certain that it was too deep a part of her to challenge the fear that moved within her like a living creature. It rose when it wanted, and controlled when it wanted. She felt shame for having allowed it entry, but honestly, she had no choice. Now she was alone.

She stood and stretched. Her joints popped and her back refused to straighten. It would. Eventually. She slipped on the pink robe Imelda sent her before walking quietly to the door. She opened the handle slowly and stepped out. She was shocked.

He sat at the table reading the newspaper. His jacket hung on the chair next to him. He wore his underarm holsters, his guns resting confidently inside. Cobby sat next to him reading the funny pages, looking like a replica of the man next to him. His holsters were visible as well, but something in the way Cobby sat made him less credible than The Dark Horse. The corner of her mouth twitched. She wanted to turn and go back into her room, but Cobby's voice stopped her.

"Are you just gonna stand there gawking?" She didn't know what to do as the panic in her throat rose. Cobby looked directly at her. "Sit down and have some coffee."

She wrapped her arms around herself. "It's late. I'm not really dressed for breakfast."

Cobby raised a brow at her. "I think he's seen women in their robe before." Then he looked at The Dark Horse with mock uncertainty. "Uhm, yeah. Probably seen women in their robe." He said with sarcasm.

She shook her head at him and turned to go back into the bedroom. "I have seen women in less than what you're wearing." The Dark Horse spoke to no one in particular. Cobby grinned wickedly.

She moved to sit across from Cobby. Thinking where it would be best to sit, she saw something out of the corner of her eye. She looked to The Dark Horse to see he was wearing glasses. She took her seat and Cobby shoved the coffee tray at her. A box of Danish sat beside The Dark Horse but Cobby did not slide that to her. She glanced again towards The Dark Horse. She couldn't see him through the paper he read.

"They're reading glasses only." With that statement he turned the page of his paper. Marie sat still and looked to Cobby who had no expression on his face. She held her coffee cup mid-air.

"I've had them since the fifth grade. You can ask Mickey." With that he bent his paper in half to glare at her. "I don't wear them because I'm old." He shook his paper to straighten it.

Cobby's mouth twitched. He put his elbow on the table and pressed a finger to his mouth. Marie still sat, empty cup mid-air, uncertainty gleaming in her eyes.

"Do you make a habit of insulting men at the breakfast table then sitting with a dumb expression on your face?" He angrily turned another page. Cobby raised his brows at her as if questioningly. She swallowed hard. She didn't know what to say.

"I, I, didn't insult you, sir," she stammered out.

"Yes, you did." The Dark Horse still spoke from behind his newspaper. Cobby nodded in agreement. Tears formed in her eyes as she mouthed, "Help me!" at Cobby. He only shook his head.

"I better get dressed. Excuse me." She muttered. At that The Dark Horse threw his paper on the table and leaned forward to stare hard at her. His glasses slid to the end of his nose.

"Well, have it out!" He shouted at her. She flinched as he yelled. He sat staring at her for a moment before she shook her head.

"Have what out?" She trembled. He sat up straight but continued to glare at her.

"Laugh."

"What?"

"Laugh!" She shook her head.

"Out with it! You better say what's on your mind and laugh it out, or I will get out of my chair!" She covered her face with her hands.

"Now!" The coffee cups rattled on the glass table top with the vibration from his loud voice.

"I had the most absurd vision of you holding a gun on someone while fumbling for your glasses." She spoke in a rush and the last words she half laughed, half sobbed out. She kept her face covered.

The Dark Horse sat back in his chair and retrieved his paper again. Cobby laughed through a mouthful of Danish. "Have a Danish before Gomer Pile eats them all."

The Dark Horse slid the box to her and she uncovered her face to see the scene was just as it was before he lost his temper. Only now, the more Cobby laughed, the more he had to laugh. Marie gave him a pathetic disheveled look.

"You gotta lighten up." Cobby said in a serious tone as he grabbed another Danish.

"Pour yourself some coffee and have a Danish, Marie." The Dark Horse spoke evenly from behind his paper.

*****

Valant sat in the back with his gun on the hunched bleeding figure. Cobby was driving while Deano sat in the passenger seat. They were headed across town, way across town, into Vinnetti's turf. It was Valant's intent to deliver the man straight to The Heart Vantino, with all hope he was where Valant thought he'd be. It was a mission that stirred his blood and he longed for a fight.

Cobby drove fast. It was an in and out kind of proposition. They had found the man down by the docks just as Pacheko had said, waiting for a boat. Valant's guys had been in and out of every boat docked in the bay, waiting to find the right one. Finally, after long days and nights of nothing, this man appeared, but no boat.

Valant and Tony both recognized him immediately; he was one of Vinnetti's. He was carrying a note, a messed up jumbled note with symbols on it. But, upon questioning, the man had no answers as to what it said, just told them that he worked for Vinnetti and someone on the inside left messages for him to deliver at the docks to be picked up by a roving boat. Valant became enraged.

So many messengers, so few message writers.

Valant tortured him awhile but that produced very little, except to confirm what Pacheko said about the boat. He began to feel that the networking of this underground take over was far too vast to really get a hold on anyone high up. Or, he just wasn't looking in the right places. He began to wonder about Mickey's guys. How many messengers were within their own ranks?

"Just stop, Cobby. Don't pull into the curb."

They had gone way into the heart of Vinnetti's home ground. He had an office there behind an upscale lounge. Valant slid out of the car and walked around to the other side of the car. He drug the man out throwing him to the street.

"Vantino! I've got something I think you may want." He paused a moment before yelling again.

"Vantino!"

The door opened and Vantino slowly walked out alone. He stood with a cigarette in one hand, and the other in his trouser pocket. He rested on one leg in a casual pose. His eyes were narrow in the bright, mid-morning sun.

"Been a long time, Dark Horse."

"Not long enough."

Neither man said anything for a moment. Vantino's dark eyes watched unblinkingly and the flat eyes of Valant reflected nothing but hate.

"Got a traitor for you."

Vantino said nothing, just took a drag on his cigarette, then threw it down and crushed it out. "Why'd you bring him here?"

"Out of respect for Georgio."

"Georgio's dead."

"If you don't listen to what this man has to say, Vinnetti will be, too"

Vantino scoffed. "You pups think you know everything."

The muscles in Valant's jaws worked. "Out of respect for
Georgio and his truce I brought him to you." With that Valant
picked the man up and shoved him towards Vantino. The man
hit the sidewalk with a deep groan.

"Is the truce still on then? I couldn't tell from our meeting
almost seven years ago. When I saw you last I was asking for a
favor, and I wasn't sure you'd carry through."

"Vinnetti's alive isn't he?" Valant turned to get into the
car.

"Dark Horse." He turned and looked steadily at Vantino.

"I already intercepted the boat. So, stop looking there. It
would serve you well to stay tight around Mickey."

It was Valant's turn to scoff. "Wouldn't it serve you well
for me not to?"

A look passed through Vantino's eyes. It was almost sad.
"Nothing serves me well anymore."

"Easy old man. Don't get sentimental." With that he slid
into the car. Cobby hit the accelerator and the tires barked
loudly as he took off down the street.

"Ah, shit. Now we're really screwed. Vinnetti already
knows what was on that boat, and we don't have a damn clue."
Valant said with hatred.

*****

Marie slipped down the side of the stage in the dark while
the band played behind her. She was done for the night, but,
she usually spent the last few songs down on the floor dancing
and interacting with the crowd. It gave Rolly a break. Rolly
sang the last two songs solo that week. The third to the last he
had a moment to catch his breath while Marie occupied the
audience and the band played John Blackburn and Karl
Suessdorf's *Moonlight In Vermont.*

She made her way to the first cluster of tables near the
stage. It was a table of men. She smiled as she approached.
"Good evening, gentlemen. Music treating you alright?"

She noticed the man on her right had a long scar across his
face. "Miss Barelli," came voices from around the table. She
smiled again and tried to remember if she had seen any of their
faces before. She could not recall having done so.

"Can I send a waiter your way? I see a few of you are a
little low on liquid libation. Can't have that can we?" She
winked at a red haired gentlemen to her left. He smirked.

"I'd appreciate a dance." The man with the long scar spoke impatiently.

"Well, I happen to be free. Would that suit you, sir?" she asked casually. She began to move around the table to him. He did not rise as she approached.

She came to stand next to him and she held out a hand. She noticed the reaction that played out across his face. He was neither surprised nor excited at the prospect of dancing with her. He reached up and took hold of her hand tightly jerking her to him. He pulled her down on his lap then wrapped his arms crushingly around her to keep her arms down. In an instant something flashed in his hand and he pressed it to her throat. She knew it was a switch blade.

"What would suit me is for you to shut up and listen. I gotta little message for your boy, Dark Horse." As he whispered his hot breath filed her ear canal with foul smelling heat. She froze in a tense position and tried not to move her neck.

"I'm gonna give you a piece of paper. You take it to him right now. You cause a fuss or make a scene, I pull out my gun and shoot you in the head. Got me?" She barely nodded. She could feel the point of the knife sting as she did so.

The man took a small folded piece of paper from the table and tucked it down between her breasts with his fore finger. "I'll kill you, Vinnetti. One shot, that's all it takes. Your head ain't nothing but a puddle."

He released her then and she stood quickly. As she turned to look back at him, he pointed to the private stage. She needed no more goading. Marie moved across the crowded dance floor, bumping in to people with each step. She shoved through as quickly as she could, but as guests began to recognize her they called out to her or tried to stop her.

"Miss Barelli. Hey, Miss Barelli." She moved as fast as space would allow, but the crush was deepening around her as she went.

"Miss Barelli, can I have a dance?" She put on a weak smile.

"Not now. Excuse me please." She shoved harder as the stairs came into view. Deano was leaning against the railing and Frankie was his opposite. Marie was in an almost deadlock now, people jamming up around her shouting her name.

"Deano!" He saw her and came for her. She reached out a hand and he took it, pushing people aside so she could pass.

"Thanks, Dean." He nodded to her as she started up the stairs.

She again passed two more men at the top of the stairs. It was not unusual for her to be on the private stage, just unusual for her to use the stairs. Marie made her way through the tables, trying to be gracious to those she passed, all the while looking for him, hoping he was there. Marie's desperate eyes found him at Mickey's table that overlooked the stage. Next to The Dark Horse was his exquisite blonde lover, Margo. She did not want to cause the scene that the scarred face man indicated would end her life, so she discreetly kept her eyes on him as she made her way to the bar. A glance of his eyes let her know he'd seen her, but he did not keep looking long enough for her to catch his attention. It would be difficult with so many around her, all clamoring for her attention.

She ordered a drink to keep a few at bay and looked to The Dark Horse again. He looked at someone across the table from him with a still expression while Margo laughed deeply. Valant took in the activity around the room. Each conversation, every face. She willed him silently to notice her. The minutes seemed like hours as she waited for him to look her way again, the note burning a hole in her soft flesh.

A man who had been watching her rose from a table to her far left and sauntered her way. She caught the movement out of the corner of her eye, panicking a little. She willed Valant to look at her and found that although she needed him at the moment, she dreaded him coming close to her. It was as if he heard her mind screaming his name for at that moment he looked up and she locked eyes with him. Marie held his gaze and refused to look away despite what her senses begged for her to do.

His was not the only eye she caught for Margo saw her, too, and a look of complete hatred flashed on her face as Valant slowly stood and left her there alone. He moved to Marie in an unconcerned way. With a look he removed the man who had come to stand next to her, attempting to get her attention. Her heart beat erratically at his approach, but she held her ground.

Valant stood next to her and leaned against the bar, shielding her partially from the views of both Margo and anyone watching beyond the stage. He stood close. He held up his hand next to her arm without touching her as he leaned his head down to listen to what she would say.

"A mmman," She clasped a hand to her mouth briefly before continuing on. He would not tolerate a weepy message. "A man asked me to give this to you."

He watched as she pulled the note from her cleavage and handed it to him. He unfolded it and read it, but nothing about him changed as he did so. She felt loath to lose the barrier he made of himself, but she knew in a moment he would leave her alone and exposed. Instead he bowed his head to speak into her ear.

"Where did you get this?" His breath was neither hot nor foul.

Her lips trembled as she lifted her face to his ear to speak again. "Table six by the stage. A man with a scar across his face."

"How long ago?"

"Just a few minutes." When he looked at her face, Marie could feel his eyes reading her expression.

"Stay here."

Cobby moved to stand behind The Dark Horse, knowing instinctively something was brewing. With a glance, Cobby was at Valant's side and in leaving they took the two men at the top of the stairs. However, beyond the stage Marie could see that table six was already empty. By now Rolly was calling goodnight to the crowd, so she turned to take a large swallow of her drink.

"What's going on?" Mickey's voice came low from behind her. She had dreaded the moment he would get involved. She turned slightly to look at him.

"A man gave me a message for Mr. Valant."

"What did it say?"

She shook her head. "I don't know. I didn't read it."

Val and Cobby came back to the bar where Mickey stood by Marie. Neither spoke until they were close. "They've gone."

"Where's the note?" The Dark Horse handed it to Mickey and he read it. Folding the piece of paper he asked, "Who gave this to you?"

"It was a man sitting in a group at table six. He had a long scar across his face."

Mickey's jaw muscle tensed as he watched her. "I can't deal with this right now. Get her back to the apartment. See what she knows." With that he walked away angrily.

"Let's go, Marie," Cobby said to her. He took hold of her arm and started toward the door. The Dark Horse followed closely behind. She couldn't help but think of Margo sitting at the table without him.

Before they left the building Cobby gave her his coat, then they plunged into the darkness outside the club. The street was alive with the sounds of people leaving, the beams of light coming from cars briefly illuminated their way as they made for Cobby's car. The Dark Horse opened the door for her, then to her surprise got behind the wheel. She had hoped he would stay behind.

The deep silence on the drive back to the apartment gave her grave doubts as to how her evening would end. She wondered what the note said. She assumed it was bad for The Dark Horse to be taking her away. Cobby looked straight ahead. She knew him well enough to know he was thinking about what came next. Unfortunately, she came next. She pulled his jacket tight around her, thinking how it was a better fit than The Dark Horse's had been. She lay her head back and closed her eyes.

Deep silence followed them up the elevator and into the apartment. When they came in Cobby immediately went to pour himself and The Dark Horse a drink. She tried to make a break for the bedroom, but Valant stopped her.

"Wait, Marie," she stopped and faced him, feeling very small and insignificant. "Sit down."

She did so slowly. He came to stand above her then handed her the small folded message she carried next to her breasts. She took it wearily and unfolded it to read its contents.

V/8 Vinnetti Keep your messenger close

She wanted to throw up. She took it as a direct threat to herself. She wondered it if was as painfully obvious to The Dark Horse as it was to her who they were referring to. She looked up at him. His face was unreadable.

"What does it mean?" she asked in a small voice.

"You tell me." The fear that he knew more of her than he let on cut into her.

"I can't." She knew an unpleasant line of questioning was about to follow. "Cobby, may I have one of your cigarettes?" He had come to sit in the armchair. He nodded.

She reached into his jacket pocket and retrieved his cigarette case and lighter. She took her time getting it and lighting it. She took a long drag while the Dark Horse watched her.

"Get it over with," She said in a tired voice. She crossed her legs and sat back. She exhaled slowly.

"Tell me what happened." His voice was low and deep.

"They caught me as I was making my way to the dance floor. The one with the scar on his face pulled me onto his lap and told me he wanted me to give you a message. Said he'd kill me if I caused a fuss. Then I came to you."

"What else did he say to you?"

She took another drag off her cigarette and looked away from him. "Hmm, something about turning my head into a puddle." She wanted to cry, she wanted to run, she wanted to scream at him how she hated him and hoped he died a gruesome death for the things he had done to other people and the things he was about to do to her. He knew more than he wanted to let on. He was waiting for her to slip up and say something to hang herself.

He held up the note and pointed to it. "What does it mean?"

"I don't know." She said it with a deep weariness, for she didn't. She did know that whoever was behind it knew her identity and connection to Vinny. She suspected that meant they were going to kill her. She really couldn't say for sure. It seemed logical.

"I find it a little too coincidental that they would put you close to Mickey twice. They are making a statement yes, but why use you?" He took off his jacket and laid it on the arm of the sofa. He then sat across from her on the coffee table. She made no move to answer him, but tensed as he sat. She looked at the two pistols strapped in their holsters beside his arms.

"How do you know Vinnetti?"

She held her cigarette between her fingers and looked at him. She knew she couldn't evade him. He wasn't like Mickey who didn't take the time to listen to her answers. This man could read her, follow her expressions and the look in her eye. In that respect he was much like Vantino.

"He owned the club my father ran."

"No. Not good enough." He cut her short.

"I met him for the first time when I was nineteen. Probably more like eighteen. He...."

"No. Don't give me that line. Don't lie to me again," his voice got lower as he spoke. Cobby shifted in his chair.

"I'm not lying to you!" She emphasized. She looked perplexed as she exhaled. "I know you think I have a connection, but," she shrugged her shoulders. "But, if that were true, I would be with him now not you. I'd be sleeping in a very different sort of penthouse suite, don't you think?"

He leaned forward and took hold of her shoulders. He pulled Marie to him until she was a mere two inches from his face. She trembled and her face grimaced.

"Mickey's gonna come through that door in a minute. When he does this is gonna turn into a very different kind of questioning. He's gonna tell me to do things that I'm not doing right now." Her whole body shook. She let out a small sob. "Tell me what I want to know and those things can be avoided." The last was spoken in a whisper. His grip tightened.

She had no idea how much she could take before she succumbed and they ended her life on account of what she would tell them. She would try for as long as she could fight the fear. Which in her estimation probably wasn't long.

"I met Vinnetti when I was nineteen..." He shook her hard.

"Don't lie to me," he ground out. A tear slipped out of the corner of her eye.

She looked at his face and he became someone else. Her father. The fear was crippling her mind.

"He owned the club my father ran....." He pressed his lips to her ear.

"I already know these things, Marie. Tell me why they picked you. Why are you the messenger?"

He looked again into her face. "I don't know. I don't. Why can't you believe that?"

It was true. She didn't know why they had chosen her. She no longer carried any connection to Vinny. He had abandoned her after he had sent her to New York. She was alone in the world. Nothing would matter to Vinny where she was concerned. Why couldn't he understand that?

"There's no reason for you to believe me. And no matter how many times I tell you the truth you won't listen to me." He pulled her to him again and he spoke low in her ear.

"I know you so much better than you give me credit for, Marie. I've known you far longer than you realize. I know what the look in your eyes means. I know your body language. I know when you're lying." She cried openly now. She hated herself for it, but she couldn't stop. She hated him for making her do it.

"If you know me so well, then you already have the answers you're looking for. Leave me alone," she whispered knowing it would enrage him. "You tell me why they picked me. Tell me what happened all those years ago that made my father Mickey's man instead of Vinnetti's. You tell me. I don't know these things. All I know is how big your hands are. How much strength they have in them. How much they'll hurt when you put them to use on me. The way when I have nightmares about you I'll smell this room and see Cobby sitting there drinking and watching. I don't know anything else." She looked at him straight on.

"I wish I knew Vinnetti. I wish he loved me. Maybe he would come through that door and gun you down before you had a chance to show me what you're capable of. He isn't going to. Not now, not ever. I'll just keep wishing while you keep hurting." She sat a little straighter and spoke a little louder. "You've already taken everything from me. My dreams, my life, my love, all that's left is the pain. So if you think you gotta a little something left to twist, go ahead and twist. I have already done what Mickey brought me here to do."

Valant exhaled heavily and his grip on her shoulders tightened. He looked into her eyes and she read no emotion there. "I took none of those things from you. I had my chance to take those things and I let you walk, remember? I let you walk. So don't you blame me for anything. I have nothing to do with your being here."

"Yes you do. Mickey didn't roll up in that big black car and take me away. You did." Her lips again trembled as she spoke. If she could divert his thinking, perhaps..... he was too intelligent for that.

"Regardless of how you got here, you belong to Mickey Delano. If you were going to belong to me I would have claimed you when I had the chance. I did not, so here you are. And you're wrong about Vinnetti. He cares for you. Very deeply in fact. Which is why I'm here, trying to get answers."

She looked at him deciding to give him one straight answer. "You're wrong. Very wrong. I have no answers. And if I do, I won't give them to you. Vinnetti had his chance too, and he let me walk, as you say. I do what Mickey brought me here to do, so he has no reason to be angry."

"Vinnetti hasn't let you walk, yet. And neither has Mickey. Don't you understand that you'll never be free? You'll always belong to one or the other?"

"Not always." She looked at him despondently. "Not always. The happy time of my life may be over, but I won't always belong to them." As he looked down something caught his eye on her neck.

"Did they touch you, Marie?" he asked in a low voice.

"What difference does that make?"

"Everything."

"No. I always carry your private messages between my breasts." She looked at him and he clenched his jaw angrily at her.

"Don't do that. Don't you get a smart mouth. I won't tolerate that." He let her go but stayed close to her. She inhaled slowly.

"Yes, they touched me. That mark is as bad as it got."

"Did he put a knife to your throat?" She nodded without looking at him. He tipped her chin with the tip of his index finger to get a closer look at it.

"Tell me who Vinnetti is to you, Marie," he whispered it to her face, his breath puffing gently against her cheek.

Her shoulders slumped in defeat. She looked at him in the eye and said, "No one."

At that moment the elevator bell dinged. He stood and moved away from her. Both he and Cobby took up a post by the bar. They looked as if they had been there the entire time, sipping their drinks and talking about something close to the weather.

"Cobby, may I have another cigarette?"

"Yeah."

Marie inhaled deeply feeling the nicotine permeate her lungs. She tried to steel herself against what Mickey would bring with him. But, he took her in then turned to the bar and told Cobby to get him a drink. He moved to her and sat down on the coffee table just as The Dark Horse had done, folding his hands together while the intensity of his eyes stopped whatever she might've said. Mickey said nothing for a time, just looked at her, noting the mark on her throat where the knife had been. His hands fairly trembled.

"They touch you?" Marie found this very ironic.

"Just that." She lightly brushed the mark with her fingers. "That's all." Again like The Dark Horse he tipped her chin with his finger.

"You know 'em?"

"No, I'd never seen them before. But I'll remember them if I see them again." He took the cigarette from her hand and raised it to his lips.

"Don't smoke these damn things. I'm sure they're terrible for women." She said nothing, just inwardly grieved for the loss of her comfort. Cobby brought his drink and handed it down to him where he sat.

"I don't understand. Vinnetti's messenger. Who the hell is that?" He stood angrily and walked to the bar. Without moving her head Marie looked at The Dark Horse. He stood lazily leaning against the bar, his cold stare locking with hers. Martin and Frankie had come with Mickey, but they didn't notice.

What's he playing at?

She found it deeply disturbing that he knew something so devastating about her and chose to keep it to himself. The only sound in the room at that moment was the tinkling of his ice in his drink cup as he took a long swallow. His eyes never left her. She looked away and said nothing.

"I won't stand for them coming in and touching her. I won't stand for that. You do something to keep her safe. Get guys posted around the stage, have somebody with her everywhere she goes. No more going around the club alone. Bastards think they can get something that means money to me and mar it." He pointed to Deano. "Keep him on her."

The Dark Horse said nothing as he rambled, just casually drank his bourbon. Something was happening here, but Marie couldn't say just what. Mickey clearly did not know what the note meant. The Dark Horse did. What it was he was going to do with that information she did not know. It made her shiver to think about the way he held her life in his hand, how easily he could decide to throw it away at any moment.

"You can go on to bed, Marie," Mickey said harshly.

"Thanks, Mick." She rose and quietly left the room as Mickey began talking in a low voice.

She closed the door behind her, the exhaustion overwhelming her as she did so. However, she knew she wouldn't sleep. She would lie there in that corner listening for the sounds that indicated they were coming for her. So, she took one of the armchairs, dragging it silently to the window. She reached into Cobby's pocket and once again withdrew his cigarettes. She lit one and sat in the chair looking down to the street below.

How much does he know, and how much did he make up hoping I'd slip up?

*****

"Ah, damn. She jacked my cigarettes." Cobby said disappointedly as he patted where his jacket pocket should have been.

"Go in and get them." The Dark Horse said with a wry smile.

"No. She's probably got the whole pack smoked by now. Either that or she's poised with a lamp ready crack the next person to open the door over the head. No thanks."

"Or, still more, she likes to smoke in the nude," Val said with a mischievous gleam in his eye. Cobby's hand paused mid-way to his mouth, the ice in his glass rattling.

"That's something to think about." Cobby held that pose for several seconds as he pictured something in his mind. He chuckled softly. So did Val. Then he grew serious.

"She ain't giving is she?" Cobby asked to himself more than anything.

"No, but she will. Mickey won't remain oblivious much longer. He already knows they have a connection, he just doesn't think it's a strong one."

"Do you?"

"I don't know. But I'll tell you what I do know. Despite her fear of me, she won't give to aggression. So, I guess I'll have to think of something else."

Cobby was quiet for a while. "I sure would hate to see them kill her. She really is something."

"Don't get attached, Cobby. All good things go in time."

*****

Valant put Deano on Marie. Mickey didn't give him a moment's peace until he had arranged some way to keep a close eye on her. At the club it wasn't just Deano who kept watch over her, Valant posted men throughout the place. For this, Marie was grateful. No matter where she went during a show, she could find one of the guys close at hand. Deano was in charge of watching out for her, and he took his job very seriously.

Deano was an unattractive man, as well as girthy, but his looks covered up a solid and loyal employee. He was a member of the Delano family, that being so, he was entrusted with jobs of great importance. Mickey felt that Marie was worth the effort. She had in fact increased his holdings single handedly, one song, one dance at a time. She was his dream.

Marie, on the other hand, was just happy to feel a small measure of security. Cobby still spent a fair amount of time following her around. He stayed at the apartment frequently to give Deano a break, but his focus was Valant. She liked having Cobby away, only for the reason that The Dark Horse was less-likely to happen by. She hated and feared him, a combination she didn't know how to deal with.

Since the night Valant had questioned her so intensely she had not seen him. Marie spent a great deal of time thinking about how she would answer him the next time he felt it necessary to question her.

The weeks passed and so did Thanksgiving. The holiday was spent at the apartment eating cold turkey sandwiches Deano brought up from a deli down the street. Marie alternated between playing poker and the piano with Cobby, Deano, Martin and Alfred. The day had ended with a lively game of spoons that resulted in Deano punching Alfred in the face. It would have been scary had it not been so funny.

On the second of December Mickey threw a huge birthday bash for The Dark Horse. It was a private party, an invitation only event. Mickey stopped by the apartment one Sunday afternoon to see Marie who was sitting quietly reading a folded up newspaper, one bare foot tucked beneath her, the other draped over the edge of the sofa. She was alone. Deano had retreated to the entry way to watch television.

Mickey came in alone and caught her by surprise. She started to rise to meet him, but he stopped her. He unbuttoned his suit jacket as sat across the coffee table from her. The shocking contrast of black on white reflecting the violence of his unpredictable mood changes. Marie watched him sit without saying anything. She merely rested her head on her hand.

"Is this what the beautiful and famous do when no one is around? Something as ordinary as reading the paper?"

She smiled slightly. "Yes. For those of us who can read. Can I get you something, Mickey?"

"No. How's Deano and the boys working out?"

"Very well. I appreciate you having them look out for me. I feel much better having them there, but I know it's inconvenient."

"Marie, I have a lot of men. And if it pleased you I would put each one of them where they could watch over you. You mean that much."

She knew he meant monetarily, but she took it as a compliment, for basically that is what it was. He seemed very relaxed and she liked this new version of him. Perhaps he only felt comfortable to show this side of himself when he was alone and beyond the eyes of those whom he commanded.

"Our boy Valant is turning forty-two. So I'm gonna throw him a party. Nothing too overdone, just a private party with a sheet cake half the size of the dance floor and plenty of naked women to jump start his elderly adrenaline system. How does that suit?"

She laughed. "Fine. As long as I'm not one of the naked women."

He grinned. "No, we'll save you for the after party."

She smiled and looked away. "Forty-two, hmm? He seems timeless. How awkward to put a number on him."

"And you've only known him such a short time. How accurately you have him pegged." There was a pause. "What about me? Am I timeless, too?"

She looked at him out of the corner of her eye and gave him a soft smile. "No, Mickey, you're ageless, and there is a difference."

He stretched his arm along the back of the sofa. "I want you to sing him happy birthday. He'll be sitting next to the floor, just come down in something spectacular and sing to him. He'll like that. He's a simple man."

She laughed quietly at this. "He's anything but simple."

Mickey cocked his head as he studied her. "Valant only pursues what he thinks is worth pursuing. If he has a hunch about something, he won't rest until he knows the answer." He had grown dark and the look in his eye was foreboding. Marie sat frozen watching the change coming like she was watching black storm clouds gather in the wind.

He leaned forward and the air chilled. "I truly pity anyone with something to hide. He'll tear you apart to get what is on the inside. I'm content to keep things as they are. I see no reason we all aren't happy. But that's not enough for him."

She looked into his eyes. The moment had come. "Ask me anything and I'll tell you the answer, Mickey. I have nothing to hide. Nothing."

His eyes narrowed as he looked at her. "No, I think we're good where we are. You please me. That's enough. We'll talk differently if you stop pleasing me." With that he stood to go. He buttoned his jacket and walked to the door. Before he left he turned, again the sunny disposition in his eyes. "Don't forget, Valant's birthday. I added a few songs to the list. I left it with Rolly for rehearsal tomorrow." With that he was gone.

So he knew more than he chose to let on. The lonely feeling of desperation settled once again on her like a cloak. She had no idea what to do, but Mickey made it clear as long as she served her purpose he would leave her alone. But if she ever stopped serving that purpose, she was done. The Dark Horse wouldn't play fair anymore.

*****

Marie did as she was told. Putting on a white sheer strapless that hugged her figure with a split up her thigh, she rolled up her hair behind her head and placed jeweled pins throughout. She had spent a lot of hours in the dark alone thinking about what Mickey had said about being pleasing. It was a long shot, but she figured it might work to please them both. So she made her plans and dressed according to his command. She put on a diamond necklace that rested comfortably between the curves of her breasts where they swelled above the gown. Marie's skin held no blemishes in its smoothness.

She waited backstage as the ensemble played through the first five numbers. Mickey had wanted her opening performance to be like a gift for The Dark Horse. She loved the opportunity to listen to Rolly for whose talent she had much respect. Mickey had actually chosen a fair number of Italian songs of which were sung in his native tongue. Mickey may have been raised in the states, but he spent a fair amount of time back in the home country as a kid. Therefore so had The Dark Horse.

When it came time for her to go, she made her way down the side stairs and met Deano waiting at the bottom. He offered his arm. She smiled at him as she took it. She enjoyed watching the roundness of his cheeks turn red. Picking out Delano men dispersed in the crowd, Marie felt comfort knowing it took Deano's consent to approach her.

Deano took her to the edge of the dance floor where they stood waiting for Rolly to finish. He sang so beautifully, his deep voice hinged with a husky tone. The floor was crowded and she caught sight of The Dark Horse dancing with his beautiful married lady. Mickey moved less fluidly with his wife, who was less than stunning when compared to Margo, but far higher in the order of things.

It took a moment for the floor to clear at the end of the song. "Now please, if you would bring your attention to center floor for something very special," Rolly announced and Marie took her cue to get to the center spot light on the floor. As she reached it, a beam of light flooded her immediate proximity and reflected vibrantly off the jewels around her neck.

She couldn't see much beyond the spotlight, but she had a general direction to follow. She walked gracefully to the table where he sat, a spray of streamers and confetti around the drinks that sat half empty across the top. Applause sounded around her as this was her first appearance of the evening. She would sing without the aid of an amplifier.

"Good evening," she spoke to those around her, then turned her focus onto The Dark Horse. "Mickey asked me to come down here and sing you a traditional birthday song. But," she looked at Mickey now, "With your permission, I would like to give Mr. Valant a more personal gift of song." She paused and waited for his say so. He hesitated only a moment before giving a curt nod. He didn't trust her not to do something foolish.

"Thank you for indulging me, Mickey." She turned back to Valant who sat leisurely on his chair watching her with something akin to interest, his eyes bright with intensity. She whispered to him, "For old times' sake." Then she smiled at him and gave him a slight wink. "If I can remember the words." She laughed softly at herself then.

She closed her eyes and left the club. She was again a child listening to that incredible performance so long ago that still sounded live inside her mind. She let the words and the tune flow from her freely, knowing that the last time she had sung the song that loudly was all those years ago when he had been listening in the dark. The record Vinny bought her played in her mind.

Alfredo Clerici's *Tu, Solamente Tu.*

She didn't open her eyes, just kept singing.

The crowd erupted at her finish, but Marie didn't notice until her eyes opened. Chairs scraped as people stood to applaud the Italian sweetheart who had vocalized a masterpiece. She bowed graciously and said thank you to those around her. Then she turned to The Dark Horse who was still seated. As was Margo.

He met and held Marie's eyes and slowly began to stand. As he did so Margo's hand latched onto the crook of his elbow with a death grip. He either didn't notice or didn't care, for he pulled away from her easily. Margo pasted on a fake smile and pretended to clap with the rest of the crowd, but her efforts to look pleased didn't quite play through.

Marie smiled at The Dark Horse, hoping that some sort of pleasure might show through his cold features. He took several steps to her; she held her ground as he approached. He leaned down next to her ear and placed a hand lightly on her bare upper arm, his fingertips brushing softly against her skin. He pressed his lips to her ear.

"Thank you, Marie. That was very beautiful." With that he placed a light kiss on her tilted cheek. As he moved away the tips of his fingers slid down her arm to her elbow. He kept his eyes on hers until she smiled at the still cheering crowd and moved away into the darkness. The spotlight was now focused on the huge cake that rolled across the dance floor toward the table. The band struck up a lively version of happy birthday. Marie turned to look over her shoulder at him again as she walked across the floor in the darkness. Although the enormous cake was now before him, The Dark Horse still looked into the shadows after her.

*****

May 1944

This was hell. Val knew that. He looked down the long tiled hallway that smelled of cleaner and despair. He sat on a hard wooden chair outside a closed door and waited like a statue for news. Any news. He kept his hands fisted together, his elbows on his knees. He had taken off his black jacket and draped it across his lap. He waited.

From inside the room muffled sobs cut into him. The nurses wouldn't let him in. He'd gone in twice already only to be forcibly removed by male staff. They compromised on the chair when they realized he wasn't going to quit. He bowed his head, sighing deeply. Mickey was still holding out hope. Val knew better.

She was fine when Mickey left her early that morning. She complained of being tired and was irritated the morning sickness had returned. It just wasn't fair considering she only had a few weeks to go before the baby was born. It was near impossible to slouch over the toilet to puke with such a large protrusion out front of her body.

Mickey kissed her softly and held her for a while before rising and getting dressed. He didn't need to leave her. What the hell could have been so important? But he had, with the promise he would come check her at lunch time. Out of love he'd called her at eight o'clock to see how she was, but she didn't answer the telephone. He figured she was still sleeping and cussed himself for probably interrupting her.

At noon he called her to tell her he wouldn't make it home. Georgio asked him to lunch with several of his business associates. A twinge of fear pricked in his stomach when she still didn't answer. As he sat at lunch the fear only increased. At length he broke away to ask Val if he'd go check on her. He knew he was probably being ridiculous, and Georgio would throw a fit if he left such an important meeting to go check his pregnant wife.

Val could go without repercussions. And Mickey trusted him completely. A wave of relief swept over him as he watched his friend leave the restaurant. Val drove alone to Mickey and Maryanne's. They lived in a quiet neighborhood far from the downtown area. It was a well-kept neighborhood, and it was Maryanne's white picket fence dream. They lived in peace there, mostly thanks to Val's vigilance.

He pulled his car up to the garage noting that her car hadn't moved, so she hadn't gone out. The front door was locked, so he went around the side of the house to the back door that wasn't. He chuckled to himself about how mad she'd be that he had shown up without calling. She hated it when she didn't have time to set herself and her home to straights before a guest arrived. Even Val, who had seen her and the house in various states of disarray.

He opened the door and put his head in. The house was quiet. He called out to her, but no sound greeted his voice. He came the rest of the way in and shut the door. He walked through the back porch and into the kitchen before calling again. The milk Mickey got off the back porch that morning was still in the wire carrier on the counter where he set it for Maryanne to put away. It was now warm and no doubt spoiled.

Val saw the phone hanging from the wall, the receiver lying on the floor. That was why Mickey could not reach her. It wasn't ringing through. Fear shot through him at that sight and he quickly pulled out his gun in anticipation of what gruesome discovery might greet him.

He went through the living room, turning to go down the hall to the bedrooms. Nothing looked amiss. The silence was cut only by the sound of a car on the street. He passed the first few doors without stopping. The door to Mickey and Maryanne's room stood open. He made his way to it. Sweat began to form on his forehead. He knew surely he didn't want to see what he was about to.

At first he couldn't find her. He looked in the bathroom. Aside from the faucet running a trickle, nothing looked out of place. The bed was unmade and the blankets were thrown back as if someone had become tangled in them as they tried to get up. He moved through the bedroom, and prepared to look elsewhere when a small sound caught his attention. It was the puff of a breath. He quickly moved around the bed and saw her there, on the floor.

The lower half of her body was under the bed, and her upper half was wedged by her large belly. He went to her repeating her name. She had clearly fallen then rolled herself up under the bed. Her face was covered in sweat and her breathing was erratic at best. When he pulled her out from underneath the bed she did not stir or acknowledge that he had done so. There was no blood, no sign of a struggle. Val cradled her head in his arms and tried again in vain to rouse her.

He grabbed a pillow and lay her head gently down on it before rising and running back to the kitchen and the telephone that lay on the floor. He picked it up by the cord and impatiently tapped the button. When he finally heard a tone he turned the rotary dial. Julian's voice answered Georgio's office telephone.

"It's Maryanne. Get Mickey and meet me at the hospital!"

"What happened?"

"No time. Meet me!" Val dropped the telephone and the sound echoed as it hit the floor.

He ran back to the bedroom and straightened the bedsheets. He picked up her heavily pregnant body and lay her on them, wrapping her up. He carried her out through the kitchen, knocking the spoiled milk to the floor in the process. The glass shattered and milk splattered everywhere. Val didn't bother to close the door behind them.

Maryanne was pale and sweat ran down her face into the black of her hair. Where once she was still, she now shook violently in a spasm. A trickle of blood ran from her mouth as her clenched jaws bit into her tongue.

"Maryanne! Can you hear me? Please. Please!"

It was the first time in a long time he didn't feel equal to the task.

He opened the door to the back seat and lay her inside. He slammed the door and slid into the driver's seat and fired the engine. He left black marks that would curdle Maryanne's blood when she saw them. She loved for things to be neat and clean. For the first time he realized he hoped she lived to see them.

She shook and convulsed the entire way, her small frame tensing, her muscles contracting with such ferocity that her back bowed and her arms raised away from her. It took nearly twenty minutes to get from Mickey's down to St. Matthew's Hospital. When Val arrived, he drove straight to the entrance. It was a struggled to get her tense frame gathered and pulled from the car. A wide streak of blood now ran down her face to her neck. The nurses had him lay her on a rolling cot as they shouted for a doctor. Then they took her from him. They turned down another hall at a dead run. Several nurses stopped Val

from following as he heard the doctor reciting unfamiliar
medical terms along the corridor.

"Please, sir. Is that your wife? Is that your wife, sir?" The
nurse yelled up at Val in an attempt to get his attention.

"No. No. She's a dear friend." He pushed the nurse aside,
but she took hold of his arms.

"Please, sir. You cannot go with her. It is hospital policy
that only immediate family can accompany a patient. They
need to see to her just now. Please be patient." He flung her
away only to have her clamp down on him again. He drug the
two women as he followed after Maryanne.

"Maryanne!"

"I know this is hard. Please give the doctor a chance to
look at her! Please, sir!"

"Val! Val!" Mickey's frantic voice sounded behind him.
Julian and Mickey had come through the entrance. Val was
struck dumb. The words would not come. He knew what he
had seen, and he knew no one, surely, could return from that.
But he couldn't tell Mickey. Julian didn't have to be told. He
knew from Val's face.

"Who are you? Are you the husband?"

"Yes. Please tell me what the hell is going on here! Val!"

"The doctor is examining her right now. Please we need
you to fill out some information on her. Please come with me."
Mickey pushed the nurse away.

"Val! What's going on?" Val just stared at him. Tears
came to Mickey's eyes. "Val! Tell me!"

A nurse turned from the hall Maryanne had been taken
into. She had a gentle look on her face as she approached. She
reached out and put a hand on Mickey's arm. "Are you her
husband?" Mickey nodded at her. "Please, it would be a great
help to us if you could answer a few questions. Maybe start by
telling us her name, and how far along she is in her
pregnancy." She looked at him in the eyes.

"I need to know what's going on here. Where the hell is
my wife?"

Julian looked again to Val. He placed a hand on Mickey's
shoulder and squeezed. "I think they don't know yet, Mickey.
Why don't you help them out and answer their questions. It
may help them treat her." His voice was steady and reassuring.
The nurse turned Mickey down the hall where Maryanne had

been taken. Val and Julian watched them go, the sad look of reality realized cleanly etched on their faces.

"God help them." It was the closest Val had ever heard Julian come to a prayer. He now put his hand on Val's shoulder.

"Come, son. Let's find a place to wait." Julian turned him in the opposite direction they had been facing walking him away.

The waiting turned into hours. Julian alternated pacing and sitting, but Val just sat, his shoulders sagging. He had grown angry and gone into the room only to be removed. He was there long enough to see Maryanne was still convulsing. Mickey was washed in a sea of grief and desperation. He was openly crying now, the tears running down his face. Val got to him once and squeezed his shoulder. Mickey didn't notice.

All told it took nine hours. By the time the doctors decided that the mother could not be spared and wheeled Maryanne's body to surgery to remove the baby, the poor child had been so stressed in the ordeal it lived only a few minutes. They had allowed that Mickey could hold it for a while. He did so with such division within himself. He had longed for this child, dreamed of it, but it was a stranger to him where its mother was not. He wanted to hold her one last time, too. It had been a boy.

He was allowed as well to see Maryanne one final time. For this Val was permitted. He had gone to support Mickey's weak body and kept a steady hold on him as his friend lie prostrate with grief over the lifeless body of the love of his life. He cried bitter racking sobs that cut into Val as Mickey rested his head on Maryanne's chest. At length, Julian said that Mickey had enough and helped Val to pull him from the room. By now Georgio waited outside in the hall. Mickey didn't notice him, either.

They called it eclampsia. Whatever that was, Val had no idea.

Val and Julian put him in the car and drove. Julian kept a quiet eye on Val, who now showed no emotion. He was like granite. Julian squeezed his shoulder. Val said nothing. He would not have been heard over Mickey's cries anyway.

Val took them to the beach and they watched the sunrise as they held their friend in the beginning hours of his anguish. After days of grief and exhaustion, Mickey buried his son and wife next to his brother, Sam. He had chosen to name his son Amato, meaning beloved.

*****

December 1955

The doorbell jingled as Marie walked into Imelda's shop. Light perfume greeted Marie like an old friend, welcoming her into a world she had a year before only dreamed of. She had not been in for several weeks and in that time Imelda had made the costumes for the Christmas shows. Mickey had planned everything down to the last detail. It was going to be grand. For the night of December Twenty-third only, two separate performances would be held at the club.

He had planned as a bonus for all his employees, as they were dubiously called, that the first performance of the evening would be a family affair. Children would be allowed, and refreshments befitting such an audience would be served; hot chocolate, Christmas cookies, and goodie bags for all the younger crowd.

At nine o'clock the adult show would begin. These were the gowns that Marie was now having fitted for the final time. This, as many had been before, was an invitation only event, for both the performances. The ensemble had been rehearsing for several weeks to get both shows correct. But, it was looked forward to with much anticipation and excitement. Even Marie was looking forward to it.

"I'll be right with you, Marie," Imelda said from above the swinging doors beyond the counter. Marie smiled a reply.

It was one of the rare times recently that Cobby had accompanied Marie. She moved through the shop to the chairs on the other side of the counter and took a seat. Cobby did as well, but he exhaled deeply as he did so. He sat back with his legs stretched out before him. His face held the look of a man who cared not for the task at hand.

Marie held her sweater on her lap, a funny half smile on her lips. How often he looked like a disobedient little boy trapped in a man's black suit. He caught her watching and shot her a look of hate. She tilted her head and rested it on her hand. The sound of voices coming through the swinging doors caught her attention.

"If you can't fix it by then, I'll go to Marquez for my gown. I don't need this kind of hang up, Imelda. Either do it right, or I'll go somewhere else." The woman's voice was clipped and condescending. Marie looked out of the corner of her eye to see the identity of the woman.

"Don't look at her," Cobby whispered low.

"I'm very sorry, Margo. I can assure this little issue will be dealt with by tomorrow. Your gown will be ready in the morning."

"Imelda, I don't care if she is your daughter. If she can't produce to the standard, she needs to be fired." To this Imelda did not reply, just stood looking at the younger blonde woman with tight lips. Although, she was not younger by much.

"I expected better of you. That you would teach her better than that."

"Well, if she has any failings, which I doubt she does, then those failings are my fault, not hers." Imelda stated firmly. "I will have your gown fixed tomorrow morning if you want to send a courier. Otherwise you can pick it up any time after we open."

Margo had reached into her clutch and produced a cigarette which she lit and blew smoke out into the confines of the shop. She looked down her nose at Imelda, and pursed her lips. "I think next time I will try Marquez. Perhaps he realizes the importance of hiring talented seamstresses." With that she turned to leave the shop, but as she did so, she caught sight of the two people sitting in the chairs next to the counter in the waiting area.

"Well, what an occasion. To finally meet up with the enigmatic Marie Barelli." Her words were laced with a faint sarcasm. She strode the few paces to stand before Marie who looked up at her from her seated position. Margo raised her cigarette to her lips again.

Marie wasn't sure if she should rise, but she did so anyway. Margo was slightly taller than she, and from such a close distance she realized that the eternally beautiful Margo had crow's feet that she was desperately trying to hide.

Marie held out her hand. "Pleased to meet you. I'm Marie."

Margo did not take her hand. Instead she took another drag on her cigarette and blew smoke in Marie's face. Marie arched a brow. Margo put a hand on a well curved hip and thrust her breasts out. "Mickey's new plaything. You ain't much."

Marie felt Cobby rise to a standing position behind her. Margo let out a chuckle. "Easy boy wonder. I'm sure there's plenty of her to go around, and around."

Margo blew another drag at Marie. "Perhaps you should smoke that outside. I doubt Imelda appreciates your smelling like an ashtray in her shop. If you'll excuse me, I have more important things to do." With that Marie stepped around her and moved toward Imelda who stood with a deeply troubled look in her eyes while watching the proceedings. Cobby continued to stand looking down at Margo whose eyes flashed like fire.

Cobby knew Margo well. He knew that Marie would pay dearly for the slight she'd just dealt. Not that Margo didn't have it coming, but the woman played wicked games with everyone; games the kind hearted had no way of winning. Marie walked to Imelda and they moved through the doors together, chatting about the fitting.

Margo watched them go out of aging eyes and plotted her revenge. But unlike what she had suffered in front of only two witnesses, Marie would pay in front of many. She shot Cobby a look of loathing and strode out of the shop.

Cobby moved through the swinging doors to approach the dais where Imelda and Marie now stood talking about the Christmas shows. Imelda stopped immediately and turned to Cobby. "Is she gone?"

"Yeah." Imelda looked to Marie and sighed.

"That wasn't smart. Not at all," Cobby stated flatly. Marie shrugged.

"Let's move on. She's not the first person to call me that."

"She'll make you pay."

Marie looked disdainfully at him. "What can she do, huh?"

"You won't even see it coming," Cobby muttered.

"Yes, I will. Women like her are predictable. Well, let's see the first, Imelda. Cobby here can be our neutral judge." Marie said cheerfully. Cobby shrugged his shoulders and stepped off the dais. He sat back into the sofa.

"Would you like some coffee, Cobby?" Imelda asked. He grunted his agreement.

"Julia, would you get Cobby some coffee, please?"

At that moment Imelda's daughter Julia came out from the dressing room behind Marie. She smiled softly at Marie and then moved to get Cobby's coffee. She was a smaller and younger version of Imelda, but did not possess Imelda's outspoken nature.

"Let's try the elf costume first. I had such a great time making this one." Imelda went to the dress rack and began to unzip a cloth garment bag. Marie undressed behind the privacy screen. "I couldn't help making a little hat to go with it!"

When they had zipped Marie into the costume, she turned and looked at herself in the mirror. It was a red sequined strapless, and it was trimmed in white fur. The pencil skirt reached to her knees with a short split up the back to allow for more movement when she danced.

Imelda smiled when she stepped back to look at Marie. "Ah, Marie, you are the perfect model for anything I make. Let's see what Cobby thinks."

When they stepped back out onto the dais, Cobby leaned back into the sofa and rested his cup of coffee on his leg. He extended his free arm along the back of the sofa.

"What do you think?" Imelda asked in her thick Italian accent.

"It'll do."

"Well, I guess if that's all we're gonna get from him, we'll just take it as a compliment." Imelda said sarcastically. "Are you going down to the South Side for Christmas, Cobby?"

Cobby leveled his gaze at Imelda. "Just concern yourself with Marie."

Imelda clicked her tongue as she fussed with the fur trim on Marie's gown. "How many years has it been since you went home, eh?"

"Imelda, this is none of your business. By now they've gotten used to me not being around."

Imelda shook her head angrily. "A mother never gets used to not having her child. She would like to know that you're still alive. How many tears that woman must have shed by now wondering what has become of you."

"I think it's probably best that she not know what's become of me, don't you?" He said hotly.

Imelda stopped fussing and turned sharply to look at him. "Go and see her. Smile like you're happy. Tell her you got an office job. Let her be next to you for a while. That would mean everything to her."

181

"I think paying her mortgage and supporting four boys when I was sixteen is really all she needed from me to make her happy. Paying their way until she met and married that prick was sufficient."

"Don't do that, Cobby." Imelda pointed a long finger at him. "You have no idea what it is to be a woman alone. If you did, you wouldn't condemn her to a life of loneliness. She has the right to be happy. Take it from a woman who has been there, sleeping alone every night and walking alone through the day grows wearying after a time. She was a young woman with a long life ahead after her boys left home, filled with nothing but solitude. Don't you dare judge her. Forgive her for what you think is a betrayal to your dead father and allow her the warmth and comfort of life."

Cobby stood and pointed sharply back. "Imelda, it would be one thing to allow her the warmth and comfort of life if she were with a man who offered her those things. He's done nothing but divide her against me from the moment they married. She has allowed that!"

"Cobby, you don't understand…"

Cobby's voice raised. "No you don't understand! You don't understand that after all I went through working for Val just to keep her and my brothers not just alive, but comfortable, she didn't even have the balls to stand up for me the last time I was there. Old man Medford pulled a shot gun on me. Called me mob trash. Said I wasn't allowed back in his house!" He pointed a finger at himself. "His house! The house I PAID FOR. The house I spent countless hours in hell to provide! And if he thought I wasn't good enough to come into the house I paid for, he certainly didn't have any qualms about my money putting three of my brothers through university! He didn't offer to pay for that! So don't you sit here and tell me she needs the comfort of my presence when she has lived quite comfortably without it!" He paused for a moment.

"Are we done here yet?" he yelled at her.

Marie looked to the floor and wondered how Imelda felt brazen enough to say the things she did. Her words ignited fire every time.

When Imelda spoke again her voice was very soft. "I'm very sorry, Cobby. I did not mean to upset you so. I just thought it might bring you peace to say good-bye to one another. Close a long and painful subject." When she turned to

Marie her voice was steady and determined. "Well, let's try the other two gowns on. Then we'll be done." Marie said nothing as they returned to the dressing room.

When they had gone behind the privacy screen, Imelda gave Marie a bold smile. "It just goes to show that no matter how important you are, how prestigious your position, you still have to contend with your mother." Imelda laughed at that. "We'll see what he does."

Marie wondered again at her. Imelda had a way of picking out the things that seemed to eat away at people then try to extract it. She was bold for a simple dress maker. Marie hoped that Imelda would not find and root out any of her short comings. Marie knew she had a few that probably needed dealt with.

The ensemble had one last dress rehearsal that morning. They went through both performances quickly. It was hoped that a little time between rehearsal and the show would afford a chance for rest. When they were able to get through, Cobby took Marie back to the apartment where she took a short nap. They went together to the restaurant for an early dinner.

As she sat alone at her booth eating, she cast a glance over to Cobby who ate with Frankie. She thought back to the things he had said to Imelda. She wondered how it was that he had come to be a part of this ring of violence. He indicated it was not entirely willingly done. But he had his reasons. Where she had been drug in, he had come in willingly from the outside. But, depending on those reasons, maybe he had been drug as well. Something inside her softened toward him a little more. He was a handsome although troubled man.

When she arrived at the club the place was bursting with energy. Cobby brought her through the front entrance since a supply truck had blocked the alley. They walked through the double doors to see the entire club had been completely transformed in just a few hours. Large decorated Christmas trees stood sentry in the main entrance. In the bar area, garland was draped along the balconies. From the garland hung glass ornaments of every color. Trees occupied all corners, some with fake gifts below, and the base of each tree was swathed in thick white cotton that looked like swirled snow. Soft twinkling strands of glass lights glowed golden from the trees.

The dance floor was no less incredible. It was a country Christmas scene. A wooden fence had been erected around the floor. Atop the posts hung pine bough wreaths and holly. Along the bottom looked as if a great blizzard had swept through as yards upon yards of pure white cotton looked authentically like drifted snow. In each corner of the dance floor stood a pine tree draped in shimmering angel hair that looked like frost.

The stage was draped in white cotton with bare space for the performers to walk safely, but from the audience it looked as though each step taken by the cast was in the snow. Enormous Christmas trees graced the sides of the stage, and were ornately decorated from top to bottom. On the top of each tree sat beautiful ceramic angels that held brilliantly shining lights. Soft golden candles shone from every banister and railing. Fake red cardinals sat perched on the railings as well. It took Marie's breath away to see such a magnificent sight that came about in a few short hours.

"Thanks, Cobby. I'll see you later." Cobby said nothing in return just walked away towards the private stage.

Behind stage was in its usual chaos. Marie laughed as she pushed through the crowd of performers, all light and gay with the prospect of the upcoming festivities. The club would be on hiatus until New Year's Eve, so many would be traveling to see family. The excitement was easy to get caught up in and everyone gave well wishes for a very Merry Christmas.

A long table was set up by the ladders that led up to the lighting catwalks. It was laden with Christmas goodies; cookies, cakes, meat and cheese trays, and candies. It was completed with a huge crystal bowl of red punch. The best of it was someone had smuggled a bottle of hooch from the bar and spiked it. Already faces were red, and laughing became more jovial.

Marie took a moment to make her way back to the table and snatched a few goodies before she had to dress. She stood back and took it all in. Not one soul was unhappy or tired. The laughter rang out and someone struck up a record player with Bing Crosby's Christmas Album. Marie sampled the punch.

"Oh, go easy on that stuff, Marie. I watched the sax section poor an entire half gallon of rum in there." Rolly chuckled when he saw her pained expression upon tasting it.

"No worries there, I don't think I could choke much of that down anyway." Rolly laughed as Marie set the glass on the table away from her.

"It was good of ol' Mick to spring for a Christmas party. Everyone is having a great time." He came to stand next to Marie and also looked out over the crowd.

"Yes." Several more of the dance company came and helped themselves to the punch. "Do you think we ought to do something about the punch before nobody can play or dance?"

"Nah, let them have some fun." Rolly drawled out.

"I don't suppose it would do to have the entire ensemble falling down drunk for the family portion of the evening." At Marie's comment Rolly laughed.

"I doubt we'd get a Christmas party next year," Rolly said.

"You traveling for Christmas?" Marie asked.

Rolly smiled at her. "Nope. Gonna spend some time with my family. You?" Marie tried to hide the wistfulness.

"Well, I'm sure I can rely on Deano for company." Rolly looked at her and gave her a half smile.

"You're welcome with us. My wife passed a few years ago, but the kids and the rest of the folks would be happy to have you." She squeezed his arm.

"Thanks, Rolly," She whispered. He looked down at her softly. "Well, I better get dressed. See you in a bit."

The dressing room was so loud Marie couldn't hear herself think. Laughter and singing rang out as half-clad girls waltzed around the room while they slipped into elf costumes. Theirs were green and less elaborate than Marie's, but flattering nonetheless. As she came in she sought out Jean.

"You're in luck. Rolly's a widower." Marie winked at her then walked over to her dressing area.

Marie's gown for the first portion of the evening was a floor length white. It had a sheer outer covering and a V-neck that didn't cut very low. She put a deep red rose in her hair. It was a nice costume for a family gathering.

The stage master's voice boomed for places as the record player was cut abruptly off. The laughter of the men in the band had grown so that Marie worried for a moment that they really wouldn't be able to play until she realized they were laughing at the children out in the audience. They rushed about looking at the decorations and feeling the "snow" to see if it were real. Waiters scurried after them in an attempt to keep the room in order. A young fellow had opened one of the fake gifts to see what was in it. He was met with disappointment and reprimand.

It was a beautiful evening for the children. Rolly, Marie, and the backup girls sang *Silent Night, We Three Kings,* and countless others while wandering out among the crowd to sing with the children. The lighting was soft and it gave the feeling of Christmas' true meaning. It had been many years since Marie had that.

Towards the end, the entire ensemble gathered on the dance floor with big red packs on their backs and went out amongst the filled tables to distribute gifts. The children squealed with delight. The faces of the gift bearers were no less excited. When the gifts had been distributed, the company met on the dance floor again and sang Mel Torme's *The Christmas Song* and Irving Berlin's *White Christmas.* They turned to each other to give hugs and wish each other Happy Christmas once again, then filtered out to prepare for the next show.

A large crowd gathered around the goodie table again and punch was served. Joyous laughter reflected the happiness performing for the children had put into everyone's hearts. Marie stopped as well, spending some time visiting with her co-performers. It felt good to belong to something so special again. It had taken a long time to feel as though she were a part of it. Stress melted as she forgot about her trouble for the evening.

Before long Deano came to whisper in her ear that she was wanted on the private stage.

"Something very important," was all he said.

She excused herself from the conversation she was having with Helen and Jean then followed Deano down the stage stairs across the now empty floor. Waiters and bus boys hurried to clean up from the first performance to ready for the second. Marie did not envy the person in charge of wiping up all the sticky spilled hot chocolate.

When they reached the top of the stairs to the private stage, Marie saw a small group of people gathered together. It was a magnificent sight. The trees here were far more elaborately decorated and there were more colorful lights on the trees. Each table top had a center piece that consisted of angel hair and a Christmas candle. None of these were yet lit, but would be soon. Holly sprigs also adorned the angel hair. It smelled of pine forest.

Deano walked her to the small gathering and within she saw Mickey crouched on the floor talking to someone. It was a small girl, not very old, but Marie could tell that something was wrong with her. Although she stood as straight as she could, her spine had a severe curve in it which made it very difficult to stand correctly. She wore braces on her legs, and leaned heavily against a metal crutch. She smiled at Mickey while he talked, but he spoke low and Marie could not hear what he said. Around them stood several people Marie didn't know, but The Dark Horse and Margo stood back from the group. Cobby stood next to The Dark Horse and made a comment to him to which The Dark Horse nodded. Eva also stood looking disdainfully down at them.

Deano leaned down and spoke into Mickey's ear, and he turned his head to look at Marie out of the corner of his eye. Then he rose. "And here she is, the lady you desire to meet."

Mickey stood and looked pointedly at Marie and she knew a warning was in that look. "I would like you to meet someone very special, Marie. This is Evelyn, my niece."

She understood what he wanted. She looked from him to Evelyn and smiled warmly. She reached down and took hold of the girl's frail hand. "I am pleased to meet you, Evelyn. My name is Marie Barelli."

Evelyn smiled joyfully up at her.

"Evelyn has something very important she wants to tell you." A smiling woman next to Evelyn said. Marie guessed her to be the girl's mother.

"Oh, an important message. I better get down close to you so I can hear it better." Marie crouched down where Mickey had been before. She took hold of the hand not holding the crutch. Her white dress circled out around her.

Evelyn battled a sudden case of shyness as she tried to speak. "I think you have the prettiest voice I have ever heard."

Marie again smiled as she squeezed her hand. "Thank you, Evelyn. That means so very much to me. Bringing joy to those around me gives me great pleasure."

"I think you are very beautiful, too." Marie smiled at this but said nothing about it.

"What do you want to be when you grow up?" Evelyn became very shy and looked down at the floor as she whispered her reply.

"I want to be a singer."

"I thought maybe you would. You look to me like a girl who loves to sing." Evelyn smiled broadly as she looked up at Marie.

"Maybe someday I could sing in my zio's club like you!"

"I think maybe so, Evelyn. All you have to do is keep dreaming, and keep singing. The rest will come with time. I think you will grow to be a beautiful woman, Evelyn. When I was your age, I dreamed of growing up to sing just as I do now. And although I had to work at it, and caught a lucky break on account of your zio is tone deaf," laughter sounded around the gathering while Mickey gave Marie a sharp look. "I still realized my dream."

"I hope someday I can sing with you."

"Me too," Marie said as she squeezed the small hand again. Then Marie withdrew hers and reached up into her hair to the rose that was pinned there.

"Evelyn, do you have a favorite Christmas song?" Evelyn thought only a moment before she replied.

"My favorite of all of them is Ave Maria."

It took Marie a moment to unpin the rose, but when she did she reached up into Evelyn's dark hair and repined it there.

"Ave Maria is my favorite, too. I used to sing it every Christmas Eve down at the St. Francis Cathedral during midnight mass when I was a girl. It isn't Christmas to me until I sing Ave Maria. Can I sing it for you now?"

Evelyn's face fairly beamed. "Oh, yes! Please!"

"Very good." Marie rose and again squeezed her hand. "It has been an honor meeting you, Evelyn. I hope I see you soon."

Evelyn's mother gently squeezed Marie's arm. "Thank you!" She whispered fiercely as tears brimmed in her eyes. The man next to her did the same. He was clearly Evelyn's father, although neither of them looked like the Delano's. Evelyn's fingers brushed the rose lightly as her face reflected exhilaration. Marie had no way of knowing that Evelyn and her mother both bore a strong resemblance to Mickey's first wife, Maryanne.

Deano moved away with Marie, following her up the stage stairs. He remained in the dark as she moved to the microphone. Hers was the only spotlight on the stage and Marie looked out to see that the staff was still busily cleaning up for the next round. She heard the joyous festivities taking place back stage.

"Excuse me ladies and gentlemen. I have a very special song request from a dear friend of mine. Her name is Evelyn and someday she will be standing where I am. So here goes a song for the future headliner of The Ruby."

As Marie began to sing, she closed her eyes and pictured the Cathedral. She did sing Franz Schubert's *Ave Maria* each Christmas, but instead of Evelyn listening, it was Vinny. She remembered the words perfectly. It was one of her favorite songs.

As her voice lifted and reached each ear, the bustling in the club ceased. Bus boys and waiters stood still and silent as they listened. Bartenders also listened and forgot about their duties. Someone came back stage and said that Marie was singing out front. The company gathered in the darkness behind her to listen as well. Evelyn stood on the top step to the private stage, completely mesmerized. Mickey himself leaned against the banister above Evelyn and focused on Marie. The Dark Horse and Cobby rested against the railing of the private stage. Time had stopped. The world did not exist in that moment. Only the voice of an angel sent by God prevailed.

When Marie had finished, no one moved. They were still lost in the sound of heaven, reluctant to go back to reality. When she opened her eyes she was shocked to see that she had brought Mickey's world to a halt. She looked up at him and for the first time, he smiled at her. She bowed her head to him and walked away.

When she got to the stage entrance Rolly smiled at her. "I'll never forget that. Not ever."

She moved into the crowd as they went backstage again to prepare for the next show.

The next show was far different from the first. Marie changed into her red costume with the white fur trim. This time instead of a rose in her hair, she wore a small elf hat. It was quite comical coupled with the seductive dress that Imelda had made. She wore open heels that were very high and the trim accentuated her bust. Everyone made great time preparing. When the band moved into position, Marie and the girls were ready.

The spotlight lit center stage on Rolly who was sitting in a large wood chair. He was dressed like Santa Claus. Next to him were Helen and Paula who were dressed as elves. The crowd cheered. The house was loaded.

"Good evening everybody! Good evening! We hope you are all ready to have a good time tonight!" More hollering went on. "I want to thank everyone for coming out. I want to take this chance to wish everyone Merry Christmas." He paused a moment as he turned to look where Marie waited in the dark. "I have a little something for my right hand lady, if she'll come out here with me. Marie?"

She was ready, although Rolly wasn't following the script. Marie walked onto the stage and into the spot light with him. More cheering sounded as she appeared. She smiled and waved to the crowd.

"Why don't you come over here and sit down a minute." Marie looked at him as if she hadn't heard right so he patted his lap. She looked out to the audience as if asking if she should. They clapped loudly.

"You can trust me," Rolly said. So, Marie walked over to him and carefully sat on his lap. It was awkward. They had touched many times, but that had been a rehearsed and planned meeting. This was not.

"Well, you got me here. What's next?" She asked playfully. Rolly just stared into her eyes.

"Well?"

He let out a discomfited laugh as he looked into her eyes. The audience was silent, waiting for his reply. "You know, I rehearsed this a hundred times in my head. Now that you're actually sitting here, I'll be damned if I can remember what I'm supposed to say." He paused as he looked up at the private stage. "Mickey, ol' boy, I've waited a long time to get ahold of Marie like this. I think I might take my chance and run with her!"

The crowd exploded. Men stood and gave Rolly a standing ovation as they cheered him on in his proposal. Whooping echoed from everywhere. Rolly laughed heartily as Marie turned a deep red.

"I'm supposed to ask if you've been a good girl and reward you accordingly. But right now, all I can think is that I hope you're not a good girl!" Again the audience roared to life where they had died some to hear Rolly's words. Marie could hear the band responding as well. She blushed deeper. Helen and Paula cheered.

"Oh fellas, look at that pretty shade of red!" Rolly yelled. Whistles sounded and Marie turned away from the audience to hide her face. Rolly was laughing a deep roar. Even the occupants of the private stage were on their feet. Women clapped, yelling as loudly as the men at Marie's embarrassment.

"Come on, Marie, honey, look at me again." She refused. She was laughing some herself now, but the sting she felt at the humiliation of blushing stung greatly.

"I'm sorry, honey. Look at me." She looked at him, her right hand resting on his collar bone, her left arm around his shoulders. He got a funny look on his face again.

"Nope, never mind. Don't look at me. I can't think when you look at me like that." Rolly was laughing again and for the first time he wasn't bailing her out of her predicament. The crowd was still going wild.

Rolly stood with her in his arms and yelled to the crowd, "I got what I wanted for Christmas, now I'm outta here! And what a pretty shade of red it came in!" The response was deafening.

Rolly put her down and stood there laughing in her ear as she couldn't look at the audience yet. She covered her face, but it was becoming funnier to her now. Rolly hugged her close to him, apologizing in her ear.

"I'm sorry. I'm sorry, this got out of hand. We can't help it. You've never lost control, ever." She looked up at him and lay her palms against his chest. She smiled at him while laughing at herself. He hugged her again. When Rolly released her, he kept hold of her hand, as if she might flee. He moved to the microphone and bent slightly as he spoke.

"Alright, let's get on with it! Lady Elves, if you please!"

Helen stepped forward with a box and handed it to Rolly. The crowd finally grew quiet and sat.

"The members of the company wanted to say a little thank you to Marie. She's worked really hard since she came on board. She has worked very hard in the performances, yes, but her greatest work has been taking the time to get to know each of us personally and care about what we have to say. Not a day goes by that she doesn't take the time to listen. We are proud of her, and what she has done for The Ruby."

With that Rolly opened the box to reveal a gold bracelet with instrument trinkets hanging from it. Tears came to her eyes as she looked at it, then Rolly put it on her wrist.

"Thank you, Marie," Rolly said. She held her arm up to look at it. She then turned to the band and wiped a tear away.

She started to talk but covered her mouth with her hand when she felt as though she might cry. "Thank you. Thanks so much. I love you all." She moved to hug Helen and Paula as well as Rolly again.

"You scamp!" She told him and he laughed. Again the audience applauded, but this time in a controlled manner.

"Alright, alright! This audience isn't here to see how many emotions you can put me through in one evening! Let's get on with it!" Marie said playfully.

With that the band started up with a very lively rendition of Gene Autry's *Here Comes Santa Claus*. The floor almost immediately filled and the party was in full swing. Marie followed that up with Joan Javits and Phil Springer's *Santa Baby*, in which she sang from the microphone on the dance floor. The dance company performed with her. She changed outfits twice, once into a golden floor length, and the second time into one of silver.

Rolly sang a solo and Marie spent that time taking a much needed break while the dance company had the floor. The spirits flowed, and by midnight the crowd was in a light hearted mood. The dancing was epic; the dance floor filled to capacity with each song. Marie noticed that the private stage didn't bother coming down anymore, but had moved tables to form their own floor.

Marie's legs began to ache about two o'clock, and she wondered if she could make the last hour. The vivacity of the audience kept them all going, and when it came time to call it, Rolly sent everyone well wishes. The ensemble received a standing ovation that lasted about three minutes. The exhausted performers gathered on center stage to take a bow together and hollered out "Merry Christmas!"

Backstage the party continued after a fresh bowl of punch was mixed up. And of course, another bottle of rum was dumped in. Fresh food trays were brought, and everyone commented on the generosity of their host. Delano was nothing if not generous where generosity paid well.

Marie took off her shoes and indulged in a tall glass of punch, feeling the effects of it down to her toes. It started out as a ribbon of warmth, then turned into a numbness she didn't bother to fight. She sat atop a prop trunk laughing with the girls about the events of the evening. How many handsome men they had seen, how many *not* handsome men they had seen. The entire company was reluctant to end such a great night.

But at length, the time came when exhaustion won out. In groups of two and three they began to leave. When Deano came for Marie, she was glad. She wasn't the last to leave but nearly so. She hugged Rolly on the way out, thanking him again. He brushed her chin with his finger and winked at her, but said little.

By the time she fell into her corner that morning, she was past exhaustion. It took no time for sleep to claim her and her dreams were filled with the show. It was like performing again, with the only difference being Alex came to be with her. It was as if they had never been apart. Her lips curved into a smile as she slept.

*****

"Well, if you aren't moving up." Cobby crouched next to Marie's sleeping form as he spoke. "And damn, why don't you use the bed? Nobody comes in here and bothers you. It's not like hiding here in the corner would work anyway. I'll tell whoever it is where you sleep before they come in." He finished out in an exasperated tone.

Marie's head pounded and her legs throbbed. Her eyes burned when she tried to open them. When she raised up on one elbow, she shot him a look of annoyance. "What time is it?" She felt certain she hadn't been asleep long.

"About seven o'clock," he said, his fine tuxedo still pressed nicely as if he had just put it on. Marie's muddled brain began to wonder if it were seven o'clock in the evening and he *had* just put it on.

"What am I supposed to be doing right now?"

"Making coffee."

"What?" She glared at him in confusion as she wondered if he were joking. She couldn't make sense of it. "What day is it?"

"Christmas Eve. Damn, Marie, maybe you should drink less." It all came back to her. Last night was the big Christmas show at the club. She lay back down on her arm.

"If it's seven, then I've been asleep for three hours, Cobby. Leave me alone."

"Just so you know, I haven't been blessed with even that much sleep. I'm still going strong. But I need coffee now to keep that going. Get up, sugar tits. Plus, I have some very exciting news for you."

"What? Mickey has decided to forgive my debt?" She asked sarcastically as she closed her eyes.

"Noooo. Much better. You've been invited to the Delano family Christmas party tonight at Mickey's."

She looked at him with blood shot eyes. "I smell a rat."

"I thought you might."

"Tell them thank you but no thank you. I have a prior engagement."

"Which is?"

"I don't know, but I'll think of something."

"Come on. I want some coffee."

"Send Deano down to the corner to get you some!"

"Nope. I sent Deano home. It's just you and me. And Val. Just you, me and Val."

Marie sat up quickly and struggled to her feet. Cobby watched with a crooked smile and didn't offer her a hand up.

"I was just kidding about the Val part. But since you're up anyway, go make some coffee." He stated the last part flatly.

Marie rubbed her face and let out a growl. "Cobby! I'll make you coffee, then I'm coming in here and going back to sleep!"

"No you won't. I brought Danish." She stopped rubbing her face to glare at him. He was grinning at her mercilessly.

"You have no soul."

"Sure I do. It's just currently in the possession of the devil. I don't actually have access to it just now."

*****

The road to Mickey and Eva's house was a long one. It wound out of the heart of the city and up into the rolling foothills above LA. It was a beautiful drive, Marie not having been in any kind of countryside for many years. The neighborhood in which they lived was a new one, with sprawling houses that were more or less the same floor plan. Each property had its own gated driveway that led up a distance to the house. The view from Mickey's was breathtaking. Far below was the city, but all around were rolling hills.

Cobby told her that LA's elite lived up there. The stars from Hollywood all had grand homes in Mickey's neighborhood. He also commented that none of them had quite the elaborate security systems though, for obvious reasons. Mickey's gate was at the bottom of a long hill. His home sat comfortably in the shade of large oak trees. There were men at the gate checking cars, and making sure each person was an invited guest. The house was a single story that consisted of huge bay windows across the front that overlooked the rolling lawn that curved down below the hill on which it sat. The house itself was made out of some type of flat rock and the retaining wall that followed the paved driveway was made of the same rock. It was well lit with little lamps.

Cars were parked all along the driveway. Most of them were black, that being the chosen color of the Delano family. Vinny's color was grey. Just as all his men wore grey suits. Mickey's boys wore black and they really did seem more offensive because of it. Men in tuxedo's escorted women clad in evening gowns and fur coats up the driveway. A line formed at the front door. The sun was nearly gone, and only a soft glow remained of the day.

Marie looked out the window and sighed. She didn't notice when Cobby glanced at her in the mirror. He parked the car to the left of the house haphazardly in a corner spot. He killed the engine and sat there looking toward the house just beyond the wrought iron yard fence. Everything was immaculate.

Marie had chosen to wear a black skirt and a red blouse, not wanting to be over extravagant this evening. Imelda had agreed. But, it didn't seem to matter what she wore, she ended up being extravagant. In that Imelda was right. Marie defined the dress, not the other way around. The blouse had short sleeves, and she wore a red sweater over the top of it. The skirt stopped at her knees. It had a split in the back that only accentuated the curves of her lower body all the way to her black heels. She had pinned her hair back into a wavy chignon. Marie kept her make-up light, except for her red lipstick. It was a tuxedo and evening gown affair. Although looking exceptional, Marie was well aware she was under-dressed.

Cobby looked at her in the mirror for a long moment before he finally got out of the car and opened the door for her. She stepped out one leg at a time. Marie stopped breathing as she stood and looked to the house. Cobby quietly pressed the door closed behind her.

"Don't make me go in there," she whispered to him.

"They'd kill us both." He whispered back. He offered her his arm. She took it gratefully. They started the long walk to the house.

It took a while to get to the front door as they moved through the line that went up the sidewalk. Women kept looking back at Marie and whispering to their partners. She was grateful for Cobby's strong arm. She kept her gaze down and tried to think of something else. Cobby looked down at her but couldn't think of anything to say. He covered her hand with his. Marie wanted to throw up. She pressed her forehead against his bicep.

The line was moving slowly through the front door. Mickey and the rest of his immediate family had formed a greeting line for all the guests. When Cobby and Marie moved up the steps into the house, she saw a large entry area. The line moved to the left down a hallway. Marie could see it led to a huge living area with a bar running the length of the back wall. Beyond this she saw nothing. She kept her eyes on her hand that rested in the crook of Cobby's arm.

A crowd was gathering along the walls in the hallway and the living room. A fair amount of whispering was going on around her. Marie noticed the line was moving along faster now. This was going to be unpleasant.

Then the room opened up, and she was standing at the beginning of the greeting line. An older couple stood looking at her, the woman with a disapproving scowl. Her face resembled a soggy and wrinkled brown paper bag, her black eyes the only animated thing about it. The house fell absolutely silent. Marie's heart beat erratically and her palms began to sweat. This wasn't fair. She had done nothing to deserve this.

And yet she had. Jealousy was a cruel wench.

Marie looked at the older woman. Cobby held firm.

"Get away from her, Cobby." Eva's voice seared. He remained rooted. He cast a challenging look back at Eva.

"Get away from her now!" Eva said firmer this time. Cobby stood like steel next to Marie.

"Cobby," Mickey's voice was low and dark.

As much as she wanted his comfort, his security, she would not have him pay a high price for it. He was her only ally. She knew that for certain in that moment. She had to protect him just as he was trying to shield her. She looked up at him and smiled. She ran her left hand down his lapel, nodding with shaky confidence. He looked down at her regretfully, and she smiled at him more boldly. While he didn't move away, he did release her. She looked back to the older woman.

The spit hit Marie below her left eye. This was going to be women's revenge. A sort of walk of shame. The older man did and said nothing as Marie wished him a Merry Christmas. The next woman was also older. She spit on Marie's other cheek. Marie took it and wished her Merry Christmas. The next woman in a golden gown threw her drink in Marie's face. Her eyes burned fiercely.

Marie said Merry Christmas and Happy New Year.

On down the line she went. Some threw drinks, some spit. One woman was merciful and blew cigarette smoke at her. On and on it went. Each time Marie smiled and wished them Merry Christmas, then moved to the next woman for punishment. When she came to Margo, the woman had obviously saved up spit most of the afternoon. It hit her blouse and Marie just tipped her head and smiled.

"You look lovely this evening, Margo." When Marie had finished speaking, Margo tossed her drink in Marie's face.

Next to Margo stood The Dark Horse. Marie neither looked at him nor wished him well. She just passed him up. He was the only one in line that she obviously avoided. She hated him so deeply, now more than ever.

That brought her to Eva. She stopped and stood before her, knowing this was the end of the line. After this she was done. Whatever relief that brought. Eva looked down her nose at Marie.

"You filthy whore," Eva drawled out then spit on her twice. Marie looked down and away while she pursed her lips. She looked again at Eva.

"You have such a lovely home, Eva. Thank you for inviting me. Merry Christmas." Marie spoke quietly through the lump in her throat. She smiled softly only to be hit with one last drink from Eva's hand. Marie stepped to Mickey.

He looked down at her with a strange look in his eyes. Could it have been regret? No. She was mistaken. Her lips trembled a smile. Her eyes glistened.

"Merry Christmas, Mickey." She whispered, then blinked back the tears.

"Merry Christmas, Marie." He extended his hand to her. She took his hand and he held it gently. "Thanks for coming."

Marie turned away and pushed through the crowd back toward the hall. Women purposely blocked her path and more than one man took advantage of the opportunity to grope her. It angered Marie so deeply that she began shoving her way through. She was done. There was no way she'd stay here. When she finally made it back to the front door, she passed into the darkness.

The night air was particularly cold with her sodden clothing. She wrapped her sweater around her, but it too was soaked and reeked of alcohol. The over powering stench made her stomach turn. She moved off across the lawn past the wrought iron gate.

Cobby stood with his hands in his pockets watching her go. He made no move to follow her. He didn't know what he'd say that would make things any more pleasant, so he just let her go. He had pulled the keys from the car when they came in suspecting that she might get desperate and make a run for it. She wouldn't get past the gate and then she'd have hell to pay. So, he figured he'd just eliminate that option. He did, however, leave a new pack of cigarettes on the dash.

Deano caught his eye from his stool along the bar and raised his head at him. Cobby shook his head to say, let her go. Deano turned back to his drink and made no further comment. The room was buzzing with talk, and before long somebody started up the sound system and loud Christmas music blasted out of the speakers.

After a while, Cobby stood at the bar talking to a young blonde haired woman. She was a pretty little thing, and Cobby liked the way she looked at him from under her lashes. She had been moving closer to him the longer they talked, and now they were nearly touching. He had no interest in her beyond that. He had no interest in any of them beyond that. He knew that this little bombshell had no interest in him beyond his position with Valant. He had no intentions of fostering a Margo for the next twenty-some years.

Val pushed his way into the opposite end of the bar and asked for another drink. He looked at Cobby who was watching him as he always did, attempting to read his intentions. Val rarely had to ask Cobby anything. Cobby already knew what he would need. It wasn't as if Cobby could read his mind, Val remained an unsolvable mystery to everyone. But, by years of learning the pattern of his behavior, Cobby could at least anticipate his moves.

Val raised his chin briefly at him. Cobby then replied by looking toward the bay windows and then back at Valant. Val moved away without anything else, and Cobby looked back to the blonde who hadn't even noticed his focus had shifted.

*****

Marie sat on the trunk of the car looking out at the view. Off to the south the lights of the city twinkled in the night. A half- moon had risen and cast a soft light onto everything. Marie felt a little comfort in it. The sky was beautiful, and she could make out the outline of the hills around her. The air was very cool, but she was content to sit and enjoy the view.

Her blouse and sweater had dried somewhat, and she kept her arms wrapped around herself. She had gotten into the car and swiped the pack of cigarettes off the dash. She now held one between her fingers and it had warmed her some. Marie thought about crying, but decided she wouldn't give them the satisfaction. She wished she had a way to blow the whole house up. What a gift to humanity that would be. If she ever saw Vinny again, she would suggest that for next year's Delano Family Christmas Bash. She knew this line of thinking didn't make her a better person.

She had never seen anything like what just happened to her at any of Vinny's family gatherings. But then, Vinny gave no cause for Nan to be that outrageously jealous. And even if he had, by the time Marie was in her early teens Nan's mind had begun to go and she wouldn't have cared anyway. Vinny refused to institutionalize her. Marie had hoped one day she'd find a man that would love her like that. She gave up on that when Alex cut her so deeply. Vinny was one of a kind.

How she missed Vinny. Did he ever think about her? Was he tonight thinking about all the times he'd gone to St. Francis Cathedral to hear her sing? How deep the regret ran that she had chosen to break contact with him in New York. She was deeply ashamed of herself for turning her back on him when he had done so much for her. Like he was her father instead of Jerry Barelli.

Like he was her father.

A tear slipped out and she didn't bother to check it. It seemed alright since now she was crying for a different reason.

Life was cruel. She didn't want to live it anymore if this was as good as it got. Was it just the evening before that the band had given her the golden bracelet? How quickly one can go from love and admiration to getting spit on. She left the bracelet with Alex's picture, too scared that something terrible would happen to it. She felt she was right, after the show Rolly made of giving it to her.

She pressed her hand to her face and sniffed slightly. She thought about running, but Cobby had been too clever to leave the car keys. She wouldn't get far on foot in open toed heels, and anyway that bastard Valant would hunt her down. What had she ever done to deserve this?

She ran her hand down the back of her neck and as she did so saw his outline. The sight of him made her jump so forcibly that she nearly fell off the car. How long had he been there? Thank God she wasn't talking out loud to herself. His height and build told her with clarity who he was.

Valant made his way to her now that she had seen him. He leaned against the side of the car out of reach of her. He seemed to know that was as far as he could get before she moved away. She just watched him with apprehension in her eyes.

"What are you doing out here?" His voice was deep and sent vibrations through the air that she could feel.

She made no reply, just turned from him and wiped the tear off her face. He stepped forward a bit.

"What are you doing out here?" he repeated, this time with less force.

"Enjoying a cigarette," she said lowly. She then raised her forgotten comfort to her lips.

"You lift those off Cobby?"

She was silent a moment. "Yes." He moved closer and she looked at him sharply.

"It's chilly out here."

"Is it?" she asked sarcastically.

He looked at her. "Come inside."

"No." He moved next to her and leaned against the car. He reached over quickly and took the cigarette that she was smoking. He brought it to his lips and took a long drag then blew it up into the air. The corner of Marie's mouth sagged.

"May I have my cigarette, please?"

"No."

Nat King Cole's *The Christmas Song* came on. She looked accusingly at him, then reached into her sweater pocket and retrieved another cigarette.

"Come inside."

Anger sparked in her as memories flashed. Her voice quavered as she spoke. "I think I've endured enough for one night." Her lips trembled as she put the cigarette to her mouth before lighting it.

He looked at her directly. "Everybody takes their knocks."

She closed her eyes and clenched her jaws, the cigarette clamped between her fingers.

"That was a pretty good snub you gave me."

"Well, I guess everybody takes their knocks." She retorted sarcastically. He raised a brow.

They were quiet a moment while Marie fumbled nervously with her matches.

"If you come in there with me, no one will bother you."

She stopped fumbling and looked at him. "No one? Or just those of the male persuasion?" She sat looking down a moment. "No, I won't go back in there. Where's Cobby?"

He looked out into the night sky and blew out another long stream of smoke. "Passing a little time with a pretty blonde. You want me to stop him?"

She looked baffled. "No. Why would I want you to do that?"

"I have no idea." He said deeply as if she were silly for asking. She gave him a deep frown. He looked back at her.

"Come inside with me."

"You're relentless." She looked away from him as tears burned again. "Please just let me be. I'm not going to run," she whispered to him. She wrapped her arms tightly around herself.

"Come inside and we'll get you something to eat."

"You already have a date. Now let me alone," she spoke harshly at him. A tear slipped out and she angrily brushed it away.

Bing Crosby's *It's Christmas Time Again* came on loud and clear over the talking and laughter within the house. Valant slipped his hands into his pockets and looked at her, but his face was in shadow and Marie couldn't read his expression. She turned from him and lit her cigarette.

"Merry Christmas, Marie," he said without much enthusiasm. He slipped his jacket off then stepped forward and put it around her shoulders. Then he was gone.

*****

Margo watched him disappear out the front door into the darkness. She knew where he was going. It ignited fire in her veins at the thought he would go, leaving her alone with everyone watching. But in reality, nobody noticed. She clutched at her drink with a white knuckled claw.

He had lovers before. Many lovers. Some had lasted a while, some only for the night. It was a liberty she had allowed him all these years. It was hard to keep a man satisfied when she only saw him once in a while. And to be truthful, if he had his lovers, then she could have hers. Nothing more than boy toys, but she was inclined to enjoy them anyway.

All of his lovers had one thing in common. None had lasted. Not like her. When she felt him slipping, she would just reel him back in. The trouble was, lately she'd been reeling, and he just kept slipping. It was not the singer who enticed him. Just her body. A twinge of jealousy hit again as Margo thought about how young she was. But young or not, she didn't have the experience Val enjoyed so much in his partner. No, he'd get bored with her quickly.

Until then, Margo planned out a little revenge.

*****

The place was in shambles. Drink glasses littered every flat surface. Food plates were strung from one end of the house to the other. Forgotten coats littered the backs of chairs and sofas. All who were staying with Mickey and Eva had long since made their way to bed and lay snoring in an inebriated slumber. The rest had gone home. The stack of Christmas records beside the record player had fallen over and lay scattered on the floor.

Mickey had loosened his bow tie, and it hung limply down his shirt. Val had thrown his somewhere but long since forgotten where. It didn't matter anyway. They were the last two. The sun was still a long way off, but it didn't seem necessary to go to bed for such a short time.

"Another year in the books," Mickey sighed. "Another year I won't remember ten from now."

"Hmm," was Val's reply.

"Then again, I may not remember what year it happened, but I'll remember what they did to Marie."

"You could have stopped her."

"Eva? Who the hell would have thought for a minute Marie would react that way? I kinda thought those women got what they deserved, myself." Mickey chuckled. "Never seen somebody take a hit like that and keep walking."

"I don't think Marie took it that way."

"Maybe not. Especially since she did nothing to earn it," Mickey replied.

Val spoke nothing. This was not a subject he trusted himself to get started on. Eva was a cold bitch, and nothing would change that. And, worse yet, that terrible look of regret in Mickey's eyes every time he dared look at Eva reminded him of that. Val just wanted to strangle her; he found himself capable of such a thing each time he contemplated it.

Mickey held his cigarette between his thumb and index finger. He just sat and watched it burn.

"She's gonna have a baby," he spoke low and regretfully.

Val sighed deeply. So many memories flooded his mind. He didn't want to look at them. That was another life. Another woman. And when she died she took with her everything that Mickey loved, made his heart beat with vitality. Now there was nothing. Just Val. Just power. Just money. And in reality, even Mickey knew that those weren't enough.

"Well, if the good die young, the spawn of the most evil people I know will live forever."

Mickey looked up at Val as the cigarette began to burn his fingers.

"Unfortunately, so will its mother." Val finished icily.

"What do I do?" Mickey said as if he were just a boy, uncertain of life's events.

"Paint the nursery."

"God, how I want her back." Mickey said in a tortured whisper. He dropped the cigarette and put his face in his hands. He had this conversation with God many times. Sometimes he yelled, sometimes he begged, and sometimes he just cried in the silence, asking for comfort.

Val gulped down his last swallow. "It's a good day, Mickey. Just think how very different next Christmas will be."

Mickey turned and looked at Val. "Yeah, I guess you're right. All I know is I don't want to make the same mistakes my father did."

"That's a good place to start."

*****

Marie woke in the back seat when Cobby cranked the engine. She lay across the seat with her top leg draped over the bottom one, and then it fell over the edge of the seat. Her upper body was swathed in Valant's coat and her head rested on her arm. She opened her eyes long enough to see Cobby, then fell asleep again. He'd wake her at the apartment.

When next she did wake, the sun was in the sky. While it was not high, it filtered softly through the window. The car had come to a halt, and Cobby let the engine idle a moment as he looked at something out the passenger side window. Then he killed the engine.

"We take the long way home?" she asked as her eyes drifted shut again.

"I need a favor, Marie," Cobby asked in a quiet voice. He looked down at his lap.

Marie opened her eyes and looked at him. A twinge of concern bit into her. "Where are we?"

"South Side." With that Marie quickly sat up and Valant's coat fell away from her. She rubbed her face trying to clear her mind for thinking.

"Whose jacket it that?" He watched her in the rearview mirror.

"Valant's." Cobby said nothing just stared ahead out the windshield. At length he slowly pulled his door open and stepped out.

Marie looked into the rearview mirror and repined her hair in places. She smoothed her face to attempt to wipe away smeared make-up. Oh, how she reeked of alcohol. She groped around on the floorboard until she found her shoes and put them on. She felt cold so she put Valant's coat back on. Cobby then opened the door and helped her out.

"You can't wear that jacket."

Marie looked down at it. "Why?"

"Because it's clearly not mine." He took it off of Marie, then slipped his off and wrapped it around her. He stood looking down at her a moment.

"Do you understand what I need?"

Marie looked into his handsome face and replied, "I think so."

He slipped his hands into his pockets, looking uncertain. He was second guessing his move. Marie took another step towards him and found his gaze.

"I appreciate what you did for me last night," She whispered. She reached up slowly with both hands and put them on his chest. Then she kissed him very softly on the lips, lingering there for a long moment. Cobby couldn't smell anything beyond her sweet perfume despite what she wore in her clothes. It was in him to take her in his arms and deepen that kiss. Every fiber screamed for him to, but something told him he shouldn't. That the heart ache it would bring them might break what he had left inside him. So when she pulled away, his eyes reflected a deep regret. As did hers.

"I'm afraid if I had half a chance I'd fall for you, Marie."

"Didn't your mama teach you about girls like me? Stay away from the woman in black."

"You aren't the woman in black. And it was girls like you my mama told me to find."

Marie smiled a crooked, sad smile. "How did someone so sweet end up where you are?"

"Because Valant took pity on me and my mother." He said it with conviction, and for the first time Marie saw how much Cobby loved and respected the man.

"Then may God bless the old devil."

"Well," Cobby said in a lighter tone, "At least you won't be the one getting spit on at this party. It will be me."

Marie let out a laugh. "That's not funny."

"I didn't say it was. You're the one who laughed."

"Someone's watching out the window now. Shall we proceed?" Marie asked.

"Uh uh. Let's get in the backseat of that car and you can kiss me again. And other stuff."

"Get in the house Cobby. Your mother is watching." He grinned down at her wickedly.

"I guess there's always the ride home."

They turned and started up the walk to Cobby's childhood home. Marie clung to Cobby's arm and pressed close. It was a great relief to her that she wouldn't be the one getting spit on. She hoped.

It was a small home. It was white and the yard was small, but everything was well kept. More than one face appeared in the window, so Marie smiled up at Cobby adoringly. She could tell he was trying to forget that his purpose today was to tell his mother good-bye. Marie hadn't loved her mother for a long time. She couldn't fathom being regretful at parting. Her life was good when her mother wasn't around.

Just as they reached the steps up to the house the door was jerked open. Both Cobby and Marie braced for the potential outcome of a shotgun, again. But it wasn't a shotgun that greeted them.

"Marty?" the woman asked in a voice that was close to hysterical happiness. She was older, with brown hair lightly sprinkled with gray, the same shade as Cobby's. She had dark circles under her eyes. Her lips trembled as she looked at him.

"Hello, Ma." At those words she burst through the door and flew down the steps to take him in her arms. At first he hugged her tentatively, then sincerely. Marie stood back and watched, trying to give them space. The woman was crying now.

"Oh Marty! Oh, how I've worried about you!" She placed the palms of her hands on his face.

"I know Ma. I'm sorry," Cobby said very low.

Several young men now stood on the steps, dividing their attention between mother, son and Marie. Cobby broke away and looked down into the face of his mother that radiated joy to behold him. He glanced to Marie.

"Ma, I want you to meet somebody." She released him and looked over to Marie. "Ma, this Marie Barelli. Marie, this is my mother, Edith."

Marie stepped towards her and smiled genuinely. "It's a pleasure to meet you, Edith."

The woman smiled warmly. "Please, everyone calls me Edie. It is wonderful to meet you, Miss Barelli."

"Please, Marie."

"Alright, Marie. Please, come in."

"Ma," Cobby began. His voice was hesitant.

"Come in. Please." She took hold of his arm with one hand and extended her free arm to Marie.

A grin spread across Cobby's face when he looked up into the steps. "Well, if it isn't the ugly twins."

"Ugly maybe, but we can still whip your ass," said a dark haired young man. Cobby climbed the steps and took hold of his brother's hand.

"Cleo, you bastard, how you been?"

"Boys!" Edie said with too little authority. "There's a lady present."

"Ah, she's heard much worse, Ma," Cobby said without looking to either lady. He had clasped his brother's hand.

The sandy haired man also took Cobby's hand and then hugged him, slapping his back as he did so. Cleo looked down at Marie.

"If she's running with you, I have no doubt she's heard worse. You always did have a mouth like a sailor! You taught me every shitty word I know!" Cleo laughed joyously as he spoke.

"Where's Mattie?" Cobby asked.

"Sleepin'. Damn kid must be narcoleptic," the sandy haired man said.

"He ain't narcoleptic. He's the baby and Ma spoils him something terrible," Cleo said. Cobby laughed.

"I do not!" Edie said firmly.

"What about Pete?"

"Sucking down coffee and eating all Ma's cinnamon rolls in the kitchen."

"Old man Medford?" Cobby asked in a tense voice.

"Trying to find shells for his shotgun," Cleo said. It was a tense moment before Cleo laughed. "Just kidding." Cobby punched his arm.

"Damn if you boys ain't ugly." Cobby grinned.

"You know, I'm inclined to think he's right after all these years. Ma must have given you all the grace and charm, 'cause I've never had something like *that* hanging on my arm." The sandy haired young man pointed to Marie with a nod of his head.

Cobby turned to Marie. She was still a ways from the steps, but he reached for her and she came forward. "Boys, I'd like for you to meet Marie. Marie, this is my brother Cleo, and my brother Andrew."

Marie stood close to Cobby, and greeted his brothers who looked at her appreciatively. She smiled shyly and knew she'd gained their favor. "It's very nice to meet you. I've heard so much about you."

"It's chilly out here, let's get Marie inside gentlemen."
Edie said after the introductions had been made. The men all
made way for Marie and Edie to enter the house first. As she
came through the door, Marie could smell the coffee and
cinnamon rolls that Cleo and Andrew had spoken of. There was
also a modest Christmas tree in the corner of the living room.
Under it were many gifts waiting to be opened.

"May I take your coat?" Edie asked Marie. She clung to it
in uncertainty for she knew once it was off, the offensive odor
of the drinks that had been hurled at her only hours before
would permeate the room. Marie looked at Cobby who was
already looking at her. He gave her a wink. She slowly
removed the jacket, then wrapped her arms around herself.

"Please sit and make yourself at home. Would you like
some coffee?" Edie asked as she draped the jacket across her
arm.

"Yes, please. That would be lovely."

Just then another young man entered the room. He was a
much younger replica of Cobby. Marie determined that Cobby
must have taken after his father in exact likeness. He stood
looking at Cobby in disbelief.

"Marty?"

"Yeah, it's me." He came forward to clasp his hand
firmly.

"How long has it been?" Cobby's replica asked.

"Oh, 'bout seven years, I guess," Cobby replied.

"Eight. It's been eight," Edie stated.

"Damn it's good to see you."

"I'd like for you to meet Marie Barelli. Marie, honey, this
is my brother, Pete." He clasped her hand politely and greeted
her with a, "How do you do."

Cobby put his arm around Marie reassuringly.

"Are you the Marie Barelli I keep seeing headlines about
in the entertainment pages of the paper?" asked Pete.

She gave a very shy smile. "Yes, that's me." She looked
down and away.

"Marie isn't the kind to brag. She'd just as soon no one
knew who she was." Marie looked at Cobby straight on. He
locked eyes with her and she knew what he was talking about.
Vinnetti.

"Please! Sit!" Edie said excitedly then bustled out of the
room to the kitchen.

Cobby and Marie settled in close on the sofa. It was overwhelming now with so many of Cobby's family looking at them anxiously. It wasn't hard to keep up the pretense. She wanted to touch him, for she wanted the comfort of his closeness. He put his arm around her and she moved comfortably next to him.

"How's the kids, Cleo?" Cobby asked in a hushed tone as it was still quite early, and obviously not all had risen yet.

"Good. They oughta be comin' out any minute."

"How old are they now?"

"Lucy is five and Martin is three."

"Martin?" Cobby asked, confused.

"Yeah. For his uncle," Cleo stated.

Cobby was silent for a while. "I got word when they were born. I'm sorry I couldn't be here."

"That's ok. Jane and I weren't even sure you knew about them."

Cobby smiled a knowing smile. "I can't be here myself, but I still know what's going on."

"What about you, Andrew? You gotta bun in her oven yet?"

Andrew flushed slightly. "The little bun will be here in March."

Cobby laughed happily. "Ah, that's great. Really great. How's work?"

"Well, I'm partnered with a guy from Sacramento. We'll be moving there in about a month. Where have you been?"

Just then a young woman came into the room and stopped and stared at Cobby. Her little round belly poked out of her pink robe. "Marty, meet my wife, Ella." Cobby rose to take her hand as did Marie. Then they again sat as Ella took a seat on Andrew's lap.

"What the hell's going on here?" Came a gruff voice. Cobby rose slowly and looked at the older man who had come into the room from somewhere and stood above them. "I don't remember inviting you. In fact, I recall telling you to never step foot into my house again."

Cobby was a fair bit taller than the older man, and Marie assumed that this was "Old Man Medford." His green eyes bored into Cobby while his bald head shown sparse wiry hairs that stuck out at odd angles. Was Marie the only one in the room who understood how foolish it was to challenge Cobby?

He was gentle, at times, but he was now accustomed to a world where life was only as valuable as your usefulness and obedience. A look came into Cobby's eyes and she had seen that look before. Only then The Dark Horse had been wearing it. She stood and took a gentle hold of his arm, not sure of how he would react.

"Cobby, honey, let's go." He didn't move so she stepped between them and put her hand on his face. Indeed the anger she saw in his eyes was explosive. "Come on, sweetheart. Come on. Don't leave them with that kind of memory of you. Come away with me," she whispered to him.

"That's right. Take your trash and go."

"That's enough!" The angry shout stunned them. "That's enough! I haven't seen my boy in eight years and I'll be damned if you're gonna run him off! So sit down and shut your mouth!" Marie turned to see that Edie, Cleo and Andrew were standing next to Medford prepared to silence him. "Please, Charles. I want to spend Christmas with my son." The last was said in a quieter voice, but it was still angry, and the tears in her eyes reflected the long suffering she'd endured.

He looked at his wife and sighed. "After all the hurt he's caused you over the years, if you want to spend Christmas with him, fine with me." With that he walked out, his powder blue bathrobe fluttering behind him.

Edie looked at Cobby. "Please don't go. Please."

Cobby shook his head. "Ma, it just isn't...."

"Yes it is. We're gonna have a good day. I hear those children getting up and we're gonna watch them open their gifts. I want my son, my Marty, here with us today." She then looked to Marie. "Please stay. I am so sorry about what he said about you. But, we don't feel that way. So, please, I beg you give us a second chance."

Marie had been called much worse in the last eighteen hours, the difference being the last person meant it, Medford was just trying to get Cobby's goat. It was working up until Edie and the boys stepped in. She smiled at Edie and put a hand on her arm. "It's been a long night. I'd love some coffee."

Tears of gratitude filled Edie's eyes as she nodded. The room relaxed, and everyone again took their seats. The silence stretched on for a great while. A scruffy haired young man blundered in with sleep in his eyes. He rubbed his face and drifted by Cobby and Marie without seeing them.

"Hello Mattie."

The kid stopped and looked at Cobby in confusion. "Who are you?"

The room erupted into laughter. "I used to tote you around on my shoulders when you were no bigger than a minute. Hated it too cause you'd try to gouge out my eyes."

"Marty?" Cobby stood and laughing gave the boy a big hug.

"Damn if you didn't grow a little," Cobby said as he ruffled the kid's hair. "Marie, this is my kid brother, Matthew, but we call him Mattie."

"He's the girl Ma always wanted!" Pete hollered out. Marie laughed as she took his hand, the boy's cheeks turning a crimson color.

"Shut up, Pete," the boy muttered. Everyone laughed again.

"Where on earth are you all sleeping?" Marie asked as she looked about the crowded room. Those without a sofa had brought chairs from the kitchen.

"Oh, Ma's got us stacked ten deep along the basement walls," Andrew said to laughter.

"Bull shit. Andrew and Ella got a bed cause she's in the family way. Those of us who are not married or replicating are stacked ten deep along the basement walls!" Pete retorted.

"Married men and women don't sleep next to other adults. It's vulgar," Edie said as she bustled in with a huge coffee tray. Marie stood and took it from her and set it on the coffee table. She then began to pour. She was used to being useful at the apartment.

"What do you do, Miss Barelli?" Ella asked as Marie handed her a cup.

"I sing. That is, I sing in a cocktail lounge," Marie said quietly. She suddenly felt inferior standing next to educated men and a married soon-to-be mother.

Cobby laughed out loud. "It's not a cocktail lounge."

"Yes, it is."

"No, it's not."

"Yes, it is. A big one, but a cocktail lounge none the less."

"What Marie won't tell you is she sings at The Ruby," Cobby stated despite Marie's glare.

"The Ruby! Oh my! That makes you...." Ella didn't finish before two children came running through the room ignoring all else but the Christmas tree.

"Children! Manners!" A black haired woman shouted. The children turned and mumbled, "Merry Christmas." Turning again, they began ransacking the gift pile. Packages were distributed among the group.

Edie drug old man Medford back in and parked him in his empty armchair. Cobby's face tensed as he did so, but kept silent. He was dressed, and his wiry hairs had been tamed.

"Alright, we're all here. Go for it children!" Edie said.

Amid cries of joy, the gifts were shredded by the two children. It made Marie happy to watch them, for she had never had the kind of family Cobby did. She lay her head on his shoulder. He lay his head on hers. They shared the joy of a moment they both knew would never come again. It would fade like a shooting star in the sky. Marie wondered how Cobby would tell them good-bye. Or if he even would. Maybe they would just go without a word, never to be seen again. Perhaps that was less cruel than just cutting the cord and walking away. Edie would have the hope every Christmas that she'd look out her window to see Cobby coming up the walk. Where hope dwelled, the heart hurt less.

They sat and watched the family open gifts that morning. It was a tranquil Christmas morning and a gift that Marie had not expected to receive. The coffee was good, the company was good, and she felt as though she were spending a Christmas her childhood had not allowed.

They visited for a while after opening presents, eating various wonderful goodies that Edie had made herself. The tension of the previous moments was gone. Cobby laughed freely and teased his brothers about everything. Medford sat quietly listening. Marie caught him looking at Edie with deep emotion in his eyes many times. It was then that she understood. It wasn't that Medford hated the fact that Cobby was mafia, it was that he'd caused his mother so much grief and suffering. He was a man who loved his wife, and he wanted to protect her as best he could from more pain. This touched Marie deeply.

Later in the morning Medford's own two daughters came with their families to share in the celebrating. The house was full, and children ran about hollering and giggling. About that time more food was brought out and Edie went in to finish dinner. Marie attempted to help, but Edie shooed her away. So, she sat next to Cobby and enjoyed the banter.

Someone broke out cards and a game was struck up. Marie declined to be involved, but Cobby teased her wickedly until she relented. He continued to tease her amid the snickering of his brothers about perhaps the possibility of some private strip poker in the basement. She then decided she wouldn't go easy on any of them. It was easy to beat Cobby's brothers, but it took serious skill to beat Cobby. But she did so, repeatedly, until all of the family, including Medford who leaned against the doorway, came to watch the thrashing she was handing out. When they had all gathered round, she said sweetly, "So, sweetheart, how 'bout that little private game of strip poker in the basement?"

Everyone laughed at Cobby's expression of contrite disagreement. "No thanks, Doll. I fear its cold down there and I chill easily."

A lively game of spoons came after that and everyone in the room was able to participate at once in that. Wrestling matches weren't uncommon among brothers as each tried to get the last spoon. It was wild and Edie stood back and watched with pride, as for the first time in a long time, all of her sons were present to play. In the end it came down to Marie and Cobby. He looked at his cards, and when he looked up again, Marie had the last spoon dangling from her nose. He threw his cards in mock anger. He leaned back and glowered at her until a grin creased his face.

"I'm gonna make you pay for that." It was her turn to grin wickedly at him.

"Not by beating me at cards."

He leaned forward and put his elbows on the table. "Perhaps with a foot race, arm wrestling. Or better yet, Indian leg wrestling."

"Martin Cobbinelli!" Edie gasped. Cobby's brothers all egged him on.

"I wouldn't get so cocky if I were you. You haven't beat me at anything, yet." Marie replied.

"Yet," said Cobby.

"Yet," replied Marie.

After the games they cleared the dining room. The women all prepared the table and brought out the dinner food. Marie helped with everything she could, chit chatting idly as she did so. She felt very welcome, although the women folk were very curious to know what her life was like. She was careful what she told them, for the truth of matters would only cause Edie more worry.

At dinner the family joked about everything. Cleo was quite ornery when it came to starting trouble. Medford remained silent until the subject of drinking came up. At that point he looked at Marie and asked, "Do you drink a lot, Miss Barelli?"

The room fell silent as they looked from Medford to Marie. "No, sir. I am a teetotaler." With that she winked at Cobby who tried not to spit out his mashed potatoes.

In a hurry to smooth things over, Edie rushed to say, "What a fine thing it is to have all my family with me today." She encompassed not only the dining room, but the table of children eating in the living room as well. "I am also very glad to have you with us, too, Marie."

"Thank you, Edie. It has been such a wonderful day." The two women smiled at each other.

"It seems a shame that we don't enjoy this every year. But of course, that would be if one of our number wasn't hiding from the law and unable to be seen in the same place twice." The sarcastic tone in Medford's voice cut into the pleasant dinner conversation. He set his fork down to fully concentrate on glaring at Cobby.

"How many years has it been? Hmm? Nearly ten?" He shook his head in disgust. "You have no regard for anyone, do you? You go off and live your fine life full of money, fast cars and free dealing women. You don't even think about your mother and brothers do you? Do you think about them here, growing up, growing old, having children and grandchildren? Or is your mind just completely buried in the bosoms of your distractions? Like this one." He gestured at Marie. She too, set her fork down quietly and pressed her lips tightly together.

"What the hell would your father think of you? Huh? You think he'd be proud that you just walked out on your mother and brothers and left them to suffer through the after years of his death? Would he be proud to think that all of his sons turned out save one? The one who lives with the devil and does his bidding?"

"Charlie, please!" Edie choked out.

He ignored her and went on. "Hell no, he wouldn't! Ain't nobody proud of you. Not your father and not your mother. You take everything and all you give back is pain. Your father…"

"That's not true." Marie's voice was steady. "If you knew Cobby, or Marty, as you all know him, you'd never say such things. I will agree with you about myself, I'm not much. But you're wrong about Cobby, as he is to me. Where you see a man who ran out on his mother and brothers, I see a man who suffered hell to keep them fed and housed. I know what kind of life he lives. Despite what you think you see here, Cobby has nothing. He has me. And I'll grant maybe that's not as much as it appears to be. His creature comforts are few. He knew when he left it meant he'd never sit here with you and celebrate Christmas. It was enough to know that *you* would. His father would be proud to know he left his wife and children in capable hands." She stared into Medford as he listened. The family had gone silent.

Cobby was glaring at Medford, but now he looked down at his plate. Then he turned despondent eyes to Marie. He smiled thinly.

"You are really something," he whispered, then took hold of her hand. "Shall we return to the life we know?"

"When you are ready. Don't go till you're ready." Cobby knew Marie meant to not say good-bye till he was ready to go forever, even if it wasn't that day. The sadness of being alone reflected so deeply in her eyes Cobby had to look away. He knew that feeling, but at least for him he had the dream of his place of belonging in south side.

"Pass Marty the ham, Cleo. He is almost out," Edie said in a desperate attempt to hold them there.

"Come with me to the kitchen, Ma." Cobby said quietly as he stood.

Edie rose silently and followed him. Medford sat still and looked at his lap.

For a long while the only sound was the soft sobbing coming from the kitchen as Cobby told his mother good-bye. Marie tried desperately not to cry. Her appetite was gone and she didn't bother to fidget with her fork. Cleo stared at Medford with murder in his eyes. No one else ate, or moved, or spoke.

When at last Cobby came for Marie, she stood with him and took his hand. They excused themselves and the family followed them out the door. All but Medford and his daughters and their spouses. Each took their turn hugging Cobby and Marie alike, wishing them well. But no one ever said anything about not seeing him again. Words of, "Next year we won't let Marie play poker," or "Summer is a great time for a family barbeque." But none of these were spoken with any hope in them.

When Marie came to Edie the woman hugged her closely. "Please, please watch over my boy. I need to know you will."

Marie pulled away and looked into her eyes. "I'll do the very best I can."

Which isn't much at all.

Cobby opened the front passenger door and Marie slipped into the car. Cleo stepped forward and said something in Cobby's ear while hugging him tight. It was then Marie remembered Cobby's jacket was still in the house. She thought better of it. It might be the last thing of his Edie would ever have.

Edie stood before Cobby again and he said, "I'm sorry. I didn't mean to ruin Christmas."

"You could never ruin Christmas. Not ever." They held each other tightly for what seemed like a long time.

"God be with you, my son. God be with you," Edie whispered.

Cobby moved quickly away from her and got into the car. He turned the engine and it fired to life. Without another look he hit the gas and the car moved swiftly away. Marie looked back to see they were standing in the street watching them go. She wondered how long it would be before Edie forgave Medford.

She looked to Cobby who stared down the street ahead, one hand on the wheel, the other resting along the door. She said nothing, for what would it be if she did? A song came to mind, and she began to sing it softly. Frank Sinatra's *Don't Worry 'Bout Me* played like a record in her head. Her deep and rich voice broke the desolate silence of the car as empty streets whipped by. She looked out the passenger window as she sang.

"Alright, I did something for you, now you do something for me." Marie said in a pause in the song.

Cobby looked at her harshly. "I am not spending any time with your family."

"HA! I want you to take me to the little Jewish bakery on Tenth Street. They sell all of their Christmas cakes for twenty cents after noon on Christmas Day." Marie continued to sing.

"You want me to buy you a twenty cent cake?"

"Yes I do."

Cobby shook his head at her. She lay her head on her arm along the seat and looked at him.

Cobby looked over at her dully. She smiled at him, then slid closer to him. She rested her head on his shoulder.

"It won't always hurt like this. Will it?" Marie asked in a soft voice.

"I don't think I'm the one to ask that."

"Have you ever been happy, Cobby?"

It took him a long time to answer. "I am happy now, with the way things are. They cannot be any other way. I fear if I had made my choices differently, things wouldn't be as good as they are now. I have accepted what is in the past. Even though I walk away from it alone."

"Well, for what it's worth, you aren't really alone. Although those of us stuck here with you aren't much."

They drove in silence for a while. Then she asked, "What did you want to be when you were a boy?"

Cobby looked down at her and in all seriousness said, "A fireman."

Marie burst out laughing and so did Cobby. "Well, I'd say you missed your mark some. Instead of putting them out, you run around starting them."

"What did you want to be, Marie?"

She sat up and looked at him square. "I wanted to be a nun for many years of my childhood."

Cobby laughed so hard he nearly hit a lamp post with the car. "Shit, Marie. What a couple of dandies we are."

Marie shrugged. "Well, it hasn't been boring."

Cobby looked at her through narrowed eyes. "What the hell kinda cake is gonna take me thirty blocks out of my way?"

Marie laughed sinfully. "Only pure delight, my boy. Pure delight."

They returned to the apartment by early evening, and brought along with them a chocolate sheet cake with fudge frosting. It had deep red poinsettia leaves on it. The price had gone up. It cost Cobby twenty-five cents. They also got caramels and peanut brittle.

Heading directly to the bar Marie broke out their treasures while Cobby poured them both a drink.

"I think you've earned this," he said, as he handed her the drink. Marie went to the kitchen and brought back two forks.

She took a long sip, then dug into the cake. It was delicious as she licked the chocolate frosting off her lips.

"You still smell terrible," Cobby said as he also dug his fork in.

"Thanks. I'm sure your family thought I was a drunk."

"Yeah. Andrew said those very words. 'Cobby, we think your date is a drunk.' I didn't bother to deny it."

She stared at him with indignation. "Well, thanks. Last time I do a favor for you."

"You know, it's really me who did the favor for you."

"How's that?" Marie asked as she took another fork full.

"Well, we were supposed to be at Mickey's today," he said sheepishly.

"What? They wanted me to go back there?" she asked incredulously.

"Well, not exactly. See, they expected me to be there, and I drew short straw to babysit you, so, you go where I go."

Marie grew very serious. "What's gonna happen to you for it?"

Cobby shrugged his shoulders. "I don't know. You're here now. They can't be too upset, can they?"

"Cobby, they're gonna have the wrong idea. They're going to think that we…"

"I know. Mickey might, but Val knows I would never do that."

Marie just stared at him while he kept eating the cake.

"What did you do that for, Cobby?" she asked. He didn't look at her, just broke off a piece of peanut brittle.

"Why did you take me to South Side?" She asked more forcefully. "Was it because you wanted to see your ma or because you didn't want me to have to be at Mickey's?"

He stopped eating and looked at her. "Oh, Cobby. How could you do that?" She covered her face with her hands. "Why would you do that?"

Acid burned in Marie's stomach. They would make him pay. If they had told him to do something and he didn't do it purposely, he would suffer greatly. It would be the general thought that the two of them were lovers. Or, he had forced her, but either way, he'd pay dearly and so would she. But, him more so.

"It's ok." He took hold of her hand. "What Imelda said was right. I needed to see my mother. You needed to be somewhere else. Two parties come out happy. I planned it that way."

The corners of her mouth drooped. "What will he do to you?"

"Valant? I don't know." He squeezed her hand. "I'm sorry I told you that. If I had known you were gonna shit your pants I wouldn't have."

"Why do you stay with him?"

Cobby looked at her and inhaled deeply. "Because aside from my father, he's the only man I have ever truly respected. Despite his capability to be so cold and harsh, inside him somewhere is the ability to understand. When I was sixteen, I needed him to understand. He did. Just as you pointed out to old man Medford, his understanding gave so much more than it took from me." He took another stab at the cake.

"When I first came to work for him, I thought he'd kill me. He wasn't afraid to knock my face in if I wasn't doing something right. One time we caught up with this bookie who hadn't been making some payments. He handed me a leather strap and told me to hit him with it till he bled. I was all of seventeen. I was too scared to do it. He looked at me and said, 'One of you is taking the hits. Better it be him then you.' I still must have looked uncertain because he took that strap and hit me across the face. It cut real deep and bled like a pig. After all was said and done, he took me back to his place and cleaned it up, put some kind of salve on it. Then he told me to save my mercy for someone who had it coming to them. Not everyone needed a beating, but those who did better get it. The first time he told me to shoot somebody went about the same." Cobby laughed at the memory.

"I wanted to run for the first few years. Then I started seeing a pattern to him. He wasn't hurting me because he was cruel, he was doing it to make me tough enough to walk with him. To live beside him and help him without getting myself killed by not being strong enough to see what is. He always looked after me. If he thought it was too much for me he left me behind. Eventually nothing was too much for me and now I walk with him just as he intended. Being sixteen he knew what I needed was guidance and food. He gave me both.

"He taught me about women, how to pursue the ones I wanted, how to get them when I chose. Mostly he taught me that respect for yourself and those around you is really all it takes to be successful. If you're surrounded by men you think fools, then what does that make you?"

Cobby took a drink and tossed his fork aside. "All in all, Marie, he is far better than the alternative I faced living and working on the streets alone. Over the years I've worked with him I've seen young men suffer terrible fates. Most of them were dead long before we got to them. We'd drive down an alley and see some kid beat beyond recognition lying in a garbage heap. That was almost me, but for some reason, he stepped in and saved me. I don't know why and I don't think I'll pursue the point. I'll just be thankful he did." With that he laced his fingers behind his head.

"I don't worry that he'll think we're lovers. He knows me too well. That's why I'm here looking out for you instead of one of the other guys. He can speak for my integrity every time."

"Then why does he hate me so badly?" Marie asked.

"It's not you he hates, it's Vinnetti. He'll tear you apart to get at him. If he thinks tearing you apart *will* get at Vinnetti. It's really nothing personal."

"Then since he's so convinced I am close to Vinnetti, why hasn't he torn me apart?"

"He's waiting for you to slip up and give yourself away."

"And if I never do?"

"Oh, you will. Eventually, you will." Cobby's voice became low and hostile. It was one of the few times he made her uncomfortable.

"Do you believe me that I have no connection to Vinnetti?"

"Marie, I think you're one of the few who doesn't have a beating coming. But like me, you'll get one anyway."
*****

It was late when Deano stepped off the elevator into the top floor apartment. Marie had long since retired and the apartment was quiet. Cobby lay on the sofa smoking in the darkness. He rose and switched on the lamp when Deano came in.

"You taking over?" Cobby asked Deano in a tired voice.

"Yeah."

"Where's Val?"

"Staying with Mickey," Deano said.

Cobby nodded.

"Night, Dean."

"Yeah. Night, Cob." Deano had taken his own jacket off. He lay down on the opposite sofa that Cobby had just been on.

Cobby headed out onto the dark street and went to his car. He took a moment to look around before getting in, then turned the key bringing the engine to life. Cobby had an apartment of his own, but the truth was he rarely used it. It was his job to stick close to Val, or to be busy doing what Val needed done. He didn't like the solitude that being home alone brought. He preferred to be where he could hear noise.

He was barely able to keep his eyes open as he headed out of town to where it all started twenty-four hours before. The men at the gate waved him on without stopping him. He wound up the hill to where he left his car. Only a few lights were on in the house, but Cobby knew that Val was awake. The man hardly ever slept, so consequently Cobby didn't either.

Val was sitting in the darkness on the patio just inside the yard gate. The only indication of his presence was the glow of the cigarette he was smoking. Cobby sat next to him but said nothing. Val spoke only when he was ready. There was no coaxing him into conversation. Cobby understood this. Being a man of great patience, he fit very well with Valant. Time passed, and Cobby lay his head back on the chair and closed his eyes. Images played involuntarily before his eyes and he knew sleep was coming.

"Do you know why they call Vantino 'The Heart'?" Valant spoke in a very low voice.

Cobby raised his head and looked at Valant.

"When he was very young, Vinnetti's grandfather told him to go down town and kill a politician that was going to run for governor. He'd been leaking information for some time, and Alberto was done with him. He told Vantino that he needed proof he'd done the job. So, Vantino cut out the man's heart and brought it to Alberto."

Cobby wasn't sure what this had to do with anything, so he kept quiet.

Valant took another long drag off his cigarette before he again spoke. "He is not a soft man and he should not be underestimated. The depth of his capabilities would shock you. He knows something we do not."

"How much?"

Valant shook his head. "I don't know. But Vinnetti went from blocking every move Mickey made to practically stepping aside. He's no longer playing offense. He is on to defense now."

He paused as he took another drag. "How was your mother?"

Cobby leaned forward and looked down at his hands. "She's fine." Valant looked over at him.

"What did they think of the stunning Miss Barelli?"

"That she was stunning." Cobby looked over at Valant. "I just wanted her to think I was better off than she imagined." Val knew he spoke about his mother.

"I'm sure Marie secured that thought for you."

Cobby looked up into the night sky for a moment, then his low voice cut the silence. "I told her I wasn't gonna come around again."

Valant sighed. "I would let you go if I could, Cob. But it wouldn't do you any good."

Cobby looked over at the man who had been the center of his life for many years. Sometimes he was hell, sometimes he was hate, and sometimes he was violence. But one thing remained true during all of these things. He was constant.

"Val, even if you told me right now I could go and I'd never see you again, I'd still be here when the sun cleared the horizon in the morning. My mother will be fine without me."

"You've paid, Cobby. For everything they have. For all that they are. Now you live this life. Is that enough?"

"It's enough, Val."

"That's good. It does no good to look back at what should have been. All you have is what is. Look at Mickey. He barely stays ahead of his past. Barely, but he does it. Life can't always be what we want it to be."

Cobby felt the feeling of impatience grow within him. He knew this already. He lived it every day.

"Do you understand what I'm telling you?"

"I guess."

"Don't you fall for her." Cobby looked sharply at Valant. "There's too many good reasons not to."

Cobby looked down at his hands again. "I just borrowed her. That's all. I needed a charming actress, and she played her part very well. In the morning she'll wake up no different than she did a week ago."

Valant let it go. Cobby was too intelligent not to realize that Mickey would never stand for it. Cobby's life was not his own. Not until he was Valant, and by then Marie would be far gone in the past.

"I'm your man, Val. Always have been."

"I know."

They fell into silence and the stars above them moved in their constellations without worry or care. Cobby felt the finality of it and remembered his brother Cleo's last words to him just that afternoon.

"God be with you, brother. I hope I can do someone the same good turn."

*****

April 1935

Thunder rolled around in the sky again as the rain hit softly on the windows. It came quietly at first, then it came in hard, angry torrents that sent rivers running down the street. It came down so hard that the droplets hit the ground and bounced back up again, making a mist that floated just above the earth. The softness of twilight didn't illuminate the scene for long before the light disappeared altogether. All that was left was the occasional burst of light from the electricity above.

Vantino turned away from the window, looking back at the small form huddled on the armchair in a blanket. She had just come back. Her face was bruised again. Not as bad as the first time, but, he obviously hadn't quite gotten his point across to Jerry. That sharpness that pierced his stomach any time the thought of physically hurting Jerry Barelli wrapped itself around his insides. Oh, he would enjoy it.

Vantino well understood why Vinny wouldn't bring Marie into his home full time. But, Vantino didn't feel like that was a good enough reason. Eventually somebody was gonna figure out she was coming around, put two and two together and come up with the answer. However, it wasn't his call to make, and since the child meant so much to Vinny, he kept his mouth shut. In a short time, the girl had come to mean something to him, too.

He smiled to himself. She was cuddled up with a little doll that Nancy gave her. Marie hated thunder and lightning. Vantino had been sitting at the desk near the window taking his gun apart to clean it when she crept in. His back was to her, and although he could hear her, he kept his back turned. She chose the armchair just out of the circle of lamp light where he worked. She said nothing. She just wanted to be close to him, so he kept quiet.

After he finished his cleaning, he rose to look out the window at the storm. He knew she wasn't sleeping, but rather watching him silently from beneath the blanket. She was such an intelligent girl. It fascinated him that she could so quickly and accurately read those around her. A lesson, he supposed, taught to her by the necessity to survive the violent changes of the man who ruled her world. Vantino burned with the desire to make Jerry pay. But that would have to wait.

"Quite a storm," he said softly to no one in particular. "Coffee would be good."

He walked from the room down the hall to the back part of Vinny's excessive home. He did so slowly, so she wouldn't have to wander the darkened halls alone in her pursuit of him. She did not know him well enough yet to take his hand and walk with him. He wondered if she ever would. Something in her longed to reach out to him and seek the friendship he offered. Men in her life weren't something she felt she could trust. He realized that her lifetime might pass without her ever coming to trust a man. That saddened him greatly.

He turned on the light switch. Moving to the stove, he took the coffee pot from the back burner, then he filled the pot with water. Out of the corner of his eye he saw her hovering just outside the doorway. She still clutched her doll. He softly whistled a tune.

He put the insides and grounds into the percolator, then turned the burner on. He disappeared into the pantry for a moment. When he did, she moved just inside the doorway to see where he went. When he came out, she skittered away again quiet as a mouse. He set the cookie jar on the counter. He pulled the handle on the ice box. He took out a bottle of milk and set it on the counter next to the stove. He lifted a sauce pot from the rack above the island. He poured milk into it and turned the burner on. Then he sat on a wooden stool and waited. Another flash of lightning with an answering boom sent her into the room and under the table.

The truth was, she was fascinated by this man. He was very powerful. She could sense that. He was greatly respected by Vinny. She could see it. He was feared by many around him, but she didn't know why. When he was in the room men either stepped aside or cowered, either way, he ruled supreme under Vinny. But, he was very personable too. He would smile at her occasionally. She accidentally bumped into him once and she cringed waiting for him to berate her, he never did. He just smiled at her. He often told silly jokes to Vinny that made her laugh behind her hand. Or he pretended to hurt himself and made weird faces to which she dared not laugh at.

She liked Vinny. Very much. But when she was really scared, like now, this was the man she wanted to be close to. This was the man who made her feel safe. But she never dared talk to him, and she never dared interrupt him. Even though he made her feel safe, he might not be willing to allow her presence. In fact she knew he wouldn't. Men didn't like little girls. They hated them. So, she stole her comfort from him without his knowledge.

Marie liked Vinny's wife, Nan, very much. She was a beautiful woman but her eyes reflected a deep sadness. She took Marie when she could, and so Marie spent a great deal of time with her. It wasn't long before Marie noticed how Nan's eyes would light up each time she entered the room. Nan never had a child of her own, and she missed the presence of one in her life greatly. Vinny and Nan had gone out that evening, but Marie didn't know where.

When the milk was warm and the coffee done perking, he got out two plates and set them on the counter. On those he put several cookies from the cookie jar. He mixed cocoa and sugar into the milk then he poured himself some coffee. When he sat at the counter again he made no move to enjoy his refreshment. Marie thought it odd he would want cocoa and coffee at the same time. She rarely got to enjoy either let alone both at once.

"Sure wish I had a friend to share this with." He said out loud then sighed deeply. Marie wondered if he meant Vinny. Do grown men really like hot cocoa? She had no idea. As she contemplated matters beyond her realm he looked at her.

Her grip tightened on her doll. Her mouth went dry. She hunched her shoulders and tried to be invisible. This was where she lost the man who gave her comfort, and gained a man who gave her fear. She was certain of it.

"Will you sit with me? I don't like lightning and I don't like to be alone."

Her beautiful eyes lit, but her features didn't change. Could it be that he hated lightning too? A grown man scared of something? No. This was a trap. She'd better run. She shook her head at him.

"You don't think I make good cocoa?" He raised a brow at her. She hid her face behind her doll.

"You must not know that I won first prize at the World's Hot Cocoa Fair, do you?" She peeked at him with one eye.

"Yep. Rode a steamship all the way to Europe. Hitched a ride on a llama up into the Swiss Alps with my cocoa and magic sugar tucked in my pocket. They had some swell cocoa there. It didn't come close to mine. I beat out everyone from the whole world on that trip. You really ought to try it." When she still didn't move he added, "I put my magic sugar in it."

She moved carefully to the counter and climbed up on the stool, wary of him the whole time. The bright honesty that shown in his face made her believe he was the World's Cocoa Champ. She took a sip and found that it was good. Delicious, in fact. He smiled at her again, that personable smile of his.

"See, told you. Eat a cookie."

While she ate her cookie she looked him over out of the corner of her eye. He wore his gun holsters beneath his biceps. His face had a hard set to it when he wasn't looking at her. She felt she should be honest with him. No man would appreciate sharing his table with someone like her. Something about him demanded honesty.

"I killed my little brother."

He didn't make any move or gasp. Just finished eating his cookie and brushed off his hands. Then he looked at her straight on.

"No you didn't."

She wasn't sure how to make him understand that such a bold statement were true.

"I did. I really did." Her voice was barely above a whisper.

"I know all about your little brother. And I know you didn't kill him."

She was taken aback. This was not how this conversation usually went. For the first part, he wasn't yelling at her. For the second, he wasn't accusing her. She sat looking down at her plate. She had carried this burden a long time. It gave her bad dreams at night that made her cry. Now he was dismissing it.

"But," she started with tears in her voice, "I was supposed to hold his hand across the street. I lost his hand."

"Little brothers do that. They fidget and fuss, then they get away from you. You didn't kill your little brother. I don't care what they told you."

She just stared at his face. He stared back. Nothing in his eyes reflected that he was lying to her. He was solid. No leaks or sugar coating. He was solid. With the innate ability of a child, she read his intentions. After a moment she looked back down at her cocoa. She resumed eating and said no more.

Vantino watched her while she ate. She was so small and fragile. She had lived through so many things that he himself had not in his own life. He knew that it would take many more conversations like the one they just had to reinforce the fact that she in no way killed her brother. It was an accident, a very tragic one, but an accident just the same. He had run into the street in front of a car. That was all.

"Are you married?" Her small voice asked.

"No."

"Why?"

"Girls say I smell funny." He made a sour face at her. Marie clapped her hand over her mouth to stop the laugh that nearly escaped. "Do you think I smell funny?"

She shrugged her shoulders. "I never smelled you."

"Well, come closer and smell me." She shook her head vigorously. It took all he had not to burst out laughing. She had a way that made him feel young.

"Come on. Just one sniff. I need to know the truth. If I smell funny, I better know so I don't talk to any more girls."

She looked doubtful. But, after some serious consideration, she leaned forward across the table, sniffing loudly. Then she sat back and clutched her doll tightly. She shook her head again.

"I don't smell funny?" She shook her head again. "Hmm. Strange." He raised his coffee cup to his lips. Marie nibbled her cookie. He lowered his coffee cup as his eyes lit brightly.

"Say, you know any card tricks?" he asked.

She shook her head again.

He reached into the top drawer on his right and pulled out a deck of cards. "Vinny and me like to sit in here and play cards and eat cookies when it rains. So we keep a deck in here hidden from Lola the cook." He began to shuffle. He knew every fancy way to shuffle and showed her.

"Well, here you are. Nancy said you weren't in bed." Vinny walked into the light of the kitchen and sat down on a stool next to Marie. "Is this old scoundrel showing you card tricks?"

She nodded at him, her eyes full of respect and admiration for a man she barely knew.

"Keep your eye on him. He'll get all your milk money." Vinny leaned over to say in her ear. When she looked at him he looked down at her softly.

It was the beginning of something. Vinny sat beside her and taught her how to hold her cards in her hand while Vantino dealt them out. They spent the couple of hours during the storm playing Go Fish, and other simple games so Marie could get the idea. Vinny was patient with her, not something he really ever was in normal life. He sat and helped her, impressed with the way her little mind grasped concepts barely touched on. Vantino kept things silly with all his childish jokes. In a while, she laughed openly at them. It was the beginning of something.

*****

1956

"This will be good, Marie. I think he will like this one for the pictures." Imelda held up a newly made gown and smiled at Marie. "He wants flashy, so we give him flashy. You and I make the perfect team. I make the gown; you wear it and make it shine." Her heavy Italian accent was tinged with fondness.

"It is beautiful, Imelda. But what do you make that isn't?" Marie sipped a cup of Earl Grey.

Imelda laughed. "You know I make all of Mickey's shirts? They are plain enough compared to this!"

Marie smiled. "Custom tailor. My, he's spoiled isn't he?"

Imelda hung the gown on a rack to wait for Marie. She had a sad smile on her lips as she did so.

"Well, I owe him. That is why I put up with Eva and Margo's baloney. If it were not for the Delano's, I would be out in the street. Or worse." Marie took another sip of her tea.

"When I came here, I was a very young bride. My husband and I left Italy a few years after we wed. He worked hard to get enough money together for us to start a new life here in America. He was so sure this was where he would make it big. We already had my oldest daughter, and on our voyage I conceived my second." Here she paused to laugh. "He called it our second honeymoon. Not that we ever had a first!"

Imelda came to sit next to Marie and she picked up her own tea cup. "When we got through Ellis Island, which took a while, we lived in New York City. It was not what my husband wanted for us. The mafia there tried to recruit him. He'd been warned not to fall for their offers. And he was a smart man. So as soon as he could, he got the money together and brought us to California." Again she smiled sadly.

"He worked in the steel yards down by the dock. We had a little house with a very small yard. I had born my second child so I was busy. One afternoon his foreman came to my door and told me a beam my husband was working under fell and crushed him. It felt so unreal. I just knew they had the wrong house, so I waited for him to come home. The foreman was a very nice man. He helped me get my husband buried. Then I was on my own.

"We lost the house a few months later. I was doing little sewing jobs for anyone who would pay me, but it wasn't enough to feed and house us. We spent three nights sleeping in the streets. My husband had always told me never to mix with the mafia that was so prevalent in our neighborhood. But, some of our neighbors had spoken often about what a generous man Georgio Delano was. So, I went to his office and begged the man there for a job. By then I hadn't eaten in days and my milk was slowly going away for the baby. We were scared and alone. I wasn't sure how long it would be before I had to turn my children over to the state because I couldn't care for them." Imelda looked down into her tea cup.

"The man refused to give me a job. No matter how I begged, he would not relent. Finally I cried to him in desperation. My two girls were crying, too. The man became very angry at us and threw us out. I held my girls tight as he did so, and when we were pushed through the door I begged him again. No, good. When I turned, Georgio was standing there watching what was going on. He asked me what I was doing there, and I explained to him what I needed. At the time I didn't know who he was, but I thought that maybe this man would help me. He did.

"He put me in a small two room apartment. Loaned me the money to buy my first sewing machine. Then he sent his men to me for shirts. After a year or so, he sent his wife to me for a few house dresses. After those, she started coming to me without being told to. She had me make her a cocktail gown and that was it. I made all of her clothes exclusively. Then she began to send her friends and family." She smiled fondly now.

"Georgio stopped by one afternoon to see how I was faring. Which was odd to me that he would take the time to check on a lonely widow and her two girls, but he did. The whole apartment was filled with fabric and projects hung everywhere. He took one look around and told me, 'You've made good. Let's get you a shop.' He had this little shop open, so he rented it to me for next to nothing. And here I am today, still sewing exclusively for the Delano family." She chuckled softly then looked at Marie.

"So you see, I owe them everything. I doubt my girls and I would have survived for long the way we were living. Especially not the baby. And while I know that he was not what some would call a "good" man, Georgio Delano had his streaks of generosity. The Bible tells us to look out for widows and orphans. He did." She again smiled with a little sadness as she looked down into her tea cup.

Marie thought about how quickly life changes without warning or a chance to prepare yourself. Hers had so many changes of course she couldn't keep track of them anymore. Nor did she want to. But, never had she been a widowed mother of two small children. That seemed more desperate than anything she had endured.

"Have you heard from your young man? The one whose picture I saw?" Imelda was prying now. She had shed a little light on herself, now she would go at an angle she felt Marie needed help with. Whether she did or not.

It was Marie's turn to smile sadly and look down into her tea cup. "He married someone else." She took a sip.

"Hmmm. I see. How long ago?"

"A few months now, I guess. I saw it in an article in a magazine."

Imelda sighed and squeezed Marie's arm. "How that must have hurt you. Why did you not tell me? I would have been so glad to have been a shoulder for you to cry on. I know you needed one."

Marie shook her head. "It's alright, Imelda. I have so much to keep me busy. I really don't think on it much anymore."

"Hmm. I think not. A young woman suffering a jilting? Not think on it? You must have a heart of iron." Imelda poured more tea into Marie's cup. Marie knew Imelda well enough to know she was working at her angle more directly now.

"You are such a beautiful young woman." She paused here. "Perhaps, time will pass and you will find yourself ready to love again." Marie waited for the rest.

"You do have the opportunity to meet other young men. Cobby, for example. He is a fine young man. Who knows, with time, and the chance you've had to grow to know one another, maybe that fondness will open a door. Then, nature will take her course as she does with all young men and women. A smile will lead to a touch, a touch to a kiss, and then you don't remember your foolish young man from New York anymore."

"Perhaps, Imelda. Perhaps." Marie said softly. Imelda smiled confidently at her.

"Well, on to other things. I have had a chance to work out that special costume you asked for. Highly unusual, but, once you explained it to me, it made sense. And not to bring Cobby up again, but his suit worked perfectly. He won't be getting it back though."

"It's ok. Not much he can do about it now. Besides, I told him that might happen." Marie said.

"Let's go try it and the gown on." Imelda said as she stood. They walked through the door into the dressing area.

"You do seem to have a way with him." Imelda stated.

"Who?"

"Cobby. He does things for you he wouldn't normally do."

Marie smiled to herself. Imelda was very good at this game. "He is a very nice person beneath all that rough exterior," Marie replied lightly.

Imelda turned, but not before Marie saw the triumphant gleam in her eyes.

*****

The Los Angeles Times had requested an interview with Mickey in an attempt to write a piece on the man behind the extreme success of The Ruby. Mickey had always been free with the press, allowing them into the club during performances. They took all the pictures they wanted of the performers at the shows. Marie had gotten used to them, and after a time the photography and barrage of questions had ebbed. She was grateful.

It's hard to maintain anonymity in the papers.

Mickey was very correct in that statement. She felt more so now that it seemed a dark influence was out there trying to get to her or Mickey. Marie didn't like having her face and schedule pasted before prying eyes.

Although Mickey had always allowed them into the club, he never granted an interview with himself or any of the performers. So, when he told Marie that he had agreed to one, she was surprised. Luckily he had decided to do all the talking, but had agreed to pictures of the performers.

Watching from the bar as Mickey and the reporter conducted their interview, Rolly and Marie sat quietly. Mickey was dressed very sharply, and he held a cigarette in his hand the entire time. He looked cool and confident as he answered all of the questions that Marie and Rolly could not hear. He was in his element. When it came to being impressive, Mickey was tops.

"How does a jerk like that get where he is?" Rolly asked in disgust.

"Well, mostly I think he was born into it." Marie replied. She was wearing the white sheer shoulder less gown that Imelda made just for the interview. She sat artfully atop a stool with her legs crossed, and her hands clasped around her knee. Her hair was swept back with a diamond comb to hold it in place. Her lips were a deep red, and her eyes shimmered in the soft light.

"Yeah, but had it been you or me, we wouldn't have made it swing for even five minutes, let alone make a life of it like he has. Look at him. He's got the world on a string."

"Have you met his wife?" Marie asked as she tipped her head slightly to look at Rolly out of the corner of her eyes.

"No," Rolly said questioningly.

"Well, Mickey might have the world, but Eva's holding the string."

"Ah. Well, I knew there must be a hitch in there somewhere," Rolly's voice had a grim edge to it. Marie shrugged her bare shoulders at his comment.

"And besides, who would want the headache of keeping track of it all? That is where his charisma comes in," Marie said convincingly.

"Maybe. But, honestly, I do feel a little jealous when I see what he has done."

"He wouldn't have done it without you, Rolly."

He sighed as he looked at her longingly. "Run away with me."

She laughed without looking at him. "No, really. I mean it. I just can't stand it that he has all of this and gets you, too. It isn't fair. I want something spectacular, too."

"You know, Rolly, what you see isn't necessarily what you get," Marie said drily.

"You are correct. That's the damnable part of it. While you are beautiful, it's your personality that gets me every time. I love the way you feel in my arms each time we dance and your body is close to mine. But it's the sound of your laughter that holds me captive. Take pity on me and hold me in your arms!" He finished out in a rush of desperation and she laughed at his comical efforts.

"I don't think Mickey will go for that. So, once again he wins out."

Rolly clutched at his heart as if it were bleeding, and gave her a look of wounded desire. "Does this mean our passion for each other can never be fulfilled?"

Marie covered her face with her hand as she laughed at him. "Sorry, love. I guess not."

Rolly reached behind him and picked up an olive fork that was laying on the bar next to an open jar of olives. He held it up.

"Then damn it all! He must die!" He said in a theatric voice. The olive fork was only a few inches long, but Rolly held it as if it were a sword. He jumped to his feet.

Marie caught hold of his arm. Through her suffocating laughter, she pulled him back down onto his stool. She couldn't speak as he too began laughing. His brown eyes watched hers dance with merriment. Marie covered her face and didn't notice the softness in his as he looked at her. At length she looked around the room through teary eyes. They had caught the attention of The Dark Horse in the far corner away from the interview.

"Oh, damn. Now you've done us both in." Rolly looked to where she was watching and snorted as he started to laugh again. He moved closer to her ear and said, "It was worth it."

"What was?"

"To hear you laugh like that."

The Dark Horse stood and slipped the small journal he had been writing in into his pocket then buttoned his jacket.

"Oh shit, he's serious now," Rolly said through short bursts of laughter. Marie lay her head on his shoulder.

"I hope you like water. Cause things are about to get real wet when we go for a dip in the bay." Neither of them could control themselves any longer.

"Marie!" Mickey shouted at them. She held her breath to stop the laughter that boiled up inside her chest. Mickey waved her over.

"Good luck, my darling." Rolly said in a nasal tone. She half turned to smile back at him and the image made Rolly's insides bunch.

She gracefully glided to where Mickey now stood next to the reporter and held out his hand for her. She took it with a smile. She felt his hand go round behind her back and come to rest lightly on her hip.

"Marie, this is Christopher Channing. He's a reporter for the Los Angeles Times."

"Nice to meet you, Mr. Channing." Marie smiled elegantly.

"Likewise, Miss Barelli. We would like to take a few pictures of you and Mr. Delano if we could. Then we'll bring Mr. Howard over. We'll get some of the three of you together." Mr. Channing began moving chairs around behind the table to arrange them for the picture.

He took several of Mickey and Marie alone. One was of them behind the table, Mickey's arm around her. Another was of them standing close together, and she wondered what this would do to the rumors that they were lovers. She suspected that was Mickey's goal. The reporter then brought Rolly over and they did them all again.

"Would you take a personal photograph for me?" Mickey asked when Mr. Channing was all through.

"Sure. I can do that."

Mickey waved Valant over and asked him to sit behind the table. Mickey then sat Marie next to Valant, Mickey taking the seat next to her, leaving her between them. The photographer readied for the shot, then lowered the camera with it's massive flash.

"You look as if your father just died. I don't think you'll like the picture very much Mr. Delano."

Mickey looked to his photograph companions. "What do you want us to do?"

"She's a beautiful woman. Get a little closer." He held up his camera again with a sly grin.

The two men moved their chairs closer. When The Dark Horse's leg brushed Marie's, she thought of the car ride that started it all. He glanced down at her from the corner of his eye looking irritated. Mickey put his arm around the back of her chair and stretched the other out front of him on the table. He was a bold ruler. The Dark Horse put his arm around Marie's waist and the heat from his palm burned into her side. The photographer still didn't look impressed.

"Come on boys. Surely we can fake a picture," Marie said as she put an arm around each of their shoulders and pulled them closer to her.

"Looking better. If we could get Mister Serious to smile now." Mr. Channing was referring to Valant.

"Nipples, knees and belly buttons, boys. It's all nipples, knees, and belly buttons," Marie stated just before the camera flashed and Valant turned his face away.

"Very nice," Mr. Channing said.

Both men stood and Marie stood as well. "All done, Mickey?"

"Yeah, Marie. We're done."

With that she moved away to the dressing room. Rolly caught her eye as she went and winked at her. She blushed softly as if on cue and waved good-bye to him.

*****

Marie saw him for the first time that afternoon. He looked so unassuming. Had it not been for the flecks of bright light in his eyes, she would have dismissed him entirely. But there was the gleam that gave him away, not to mention the fact that he was still. Nothing about him quivered nor tensed as he spoke to her, but she knew this was who they were looking for.

Marie left the club with Deano after the interview with the Times. By then it was late, so Deano took her back downtown the few blocks to the restaurant for an early dinner before it was time to get ready for the night's performance. There was no space in front of the restaurant to park the car, so Deano double parked for a moment to let Marie out. Then, while she walked to the door, he left to park the car around the side of the block. She saw a man walking down the street alone. She assumed he was on his way somewhere. But as their paths crossed, he spoke to her.

He tilted his head at an angle as he looked at her. He stopped walking and watched her cross in front of him. "Miss Barelli?" he asked in a polite fashion.

Marie was used to people recognizing her and stopping her to talk, but this was different. She was for all purposes alone, despite the fact that the doorman stood waiting for her. "Hello," she answered back.

"Forgive me, I'm sure you get this all the time. I can't pass up the opportunity to say hello to the shining spark of The Ruby." He spoke in a confident manner. His eyes didn't stray from hers. His posture was nonchalant. He had black hair combed straight back from his face and a lock of it fell across his forehead. His skin was smooth from where he had shaved that morning, and his brown suit was well pressed.

"Oh, no problem." She held out her hand to him and he bowed gracefully over it when he took it in his. He never looked away from her. They were cunning eyes, calculating eyes, and the depths were black as night.

"It really is an honor to meet such an important person. And alone on the street, no less." As he spoke his face reflected the ironic tone in his voice.

"I doubt I'm as important as you think." He let out a light laugh when she finished speaking.

"Come now, don't be so modest. What you are no one else could be." The corners of his mouth quirked as he said it.

"Oh, I'm fairly common back in New York. But I am grateful to be here. Have you had the chance to spend an evening at The Ruby?"

His mouth curled into a vicious smile. "I must admit I've been following your career for some time now. I feel I know you without actually having met you. You are a spectacular performer; particularly now that you work for Mickey." He arched a cynical brow. "And, the performance has paid off very well so far."

Marie said nothing, just watched him for a moment. Nothing he said would indicate anything was amiss, but as she stood there she saw it. The subtle change that he made. His mouth pressed thin for a split second and his eyes fairly gleamed. But then it was gone. This was a man well versed in controlling himself. More so than Mickey who barely kept himself in hand. This man was acting and he was very good at it as he hardly gave anything away.

"Well, thank you, Mr.?"

He lurched forward and offered his hand again. "Danny G. My friends call me Danny G."

"Well, Danny, it was nice to meet you." She took her hand from his and made to step past him. She was relieved to see Deano coming up the sidewalk.

"Just one thing, Miss Barelli," he moved to block her departure. "Could I trouble you for an autograph?"

"Certainly. But, I have no pen or paper. Perhaps we could step into the restaurant." She moved past him again.

"No problem. I have a pen and a piece of paper." He reached into his pocket and her breath caught. Deano was next to her now.

"Silly me. I made a few notes on this. But, it will still work." He handed her the paper as well as the pen.

Marie looked down as she unfolded the paper. It was as if history was repeating itself, only this time, The Dark Horse was nowhere near to step in. She placed the paper on her leg to sign it and as she did so read the scribbles he had referred to.

V/8

She quickly signed her name and handed it back to him. His eyes were fairly glowing and his face was taught.

"There you are. It was nice to meet you, sir." Marie spoke as she handed him the autograph and pen. She was fairly certain from his vantage point Deano had not seen the note. She moved away from the man who called himself Danny G, but as she did so she looked back at him and saw his emotions laid bare. His intent was obvious. This man knew something about her he planned to use.

Inside the restaurant she thought about what had just transpired. This man had revealed himself to her. Why? She contemplated going to Mickey, but that was suicide. She'd have to come clean about why he might have an interest in her. That might compromise her position worse than it already was. Perhaps that's what Danny G wanted. To manipulate without ever lifting a finger. She decided from that moment on she'd stick closer to her escorts.

*****

Mickey's uncle was a repulsive man. Not so much for the fact that he was a rather robust individual, but because of his mouth and the drivel the salivated from it. He spent part of his time trying to tell Mickey his business, the rest was spent on orations of the female body and the parts of which he found particularly satisfying. He was rarely invited anywhere, and when he was he was kept from Valant, who kept his gun loaded for any opportunity. Valant had many a satisfying daydream on the demise of that one uncle.

Mickey left him alive because he was the last remaining relative on his mother's side. Sometimes he wondered at the prudence of it.

But at that particular moment, he himself was about to pull out the pistol he kept in his own jacket and pull the trigger. Who would really care? His own mother had refused this man's company even after he was all she had left.

"This club isn't where you are gonna make your money, boy. The Stock Market. That's the place." He paused to take a drink then choked on it. "Oh shit. Did you see the knockers on that little gal?"

"Uncle Remmi, that's my wife."

Uncle Remmi laughed crudely. "I bet those make for a good time, eh?" His fat face stretched into a lecherous grin as he elbowed Mickey in the ribs.

Cobby, who was standing by to cover Mickey, discreetly covered his mouth with his hand and looked away. It never failed to amuse him the reactions Remmi got from Mickey and Valant. It was also hilarious to him that Remmi really didn't know he was lusting after his nephew's wife. When he did know it, the impropriety of it didn't bother him. Mickey caught the movement out of the corner of his eye.

Mickey held out his arm to Cobby. "Uncle Remmi, have you met Cobby?"

All amusement in Cobby died. Of course they had met. Hundreds of times. Remmi still called him Cody.

Amusement glittered in Mickey's eyes as he introduced them. Again.

"Why don't you fellas visit and I'll send a tight little waitress with another drink for you, eh, Remmi?" Remmi didn't notice Mickey's sarcasm in the elbow he gave him to the ribs.

"Oh, sounds good, Mick." He took another sip of his drink. Half of it went down his chins. Mickey pointed and laughed at Cobby as he walked away.

Bastard.

"Well, young man, I'll bet you enjoy yourself each night here at the club." He gave Cobby a wink. "New recruit, eh? How long have you been working for Mickey?"

"Thirteen years, sir," Cobby said in a flat tone.

"Thirteen what?" Remmi was distracted by a brunette in a low cut gown.

The music had stopped and the lights on the floor dimmed. Couples left at the signal. It took several seconds while the band waited for everyone to take their seats. Remmi was saying something repulsive about the brunette, but Cobby kept his eyes on the floor. It was taking a very long while for the band to resume. He glanced up and saw that Mickey noticed as well.

Remmi was still talking, but Cobby cut him off. "Excuse me a moment, sir."

He made his way to the balcony. Valant, who left Margo, was also looking out onto the floor. They met eyes and Cobby moved to him.

In a sudden flash of light one spotlight came on at the edge of the floor near the stage. Into the light walked a man in a black suit. His hands were in his pockets and the white cuffs of his shirt were rolled up over the cuff of the black suit jacket. He wore a fedora on his head, and the point in front was pulled low over his face.

This man struck Cobby as odd. He was of a small build, and he walked as though he were strolling in the park. From the distance Cobby couldn't tell if he were wearing shoes. The balcony around had filled up as curious people watched what was about to unfold.

The band started playing but the lights didn't come back on the stage. Rolly began to sing, the sound of Alan Jay Lerner's *On the Street Where You Live* seeming to reach out from the blackness of the stage like a vocal manifestation.

As the words came from Rolly, the small man in the suit began to walk with more of a dance to his step. He turned and skipped, then spun in a tight circle. It became obvious to Cobby this was no man, but Marie, dressed in the suit she had borrowed from him. Just then, he noticed her toes underneath the hem of a pant leg, and the spike heels that went with the toes. He chuckled to himself.

Marie's step was barely making contact with the floor as she went along, dancing with herself. Into the spotlight came one of the company dancers who happened by her in a small sequined costume. Marie pretended to watch her pass with interest, then grabbed hold of the front of her hat as if to offer courtesy. She made several dance steps as the girl went on.

Marie spun quickly to the center of the dance floor. There she was met by two of the dance company. They were both dressed in the same sequined body suits. They stood on each side of Marie, as they moved as one to the left crossing their right leg in front of their left. Then when they came to a stop, they ended on the left leg. They stretched it out before going on to the right side of the dance floor, crossing the left leg in front of the right. As they came again to a stop, they stretched out the right leg.

The two girls moved from Marie, and she again walked jauntily along, this time two new dancers appeared in separate spotlights. They came to halt to watch Marie as she walked by.

As an instrumental segment began and the pace of the music picked up, the spotlights around Marie lit up to reveal the four dancers around her. They all spun at once, and in doing so came to stand in a line, two on each side of Marie. They walked forward together, each step crossing over the leg of the girl next in line. Marie made a stark contrast to the dancers next to her. She was bold in her black suit, and played the masculine part well, although nothing in her feminine form lent to the charade. As they stopped together, they kicked their legs up at eye level multiple times before the music slowed and Rolly began to sing again.

One by one, the company dancers spun out of the spotlight leaving Marie to spin alone. She came to a stop when the last girl left. Marie jumped and clicked her heels together and the crowd was no longer seated. The sound came as one as both the applause and the cheering began. Marie again strolled along the floor as if in a park, looking at objects that weren't there, nodding and bowing her head to imaginary people.

Marie made a small bow and tipped her hat to the raving crowd then disappeared from the light. The crowd continued to roar, broken only by the shrill piercing of whistling. The crowd was chanting for an encore. This was the hook that brought them back the next night. Marie knew this well. It was a full five minutes before the crowd began to simmer, and even then the excitement in their voices as they left reverberated along the walls and the ceiling.

Valant looked at Cobby. "I wonder where she got the suit." He said it flatly with sarcasm.

Cobby slid his hands into his pockets and shrugged.

Mickey stood with an amused expression on his face at the balcony. His hands were in his pockets, and the way the corners of his mouth quirked spoke of his pleasure at her impromptu performance. Mickey wasn't a man to like deviation from the plan he laid out, but in this case he looked pleased. He met Valant's eyes, and then turned to find Eva.

It wasn't what Mickey had planned. Marie changed the costume as well as the choreography. Not to mention the fact that she wasn't supposed to be a woman in a suit playing a man. But, she had done it beautifully. Anyone who watched it would agree. Mickey would no doubt get over it when he read the reviews the next morning. Marie had stepped out of bounds to define her talent and was successful. But, that didn't mean Mickey would give her free run on artistic license.

She was very tired as she climbed in the car behind Deano. She slept all the way to the apartment; didn't bother to change out of her suit before going to bed. She lay down in her corner watching as the last of the days images floated before her mind's eye. Her legs throbbed something terrible.

Marie had done it. She had done it and the crowd had loved it. Now she would have to brave Mickey. But it was worth it.

*****

The sky above was nothing but a black hole. No stars were visible through the layer of clouds that had gathered sometime in the evening. The lights of the city didn't reflect off them, either. Valant moved along the alley way silently. He kept close to the building. His eyes adjusted to the darkness surrounding him and he didn't need direction.

They had chipped away at this for weeks. He and Cobby spent countless hours looking and asking questions, always eliminating whoever it was they questioned. They left no tracks, no one to identify them. Eventually it paid off. Whoever it was they were up against made sure that no one had any idea of who he was.

Valant never fought against someone he didn't know. He knew everyone. Absolutely everyone. Who worked for Mickey, even on the lowest levels, and he knew who worked for Vinnetti. Nothing was a mystery to him. Anything that happened he knew about it. But this was something different. It was hard to fight an opponent that didn't exist.

It seemed odd. To plan a takeover when nobody knew who the leader was. Valant sorted through layer after layer of lower level guys, mostly couriers, until he finally met a man who could give him answers. That man informed Valant that who he sought had an office of sorts down by the docks in Vinny's territory. It was an old run down warehouse, but it was more than met the eye.

Valant brought his best with him; Cobby, Deano, Martin and Frankie. They spread out, one on each side of the building. A small warehouse in comparison to those around it. Each man held two gas bombs, one in each hand. Their orders were simple. Find a window to throw them in or some other flammable spot. Light the rag that was jammed down into the glass bottle neck. Yes, this would be easy.

Valant himself waited to light his. By now he could hear sounds of bottles breaking. Around the front of the building he could hear the fire taking root. Beams moaned and popped under the intense heat. When he was certain that all of his men had lit their side of the building aflame, he lit his own and stood just to the side of what he knew had to be the main entrance. It stood slightly ajar and he threw his lit bottles into the building, then waited. It was a long time, but finally he heard voices inside. By then, his men had joined him.

He reached into his jacket and pulled out one of his guns and aimed it, waiting for the first man to come out the door. The voices now were shouting. Cobby came to stand beside Valant and held his gun as well. The shouting was near the door. Valant could feel the heat slowly moving through the bricks in the wall. The alley was lit from the flames that reached out the windows above.

The first man was on fire. Flames ate away at his back as he ran frantically trying to find a way to put them out. Valant shot him instantly. By now the sound of the fire drown out any noise his gun made. The next man Valant hit as he sailed into the alley. Cobby shot the next and Valant hit the next two. It was a long moment before the last two also came through the door and fell to a quick trigger.

The intensity of the heat was beyond bearable in the small alley. Cobby's instincts drove him to leave the cramped oven he was standing in. Valant stood studying the faces of the men who lay lifeless on the ground. Cobby took hold of his arm and pulled.

"We gotta go, Val." Valant seemed not to notice the intensity of the heat. It struck Cobby that perhaps he was right at home in it. The rumors he had heard about The Dark Horse being the devil might actually be true.

But, Valant turned with him and they fled the alley. They walked the several blocks back to the car and heard sirens in the distance. They met up with the rest of the guys as they moved along.

"A dirty deed done," Deano said as they slipped into the car and Cobby cranked the engine.

"It will either end it, or start a war," Valant stated.

"Did you know any of them?" Cobby asked as the car moved along.

Valant was silent a long time. "No."

*****

"Wake up." Cobby's voice was soft and it took Marie several tries to decide if it were really him or just another of her dreams. She covered her face with her hand.

"Come on. Wake up, sugar tits." That gave it away. She despised that name.

"Leave me alone," She moaned. He pulled her hand away from her face.

"We have this same conversation every morning. And every morning you tell me to leave you alone. Why not get a new line?"

"Alright, piss off."

Cobby chuckled. "You're so angry when you're sleepy." Then his voice went stern. "Don't you get sassy with me. By changing the conversation I meant maybe you could be pleasant and accommodating."

Marie covered her face again. "Pleasant and accommodating starts at eight."

Cobby pulled back his jacket cuff to look at his watch. "Well, we are fifteen minutes into pleasant and accommodating. Get up, sugar tits."

She growled at him. "How would you like it if I called you sugar nuts?"

Cobby snorted a laugh. "Come now, Marie. It's a term of endearment."

"More like a term of endurement," she snapped.

"I only say it because it's super effective in waking you up. Come on, sugar tits."

"I hate you."

He bent low and whispered to her in a husky voice, "You don't mean that."

"Yes, I do!"

"You look real nice in my clothes, by the way."

Marie slowly stood without his help and looked at him. She had taken the pins out of her hair the night before. Now it flowed around her face and down her back. Beyond that, she still wore the suit from Cobby. She stretched her arms above her head and her lithe dancer body was firm. When she looked at him again, Cobby had a deeply amused expression on his face. She cast him an irritated glance and walked out of the bedroom.

As she passed through the door she stopped. The Dark Horse sat reading the morning paper at the dining room table. Cobby moved past her. As he did so he bumped into her shoulder knocking her forward. He looked back at her with that highly amused expression while rubbing the side of his nose with an index finger.

"Coffee, Marie," Cobby said as he removed his suit jacket and sat down.

Valant said nothing as she passed and went into the kitchen. She took her time. She waited for the coffee to perk, making up the coffee tray. When at last it was done she moved into the dining room with it. They sat as they had before, only now Cobby was reading the funnies. Marie looked at them and smelled the strong acrid smell of smoke between them. She set the tray down and looked between herself and them.

"Well. I feel appropriately dressed for coffee with the boys this morning." Both men stopped reading and raised their heads to look at her. She poured.

"Have you said good morning to Mr. Valant?" Cobby asked sarcastically.

Marie stared hard at Cobby. *I hate you* she mouthed.

"Good morning, Mr. Valant." She said in a respectful tone. Valant merely grunted.

Marie sat quietly sipping the hot coffee, avoiding looking at Valant who held his paper up before him. She was afraid to draw attention to the fact that he was again wearing his reading glasses. That was one of the worst moments in her life the last time he had read at the table.

"I'm guessing I don't get my suit back," Cobby said as he leaned back in his chair and eyed her. He made her uncomfortable when he was like this. She never knew what he would say that would set The Dark Horse into an angry fit at her.

"Imelda said she can fix it so it is the way it was." She took another sip of coffee. She would drink a quick cup and get out of the horrid room with its horrid acrid smell.

"No. You fill it out rather nicely. It went for a worthy cause." He laced his fingers behind his head. He eyed her with extreme amusement now. She deeply feared where he was going with this.

Cobby, she mouthed at him. She was going to run. Right then. Just up and go. His mouth stretched into a grin.

"Hell, you could be one of us, with that suit."

Valant sighed deeply and turned the page of his newspaper.

"How are you with impressions?" Cobby asked.

She cocked her head at him and a twinkle came into her eyes. "Well, let's see"

She scooted to the edge of her seat and then leaned way back. She laced her hands behind her head and eyed Cobby with amusement. In a falsely seductive voice she said, "Wow, you fill out that suit real nice."

She tried to pull her bosom into her chest more. "Come on, sugar tits. I want some coffee." Cobby snorted as he started to laugh. She continued on.

"Yeah, that's right. I'm an important man. You bet. I can drink scotch and eat cake without puking. Oh, yeah. Work for the big man. That's right. Work for The Dark Horse. They call me Sugar Nuts." Her voiced carried a sultry and very fake masculine tone. Cobby was laughing.

"Deano. Do Deano." Cobby said between guffaws.

Marie sat up and eyed the Danish on the table. She cast a questioning look at Valant who nodded. She took one and then looked at Cobby. She raised the Danish to her mouth and took a really large and aggressive bite. Part of the Danish hung from her mouth as she tried to chew it. She stopped chewing abruptly and looked at the Danish on Cobby's plate.

"Yooughah eiat aaaat?" She asked him. Cobby could hardly stop laughing to ask her to repeat herself.

She moved the Danish to the side of her mouth and said again rather loudly in an Italian accent, "You gonna eat that?"

Cobby burst out and slapped his hand on the table. By now Marie was laughing a little too. It took some time to chew and swallow the Danish in her mouth. She looked at Valant and his eyes were narrow slits of disapproval over the rim of his reading glasses.

"Oh, shit. Mickey. You gotta do Mickey."

Marie sat with her back straight. She stretched an arm along the table in front of her, the other she bent at the elbow. She brought an index finger to her lip. She took on a stately air as she looked down her nose at Cobby. He snorted again he was laughing so hard. She kept this pose for a long while, then with great fear, pretended to see something across the room and cowered looking like she would run.

"Oh no. Was that Eva?" She then broke into laughter.

"Oh no, you didn't. No, you didn't!" Cobby said, but laughed just as hard. Valant laid his paper on the table and looked at her. His face showed no amusement as he removed his glasses.

"Now me." His deep voice cut through the laughter like a freight train. Both Cobby and Marie stopped laughing to stare at him.

"Now me," he repeated. Cobby looked surprised. He looked to Marie to see what she would do.

"No. It was just a joke." She looked down into her coffee cup. He leaned forward and put his elbows on the table.

"Me," he stated firmly. Something about it irritated her. He was the spoiler of all fun and it grated on her.

She looked at him challengingly and said, "Ok. Give me your glasses."

He handed them to her without looking away from her eyes. He seemed to be daring her to insult him. She was just ignited enough to do it. She despised him for the way he treated her, for the way he treated everyone. He was not the god he thought himself to be.

She took the glasses and slid them onto her face. They rested on the tip of her nose and she avoided looking through them for they made her eyes blur. Lifting her hair and tossing it over her shoulders, she sat back in her chair with her spine straight, then extended one arm onto the table. She took his paper from him and held it up as if to read it. She secured her face into hard lines of disgust and sighed a heavy, dissatisfied growl. Then she lowered her paper, looking at Valant like he was for all the world the most loathsome creature ever to suck air. The room was silent as she glared at him.

"Nailed it," Cobby muttered.

"Give me the glasses." Valant ordered, his voice reverberating throughout the room. She did so with a look that said, *you asked for it.*

"Well, if you boys don't need anything, I better get dressed." She waited a moment before rising to leave. Valant was back to reading his paper. Cobby was watching them both with caution.

After she left, Cobby chuckled to himself again. "She really is something."

Valant gave him an irritated sideward glance. "Yeah. A real piece of work."

*****

The crowd was particularly large that night. It had been overwhelming at times, but this topped all those nights combined. After Marie's particularly spectacular dance whilst wearing a man's suit, the place had climaxed into an all-out show. Mickey couldn't have been happier with the performances and had spoken to Marie on several occasions about trying out more of her ideas. It seemed she could do no wrong. But then, he was making money faster than any other venture within the city. He was doing it with very little expense to his own pocket book.

He felt he owed Marie more than he was giving, but he also feared if he changed anything she would lose her grateful attitude. It was a buried fear of his that she would one day leave him high and dry, struggling to replace her. Which would be impossible. It would take years to find the kind of charisma that she carried even when she was silently eating her lunch. She took a little more of his soul every time he looked at her. She was not Maryanne, but she was a close second. She made him look at Eva with even deeper regret. But he made his promise, and if Georgio taught him nothing else, it was keep his promises. Now there would be a child. Mickey refused to think of the child.

The press was always present. It became normal to see them each time Marie entered the club in the morning. They all wanted something from her, a small scrap of gossip that they could take to the printer to set the world on fire with. She was never more than charming, and she never spoke to them. She had come a long ways from the night The Dark Horse had to escort her in. Mickey allowed such nonsense outside the club each day for he knew that it was only increasing his business.

Mickey had professional photographers come in and take pictures of Rolly, Marie, all of the band and dance company. He hung the portraits in the entry way. He found himself stopping to look at them each time he entered the club from the front. They were huge, making the performers larger than life. Which they already seemed to be anyway. Despite this, Marie never changed. She kept being respectful and polite, charming and engaging. After a time, Mickey forgot that she might be anything else beneath all of the glamor.

Marie was always kind to everyone. It seemed to each man that she surely must be in love with him. However, she never focused on anyone in particular more than she did anyone else. It was part of what made her so grand; she simply made each person feel wonderful. It was only a few, like Cobby, or Imelda, that realized she was far deeper than she appeared on the outside. She carried something heavy deep down inside that she never let show. She was an actress, and she was damn good at it.

After she learned of Alex's engagement, she grieved over her lost love alone in the dark and never made a reference to him again. Only when Imelda asked did she speak of him out loud. He had killed a dream so effectively that she accepted her fate with Mickey completely. She would ride the wave until it was gone, and she knew when that happened, she would be, too. This was why she was kind to everyone, and no one in particular all at the same time.

She thought well of Cobby, and while he was very handsome and likeable, to love such a man was certain death for them both. She knew what heartache this would be right up until the last moments of their lives. So, she loved him as well as she could and left it at that. Hers was a life destined to be short. As was his.

That was not to say, however, that she wasn't happy where she was. It had taken sometime to realize that. Although not the success she had dreamed of, she was indeed living the dream she had cherished since childhood. Begrudgingly, she knew she owed this to Mickey. It was he who made all of it possible. Without ever speaking it out loud, they each knew their dreams were made reality through each other. Mickey went from barely keeping himself under control in her presence to always smiling softly at her. He maintained a relaxed demeanor. Although he was full of mystery, Marie began to like him, but realized quite effectively that like herself, he was carrying something heavy way down deep.

Deano stayed at Marie's side constantly. She saw less of Cobby because of this, but she felt better having Deano there all of the time. Martin and Frankie alternated helping Deano. She was well covered. She moved freely around the club during performances knowing any number of men were prepared to step in at any time. During a particular show, a drunk man had gotten fresh with her and grabbed her butt. Deano stepped up and hit him in the face with the butt of his pistol. That had ended most all foolishness. She saw no more of the man with the scar on his face.

She realized the danger was not gone.

Marie thought of the man she met on the street now weeks past. She knew that his appearance had been a warning of sorts. He was simply telling a wiser person that he was aware of her and her connections. Why did the men who surrounded her have this notion that she held some kind of value to Vinnetti?

She was a woman alone in a dangerous situation beyond her control; merely a pawn in a much greater game. That was life. Even the free live under the controls of situation and emotion. Fear of losing what means the most, precious and fragile life.

She knew Danny G would eventually make his move. She wondered how much Vinny and Mickey knew about what was going on. And more importantly, would either stand to protect her? She did not know. She had gone over the possibilities many times, but she always came to the same conclusion: if she was going to survive, she would have to do it herself. Hers was the only move she could be certain of.

The band played Glenn Miller's version of *American Patrol* and the floor was packed. It was one of those rare occasions when both Rolly and Marie were free at the same time. They watched from behind the stage at the dancing couples, laughing along with the dance company at the goings on.

"Mickey's down front tonight. Why is that?" Julie asked.

"Oh, he said something about a private guest wanted to be down there," Rolly replied.

"I wonder what a person has to pay to sit at a table on the floor." Helen wondered out loud.

"I heard once it's a thousand a night," Rolly said. Everyone collectively groaned.

"That's several month's wages for me!" Julie said.

"You know, one of the door guys told me Bing Crosby was here last night?" Rolly stated and everyone turned to look at him.

"Really?" Helen asked in awe.

"That's what he said," Rolly replied as he shrugged his shoulders. He then turned to Marie.

"Since we got Mickey down on the floor anyway, let's bring him out for a little recognition." Marie nodded her head.

When they took the stage the floor was still clearing. Marie quickly found where Mickey was seated then watched the couples leave the floor. The Dark Horse had the beautiful Margo. They made their way to the table where Mickey sat. Mickey's guys were stationed everywhere. Mickey wasn't taking chances anymore.

The spotlight came on Rolly and he began to speak, allowing the band time to catch their breath.

"I just want to thank everybody out in the crowd tonight. What a great crowd we've got going. I don't know if this club has ever been this packed." Rolly looked around the expanse. The balconies were full.

"Is everyone having a good time?" Rolly's response was several seconds of cheering. "Alright! Glad to hear it! But you know, I think we might need to take a little time and thank the man that has made all of our good times possible. Mr. Mickey Delano!"

Another spotlight came on Marie as she made her way across the dance floor to where Mickey sat. She was wearing a white dress that softly followed the contours of her figure. The trim across the top of the bust was gold. Her olive skin darkened even more when next to the soft fabric. Her hair was swept back and held with a diamond comb. She approached Mickey with a sensuous smile.

Mickey rose from his place at the table to meet her. He walked out onto the floor while buttoning his tuxedo jacket. He looked very handsome. He offered his arm to Marie and they went to the center of the floor.

"Here he is ladies and gentlemen, the man who made it all possible, Mickey Delano!" The crowd stood to give him a standing ovation to which he smiled and waved. The room was deafening as they stood there, Marie clapping along with the crowd.

Mickey turned to Rolly and nodded to him, so Rolly started up the band. The crowd began to subside with the music.

"Well Marie, may I have this dance?" Mickey asked as he looked softly down at her.

"Certainly." She moved into his open arms with ease. The band played another of Glenn Miller's best, *Moonlight Serenade.*

Mickey clutched her close to him, and when he spoke it was into her ear. "You are truly something special, Marie. The likes of which I never thought I'd see again."

She smiled and replied, "Thank you, Mickey. I hope I have been all that you were hoping for."

A crooked half smile graced one side of his mouth. "Oh, yes. And then some."

"I have to say, you are a fine dancer, Mr. Delano." A rumble from deep inside his chest formed.

"We've never danced, have we?" A dark and wicked smile crossed his features and reflected only shadows deep in his eyes.

"No, we have not. Tonight is a treat for me," Marie replied. "It seems a shame to possess something you never enjoy."

"Oh, but I have enjoyed you. The splendor you've brought far outweighs anything else you could give."

"Then I am glad."

His face grew pensive, then he said, "Besides Valant, no one knows my secret."

"Dare I ask what it is? No, I don't."

He smiled at her. "Eva is going to have a baby."

Her face immediately beamed at him. "What a wonderful secret! Congratulations!"

"Ah, see, that's what I wanted. To tell someone who would be happy for me. And when I thought of who would be, yours was the only face that came to mind."

Marie squeezed his shoulder. "I think it's wonderful."

His face clouded when he looked into her shining eyes. "I was nearly a father once before. It was not to be. Now the thought of losing like that again makes me a coward."

She smiled a sad and understanding smile. "Not this time. This time will be different."

"What if I don't love it like I would have the one I lost?"

Her face went dark and sad for a brief moment. His brows knit together as he watched the change roll across her features. "I cannot imagine holding a child that is your flesh and blood, and not loving it." It was more of a question than an answer. But when she finished she smiled again.

"Nothing replaces what you lost, and nothing is meant to. It's just the opening of a new door to bring a new joy."

He looked at her in deep contemplation. "Thank you," he whispered as he drew her closer to him. She relented easily. It was a rare glimpse into a hurting soul. Marie knew he was merely seeking comfort from someone who had not been there to share the burden of grief the first time it tore him down. In a way, it was comforting to her, too, to be held in such a manner.

The music so perfectly played wrapped itself around them. Time seemed to stop. The warmth of her artful body warmed his soul while he relished in the feel of a memory. He closed his eyes and went into the past for a brief moment of comfort that could not last. As for Marie, she forgot that she was dancing with Mickey in the spotlight. She thought of Alex. Mickey was so much taller than Alex, but it was as if she were free for a moment to relive her own past happiness.

The music played on in her mind long after the notes stopped and they reluctantly parted. She smiled at him and gave him a wink, his eyes full of gratitude. It was in this state that she had passed the rest of the evening. When the flash exploded before her eyes in the darkness of the alley, it ripped her into another reality. The sound deafened her, and the warmth of Deano's heavy body beside her disappeared.

She turned to find at him on his back, blood throbbing out the gaping hole where his heart should have been. He grasped for her hand, mouthing something she couldn't hear. *Marie.* She screamed his name and took his hand. He looked beyond her to something she couldn't see. Now he mouthed something else.

Run.

Hands tore at her from behind and she desperately clung to Deano. He was trying to get up but the blood spot on the front of his shirt was now a puddle surrounding him. She was being violently yanked from him. She again screamed trying desperately to hold on. The strong arms won out and her hand slipped from Deano's. He weakly reached for her. Marie's last glimpse of him was of nothing but a blood covered hand. Then he was gone.

Marie fought and writhed in an attempt to free herself. They turned her over to face them, tears running down her face, knowing this was it. There were four of them, among them was the man with the scarred face. He sneered down at her. She turned to run, but was easily grabbed by a man beside her. He pulled her arms around behind her back and held her there.

Cobby. Where is Cobby? He was supposed to be waiting for me!

The circle of men closed in tight around her as the man with the scarred face reached into his pocket and pulled something out. It was a knife. Marie could no longer control the fear inside. She jerked wildly like something gone mad. Another man covered her mouth after she frantically screamed. Her ankle buckled as her spike heel bent. The man with the knife came closer. She jerked and fought all she could, but four was just too many to get the better of.

Cobby!

"You take something from Danny, Danny takes something from you. Now we see if your beauty is only skin deep." His scarred face was hideous. Marie's mind started to shift. His image began to blend with those from her childhood. It was as if a fracture was splitting her sanity. She had felt fear before, but this was all consuming. He brought the point of the knife closer to her face. She felt it pierce her delicate tissue as the man holding her crushed her skull against his chest.

"I'm gonna carve you up. Every last inch of you," Scar face hissed at her.

The knife plunged all the way to her cheek bone as it traveled. It cut her gums and ground against her teeth. The pain seared and she could hardly breathe until the hand clasping her mouth released. She gurgled a howl but it was hardly audible in that dark alley. She felt the knife cut her lips.

*****

Valant stood and slipped into his jacket. Margo had left some time ago after Val declared he would be staying with Mickey at the club for a while. He wanted to play cards, he'd said. So, she went on without him to wait at his apartment.

He and Mickey met eyes across the gaming table and Mickey nodded. Val turned to go and as he did so, buttoned his suit jacket. He stepped out the side entrance and scanned the dark parking lot. When he looked to the left he saw Cobby's car still where it had been parked all evening. Valant's gut clenched down hard. Cobby was supposed to take Marie home.

Valant moved cautiously, staying in the shadows as much as possible. When he came nearer to the car he could see that the driver's side door was ajar. Val went closer with greater attentiveness, looking around him continuously, straining his ears to hear any slight sound. He looked through the driver side window and saw what he dreaded seeing. Cobby was in the car, slumped across the front seat, face down. Valant opened the passenger side door and knelt before Cobby.

"Cob, hey." It struck him as odd how afraid he was to touch the still form of the man who had been by his side for thirteen years. The only reply was the steady *pat pat pat* of the blood that dripped from the seat to the floor. This gave him hope. A still heart did not pump blood out of the body.

"Cobby." Valant said louder. He reached down and touched Cobby's shoulder. Although he was still, he was not rigid.

"Cobby. Wake up boy. Where's Marie?" Valant shook him slightly. "Cobby! Where's Marie?" he spoke louder. The next time he shook him he did it with great force. He did not know the extent of Cobby's injuries. He didn't want to turn him over and see.

A small choking noise bubbled in Cobby's throat. "Cobby! Wake up!"

Cobby jerked suddenly, but did not lift his head. "Where's Marie?" Valant growled at him. "Damn it, boy! Where is the girl!" He shouted angrily.

"I don't...... I .... Phummmm."

Valant rolled Cobby over none too gently. Cobby's face was gone underneath a layer of crusted blood and swelling. Clearly his right eye would not open. Blood was matted into his hair. Clots streaked across the seat where his face had been.

"Where's Marie?" Valant asked in a quiet voice but still with great force.

"I can't remember.... I can't...." Cobby searched his blurry mind and tried to remain conscious.

"Did you see her? Was she in this car with you?" Val shouted.

"No. No, I don't think so."

That was all he needed. Valant slammed the car door and jumped across the hood. When he slid into the driver's side door he shoved Cobby out of the way.

"I need you, boy. Keep your head on." The keys were in the ignition and he cranked it with great force. Before the engine quieted Valant hit the gas and jumped the curb. Cobby hit his head on the window when Valant turned the car onto the street in front of the club and left black marks in his wake. Cobby fought desperately to keep his good eye focused as he held tight to the dash.

Valant again turned the car with great speed into the alley way where Cobby was supposed to meet Marie and Deano. The sight that greeted Cobby's eyes jarred him into full consciousness.

"Cobby, get your gun."

*****

Marie felt the point of the knife thump each time it raked across the bones that surrounded her sternum. When the scarred man had finished with the right side of her face he had hit her hard with something across her eye socket to stop her screaming. It had worked. She could neither see out of that eye nor rouse the strength to scream any more. The cut job had only just begun. Then he had moved on to her chest.

"Heads up, we got company!" The man holding Marie rasped out. She could hear nothing else.

She was flung violently to the side as a car sped down the alley towards them and hit the brakes just before striking her. Shots began to ring out as she clung to the brick wall of the club. Glass shattered and men shouted angrily.

Valant started shooting before the car came to a halt. Cobby opened his door and rolled to the ground firing under the car, hitting and splintering an ankle. The man fell down screaming. A shot hit the window next to Valant, just missing his midsection. Clearly these men were going for slow and agonizing in the way of death. Valant started to fire rapidly and one fell, but another took shelter behind a dumpster. Cobby stood and fired at him after he left his dumpster, sprinting off down the dark alley. Cobby pursued.

Valant saw Marie standing next to the wall just before he was hit from the side by a man running fast. It knocked his air out. Valant took his neck in the crook of his arm. He struck repeatedly into the man's temple with his fist. Valant's knuckles cracked and popped as he did so. So many men made the mistake that The Dark Horse was not a man to use his fists. The truth was, when the beast inside his soul demanded that he kill, he did so however he had to.

The man he held retaliated by punching Valant in the back and kidneys. Valant braced against the pain and kept striking. There would be time to lament the hurts later. The man who had been shot in the ankle groaned. It was Scar Face. He looked violently at Valant, the rage turning his face red. He was not far from Marie, and when she saw him looking at her she lunged away to Cobby's car.

Her eye wouldn't work and the other was so very blurry. She couldn't see far in front of her. Grunts sounded from the two men fighting for their lives just to her left. The man with the scarred face looked at Marie with all the hate he could summon and reached down into his pocket. He stretched low on the ground unable to hold himself upright anymore from the blood loss. It ran down what was left of his foot in rivers. A shot rang out from up the alley.

The man's face was twisted as he fished for something. Instinctively Marie knew it would be a gun. She had been crouching, but now straightened herself and watched with no emotion. This was it. She was checking out. The vision of herself in the portrait hanging by the entrance to the club flashed in her mind. The feel of Mickey dancing with her warmed her skin. She watched as Cobby laughed at her from across the breakfast table. Vantino grinned at her as she slid the car into drive.

God forgive me. God understand me.

He found what he was looking for. It was just what she expected. He pulled it out and aimed. Then he was gone. In his place was a black suit jacket. Marie inhaled sharply and heard the gun fire. The suit jacket did not move or falter. Instead, Valant turned to look down at Marie and hatred reflected deep in his eyes. It was the only emotion she had ever seen in his features. Valant then looked over to where Cobby was standing still holding his gun on the scarred face man.

Valant took another round of bullets and reloaded his gun. He walked slowly to the man he had been fist fighting and stood over him. He was alive. Looking up at The Dark Horse, his breathing became heavy and rapid. They were a few feet from Marie. When The Dark Horse shot him in the head, the blood sprayed across Marie's seeping face and melted with her own. She jerked and cried out sharply as the gun sounded. She covered her face.

Valant walked to the man who lay face down from the first shots he'd fired when he exited the car. The man wasn't moving, but Marie saw the determined and ugly expression on The Dark Horse's face. She closed her eye just before another shot rang out and a bullet met with another head. Valant repeated this action with the scarred face man.

Marie was crying openly now, her body jerking with her sobs. She fought the urge to throw up until it became too much. She wretched the few contents of her stomach onto the hard concrete. She choked and coughed and caught the cold eye of The Dark Horse. He and Cobby were bent over the scarred face man, looking at something they had found in his pocket.

Marie wiped her face and burning pain flashed. She tried desperately to wipe what she thought was the other man's blood from her face only to realize it was her own blood she was wiping. It was now coming in torrents. She looked down at her hands to the sticky wetness that gathered there, then glanced to the now faceless man next to her. This world was ugly. It was full of hate and violence. She was caught in an evil man's game. She was no match for what she was fighting, and the odds no longer seemed fair in any way. She knew her face was gone, and so was her usefulness to Mickey. Her life was over. She just wanted to be free.

She saw The Dark Horse glance at her again then turn back to what he and Cobby were looking at. Marie slowly bent down and slipped off her heels, one at a time. Then she stood. The Dark Horse looked at her again, but something about her posture made him do a double take.

"Marie…" he spoke low and warningly.

The blood on her once white dress with the gold trim was now deep red tinged with rust. She gathered up the sticky skirt in her hand and lunged away down the alley barefoot.

"Marie!" Came the angry shout of The Dark Horse. The darkness enveloped her.

He stood and tore off his jacket. "Cobby, bring the car!" Then he was away after her.

Her heart burst into speed as her swift dancer's legs carried her off and away. The tightness in her bodice did not allow for the proper breathing room. Her chest expanded and retracted forcefully as she tried to loosen her restraints. But she kept on. As she neared the street Valant's deep and panicked voice sounded again.

"Marie! Stop!" But she would do no such thing for she had ground on him.

As she tore from the alley way and into the street the bright lights of a car shone on her briefly before she was struck. The car was not moving along very fast, but she rolled across the hood. A man jumped out and shouted fearfully at her. She hit the ground running. The pain in her left leg burned like a furnace. This was her one chance to run, so she took it. Her bare feet pounded down along the sidewalk.

The Dark Horse ran out of the alley just in time to see her hit. As she started off up the sidewalk he jumped and slid across the hood of the car landing on his feet on the other side.

His own heart burst with the demand for more speed. She was damn fast.

Marie's feet bruised and ached with each pounding they took as she bounded down the street. Her lungs burned and her heart was at capacity, but she pressed on. She could feel him closing the gap between them. She refused to be the loser in this race.

If I can make 42nd, he'll quit the chase for fear of being seen.

She hammered on and lunged desperately when he made a grab for her. She could hear his steps falter as he did so. She pushed harder to put more space between them. A patrol car stopped when they saw them both running in the dim light. The Dark Horse waved them violently on. The hope that flared sputtered and died as she saw them do his bidding. But, in waving them on she gained some ground on him again.

Ahead she would have to make a sharp right and run another two blocks up to 42nd. Once there, she could get a ride back to Vinny. Back to Vantino. If they would have her. She slowed as she made the corner, her feet slipping on the concrete. She felt the brush of his fingertips as he made another grab for her. She lunged again and pushed away with great force.

She could see the cars on 42nd now. It made the hope surge again and the sound of Jerome Kern's *Long Ago and Far Away* engulfed her mind. It was as if what was happening was a dream she was watching from some safe place. It was not her life she was running for. She knew her brain wasn't getting enough oxygen. She felt his fingers across her bare skin again.

"Marie!"

She cried out in desperation and agony at the frustration of it all. Why could he not just let her go free? Was it so important Mickey extract his payment? Tears flowed from her good eye as she saw a vision of Vantino at the other end of the block. Just one block to go and she'd be in his arms. He was reaching out for her.

"Vantino! Help me! Vantino!" She screamed in horror as she felt The Dark Horse's hold take root. He began to drag her down. She pulled with everything she had.

When her speed began to ebb, she turned and did what was left to her. She had waited a long time to fight the men who abused her. Now she took all the hate and fear they had caused her and threw it at him. Her right hand met with the side of his face with great force. He grunted with the impact. He did not loosen his hold on her. She kicked and struck wildly. He took her hits without any retaliation. Her lungs felt like a thousand needles bored into them.

"It's me," he spoke low and easy. She continued to hit him with all she had left. When she struck his ear, his eardrum rang violently.

"Stop, Marie. It's me." He spoke again. Her hits faltered and he knew she would soon lose consciousness.

Her vision blackened briefly. Her hands stilled, but she shook her head clear and looked up at him. She pushed against him and continued her fight.

"Stop. Please, stop. It's me." His voice was low and sad as he looked at her unrecognizable face. He tightened his hold on her waist when she stopped and began sobbing dry, racking sounds.

"Just let me go," she shook out. "Please let me go. He's waiting for me."

"There's nobody here but me," he whispered.

With great sadness she realized he was right. Vantino was a vision, as the music had been. She looked up at him. She stopped crying and her body tensed.

"Stop, Marie." Her body trembled.

"Help me," she whispered. "I am so afraid."

Her heart could pump no more. When it slowed, she slumped forward and smeared blood down the front of his white shirt. He lifted her into his arms and against his chest. He turned to walk back the way they had come. Cobby met them at the corner. He jumped out and opened the back door.

Valant slid into the back seat still holding Marie. Cobby shut the door and hurried around and got in the driver's seat. When he looked back, Valant was still holding Marie against him. Cobby could hardly see anything his head hurt so badly. Blood was soaking up his jacket again.

"Where?"

Cobby kept his eye on the mirror. Valant looked down at Marie's face.

"The only safe place I know."

Cobby's heart filled with dread.

*****

Gathering Storm

It was a long drive out of the city to Valant's safe haven. It was an excruciating drive for Cobby as he fought the line between reality and oblivion. Several times he jerked himself back only when the car tires left the road. Valant never asked him if he were alright, just trusted him to get them where they were going. Each time Cobby glanced in the mirror Valant was patiently wiping what blood he could from Marie's face and staunching the flow from the deepest cuts. He said nothing about her condition, just kept at what he was doing. Valant knew more of her had been cut, but he figured those parts could be covered later with clothing. Her face, however, could not. So he kept up with it.

When Mickey lost Maryanne, the two of them had gone to Mexico for several months. Mickey always had a razor sharp temper. When bar fighting became boring, Mickey picked up prize fighting to help temper the anger that grew within him. Valant was his cut man, and so he sought the best to teach him his trade. He was a small Mexican man by the name of Julio. Julio had no teeth and spoke very little, but he spent a great deal of time teaching Valant how to treat every facial wound a boxer could sustain. It was now he needed that knowledge the most.

When at last the nightmare was over, Cobby was able to shut off the engine inside the garage of the safe haven. Cobby decided just to lay across the front seat atop the dried and flaking blood that his own body let earlier in the evening. Valant's voice stopped him just as he was lowering himself down.

"You can't sleep now. If you sleep like that, you'll never wake again. I need your help."

It took Cobby some time to find the key and open the door while Valant kept up with Marie's face. She was still and silent as death, but Valant could feel her breathing against his chest. Every so often she would let out a very faint moan. He wasn't sure yet if her leg were broken. He guessed not after the dash she made on it.

Cobby helped get her out of the car, then went ahead and turned on the lights. The house was dark and it seemed they were disturbing a tomb. They walked past the bar and living room area straight to the back of the house into the bedroom. Cobby turned on the lamp with a shaking hand.

He needed a drink badly.

Valant laid Marie on the bed atop the white fitted sheet. She was a grotesque sight. Cobby closed his eyes and covered his face with his hands. There was very little white left on the front of her beautiful evening gown, and the gold trim along the bust line was unrecognizable. Across her chest just above her breasts was a gaping wound that gleamed white from the bone underneath. Then her face. Oh, her face.

Dear God give me strength.

Cobby rarely prayed anymore. He felt too guilty to do so. He knew this was beyond his capabilities.

"Cobby. Help me." Valant's voice was low but strong.

Cobby slowly lowered his hands and again looked at her face. The soft and beautiful curve of her jawline was gone. It was replaced by hideous mottled swelling. The red and angry flesh had been so cruelly cut. Her eye socket was gone, filled in with fluid beneath the skin. It was a deep shade of purple. Blood encrusted her hair, her neck, her arms and hands. Her feet, too, were scraped and bleeding.

"We gotta get the dress off." Valant rolled her gently onto her side and began to unhook the garment all the way down to her buttocks. It was no longer soft and molded to her delicate curves, but stiff and disjointed from the dried blood.

"Pull it gently off." Cobby took hold of the dress and thought back to all the times in a haze of cigarette smoke he had imagined her naked. This was not how his dreaming went. This time she was not willing, not unwilling, just absent.

He took hold of the dress and pulled it gently down her body. When it was free he tossed it into the corner by the bed. She still made no sound. She lay in her under garments, and these too Valant began to unhook. Suddenly Cobby could take no more. He did not want to see her naked, to see more of what they may have done to her while he bled away in orbit. Something tore his insides as he realized she must have been waiting to see him coming. Praying he would come. All the while he was unavailable. This reality was more than he could carry and he clasped his hands behind his throbbing head.

"Stop! Stop, stop, stop! No more! No more! Just let her die!" Cobby said in a panicked voice. Valant stopped what he was doing and looked up at him. He said nothing. Cobby began to rock back and forth.

"Oh shit. I can't see this. I can't see this."

Valant softly rolled Marie onto her back and stood. He moved easily to Cobby and took him by the neck.

Cobby's mind reeled back to the note they had found in scar face's pocket.

V/8 Nice little scrolling. Beauty is only skin deep, flesh of his flesh, blood of his blood.

"We did this. We did! That warehouse. They got Marie for that warehouse!" Valant got within a few inches of Cobby's face. He squeezed Cobby's neck tightly to get his attention.

"Listen to me. That doesn't matter right now. What matters is Mick's gonna come through that door. When he does, he's going to look at her. If he sees what you and I see right now, he's gonna take out a pistol and end her. Do you get that? If she looks like this he'll consider it a mercy. So, pull your shit together like I know you can. We've got very little time."

He released Cobby then. Moving back to the opposite side of the bed he resumed unhooking Marie's underthings. Cobby took off his jacket woodenly and tossed it away.

"There should be blankets in that closet." Cobby moved away. When he returned with blankets in hand, Marie lay in nothing but her panties. A large and angry bruise engulfed her left leg.

"What happened to her leg?"

"Car hit her when she came out the alley. Get me a shirt from the bureau."

It took them both to slip the white undershirt over her head without disturbing any of the cuts and welts on her skin, then put her arms through the arm holes. She began moaning and moving her legs as they did so.

"Bring bandages and chloroform from above the bathtub. Water and my stitch kit, too. Then go boil water. Everything has to be sterile." Valant was carefully laying her back on pillows as he spoke in a low voice. It would be dangerous for her to resurface now.

It took time for Cobby to get the water boiling and the necessaries gathered up. As he did so, Valant sat over her and painstakingly washed all of the cuts. He rose for fresh water and soap many times. Fortunately she did not stir. When everything needed to stitch her up was gathered and sterilized, Valant told Cobby to stand by with the chloroform. The pain of the needle would no doubt drive her to the surface.

She cried softly as he stitched but she did not wake. It took time trying to fix where the knife cut her gums, but he did the best he knew how. He carefully finished her face before moving on to her chest. It took nearly as much time as the cuts on her face, all the while his glasses perched on his nose. When Valant finished, he lowered the shirt over her breasts and covered her with a blanket. The right side of her face was swollen to the point her skin was shiny from the tension. He had a hard time getting her lips back together, but when he was finished they looked alright. She would now be fighting the massive scarring that would try to develop while she healed.

As Cobby picked up the bloodied bandages from around the bed, the vision in his one good eye blurred and he stumbled, hitting the bed with his knee. The jarring caused her to start thrashing. Valant was there immediately to hold her down, afraid that she would tear her stitches. Face work required such fine and delicate stitching to prevent scarring.

"For shitsake! Get a damn drink if it will steady you!" Valant hissed. Cobby didn't have to be told twice.

He moved slowly through the darkened house to the bar opposite the kitchen. He felt his way rather than used his one good eye. The throbbing it caused just trying to focus made his brain immediately try to shut down. How badly he wanted to pass out.

He couldn't remember anything. No matter how he tried the last vision he could summon was standing along the balcony watching Marie and Mickey dance. The next he really had a hold on was Valant telling him to get out his gun. When Valant had hit the brakes he'd nearly hit the dash and that had thrown him into action. He had no idea how he came to be in his car, face down and bleeding, nor how Marie had come to be as she was. He didn't want to know. Didn't want to live with a vision hearing the story would bring. He'd never forgive himself.

He fumbled until he came to the decanter that sat just where it always did. He pulled it out from under the bar and jerked the stopper. He didn't bother with a glass, just lifted it to his lips and felt the burn as the liquid poured down his throat. He'd been at the safe house before. A few times. He hated it there.

His first trip to the safe house was when he was just twenty. Valant had taken him to do some job, Cobby couldn't even remember what now. Valant handed Cobby a pistol and told him to finish it. Cobby refused. Valant gave him a very lethal look and repeated to finish it. When Cobby balked again Val put the gun in his hand and aimed it for him. He still couldn't do it. Val had said a few choice words in his ear to encourage him on, but still his hand trembled. When he did finally pull the trigger the shot missed entirely.

Valant then growled deeply, taken the gun from him and passed it over into his own left hand. Then without looking or aiming with his offhand, proceeded to fire at Cobby. The bullet tore through his abdomen, entering in his side and exiting near his belly button. He had been very fortunate it damaged only muscle and nothing serious. Valant brought him here to clean him up and let him heal.

Cobby remembered Valant putting him in the bathtub to clean him up. There was blood everywhere. The pain and agony of those days still stayed fresh even after ten years. It was a valuable lesson and Valant dearly loved teaching valuable lessons. He did an exceptional job taking a shitass kid from the docks and building him into what he was. Cobby took another long pull from the decanter. As he did so headlights danced on the wall next to him.

It was Mickey. The moment Cobby had been dreading finally arrived.

Maybe it would be best if they ended her. She was so clearly never going to be the same again. Her face was unrecognizable. Not to mention the emotional damage going through something like that was going to be. Each time Cobby thought it'd be best for her, he'd see her sitting at the table in the apartment, her hair flowing down around her shoulders as she laughed at something he'd said. Or see her sleeping form curled in a tight ball in the corner of the bedroom. Hear the sound of her rich and harmonious voice as she sang Frank Sinatra's *Don't Worry 'Bout Me* as he drove away from his family for the last time. The way she'd felt when she laid her head on his shoulder.

This was one time he knew for certain he could not pull the trigger. The one time he would not stand beside the man he greatly respected when Valant pulled the trigger. Indeed, he hoped to be long gone by then, even if he had to steal Mickey's car.

*****

Mickey stood at the foot of the bed with his hands in his pockets. He'd been standing there for a very long time, just looking. His shoulders sagged and the corners of his mouth drooped. In his eyes was a look that hadn't been there since the day he watched his wife slowly slip away from him. He could not speak.

Marie lay unconscious under a blanket in Valant's safe house, and he had no idea what to do about it. He could see from the extent of the damage that she would never be the same. Her soft and sensual lips were now marred with ugly red tissue and were swollen twice their regular size. The right side of her face was etched in a horrific pattern carefully stitched by Valant's competent hand. But that would not be enough. It would take a miracle for her to heal to a point she would feel comfortable being seen in public again, let alone stand before hundreds and perform. He did not want to see the look of devastation in her eyes when she finally awoke; all that she was swiftly taken from her in a dark alley.

And so was his dream.

This beautiful and unearthly creature had given him such delight, such excitement and joy. Amused and amazed him with her class and grace, resilience and kindness; was now reduced to this. He finally turned away. Never, if he searched the world over, would he find another Marie Barelli. She was the only one of her kind.

"What are you going to do?" Mickey asked in a devastated tone.

"Give it time, I suppose," Valant replied in a low voice.

Mickey shook his head. "Don't do that to her. Don't make her live through this. That's not fair."

"How can you go from your life is mine, you owe me, to just let her go? Is she worth so little?"

Mickey looked at Val. "Worth so little? How can you ask me that? Have you not been here since she came? What will be left of that beautiful creature that enchanted us all and gave us such delight? Is it right to make her open her eyes to what her life is now? Is it right to take her from the top, down to the muck of life?" He paused a moment. "If she were one of your fine horses, and were suffering the fate of never being great again, would you make it live anyway? Just to give it a chance?"

"Don't throw her away. She deserves better than that."

"And who will look after her? Huh? Who? You? You gonna look after some maimed woman for the rest of her life?" Mickey said defiantly.

"You can't let her die. You know that."

"Why? 'Cause she's Vinnetti's? Has she ever said anything that would make you believe she is in any way tied to Vinnetti?" Mickey asked forcefully.

There was a long pause. "No."

"Then I have no reason to think she is. What the hell does that old bastard care if some lounge singer gets bumped off to spare her some agony? What the hell does he care?" Mickey pointed to Marie. "How you gonna look into those soft eyes and tell her it's over?" He finished quietly and tears appeared on the rims of his eyes.

Valant slid his hands into his pockets. When he spoke it was in a low voice. "I've never asked you for anything. Never. I've always respected your position over mine. I've never gone against you. I'm asking you now as a favor. If we kill her, it may be the biggest regret of our lives."

Mickey rubbed the back of his neck. "It would be so much easier now, while she's out and won't see you coming."

Valant remained silent.

Mickey appeared to be battling with himself. He sighed deeply then shrugged. "You'll regret it when it ends up the same. Just let her go now, that's my word. But if you think you can save her," he gestured towards her. "Then by all means try. In the meantime, I've got to bury Deano."

Both men were silent at this. Deano had been with them for many years. He was a trusted friend and partner. Now he was gone.

"The warehouse was not enough, Val. Find him."

Valant's eyes moved over the still form under the blankets and his eyes went cold and hard once again. "I will. Oh, I will."

*****

Marie fought to bubble to the surface. She kept having the same strange dream where she was eating lunch at the restaurant. Alex would come in smiling at her, then take her by the hand and tell her, "Come on sweetheart, you've been here long enough." She would roll back through a series of dreams blended with memories, one in particular of running down the street in the dark. That one was very vivid.

She could hear voices in her sleep, voices that were warring with each other. Something about letting a great horse die. A great horse who would no longer be great. Then burying Deano. But she knew that wasn't right because she had just seen him. He had come and sat beside her for a while, holding her hand and smiling at her. Which was odd, because she was in a bed in the dream, but didn't know where. Deano told her to sleep, but she was asleep, or at least she thought she was.

She couldn't hear anything but her own breathing. She tried to open her eyes, but for some reason one was stuck shut, and the other didn't want to focus real well. She was in bed and nothing about the smells around her were familiar. She reached up to rub her eye open only to feel a deep and searing pain that came with touching her own face. She jerked her hand away and struggled to sit up. Her entire body hurt. She forced her eye open and saw through the haze the bed she was laying on.

It was covered in blood. The sight started her heart to racing which in turn made her head throb with intensity. Dried blood covered her hands and she threw the blanket off of herself and tried to stand. Her left leg screamed when she put weight on it, so she just stood there on her right leg looking around herself in great confusion. She had never seen this place before. In the dim lamp light she could see nothing beyond the door. She looked down to see she was wearing a shirt she didn't recognize.

She searched the floor frantically for clothes she might identify. She saw the white of a skirt tossed in a corner by the head of the bed. She moved to get it but then stopped. Only the portion she had first seen was white. The rest of it was a rust red and it was crusted over from dried blood. An image came to her mind just then. Deano lying on the ground and reaching for her with a bloodied hand. He was mouthing something to her, but she couldn't make it out. She lurched backwards into a pile of bloodied bandages. She gasped. What was happening to her?

*****

Valant finished stitching Cobby's right cheek and carefully wiped away what was left of the dried blood. The hit both Cobby and Marie had taken to the face were identical. The same person struck them both. But, that person was now dead. Valant had wondered briefly if one of the men they just killed could be the leader. But, he dismissed that. Surely a leader who

had master minded everything to date wouldn't get caught in
an alley so easily.

"Can you see out of your good eye?"

"Yeah."

"Have you tried the other?"

"No. I can't get it open."

"Well, leave it then." Valant sat back in his chair and
began to put his stitch kit away.

It had been such a terribly long night. After Mickey left
Valant sat Cobby at the bar and began stitching up the gash that
he received. Valant asked him what happened, and Cobby
answered truthfully that he couldn't remember. Valant's body
went taut and he sniffed loudly as he looked down at the stitch
kit. He said nothing, but Cobby knew he was deeply angered.
Very deeply angered. It was the times that Valant went silent
that Cobby had the most to fear. He blamed Cobby for being
caught like a fool kid.

"You can sleep now. I'll wake you in an hour." Valant's
voice echoed in the silent house of horror. Cobby nodded.

"Take the room…….." Valant stopped speaking and sat
still, listening. He stood and walked to the bedroom without
saying anything else.

She was up. She stood next to the bed on one leg looking
down at what once was a very beautiful show gown. She
looked very confused. He entered the room silently and stood
just inside the door. She looked down at her hands.

Blood pounded through her throbbing head and she tried
to make her fuzzy brain come up with an answer. Somewhere
deep inside a voice begged her not to, to leave it a mystery for
she would not like the answer when it finally came. A tentative
hand reached up and felt her face, but the pain was so great she
gave up. A terrified cry escaped her throat. She looked up to
find a way out and saw him.

He watched her with a look of caution, as if judging her
reaction. His body was tense and she knew he waited for her to
make some move. Another image flashed in her mind. She was
running and he caught her and drug her down. Why was she
running? Presumably from him. Had he done this to her? He
must have. His entire white shirt was stained a crimson red. A
great streak of it went from his shoulder down. She stumbled
back to get away from him and hit a dresser. Pictures fell to the
floor.

Valant tensed before taking another step into the room. "What happened to me?" She asked in a fearful voice while a tear slid down her cheek. His lips stretched into a grim line, but he said nothing. "Did you do this to me?" She choked out in a whisper.

He slid his hands into his pockets and shook his head. He was lying. He had done this to her. Who else could have? She let out a long sob. She looked down at herself again. He moved closer to her. She stumbled backwards into the corner where her gown lay. Her left leg just didn't seem to work very well. She pressed her back against the wall and watched him. He stood there, looking down at her.

Her mind once again shifted. She was back home again. She looked around to see that she was in her old bedroom, which meant her father must have been near. No, that wasn't right. She shook her throbbing head trying to get it to make sense. She was in New York. That was it. She breathed a deep sigh of relief. What had caused such an awful nightmare? And why The Dark Horse? She hadn't thought of him in years.

Alex. For some reason she had the notion he was close by. "Alex. Alex where are you?"

He appeared at the door. "Oh, Alex." She tried to smile at him but her mouth wouldn't stretch.

Her mind flashed again. It wasn't Alex in the doorway. It was Cobby. Only not Cobby. This Cobby was missing his face. She cried out in fear.

"Cob, get the chloroform. Couple drops on the rag next to the bottle," Valant said quietly to Cobby.

Valant took another step towards Marie and now he was within arm's length of her. She pressed into the wall and shook violently. She was about to fight, he knew that.

"We're not gonna to hurt you, Marie. We just want to help you." Valant's voice was low and soft. She shook her head violently in an attempt to remain conscious.

"Here, Val." Cobby passed a cloth with chloroform on it over his shoulder into Val's waiting hand.

Val stood a moment and watched Marie as she started to crowd into the corner and sob uncontrollably. She let out little screams while she looked at Cobby. Val lunged for her and took hold of her upper body with his and wrapped his arms around her, pressing her into the wall. She screamed loudly, pushing with all her strength. Valant pressed the cloth against her face and waited for her to slip away. It took time, longer than he would have thought. He picked up her limp body and put her back on the bed, covering her with the blanket. He scratched his forehead with his thumb as he looked down at her.

"Call me if you need me. I'll be on the couch," Cobby said in a defeated voice, then he was gone.

Val took a moment to check her stitches, making sure she hadn't set any loose in her struggle, but they looked alright. He gently rubbed more salve on all of her wounds and listened to her shallow breathing turn into the deep breaths of sleep. He was exhausted. More so than usual. He stood and walked around to the other side of the bed and took off his shoes. He very gently lay down next to her. It smelled of dried blood. That didn't matter. He was used to that smell.

He reached over her and switched off the lamp. Dawn was coming, and with it the problems of a new day.

*****

Marie struggled to wake. She kept dreaming that she did wake. That she would rise from her corner in the apartment then go on about her usual business of making coffee and getting dressed. She'd get all the way through the morning routine only to find something not right. Like Cobby wearing a clown nose while reading the paper, or Mickey walking in and playing the baby grand. She would then know she was still dreaming and drift back to start all over again.

She dreamed of Vinny. Of how he would tell her she needed to be strong. That this wasn't as bad as it could get. Like he was talking about the weather. Then they'd suddenly be on the beach and he'd pull out his umbrella to block out the sun entirely. She would be singing at the club with the band to a packed house only to look out into the darkness to the one lit table where her father sat. The rest of the crowd had disappeared. Then the band would vanish too, and she was alone singing to her father who just got angrier the longer she sang.

She kept seeing Deano. Again and again. He was always at the restaurant or the club, and he would always turn and smile at her. Something about this made her heart break, but she couldn't figure out why. Just the sight of him made her start crying in her dreams. No matter how she would call out his name or try to get to him, something would block her or her voice just refused to work. Then he would walk away, whistling a tune while she tried to get him to turn around.

Music exploded in her mind. Song after song would play. She fought and pushed to make her body work, but it would not. She just remained trapped in her own mind. She relived all the times her father had so cruelly beat her. The first time she ever met Mickey. Images flashed of a dark alley and searing pain, but she refused to follow that one. It was an involuntary trip down a pain filled road.

At last, she slowly drifted to the surface, like rising out of deep water. Nothing smelled familiar and everything was quiet. She lay still for a moment, listening. Then she heard it. The sound of a breath. She tensed as she listened. It had been unbearably close to her. She was scared to move for fear whoever it was would know she was awake. But the breathing stopped.

Her eye wouldn't open, not matter how she tried. Finally, she raised her head just slightly so she could see out the eye that did work. There was hardly any light in the room, but she could see him clearly. He was not a foot from her, lying absolutely still watching her. When she saw him she screamed and jumped from the bed, crashing into the dresser and sending its contents once again flying. She screamed out in pain from her leg and face when she tried to run.

Valant sprang from the bed to block her departure. He made a grab for her. She wrenched back violently and crashed into the corner again. She knocked the lamp from the nightstand and screamed. Her chest heaved from the fear that pulsed through her like electricity.

Damn, the chloroform hadn't lasted long. "Cobby!" Valant yelled.

Marie leapt from the floor to the top of the nightstand in one athletic move. Val made a grab for her but she cleared his arms and landed on top of the bed. She bounced from there to the floor on the opposite side.

"Cobby!"

"Working on it!" Came the reply from behind The Dark Horse.

Marie made for the open doorway and nearly made it since both Cobby and the bed blocked Valant. But then something caught her eye. At first she thought there was another person in the room, but then she looked at it straight on and realized it was a reflection in the vanity mirror. It was hideous. The face was swollen and mottled. The shining eyes reflected deep madness. There was a fiery red gash across the chest where the man's undershirt was too large and gaped open. She froze. So did the men.

She stopped breathing as she stared. Then a sob broke loose. Her hair fell across her face and tears squeezed out of her eyes.

"Dear God, what happened to me?" Her voice was barely audible.

As she stood there it all came back to her in a flood of memory, all except the part where Valant had run her down. Then, the new memories meshed with old ones and it became her father in the alley, not Scar Face. She cried violently now. She didn't notice Valant had carefully made his way to her and now stood just a few feet away, chloroform in hand.

"Let me help you." He whispered.

Her head jerked at the sound of his voice and she again leapt from the floor to the bed. He grabbed her. She fought and struggled and screamed at him as he tried to hold her down. Cobby took hold of her legs. She bucked and writhed against the two of them and it was difficult for Valant to get a hand free to press the rag over her face. It took longer for her to go under, she was fighting so hard. She'd torn open the cut on her chest and Valant sighed as he lay on top of her studying her wounds.

"Get the stitch kit." Cobby rose heavily and moved off.

*****

Mickey told the band himself.

After he left Marie in the hands of Valant and Cobby, he had gone home, only to sit in the darkness and stare. The grotesque image of the once enigmatic Marie would not leave his mind's eye. He could not sleep, he could not move, he wasn't aware if he was breathing. He just stared into the darkness.

Eva came in and tried to talk to him, but he ignored her. The firm lump on her belly was beginning to show through her soft cotton night gown. It struck a wildly painful chord in his chest. Eventually he pulled her close to him and kissed her softly, smoothing her hair that was feathery from sleep. For once she remained quiet and asked nothing of him, just lay pressed against him. When dawn came, he rose and carried her back to their bed, then left for the club.

It was not easy to cover up five homicides in an alley. But, by the time the sun had risen, there was nothing left to give any idea blood had been shed. Mickey stood looking down on the spot where Martin found Deano. Mickey himself had come out to look the scene over. He'd taken charge of the cleanup before he drove out to the safe house. Standing there looking down on the spot where such tragedy had occurred, old scars within Mickey started to bleed again.

Deano.

He was ugly, but he was family. Not to mention loyal to Mickey, not just the Delano family. They'd put him in the family cemetery in just a few days. What a mess.

There were rumors that morning among the company something was amiss, but nobody really acted differently. Working for Mickey meant that every morning something had happened the night before. Mickey walked out onto the floor when both the band and the dance company had gathered for rehearsal on the main stage. They were milling about waiting for Marie who was never late.

Mickey stood before them for a minute or two while they found a place to sit and listen to what he had to say. He looked down at the floor for a long time before attempting speech. Mickey's hair fell forward and across his face, his shoulders slumped. It was the end of an incredible dream. Somehow he just knew that. No matter if by some miracle Val was able to recover even a fraction of her face, he knew it was over.

He told them the truth. Rumors would spread in the papers when Marie suddenly did not show back up. Mickey felt that they deserved to know what they were up against. He said that she'd been attacked in the alley behind the club the night before. That she was not doing very well. That more than likely she would not ever be capable of returning, if she survived, which he also held out little hope of.

They listened in stone silence. No one moved or spoke, they just sat speechless. It did not help matters that he had been blunt, so obviously shell shocked himself. He knew they doubted the authenticity of his statements, because in reality he still doubted them too.

Rolly took it the hardest. He listened with his head bowed. When Mickey was through, he quietly walked out of the club and did not return until that night at show time. It was obvious to all but Marie the depth of his feelings for her. Most doubted he would come back now that she was gone. He did, but all the spark that made him great was gone. It was only his respect for those he worked with that made him come back.

It was a terrible performance. The show had to be rewritten as Marie was no longer there to play her part in it. The company struggled to fill her shoes. Which was impossible. Mickey didn't attend, the once great Ruby was reduced to rubble like The Lamplight Lounge.

*****

Valant did not think she knew who he was.

He carefully stitched her chest again then removed all traces of blood within the room. Valant wiped the wall and burned the bandages, took down all the mirrors, and covered the one in the bathroom. He returned to the bedroom to wait for her to wake again. He took out his leather bound book to finish some notes while the sun crept higher in the morning sky.

When she did wake, he sat silent and watched her go through the same thing again. The confusion, the registration of pain, trying to get her mind to focus on the present when a black sucking hole kept pulling her into what was obviously a very devastating past. Then she noticed him again.

Marie rose in one deft movement from the bed and cleared the footboard when he came close to try to calm her. She ran into Cobby only to relive the horrifying nightmare of seeing his battered face. Valant came up behind and took hold of her to keep her arms down. She fought and screamed like a wild animal that was wounded. No matter how gentle he tried to speak to her, how he tried to reach her, she was gone. The person in her midst was no person at all.

So they drugged her again. Then they stood there looking down at her for a long time, Cobby waiting to see what he dreaded was coming. That Valant would lift her up and carry her outside. Then he would wait the long seconds for the sound of the gun. She was so messed up. Cobby had no idea this was what she carried. She was so good at keeping it all hidden. Even from him.

Cobby looked to Val who stood with his hands in his pockets, his legs apart. There was a deeply contemplative look on his face.

"I want you to tell Mickey I won't be back for a while."

Cobby's jaw muscle worked as he looked at Val who was silent for a long time. Just how long was a while? Did he mean days or hours?

"That means you're me." Valant's deep and gravel voice added. He had waited a space of time to inform Cobby so that the realization would come.

Cobby shook his head sharply. "No. I won't go."

For Cobby it hung in his mind like a noose. He was so out of it when he drove them to the safe house. It had taken all he had not to slip away and drive off the road. He hadn't done any looking for a follower. It was possible that they could've been followed from the club. Whoever had ordered this done to Marie was obviously set on revenge, so who could say that they didn't know where the safe house was? Cobby knew that Valant could hold his own, both physically and with a gun, but not forever. He would not leave him to fight alone. The thought made his insides twist and knot. He made a vow to stand with Valant long ago, and meant to keep it.

"I won't leave you here alone. Not this time."

"You've got to. I can't be here and there both. I know you can handle things with Mickey. I don't think you can handle things with Marie."

Cobby's brows furrowed. It was an unfortunate truth. He could always handle things where he had no feeling. Where Marie was concerned, Cobby had feeling. Valant knew this, he had made the assessment many times. Cobby could be Valant, but only if he weren't caring for Marie. He sighed.

"I won't leave until tomorrow. If anything is going to happen, it will in the dark tonight. Let me stay through that."

Valant thought a moment then nodded his head. "Alright, in the morning then. I'll make up a list of things I'll need."

*****

Marie was playing cards at the island in the kitchen with Vinny when Mickey walked in and asked for some milk. She was shocked when all Vinny did was tell him not to drink from the glass jar. She writhed and tried to extract herself from the grips of blackness that held her. She fought and struggled and tried to cry out but all that would come was a moan. A moan no one heard.

When she was close to waking she'd fall down into the realm of oblivion she had been swimming in and start all over.

Sometimes they were memories of things that actually happened, sometimes they were nightmares of things she feared were yet to come. She did not understand if this was death. Perhaps she had passed through the gates of hell and now this was eternity. She cried out to God and hoped He would listen.

*****

She woke to silence and the unfamiliar smell of the pillow and blankets around her. She lay still for quite some time as events rolled through her mind. She then began to wonder what to do. Her body felt shattered. She knew moving was going to make it worse. She couldn't remember how she might have gotten where she was, but an image of The Dark Horse kept coming up in her mind. She was clearly trying to out run him, but he was gaining. She could also hear the sound of his enraged voice as he yelled for her to stop.

Had she out run him? Maybe she had made it back to Vinny? This thought brought her hope. She rose to a sitting position as quickly as she could. She could see to her right a tall dresser and beyond that a vanity table missing the mirror. There were pictures on top of unfamiliar people. The blankets were clean despite the fact that she was certain she had seen them bloodied. Her good eye moved to the iron that made up the foot of the bed before she saw something in the corner.

He was near the door sitting on a chair, a small leather bound book in his lap. He was watching her with interest as if he were unsure of her next move. She let out a small gasp at seeing him and moved to the edge of the bed. Her hopes were dashed at seeing him there. The memory of her lungs on fire as she pounded down the street away from him flashed. She was filled with agony born of twice being caught in captivity. She sobbed out loud at the very sight of him and she sunk down onto the bed and wept.

He was relentless.

She fought him. Marie could remember that. She felt the sting in her hand from slapping him across the face. He didn't flinch nor loosen the hold he had on her. Marie felt as if she were a tiny boat lost in the giant waves of an angry ocean, and The Dark Horse was that ocean.

What would he do with her now?

She was caught running. Now she was his.

"Marie." His voice was close. She looked up to see him standing above her looking down.

Despite the pain in her body she made a lunge for the opposite side of the bed. Fear rushed through her yet again. It owned her completely, ultimately. What he had in store for her she did not care to know. One more of the kind of experience she known with men would be the end of her mind. She felt the bed sag behind her under his weight and she cried out. She grabbed hold of the bedside table and pulled with all she had hoping to make up for her useless leg. He came over the top of her and grabbed her hand to pull it free. Adrenaline fired and she rolled quickly slapping him hard across the face, then came at him just as hard with her other hand. She made contact with his opposite cheek and he jumped to straddle her and take hold of her hands. She screamed at him then raised her knee to it drive into him in the one place she knew would stop him completely. She hit him, but he was close and she didn't have enough force as her knee met with manhood.

He groaned an angry sound that came from deep within his chest. He settled on top of her and pressed down forcing all the air out of her lungs. She still fought wickedly, but he was now seated firmly. He bent his head and took a few moments worth of maddened breaths before he opened his eyes and slowly looked down at her. Her face was a deep red and tears fell freely down her cheek and across her nose. Her lips were bleeding again.

He sighed very deeply. She sobbed and turned her face from him unable to look into his blazing eyes any longer. She had never had a man force himself on her, but that was about to change. She felt the fight go from her and in its place came the urge to beg. Something she had once told herself she'd never do again for it yielded very little results.

"Please! Don't do this to me," she sobbed out, her face turned from his. "Please."

"Don't do what to you?" He spat. "Stitch your face, clean you up? Hmm? Look out for you where you'll be safe? Just which of these things do you want me *not* to do?"

She lost it entirely. She cried silently into the mattress as horrifying images played in her mind's eye. "Don't hurt me, not again."

"I didn't hurt you the first time. If you want me to drug you again by all means keep fighting."

She looked up at him then. "No. No. Please. Don't send me there again." She held her breath to stop the sobs. She made a snorting sound as her body involuntarily tried to sob anyway despite the way she had clenched her lungs shut.

He shifted on top of her and felt the ache in his groin where she had kneed him. He clenched his jaw and the muscles flexed at his anger. "You are one hell of a fighter."

She again turned to bury what she could of her bleeding face into the mattress. Her body shuddered uncontrollably beneath him. Valant gave her a grim look.

"Marie, look at me. Now." Her arms had gone limp. He reached over and raised her face to him. Her eyes fluttered open and the brown depths reflected a pain he had never felt.

"Marie, let me help you." Her body tensed for fight. She didn't understand what he meant. What would he take if she agreed to his offer? All men took, so would this one.

"Marie, I won't hurt you. I just want to help you." Nothing in his voice offered any suggestion of truce.

She went to turn her face away again but he stopped her with her own hand. "When have I ever hurt you?"

Her mind immediately went to the night he had so firmly questioned her about Scar Face in the apartment. He had demanded to know who Vinny was to her. At the thought of Vinny she felt her mind start to shift.

"Never. I have never hurt you. I may have intimidated you, but I never hurt you. I want you to think of all the opportunities I've had to do with you as I pleased." He shook his head at her. "Not once did I. Not once. You have known me a long time, Marie. I could have had you when you were nineteen, but I didn't. You have no reason not to trust me, despite what all those other men have done to you."

He kept his gaze steady with hers and a tear rolled down her cheek. The sharp stinging pain of her cuts and stitches began to register and stars gathered in front of her eyes from the lack of air. An image of The Dark Horse rose in her mind. He was standing half in the shadows smoking a cigarette telling her goodbye in his own way the night before she left for New York.

She looked at him steady. Fear started to gnaw at her insides. The left side of her face crumpled as she began to cry, deep and sorrowful. "I'm not who you think I am. In a moment

you will melt into my father, then into Mickey, then into Scar
Face. I can't hold myself together," she cried.

The corner of his mouth twitched. "I know."

"You can't help me. Nobody can," she whispered.

"Let me try."

"I won't pick up the pieces this time. Just let me die,"
Marie choked out.

"No." His answer was firm and cruel. Her body went limp
and her mind refused to hang onto him any longer. He became
Vantino, then Vinny, and finally her father. Valant watched the
changes roll.

"Marie. Look at me." He shook her slightly. It took a
moment for her to register him as himself.

"Stay with me. Look at me." She did, so he stood and let
the air come back to her.

"I'm scared of you," Marie breathed.

"I know that, too. Let me help you," he said in a deep
voice.

"Please don't leave me with them. I can't stop them from
taking over."

He held out a hand to her. "I won't leave you with them."

Marie looked at him out of her good eye and nothing but
distrust reflected from it. Her borrowed undershirt was
crumpled and pulled low. Her hair spread around her in a crazy
mass. Her legs shivered from fear and the coldness she felt
within her soul. She licked her lips and tasted blood. Her
breathing slowed as he looked steady into her face.

She reached up and took his hand.

*****

Mickey stood watching the sun go down from his office
window in his great house on the hill. The deep purple of the
sky above stretched until it met with the burning orange that
hovered along the horizon. A few stars caught his attention. He
sighed before turning to look at Cobby.

He shook his head before he spoke. "You know, the last
time he rescued an alley dog we got stuck with you." Mickey
looked hard at Cobby now.

Cobby stood looking out at the same sun set, his hands in
his pockets, his black suit jacket falling down to cover them up.
He said very little. That was the way Cobby was. He was not in
a position to ever make his opinions known, until now. "I've
done my best."

Mickey smirked. "He has a knack for picking out the ones worthy of being saved. The bigger the mess, the deeper he believes in them. Take you for example. I would have just run you until you finally got beat to death in that alley. I didn't give a shit about your ma, I didn't give a shit about you. But something about you caught his attention. Now look where you are."

Cobby looked down for a moment. Mickey looked back out the window.

"My opinion hasn't changed. In the end, she won't hold together. No matter what he glues her back together with. However, he asked as a favor, so I let him try. But he'll be stuck with her until he finally tires of it and does away with her. No mistaking that. Then you come to me. You tell me that he has sent you to replace him in his absence." Mickey pursed his lips. "Nothing ever replaces Valant in his absence. Not ever. He is my brother. Nothing ever replaces him. Especially you. So don't tell me you're gonna do his job, cause you won't." Mickey's angered voice spurned.

Cobby bowed his head and turned to leave. Before he reached the door Mickey stopped him. "Where you going?"

Cobby turned to look at him. "Mexico. Just across the border. Frankie found the boat we've been looking for docked down there."

Mickey walked to him and stood a foot away. He reached up and took hold of Cobby's face and looked at his right eye. "There's an old Italian belief that when two people suffer the same fate, their lives become intertwined." Mickey dropped his hand and stood there looking at Cobby.

"I'm not responsible for her."

"Not responsible. Just intertwined," Mickey replied.

*****

Valant took her into the bathroom and sat her on the toilet. It took him a moment to rummage around and find what he was looking for. She had no idea what that was. She was shivering violently. She began immediately after she realized she was all but naked. Deep humiliation burned to realize he already had a full view of her naked body without her consent. But, there was nothing she could do about that now. Her palm remembered the feel of striking his face.

She looked down at her hand saw that it had been cleaned thoroughly. All the blood was gone from it.

All the blood was gone from it.

Marie saw Deano clearly. He was walking beside her one moment, chewing his gum and snorting impatiently at her as he always did. Then he was on the ground, gasping for air. His bloodied hand reached for her. She felt herself take hold of it, then felt it slip away from her. He told her to run, but it was far too late. Far, far too late.

She trembled as she recalled the desperate look in Deano's eyes when he saw them drag her away. She could not recall a second shot, so perhaps unlike The Dark Horse they did not bother to shoot him in the head. All she could see was Scar Face.

Valant sat down on the tub next to her and opened a tin full of foul smelling salve. He took a soft cloth and wiped away the blood that was seeping from the gashes. The pain was excruciating. When he wiped on the salve it seemed to numb it for she could no longer feel the sting of each delicate stitch. She looked at her hand again.

Valant wasn't looking at her, but was instead screwing the lid back on the salve, rinsing the cloth to clean up her chest wound. Tears began to flow again as the dreams of Deano floated through her mind. Valant stood above her wringing out the rag.

"Deano?" she whispered. He heard her but did not answer. He sat down again and without consent pulled her shirt low and started wiping blood away. Marie watched him with huge frightened eyes. She tried again.

"Deano?" At her sharp intake of breath he looked up at her face. He just looked at her for a moment, then very slightly shook his head. He went back to his task without any comment.

The vision of Deano walking away from her in her dreams came to hit full force. Him telling her to sleep although she already was. She rocked back and forth with the impact of it. Deano had been part of her life for a short time, but like Cobby had been there day and night. He was gruff and he was mean, but he watched over her like a hawk. He never would have let them get her had they not shot him like they did.

She was crying hard now. Nothing she could do would stop it. Valant did what he could for the wound, then sat and looked at her losing her mind yet again.

"Don't cry. Don't cry over him. He was just a thumper anyway." His voice held very little comfort. "You've got to stop feeling, stop thinking. What is in the past cannot be made right. You have to start over from here."

She covered her face with her hands. "Why do I keep on living?"

He pulled her hands away from her face. "Because life and death are not up to us. Until your heart has beat the number of times it was wound for, you keep living. Now start over."

She saw her own image flash in her mind. It was the picture of herself that Mickey hung in the great entry way of the club. Then she saw herself in the vanity mirror, the look of madness, the swollen and grotesquely disfigured face and chest.

Start again. As what?

No more starts. No more try again. This was more than anyone should have to carry. To once be great and magnificent, then to plummet to the depths that children's nightmares were made of. Not even Alex would want her now, if he weren't already married.

"They took something. Yes. But they didn't take what makes you Marie. You still have that. Find it and hang on." His voice was firm and commanding.

She shook her head no. She looked up at him and bitter angry tears fell freely. "No. No, they took the most important thing I had. Not my beauty, not my voice. They took the wall I built that kept my demons in. Now they fly free and I'll never get them caged."

He sighed and looked down at his lap.

She whispered to him, "Do you have demons?"

"Yes. A guilty conscience. That's the worse demon you can have."

Her eyes glittered and she exhaled a sob.

"Then you do know me better than I thought."

*****

It was a long night. Marie laid on the bed for several hours, fighting the urge to seek shelter in a corner. At last the night visions won out. Slinking off the bed and to the corner across from the one her bloodied dress had lay in, she crawled silently. She cowered behind Valant's chair. The pale light from the window did little to protect her imagination from shadows. At last she buried her face in her knees and remained there in a tight ball. Tears fell soundlessly for fear her father would hear and drag her by the hair to the closet.

About midnight she started talking to herself. Valant lay in the dark on the sofa in the living area of the open house smoking. He strained to hear what he thought he heard. Rising he crept into the bedroom and his stomach burned when he could not find her on the bed. The room had gone quiet and still. Perhaps she found a way out. He checked the window but it was closed. Surely he would have heard her open it anyway.

"Shh. He's coming." He turned when the barely audible whisper met his ears. He could just make out his white undershirt crouched in the corner. He moved around the bed and knelt before her.

"Quiet, Alfred," she said to no one. Valant remained behind the chair watching her. She reached out to take hold of something in the air and then pulled it onto her lap. There was nothing there. She rubbed her good cheek against something, smiling as much as her damaged lips would allow. She wrapped her arms around whatever she held.

"I missed you. Nothing smells like you do. What sort of games have you been playing?" She rubbed what could have been a very small back had it actually been on her lap. "No, he doesn't put me in the closet anymore. But, I have lived many times over since then. Where are you going?" She grasped out in the air and fell forward as she tried to reach something. "Alfred!"

She fell backward into the wall and braced herself for something. She struggled and pushed against the wall trying to free herself, then rolled up into a tight ball and covered her head. She stayed like that for a very long time. Valant wondered if she had passed out. He began to reach for her, but just as he did she raised her head and began whispering again.

"He came to see me, Vantino. Many times. I never told you, did I?" She looked up at the wall and traced her hand down it slowly. "He stood in the dark and listened to me sing. What would you have done to him if you had known? What would you have done if you knew he was the only one who truly heard me? Can we go to the kitchen and play cards? I hear the thunder rolling again."

Valant glanced out the window to see bright stars blinking in the night sky. When he looked back at her she was again holding something. "Dignity. That's what separates us from them. Isn't that right, Vin? What happens when you have no dignity left? Does that make me one of them?" She buried her fingers in her hair and rested her forehead on her knees.

A great sadness settled over Valant then. He could have no idea of the things she was haunted by, nor would he ever understand the depths which they tormented. But before him sat a twenty-six year old woman who had lived lifetimes to his one. She had been great, unbelievable at times, and she had strived over everything to become great. Now she was broken, more so than she must have ever been.

"Marie," he whispered as he pushed the chair aside. At the sound she jerked her head up and pressed into the corner. "It's alright. It's just me." He held out a hand to her. "I said I wouldn't leave you, didn't I?"

She looked confused. Her face registered that she was seeing multiple people instead of him. "Oh, Vantino. I heard thunder. I was so afraid. I decided to hide here until you came." With a relieved smile she reached for him, but then pulled her hand back. "But you're not Robert Vantino, are you?"

"No," he replied in a deep voice.

"Then who are you? I've never seen you here before."

"I've been listening in the dark to hear you sing."

She let out a rapid fearful breath. She pushed back away from him. "Oh, no. Oh, no! No, not you."

"Then I'm Vantino. I came for you when I heard the thunder."

She slunk down some and looked at his face. "Do you remember, Vantino? When you took me to see the man they call The Dark Horse? Do you remember?"

Valant hesitated for a moment. "Yes."

"It was so long ago." She looked past him as if recalling. Then she looked straight at him again. "I have seen him again. Many times. He is all you said he would be in time. I dream sometimes that he'll kill you."

Valant's jaw clenched. "Don't worry 'bout me. I'll be fine." A great change came across her features then. When she looked at him he knew she was seeing Valant.

A tear slipped out of the corner of her eye. "I sang that to Cobby, not so very long ago. After I kissed him and he told me he could fall for me if given half a chance. Then we walked in and he said goodbye to his mother for the last time." She paused a long moment as her eyes glinted with apprehension.

"Where is Cobby now? Is he dead, too?" Her face filled with dread as she waited for his reply long in coming.

"No. Cobby isn't dead."

"He told me you were hard on him," she whispered slowly.

"Yes, I was. For his own good." He paused. "I told him not to fall for you. That you could never be his."

She let out a small, sad laugh. "He would do anything for you, you know that?"

She had a strange look on her face and she was greatly confused again. "Who are you?"

"Vantino. I've come to play cards."

*****

When Cobby came back, he brought Imelda with him. She had to lay blindfolded on the floor of the back seat, but she insisted that Marie would need another woman. That two non-understanding men couldn't possibly give her the comfort she needed. Imelda was not prepared for what met her.

Valant listened to Imelda's reasoning while studying the large suitcase full of clothes his hastily penned note had ordered. Despite what he thought was better for Marie, he at last relented and went into the bedroom and carried Marie out. She lay limp in his arms. When Imelda saw what was left of her face she immediately began to cry. Valant gave her a very harsh look as he set Marie down. Imelda attempted to control herself.

Marie stood on one leg staring at Imelda. Gone from her eyes was the light that shone brilliantly. It was replaced by dullness that reflected an empty mind. That look was far more disturbing than the cut job. Imelda began to tremble as she dropped the suitcase and went to Marie.

"Oh, child. Oh, dear child." She took Marie into her arms and cried. She clung tightly to Marie as a mother holds a grieving child. Valant had braided Marie's long black hair and replaced the undershirt with a white button down dress shirt. It hung down past her buttocks but left her legs showing.

Imelda clenched her jaws as she took this in. "Bathroom?" She asked as she took control of the situation.

Valant nodded toward the bathroom door next to the bedroom in the short hallway. Imelda gathered up Marie as best she could and like an oak half carried her to the bathroom. When they reached the door she turned back to Valant and said, "Bring the suitcase to the bedroom." Then she quietly closed the door behind them. It was only a few seconds before Valant heard the faucet in the bath tub turn on and the water rushing out.

Imelda undressed Marie and helped to lower her into the warm water, then she left the bathroom to get into the suitcase Valant set on the bed. She took out soap, shampoo and a brush. She returned to the bathroom and hummed softly as she washed Marie. First her hair, then her body. She was careful not to hurt her wounds. Imelda kept up with the soothing sound of her voice until Marie closed her eyes. The hot water warmed Marie's blood while Imelda brushed her hair.

"I brought you clothes, Marie. Proper ones. To make you feel like a woman, not a waif in an oversized man's shirt." Marie could hear the irritation in Imelda's voice. Imelda was silent for a time. "I know he is not a gentle man. But, Valant can be a good man, when he wants to be." Her heavy Italian accent stressed her words.

Marie knew Imelda was struggling to say something, but she didn't know what. "There. Let's get you out and into something soft and warm." Imelda lifted her from the tub and wrapped her in a dry towel. Then she helped her into the bedroom, not bothering to see if the men saw Marie. She felt it mattered little. They had already seen all Marie had. She dressed Marie in a simple light blue house dress, then braided her hair back much the same as Valant had.

"I think you have the most beautiful hair I have ever seen. Even when I was young I didn't have hair like that." Imelda smiled as she ran her finger tips down the braid. "You know, after my first husband died, I wanted to die with him. There was a time when I wished I didn't have my beautiful girls. Then I could throw myself into the sea. But I knew if I did that, something dreadful would happen to my babies. I regretted them for a time. But only for a time. I did not want to hurt them, so I got up every day and kept sewing. Even when all I really wanted to do was die. I was far from my home and people. I didn't even have my mother to comfort me in my grief. Then Georgio came along."

She tied the end of Marie's hair and sat down beside her on the bed. She pulled Marie to her and then held her as she spoke. "After Georgio rented me the shop, he would stop by every now and then. He started to stop by more frequently. I never thought much of it, I just offered him coffee. I could see he was sad himself. I knew his son had passed and things with Mickey were bad. Not to mention his wife had all but left him in her grief. So, I sat quietly and listened to him talk about small things.

"I found myself looking forward to his visits as time went on. I even started coming to the shop early so I could have coffee ready. He was so good to the girls, he always spoke to them. I could see the regret in his eyes each time he looked at them. I never thought for a moment that he was handsome. I still thought of my husband that way. And then, one day, I was talking to him about something funny one of the girls had done. When I looked at him, he had this funny half smile on his face. It struck me then just how handsome he really was." She stopped for a moment.

"I felt myself slip a little more each day. Each time I saw him. I started to dread our little visits. One morning he and Julian stopped in. Julian asked if he could take the girls to the restaurant for a pastry. I agreed. As I poured the coffee I looked up at Georgio, and everything I was feeling about him was in his eyes as he looked at me. I had been alone a long time, and the wants I had only grew stronger each day.

"He was as regretful as I that he was married. I told him I couldn't be with him, that the shame I would feel if my girls ever found out would be the end of me. So, we agreed to stay away from each other. Might as well tell water not to run downhill." Imelda sighed again.

"The next time he came to me and Julian took the girls, I was not so strong. I fell into temptation and the love we made was passionate." Her voice broke a little. "I know I will have to atone for what we did. I hope God will understand that we did what we did out of a great love for each other. It was hard to feel it was wrong, but I know it was. Georgio watched over the girls and me as if he were our husband and father. I loved him as such. It is pointless to say his wife didn't love him, for that didn't make it right in God's eyes." Imelda stopped and raised Marie's face to her.

"I know these boys are hard. I know they are cruel and violent. But the truth is, they have the capacity to be kind, too. Maybe not the type of kind we women desire, but they can be very loyal when they want to. Valant is no different. In all the time I have known him, I have only seen him help a few people. But when he does, it is with everything he has. You can trust him to help you, too. He has chosen to help you."

Imelda gently took Marie's hand. "Oh, I know you don't like him much. He is a very intimidating man. But, take what he offers you, and then go on with your life." Imelda covered Marie's hand with both of hers. "Take it, and go on."

"I brought you all the things you will need. When you need more feminine things, just send a note with Cobby and I will make up another package." Imelda smoothed Marie's loose hair from her face. "Let him care for you, then you can go."

There was a soft tap at the door before Valant opened it. "It's time, Imelda."

She turned to Marie. "I've got to go now. But, I will come back when I can. I promise you that. As soon as Val lets me, I will be back." Marie clung to her. Imelda wrapped her arms around Marie and held her tight until Valant returned and insisted she go. Imelda lay Marie down on the bed and covered her with a blanket, then smoothed her hair down again. She left quietly.

When she reached the front door she turned to Cobby and Valant. "Are you sure you can handle this? Because as of now she is going to take a lot of understanding."

Valant just looked at her. "Do you doubt my dedication?" There was accusation in his tone.

"No. I would never doubt your dedication. But that girl needs someone who will hold her and distract her. You can't leave her alone all the time sleeping in that bed. She'll be catatonic. I will stay. My girls can handle the shop."

"No." Valant's answer was firm. "It may be just a matter of time until we are found here. I won't have you in the middle of things if they do."

Imelda looked at the floor. She knew better than to challenge him. He was the only one she wouldn't challenge. "Then keep in touch with me. I will get you whatever you need. Don't hesitate to ask for something." Imelda looked up into Valant's face. "This is not the time for harshness, Val. She needs a gentle hand."

Valant's jaw ticked. "I think harsh is the only thing Marie understands."

*****

Marie lay still under the blanket and listened to the silent house. She was wrapped up in a tight ball with her arms tucked against herself. Imelda had comforted her greatly. She was saddened to know that she was gone. Marie was stuck in a void of reality. Imelda held her concentration.

"Marie," the sound of Valant's voice startled her. She turned her head to look at him with her good eye. "Time to eat."

Without waiting for her to answer, he gathered her in the blanket and lifted her from the bed. He carried her out into the open area that was the living area, dining, and bar. It was a vast house with a vaulted ceiling. Great beams ran the width of it. The walls were wood paneling. An extensive library corner held several hundred books neatly tucked away. Arm chairs and a coffee table offered a comfortable reading nook. Much like the apartment, the kitchen was held in by cabinets and a counter.

He set her down at the counter on a stool, then wrapped her blanket around her. The kettle was already whistling, so he moved through the door and gathered a cup and loose tea. Bags of groceries sat on the counter holding all the supplies that Cobby and Imelda had brought. Marie looked down at her dress. It made her feel secure somehow to have a house dress instead of a man's shirt.

Valant wore his usual attire, but the black jacket was gone and the sleeves of his white shirt were rolled up. He moved with familiarity in the kitchen, never needing to look for something or blunder as to what needed to be used for a particular purpose. It was a functional kitchen, but void of anything feminine. Marie thought of Margo. She guessed that they never spent much time together here. She thought of herself and wondered how much time she would be spending with him.

Valant stirred in a teaspoon of sugar and handed Marie the cup on a saucer. He sat down across from her and folded his hands in front of him. She couldn't make her arms move to pick up the cup. She hated his scrutiny.

"I don't make a lot of tea. I need to know if it tastes like dog shit."

She withdrew her right arm from the blanket and reached out to take the cup. Her hand was shaking so badly tea sloshed from the cup and hit the saucer. She used both hands to bring it to her mouth. It took great effort to get the hot liquid past her torn lips. It was bitter and hot, just slightly over steeped. She nodded at him and set the cup down, it rattled as she did so. It burned her swollen gums and she winced.

He sat a moment and watched her, then stood and began to go through cupboards taking down bowls and ingredients. He moved with ease and without urgency. Marie watched him through dark, fearful eyes. The swelling was down in her socket just enough she could open her eye a slit.

"I make pasta. I make it very well." He measured various things into a big mixing bowl.

"Julian Delano was a very good chef. He took the time to teach me some of what he knew in the culinary arts. At the time I despised it, but now that I am older, I enjoy it."

He worked silently for a time, his forearms flexing as he mixed and then rolled out the dough. It was such a contrast to what she knew of him. "I was in grammar school when I met Mickey. We spent much of our time together. When I met Julian, I was deeply afraid of him. It was many years before I felt differently. So, contrary to what you may think, I understand fear. He was harder on me than I was on Cobby. There were times I knew I wouldn't survive him. In time, I became what he called his masterpiece. For all that was worth."

After that he went silent. Marie spoke nothing, just watched as he finished his work. Her mind was easier to control with something to focus on, but her emotions still ran free. At times he would look at her and she was still, others she would be crying silently. Valant made no mention of it, just kept working.

"I remember Julian," Marie spoke as she looked beyond Valant into her memory. "He killed my oldest brother."

*****

Valant lay in the dark and listened to the sounds in the night. It had been a long time since he had stayed at the safe house. It was hard for him to distinguish which sounds were normal, and which might be an intruder. He'd already risen twice to go and check sounds he couldn't identify. He listened to the sound of Marie's breathing, sometimes fast, and sometimes regular. He knew she was asleep, but her dreams must have been bad for she trembled and cried out frequently.

He had chosen to sleep beside her, without touching her. He told her he would not leave her to her demons. He did the night before and she had a terrible time of it. The things she said in her delirium made him think. She said nothing when he lay beside her, just watched him through a fearful eye. He slept in his clothes, and he was glad when the first noise concerned him. Marie buried her face and lay still for a long time, but at length she fell into a troubled sleep.

Valant didn't sleep much. Never had. It seemed odd to lay in one place for so long. The light of the half-moon filtered through the window and cast a soft glow on the foot of the bed.

"I don't want to dream of him anymore." Marie's faint murmur drifted endlessly in the vast openness of the house.

"Who?"

"Alex."

"Eventually you won't."

She was quiet after that and Valant wondered if she had been hallucinating again. But then she spoke.

"It hurts so desperately to know he didn't love me, just the promise of what I'd become, and all that went with it."

"Yes it does." Valant's voice was low and deep.

"Why do I still care?" She turned her head to look at him out of her good eye.

"You'll let go when you're ready. You're just not ready yet."

She hesitated before asking, "Why didn't she marry you?"

Valant sighed. "It's complicated." He, too, paused a moment. "That's not true. It wasn't complicated at all. She wanted my power and his money. She ended up with both."

"Did you ever meet anyone else? Did the pain of it go away?" She asked in desperation for herself.

"Yes," he replied slowly. "I met someone else. But by then I wasn't the optimistic young man I had been. You are better off the way you are. I kept up with Margo, so the reality of it never seemed to fade. Had I been like you, and she was just gone, when I met someone else I wouldn't have been so cynical inside."

Marie inhaled shakily. "Why do I feel the knowledge you have I am acquiring?"

"Marie, you are a talented young woman. I have watched you a long time. No matter which way you fall in, you always come out heads up."

She raised her head again and looked at him. "Why am I here? Why are you here with me?"

He tilted his head so she could see both his eyes. "Tell me, Marie. Since the first time I met you all those years ago, when have I not been there when you needed me?"

*****

Marie lay in the dark and listened to the ringing in her ears. The kind of ringing heard only in absolute silence. Her pillow beneath her good eye was soaked with tears that seeped out at will and she chaffed at the fact she could no longer control her emotions. Valant lay beside her and his regular breathing was barely a whisper. She wasn't sure if he were sleeping or not.

She kept seeing her own image in the vanity mirror. It plagued her constantly. She desired more than anything to look at her reflection to ascertain the amount of damage done. She knew it was the vain streak in her that cared so deeply, but the truth was she wasn't in some grisly accident or born deformed. Those instances were beyond a person's control. What she lost was taken from her violently.

She didn't want to think what would have happened if they had finished what they started. She would no doubt have slowly bled to death from the deep cuts. She wasn't so sure she didn't regret that they couldn't finish. She wouldn't be in the pickle she was now.

She thought of the man who lay a mere two feet away. She was terrified of him. His manner had been slow and deliberate, but he hid something from her. Something that made her afraid. She had no idea how long he would put up with her. She had no control over her mind and when it shifted. She also became increasingly afraid of what she was saying during those times. Her dreams of Vinny and Vantino were so vivid, she knew she was more than likely talking out loud to them.

The Dark Horse was a man who had a reason for everything. He didn't do things without first mapping out the possible outcomes and rewards. He was purposely keeping her alive, but for what? He had spoken of always being there when she needed him, and a very disturbing image had immediately flashed in her mind of Scar Face raising his gun to kill her. The Dark Horse stepped in front of her. She couldn't recall if he even had a gun to defend himself with. So much of that night were mere bits and pieces. Marie refused to delve deeper to sort it out. The important thing was she had run, and obviously failed miserably. What The Dark Horse had meant about always being there she didn't know. She did know he showed up at the strangest of times, but she couldn't find any rhyme or reason to it.

Which brought her to the next troubling thought. Why had she been attacked in the first place? As a way of getting at Mickey? Or was there something deeper going on there? She clearly had a connection to Vinny, if anyone were casual enough to look. So did they strike at her to get to Vinny? The worst yet was something else entirely. Did they think that if they stopped her they'd stop Vinny?

*****

Cobby's tired, bloodshot eyes looked down the long stretch of road as far as his headlights shone. He was eased back in the driver's seat and he had one hand draped over the wheel. It was a long ride from the border in the middle of the night. Martin slept in the passenger seat next to him with his head tipped back at an awkward angle. It seemed very severe and Cobby suspected he wouldn't be able to move his head when the sun came up.

That reminded him of Marie. He wondered how she was doing, or if she was doing at all. He still figured at some point Val would put a bullet in her just to end her agony. It did not appear she would be reachable in the dark recesses of her own mind. A terrible twinge hit him with that thought. She was suffering so deeply. He thought back to the times she slept in the corner of the bedroom. At one time he wondered why she did it. He was currently afraid to know the reason, having seen the hell that lived just below the surface.

The traffic was thin and he was trying not to drift off. He had not slept much since the night Marie was so cruelly cut up. His body was exhausted and he longed for the comfort of sleep.

The reflection of headlights behind him glared off the mirror. So, he moved over slightly to block the light from piercing his eyes. The car had just turned a corner behind him, but was moving rapidly. Cobby watched them in his rearview mirror.

"Martin. Wake up." Martin woke with bleary eyes and indeed had a difficult time getting his head up.

"We got company." Cobby put his foot into the floor but the car behind them already had a lead. Cobby didn't have time to debate it before the car struck the back end of Cobby's '56

Cadillac. It lurched forward, but Cobby kept the wheel steady. He saw the car fade back and then pitch forward for another hit. Cobby swerved hard to the left and the car missed.

"Who the hell is that?" Cobby yelled.

"I don't know. All I can see is headlights!"

"Well for shitsakes fire at them!"

Cobby's eardrum spiked when the revolver went off in the tight space. The back window broke out and shattered all over the seat. The car kept right on them.

"He's coming again." Martin warned. Cobby glanced down to the speedometer which read ninety-six. He demanded more.

"He's trying to come around!" Martin yelled. Cobby swerved to the right and cut the car off. Cobby then had to focus on keeping it dead center so the car couldn't get around. It was trying forcefully anyway.

"Don't let him come up beside! He'll have us then!"

"No shit, Martin!" The violence as Cobby jerked the wheel whipped both the men. "Why not try another shot!" Cobby yelled sarcastically.

Martin fired again but nothing changed. Cobby dodged to the left again to block the road, but this time his tires left the pavement. He over corrected and began to fish tail down the highway. Shots entered the cab as Cobby dedicated all his strength to straightening out the wheels.

Martin shot rapidly behind him. With the movement of the car nothing was likely to hit a target. Cobby was able to get the wheel under control about the time the car came up beside them and hit them hard. It pushed Cobby off the road again, but he came back fighting. He swerved right while accelerating, hitting the car with as much power as he could muster.

Cobby looked over in time to see the next hit coming and braced himself. He looked at the speedometer. It read one hundred ten. The hit didn't affect them much, but Cobby wasted no time in retaliating.

"Shoot them!" Cobby yelled. Martin struggled to reload his gun. "Take mine!"

Martin raised his arm to fire. A bullet shattered the passenger window and ripped through his neck muscles. It was then very hard for him to breathe. He gasped and sputtered as blood poured out around him.

"Martin!" Cobby yelled just before the car was hit again. Cobby held the wheel. This time the car stayed with them, forcing Cobby farther off the road. Cobby looked over for a brief second and saw "The Heart" Vantino. Then he hit the brakes in an attempt to shake them free, but Vantino only pushed him harder. A wall of dirt sprayed up from Cobby's tires. The car began to slow, and the wheels went with the force of Vantino's push. Cobby fell forward as the front of the car struck something solid. Cobby couldn't see what as his chest hit the steering wheel. Martin flew forward as well, striking the dash, but Cobby wasn't sure Martin was alive to feel it anyway. Martin landed in a heap on the floor, blood running everywhere.

Cobby's vision blurred for a moment as the sunrise loomed on the horizon. His chest hurt and refused to expand with each breath. He heard yelling. Cobby was moving in an instant, trying to find the gun he had given to Martin. If it lay beneath him, he had little chance of reaching it. Out of the corner of his eye he saw two men approaching the car. Time to fight.

He jerked the door open and tore off his jacket. As two men in gray came around the back of the car, Cobby plunged into his pocket and found the only weapon he had besides the knife down by his ankle; brass knuckles. He slipped them on and braced for it. They came at him without guns drawn, so he knew he had the chance to fight.

The man on the left dove for him. Cobby swung hard. He struck him in the ribs just below the shoulder. He turned to the man on the right, swinging again. Cobby missed when the man jumped back. The one on the left came again, hitting Cobby in the stomach. He hardly flinched before firing back with a blow to the face. The man on the right advanced.

Cobby drove his fist into the man with all he had. It was enough to knock him down and leave him gasping for a moment. Cobby had no time to rejoice in it. The next man came at him full force, knowing if he could get Cobby off balance he wouldn't be able to use his fist with the brass knuckles. Cobby saw him come and take hold of his mid-section. He braced as best as his precarious position would allow. He felt his feet leave the ground and the odd sensation of flying registered in his mind.

Cobby didn't wait for the blunt trauma of hitting the ground. He bent his elbow and began hitting as he fell, his hand connecting with the man's head as he swung. The two men made a collective grunting noise as they hit the ground. Dust filtered up around them. The man kept hold of Cobby's lower back, his arms tightening like a vise grip despite the force of the fall. Cobby swung again, this time unable to hit with as much force as before, but still making contact. It broke the man's determination. Cobby rolled quickly away, only to be hit full force in the kidneys from a blow that came from above.

Cobby kept going. He jumped to his feet bracing for the blow that hit his stomach and forced him to expel a loud groan. This was his life or death, and Valant had trained him well to fight for his right to live. He had been fighting for his life long before Valant killed three men in an alley to save him. He knew how difficult living was.

He growled at the pain and looked to the man who was coming at him a third time. The man who was down was struggling to get up. Cobby knew he would soon be contending with both again, if Vantino didn't pull out a gun and end it all. He inhaled deeply just as the blow to his left side made contact. His breath rushed out of him in a gagging sound. He returned a blow, and the man crumpled to the side. Cobby took the opportunity and fired hard again, this time hitting the man in the ribs. He felt the pop as one broke.

The second man had gotten up. This time the exhaustion deep in Cobby's muscles turning to sludge that wouldn't move. Cobby raised his fists to block him, but his body just didn't seem to cooperate. He took a blow to his face and stumbled backward. He flung himself to hit the man in the stomach. It was like striking granite, but the man felt it.

"That's enough." The voice was loud in his ear.

Cobby didn't stop. What came next was death. He wanted to go down fighting with everything he had. One man got behind him while his focus was on the man in front. Cobby felt the crushing weight come down on him hard and his knees nearly buckled before he straightened himself out. The man before him drove hit after hit into his mid-section, paralyzing Cobby.

"That's enough." The three men stood panting and sweating, blood pouring from open wounds, dust caking in the perspiration.

Vantino came to stand before Cobby, a cigarette in his right hand, his gray suit unsoiled from the fight. His face had deep lines etched in it, but neither his thick hair nor moustache were tainted with any gray. He stood quietly looking down at Cobby, who was sagging on purpose trying to make it hard for the man behind him to hold him up.

"Well, you must be Cobbinelli." Vantino pursed his lips when he finished speaking. He flicked the ash off his cigarette but didn't raise it to his lips. "I've been hearing about you for years. It seems none of the things I heard were true. You do have fight in you. What the hell happened to your face?"

Cobby raised his head to glare at Vantino whose dark eyes glittered.

"Didn't find much in that boat, did you?"

Cobby didn't say anything, just slumped there and felt the deep penetrating ache that reverberated throughout his battered body.

"I already cleaned out that boat. I took everyone I found on it and tied cement blocks to their feet and tossed them overboard," he paused a moment to take a drag on his cigarette, then tossed what was left away from him. "The Dark Horse seems to be losing his touch. I took care of that boat a full two days ago. Now I find you picking up the slack. Just what seems to be keeping him busy these days?" Vantino looked down at Cobby.

"He's got better things to do than bother with you."

"Does he? Well, then that brings me to my next point," Vantino's voice got low and dark as he spoke. He came closer to Cobby. "He hasn't kept up his end of the bargain. I kept my end. Now I hear something happened to the girl. The Dark Horse drops off the earth. Is he such a coward that he has gone into hiding?"

"What girl?" Cobby hissed out.

Vantino drove a fist into Cobby's gut. "You know what girl. What happened to her?"

"She took a vacation," Cobby gasped out.

"I swear, you little piece of shit. I will cut off your arms and legs while Patrick holds your head up and eyes open so you can watch. Where is the girl?"

Cobby said nothing, just braced for the next blow. Vantino hit him twice in the stomach, then grabbed a handful of Cobby's hair and pulled his head back to look at him.

"Is she alive?"

It took a moment for Cobby to decide what to answer, but at length he said, "She was when I left her." Vantino released his hair.

Vantino took out a piece of paper and slipped it into Cobby's breast pocket. "I want you to give The Dark Horse a message for me. It might be good for you to know that the warehouse you assholes burned down was his headquarters; in America." The last bit was said with sarcasm. "Tell Valant that I intercepted that boat, and now the lines are silent. Tell him whatever is coming will be big, if the coward ever comes out of hiding." With Vantino's nod the two men threw Cobby to the ground and spent several seconds kicking his ribs.

Cobby lay there with stars floating before his eyes and dirt turning to cement in his mouth. His face stung from the cuts as more dirt packed in there as well. He waited to hear their retreat, the sound of a motor turning over, and tires slipping on pavement before he attempted to get up.

He pushed himself onto his knees, the jagged edge of pain registering in every part of his body. He felt of his already damaged face to find more lumps and the deep gash Val had stitched was again gaping open and muddied blood crusted over in it.

Cobby rose slowly to his feet and stumbled half bent over to his car that was, miraculously, still running despite the hit it had taken. He did a quick examination of the damage done to it, but there was only a large dent where it had hit a post. The deep sand had slowed the car and for that Cobby was grateful. He had no desire to see what it felt like to break out a windshield.

He slipped into the driver's seat and struggled to pull the door closed with his fingertips. He knew multiple ribs were broken and he felt the sharp pain as he forced them to move. Down on the floor in a bloodied heap Martin groan softly. Cobby looked down at him in surprise.

"Martin, next time I tell you to kill someone, get it done. I swear, if you don't, I'll shoot you myself."

*****

Cobby took Martin back into the city and did the best he could to patch him up. Martin was fortunate that the bullet had not hit the artery that ran so delicately close to his esophagus. All that was torn was muscle, and it would likely never be the same again. Martin had taken quite a hit when he met with the dash, but he was conscious again and making a fuss over his neck getting sewn shut.

Cobby sat directly under a bare light bulb, covered in blood, his sleeves rolled up past his elbows. He worked with a deep frown echoing from his lips to his forehead. Occasionally he would jerk his line of thread when Martin would get to shifting too much in an attempt to still him. More often than not it worked.

Mickey sat in a chair a few feet away, casually slumped at a comfortable angle. He watched Cobby work despite what he knew must be broken ribs and deep hurts of his own. He had nothing to say at the moment, just watched as the grueling process of stitching muscle to muscle went on. It wasn't a job for an untrained man. Which was why Cobby was doing it. He had assisted Valant many times. Not that Valant was a doctor, but the possibility of getting one wasn't realistic.

"There. Carry on your crying somewhere else you tit." Cobby spat as he threw the needle and thread into the dish that sat next to him. Martin stumbled to his feet and made his way to the cot in the corner. He moaned loudly as he lay down on it.

Mickey stood and removed his jacket. Cobby started the cleanup process. "Take off your shirt," Mickey ordered.

"I'm alright, Mick," Cobby replied without stopping his task.

"Yeah, you look it." Mickey rolled up his own sleeves.

"I've had worse."

"Maybe, but those cuts need cleaned out. Sit down." Cobby turned and looked at Mickey, then sat down slowly. Vantino's boys had popped all of the stitches Val worked hard to get into his face. Now everything was packed with dirt and oozing a strange yellow liquid. His ribs hurt and he really didn't think he could sit still for another minute, let alone long enough for Mickey to clean him up. He just wanted to sleep.

Mickey worked slowly, taking his time to clean everything out. It was strange to Cobby. Mickey never bothered with anything. Only where Valant was concerned, and even then it almost seemed as if Mickey couldn't take the reality that someone might actually be mortal.

"What did you tell them?" Mickey asked.

"Nothing. Vantino wanted to know where she was. I told him nothing."

"She's held tight to the story she doesn't know him. Has she told you anything?"

"Only that she knew Vinnetti from her father's club. That and she was afraid of Val because she knew he would pursue information she didn't have." Cobby winced as he spoke from the pain.

"I'm afraid there really is no way for me to restitch this. It's pretty ugly."

Cobby shrugged.

"It really doesn't matter what she tells Valant. I'll keep her just for sentimental reasons." Mickey's voice trailed far away.

"He means it, Mick. He wants her back. Valant told me never to underestimate him. I believe that now. He may be getting old, but none of his fire has died."

Mickey worked silently. When he was done, Cobby stood and looked at him. The pain in his rib cage making it impossible to breathe.

"If it's all the same to you, I'm gonna go out there."

Mickey nodded. "Yeah. Tell him Vantino's coming. But, I doubt it will make any difference to him either."

*****

She watched him all day. He never faltered. He was like a train, just moving along the tracks without taking account anything around him. He didn't speak unless necessary. Then he made his point and resumed whatever he was doing. When she took a bath he ran her warm water. He reached to undo the buttons on her dress and she had forcefully pushed him away.

She had no intentions of being conscious while he saw her naked body.

"I've already seen you naked, Marie. I didn't lose my mind then, and I won't now." He looked sharply at her.

She looked at the floor and wrapped her arms tightly around herself. He sighed heavily and his jaw ticked.

"You don't cut any slack do you? Once you form an opinion, you never do give to evidence."

"You are not my keeper," she whispered.

He bent over to look into her face. "Yeah, actually. That's exactly what I am."

He moved to the door. "Get yourself cleaned up."

She sat and soaked for a long time, thinking about what he said, about him, about herself. She didn't want him for a keeper. She didn't want any keeper. She wanted to be free, to roam as she pleased, to return to New York, walk the streets of LA without wondering who would come for her. She wanted to walk into Imelda's and buy whatever she chose for herself, not be beholden to some man who provided for her just to suit his purposes.

Freedom.

It was a word. It was a feeling. It was not in her lifetime. Valant was right. She did understand that even if she somehow escaped him, she would still have to answer to Vinnetti. Now Valant knew of a fine thread of a connection to Vinnetti and would use that to Mickey's advantage. The familiar surge of anger erupted.

When she rose from the bath tub, she determined to get herself out and dressed. Her leg ached fiercely, but she was able to get dried off and dressed with some difficulty. It hurt her chest greatly to raise her arms, the skin feeling as if it would literally rip at the seam. She didn't have a brush with her either. It was on the dresser in the bedroom.

When she opened the bathroom door and limped through it, Valant stood from the dining area table where he was sitting. He slid his hands in his pockets and looked at her, waiting. Marie's good eye looked next to him where Cobby sat. He was as grotesque as herself.

She gripped the door jam and shuddered at the stream of images she saw. She was right back in that alley way. Blood was everywhere, some of it was hers, and some of it was someone else's. She watched Valant shoot those men point blank one at a time, not bothering about her reaction. She also saw Scar Face raise his gun to point it at her. She remembered running.

Cobby watched her with great hesitation, judging her reaction. The last time he had seen her she was still a mess, unable to speak or function on any level. He saw the apprehension in her own eyes as well. He attempted a half smile, but she just looked at him. Her hand drifted to her own face and the identical wound they had in common.

"Intertwined," he whispered to her.

She looked sharply into his eyes. She understood.

"Well, if we're done with the happy reunion." Valant's sarcasm reached them both.

Valant helped Marie into an armchair not far from where they stood. Valant then moved away to the kitchen. Cobby sat across from Marie on the sofa. He sat with his elbows on his knees.

"How are you, Marie?" he asked softly.

She said nothing, just looked away from him and lay her head against the armchair. She heard Cobby exhale slowly then sit back. Valant returned with a glass of water and handed it to Marie, who took it and held it close to her. She sipped at it sparingly, not looking at either man.

"We seem to have a small problem, Cobby." Valant started as he stood a few feet away. His hands were in his pockets and he looked down at Marie as he spoke. A sharp look of consternation reflected in his eyes.

"Miss Barelli seems to think it's unfair we've seen her naked. While I seriously doubt that either of us enjoyed the moments her body lay exposed to us, she has taken it personally." He began to unbutton the cuff of his shirt. Cobby looked from Valant to Marie with a growing look of suspicion.

"She doesn't think we are fair or just men. We can't have that." He unbuttoned the opposite cuff. "Stand up, Cobby." Valant's eyes bored into Marie as he spoke.

Deep mortification graced Cobby's attitude. Valant's hands moved to the button just below his throat. Marie's dark eyes shone with disbelief. She put her glass of water next to her on the table. Her hair fell across her face and she shoved it away.

"Cobby!" Valant barked to the younger man who sat like granite, his eyes focused on the man before him. It was Val's unpredictability Cobby feared most. Knowing what he did about Valant, he slowly rose and slid off his jacket. He laid it on the chair behind him, his ribs screaming their disapproval.

Valant finished the buttons of his shirt front and now he jerked the tails free from his pants. He cast the shirt aside behind him without ever taking his intense eyes from Marie. She covered her face and let out a small cry of anguish. She looked to Cobby and her eyes pleaded with him to do something. But, his handsome and scarred face looked away from hers. There was nothing to be done. He started on his shirt front.

Valant pulled his undershirt over his head and lay it atop his shirt. He began to undo the black belt that rested snuggly against his pelvis. His chest was covered in salt and pepper hair that moved down his torso. He slipped his shoes off. Cobby was pulling his shirt free from his pants, then reluctantly took it off. He too slipped his undershirt over his head. On his face he wore a look of pure disgrace. He would not look at Marie.

"Stop it. Right now!" Marie spat at him. Nothing in Valant's expression changed, the intensity of his pale gaze was accusing as she shot him a look that mirrored Cobby's mortification. The belt hit the floor.

Cobby stood naked from the chest up, the deep bruising shadowed his torso in a black ink. His hands were scuffed and scabbed across the knuckles and more than a few fingers looked dislocated. Marie looked away from the well-formed body that moved with reluctance.

Valant's black slacks hit the floor. He stood before her in nothing but a pair of light blue boxers. His body was not the blackened mass that Cobby's was, but when it came to definition, there wasn't much difference between the two. Valant's skin was just a shade or two paler than Cobby's. Marie had never seen a naked man in the flesh, let alone two at once.

Cobby let his pants drop to the floor, but he didn't step out of them as Valant had. He stood in his white boxers, the corner of his mouth twitching and a humorless stare on Marie. Valant's hands were resting on his hips, his jaw ticking as he stared at Marie as well.

"Do you feel vindicated?" he asked sharply. Marie looked up at him with brilliance in her brown eyes. He was making a mockery of her and her feelings of violation. He moved closer and bent down to look directly in her face. "Do you?"

Marie's chest rapidly expanded and retracted as her body trembled slightly. "No," she said quietly but firmly.

"Well, this is all you get. Because neither of us removed your panties. We did not look at you in your entirety. Not to mention, we did what we did in an effort to save your life. To care for you in the best way possible. So if you want to take offense at something, pick something valid."

Marie's mouth trembled as she looked into his cold eyes. Her bad eye was open a slit and tears banked on the rim. She refused to let them fall. Valant straightened and stood looking down at her. She pushed from the chair and stood with difficulty balanced on her right leg. She looked up into his face for a moment, then turned to go. She moved slowly and unevenly.

"Marie." His voice cut off her retreat and she stopped to turn her head. She didn't look at him square on.

"I'm not here because I want to be," Marie whispered before moving on.

Marie gently closed the bedroom door behind her. She went to the bed and lay down. She covered herself with the blanket, burying her good cheek in the pillow. She thought about the multitude of people she had known not so long ago. Now she was down to two. Cobby, who had lost what little carefree air he once possessed, and Valant who had taken on the role of disgruntled caretaker. Marie, well, she was no longer the beautiful and talented young woman she had been. The very thought of using her voice to sing, or her body to dance brought her such a surge of regret.

She kept her thoughts from anything she had been before the night in the alley. Several times she thought of her picture of Alex and the bracelet the band gave her at Christmas. She knew she'd probably never see those things again. It pierced her heart to think of Rolly and the good times they shared. She tried not to think of what his expression might be if he were to see her now.

Everything changed so abruptly.

Now she was the ward of The Dark Horse, to what end she did not know. She suspected that it would be a bad one, regardless of how he treated her now. Bad things always happened to those who surrounded men like him. Whether he helped her to meet her end, or just the association with him did it, she would pay a price. She had no family, no home, no country. She was adrift.

Vinny still ate at her.

*****

Cobby waited in the driveway for Valant a long time. He smoked a cigarette, releasing smoke rings up into the starlit sky. He felt restless and longed to go, but felt the urge to stay. It was two feelings at war with each other within himself. The memory of her face burned in his mind, and he couldn't see anything but marred perfection. She was indeed doing better than the last time he saw her, but she really wasn't much above catatonic.

Valant was a mystery. The things he chose to pursue, and the things he did not were difficult to identify. He was taking great care of her, but why, Cobby couldn't fathom. He doubted seriously that Val could be in love with Marie. Val was not that kind of man. He never had to pursue women, he just chose one for the moment, used what he wanted, then pushed her aside. Margo was just for appearances sake, and perhaps for the sentimentality of it, but Cobby never could see where Val really cared about her. And anyway, Margo was such a wretch, who could love that?

Cobby did know, however, that Valant enjoyed Marie's voice. He took time each chance he got to listen to Marie sing. Whether that was at rehearsals, or stopping in at the club each evening. But that wasn't enough to justify what he was doing for her now.

Cobby heard the scrape of the door opening behind him, then softly closing. Val moved silently into the dark and came to stand beside Cobby, who hadn't moved. Valant still had his sleeves rolled up from his dinner preparations, then the cleanup.

"Cigarette," Val stated in a low voice. Cobby took out a pack as well as a lighter and handed both to him. Val lit one and inhaled deeply, forcing the smoke out his nose.

"I have a message for you," Cobby reached into his pocket and pulled out the slip of paper Vantino had put there the night before.

Valant hung his cigarette between his lips and took the paper. Cobby flicked the lighter and brought flame to life. He held it next to the note so Valant could read it. Val squinted as he attempted to do so.

Vinnetti wants the girl. Truce be damned.

Val said nothing as he took the cigarette in his fingers again. Cobby closed the lighter and snuffed the flame, then waited for Valant to voice his thoughts.

"Where did he catch up with you?"

"Just this side of the border. Before sun up."

"By the looks of you and the car you put up one hell of a fight."

"Yes, sir."

"Was he everything I said he would be?"

Cobby nodded his head and remembered a moment. "Yeah."

"Well, brace yourself. He's going to get worse. They want her back."

Cobby lit another cigarette. "He's asking for you, specifically. Don't think he'll accept me as your replacement."

"No, he won't. Make no mistake, Cobby. Next time he'll kill you to clear the road to me." Val stated firmly. "Vantino came to me and asked in the name of the truce that I look out for Marie. I said I would. They obviously know something happened to her."

"Why? What is she to him?" Cobby asked.

Valant exhaled a stream of smoke. "Marie thinks nothing, and I believe her. No matter how deep I dig, she keeps coming up with the same answer. They met by chance, and are no blood tie."

Cobby scoffed. "Well, they obviously have some tie, despite what she thinks. You think Vinnetti will start a war over her?"

Valant thought a moment. "No. He put her here to hide her, I think, from The Underground. He put her where he figured they wouldn't look; with Mickey. Either Marie is a much better liar than I give her credit for, or she genuinely doesn't know what is going on. If Vinnetti starts a fight for her that will leave her open to identification by the Underground. He won't risk that since he has tried to keep her identity hidden."

Valant and Cobby both fell silent for a time, each concerned with his own thoughts. The soft sounds of the night echoed around them, the darkness lending a protective cloak to everything. Valant had lived his life in the protective cloak of the dark. Done most of his work in the dark.

"What about the boat?"

"Nothing. Vantino got there first and wiped it clean. Not a trace of anything."

"There's a man down in Vinnetti's area. His name is Arthur. He runs a fabrication shop out of an old warehouse off of Clement Avenue. Go to him and tell him I sent you. Ask him how the weather is in the Bahamas this time of year." Cobby nodded. He knew Arthur, but it had been years since Valant had gone to him for information.

"How's Mickey?"

"Fine. At least he seemed normal."

Valant took another drag before dropping the cigarette and snuffing it out with his foot. "Watch your back, Cobb. There are two separate groups gunning for you now."

"Yeah, I know."

*****

Marie sat at the counter watching him. He had insisted she come and drink a cup of tea. When she hesitated he picked her up and carried her to the counter. She was reluctant to be near him since he and Cobby stripped down in front of her two days before. Now Cobby had gone back to the city and Marie was left alone with him.

He gathered up bowls and utensils and set them on the counter. He didn't look at her. She sat stoically sipping her tea, trying to avoid any action that would cause him to take notice of her. It was impossible. He glanced at her every so often, almost as if to make sure she was still there. She avoided his looks like the plague.

In her life Marie had been taught to respect men. The action of subservient avoidance had always worked before, but now it seemed to draw Valant's unwanted attention. Marie could read almost all men by the way their hand moved, the tick in their jaw, the tension in the forearm. Not Valant. Nothing she read from him was correct. When he was tense he was relaxed and left her alone. When he was quiet and his movement soft, he was usually filled with rage.

He made no sense.

He glanced at her again. She took a sip of her tea, and kept her head down and away. He didn't understand anything about her behavior. Most men would have left her alone when they saw she was conceding. Not this one. It made him pick away at her more. She wasn't sure what she had to do to keep him off her back.

"Vinnetti." Marie lowered her cup and set it in the saucer. She looked up at him with apprehension.

"It's time you did something with yourself." He unbuttoned his cuffs and rolled them up without saying anything more. Had he just called her Vinnetti?

"Do you cook, Vinnetti?"

She just stared at him without blinking. He stared back. "Well?"

"That's not my name," she said lowly.

"Sure it is." He continued to stare at her. "Do you cook?"

She wanted to rub her face, to press deep into the creases and massage away some of the tension. But that would make the screaming pain return. "Some."

"Like what? Boil water? Scramble eggs with a sprinkling of shell? Burn the toast? What?"

She looked at him and her mouth twitched. He was just so sarcastic. "I bake mostly."

He turned back to the counter and moved a bowl closer to him. "Huh. Well you'll mostly starve to death then."

Marie spent time in Vinnetti's kitchen and had learned many things, but they were mostly related to baked goods. She could make a few things to keep herself alive, but while in New York she had eaten at diners and such. She definitely did not have the opportunity to further her culinary skills while with Mickey.

"Come here," he didn't look at her when he gave the order. She wanted to cry.

At length he turned and looked at her. "This is about to be your problem. So you best come over here and learn something. The first time you try to serve me Petite Fours for dinner, I'll throw a shit fit like you've never seen."

Marie pursed her lips, then stood and moved around the counter. She limped, but it seemed as though her leg was slowly getting stronger. The swelling in her face was also down and she could see out of her bad eye that was open. Her face was an ugly red and deep purple. The gashes were irritated lines that shone from the salve Valant rubbed on them multiple times a day. Marie smelled like a cross between an herb garden and a hospital hallway.

Valant moved aside to make room for her. He took a plain white cotton apron off the counter and slipped it over her head. It came to rest against her light green house dress. She tied the strings behind her then glanced up at him. He was looking down at her with that same disinterested gaze he always wore.

"Alright, Vinnetti. Let's see how hopeless you are."

"I am not a Vinnetti," Marie whispered fiercely as she looked down at a wooden spoon on the counter.

Valant moved closer. "Vinnetti." He moved closer still. "Vinnetti." Marie sighed deeply and pursed her lips again.

He came within an inch of her ear. "Vinnetti." He tilted his head to look at her face. "Shall we start with the egg noodles?"

He moved away and folded his arms. "I like a lot of noodles in my soup, so I triple the amount of dough when I start. Break three eggs into that bowl, then scramble them."

The truth was, it did help. Marie was so occupied trying to keep up with Valant so he wouldn't get close to her again that her concentration blocked out all other thought. He took her through the process of making the dough for the noodles.

"Sprinkle flour on the counter. Put the dough on the flour and roll it out." It was very difficult to roll out the stiff dough and Marie had to push hard to get it done.

"Here." He moved her aside, then rolled it out for her. It was easier for him, his upper body strength working to his advantage. "We let these dry for several hours, while we make our stock. Fill that pot with water."

She peeled the carrots while the water boiled. Then he showed her how to chop the carrots quickly. His hands worked so fast she couldn't see the knife. Marie found that to be accurate. He was damn fast with a knife in all other situations.

"Put those chicken thighs in the water. We let them boil down awhile. Go rest your leg." Marie was glad to escape the close proximity of the kitchen. She moved to an armchair and sat down. She lay her head back and closed her eyes a moment. Her head hurt greatly, but she couldn't be sure if that was because of the injuries or the experience of cooking with Valant. She let her mind drift back to the days helping Nancy in Vinny's kitchen. It was a pleasant memory, filled with good food and company.

"Here." Valant's voice shattered her tranquility.

He stood above her with one hand in his pocket; the other held a book which he offered to her. She raised her head and reached to take it. He pulled it back from her.

"You can read, can't you, Vinnetti?"

"Mostly sheet music," She replied sarcastically. He narrowed his eyes at her.

"Did Vinny Vinnetti bother to teach you anything? Or would you rather not discuss the things he taught you to do?" His eyes changed as she inhaled deeply and tensed. He thrust the book at her again and she stared at him incredulously.

"Try reading. You might learn something else. Something less invasive."

She hated that man. She stared at him with indignation as he moved to an armchair not far away to sit down, picking up a book of his own. He picked up his reading glasses from the table between them and slid them onto his face. He didn't look at her again. He appeared as though he could be someone's father. She hoped he wasn't.

Marie sighed heavily and looked down at the book he gave her. It was Charlotte Bronte's *Jane Eyre*. Marie had never read it, although she had heard of it. She opened the cover to the first page to see an inscription written there.

To Hazel, love you, John

Pressed between the next pages was a photograph. It was of a handsome man leaning on a doorway. His hair was black, and his eyes were lit with mischief. His arms were folded across his chest, and in one hand a cigarette burned. Marie didn't recognize him in the slightest.

"My father, John Valant, Senior. That book belonged to my mother. Please don't damage it." Valant irritatedly looked back to his own book. Marie pressed the photo back between the pages.

Marie began to read, but found it was hard to concentrate. Words would set her mind to drifting and she would find herself back in New York. She spent time reliving those nights she had performed as headliner. She would see Alex's charming smile, hear the rich sounds of his trumpet. Deep regret filled her insides until nothing else remained.

It was over. All that was past. Now all she held were memories golden and happy. After a time she quit bothering to turn the pages of her book. The lines written there became blurred and unreadable. She longed to see the picture of Alex that was lost behind the bureau. To see the contours of his face again. Just one last time.

They ate in silence. Marie kept to her own bowl and avoided looking at him directly. Valant seemed content to leave her alone for the moment. His only comment was that the soup wasn't a total loss. She took it as acceptable and left it at that.

She cleared the dishes and washed them. It took her time to figure out where everything went, but he had allowed her space, having gone out on the patio to smoke. By the time she was done, her leg was aching and her body was exhausted, both physically and spiritually. The constant silence of the house was getting to her as well. She longed for Cobby to return.

She didn't bother to slip on the cotton nightgown Imelda brought for her, just lay on the bed and pulled the blanket up over her dress and buried her face. She had no idea what the rest of her life would be, but this was unbearable. The last image to drift into her mind before sleep took her was the look in Valant's eyes when she sang to him at his birthday bash.

*****

Cobby sauntered across the crowded restaurant and nodded to the people he knew. He knew the majority, but he only wasted his time on the important ones. His attention lingered on a table where a brunette dined with an older gentleman. He smiled at her and she blushed shyly, looking out the corner of her eyes at him. The older man didn't seem to notice.

Mickey spent a fair amount of time hiding out at the restaurant. The club was a pit of loss and regret, and home was nothing but despair. So, he held neutral ground and stayed at the restaurant where his memories weren't disturbed.

Cobby walked through the door of the office to several card games in full swing. Mickey sat at his desk blowing smoke rings at the ceiling. A plate of half eaten ravioli sat in front of him, but obviously his cigar held more fulfillment. When Mickey saw Cobby, he lowered his hand with the cigar and lifted his head from the back of the chair.

"Well?"

Cobby stopped in front of the big oak desk but didn't bother to sit in one of the two empty chairs. Instead, he slid his hands into his pockets. "It's a New York address. And, interestingly, not far from where our girl used to live."

"No shit?" Mickey sat forward and stubbed out his cigar in the ash tray. "Her fella?"

Cobby shrugged. "Don't know yet. Can't find him."

Mickey shook his head. "Outta the frying pan into the fire."

Cobby waited a moment for Mickey to give some indication as to what he wanted done next. He folded his hands in front of him and fisted them together. He pressed the fist to his mouth as he thought. When he had decided something, he lowered his hands and looked at Cobby.

"How is she?"

"Why don't you drive out and see for yourself."

One corner of Mickey's mouth pointed upward. He looked perplexed, but only for a moment. "No. Valant will tell me if she's ever ready. Which I doubt. You can keep me posted."

Cobby raised an eyebrow. "I'm not going back out there."

Mickey's brows knitted together. "Why not?"

"I don't know which of those two is less predictable."

Mickey looked at Cobby for a moment, then let out a loud laugh. "Oh shit. What did he make you do?"

Cobby looked from side to side, then quietly said, "He made me strip down in front of her."

Mickey burst out with uncontrollable laughter at that, clapping his hands together in merriment. "Valant. Priceless every time. What for?"

Cobby's mouth set into a grim line. "Something about her being pissed we saw her naked."

Mickey laughed harder. "Oh, hell! Valant never had any patience." He paused a moment and enjoyed the look of disgust on Cobby's face. "Well, I'm afraid you have to go back one more time." Mickey pointed to a table near the door. "You've got to take him that."

*****

The morning sun filtered through the windows and radiated off the polished wood floor. The smell of coffee filled the house like an old friend come to brighten the day of the down trodden. Valant sat at the dining table with his chin in his hand watching every limp Marie made like a cat watches a sparrow. He was waiting for his chance.

Marie put his plate of sausage and eggs on a tray, then moved to put a smaller plate of muffins on. She hated the way he watched her. He never ceased. He judged each thing she did, weighed out the choices she made, amused himself at her expense. It chafed like a pair of starched panties. She picked up the tray and made her way to the table. His jaw tensed as she approached.

She set the tray before him and then smoothed her white apron. "Coffee, Marie." He took hold of his napkin and shook it out before laying it across his lap. She nodded, then moved to get the coffee.

She put together another tray with a coffee carafe and a cup with a saucer. Valant liked for things to be restaurant quality. He liked to be served from a tray. Unfortunately Marie had no experience with that. She had never even eaten at the caliber of restaurant Mickey operated each day.

Marie heard something near the front door and she turned to look at Valant who now sat with a newspaper in hand and glasses on his face. He had lowered his paper and he looked at the door as well.

"Morning," Valant stated in a rather unfriendly voice. Cobby strolled to the table and looked around until his eyes met Marie's. He nodded to her and she dipped her head to him.

"Have a seat," Valant said as he turned a page of the paper. It was from several days ago. The last time Cobby came he had brought several. "You're just in time for Marie to make you breakfast."

"Oh, no thanks," Cobby said as he took off his jacket and draped it over a chair, then sat in the seat next to Valant facing the kitchen. Cobby's ribs were still sore and he sat stiffly.

"You're just in time for Marie to make you breakfast." Valant repeated without looking at him.

"Really, I'm…"

Valant lowered the paper to glare at Cobby. "You're just in time for Marie to make you breakfast."

"I'll have breakfast," Cobby said taking the hint.

"Vinnetti," Valant ordered.

Marie stepped from the kitchen and looked to the table. "Cobby just expressed his desire to eat something."

Marie looked to Cobby. He shrugged his shoulders. "I'll have a Belgium waffle with a mixed berry sauce on top and a side of bacon." Cobby folded his hands together on top of the table and looked at her expectantly. Marie's shoulders sagged.

More than likely Valant would use it as a teaching opportunity.

"Cobby," Valant's voice held a warning.

"I'll have what he's having."

"How do you like your eggs?" Marie asked with dread. If she didn't know how to make them, Valant would show her. Cobby read her expression.

"Runny?" Cobby asked. Marie shook her head slightly. "Over easy?" She shook her head again.

"Hard?" Another shake. "Just like Val's?"

Marie nodded her head and turned toward the kitchen. She had no idea what snotty yolks were called, other than gross. She was thankful that she had spent time with Cobby and he knew her well enough to judge her limitations. She took him a cup and saucer.

Cobby's eggs weren't just like Valant's, in fact, they were nothing like Valant's. But, she got them done along with the sausage, then she put it all on its own tray and carried it out to Cobby. He gave her a funny half smile as she set it before him.

"Thank you." He waited until she was done to reach for anything.

"Sit down, Vinnetti." Valant ordered as he took another bite of egg dredged sausage. Marie looked at him for a split second with apprehension before sitting. He then stopped to look at her. "Get yourself a cup and whatever you would like to eat."

Her eyes met Cobby's before she stood and moved to the kitchen. She put a muffin on a plate and then turned another cup upside down on a saucer. She went back to the table and sat quietly as she poured herself some coffee. She didn't bother with the sugar that sat in front of Valant, just sipped the bitter black brew.

Valant lowered his paper and looked at her intrusively before taking the sugar bowl from the tray in front of him and setting it in front of her. He then went back to his paper. Cobby's eyes moved between the two.

"This is good, Marie. Thanks for breakfast." Cobby's hand was paused mid-air between his plate and his mouth. When she raised her eyes to meet his she saw a look of sympathy there. Of everyone in the world, he knew how hard Valant was, how difficult to please. It was then she noticed how over-done his eggs were.

She flashed back to the night of the Christmas party and how firmly he had stood with her against the coming onslaught of bitterly jealous women. Of the way he looked at her the next morning at his mother's house. Cobby was as loyal a friend as God ever made. Marie's eyes glistened.

"Thank you," she whispered.

Later, when Marie had started the dishes, Cobby brought her his plate. He set it down next to the pile of other soiled utensils. She stopped him when he turned to leave. "Cobby."

He half turned to look at her. "Yeah?"

"Can I ask a favor?"

"I suppose."

She stepped closer to him. "In the apartment, behind the bureau, I have a few things, I'd... I'd appreciate it if you'd bring them to me," she said with uncertainty.

"Like what?"

"Nothing much. Just a picture and the bracelet the band gave me the night of the Christmas show. They are the only things in this world that are truly mine."

"A picture?" Cobby's brows knitted together for a moment. Marie nodded her head.

"I don't go to the apartment anymore since you aren't there, but I'll see what I can do."

*****

Marie was pretending to read again. It was a difficult process. The page turning had to be timed just right or he noticed. In her mind she had gone off to places unknown. The great urge of her mind to shift and take her to nightmares too unspeakable to be put into words was waning somewhat. As long as Valant was around she was fine. She was too scared to be anything else. But her nightmares didn't cease at night.

Her face was still extremely painful. The swelling had lessened and she was able to keep her eye open all the time now. When Valant cleaned her up and put salve on her a few minutes before, she felt his closeness like the Black Death. When he had finished, she asked if she could look in a mirror.

"No." It was a solid and an unyielding reply. She knew then, that even after the three weeks that had passed her features were still so grotesque he didn't feel she could handle the truth. Without another word, he stood and put things away.

So there she was. Pretending to read. She knew he probably knew, since she could feel his eyes on her every now and then. She disliked the feeling of hiding in plain sight, much like a rabbit would. After a time, he rose and left the soft circle of lamplight and headed towards the bar. He made very little noise and she couldn't tell what he was doing. He turned on the light above the bar.

Marie's head lifted in surprise when she heard the beginning notes to Glenn Miller's *Moonlight Serenade*. The sound changed the entire atmosphere of the darkened house. It was the arrival of a long missed friend. She closed her book and slipped off her shoes. Marie curled her legs beneath her and rested her head in her hand. She closed her eyes and drifted away, focusing only on the sound. The power of that music greatly eased her burden.

She felt him rather than heard him, and when she opened her eyes he stood before her with his hand extended to her. "Dance with me."

"No." She shook her head. The surge of pain and loss hit her full force. Dancing was no longer a part of her life.

He reached down and gently took hold of the wrist that held up her head. He pulled her arm to him and continued pulling until she stood. "Valant, you get your way every other time. Let me alone this once."

He said nothing in retort, just kept pulling her toward the radio that she didn't know Cobby brought to her that morning. Tears burned hotly as if she were facing the end of a good thing head on. Valant pulled her to him and his body heat seared. His palm slid a few inches just to the right of the middle of her lower back. He put her left arm around his neck, then took her right hand in his left.

"Don't make me do this," she whispered to him.

He forced her to move. He used his strength to manipulate her movements, and when that became too awkward for her, she began to move with her own, slow, choppy movements. She stared at his shoulder beneath his gleaming white shirt until her vision blurred. He just kept going, not stopping for the emotion that took hold of her. Memories hit her, one after another, and it occurred to her this must be the grieving process.

"It isn't the end, Vinnetti. Just the start of something else." His voice held no emotion, just a matter-of-fact quality.

She let out a sob. She didn't want something else. She wanted what she had before. "It's over. All that I was is gone."

"Not gone, just different."

"A great horse......" Her mind clung to that, although she wasn't sure where it came from.

He stood still and looked down at her. "Great horses may never run again, but they go on to other things, and no matter what, their greatness never changes or disappears. It lives inside them."

She looked into his eyes. "How did you go from John to Valant?"

"It was become Valant or die. Now you'll do the same. You'll transition to whoever comes next. That's just the way it is."

"Who's next? Who am I to become?"

"Time will tell, Vinnetti." He tilted his head slightly as he said this to her. His eyes held hers firmly. She got the feeling he was telling her something. "Dance, Vinnetti."

He moved again, this time Marie followed his lead. The radio started over with a new song. Jo Stafford's voice came out smooth and elegant, with a hint of regret. *Red River Valley* seemed somehow appropriate to the mood Marie was in. She looked up at her partner and found him already watching her.

"You're miserable," she stated flatly.

"So are you." This made her let out a small laugh.

"Well, at least I've affected less people."

"You think so, huh? I know a band leader near suicide over you."

"I know a lot of people just went ahead and died over you." Her voice was only slightly accusing. Valant made a strange noise.

"You're a merciless tease." Marie's jaw dropped at this granite sounding accusation.

"I am not a tease!" Marie's voice raising slightly.

"No? I think I know a few men who would disagree with that."

"Like who?" She asked caustically.

Valant spun Marie without her missing a beat, her eyes burning. "Like poor Cob. Mickey. That ridiculous band leader, Deano, that damn trumpet player that's always kissing you. More than likely that piece of shit you were engaged to, and....."

"What did you just say to me?"

Valant looked challengingly down at her. "I said that piece of shit you were engaged to."

"Well, let's not discuss pieces of shit we were once engaged to."

"Not valid, Vinnetti. Pick things that are valid."

"Don't call me that! And how isn't *she* valid?" Valant's eyes glittered. He stopped dancing long enough to reply.

"We were never engaged."

"Which brings me to my next point! Who the hell is she to spit on me!"

Valant shrugged. "Oh, I don't know. A good judge of character?"

"A good judge of character! Obviously not if she has been hanging around you all these years! You're both miserable! And you! All that drivel about, 'When haven't I been there when you needed me?' What garbage! Where were you when every Delano woman insulted me? Huh?! Poor Cob was the only one brave enough to stand up to that line of bitches. A line *you* were standing in!"

The corner of Valant's mouth twitched. "I still can't believe you snubbed me. After that lovely rendition of *Tu, Solamente Tu* you gave me for my birthday. I thought surely that was a confession of feeling." His voice was thick with sarcasm.

"What? Stop avoiding the point!"

"What is the point?"

"The point is….. the point is you left me to that pack of wolves!"

"We're back to that again." His voice was deep.

"That's the point!"

"I thought you were attempting to prove you aren't a tease."

"I'm done with you." Marie tried to move away but he held her firmly.

"I had nothing to do with what those women did. But, you being a Vinnetti, you decide to blame me for all your misfortune." He stopped moving and held her gaze. "You not giving an inch in the face of those women hurt more than anything I could have done. So, once again, Vinnetti falls in anyway, and comes out heads up."

Marie closed her eyes and pursed her lips tightly. "Don't call me that. I am not a Vinnetti."

"Oh, I'm not so sure. The longer I know you the more you act just like them. I would rather be a Vinnetti than a Barelli any day." She stared up at him.

"Well, I think I'd rather be a John than a Valant."

"Ok, you be John, I'll be Vinnetti." He raised a questioning brow at her when he finished speaking.

"No. You try being John, and I'll try being a Barelli." He let out a snort of disgust.

"You have never been a Barelli, but if you start, I will put a bullet in your head."

"Then that leaves you as John." She stated. She stood firm for a moment, then let out a chuckle. Valant took on a defensive look.

"What?" He said agitatedly. Marie smiled slightly.

"In all the times I have thought of you, feared you, hated you, you were The Dark Horse. It never occurred to me you have a first name."

*****

Marie lay in the stillness listening to the sounds of the night. She had been lying like that for some time, not moving nor sleeping, just waiting for the time to filter by. She assumed that Valant was sleeping, for she heard nothing from him after he had turned out the lamp on the table where he always read. He moved quietly across the floor to the couch he slept on and then the house had gone still.

In her mind, Marie had cleaned the entire house, fixed the several meals Valant taught her to make from scratch, and then she moved on to songs. She picked ones she had never performed, for the painful memories were nearly as bad as the nightmares. If she kept her mind busy long enough, the night would pass and she would be fine. But, it was hard to deny her body the rest it craved, although sleeping never gave it what it needed anyway.

She heard a noise near the kitchen and she stopped her breathing to listen. It had been so faint she thought she hadn't heard it. After a moment she heard a faint scrapping noise near her door and she moved slightly to see the outline of it. She thought she saw a movement there. She wondered briefly if Cobby had returned, but then dismissed the idea. He would not have come to check on her and Valant would have been up and speaking to him.

Someone stepped into the room. It was a short figure, and she didn't recognize the stature in her mind as anyone she knew. Her heart exploded into action, but she lay still, as if the muscles in her body wouldn't respond. She wanted to jump, to fight, to scream, but nothing happened. The figure moved toward the bed, and as it came to stand next to her she rolled over to look up at him. His face changed shapes and identities as he looked down at her, and she knew her mind had slipped again.

She tried to force out a scream for Valant, but only air came out of her mouth. She tried again as the man bent down to get closer to her. "Don't bother calling for him. He's already dead."

The man whose face still wasn't clear made a lunge for her and she moved into action. She let out a scream at the thought no one was going to hear her. The man took hold of her and held her arms down at her sides while she jerked and writhed furiously. He was trying to press her down onto the bed. She knew she had to avoid that with all she had.

"Stop fighting me." The man's voice blended with that of someone she knew and she fought harder against him.

"Marie. It's a dream!" Valant lowered his weight completely on top of her in an effort to subdue her struggling. He knew she couldn't breathe that way, but he had no choice.

"Valant!" she screamed.

"I'm here! Right here!" He said into her ear. "Just look at me."

She still moved and shook, but she forced herself to look at him. It took a while for her to recognize him, but eventually she did. She went limp and sweaty, still struggling for air. He released her, but remained over her in case she wasn't completely convinced who he was and decided to fight again.

"This is no way to live," she whispered into the blanket.

"No, it's not."

"I fell asleep. Damn I fell asleep." She still lay gasping for air, the sound of misery evident in her voice.

Valant moved to stand but she took hold of his arm. "Please don't leave me, John."

He froze and looked down at her.

"Don't leave me here. Alone. He said you were dead."

"Marie, even if they found us out here, and then somehow got into the house, I would never let them get to you. I would never let them touch you. Do you understand?" His voice was low and certain.

"Then do your damn job and stay close," she spat at him.

"I've been here night and day. Every second. How much more do you want?"

She looked deflated. "I want you to find some way to keep me awake permanently."

"I can't do that. You just have to sleep knowing I won't let anyone get you. Whatever you see isn't real."

"I hate sleeping in the bed. Let me sleep on the floor."

"No."

"What difference does it make!"

"I know where you are in the bed. If I need to get to you fast I'm not looking around for you."

"I don't need Valant, I need John." She looked at him steadily.

"I'm not sure he exists anymore. If he ever existed, and if he did, he was just a boy."

Marie didn't look at him, just crawled back up onto her sweat drenched pillow. Valant pulled the covers back up over her body. As he moved to leave she caught his arm again. "Don't leave me."

He sighed heavily. "You're asking me to get personal. I don't do that."

"All I'm asking is that you don't leave me. You're hard and indifferent, surely a few hours won't ruin that." She held him firmly.

He moved around the bed and lay down on top of the blankets. He looked at her and found her dark eyes watching him. He folded his arms across his chest and tensed. "Get some rest."

"Thank you, John."

"That's a first."

"What?" Marie asked as she raised her head to look at him.

"The first time you thanked me for any of this."

*****

Cobby returned at breakfast the next morning. He was quieter than usual. When he came in, he sat at the table next to Valant who was reading the same paper for the third time. Cobby didn't have time to bring him a new one. Cobby didn't take off his jacket either, just sat down and nodded to Marie who looked at him from the kitchen doorway.

When she turned and went back in, Valant asked Cobby if all was well as he turned the page of his paper. Cobby shrugged as he watched Marie bring out the coffee tray and three cups. Cobby took note of this but said nothing. Before it was only the necessary number, excluding herself.

Her face was an angry mat of red welts and scarring flesh. When she looked back at him over her shoulder, the left side of her face showed nothing about her had changed, but the right side was unrecognizable. She knew this, and anytime she was sitting she kept her hand discreetly over it. Valant still had all the mirrors either removed or securely covered, so Cobby wasn't sure to what extent she knew about her features. She kept her house dresses buttoned to the top, so he had no way of knowing how her chest was. But, judging by her face, it wasn't good.

Her eyes darted nervously, hovering only for a moment on anything she glanced at. The only thing she gave attention to was her coffee cup. Valant kept a watchful eye on her constantly. Cobby figured that was what caused most of the nervousness. Valant was not a man anyone wanted the full attention of. Cobby knew what it was like to be Valant's right hand, to feel the weight of Valant's disappointment, his punishment, his unpredictability. He could not imagine being trapped with him as Marie was.

Marie stirred sugar into her coffee, then set the spoon down silently on a saucer. Her right hand squeezed into a fist before coming to rest against her jawline, her fingertips barely touching the rim of her eye socket. She tried to look relaxed, but her constant shifting belied that. Valant watched her over his glasses. Unless Cobby missed his guess, it had been a long night.

The only sound in the room was the ticking of the clock as Valant slowly leaned forward and took Marie's hand away from her face. She looked at him with dread and misery, afraid of his next move. Valant laid her hand in her lap.

"Cobby and I already know what your face looks like. Don't try to hide it." Valant's flat eyes held hers for a moment before he looked back to his paper. Marie's right hand came up again but this time it laid against her neck, the awkward look in her eyes echoing the feeling in Cobby's own mind.

Without looking away from his paper, Valant asked, "Cobby, do you feel any different about Marie now that her face is grotesquely disfigured?"

Cobby looked sharply at Valant, shock in his face. He blinked a few times before answering, "Well, no. And I don't think........"

"So you would still find her an attractive female, worthy of the energy it would take to screw her?" Valant turned the page of his paper, but never looked away from it.

Cobby sat speechless, his cup hovering a few inches above its saucer. His mouth opened and closed several times as he tried to think of a way to respond to the damage Valant was doing.

"Come on. If you saw Miss Vinnetti here on the street for the first time, and recovered from the shock her face brings, would you take the time necessary to give a grateful girl a hump?" Cobby coughed discreetly.

"Her body still maintains the heart stopping figure it did several months ago, nothing changed that. Her empty head still rumbles around various ideas that are unworthy of mentioning, and, let's admit it, whatever fantasies you had about her before are easily achieved in the dark, where viewing her face and chest don't have to happen." Valant turned another page. A tear slid down Marie's cheek as her body trembled.

"In fact, why don't you take Miss Vinnetti here into the bedroom? Work out a few of those fantasies…"

"Shut up." It was barely a whisper, but it was enough to make Valant fold half of his paper down to look at her.

"Shut up." This time it was spoken a little louder. It passed through trembling lips as tears smeared across her cheeks. "Shut up!" she sobbed out. Her body shook with the effort it took to either restrain herself, or, force herself to be heard. Cobby wasn't sure which.

"You… miserable….. asshole!" Marie made a wheezing sound as she sucked in air between sobs. Valant's eyes fairly gleamed.

"I'm not nothing! I am something and I don't deserve *you*!" Her body shook with unspoken words that refused to untangle in her mind and come out her mouth. "I'm not stupid! I'm not ugly! This isn't my fault!" She stood to go and like lightening Valant had a hold on her arm. He set her roughly down on the chair again and got in her face. She flinched and cried harder.

"No, you're not nothing. No, you're not stupid. No, this isn't your fault. When are you gonna wake up and realize that what made you great, wasn't located on the outside of your body." He tipped his head as he continued. "When are you going to realize that nothing changed what made you great except you? You let it get to you."

Valant sat back in his chair and picked up his paper. He shook it out and replaced his glasses on his nose. He was calm as if nothing had happened. "Coffee, Marie."

Marie looked at him completely stunned. Tears still dripped intermittently, but something in her eyes changed. She was no longer looking at Valant with apprehension, but something closer to hate.

"Coffee, now." Valant barked.

She blinked a few times, then stood and took hold of the carafe in front of Valant. He grabbed her wrist as she did so. "Don't ever call me an asshole." The look in his eyes was cold and unforgiving. "And don't tell me to shut up." He glared at her a moment before returning to his paper in silence.

Marie didn't look at Cobby, just turned and walked into the kitchen. Cobby said nothing, merely took another sip of his coffee and wondered why he came out to see them. He couldn't deny that he spent his time in the city thinking about them and how they were getting along, but to come and witness it was a painful experience.

But, to Valant's credit, she was no longer catatonic.

Slowly but surely, life was coming back into her eyes, and although he was the worst person ever, Valant was making headway. Cobby considered a moment whether or not Valant said things like that to her all the time, or if he waited until Cobby was around to use as a set up.

"What's new?" Valant asked from behind his paper in a low voice.

"Arthur had an address. Checks out in New York, just up the street from where Marie lived," Cobby replied from behind his hand.

"Who is it?"

"A guy they called Plato. He was some kind of watchman. He moved in right after Marie, left immediately when she did. Didn't bother to pack his shit, just left."

Valant looked to the opposite page. "How many different addresses did she have in New York?"

"Two. Just two. I'm looking in to the first address where she lived alone for the first year or so. I wouldn't be surprised if she had a watchman there, too."

"Does Arthur think they were onto her before New York, or just when she got there?"

"I don't know. I think if she ends up with a watchman on her first address, then yes, they undoubtedly knew about her before. If no, then not until New York."

"Do you have a man in New York?" Valant asked.

"Yeah. A good one."

"You sure you can trust him? He's got no ties back there?"

"No, I sent him from here. He's good."

Valant folded a corner of his paper to look at Cobby. "Who is it?"

Cobby looked back at Valant. "My brother, Cleo."

Valant's brows knit together. "Would you rather I go myself? I'm pretty sure they know me."

Valant didn't hesitate. "Out of the question. Just remember what they'll do if they catch him."

"They won't. Cleo is very clever. He's in, and he's out."

Valant sighed. "I trust your judgement. And, you've gotten farther than myself."

They were silent a moment, listening to the sound of Marie in the kitchen, who had obviously composed herself and moved on to her task. "There's one more thing. That kid Marie was engaged to?"

"Yeah?"

"Can't find him. Cleo has been everywhere, nothing. The club said he left about two months ago to do a tour in Georgia, never came back."

"His fiancé?"

"Gone, too."

Marie came towards them carrying the coffee tray, her eyes still red, but a determined look in her eyes. She set the coffee down on the table and looked at Valant. "What do you want for breakfast?"

"The usual."

"Cobby?"

"The same, please."

Marie returned to the kitchen and pulled open the icebox and took out the sausage and eggs. She closed the door and reached up to the cupboard next to the icebox and took down a glass bowl to mix in. When she turned around, Cobby was standing there, watching her. She stopped short and looked at him with a confused expression.

Without saying anything, Cobby reached into his jacket pocket and pulled out a magazine. He handed it to her and said nothing, just looked in her eyes as he waited for her to take it. Marie did so, and it was then that she noticed something hanging from it.

Her bracelet. The tips of her fingers brushed over it and she pursed her lips to stop the emotion. "Thank you," she mouthed at Cobby. He nodded and walked away, leaving her staring at the magazine. Inside, she knew Alex's picture would reside as well. She thought about how thoughtful Cobby was to bring her a music magazine, but something about the cover looked familiar. Then she looked at the date. It was from months ago. It took her a moment to realize what it was.

It was the magazine Valant had given her on the street. When he had opened the car door and thrust it at her without a word. Valant was there, amongst the people her memories were comprised of; Alex, the band, and Valant. He was nowhere in her life, except everywhere.

*****

For Marie, each day was the same. She found in the monotony of habit a way to keep her mind clear of all the things that made her mind shift. She rose early each morning to make coffee, padding her way in her cotton nightgown past Valant who remained on the couch for sleeping. She started the coffee, and while it percolated she padded her way back to the bedroom to dress in one of her four house dresses. She brushed out her hair and pulled it back in either a bun of some kind or a braid, depending on her mood.

Then it was back to the kitchen to make breakfast. By then Valant would be dressed and sitting at the table waiting for her to bring his coffee, looking at some type of reading material. He read all the time. When he wasn't reading, he was working in his leather bound pocket ledger. Marie would bring his coffee, then get his breakfast. After which Valant would doctor her face and chest.

She spent the remainder of the morning doing laundry, cleaning around the house, or ironing. She would fix lunch, then in the afternoon finished whatever she hadn't in the morning. She also liked to bake. Valant wasn't much on eating baked goods, but Cobby loved her creations. Then she would sit and force herself to read a while before it was time to start dinner. After dinner, Valant doctored her face again.

The objects in the house became familiar after dusting them each day. Marie made up in her mind the stories behind each, the photographs, the books, the knick-knacks. Most of everything was very old, and she knew they had not been Valant's for long. The books were stacked neatly and in alphabetical order on the library corner shelves. The cross beams in the ceiling were fodder for her to ponder in her slowest times. Everything fit into an order made by someone else.

There weren't many photographs, but the ones on display were mostly of Valant and Mickey. A few she assumed were Valant's parents, and then several on the library shelves of a very young Valant and Margo at the beach. She was smiling wildly, but Valant was as serious as ever, just with no gray in his hair. For some reason each time she looked at the boy he had been she smiled. It was odd to see him in such a way, for she couldn't picture him at the beach the way he was as she knew him.

One afternoon while she dusted the library shelves a large book slipped from her hands. When it hit the ground, photographs and newspaper clippings scattered. Marie looked around in fear, but Valant was still smoking on the patio. She hastily picked up the contents, turning the pictures over in her hands and stuffing them back into the book. The pictures were of Mickey and a young woman, the caption on the back reading, "Mickey and Maryanne, 1940." There were several of what she guessed were Mexico, for the women sitting on Valant and Mickey's lap were very dark.

Again there were photographs of Valant and Margo at the beach, only in these they were kissing passionately, Margo's blonde hair ruffling in the breeze. Another was of Mickey on his wedding day, to a woman Marie didn't recognize. She must have been the loss Mickey couldn't bear to face again. A very young Valant stood next to an older man, both striking in their black suits. The back simply read "Julian."

Marie heard Valant moving outside, so she hurried in picking up the pictures and clippings. Then something caught her eye. Her own name. It was on a clipping from a newspaper, which one she couldn't tell, but the headline read, "Marie Barelli takes New York- Headlining at The Diamond." She didn't bother to read the article, just picked up another clipping. This one was from a New York City magazine, and her picture accompanied the article. She was on stage performing. She recognized the stage as that of The Diamond. A third clipping was recent, it announced that Marie Barelli, headliner for The Diamond in New York City, was coming to perform at The Lamplight Lounge on the lower east side.

Valant was moving toward the door. She crammed everything back in and put the book back on the shelf. Valant came in to find her dusting quietly, minding her own business. He moved away again and went into the kitchen. Marie's mind was jumbled.

*****

Mickey rose early and left the house long before the sun was on the horizon. He drove in the starlit stillness into town. He walked down the silent hallway to his office slowly, pausing to look at the pictures as he passed. He thought momentarily about the men who had founded the empire upon which he now sat. When he came to the picture of his brother Sam, he stopped and slid his hands into his pockets. His shoulders sagged a bit.

He remembered the jealousy he had felt for his older brother as a child. Sam could do no wrong. Sam made no mistakes. Sam was golden. Mickey, however, was nothing but trouble, and he constantly disappointed with his decisions. Only Julian understood him, and when Val came along, Mickey turned away from his own family. In truth, Mickey and Valant raised themselves with Julian's guidance. Mickey had respected Julian's authority, while he never respected his father's.

When Sam died at age 19, Mickey became center stage. But, at that time he was 14, and he already knew he wouldn't play second fiddle. He would gladly take the empire, his father be damned. Mickey knew his father harbored serious regrets about the way he had raised Mickey, but Mickey was beyond making amends. He wasn't that kind of person. He was full of hatred and bitter disappointment himself, so he turned his back on his father.

So, when it came to influencing Mickey, Georgio Delano used Valant. He would talk to Valant, and then Valant would slowly bend Mickey in the direction Georgio needed Mickey to go. It didn't always work. Not to mention the fact that Valant often refused to cooperate himself. Georgio sat without options most of the time. Julian had his own opinions on the subject, and had always warned Georgio about the way he treated Mickey as a boy, but wasn't heeded.

Mickey stood looking at Sam and a pang of regret hit him. He never knew Sam very well. The distance in their ages was great enough they never grew close, and Sam being the apple of his father's eye, he rarely bothered with Mickey. Besides, Valant was Mickey's brother. That was how he saw it. But, maybe, just maybe, had Sam lived, Mickey might have been home the morning Maryanne so desperately needed him. Maybe, just maybe, she might have lived. Mickey lowered his head. How deep that cut went.

Mickey looked into his office at the pale light just starting to brighten the room and saw his large desk, the same desk his father sat at. He envisioned his father sitting behind it, that same look of disappointment in his eyes. Then he saw Julian next to him, the expression in his eyes saying, "You're more than that." Mickey sighed. He couldn't face the pain in that room, for tucked in the top drawer was a picture of Maryanne. It had been so long, but he could still feel her body against his, her breath on his neck. He could remember the way her eyes lit when she saw him come into the room. No one had ever looked at him like that. Not before, not since.

He missed Valant. He felt naked without him.

He turned and walked back out onto the street. It was one of those rare times he was alone, having shrugged off the boys at the gate. He took in a deep breath, smelling the scent of the city in early dawn. The street was quiet. He looked up the street and noticed that the lights in Imelda's shop were on. He sauntered slowly up the walk and looked in the window. Imelda was there, putting a new gown on a mannequin in the window. He watched her work for a minute or two until she must have sensed him there. Imelda looked over her shoulder at him. Her brows knit together.

"Mickey?" she said without his hearing.

She left her work and went around to the front doors. She took out a key and unlocked them, then opened the door to look at him. He hadn't moved. He looked lost.

She tilted her head at him. "Mickey? What are you doing out here?"

He shrugged. "Well, come in here." She opened the door wider and moved aside to make room for him. He looked down at his feet, then slowly moved towards her.

"Are you alone?"

"Yeah."

"Everything ok?" He nodded. She looked at him disbelieving. She had seen that look on his father's face.

Although she knew Mickey would hate to know it, he and Georgio were much the same.

"Coffee?"

"Yeah. That would be good." She motioned for him to follow her into the back, then sat him on one of the couches. He sat and looked around at her beautiful items, most in the current room of the soft and underthings variety. Those sensual things never made Mickey nervous.

Imelda watched him with intermittent glances and tried to decipher his thoughts. Much like Valant, Imelda had learned to read Mickey. He was rather predictable if you knew his story. But, only a few left knew that story.

"You are out and about early today. How did you slip your entourage?"

"I told them to go to hell."

Imelda smiled to herself. "I see." She walked to him and handed him a cup of black coffee.

"Perhaps you needed time to yourself. You won't get much of that in the near future."

"Maybe."

"Where is Valant?"

"Still gone."

Imelda pursed her lips together. She knew well where Valant was. "Will he be back soon?"

Mickey shrugged his shoulders. "Don't know." Imelda nodded slightly.

She sat and looked at Mickey who wasn't drinking his coffee. His eyes wandered the room as he took in everything around him. Imelda hadn't been around Mickey by himself in quite some time. Imelda had his sizes for anything she might make for him. He no longer accompanied Eva when she came in like he did before they were married.

"How long until fatherhood?"

Mickey looked at Imelda. "About two months, I guess."

Imelda looked down. "You will be a fine father, Mickey."

"What makes you think that?" he asked, doubt in his face.

"You do everything opposite to what your father did. He wasn't a very good father to you." Mickey sighed. "And, I say this because, you will be a good father, as Eva won't be a good mother."

He looked at her steadily. Her lips were firm and serious, the small lines around her mouth deepening. Imelda rarely looked her age, but at that moment she did.

"What do I do?" he asked quietly.

"I suppose if you wait patiently, that answer will come to you without your helping it."

Mickey rested his elbow on the arm of the sofa. He pressed an index finger to his lower lip.

"What is really troubling you, Mickey? It can't be that your wife is less than perfect. Surely time has resolved you to that."

He pursed his lips together. "Nothing is as it should be."

Imelda smiled and looked down. "Your father said the same thing," she said softly.

Mickey scoffed. "Did he long to be free of my mother as I long to be free of Eva?" The sarcasm was evident in his voice.

Imelda grew serious. She looked away from him, aware that she should not have spoken.

Mickey looked reproachful. "I knew Imelda. Almost immediately. Of all the things I hated him for, you weren't on the list. If you had been, I would have thrown you out as soon as he died." Imelda nodded.

Tears were in her eyes as she looked up at him. "I loved him, you know. Even if he hadn't given me the shop, hadn't saved us from destitution, I would have loved him anyway." She sniffed slightly. "He was so good to me, after I thought that I could never love like that again. He was patient, and he gave me the kind of love only a man who understands loss can give." She paused a moment. "Georgio was not my first husband, nor did he replace him. He was Georgio, and I loved him as Georgio. When he died, I grieved for him just as I did my first husband. The losses were separate, but equally as devastating."

"What do I do with a woman I don't love?"

"Admit the mistake, and go on with it. She is the mother of your child."

*****

It had opened up a whole new realm of contemplation. Marie was not very comfortable with this train of thought. It meant admitting to a greater depth to The Dark Horse, and that was unpleasant. It was easier to think of him as nothing but a black hole which nothing filled or brightened. He neither had thought or feeling, and making life hell for those around him his only passion. She didn't want to admit he might be human.

It made pretending to read very difficult. She just kept glancing up at the book where it sat on the shelf, its contents tucked neatly away, like they had never been disturbed. She was filled with a great curiosity as to what else may pertain to her in that leather bound book of memories. But at the same time, she was filled with dread to look.

He never looked at her with anything more than indifference, so she concluded that it had been her voice that drew him. It seemed surreal to think back on the times he had come to listen to her sing at her father's club. Could the talent of a nineteen year old girl draw a man nearly twice her age? It seemed so. But then, he seemed determined to prove she was somehow connected to Vinny.

Marie began to watch him as closely as he watched her. His actions weren't out of the ordinary, and he never treated her with anything beyond annoyance. She knew he felt her a total waste beyond her performing abilities. He made that clear repeatedly. He must have a good reason for keeping her around.

She wondered if he were suffocating in the monotony as she was. Valant was used to a life of continual action, and being trapped with a woman far away from the city must be maddening for him. But, true to form, he never showed signs of listlessness, boredom, or angst, as she often felt. She could never guess at anything he was thinking. Unless he got that firm look in his eye, and then she knew he was about to draw blood, and the cut would run deep.

She had never known a man who, unlike her father's approach, would take what he knew was a raw emotional nerve, and then crush it with pliers. He did it repeatedly. He could read her thoughts, then take them and use them to grind her down. It was worse than what her father did, which was to just use his fists. At times she thought of the words that Valant himself had used to describe his own life with Julian.

There were times when I didn't think I would survive him.
Marie felt the same way about Valant.

She also doubted what Imelda had told her. That she should take the help Valant offered her then get on with her life. She wasn't so sure there would be anything left of her when he was through "helping" her. In her own heart she felt a hardening. Like a small stone was starting to form there, and her ability to openly show kindness was going. He was slowly hurting her to a point that she felt she could no longer take anything from anyone. There was not a subject Valant wouldn't use.

He pestered her relentlessly about Alex. Made snide comments about their sex life, which didn't exist for Marie was old fashioned and thought a wedding was near. It embarrassed her so to think that Valant would force his way into such matters, so she kept her mouth clamped and refused to let him get to her.

He called her Vinnetti, Vinnetti's lover, Vinnetti's illegitimate daughter, and his prostitute. Anything he could think of. She turned her back on him and braced herself, her hands trembling, her breath ragged. She hated him. She wanted him to die. Not just any death, but a horrible grisly one.

He made remarks about her looks. Insinuated she was unintelligent. Pushed her every moment.

Then one day, he pushed too hard.

It was after a particularly deafening lunch of silence. He told her it was unacceptable after she had worked on it the better part of the morning. He'd thrown his napkin onto his plate and indignation flared in Marie. She bowed her head and stood to gather up the plates when he said it.

"I guess I should have just raped you and left you in an alley when you were nineteen. That was the best there was ever gonna be of you." She glanced at him out of the corner of her eye to see him sitting with his head cocked and an eyebrow raised.

She found it no longer hurt. A rage inside exploded so fiercely that it lit her eyes with hatred. It burned down the length of her arms and just as she had to restrain herself from hitting her mother that last day so long ago, she forced herself not to lunge at him with a knife.

His eyes flickered.

"It would have been so easy. You would have been too chicken shit to fight back. All I would have had to do was take you outside, drag you into the dark, press you up against the wall. No doubt spreading your legs would have been easy, too, the fear making them limp. All that would stand between us was one button..."

In one swift movement, Marie swept the stack of plates on the table to the floor with an ear splitting crash. The echo of shattering glass reverberated on the wood paneling long after the breakage stopped. She snatched up a knife that lay before him and thrust it at him as he jumped to the side. He didn't quite clear it as the blade punctured his arm just above the elbow in the muscle. She reached for his coffee cup without looking and took hold of it. He was still taking hold of her hand that thrust the knife when the coffee cup shattered against his head. When he was momentarily stunned she back handed him as hard as her arm would swing.

In a flash of movement he took hold of her body and trapped her arms at her sides. She let out a scream into his face and squirmed to get away. His eyes lit furiously with something she couldn't fathom and he clenched down on her with all of his strength. Her lungs were crushed and no air could expand them.

"It is the meek who suffer wrath." His voice was deep and rigid.

He released her then and moved away. She covered her face with her hands when she saw the mess that she made. Shards of glass littered the floor and food remnants as well. Valant moved off to the bathroom to survey the damage done to his arm, blood trailing down his sleeve and covering the back of his hand.

She kept an eye on him.

She could not read him very well, nor his intentions at any given moment. She kept herself braced for anything he might choose to say or do. When she looked at him her eyes were hard and no emotion could be seen there. She didn't speak unless spoken to, and when it came time to serve a meal, she did not wait for his approval, merely ate her food.

He still kept watch on her, but his eyes had changed.

At night Marie would pull out her picture of Alex and study his face in the pale light. Something inside her heart went from grieving about him, to thinking of what she would say if she ever saw him again. In Marie's soul something burned bright. She lay long into the late hours staring at the ceiling clenching her jaw. She began to replay that night in the alley, looking at every image, everything that was done to her, to Deano, to Cobby. She saw Deano lying in a deepening puddle of his own blood, reaching for her, telling her to run.

Her hands and arms trembled from the tenseness that ran down them. The muscle in her groin ached in the morning from the rigidity in her legs all night. There were times she would see Scar Face so plainly coming at her with a knife. She would hold his image in her mind then rise from her bed and spend a good ten minutes driving her fist into her pillow repeatedly. She breathed fire from the anger stoking up within her.

Valant didn't have to openly accost her anymore. Just one well-placed comment set her blood pumping. She would look at him with an indignation that was rivaled only by the acid in her veins. Cobby sat in awe struck silence now when he came to visit. She had asked for cigarettes some time back, and now he never forgot to bring them for her. Valant threw them out if he found them, so he hid them in locations all over the house.

Cobby watched Valant study Marie, waiting for an opportunity to bait her, but few opportunities arose. She was respectful, but very few things hurt anymore.

Late one night, Valant stood in the shadows next to the library window, watching Marie out on the grass. Her white cotton nightgown pressed against her body in the breeze, her hair floating and shining in the moonlight. She looked out into the sky for a long time, her bare feet getting cold in the soft grass. She held something in her hands and after a while, she lifted it up to look at it one last time.

She then flicked the lighter and Valant could just make out the form of a piece of paper and that it was a picture. She lit the edge of it, then held it in her finger tips as it began to burn. Just before the flame reached her flesh, she let it go and watched as the flame floated on the breeze a moment before disappearing. She remained there a moment breathing heavily, then tipped her head back and closed her eyes.

Valant pressed a thumb to his lips as he watched her with intensity.

Her face was healing. It only hurt when she applied pressure to it, and even then it was something she did to keep the fire burning, to remind herself of a debt she was owed.

A debt *she* was owed.

It was not the same as owing someone else. A man out there would pay for what he had done, what he had ordered done to her. She saw his face, his devil smile, heard the sarcasm in his voice each time she recalled their meeting on the street. Danny G. She would set herself free. He would pay his debt, and so would she. She thought constantly about how she would do it. It became an ambition.

She moved restlessly one afternoon dusting an already spotless house. She was beginning to chafe at the monotony of her responsibilities and wondered how long Valant intended on wearing her away like this. They rarely spoke, but he watched her like a hawk, a giddy gleam in his eyes when she caught him. She would narrow her eyes in return with a subtle, *go to hell,* written within their brown depths.

She stopped to look out the window into the green yard at the row of lilacs that blocked her view. She ran the feathers of her duster through her fingers as she tilted her head to study the contrast of the blue of the sky against the green of the bushes. Her eyes followed the line until they reached the roof of the shed and the beauty of the contrast ended.

The roof of the shed.

She had seen it before, but had never really stopped to think what might be in it. It was always one of those things that just was. Never really a curiosity trap. She had studied everything else that was a staple until surely her eyes had worn a hole in those objects. But not the shed.

It was the same gray color as the house, its roof the common color of shingles. Nothing about it screamed out its uniqueness, but it caught her attention like nothing else had in days. Valant sat behind her, his glasses perched on his nose in familiarity, reading a book he pulled off the library shelf.

Marie ran the wooden handle of the duster down her cheek. "What's in the shed?"

Valant sighed and without looking up from his book said, "That's where Mickey and I take beautiful young women we pick up off the street and sexually torture them."

"Sounds lovely."

In a low and husky voice Valant returned, "Want to see it?"

Marie turned to look at him, annoyed. "If that were your intention you would have done it by now."

Valant looked up at her with mock surprise. "Well. Marie Vinnetti forms her very own opinion." He tossed his book on the table beside him.

Marie looked down her nose at him.

He removed his glasses and set them on the book.

"You want to see the shed? I'll show you the shed."

He walked to the closet by the front door and retrieved a key while Marie stood where she had been, watching him. He stopped at the front door and looked back at her. "Well, you coming, Vinnetti?"

She thoughtfully set down her duster and walked to the door. He stood looking down at her as she walked past him and through the door he held open for her. He watched her out of the corner of his eye as they walked to the shed. Something about the way he watched was challenging. She stared back resolutely.

He bent and unlocked the handle, then pulled the door open in one swift movement. Marie peered into the darkness as disturbed dust sifted out. It was nothing but a black hole, but as her eyes adjusted she saw something draped in canvas near the back. Valant slid his hands into his pockets and studied her face. She raised a brow as she looked at him. Nothing in his face changed.

She moved forward to the canvas. It covered a long rectangle and Marie figured it must be some kind of car. Valant came up beside her, and his arm brushed hers as he took hold of the canvas, slowly pulling it off. It came free and fell in a heap just before the bumper and Marie stood in awe of what she saw.

She moved past Valant, who watched her expression with curiosity. Marie gazed down at the wonder and held her hand just an inch or so above the pearl white paint that gleamed in the low light of the shed. Valant slid his hands into his pockets. Marie moved slowly up the side of the car, following the contours, bending to peer into the window of the interior just below the soft top. It was beige and the tandem seats sat close together, the shifter on the floor between.

"Jaguar XK120 if I am not mistaken?" She asked as her hand continued to follow the contours around the back of the car, still without making contact.

"Ummhmm," was all Valant replied. He moved to get a full view of Marie moving around the opposite side.

"Coupe convertible. Named the XK120 because it tops out at 120 miles per hour. Hails from Great Britain." She was talking softly and to no one in particular. "She's a rare beauty. Made just after the war in '46. Very few came out of production that year."

Marie came around the front of the car and stood looking down at it. When she glanced up at Valant he was watching her with one eyebrow raised. She smiled softly at his expression. She moved around him again to take another look through the window at the interior.

"Are we gonna drive it, or make love to it?" His voice was low and deep.

Marie looked up at him in surprise. "Isn't that against the rules?"

"What rules?" He walked to the door she was bent looking in, and as she stepped aside he opened the door for her deliberately. After she slid into the interior, she looked around her as Valant came around and got into the driver's seat. He studied her a moment before putting the key into the ignition.

It roared to life almost immediately. A thrill surged through Marie to think that she was about to make a form of get away. Valant put it into gear and eased the car out of the shed into the daylight. The brightness of the sun reflected off the immaculate white of the car. It purred softly as it moved up the small graveled lane beneath the trees and shrubs next to the yard.

Valant took it easy, going at a turtle's pace up the lane and onto the highway. Marie was seeing things she had only looked at from the confines of the house. Everything looked different from the inside of the car. It smelled of leather and shed, but sounded like a race car in disguise, just waiting for the chance to fly.

"Can you drive, Marie?"

She looked at him and innocently replied, "A little."

When hitting the pavement he stopped the car, got out and put the top down. The sun instantly warmed Marie's face and arms. Between the beautiful day and the car, she felt radiant in her simple red house dress.

Valant opened her door and held out his hand to her. She just looked at him for a moment, then said, "Are you sure you trust me?"

"I'm positive I don't trust you. Are you going to drive or not?"

She smiled as she took his hand. She looked back at him, the good side of her face looking cunning in the light. His mouth twitched. He didn't get her door as it was already open, and he thought it best not to leave her unattended in a running car. It was possible the last sight of her he'd have was nothing but his car driving away.

He stretched his arm across the back of the seat, looking at her coldly as she got in and gave him a wicked smile.

"How do I make it go?" She asked unknowingly.

"You have to put it in gear. Like I did. Then push that big pedal to give it throttle."

"How do I make it stop?"

He looked at her doubtfully. "Push the smaller pedal to the left."

She reached under the steering wheel. "Not with your hands, stupid."

She narrowed her eyes at him, then handed him one of her heels. As she handed him the other she said, "Here, stupid."

He arched a brow and looked out the windshield, put her shoes on the floor beneath him, then returned his arm along the back of the seats. "Put it in gear."

"Like this?" She asked as she smoothly executed the maneuver and the car rolled easily down the pavement.

"Now move it up another gear." Valant said.

Marie turned and gave him a mischievous grin. She hit the accelerator and the soul of the car surged to life. Like a kindred spirit, Marie shifted easily at the sound of the engine. The speedometer climbed steadily as she moved through the gears effortlessly. The wind threaded through her hair and pulled several pins out.

Marie took a deep breath and tipped her face into the wind. She laughed at a memory of Vantino who had loved speed more than he loved any woman. It made his eyes light, his face beam with excitement. He had taught her to drive, starting back with Vinny's Sunday car and that marble lawn statue. He had kept at it until Marie was one of the best defense drivers he had ever met.

It was Vinny, however, who had taken the time to introduce Marie to the world of automobiles. They looked at magazines, perused rare dealers together. Although he had never given her a car of her own, he made sure she knew everything she could about them. Vinny had not been aware the depth of her education from Vantino, however. But, as with most things with Vantino, Vinny didn't know the lengths he went to in an effort to get to know Marie. She was a rare gem.

The speedometer met with ninety, and Marie laughed out loud. Her eyes left the road to meet with Valant's. He had a strange expression on his face, his eyes light with what? Possibly amusement? The corner of his mouth twitched again. Marie laughed harder.

As the miles dissolved into bliss, Marie pushed the car harder, slowing only for corners and road changes, taking Valant's directions. Her face became a mask of delight, her eyes shining. Valant only glanced at the road now, having traveled it before. His contemplation now for something else.

He directed her around the city to a smooth highway that ran next to the ocean. She showed no fear, and passed slower vehicles without slowing the brisk pace of one hundred thirteen miles per hour. Marie took risks of passing without ample room, but not once did she falter in her confidence, nor did the expression leave her face.

She was at home in possibility.

The terrain of the sea shore began to change as the road left sea level and climbed up the face of the rock cliff. Marie took the switchbacks with ease and slowed only when necessary, which was becoming more often. The road wound until the ocean was far below. There was several places where the cliff fell away just beside the asphalt, and the ocean lay hundreds of feet beneath. At last Valant moved his arm and asked her to slow. By now the sun was far west. The late afternoon light was a deep golden color.

"There's an overlook up here, pull in."

The engine again purred softly as Marie turned off the pavement and the tires crunched on gravel. She stopped the car and stared out to the western sea and the sky so clear above it. The smile was gone from her lips as she sat regarding the beauty of it. After several minutes, Valant reached over and shut off the ignition, then rested his hand on his knee.

Marie's face was set in lines of contemplation, but when she turned and looked at him, she seemed to remember where she was and gave him a self-conscious smile, her black hair falling across her face. She looked down and away, back out to the ocean. Valant softly opened his door and slid out. He moved around the front of the car and came to her side, then opened her door as well, holding out his hand to her. She took it and stood.

She walked to the edge and scrutinized the sight below. Waves crashed into rock and white walls of sea water exploded with the tide. The sound of it was still immense from such a great distance, so she imagined it was deafening to be near it. She wrapped her arms around herself as she contemplated it, the fall, the impact. As if he read her mind Valant appeared beside her.

"You're not going to do something foolish are you?"

She looked at him, nothing but seriousness in her features. "Would it matter if I did?"

"I think you know it would. There is more out there waiting for you than this."

After a time the height made her eyes blurry and she felt almost dizzy as she gazed out at it. So, she turned away and went to stand next to the car. Valant moved with her, and as she began to move for the passenger side he stopped her.

"Who taught you to drive like that?" His face full of deep suspicion.

Marie looked down and away from him, then said softly, "Robert "The Heart" Vantino."

He slid his hands into his pockets and clenched his jaws together. She smiled a sad smile, then let out a small laugh. Marie turned and kept walking.

"Why?" His voice was hard.

Marie stopped and shrugged her shoulders before turning to him. "I don't know. Maybe he couldn't find the right woman, so he thought he'd train up his own."

"Bull shit."

Deep hurt filled her face and she brushed her hand across her scars. "I'm not who you want me to be, John. You want something from me I don't have to give."

"Then tell me the truth," he stated flatly.

"The truth." She laughed softly again, then looked at him with despair in her eyes. "I had a little brother." She stopped short and looked down. She tried again. "I had a little brother. He was just two when I was seven. He was male; I was not." She looked out to sea again.

When she looked back at him, the despair had been replaced with regret. "I was born female, the only one of nine children. I was not loved, I was not wanted. So, when he pulled away from me one afternoon and ran in front of a truck, I took the blame." Images of the scene flashed in her mind. She heard her own screams and that of her brother, Gabe. Then she saw her father and mother.

Marie covered her face with her hands. "My mother took his broken dead body into the kitchen, my father took me to the bedroom. He took off his belt and hit me until I couldn't see anymore. Then he drug me by the hair into the closet and locked me there for days." She looked ashamed.

"When he wasn't passed out, he came and beat me all over again." She raked an impatient hand through the hair the wind had freed from her bun. "My oldest brother tried to stop him, but he got the same treatment. So, when he could, my brother went to the only person he could think of. Vinnetti; whom he was working for at the time. My brother never came back after that, but that one move saved my useless life.

"The next I saw was Vinnetti, who had decided, for what reason I don't know, to come and check things out. Somehow, he found me in that closet, picked me up and took me home. I am no relation to him. He is neither my father, nor my lover. Just a man who helped me when I needed it. If we still had a connection, I wouldn't be here with you now." She stood looking at him across the car. His hands were still in his pockets, but his body had gone rigid, his eyes the cold flat blue she was most familiar with.

As she opened the passenger side door, her hair fell in her face again. She brushed it away, and as she did she glanced at him. He was standing there, looking at her, his face a granite mask, but something in his eyes made her shiver slightly. She stopped.

"Does this mean you're done with me?" She asked, a casual acceptance of his whim.

"I already told you. When you die isn't up to me." He said it matter-of-factly, so she wasn't sure if he was referring to God or Mickey.

Marie looked at him dejectedly over the interior of the car. "Who are you? Really?"

"Just a man. Formed and built to be what you see."

"Why are we out here?" Marie asked quietly.

Valant shrugged his shoulders. "Taking a drive."

"Then let's get on with it."

She moved into the car and gently closed her door, but Valant remained standing, looking down at her for a moment. He slowly opened his own door and slid in next to her. She didn't meet his eyes, just kept gazing out to sea, her hand pressed to her chin, her fingers resting lightly on her lips. The look of shame was still evident.

"Vantino was the only person who ever told me it wasn't my fault," she spoke faintly. "He must have told me a hundred times." She sighed lightly as she lowered her hand. "I still don't believe him." A tear fell down her cheek and she impatiently brushed it away. She closed her eyes to see the many faces of those whom she had loved in her life that were no longer present.

"My parents died when I was twelve. I had an aunt that took my sister, but she wanted nothing to do with me. Mickey and I had been friends since grammar school, so at the funeral Julian Delano was the only man who stood and agreed to take me. That's how I came to be who I am."

Marie looked at him for a long moment, studying his sharp features, taking in the bare arms beneath his rolled up white shirt. He wore no jacket, and Marie realized that this was as relaxed as she had ever seen The Dark Horse. It was hard to picture him as a little boy in grammar school. He took his turn staring out at the ocean.

"What did you want to be when you were a boy?" Marie asked.

Valant sniffed before he turned to look at her in all seriousness. "A policeman. Mickey and I both."

Marie began to laugh as she covered her face with her hand. Valant remained watching her reaction. "What did you want to be?"

She quit laughing and returned his serious gaze, the loose hair falling in front of her eye again. "I gave some solemn thought to being a nun."

A strange rumble came from Valant's chest as he turned the ignition and slid the car into gear. "I guess they call that victim of circumstance." His voice full of irony.

*****

Cobby made his way across the dark parking lot outside the warehouse. He had been trying to keep things quiet since he traveled alone most of the time. He just couldn't seem to find someone whom he wanted to have with him. Taking Martin had ended in disaster. So, when he could he went alone, the rest of the time he was usually with Mickey. It seemed odd, how Mickey said Cobby couldn't replace Valant, yet Cobby was the only one he wanted close. Things had gotten to the point where neither of them ever wanted to be recognized.

Cobby came up to the side entrance and spent some time listening to see if he had been followed. He now knew why Valant did so much work in the dark alone; it was far easier to remain unseen. When he felt the coast was clear, he opened the warehouse door silently. He peered into the dimly lit expanse that had once been full of crates of booze. Now, however, Mickey moved product so fast the warehouse was rarely full anymore.

Cobby cautiously moved through the door and looked around. He found Tony standing next to a table, clip board in hand, reading something written there. More than likely the ship dates for product from Mexico.

"Hey, Tony."

Tony looked up in surprise. "Hey, Cob. I didn't hear you come in."

"Which is probably a good enough reason to keep the door locked."

Tony shrugged. "I knew you were coming."

"Not a good enough reason to not lock the door. What's going on?"

"Just moved a shipment out, literally about twenty minutes ago."

"That's why it looks so bare."

"Yeah. Ah, Mickey's got so much shaking these days I can't keep him stocked. Last round I bought came from damn near South America. That takes too long to get the booze here, then redistributed. But, one hates to stray from suppliers. You just never know who's on the other end with a new one these days."

Cobby nodded. "Had any problems?"

"No. But I'll tell you Cob, I don't like the rumors I'm hearing."

Cobby tipped his head back in anticipation. "Oh yeah? What have you heard now?"

Tony shook his head. "This Underground business. Not that I'm rooting for Vinnetti, but I've heard they've got him driven into hiding. They've been burning his holdings right and left. Not to mention killing any of his guys they catch. Vantino's executing anyone with a possible connection to the

Underground. That isn't stopping it. My question is, if they get Vinnetti ousted, how long till they come after us?"

Cobby looked thoughtful. "Well, they have a long way to go to get him ousted. If anything I know about Vantino is true, he's a force to be reckoned with. But all the same, keep the damn door locked. And, maybe, know your escape routes, just in case."

Tony nodded. "Alright."

"Beyond that all is well?"

"Yep. Making money faster than Mickey can spend it."

Cobby let out a snort. "It helps his delightful wife is in her seclusion just now."

Tony chuckled.

"I'll be back in a day or so. Call me if you need me."
Cobby turned and left the warehouse, evaporating into the dark. The lights in the warehouse had been dim, but enough to make seeing in the dark very difficult.

Cobby left his car about a block away, not wanting to get too close if he were being followed. It was hard to be so cautious all the time, especially without Valant. He turned a corner and could see his car sitting in the street, the pale embers of light from lamps up the street glinting lightly off the windshield. Cobby stopped.

Cobby had been silent and he was glad. He could just make out the shadow of someone leaning against the hood of the car. A tiny red flare indicated a cigarette. Cobby reached into his jacket and pulled out his gun.

"No need for that," came a low reply.

Cobby stood without saying anything. The hair on the back of his neck stood rigidly and his stomach burned as adrenaline coursed. He doubted this man was alone.

"You're good, Cobbinelli. Far better than I gave you credit for." Cobby recognized the voice as that belonging to Vantino himself. Fear surged as he remembered the fight that ensued the last time they met. He dreaded another beating like that.

Vantino took a long, last drag on his cigarette, then threw it down and crushed it out with his foot. "It's hard isn't it? Making your way in the blackness, then having the courage to turn the key in the ignition. Wondering all the while if the blast will hurt, or if it will be over in an instant. Makes a man reluctant to drive anywhere."

Cobby understood what he was saying. He had these same fears on nights like these. "I suppose."

"Well, rest easy. I've been here since you left. I know nothing has happened to your car. Not having done something myself, naturally."

"What do you want, Vantino?" Cobby asked in a low voice, straining his ears for the sound of other men who would be closing in on him.

"Did you give him my message?"

"Yes. Can't say it made much difference."

Vantino stood. "Well, I guess I want the same thing I wanted last time we spoke. Is she alive?"

Cobby hesitated as Marie's image appeared in his mind. "Yes, she's alive."

"Where is she?"

Cobby snorted. "I really don't know why you bother asking."

Vantino slid his hands into his pockets. "Well, because I'm offering you the one easy out I allow. And, because I think you are reasonable, unlike Valant."

Cobby sighed. "I won't tell you where, but I can tell you she is safe. I can also tell you Valant will die before he lets anyone get to her."

"That doesn't make me feel better."

"I think she is better off with him guarding her and you and I out here keeping the line pushed back. Wouldn't you say?" Cobby asked.

"The line is getting blurry."

"Well, keep on killing. Eventually they are bound to take a step back." Cobby paused a moment. "Where is her fiancé?"

Vantino shrugged. "I watched him myself for a time in New York. He was a loose end she didn't need. So, I beat the shit out of him and told the crying little pussy he wouldn't see her again. Problem solved. Marie needs a man, not an invalid. Not to mention I did him a favor since The Underground was already following him. I told him he best spend some time elsewhere."

"Well, I guess that proves my theory. The Underground was on to her in New York."

Vantino clicked his tongue. "Yes, I guess it does. Nonetheless, I don't think Marie will appreciate that I ran her boy off. Even if it was for her own good."

Cobby took a moment to think on how true those words were. "Why? Why not let her have him? What difference did it make?"

Vantino shrugged. "Marie doesn't get to choose her path."

Something burned in Cobby at hearing this. His jaw clenched and in his mind he saw the half-picture that had rested behind the bureau in the apartment. He thought of the young woman who had so bravely asked him to get it for her. Who had been with him the last time he saw his family, including Cleo, whom he had only spoken to on the phone since then. Cobby thought of himself.

"What now, Vantino? Is this where I beat the shit out of a couple of your guys? Maybe save myself some trouble and start shooting in a circle?"

"Afraid to take another beating, Cobbinelli?" Vantino's voice was condescending.

The explosion up the street sent a blast of hot air and compression past Cobby and Vantino that hit like a freight train. Instinctively Cobby turned his body away from it as the entire street lit like the coming of the sun. Vantino bent to hide behind Cobby's car. When it passed, Cobby shielded his eyes as he looked back up the street.

The warehouse was burning. He moved toward it, but Vantino caught his arm.

"It's too late boy. And no doubt they've stayed to view their handy work. Let's go." Vantino pulled Cobby back as he thought about the mere minutes that had passed since he himself had been standing near the bomb blast. He thought of Tony, and hoped that the man had gone, not staying to die a horrible death.

"Let's go." Vantino pulled Cobby insistently, and finally Cobby turned unconsciously moving to the driver's side of the car. Vantino was already sitting in the passenger side as Cobby slid in.

Cobby looked at the older man beside him and as he turned the ignition asked, "Who are they?"

"They'll be you, if we don't get them stopped."

Cobby flipped his black Lincoln around and headed back up the street and away from the fire. He hit the accelerator and ignored the stop sign. "Where's your car?"

Vantino looked at him with a firm expression. "I'll buy new one."

Cobby looked at him. Vantino broke into a grin. "I haven't lived this long cause I'm stupid."

"That means you're at my mercy." Cobby edged a little more on the accelerator. Vantino reached into his jacket and pulled out his gun, then aimed it at Cobby.

"I trust you." Then Vantino started to laugh. "Laugh, boy. Laughing about horror is the only thing that makes it bearable."

Cobby thought about the strange turn of events. How he was currently running with an icon he had only heard about until Marie. Then he took into consideration himself, and how far he'd come since his father died. He chuckled softly.

"Ahh. That a boy. That damn Dark Horse must have a cob jammed up his ass. Takes himself and everything around him too seriously." They laughed for a moment.

"I'm not taking you downtown. Your guys will gun us both down if they see this car. And what the hell are you doing out alone?" Cobby questioned.

"Oh, just inquiring about an old friend." He paused a moment, the gun never wavering. "How bad did they cut her up?"

Cobby was silent. His face drooped into a grim set of lines and he gripped the wheel. Vantino sighed wearily. "That bad."

"Valant really is doing the best he can."

"He better, or I'll kill everyone that was ever important to him. Cut up that pretty Margo he's always kept around."

"I'm not sure that is real motivating. That bitch needs cut up. I think even he knows that."

"I could cut you up. Surely that would sting."

Cobby shrugged. "You do what you have to."

"You are far more than I gave you credit for, Cobbinelli."

"So you've said."

Vantino cocked his pistol and put it against Cobby's head. "Take me downtown."

"That won't work, Vantino. You shoot me in the head and you die in the crash."

Vantino let out a maniacal laugh. "You assume I have a fear of death. No such luck. But, you being young, I'm sure you have something you think you want to live for."

"This will end in death for me either way."

"You have no faith in me, Cobbinelli."

"Why should I?"

"Because I could have killed you any number of times over the years, but I let you go. I will kill you now, if you don't do what I say."

"Well, that's nice. I mean it really is, but, we got us a tail. So you might save the bullet you meant for me for whoever is in that car." Cobby kept taking glances at his rear view mirror. Vantino kept his gun on Cobby's temple as he looked back at the car gaining ground on them.

"Oh shit." Vantino laughed loudly. "This is something. They got us both in one place. Lucky bastards. Put it in the floor, boy!"

The warehouses and alleys began whip by as Cobby reached eighty-seven miles an hour. Vantino had taken the gun away from Cobby's head and was watching out the back window. He looked at Cobby.

"I say we get a look at them."

Cobby looked over at Vantino. He was met with complete seriousness. Cobby let off the accelerator. It occurred to him that it might be Vantino's men in that car, but as they passed under a street light he could see that the car following them wasn't the usual variety of Vantino's.

"How do I know those boys aren't yours?"

"How do I know they aren't yours?" Vantino fired back. Cobby's mouth drew into a grim line. "Trust me boy. I came to you alone."

It appeared Cobby had no choice but to trust him, and, at least Vantino had taken the gun away from his head. That seemed promising.

The car slowed and they came up from behind. Vantino had reached behind his lapel and pulled out another pistol. He handed it handle first to Cobby. "Keep this. Use it if you need to, otherwise I might need it." He rolled down the window as Cobby braced the wheel, his knuckles turning white. He took deep breaths to slow his heart. The form of the car came into his peripheral vision on the right side of his own vehicle. He looked over to see Vantino stretch his arm out the window and fire, hitting the windshield of the other car. The car swerved only slightly.

"Get down!" Cobby just had time to slouch in his seat before a bullet broke out the window on his left. He managed to keep the car going straight, but let into the accelerator again. They were dead even with them now, and Cobby looked up the road to see nothing but a straight shot. He took a chance to look over past Vantino into the pursuing car that now locked with them, speed for speed, maneuver for maneuver.

The car was full. Two in the front, two in the back. "Shit, Vantino." Cobby heard Vantino's gun fire again, felt another bullet go past his head. They were gunning for him in an effort to stop the car. Possibly, they were interested in Vantino. If they caught him, what a great coup that would be. Cobby glanced at the street ahead of him again. A car was coming at them, but it swerved onto the sidewalk in order to get out of the way.

Cobby looked over again as a bullet left a hole in his windshield in front of him. Vantino had obviously hit the front passenger, who now sat clutching the side of his face, blood running out between his fingers. The driver was an ugly man, his face scarred clear up past his hairline, his lips nothing but gnarled mounds of flesh. Cobby couldn't make out the features of the rest.

"I've seen what I want to. Finish them." Vantino ordered. Cobby raised the pistol Vantino had entrusted him with and aimed behind the seat towards the back of the car opposite him. At that moment he felt a bullet rip through his right shoulder and stop when it hit bone. The car jerked furiously and Vantino looked at him for a split second to see if he were dead. Knowing the pain would soon register, Cobby again raised his gun and fired, the glass of the rear passenger window shattering. The bullet flew out into space unknown. Cobby stilled himself again as another bullet struck the dash in front of him. He aimed as the sound of Vantino firing again pierced his ears. Cobby fired and the man next to the passenger window jerked forward and did not recover. His arm started to sting. He fired again, but his aim was bad now.

Vantino raised in the seat next to him and Cobby watched in shock as Vantino moved through the window and into the car next to them. He waited for Vantino to fall, dead, but he heard the sound of only one shot, and Vantino jerked violently, but instead of falling, he kept on with it. It took all Cobby's concentration to keep his car locked with the other, to hold Vantino's precarious position.

The Underground car began to swerve violently and Cobby couldn't mimic its unpredictable movements. The gap between the two was widening. Just as Vantino slipped, the upper half of his body starting to fall, Cobby leaned over and took hold of Vantino's jacket, pulling with the last strength his arm had, dragging Vantino in. The car was no longer beside them, but now smashed into the wall of an abandoned warehouse. Vantino looked back for a long time for any sign of movement. There was none.

Vantino opened his jacket and put his pistol back in its holster, then reached up with both hands and smoothed back his hair. Cobby flung his pistol at him with his good arm and then took the wheel with it again. Vantino picked up the gun and put it back as well.

"I think I have one bullet left for you," Vantino admitted before laughing loudly. He looked over at Cobby whose face was turning pale. Vantino reached over and gently moved Cobby's jacket to get a look at his wound. He clicked his tongue. "Ahh. That one is deep. Hit bone?"

Cobby nodded as he edged on the accelerator.

"You gonna pass out?" Vantino asked.

Cobby looked at him squarely. "No."

"Atta boy." Vantino gave Cobby a strange half smile.

"Take yourself to Mickey. I'll do what I have to." Cobby nodded again as beads of sweat formed on his forehead.

Cobby drove on for what seemed like forever. His mind was consumed with the pain that now radiated down his torso and into his hip joint. Things that weren't damaged began to scream in sympathy. Cobby licked his lips only to find his tongue dry. Vantino kept a watchful eye on him, knowing full well where they were headed.

Finally, Cobby pulled the car over to the curb outside headquarters in the soft light of dawn. He was overwhelmed with the prospect of getting out of the car, then bracing himself for the process of having the bullet dug out. Blood was soaking up his trouser leg. He looked over at Vantino.

"I'll send your car back." Cobby just nodded as he pulled the door lever. He placed his left foot on the pavement.

"Hey, boy." Cobby barely moved his head as he looked at Vantino. "Valant won't think much of you not pushing me out the window." He then paused a moment. "Check in on her for me."

Cobby looked at the dash for a long moment before nodding. He placed a hand on top of the car and used it to help pull himself out without moving his injured shoulder. He stood in the street and watched Vantino slide over and take up the vacant driver's seat. He wasted no time in cranking the engine and he shut the door as he shot away from the curb.

Cobby looked up at the restaurant to see Mickey appear in the window, along with about fifteen other guys. Cobby just stood there, the corner of his mouth twitching. He watched as Mickey slid his hands into his pockets and clench his jaws.

It might be difficult to explain.

*****

"There's not much left for me to do. Now we wait." Valant said as he smeared the last of the foul smelling salve on Marie's face. The evening sun shone through the window above the bathtub, elegant in its golden light, but too weak to warm the tiles.

Marie took a deep breath. "Then I want to see it."

Valant made as if to ignore her, but then he sat down on the tub and put his elbows on his knees. He looked at her steadily, the cold look freezing the blood in her veins. She braced herself for whatever was about to come out of his mouth. It had been a long time and she was tired of wondering.

"Alright," he said hesitantly. "Wait here." He stood and left the bathroom.

She waited in apprehension, wondering if maybe she should just keep living oblivious. It seemed realistic that she could be Valant's maid forever. But, she knew eventually something would force her out into the world alone. Possibly even Valant.

After a minute he returned carrying a small hand mirror. He again sat on the edge of the tub, his eyes revealing nothing of what he might be thinking. Marie swallowed hard, and again wondered if this were best. She had grown quite accustomed to fixing her hair without the aid of a mirror.

No. It's better to face it head on.

Valant handed her the mirror. She inhaled deeply and then forced the air out of her mouth. Marie closed her eyes and raised the mirror to her face. She debated with herself for a second before she opened her eyes. She tilted the mirror slightly to see. Valant watched with trepidation.

Marie's breath hitched.

She knew it was better than it had been. That was just a matter of course. Perhaps if she had been seeing her face throughout the healing process it would not have been so shocking to see the red, scarring lines that crisscrossed her cheek. Her lips that had hurt so very much were now large and uneven. The side that had not been cut did not close properly due to the swelling and scarring on the side that had been. Her gums that had taken an agonizingly long time to stop burning gave her a permanent chipmunk look. The physical pain Marie endured was better, but the emotional damage would last years.

The mirror began to shake. She was no longer able to see the wreck that was now her face. She lay the mirror on her lap as her breathing became ragged and increased. Unlike Cobby whose face showed only a few scars, mere lines in his flesh, Marie's face was gone. Her looks had been dramatically altered to a point she would not recover. Underneath her eye was puffy and black as if she hadn't slept in weeks, and now she felt that way, too. In reality, she hadn't slept in weeks.

Marie held her breath and closed her eyes. She didn't want to cry about it anymore.

"There's still swelling. Not all of it is gone. In time, you'll look even more different. When the swelling goes."

She opened her eyes to reveal the violent emotion underneath, the tears threatening to spill, but she held them back with sheer determination. "What swelling?"

Valant took a deep breath, then said in a low voice, "Beneath your eye." He reached up and with the tips of his fingers brushed the dark circle. "Along your cheek bone." His fingers traced over the petite bone that made up her face. "Your lips." He ran the pad of his thumb across her disfigured lips, then returned his hand to his knee.

Marie looked down at her lap. She started breathing again, but her breath came in short gasps. "I wanted to see. Now I know. I'll get dinner on the table."

"Marie. You will always be beautiful," Valant said with little emotion.

Marie closed her eyes again. "I hate myself for placing so much value in it."

"I think it would have been far more devastating to have lost your voice."

"They would have had to cut my throat for that," Marie stated.

"That's what I mean."

She looked at him. "In time, everyone would have found someone else to listen to."

"Maybe some." His eyes were cold, nothing within their depths giving any clue as to what he meant. She knew full well that singers came and went. Damn precious few were ever remembered.

As they sat looking at each other, Valant heard a car coming up the road. He quickly stood and moved past Marie out into the dining area to look out the window. He remained there and slid his hands into his pockets when he recognized Mickey's car. Marie had come to stand near the entrance to the hallway, watching Valant's reaction.

Valant turned back and looked at her before moving away to the front door. He watched to make sure it was Mickey, then closed the front door behind him as he went to open the garage for Mickey to park in. Cobby sat in the passenger seat. Valant lowered the door closed behind them. Mickey shut off the engine. He glanced at Cobby before easily sliding out and standing. Cobby did not move so gracefully.

Mickey buttoned his jacket as he stood looking at Valant. "Val."

"Mick."

Cobby stood awkwardly and moved to close his door with his left hand. "What happened to you?" Val asked.

"Little run in." Cobby said.

"Well, come in." They moved through the door to the house and stopped in the bar area. Marie came out of the kitchen and waited apprehensively. Mickey nodded to her and she returned the gesture, then disappeared into the kitchen.

Valant poured everyone a round, Cobby taking his and gulping down half the glass in one swallow. Valant took note of it as he and Mickey watched. "How bad?"

Cobby looked at Val. "Shoulder. Hit a bone."

"Well, I need you. You think you can swallow it and make a little run with me?" Valant queried.

Cobby's face was pale as he nodded. "I need you to stay with her, Mick." Valant said quietly.

"Alright," Mickey replied.

The sound of Marie's heels echoed off the wood paneling as she stepped out of the kitchen. "May I get you something to eat?" She asked cautiously. Valant inconspicuously took a drink.

"That would be nice," Mickey replied. Marie nodded and retreated into the kitchen.

Mickey looked at Val. "They got one of the warehouses last night."

"Which?"

"The one down near the docks. Luckily Tony had just shipped most everything out." Mickey took another drink as he leaned on the bar across from Valant.

"We lose anybody?"

"Tony's burned up pretty bad on his back and legs. He was the last one there and he was getting into his car when the blast went off."

Valant turned his unwanted attention to Cobby. "So, what happened to you?"

Cobby glanced at Mickey who arched a sarcastic brow. "Yeah, Cobby, what happened to you?"

With reluctance, Cobby explained what had happened. His face was etched with a trace of guilt. He avoided eye contact with Valant and the disgust he knew could be found there. Cobby had Vantino. Could have ended the entire affair. But he didn't. He let him slip through his fingers.

In the end it was Marie who saved him.

She brought out table service and began to set the table. She moved as silently as possible, setting each place as perfectly as she could, moving the forks a fraction of an inch as to be symmetrical to the plates. She kept her face turned at all times so that her scars weren't visible. She returned to the kitchen and Valant's focus was back on Cobby. His eyes narrowed.

"Well, I guess he lives another day," Valant said with deep cynicism.

"Ah, come on. I think that one can slide. More than likely they would have killed him had he been alone. I can't afford to lose him right now." Mickey stated as he looked at Val. Cobby knew intervention wasn't going to save him just now.

"Dinner, gentlemen," Marie said softly as she moved into the kitchen again.

Cobby kept his head down under Valant's glare. Mickey put a hand in his pocket and raised his drink to his lips while he strode to the table. He stood at the head of the table watching Marie as she brought out the last of the dishes. Valant sat to the left of Mickey and a downtrodden Cobby sat across from Valant. Marie had not set a place for herself.

She set the bread bowl on the table and turned to go back to the kitchen. "Get a plate, Marie." She froze.

"Oh, no. I'm sure you have business to discuss." She had turned only the left side of her face back to look at Valant. Even then, their eyes did not meet. Her body filled with dread at what sort of spectacle he would make of her in front of Mickey. Cobby looked at her from a dipped head.

As she started to leave again, Valant said, "Get yourself a plate, Marie, and come sit down."

Her eyes met his and he read the pleading there, the begging to be left alone. His hands were in his pockets, his face firm and steady. She could read no intent there, but then, she never could. She knitted her brows together slightly for a split second. The corner of her mouth tugged.

"Get a plate. Come and sit down," he said it quieter this time. She knew she had lost. Marie lowered her eyes in a look of conceding, then got herself a plate. Mickey watched the whole scene with interest. It was few the number of women who would take the time to question Valant, to plead for him to change his mind. Mickey had known only one woman though, who had ever convinced him to change his mind. She was not Marie. In that instance, Margo had used her body. Mickey doubted Marie ever played that way.

Marie sat next to Cobby, and the two of them glanced at one another, mutual misery and desperation evident. Neither offered a half-hearted smile. They began to dish up. No one spoke during the task. Marie took very little, knowing she probably wouldn't eat even that.

As Mickey and Valant both began to eat, Marie's mind began to fill with dread. She was so afraid the meal wouldn't be good enough, that Valant was searching for fault. Her body was rigid and her palms were sweating. Valant would tolerate no defense of herself with Mickey present. Whatever he dished out she'd have to take, no matter how degrading.

"This is good, Marie," Mickey said as he looked at her speculatively, his fork paused mid-way between his plate and mouth. Marie cast him a sideward glance.

"Thank you," she said quietly.

Valant considered her as he ate his food, but said nothing. After several minutes of silence, Marie gained the courage to ask, "How is Eva? Is she miserable yet?"

Mickey looked squarely at Marie. "Yes. She is miserable. But the pregnancy doesn't bother her much."

Cobby made a choking sound as he clasped his napkin over his mouth. To Marie's utter shock and dismay, Valant chuckled. A short, rumbling sound that came from his chest. Nothing in his face changed except the light in his eyes. When Marie looked to Mickey, he sat grinning at her.

"Eva is fine. Thank you for asking." He returned to eating his meal.

Cobby struggled to eat with his left hand and his face was deathly pale. Marie watched him out of the corner of her eye. His right arm lay limp in his lap. If it were possible, he had eaten less than herself. Marie looked down at her plate again before casting a glance at Valant who was still watching her. She locked eyes with him for a moment, the brown depths of hers reflecting her agony. He still said nothing.

After the meal concluded, Valant rose and left the room for a time. When he returned, he asked that Marie make coffee to go with the small angel food cake she had made for dessert. She nodded and taking a stack of dishes started the pot. She could hear the men talking quietly from the living area as she worked, but she could not make out what was being said.

He insisted she drink coffee with them. She left to get another cup. Then she poured coffee under the scrutiny of the three men, passing out the cake as well. The conversation turned to trivial matters during dessert, and Marie found herself becoming very tired. The urge to sleep was overwhelming and eventually she asked if she might retire. Valant merely nodded.

She barely made her way to the bed, the last thought in her mind the oddity of it. It didn't seem likely she would become so tired so fast. But, Vantino was waiting for her at the entrance of her dreams, so she went willingly.

Valant gave her an hour or so to fall into a heavy sleep. He knew she would. She rarely slept anyway, and her body would no doubt welcome the excuse. The three men stood at the foot of the bed and watched her sleep far from peacefully.

"I just sentenced her to a night of hell. So be prepared for whatever comes," Valant said to Mickey.

Mickey nodded. "I know all about nightmares."

The two men looked at each other. "We'll be back before dawn."

*****

Cobby's face glistened with a thin layer of sweat that had been forming since he slid into the car. He licked his lips and tried to wet them, but his mouth was dry. He felt weak and tired, not having slept in almost thirty-six hours. His wound was giving him trouble requiring rest. He sat like a stone next to Valant who drove on into the night bent on the task he had set his mind to. He didn't look at Cobby.

Cobby watched Valant's hand tighten and loosen repeatedly on the steering wheel. Cobby knew well that rage burned within Valant like a conflagration. When he was like that, there was no stopping him, just moving in an effort to keep up with him. Whatever was eating at Valant had been doing so for some time. Cobby knew the pain that he would endure carrying out Valant's wishes.

They drove on for what seemed like forever until darkness melted away one street light at a time. They avoided Mickey's side of town. Went well past where his warehouses sat. They moved along through the line into Vinnetti's turf. Still Valant drove on.

Then things began to look familiar to Cobby.

He looked at Valant who didn't acknowledge him, just stared ahead, the vicious intent clearly etched into his sharp features. The streets darkened once again as they entered a residential part of town. A poor part of town. The hour was well past midnight and all the houses were black inside. The occupants no doubt sleeping. This was the hard working class, those who suffered and survived the factories and docks, boats and refineries. The backbone of the country.

All but one house.

Valant stopped a few homes down, not wanting to be seen before they were ready to be. He had grave doubts that anyone in the neighborhood would call the police if they saw something strange at the house they now walked up to in the cover of dark. Cobby had drawn his gun in the car knowing his right arm would not be able to reach for it quickly if need be.

Valant gazed at Cobby with ice in his eyes. Cobby knew to follow his lead. Keep his back clear so Valant could do what he came for. Valant walked around to the back of the house and quietly opened the gate into the backyard. Piles of trash and several old cars lay about in the weak light. They made their way to the back door, climbing the cement steps that were crumbling.

Valant looked at the barred windows and tried the door knob. It was locked, so he looked to Cobby and moved aside. Cobby took aim and fired. The rotten door swung easily and both men passed inside. Valant took out his own pistol as he moved through the laundry room into the kitchen. He heard movement upstairs and began looking for the stairs.

"Kill everybody but the old man."

As they rounded a corner into the hall Valant saw the stairs ahead. Cobby saw movement in a dark room. He took aim and fired without stopping to see if he had hit his target. They reached the stairs to hear a woman screaming. Valant aimed his pistol for the top as he moved up. At the first sight of a human form firing and dropped a man dead. More screaming ensued. Cobby kept an eye on the stairs behind them. His shoulder burned with intensity.

Valant and Cobby stepped over the body of the man just shot, following the sound of screaming. A door at the end of the hall slammed shut and the screaming was muffled slightly. Neither man bothered to check the rooms upstairs. They kept moving for the door at the end of the hall. Valant kicked it in. As he came into the room, he heard the explosion of a gun just before he felt the bullet go past his head. The rage inside him flared to new heights as he searched in the dark for him.

Jerry Barelli.

Marie's mother screamed for all the world like she was being dismembered. It grated on Cobby's nerves like nails on a chalkboard. So, he made his way to her and raised his right arm despite the pain. Then, put the butt of his pistol through her front teeth. She reeled and staggered, so he hit her again in the cheek bone. She fell, stunned, clutching her mouth. She was quiet except for the occasional whimper.

Valant lunged at Jerry before he had the chance to get off another shot in the dark. He put his pistol against Jerry's right clavicle, pulling the trigger and feeling the pop as the bone was shattered. The bullet moved on through Jerry's body, embedding itself in the wall behind him. Now Jerry screamed.

Cobby grabbed an old sock off the floor and gagged him with it. Jerry made retching sounds as the sock was driven down into his throat. Valant picked him up by the collar and threw him to the floor, blood splattering as he did so. Jerry made loud snorting sounds as he hit, unable to gain air or withstand the pain he deserved. Valant pulled out a long knife from beneath his spotless black jacket.

Valant knelt down on him, forcing more blood out his gaping hole and shutting off his remaining air supply. He grabbed Jerry's face and held it steady, crushing his jaw under his grip. A shadow moved in the doorway. Cobby fired from where he was standing above Valant, hitting another man.

"You listen." Valant's voice was low and full of hatred. "Vengeance is Mine, says the Lord. This is just a reminder that He will have His Judgement Day."

Valant took his knife and sliced Jerry's forehead, making gaping lines that formed the triple x. "Everyone will know that you are a child abuser, liar, and murderer. A murderer for selling your own flesh for death to pay a debt." With that Valant spit into the wound, finishing off the punishment. He rose and straightened his jacket, moving toward the door. Cobby followed.

They left the house that was now filled with silence. No footsteps moved to block their retreat, nor act upon justice. As they walked out the front door and into the night air, dogs in the neighborhood barked, but the sound of sirens did not wail out into the stillness.

It was as Valant expected. No one was going to bother standing up for the Barelli's. At least no one would stand up for one that wasn't Marie.

*****

It had been a very long time since Mickey was entirely on his own. In fact, he was having a hard time remembering when that might have been, aside from his early morning visit with Imelda. Recently, without Valant, he had begun to long for solitude. This was different. As the long hours of the night wore on, sounds made him anxious, shadows made him nervous. He wondered how Valant took it night after night, waiting, listening. It gave Mickey a deeper appreciation for the men who kept watch over him all the time.

Valant had not exaggerated when he said that he had sentenced Marie to a night of hell. She thrashed and moaned, fighting with someone he could not see. It was miserable watching her. It disturbed him to realize that she knew she was stuck in that other world, for she cried out for help often. It was hard for him to divide his concentration between listening to the house and watching Marie in her agony.

Eventually, Mickey pulled a chair up next to the bed after he had again checked the house and all its entries. He looked at Marie in her unreachable state and the memories flooded back to him. He could see Maryanne clearly. Fighting and thrashing just as Marie was, moaning and sweating, trying to make her way back to him. But she had not. Nor could Marie.

Mickey bent forward and rested his elbows on his knees, his head in his hands. So often since Marie had come she evoked these kinds of memories. Some happy, some tragic, but all of them Maryanne. They were so alike, it gave a jolt to Mickey sometimes to look at Marie. Maryanne, however, had not lived to see twenty-six. The pain seared. Marie whimpered out a name. Valant's name.

For a moment Mickey wondered if she were looking for him, or if he was her nightmare. But, again she called for him, this time louder, her voice more tormented. Something in the house creaked. Mickey felt like snapping.

She asked for Valant again.

Mickey took his gun and put it on the small table next to the armchair in the corner. He wrapped Marie in a blanket, picked her up and carried her to the armchair. He sat with her pressed tightly to his chest, the blanket covering them both. He held his pistol in his right hand.

"John," she whispered. It had been many years since Mickey had heard that name.

"He's coming," Mickey whispered back. "He's coming."

Suddenly Mickey knew how Valant felt the day Maryanne died. Mickey sent him to do *his* job, and when he found Maryanne, who no doubt had wanted only Mickey, Valant must have tried to promise her the same thing. How helpless he must have felt, watching her, knowing she was going to die, quite possibly before Mickey arrived.

Marie shook and trembled. Mickey set his gun aside, then smoothed the hair away from her face. Slowly he took her hair pins out. He threaded his fingers through her coal black tresses and combed away the tangles as best he could. She jerked violently.

"He's coming."

*****

Valant and Cobby moved through the silent house at dawn. He had expected to see Mickey somewhere on the sofa in the living area, maybe by the library, but the space felt void of life. They made no sound as they entered the house, knowing Mickey would be watching, but he was not. Valant moved to the bedroom and passed through the open door, looking at the disheveled bed without Marie. Then he saw them.

She was still out, her head resting against Mickey's shoulder, a blanket draped around them both. Mickey held a steady gun on Valant, his eyes dark and imperceptible.

"Rough night?" Valant asked quietly.

Mickey slowly lowered his gun to the arm rest. "What did she say to you, that last morning?"

Valant looked down at the floor and sighed. "Nothing. She was so far gone."

"I'm sorry. I'm sorry it was you," Mickey said in a shaking voice.

"Let her go, Mickey. Don't keep her tied here. Let her spirit go."

Mickey looked down at Marie. "She asked for you. It better be you she sees when she wakes up. Where's Cob?"

"Sleeping by now."

"Did you get it done?"

Valant's eyes blazed. "Well, I feel better."

*****

Valant let Cobby sleep until noon. Mickey had taken Valant's Thunderbird and headed back to the city shortly after breakfast. When he woke Cobby, it took Cobby several seconds for his eyes to register Valant, the glassy depths reflecting the fever he was feeling. Valant told him to rise, but it took both men to get him up.

Marie made soup at Valant's request. She watched with interest as Valant helped Cobby out of the bedroom and to the table. He sat Cobby in a chair, removed the young man's button down shirt, and then cut off his undershirt. The wound was purple and swollen. The scab where the bullet pierced was a crusted red, but it was obviously clean. Mickey had done well to keep the infection out of it.

"Get me something cold, Marie. I need to ice this." Val requested.

She did so. While they sat and ate their meal, Cobby fought back his fever and the pain. Valant gave him several pills. Marie did not know what they were. After he had eaten, he looked less flushed than he had before, but still not great.

After the meal Marie went into the kitchen to wash the dishes. Valant came in and said, "Leave those." He pointed to the door with his head. "Let's go."

Marie's eyes were light with surprise. She was reluctant to go. "Come." He insisted.

They moved out to the driveway where Cobby was already waiting in the passenger seat of Mickey's black Lincoln. Valant opened the back door for Marie, and as she slid in behind the seat she looked up at him with distrust. He made no comment, just put the seat back and climbed in behind the wheel.

Valant was wearing his usual black suit jacket once more, and it almost looked strange to Marie. It had been so long since he had worn it. He slid the car into reverse and stretched his arm along the seat as he backed out the driveway. Cobby said nothing, just sat quietly, his face revealing nothing.

Marie wondered as they headed down the road and away from the safe house. Fields and farm houses dotted the countryside, few and far between. She recognized some of it from when she herself drove this road, but then she had been filled with excitement. Now she was filled with dread.

Valant drove to the southwest side of the city. When he pulled into a waste site, Marie's stomach lurched. Her eyes darted around the car until they met Valant's in the rear view mirror. His gaze was cold. She didn't like the dark intent she read there. He was determined to accomplish something.

The car moved around to the back of the heap before stopping. Valant stood before assisting Marie out. Valant buttoned his suit jacket resolutely as he moved around to the trunk. Cobby got himself out, not looking like anything was wrong. Only the circles under his eyes lent evidence to his situation. Whatever Valant had given him had worked.

"Marie," her eyes met Cobby's for a moment, taking in his relaxed stance before looking to the trunk where Valant was standing, hidden from view.

"Marie, come here," Valant's firm voice sounded again.

She moved cautiously to the trunk, her heart pounding, images of her life flashing before her eyes. He came into view. Just as she suspected, he was holding a gun, his steady fingers loading it successfully before looking at her pale and stricken face. When he raised it to her, she stumbled backwards and let out a small scream. His jaws clenched angrily as he moved after her.

He grabbed her by the shoulder painfully and held her still. She folded her arms around herself in a measure of protection. Valant put the pistol in her face, barrel pointed away. "Hold this."

He shook his head at her bitterly as he turned and walked back to the trunk. Valant pulled out a shot gun and closed the trunk. He shot Marie an annoyed look before walking toward an old fence lined with bottles. Marie looked at Cobby who stood smirking at her. He extended his arm.

"After you."

Marie kept her head low as she followed after Valant, Cobby close behind her. Valant lay the shotgun on top of a barrel and took out one of his own pistols that rode beneath his jacket. Without checking the weapon, he took aim, breaking the bottles one by one. He didn't miss any. It was done as if he were pulling on his trousers. When he finished, he didn't look at his companions, just reloaded as Cobby lined up new bottles from a nearby bucket.

"Marie," Valant said it without looking at her.

She stepped next to him, feeling more confident now that she was carrying a gun. Valant returned his own gun to its holster, then stepped behind her. "Raise the gun in your right hand."

She did so, and he moved closer to her, his body coming in contact with hers in several places. "Close your left eye and look down the barrel. The butt of the pistol should feel comfortable in your palm." She nodded.

"Take aim by looking down the barrel, then when you are ready, squeeze the trigger until it fires." Valant extended his arm down hers to steady her, holding her wrist lightly in his hand.

"I'm not sure I can do this," she stated.

"Why not?"

"It seems wrong, a woman shooting a pistol like this. It feels unnatural."

"Oh, come on Marie. It's completely unnatural for men to dance, but we do it." Cobby stated sarcastically.

Marie cast him an unsure glance. "Well, dancing isn't like this. This has the potential to kill someone."

"Oh grow up. Don't be such a tit," Cobby spat.

"Do you think I'll be able to hit something?" Marie asked with doubt as she looked to both men.

"I tell you what. You hit anything and I'll buy you dinner." Cobby said equally as doubtful.

"Anywhere?" Marie asked with surprise.

"Anywhere."

"Ok." she sighed out. Without hesitation Marie gripped the gun with both hands and took aim, beginning to fire the pistol. Just as Valant had, she methodically hit each bottle and it shattered on impact. After the first shot Valant dropped his arm and stepped away from her to watch. When she came to the last bottle, he reached over and picked up the shotgun and handed it to her.

"See the bucket?" She nodded at the old rusted bucket sitting on top of a heap of cans.

She cocked the shotgun, then took off her heels. As she braced herself, Valant moved to stand next to Cobby. Marie looked down the barrel of the gun and fired, never at any point of the severe impact to her shoulder closing her eyes. Her upper body tensed as the gun kicked and struck her, but she took the hit without flinching. The bucket rose in the air before falling out of sight behind the trash pile.

She lay the gun in the crook of her arm and turned to the men. Cobby lunged to the side to avoid the gun, but Valant stood still, his eyes hard and unyielding. Marie looked at Cobby and tried to remain professional, one corner of her mouth tugging severely.

Marie tilted her face to the sun. "I'm thinking expensive. Probably steak. Nice bottle of blush, lots of dessert." She turned a serious face to Cobby who stood with his mouth open, his look incredulous.

Marie began to laugh. "You're a sucker, Cobby!"

Cobby shook his head and then started to laugh.

Marie turned serious. "I never said I couldn't protect myself in that alley. But you boys are always clamoring to protect a helpless girl, so much so to the point something terrible happens to her. If I would have had a gun, things would have been different. Don't assume you know me just because I look pretty in a dress."

Cobby was still shaking his head. "I never thought for a minute you possessed that."

Marie smiled softly. "Well, you would have been right had you been there for the initial lessons." Marie laughed openly now. "I was eight when I first fired a shotgun. Knocked me back four feet, then rolled my legs up over my head! What a sight." The picture of Vantino and the boys hooting brought another chuckle. Cobby chuckled too.

Valant opened the trunk and looked at Marie. "Vantino?"

Marie looked at him seriously as wisps of black hair traced her cheek in the breeze. "Who else do you know that can shoot like that?"

It became a standoff. Valant stood with dark hatred in his eyes as he stared at Marie. She crossed her arms over her breasts and stared back, not with hatred, but with sadness. She was not accepted for her talents. The more The Dark Horse came to know her past, the less he liked what he saw. Again she wondered why he was bothering to keep her around.

"What's gonna happen, Marie? What's gonna happen when the day comes we go head to head?" Valant asked in a low voice.

She shook her head. "I don't understand."

"Yes, you do." He cut her off. "Are you gonna have the balls to point that pistol at my head and fire?" Her brows knit together. Valant looked at Cobby. "What about Cob? Can you do it?" He moved to her and took hold of her arm. He reached into his jacket and pulled out one of his own pistols.

He jammed it into her hand and crushed her fingers with his. "Point it at him." Marie winced as he shouted in her face. Angrily he grabbed his second pistol and jammed it into the soft roundness just below her arm pit behind her breast.

"Shoot him. Shoot him or I'll kill you." His voice was granite. She knew he meant it. With terror filled eyes she looked at Cobby who was neither afraid nor moving. He stood with his hands in his pockets, his black jacket fluttering open in the breeze. His head was bowed slightly and a look of great pity radiated deep in his face and eyes.

"Do it," Cobby whispered.

Marie's face crumpled. Valant jammed the gun harder into her ribs. "Get after it. Decide whose life is more valuable. Yours, or Cobby's."

Marie went completely still. The trembling stopped and a strange look passed through her eyes. Cobby waited, the gun ground into her ribs. When she opened her mouth to say something, her musical voice came out instead. Her deep and rich voice poured out hauntingly sad with Jo Stafford's *I Should Care.*

Marie lowered her gun and waited for Valant to fire his. She squeezed her eyes shut tight, her senses taking in everything around her. The sound of the wind, the song of the birds, the smell of the grass mixed with that of the waste. She could feel Valant's breath on her cheek, increasing in speed as hers slowed.

"Do it, Valant. We haven't got all day," she whispered.

"Damn you!" came his fierce voice, also a whisper. "Damn you to hell! Damn your beautiful soul into the fires of eternal damnation!" He pushed the gun until her ribs made a popping noise. "Don't you know? Don't you know what they will do to you? They will take you and do unspeakable things. Things that make getting carved up look like vacation. Can't you see what Vinnetti has done?"

"There's nothing I can do about that."

"Vinnetti can't honestly believe a woman can take over his empire. Especially not you. You're weak, you're soft, and you haven't got the capacity to shoot a dog. Vinnetti is gonna get his most prized possession raped, tortured and murdered."

Marie let out a laugh as her ribs began to separate slightly. "So?" She looked into his hard eyes. "So? Live and die. Take your knocks. Remember? Well, I've been taking mine a long time now, so a few more won't matter. Pull that trigger if you're going to."

Valant pulled the trigger. The sound of the hammer clicking into an empty chamber made her flinch. Valant pulled the gun away. "First rule. Make sure they shoot you in the head. Lung shots take way too long to die from. Second rule. Never look at the man holding a gun on you. He'll shoot you just to get you to stop looking at him."

Valant took both guns and holstered them. Marie remained where she was, still not breathing. "I meant what I said. About Vinnetti's empire." He shook his head at her. "You won't last a day."

Marie had considered this. But, she didn't really believe either that Vinny would put her at the helm. Looking back, it did seem she had a fair amount of training that most young girls didn't. Once it occurred to her that maybe he let her go to Mickey just so she could learn the way he worked.

Lyn Miller

"What about you?" Valant turned and looked at her from where he stood by the car door. "When the day comes and we go head to head, will you be able to kill me?" she asked.

"I'm gonna do what I have to." Valant said matter-of-factly. Marie nodded as she looked down.

"What about you, Cobby?" Marie asked, her head tilted slightly.

"I'll do what I have to."

"Then I guess we understand each other. Why not end it now? If Vinnetti ends with me, why not end the line?" Marie demanded.

Valant raised his head and looked down his nose at her. "Because of the truce."

"What truce?"

"The truce struck between two cowards. Vinny Vinnetti and Mickey's father, neither with enough balls to go against each other and see who would win. Some panty waste scheme to keep the peace."

"Why? What is the point of keeping words spoken between two men so long ago? Why not do what it is you burn to do and end it all?" Marie shouted.

"When Mickey says, there won't be a Vinnetti left standing. That includes you." He pointed at her. "Get in the car."

They drove into the city and Valant chose a small but nice Italian restaurant in the heart of Mickey's territory known as Little Italy. Within these confines there was no way for any of them to remain secure in anonymity. Valant was known on sight every time, as well as Cobby. Marie was considered an Italian sweetheart to all who had ever heard her sing.

They sat in a booth in the back, the establishment wasn't terribly busy as the hour was early. The young waiter had worked hard to see that they were well cared for. Looking at Marie, he instantly recognized her and a look of sadness had passed his features. But, he smiled charmingly at her and made a point to look directly at her. Valant was impressed, as he doubted she would get that kind of reaction very often. When they left, Valant placed a three hundred dollar tip under his plate.

Marie sipped her drink with a soft smile on her face. She was sitting across from Valant, between Cobby and the wall. Both men were keeping a vigilant watch on those around them.

Marie well understood the chance they were taking being in the open like this. She figured it was a wise idea to eat quickly.

When they had finished eating, Marie asked to be excused. She had intentions of visiting the ladies room. Valant looked doubtful as he agreed. He stood and watched her as she went, only returning to his seat when she disappeared up the short hallway. It made Valant very uneasy for Marie to be so accessible in an open area.

Marie washed her hands and looked briefly at herself in the mirror. She brushed back a few wispy strands of hair and then looked away. The scars stood out so loudly she didn't want to look at herself. She left the ladies room only to bump into a man standing in the hall.

"Oh, excuse me," she said politely.

"No excuse for trash like you, Vinnetti."

She looked at him in shock for only for a moment. He was tall and ugly, a prerequisite for Danny G. His teeth were uneven and rimmed with a slight tinge of green. His suit was ill-fitting and a dirty color of brown. He leered at her from his height above her.

"Nice to see you made it, although your pretty face is gone. Now you're just as ugly as the dog you are."

Marie's heart pounded as she looked down the hall toward where Valant and Cobby now sat, but she couldn't see them. "Yeah, that's right. Your boys can't see you, but Danny G can." The man took hold of her shoulder and squeezed it hard. He turned her roughly and pointed, extending his arm over her shoulder and she could smell the scent of stale cigarettes. She looked down his arm to where he pointed.

Danny G sat in a booth even more secluded than the one Valant had chosen. Marie's stomach flopped. He had all three of them. Her brows knit as her mind ran through the possibilities. Danny G raised a napkin to his mouth and dabbed at the corners before tossing the cloth aside. On his mouth he now wore a triumphant grin.

"Marie." He mouthed.

A deep and hot hatred raged out of the furnace of Marie's soul. The night she was carved up flashed through her mind, and she thought back to all the things this man had taken from her in one move. His intentions had been to also claim her life, but Valant had stopped everything before they got to that. She knew she should be afraid, for she knew Valant was right.

Danny G wanted some kind retribution against Vinny, to make an example of her to Mickey. That way Mickey knew what was coming to him. It was just pleasure that drove Danny G to reveal himself to his arch rival, Marie herself. A mere club singer. How that must have grated on him.

Marie stood straight and glared at Danny G who only laughed. Marie's hands folded into fists. Valant was wrong about one thing. It was not he that she would have to go head to head with, maybe even right in that small but fine Italian restaurant. Another thing was for certain. She was tired of being caught without a gun.

Damn men! Let me protect myself!

It then occurred to Marie that perhaps it wasn't that they felt she couldn't protect herself, but rather that they feared she would.

Marie raised her arm and made a gun out of her hand. She pointed it at Danny G whose expression went from laughing to serious. His face mottled with the same hatred that marred Marie's. He well understood what she wanted. She was inviting the fight he had every intention of bringing to her. With black eyes gleaming, Danny nodded his agreement. A hideous grin of intent spread across his mouth that reflected in his eyes.

Marie stood her ground, despite the fact her mind tried desperately to shift. She held on, knowing if it went she was dead, and so were Valant and Cobby. She fought to deal with the power struggle her consciousness and her torment played. She kept her eyes on Danny G. At last, Danny accepted her invitation to go head to head, bowed his head and stood. He buttoned his jacket, then left the restaurant.

The man behind her laughed lowly and moved around Marie, shoving her as he went. She stood and watched them go. After they'd gone, she clasped her hand over her mouth and leaned against the wall as she moved up the hall. She composed herself before going around the corner, knowing Valant was watching for her and would know instantly she was off.

She thought of Cobby laughing about her undisclosed ability to shoot. She pictured Vantino from her vantage point as a little girl with her knees rolled up over her head. He was laughing joyously at her plight, the shot gun laying just above her head where it had fallen after knocking her backward. She thought of the permanent freedom soon to be hers.

She rounded the corner, and just as she suspected, Valant was tensed until he saw her. She watched them both on the ride home. She had not feared Danny G would strike at them at that time, for she knew he was in the game of spilling her blood where the most people, the most important people, would be present to witness it without being able to stop it. A restaurant wasn't that place.

Valant met her eyes in the rearview mirror as he watched her intently. She looked down and away. She looked to Cobby and his hardened features. It occurred to her then that it wasn't perhaps that Valant wanted to go head to head with the Vinnetti's, and in particular her, but rather that he might have to that bothered him.

*****

In the days that followed, Valant began spending time in the city. He would come and go, but always he or Cobby was with her. Cobby became more silent and withdrawn, and she would catch him watching her in great speculation. She always smiled at him when she caught him like this. She knew that they were coming to the end of something. They had a plan. What it was she had no idea. But, she knew it was in place.

Valant spoke to her less. His demeanor changed as well. He wasn't as hostile and no longer sought out situations in which to torment her. He spent his time with her quietly reading, or cleaning his guns at the table. She began to realize that he was troubled. She no longer caught him watching her, and it was as if she was free to be herself.

She was hauling a wicker laundry basket past the dining room table when it caught on one of Valant's jackets that was draped on a chair. Not seeing it she pulled the whole chair over. "Damn," she whispered as the clattering echoed off the walls. She set the laundry basket on the table and stooped to pick up the chair and jacket. As she righted it, something fell out of the jacket onto the floor.

Valant's leather bound book lay open face down on the hardwood floor. A sting went through Marie as she realized whatever was in that book she wasn't supposed to see. Marie looked around for Cobby, but he had gone outside, probably to smoke. She slowly turned it over to look, but something else on the floor caught her eye.

She saw herself.

She had never seen the picture, but she remembered quite well the day it was taken. This had been the last of a series of shots taken the day Mickey consented to an interview with a newspaper. One of the last times she and Rolly had joked so freely together, about Valant, no less.

It was the three of them, Marie in the middle, her arms around both Mickey and Valant. She could still see Valant turn his head just as the flash went off. She never thought of it again, until now. Mickey was grinning. What had she said? So was she. But Valant, the camera had very effectively caught his look. The slight turn of the head. The grin that stretched across his face. The way his eyes slit into little half- moons and the twinkling behind them. His hands sat relaxed atop the table, folded together.

He looked young.

After a moment of staring she looked back to the leather bound book. She finished turning it over. Her breath caught in a little sucking noise as she looked at it.

He was an incredible artist.

The tone of her mood, the light on her hair, the softness of her lips. She could not have been more than nineteen in that particular sketch. It might even have been the very first time she had ever performed. She turned the page to see Cobby, smoking a cigarette leaning against a brick wall. So cool, so calm, so Cobby. She turned another page to see Mickey standing over a grave. How Valant had accomplished such artistry in each pencil stroke, she couldn't fathom. Mickey's shoulders slumped and his head hung. He was a man with a heavy burden.

With trembling fingers she turned again. She was there, alive on the page. This time maybe before she left for New York. She skipped ten or so pages to see herself walking down the street. It was a perfect backside view. Again how Valant had accomplished the lighting with a black pencil was incredible. She turned again to see herself looking longingly at a magazine, then herself on stage in the dark blue gown she wore opening night. She skipped more pages to see herself the first time Valant had taken her back to the apartment. The fear of him was evident in her eyes. That particular page was marked with the hair pin he reached up and gently pulled free, just after commenting on how she respected men. Marie remembered it so clearly.

The next was a picture of her sitting at the bar, in conversation, her head in her hand, smiling about something outrageous. After skipping some again she found herself naked, at least her top half anyway. Her head was turned so that the cuts didn't show, her eyes closed, but the torture of it clearly etched in her face. Marie's hair curved softly beside her breasts, the softness of her hips there despite the panties. It occurred to her that something was wrong with the picture.

Her chest.

There was no cut, no blood, no scar, not even a slight mark. It was how he had seen her, she supposed. She found another of her sleeping, her face buried in the pillow. Although this one did have her scarring, it was minimal. The next was of her sitting and obviously looking at him, her eyes wide and full of fear. Under it was the only inscription she had seen so far.

Marie, could you ever trust me?

A few pages farther on had her driving, laughing as the wind blew through her hair. Then she was standing across the car from him, her look serious, a lock of loose hair over her eye.

"Used to scare me shitless when he would go and listen to you." Marie jumped at the sound of Cobby's voice. She looked up at him and tensed. He stood relaxed, his hands in his pockets, his white sleeves rolled up.

"I followed him every time. I knew where he was headed when he gave me the slip. The way he watched you," Cobby shook his head. "I never told Mickey. Val clearly didn't want him to know. But I feared Vinnetti would get him. I guess he thought you were worth it." Cobby merely regarded her.

Marie rubbed her forehead. "What is this?" she asked holding up the book.

"I think you know what that is. All the words he's never gonna say to you."

Marie looked solemn as she gazed down at it. "He is very talented."

Cobby looked at her steadily as if waiting for something to come to her. Marie smiled and let out a sad laugh. "I guess it should have been obvious," she said to no one in particular.

"I watched him look for you in music magazines."

Marie closed the book and ran her finger tips across the cover. "All that time I hated him. All that time he was sketching me. What now?" She whispered the last to herself.

"Why is he so cruel?" she asked fiercely.

"I really think the only thing that scares him, is that when you'll need him most, he won't be able to help you." Cobby looked down a moment. "God help you, Marie." She looked sharply up at Cobby whose face was drawn and sad. "God help you, for Vinnetti has marked you, despite his attempts to hide you."

"Tell me what you know."

"You don't want to know," he said as he slowly shook his head.

Marie cocked her head at him. "I am not so naïve, Cobby. I know they plan to use me as bait. I've known that for some time. Why else would Mickey have consented to me living?"

"It isn't just that anymore. It's the depth of the Underground. How far they have gotten to you."

Marie swallowed hard, then pressed her lips together. "I'm going to do it."

Cobby's head lifted in surprise. "Why?"

She was quiet a moment. "Because, the truth is, there is no way I can win. I know it's me they want. Vinny's line goes with me. Mickey has a child to carry on for him. And regardless if Mickey dies, Valant can raise the child. Either way, Mickey's covered. Vinny dies with me." She looked down at the book again. "Valant is right. Vinny isn't going to put a woman at the helm. I know that. I would rather see Mickey run LA than The Underground."

Cobby's shoulders sagged a bit. "He's looking for you."

"Vinny?"

"No, Vantino."

Again Marie let out a sad laugh. "I know I won't die alone. Vantino will be right there. We'll go together." Marie smiled at Cobby. "Don't look so sad. I've been nothing if not a pain in the ass since the first time you saw me."

His brows knit together. *I Should Care,* he sang softly to her, the same Jo Stafford song Marie had first sung to him.

*****

Mickey lay awake listening to Eva breathe. Her breaths were deep and came at a steady rate. Mickey didn't sleep much anymore. His mind constantly went round and round with everything. He would rise and walk through the darkened house, looking out at the night sky and the stars that shone down like diamonds. Eva had insisted on bay windows throughout the house. Having come from a two room apartment jammed with twelve people, Eva wanted to be able to see space as well as feel it. She wanted nothing to remind her she had come from poverty.

It was now, in these moments when he found himself alone, that Mickey pondered Marie. He wondered how it was that she had come from worse conditions than Eva, and still came out a better person. She was not wrought with the desire to erase who she had been as a child, she simply became who she wanted to be. Marie had come through for him before, would she again?

Mickey was gravely doubtful that Valant could get her back where she needed to be to make a return to the club. No woman he had ever known would be seen in that setting again after such a terrible experience took her beauty from her.

Valant didn't have the touch with women either. His dark side was alluring to a particular type of woman, but Marie wasn't that type of woman. Not to mention she was clearly terrified of him.

Mickey exhaled and ran a hand through his tangled hair. The Underground was getting out of control. They weren't just hitting Vinnetti anymore. Drive-by's had become the norm in the outskirts of Mickey's territory as of late. The Underground would slowly make their way in, just as they had Vinnetti's turf. Mickey had more guys watching the house, but he wondered how that would help, and if he should move Eva elsewhere. It was just a matter of time before they made a pass at his home.

His thoughts turned again to Marie. He stared out at the night sky and thought of her tenacity. He hoped it was going to be enough, and he hoped for once that Valant went easy. This was not the time to push a sinking ship.

*****

Marie began to watch him. She studied him all the time. She went from avoiding him, to seeking him out. He still rarely spoke to her, and he quit watching her. It left the field open for her own curiosity. She would hold up her book and look at him, his legs stretched out before him, his glasses perched on the tip of his nose. She would contemplate the women he surely had known. The beautiful Margo, the countless others he must have claimed even if only for a night. It was odd to consider him in such a way.

She thought about the way he had diligently cared for her in the hours of hell, never giving up on her, or her extreme issues. She compared him to Alex, and found she really didn't remember much about him, other than he played the trumpet. The feeling of his kiss had gone from her, the feeling of his breath on her cheek was replaced with Valant's thumb as it ran across her disfigured lips.

She used to lie on the floor of the apartment and remember the way Alex's laugh would ring out loud and frequent. Now, only one thing could be heard, and that was the small distorted sound coming from Valant's chest the one time she had made him laugh. The few light touches Valant had ever given her were burned into her memory, and for what reason? If she had truly hated him, she would have discarded them immediately.

She looked at him and saw The Dark Horse, but then would look to his behavior and knew he was John. Despite what he had hoped to keep from her, he had revealed instead. He was not a man who would ever be tender, but in fact he was, in his own coarse way. He was a mystery, completely unsolvable, and Marie found she liked that about him. He was unpredictable, and for having no feeling, his emotions raged constantly. He just had different ways of dealing with them.

Marie reminded herself he was a killer, but then, she didn't dwell on it. She had finally come full circle, and she looked back on her life to realize she had been surrounded by killers all the way. She was broke to them, their behavior, had more experience with them than most people. She'd seen the darker sides to their existence, lived among them as both friend and enemy. If anyone was made to tolerate Valant, it was her. God had been training her for this all her life.

Marie kept going back to Margo. She asked herself again and again why he would've tolerated her all these years. She had no answer for that. Perhaps he still loved her. Or, she was now merely habit. When Valant helped her in the kitchen, or sat at the table cleaning his guns, as he frequently did, she would watch his forearms flexing against his white shirt. If his sleeves were rolled up, flex in general. His hands moved about whatever task he set them to with ease and competence. Why would a man so loyal, who dealt in matters of respect, not demand his woman do the same?

She had seen him dance with other women besides Margo at the club, but they seemed to annoy him. To be honest, even the last she had seen him dance with Margo before the attack, he seemed annoyed with her as well. He was a mystery. The more she watched him, the more she wanted to watch him. She started to wonder what his thoughts were, or if knowing them would only terrify her.

One evening after several days of just the two of them, Marie turned on the radio just to break the silence. She walked across the wooden floor to the bar in her bare feet and turned on the knob. She looked at him for permission. He merely watched her over the rim of his glasses from his favorite reading chair. Looking at him made the pit of her stomach burn.

She took her time washing the dishes and putting them away. During the chore she thought of the last time she danced with a man when it had been her choice, and not required as part of her job. It was sometime back when she was in New York. Marie tried to stay out of Valant's way, as he so clearly wanted her to. It didn't seem fair to stay holed up in the kitchen. She shut out the light behind her. The only remaining light a lamp next to Valant, the other near the bar.

As Marie stepped out onto the hardwood floor, Jo Stafford's "The Nearness of You" came over the radio waves. It was a favorite of Marie's. She stopped and looked at Valant who read his book as he raised a glass of brandy to his lips. He took a sip, then returned the tumbler to the table next to him. Marie ran her right hand down her bare left arm as she looked away from him and smiled.

She moved silently on bare feet. She came to stand before him, and he looked up at her over his glasses, looking like a cranky father. She slowly took his book in her hands and closed it, laying it gently on the table next to him. His eyes changed, but she didn't know to what. Very softly, she placed a hand on either side of his face and carefully pulled off his glasses, her finger tips lightly brushing his face. She folded them and set them on his book.

He sat unbreathing, watching her out of cold eyes as she trailed her fingers down his left arm, barely touching him, until she came to his hand. She took hold of it and raised it to her, "Dance with me," she whispered.

"If I say no?"

She smiled at him as he stood. "You won't."

She walked backward as she led him to the open floor near the bar, all the while watching his eyes that never left hers. She moved willingly into his arms, his hand settling just above her hip, his fingers spreading to take up more of her flesh. She put her arm around his shoulder, realizing how much difference her heels made. Without them she was much shorter than he. He took her hand in his.

She moved against him. Looking up she saw the familiar unkindness in his eyes and wondered if he was hiding something. They moved to the music, and when she looked up at him again, she found he hadn't changed. He watched her closely.

"What?" he asked in a low voice.

"I don't want to be one of those girls that annoy you," she whispered to him.

His brows knit together for a moment. "Girls that annoy me?"

"I've watched you dance with girls that clearly annoy you. I don't want to irritate the only dance partner I've got." She gave a small uncertain smile when she finished speaking.

"Well, then maybe you don't talk about your hair, your gown, how attractive you think I am," he said flatly.

"That should be easy. We both know my hair is gorgeous, I'm wearing the same dress I fried bacon in this morning, and I don't find you attractive," she replied just as flatly.

"Now, you've annoyed me. You covered all three topics in one sentence." Valant kept dancing.

She laughed at him. "What irritated you the most? The part where I said I don't find you attractive?"

"No. You said bacon. Now I want some."

Marie laughed up at him. The corner of his mouth twitched. "You really are funny. Once I wade past that deep sarcasm to the heart of the cynical tormenter, I find you really are much worse than I anticipated." He spun her away from him.

"Am I?" He asked as she smiled at him. "I thought the point wasn't to annoy me?"

"Well, then let's take neutral ground. Handguns. Let's talk handguns." His hand slid just an inch lower on her hip, ever so slightly pulling her to him. "Or maybe the wonder that is the all-new 6 cylinder coming out of Detroit?" she whispered into his face.

He slowly shook his head at her. Marie looked into is eyes for a moment, then closed hers and pressed her cheek to his. He readjusted the hold he had on her and pressed her tightly to him. Marie didn't move away, just kept up with his lead. He smelled of aftershave and cigarette smoke, the combination a deadly intoxication of manhood. The way his fingertips moved slightly over her hip sent tiny shockwaves along the surface of her skin.

He had shaved that morning. His skin was smooth with just the slightest hint of stubble to account for it. Every move he made was powerful, executed with grace and experience. For the first time in her life, Marie felt the impact of a man. Not just a young boy out to gain experience along his way to manhood. Valant was done acquiring experience, he was now making use of his past encounters. He was well aware of the effect of the slightest movement of his hand, the way breath on her neck would send chills to her mind.

He knew a move could be made without any move at all, just by merely brushing his lips against her cheek. Marie found her breath refused to come out without a slight shudder and music was optional. Valant's leg brushed against hers when he bent to dip her, but kept her pressed tightly to him. When he returned her to an upright position, her body felt weak enough to be pliable in his arms. None of her movements were now dictated by her own mind, but rather as a compliment to his.

He settled his lips against her ear and whispered, "I find nothing about you irritating."

Marie slid her hand over to rest it against his collar as she closed her eyes. The movement of the muscles in his neck and shoulder played out beneath her hand. She turned her face slightly to feel his neck against her cheek and nose despite the scars. Marie thought she understood the power of desire between a man and a woman. Thought she had played with its fire and felt the electricity it held. She knew now that was wrong. She had been attracted before, that was undeniable, but for the pull of a man who knew well the game and all its intricacies, she felt an inadequate amount of understanding.

"You'll get yourself into trouble, dancing with me like this," he whispered again.

Marie melted against his neck. If she could have, she would have moved closer to him. He was in total control now, and she had no say in what he did. Nor would she allow herself to stop him. His palm drifted farther down until the tips of his fingers brushed along the swell of her hip.

"You have a talent for conversation," she whispered back to him.

It was then that the notes of a soap commercial reached Marie's ears. Valant stopped moving and stepped away from her. She watched him go in a trance, as if she weren't even in the room. He slid his hands into his pockets and looked down at her, a look of triumph gleaming in his eyes.

"I think it's time for all little girls to be in bed."

The corner of Marie's mouth twitched as she nodded in agreement. She looked up at him from under her dark lashes, her brown eyes reflecting the wave of unpreparedness she felt when he touched her. He looked knowingly at her. She turned and left him there. She closed the door behind her, unsure of herself. It had been so easy for him to manipulate her. That was not an ability she had expected him to possess. Nor an ability she thought she would so easily succumb to.

*****

Valant struck a match and raised it to the cigarette that was held firmly between his lips. He inhaled deeply and then blew a stream of smoke towards the ceiling. It was dark outside the office. Mickey sat in his great leather chair behind his desk and slouched.

"We can't wait anymore. They are hitting us right and left now. I can't afford to let anymore guys get killed, or run the risk of hiring out new ones. Nobody but the dead can be trusted in this game." Mickey stated in exasperation.

"I know."

"Then no more time. No more. We move on with the plan," Mickey spat.

Valant exhaled and nodded slowly. "When?"

"Two weeks. That gives us time to get the word out. I can't afford any more than that."

Valant rose and made his way over to the mini bar and poured himself a drink. He took a long swallow before returning to his seat. "What else have they hit?"

Mickey shook his head. "They've been by the house. Shot up the guard gate, wounded one guy pretty seriously. Eva is scared shitless so I sent her to my Uncle Remmi. If that doesn't cause divorce nothing will." Mickey finished sarcastically. "I need you here. Now. No more playing the faithful doctor."

"I know."

"No, you don't know!" Mickey said as he shot forward. "That shitass kid Cobby has been doing your job. It's just a matter of time until they kill him, Val. Are you prepared for that? Are you ready to let him go?" Mickey jammed his finger into the table. "The time is now!" He calmed some and sat back in his chair. "I set the ball rolling today. No more waiting."

Valant looked down and nodded again. "Monday morning."

"Alright. Monday morning."

*****

Marie stood at the sink running water to wash the breakfast dishes. Cobby sat at the dining room table looking at an old newspaper. The morning sun shone across the yard outside and Marie took a moment to stand on her tiptoes and look out at it. When she had awoken the morning previous she had found Valant gone. Cobby was sitting at the table as if he had been there all night.

She knelt and opened the cupboard door to get the dish soap. She watched as bubbles formed in the hot water. She turned slightly to get the coffee pot from the stove when Valant himself caught her eye. He was leaning against the doorway to the kitchen, his hands in his pockets, a strange look in his eyes. Her breath caught as she looked up sharply at him.

She clutched a rag in her hands as she turned to him. "What?"

He tipped his head slightly. "Come here."

It was as if she could read him for she moved cautiously to him and stopped just out of reach. He didn't move, just glanced down at a long white box that rested on the counter next to him. "Come with me."

"Where?"

"It's a surprise." He indicated the box. Her look was confused. "Open it."

She wasn't sure she liked the prospect of going out with him, since most other times didn't pan out well. "Open it."

Marie licked her lips and stepped to the box. She untied the string that held it closed, then slowly lifted the lid. She pulled back the white tissue to look down at a pastel yellow dress. It was high, covering her shoulders and her chest, with a roll of the soft fabric just below the hollow of her throat. It was a beautiful and soft hued dress. She liked it immediately. She didn't have anything in such a gentle color.

"John," she whispered as she traced the fabric with the tip of her finger.

"Go put it on." He returned in a low voice. She looked up at him.

"Where are we going?"

He shook his head at her, his eyes hardened with secrecy. "You've got twenty minutes." He left her then. She replaced the lid on the box then went to change.

As she walked by Cobby who still sat at the table, he winked at her.

Marie tried to hurry, but something told her with a dress like that, he intended for her to be seen in public. She relished the feel of the silk underwear that Imelda had included in package, looking at herself in the vanity mirror. As she took time to put on make-up, she realized that Valant had been right.

Her face was changing.

The swelling had gone down more in her lips. They were less jagged and ill-fitting. They pressed together almost evenly. The gashes along her cheek were less angry then they had been. While she wouldn't be the Marie she had been before, she wasn't the grotesque figure she saw in the mirror the night of the attack. Make-up served to cover it all, even if not very well. Valant had indeed done something incredible for her, how he had done it, she still wasn't sure.

She slipped on her white heels and looked at herself one last time. Her hair was loosely rolled into a bun, the dark hair around her face shining in the early morning light. She smiled softly to herself as she remembered the way she used to look. She was far from it now, but she was still pretty, to her own mind. Valant's words echoed in her ear of when he told her that what made her beautiful wasn't located on the outside of her body.

Perhaps he was right. If Valant could be trusted.

She left the bedroom with make-up in the small clutch Imelda had provided. Valant had not returned. When she looked at Cobby who was still sitting at the table she found him smiling softly at her. "He's waiting for you out front."

Marie nodded and continued on to the door, pausing only a moment when she opened it. He was leaning on the hood of the Jaguar. As soon as he saw her he stood slowly. He took in a slow breath as he watched her walk to him, his face saying nothing about what his mind must have been thinking. Marie stopped just before she reached him, the clicking of her heels slowing before ceasing. She reached down and grasped her skirt.

"It's lovely. Thank you." She looked up at his face then, uncertainty in her dark eyes.

"My pleasure," he moved closer and held out his elbow. She gracefully took it. He escorted her around to open the door for her.

Before she got in, she looked up at him and innocently said, "I don't get to drive?"

The corner of his mouth twitched as he replied, "No, don't want to be too early."

Marie was looking at him coyly as he got into the driver's seat. He had left the top up, knowing she wouldn't want to have the wind messing her creation of self. Marie liked the way he looked in his black suit, so dark, so cool, so handsome. It surprised her to realize she thought so, after all the times she had thought him ugly. She smiled to herself.

He looked over at her as he pulled onto the pavement. "What?"

Marie looked at him square. "Where are we going?"

He shook his head at her. "Guess you'll see."

"Why didn't Cobby just ride with us?"

Valant looked at her, annoyed. "Well, then it wouldn't be like we were alone."

She laughed at him, then looked shocked. "Are we on a date?" He didn't look at her. "We are, aren't we?"

"No," he kept looking at the road.

Marie sighed. "Think of the story. 'Yes, girls, I once dated the incredible Dark Horse.' What a mark of distinction."

"As if you don't already have enough talent to distinguish yourself." He said derisively.

Marie smiled and looked out the window. They drove on for a long while, passing the city and ending up on the outskirts on the northeast side. Valant drove with certainty, so she guessed he had been where ever he was going before. The spring sunshine was bright and cheerful, full of promise of a beautiful day and memories to be made. The joy of being alive surpassed all of her regrets at that moment, left her future to the forthcoming. Perhaps tomorrow would be painful, but at that instant she was happy again.

He pulled into a parking lot that was filled to the max. He drove to the front and left his car next to a building. He opened her door and took hold of her hand. Marie didn't bother to look for Cobby, whom she knew was close. She rather liked the feeling they were alone. Valant took them to the main entrance of a great stadium. They walked under an archway that said, Santa Anita Race Track. There were people all around, couples moving in through the same doors as they, brightly colored dresses decorating the surroundings.

Marie held onto Valant's arm as he produced several passes at the gate. Instead of following the line of people through the main entrance to the stadium, Valant was directed to follow a different walkway. The sign said reserved seating, and curiosity piqued in Marie. She longed to know what they were about to see as a voice came over the sound system.

Valant was looking down at her with an amused expression. "Have you ever been to the races, Marie?"

"No."

They walked down a hallway and climbed a set of stairs to emerge in a very fine seating area. It overlooked the track and infield, and tables were set up with white table cloths. Valant moved to a table behind a roped-in area. A man in a vest and tie greeted them and asked if they would like some champagne. Valant nodded. He pulled out a chair for Marie and she held her skirt as she sat. Valant sat next to her, looking out over the track. There wasn't an inch of the finely groomed track and infield Marie couldn't see from the comfort of her chair. A small pair of binoculars sat on the table for seeing across the great expanse.

"Ladies and gentlemen, please place your bets for race one. Post time is fifteen minutes." The voice boomed in the sound system. The tables around them were sparsely occupied and Marie liked the feel of it. Waiters moved around serving drinks and assisting people. It was very different where Marie sat as compared to the seating below where the occupants sat next to one another and there were no tables, just rows of seats.

"Would you like to bet?" Valant asked.

"No. I wouldn't know the first thing about it."

They watched the first four races while sipping champagne, and enjoying the races from a detached setting. Marie was fascinated with the horses. They were great beasts with speed and power, the likes of which she had never been close to. She loved their grace and elegance, yet admired their ruthlessness when it came to winning.

"How do they know which horse to race?" She asked as she watched a string of horses being led in front the stadium at the sound of the trumpet.

"Mostly it's done by bloodlines. Horses are bred out of champion lines. Literally built to do their job." He took a sip of champagne. "But, I think there's more to it than that. Unlike people, horses wear their potential. It is obvious by the look in their eye, the way they carry themselves, the way they act. I have found, that color plays a part as well. Something about gray horses makes them run harder, even to their own detriment."

"Hmmm…" Was all she said when he had finished speaking. She began to watch the individual horses, trying to pick the ones that looked like they might win. She found it harder than Valant made it sound.

Valant watched Marie more than the racing, his intent eyes revealing nothing. He kept his observations covert, answering her questions when they arose, but never spoke unless spoken to. He did not want to disturb her entertainment. Just before the sixth race, he rose from his chair.

"Alright. Enough of merely being a spectator. It's time to place your first bet." Marie stared up at him with great doubt.

"How on earth am I supposed to pick a horse?"

His mouth twitched again. "I'll help you." He reached for her hand.

They stood in the betting line and looked over the dossier. Valant rattled off odds and statistics which really meant nothing to her untrained mind. She tried to pick with discern, but she really had no idea how to.

"Look. This one has the highest odds." He pointed to where he was reading.

"What color is he?" Marie asked as she looked at him.

Valant gave her a look of disgust. "He's gray."

"What's his name?"

His look deepened. "Full Fury."

Marie smiled. "I like that. I'll go with that one." Valant snorted his disapproval. They placed their bet and returned to their seats.

The trumpet sounded as the horses entered the track. Marie stood to watch them parade by. "Which one is he?"

"The dark gray, there." He stood close behind her and pointed. "Number seven."

"Oh, he's pretty. I think I chose well." Valant shook his head at her.

They watched as the horses were warmed up and then loaded into the gates. The anticipation built in Marie until her pulse raced and her stomach clenched. She rubbed her hands together as the feisty gray fought at being loaded. He stood with his head up, waiting to hear the bell and see the gate thrown. Marie wondered what it was like to be the jockey.

The bell sounded.

They became a mass of surging power and energy, reaching and pushing, roaring and thundering. It made a shock that reverberated through Marie as they fired harder down the track. The gray chose his place in third, then stayed there. The two leaders, two bays, coursed along ahead of the rest. The fight became personal between them. Full Fury remained behind the fight.

The singular form of the two charging horses locked together hurled down the track. They kept up neck and neck for a while, then one would lunge ahead, only to be over taken by the other. Neither jockey could out maneuver the other.

"Oh," Marie groaned out. Valant looked at her out of the corner of his eye.

As they came to the final turn, Full Fury moved. His great body fired into another gear, as if he had merely been traveling along, waiting for an open stretch of road. Around the turn he took his time, inching forward through the apex. As the final leg of his journey opened up before him, he fired hard, his legs bunching then stretching out beyond what they had been.

Another horse behind him made his move, but Full Fury closed the seven lengths like he was walking to the mail box.

"Oh, my." Marie muttered, then covered her mouth with her hand.

The dark gray rushed past the two bays and started to eat up ground. The horse behind him who had moved with him pounded behind him at five lengths. When Marie began to see what was happening, she let out a small squeal as she stepped to the balcony to watch Full Fury close the last bit of gap between him and the finish line.

The crowd below had risen into a great sound of rejoicing at the sight of the gray beast hurtling himself as well as dirt down the track. The two bays were now in the distant past, as well as his challenger. Marie let out a cheer as Full Fury sped past. She clapped her hands joyously and laughed. She clasped her hands together as she watched the jockey stand in his stirrups and begin to slow Full Fury.

Laughing, Marie turned to Valant who still stood next to his chair at the table. Marie stopped laughing as she looked at him. He had his hands in his trouser pockets, but his body was rigid. On his face was an old expression Marie hadn't seen since the night before she left for New York. The same expression that made her think she'd never see New York. She swallowed.

He held out his hand to her. "Come. Let's meet your champion."

She picked up her clutch as she stepped back to him and threaded her arm through his. She walked beside him and felt his power, his presence, felt the way he moved to make way for her. Something about it made her heart stop and her stomach flip. She felt misplaced, like she wasn't quite good enough to feel the protection of such a high profile man. They must have made a striking couple, for men and women alike turned from conversations to watch them leave.

The late afternoon sunshine caressed her skin as they made their way to the stables. Marie was once again enraptured by the sight of it. Horses moved about everywhere. She let Valant guide her. She was too busy looking around at all of them, admiring their beauty. Valant moved through the congestion straight to a particular set of stables where Marie's eyes went to a dark gray that walked on the hot walker.

A man in a brown suit and fedora stood talking to the jockey as they watched the horse prance on the line. The jockey was still wearing his purple silks, and she marveled at the fact that he was smaller than she.

"Don," Valant called. The man in the fedora turned to him and smiled broadly.

"Ah, Mr. Allen." He reached a hand out to Valant, then shook it vigorously. Marie was trying to catch up on what was going on. Clearly these two men had business, but not with Valant as himself.

"That was a great race. I am so glad you were here to see it. Each time we run him he just comes on hotter." Don turned to Marie and removed his hat and bowed. "Lady."

He had an Italian accent, and his skin was a dark olive color. He returned his hat onto his head as he looked back at Full Fury. Valant's eyes studied the gray as he moved along. "What do you think? Turn up the heat?"

The two men began converse on strategy, so Marie moved away to get a closer look at Full Fury. She stayed out of his way, but when he came by her he tossed his head and snorted. He swung around to side step, keeping her in one eye or the other. As he walked around again, he charged against his line, snorting and reaching for her.

"He would like to meet you, Lady." Don had left Valant and was now just behind Marie. Full Fury lunged forward and tossed is head at her. Don looked at her for permission. She looked at him with uncertainty, then nodded her head gently. Marie looked back at Valant who nodded as well. She took Don's hand and stepped to the horse who was now held in place by a groom. Full Fury reached again for her.

Marie was nervous about him as she came to his head, but Full Fury stilled and lowered his muzzle to her hand. At the gesture, she raised it to him. His nostrils puffed air ever so gently, then he raised his elegant head to hers. She stood still as his breath puffed gently again, this time leaving traces of moisture on her skin. He lowered his head to her open palm and nudged his nose against it. Marie tentatively touched his soft hair. He no longer moved, just stood as her hand stroked his face.

"Much like Mr. Allen, Full Fury has an eye for a beautiful woman." Don said to her as he smiled. Marie flushed and bent her head. Don looked to Valant. "Do you not tell her she is beautiful?" he said it almost reproachfully, but only grinned as he looked back at Marie.

"It was a pleasure to meet you." Marie whispered to Full Fury. She moved away from him and he tossed his head at her. She smiled and moved back to him. "You are a champion. And you know it, don't you? It is true. I can see it in the way you carry yourself." This time she stroked him with both hands down the sides of his face. "I will see you again, someday."

She moved back to Valant who took hold of her like a lost possession. He looked down at her. "What did Full Fury have to say?"

"I have no idea, but he was adamant he get it said," Marie replied. They both looked back to Don.

"Marie, this Don Delosa, my trainer. Don, this is Marie Barelli." Don removed his hat again and gently took hold of Marie's hand.

"A pleasure, Lady."

Marie smiled at him, then glanced to Valant who studied her. She blushed slightly under his scrutiny. "Well, we have another engagement we can't be late for. Thank you, Don."

"Again, I am glad you were here to see it." Don said as he replaced his hat.

Valant turned Marie away. They walked leisurely back across the grounds. Marie smiled to herself as she lay her head against his arm. He looked down at her and she wrapped her right hand around his arm just above her arm that was linked in his.

"Thank you, John. That was wonderful," she said lightly.

"I'm glad you enjoyed it," he replied in his deep voice.

They drove away from the track, and Marie was surprised when he headed back into the heart of the city. It was now early evening. He gave her an uncertain glance. She looked at him in curiosity. He reached over and brushed a lock of hair from her forehead.

At length Marie began to fill with dread as the sights became more and more familiar. They were back into Mickey's turf. She tensed in her seat, leaning away from him towards the door. She became very agitated when it was obvious where they were going. Marie turned in her seat to look behind them for Cobby. He was there, a ways back, but he was there.

"Don't. Please don't do this to me." His face had hardened into his usual mask. He didn't acknowledge her. He slowed the car and pulled into the alley behind Mickey's restaurant. His body was rigid as he exited the car, standing briefly to button his suit jacket. He looked up the alley as he moved around the car to Marie's side. Opening the door, he saw that she was near hyperventilating. He reached down for her.

She looked up at him with betrayal in her brown eyes, her fine features as hard as his. "No. No, I won't go in there."

"Yes, you are." He bent and took hold of her arm.

Her look immediately shattered when she realized he would force her if necessary. "Please, John. Don't ask me to go in there." Her eyes filled and she sought his face, but he kept his eyes from hers. He pulled her forcefully from the car. She alighted very improperly. Marie jerked on his iron grip, but he was angry now and gave nothing.

Marie looked for Cobby who was standing next to his car, his face drawn. They moved through the private entrance after Valant knocked and the guard let them in. Valant pulled Marie down the hallway that lead to Mickey's office and through the kitchen. Chefs stopped to watch them as they passed, but all knew better than to say anything. When Valant saw a young waiter by the double doors, he demanded a table up front. A place Valant himself never sat.

Valant's grip bruised her upper arm as they waited. Marie's breath came in short raspy sounds as she stared up at him. "John Valant. Don't you humiliate me. Please!"

He stared ahead, his jaw clenching and unclenching. The young waiter returned and asked them to follow him. Marie knew that if she drug along, Valant would hit her, in front of everyone. He wouldn't allow himself to be made a fool before the entire restaurant. So, Marie covered the right side of her face as they walked through the doors amongst the crowded Sunday evening diners. As soon as patrons recognized Valant, they stopped talking and gaped, noting the look on his face as well as the young woman he was escorting forcefully.

Marie kept her head down, but she did notice Mickey as he sat eating dinner with Eva at a table near the back. Mickey sat in shock after he lay his fork down. Marie couldn't bring herself to look at Eva, and her reaction to the hideous woman Valant was towing. The old hate returned.

Several women gasped as she passed and turned to whisper to their dining partners. A man muttered, "Good Lord!" as she slunk by. Valant was determined and retained his hold on her upper arm. The restaurant was silent now as all gawked in open disbelief. In the far corner Marie heard a woman ask, "Isn't that Marie Barelli?"

Shocked gasps and murmuring followed the comment.

They reached the table, which was, front and center. The waiter hurried to pull out a chair for Marie. She sat resigned into the waiting seat, and kept her face covered. Valant sat next to her, so close that their legs touched. She moved away from him, but he took hold of her leg, pressing it back against his firmly.

"Champagne." He barked at the waiter as he opened the menu with his left hand. Sounds around the restaurant began to return to normal. Waiters and busboys moved again. But, all eyes of the patrons remained on Marie.

"Don't touch me," her broken whisper shot at him. With that he moved his hand farther up the inside of her thigh and dug in harder.

"What are we having, Vinnetti?" He asked harshly as he scanned the menu that he knew well.

Her shoulders dropped at the sound of his chosen name for her. "I hate you." She sobbed out. He forced his hand farther up her leg until it rested against the delicate place considered most personal. He squeezed her thigh.

"No, you don't," he stated. "I think the Rib Eye. That sounds good."

The waiter returned and poured the champagne. Valant ordered steaks, all the while his hand cushioned between her legs. Marie was flushed so deeply. She knew it made her scars all the more obvious. When the waiter left, Valant took a long drink of his champagne.

"Have a drink, Vinnetti."

"I am such a fool. A stupid fool. All day I kept thinking how charming you can be. How wonderful. That it was nice to have you treat me like an attractive woman. I ate it up. Just like a stupid woman would. I ate it up and you just kept it up. All the while laughing at me and planning this." Her voice broke then.

Valant took another long drink that finished off his champagne. He reached for the bottle that was chilling in a bucket of ice. "Get your hands off of me," her voice was still a whisper, but it was firm now.

He turned his hand and took hold of her most sensitive place, her legs bracing against him. Marie's free hand clutched and pulled at his. She covered her entire bowed face with her right hand. She lost it and began to weep.

"Which part don't you like, Marie? Do you hate people staring at you? Now, not because of your face, but more because we are engaged in a very private act in plain view? Or is it that everyone is about to watch you enjoy it?"

Marie looked up at him, pure hatred in her face. She made a grab for her glass of champagne, but he latched on to her hand. His hold hurt her wrist.

He shook his head at her. "No. You don't get to play that way. You play by the rules of propriety. You want my hand gone, you keep your head up and act like a human instead of a guilty monkey."

She blinked back angry tears. "The only opinion you have to fear is mine," he affirmed.

Marie rubbed her eyebrows with her thumb and index finger a moment. If his purpose was to distract her from the gaping stares, his tactic had worked. Marie sat up and dropped her hands from her face. She took hold of her napkin, then unfolded it along her lap. She took a long drink of champagne and watched Valant tense beside her when she took hold of the glass. She set it down gently.

She looked down at the fine china and cutlery set before her. She licked her lips before speaking. "I'm afraid I've never had the pleasure of dining in such an elegant setting. I have no idea which forks are for what."

Valant glanced over at her. "Don't worry. Nobody will notice which fork you're using. They'll be too busy staring at your face." At her crumpling look Valant let out a snort and set down his champagne glass. "The point is, do you care if they stare at something beyond your control? The more you cry and carry on, the more they're going to stare. Act like a beautiful woman, and they will see a beautiful woman."

He removed his hand from the apex of her legs, and extended his arm across the back of her chair. "Smile, Vinnetti. That way they think you enjoyed it. I have a reputation with the ladies to uphold."

Marie smiled weakly. "You are crass. Beyond comprehension."

Their meal was brought to them and Marie focused on eating rather than on what the crowd around her was thinking. She found it easy to distract herself, because the first time she unconsciously covered her face his hand was back, wedging itself between her thighs. She dropped her hand into her lap. He removed his.

They had dessert with coffee, and it occurred to Marie this was the longest she had ever seen him linger anywhere. She was indeed more afraid of his opinion than that of the others around her. While they would whisper, she couldn't hear their remarks. She felt the repercussions of his.

When they finished their meal, Valant stood and took her hand, gently this time, bringing her to her feet. He took off his jacket to put around her shoulders. She looked uncertainly into his eyes. "It's dark out now. It may be cold." With that he put his arm around her waist and guided her through the restaurant.

Marie wasn't sure if she wanted to push him away or move in closer. He was impossible to understand or predict. They moved past Mickey who now sat alone, Eva having gone. He slouched back in his chair, his index finger pressed to his top lip. Valant nodded at him. "Mick."

Mickey didn't reply, just watched them pass.

When they entered the alley again, Cobby was already parked close to them. Valant didn't acknowledge him with anything more than a look. He handed Marie into the car, then moved around and got in. She settled back into his jacket and looked out the window. Valant had that silent determination about him again.

Marie's head fell back on the seat when he pulled into the club parking lot. It was empty, as it was Sunday night and the club was closed. Valant parked at the side entrance. Cobby parked in his usual spot near the building, but didn't get out of his car. When Valant opened Marie's door, she knew better than to fight him. She took his hand and stood, looking around the dark parking lot, memories filling her mind. She pressed a hand to her face. Valant held her hand as he knocked on the door. A guard opened it to peer through at them, but had obviously been expecting their arrival.

He led her down the private hall, past the private stage and down the steps that were barely lit, out onto the floor. He kept going even after Marie closed her eyes and refused to see anything. It hurt so deeply. She felt him step up onto the first stage, then move up to the next. He took her straight to the microphone center stage and stopped. He looked down at her in the faint light, and slid his hands into his pockets. At that moment the spot light flooded them both. Marie visibly jerked.

She looked up at Valant and backed away from him. "Is this it? You rebuild Mickey's dream?" His jaw clenched. "Why you? Why not someone a little better suited to the job?"

"Who? Cobby?" He asked in a hard tone.

"I'm not stupid, Valant. You need me. Mickey needs me. Now you just have to find a way to paste me back together. Just long enough." Her mind flashed back to Rolly standing at the microphone smiling at her as he sang. She looked away from Valant.

The room filled in her mind and she could see herself, so elegant, singing before them. Her voice reaching high and distant. The floor began to dot with couples moving in unison to the sound the band was making behind her. She closed her eyes, but the scene only became more real. She stepped away from Valant in a silver gown. Marie looked down to see her smooth skin was unmarred, and her cleavage was nothing but perfect. Her fingertips traced her cheek to feel the radiant skin she once had.

The smiling faces of the back-up girls reflected at her from the smaller spotlight she didn't stand under. Rolly gave her a wink as he began to sing the song made so popular by Frank Sinatra. *All the Way*. With a joy she hadn't felt in a long while, she smiled, moving in her spike heels and gown down the steps to the lower stage. She stopped there and heard the crowd clap for her. She took a moment to remember the way her voice felt as she sang. The audience watched in rapt fascination just as they had before. She continued on to the center of the floor where she sang a few lines to a song she'd sung a hundred times before.

But, as she stood there, something reminded her all was not well. The dancing couples began to drift away from her, and her voice faltered some. She looked around her for someone to dance with, but found no one who came forward to claim her. The joy she felt at returning to happiness ebbed some. The first pang of fear crept into her mind.

He was dressed in his tuxedo, the same one he had worn so many times before when he danced with the beautiful Margo. He made his way through the crowded couples to where she stood, confused, and took hold of her. He looked down at her confidently as he slipped his arm around her waist. He was handsome as he looked down at her. She smiled, relieved, up at him.

"Hello, John," she whispered.

"Hello, Marie." He said back as if seeing her for the first time in a long time.

She pressed her cheek to his lowered one, and moved closer to him. The couples around them moved in again, and she could hear the band playing flawlessly. Rolly's voice rang out strong and wonderful. Valant lay her hand against his chest, then covered it with his own. Marie moved her face into his neck when he did so, smelling the familiar sent of bourbon and aftershave. She smiled against his skin. Laughter and conversation echoed in the great room.

Marie relished the feel of the strength in his arms, the way his hand moved lower on her back, how he tipped his head to cradle hers in his neck. His breath caressed her neck and shoulder. Her body molded to his perfectly. Every move he made sent intense sensation across the surface he touched.

"John…." She whispered faintly.

He moved his head and she raised hers slightly. He traced her cheek bone with his lips, and she tilted her head to offer him more of her face. Her breathing stopped and she closed her eyes. He traced along her forehead and down her other cheek. She didn't remember the scars he was touching. He caressed down to her lips, and she inhaled lightly when his lips met hers. Their warmth was light at first, unintrusive, but when she didn't move away from him he pressed in closer. Marie melted into him further as he deepened the kiss. Her hand unconsciously moving to his neck. He gently broke the contact and she again moved to the security of his neck, inhaling his scent.

His lips brushed against her ear and he whispered, "Tu, solamente tu, my beautiful Marie."

Marie wrapped her arms around his neck and nestled in again. Marie's mind was easy, she closed her eyes and saw nothing waiting for her. She could hear the music, Rolly's voice steady as he sang. Nothing tormented her, worried her. She was content, even if she were locked in a dream where nothing but dancing with Valant was real.

Mickey watched from the balcony next to Cobby. He spoke nothing as he looked to Cobby who stood with his hands in his pockets, his face firm. Cobby looked over at Mickey after a moment, and the two men exchanged a look of regret. Mickey reached up and squeezed Cobby's shoulder. Cobby looked back to the two lone figures that moved together as one in the silence. Mickey turned and walked away.

*****

Mickey didn't bother going home that night. After he left Cobby standing there looking down at the two people who centered his universe, he went out to the entrance hall and paused to look up at Marie's portrait in the gallery. Mickey felt a horrible crushing weigh of condemnation. He closed his eyes and exhaled slowly.

He went back to his office and spent the night drinking and playing cards. Eva had begged him to come to Remmi's, but Mickey refused. She rose from the table to go with her escorts and looked back at him with tears in her eyes, her huge belly making her cumbersome. He didn't want her just now. She was a painful reminder of things he couldn't change.

A few hours before dawn, Mickey wandered out into the street, which he knew was a terrible idea, and made his way to Imelda's. For a moment he wondered what his father would say. He guessed his father wouldn't care. His mother on the other hand, would care very much. She was never particularly attached to anything except Sam, and when he died she spent her time finding ways to torture Georgio. Enter Imelda. It made sense. Mickey knew well the difference between making love for lustful purposes and making love wrapped in the softness of a woman who loved him. One was easily cast aside, the other brought him back again and again like a powerful drug.

Mickey stopped to look into the shop window. A young woman was moving mannequins by a rolling hanger. She bent to the task of changing a dress on one. She looked like Imelda as she concentrated. But, when her head raised she looked like someone else entirely. Mickey watched her for several minutes. Imelda came out of the back and joined her.

Mickey walked to the door and knocked softly on the glass. Both women turned in surprise. Imelda smiled as she moved to open it for Mickey, pulling a key out of the pocket on her apron. "Good morning! What brings you out so early?" She looked at his eyes and then said, "Or is it still yesterday for you?"

Glenn Miller's *Star Dust* played softly from a small radio on the counter. "Have some coffee, won't you?"

"Yes. Thanks." As Imelda moved away through the swinging doors that led the way to the back, Mickey looked to the young woman who watched him from the corner of her eye. She flushed slightly when he noticed her. She turned back to her task, her back to him. Mickey slid his hands into his pockets and sauntered to her.

"You must be Imelda's daughter."

She turned in surprise to find he had come so close to her. She looked flustered. "Uhm, yes. I'm Julia."

Mickey tipped his head in recognition. "Ahh, the newly wed."

She smiled softly. "Yes." Mickey watched her a moment as she pulled a red dress over the mannequin and secured it into place.

"Last time I saw you, you had pigtails."

"Last time I saw you was yesterday." Julia looked pointedly at him, then returned to the dress.

Mickey chuckled. "Point taken."

Imelda came in carrying a coffee tray. She set it on the counter and began to pour three cups. Mickey left Julia and went to claim his cup of steaming liquid. "She looks a little like you, Imelda."

Julia turned to look at them both as they studied her. She said nothing, just turned back to her work. Imelda smiled. "One of the only two things I ever did right."

Mickey took a sip of coffee. "She is like you in that she isn't afraid to voice her observations," Mickey said with irony.

Julia looked at him for a brief second. "Oh? What observations has she made?" Imelda asked.

"That I'm *not* observant."

"Well, you aren't," Imelda said flatly.

"I have a lot on my mind." Mickey said defensively before taking another sip. "Besides, what the hell else has she got to do all day but notice me? Day dream of her knight in shining armor?"

Imelda again smiled softly at her daughter. "I remember those days. Do you Mickey? Do you remember what it was to be consumed by someone?" Mickey said nothing just inhaled and looked at Julia.

"To be young again," he muttered.

"You are not so old, you know." Imelda gave him a knowing look.

"Yeah, thank God I'm not ancient like you." Mickey said with mock relief.

She shot him a disgusted look. "Yes. What am I? Eleven years your senior? So ancient."

Mickey's eyes went dark.

"Is she ready?" Imelda asked apprehensively. Mickey said nothing for a moment, his eyes on Imelda's young daughter.

"I hope so."

*****

"Don't bother with coffee," Valant said in a low voice as he looked at her from the dining room table. He and Cobby both sat in their suit jackets in the pale light of dawn.

Marie had come out of the bedroom in her soft cotton night gown just as she did every morning, her long black hair spilling over her shoulder. She met his eyes, a look of happiness in hers, a look of hardness in his. She knew it then. The closeness she had dancing with him the night before was gone. When he stopped her, she saw the suitcase next to Cobby.

There were no lamps on in the faint light, but she hadn't needed them to know what was coming. "Get dressed and pack your things."

Her mouth twitched as she looked at Cobby who wouldn't look back at her. "Am I coming back?" She managed to ask in a small voice.

"No." Valant's reply stung.

Cobby then stood and walked the few steps to her, holding out the small suitcase. He finally met her eyes, a look of deep regret shining out of his. It hit like a rock. When she took the case he backed away from her as if she were the walking dead. Marie pressed her lips together briefly. The brilliance of her dark eyes were enhanced by the tears that now glistened in them.

She looked at Valant, but his face was a mask of granite and she found no solace there. Panic seized her heart, and her hand trembled as she turned from the two men who had been her steady and constant for the past few months. They fully intended to use her as they found convenient. What was worse was that she fully intended to go along with it. Not because her empire was at stake, but because somehow in the past weeks her purpose had changed to giving her life so that she never had to see Valant's bloodied and shattered body lying lifeless. She wanted him to live. Of course there was Cobby too, and Vantino and Vinny, but each time she closed her eyes it was the form of The Dark Horse that haunted her.

His touch burned her, lit fire across the nerves of her body. But that wasn't it. He had meticulously torn down each of her issues and put the walls back up. This time with firm brick so that what was behind those walls wouldn't be seen or felt. In his callous way he stood up against her every time she tried to break down. Forced her to toughen her resolve, showed her in every unkind way that the only things that break you, are the things you turn yourself into glass for. He raged against her, melted against her, pouted against her, patiently taught her, methodically wrenched her each direction. He had taken the time to awaken the desire in her which had long laid dormant.

Now he cast her aside in the same cruel manner in which he did everything else.

Marie took her time dressing and packing her things. She didn't cry, although the possibility edged closer to the surface with each passing moment. It was past time for begging. Now she channeled her energy into moving her body along in its task. She moved like sludge. It seemed the task of folding five house dresses, and as many sets of undergarments, might as well be single-handedly pushing the Titanic out to sea, and being twice as doomed.

She wanted to pray, but she was afraid that she would get the same cold feeling from God. She hadn't proposed her plan to Him, and she feared He wasn't going to be pleased with her for it. So, she ducked her head in shame and kept going. She had no say anyway.

She brushed her hair and rolled it into a bun, looking in the same vanity mirror she had seen herself in that horrible night when she was swollen and bloodied beyond recognition. She took time with her make-up, not sure where she was bound and who may be there. The memory of the night before was so real in her mind. She thought surely she could close her eyes and be back in his arms again, his lips pressed so wonderfully on her own. He had come out of the crowd and taken her into his arms as if he could wait no longer to hold her against him.

Then her mind flashed to the restaurant. The deep burn of humiliation still bore its sting. He was a man of many characters. She wondered which of them he was truly, and which ones he had to work at to be. She feared the attractive man who held her so possessively was the mere act.

She stood and looked around the bedroom for a while, her eyes resting on the pictures and objects that had become so familiar to her. Almost as if they belonged to her in some way. Her knees were weak and threatened not to carry her despite the fact that she had been prepping herself for this for some time. But, after the night before, she felt she couldn't go. Didn't want to go. She wanted him to hold her, to kiss her, to make her forget that he was turning his back on her.

She shuddered violently as she inhaled, and knew she had to go. God help her she had to go. Now, before she broke apart. There would be the long hours of the night to cry. If night came for her at all.

She walked gamely out of the bedroom to where they still sat silently at the table, Cobby with his elbows on his knees, bent forward looking down at his hands that he rubbed together. Valant, who slouched in his chair, his chin resting in his hand. His eyes raised to her, but nothing changed. Marie's heels were the only sounds in the house.

Cobby stood slowly as she approached him and set her suitcase at his feet. She looked down as she stood before him and licked her lips. Her red dress and black hair complemented each other in a rare and deep beauty that most men never saw.

"Will you leave us a moment, Cob?" He nodded slightly as he bent to take hold of her suitcase. With her head bent she looked sadly at the small case that carried the entirety of her life. Her lips trembled viciously, and she covered them with her hand. Valant stood and walked to the stool at the kitchen counter and leaned back on it in a casual pose.

On shaking legs she walked the few steps to stand just out of reach before him. She raised shining eyes to him and saw his look of indifference. Her mouth twitched as she bravely looked into his face. He slid his hands into his pockets, but said nothing.

Marie blinked back tears and in a broken voice asked, "Do.... D...... Do yyou have anything you want to say to me?"

She searched his face as she waited for his answer. He stared at her for a long time, the coldness in his features unrelenting. Finally, he shook his head, barely.

It cut so much deeper than she had anticipated. Her face scrunched as one tear fell onto the hardwood floor. She bowed her head and bit her lip to get a hold on her emotions. This wasn't one of his lessons. This was real. He was done with her.

Valant watched her as her body tensed and she literally swallowed all the emotion that was raging freely in her face. She inhaled deeply and raised her head to him and looked into his eyes. She stepped to him slowly until her legs brushed his. She reached up gently, taking hold of his face. Marie smelled that wonderful scent of bourbon and aftershave. Then she whispered to him.

"Thank you could never be enough." With that she raised her lips to his and pressed them softly together. She held her position, savoring one last time the feel of his mouth against hers, his body heat reaching out and caressing her skin, the lean strength he possessed. He didn't pull away or tense.

She pulled slowly away and looked into his eyes. "Goodbye," Marie whispered faintly, then she was gone, the sound of her footsteps echoing mercilessly off the wood paneling she had cared for each day. The silence that followed Marie took possession of her newly vacant inhabitance, crushing like a tidal wave. Valant closed his eyes.

Cobby stood next to the car door that hung open for her. She refused to meet his eyes as she slid into the cold interior. He closed the door softly behind her. He looked at her in the rearview mirror to see the right side of her face, the scars evident despite the make-up. Marie waited until they had hit the pavement before she slowly lowered herself onto the seat, her entire body aching with sudden age. She spent the rest of the drive succumbing to the shifting of her mind as images of hell tore at her soul.

*****

Lyn Miller

Revenge

Instinctively she already knew where they were going. She didn't have to raise her head to know she was being followed by an entourage. She was far too valuable now for them to leave her exposed. They had one shot to bait Danny G. They had to use it carefully. This was as close to royalty as she would ever get. She knew though, she was safe until Danny G could get her in front of everyone.

When they got close to their destination, Marie sat up and looked out the window at the city streets. She smoothed back her hair and rubbed her scars to get the reality to come center front. She had no idea how she would hold on when it came to facing everyone.

Cobby pulled into the alley behind the club.

Marie shattered. Deano reached out for her with a bloodied hand, she smelled the rank body smell of the man who held her, felt her heart come to exploding point as she made her way down the street and away from Valant.

If you run……..

She had run. In honesty, she was worse off than if Valant had just tortured and left her for dead. Now he took what was left of her soul, and turned her back out on the streets. Cobby now stood with the door open reaching down for her. She hadn't noticed. She inhaled deeply trying to steady herself. Part of her feared greatly that Valant would materialize out of nowhere and take control of the situation. So, she took hold of Cobby's hand and stood on shaky legs.

"Don't leave me, Cobby," she whispered in a terrified voice. Cobby took hold of her hands as he stepped closer to her.

"I won't. I'm with you now until the whole thing is over. I've got your back." The vision of Deano ripped again through Marie. As Deano disappeared and Cobby took his place, his own bloody hand reaching for her instead of Deano's.

She started to sob, and Cobby produced a handkerchief from his pocket. She took it and dabbed at her face, trying not to ruin the make-up she had carefully put on. She composed herself as best as she could, watching the cracks in her vision as her mind demanded to take full control of her. She stood rigid against it.

"Let's go in. It won't be so bad in there," Marie said quietly to Cobby. He put an arm around her and took hold of one of her hands, leading her into the building. She was correct in the assumption that being away from the place her life had ended would be better. She was able to shake the shifting and hold herself up again.

Now to face them.

She stepped away from Cobby and looked up at him uncertainly. He smiled at her, all the previous pity and concern gone. He was like he was from before. "Damn, you look good, Marie."

Marie's mind shifted. She became herself again, not the shattered and ruined Marie, but the Marie who had stunned and dazzled. Cobby watched as the change crossed her face. He struggled gamely on.

"Hurry up Sugar Tits. You're gonna be late," he said teasingly. "Damn. What the hell. Are you fundamentally against breakfast or something?"

She frowned. "Take it up with Mickey. He thinks I'm too fat for breakfast." She walked away from him up the hall and past the dressing rooms. She turned and looked back at him coyly. Cobby made sure to be smirking at her. Then she rounded the corner, and was gone.

Cobby broke when she disappeared and he heard the roar of applause as she entered the stage. He covered his face with his hands and leaned against the wall. Valant had been right. She would shift back to another time, completely unaware she was anything but who she had been before. He felt like the biggest asshole that had ever lived, forcing her to shift like that. Val insisted Cobby make her shift. The truth was it was easy, and although this Marie wasn't real, it was far better than the suffering Marie that had ridden into town with him.

God help them if the shift didn't last. What he had told her about being by her side constantly was true. He just hoped he would be able to protect her when the time came.

*****

The shift didn't last. In fact, it was gone the moment she looked back at Cobby. But, she kept her strength with sheer determination. Valant's words came back to her repeatedly as she made her way to the stage door.

Act like a beautiful woman and they'll see a beautiful woman.

She nearly crumbled when she first saw Rolly waiting for her by the entrance to the stage. He turned and looked at her with such apprehension, and then relief at just being able to gaze upon her. He moved to her quickly and took her in his arms, holding her tightly. When he looked down at her with sad eyes, she tried to offer him a strong smile in return. He almost believed her.

"As beautiful as the first time I saw you. You just never do change."

"Hello, Rolly," she said softly.

"Hello, sweetheart," he held her tightly to him again. "We best go see them. Everyone is dying to see you again." She nodded.

As she entered the stage the band and dance company exploded into applause and cheering. She smiled bravely and felt Rolly's strong arm around her waist. Marie began to hug and kiss everyone who came to welcome her back. Steven gave her a strong hug, and she relished the feel of the friendship he offered out to her. All of the dance company told her she was looking so wonderful. It was then she knew Mickey had prepped everyone.

She saw sadness and shock reflecting in all eyes, but no one made mention of it. They just moved on, and acted like she had merely been gone, not destroyed as well. Marie was grateful for their kindness, but it just solidified in her the fact that in a short time she wouldn't be among them anymore. In attempt to bring her in and make her feel as she had before, they only made her feel like the marked.

"Well," she said finally as she looked at the crowd around her, "I hope I haven't held up rehearsals too much?"

Rolly smiled at her. "Nope. The show never starts until we have Marie."

*****

Mickey stood beside Valant on the private stage and watched as the company welcomed Marie. Neither man spoke as they watched, just took in everything. Valant looked around the room to the men posted everywhere, and made mental count of the men outside. His eyes drifted to Cobby who stood just off the dance floor with his hands in his pockets. As if he could hear Valant's thoughts he looked up at him. Valant nodded to him.

When he looked back at Mickey, he was already watching Valant. "It's for the best, right?"

"It's for the best," came Valant's hard reply.

*****

Marie would not be performing at the club for several weeks. She learned from Rolly during rehearsal that Mickey had scheduled a huge debut for her two weeks from then. It was generally agreed that this would give her time to slip back into the grove of things. Give both herself and the band confidence she had the performance memorized. To Marie, it seemed silly. Odds were, she wouldn't even get the performance rolling before it was ended.

The long day finally drew to a close, and although it was clear Marie wasn't firing with her usual enthusiasm, she made the first rehearsal back. She would glance to Rolly and catch him watching her, something sad and yearning in his eyes. He would smile at her softly, then she would look away. He was such a nice and good man, why hadn't he claimed her heart? Then, Valant would flash into her mind, and she would want to drift away into the dark somewhere to lie down. The burden in her soul too heavy to lift and carry anymore.

But he was gone. As if he had never been. As if the torment he had put her through was a dream. It was the only thing her mind wouldn't let her flash back to, no matter how hard she tried. She stared at the dance floor and saw herself there, his warm lips pressed to hers, her arms caught around his neck. His arms holding her possessively. Had it really just been the night before?

Cobby came out of the darkness surrounding the stage to claim her, just as he had all those months ago when she had first come to meet the band. This time, she took his hand when he led her away. When the dark claimed them, she lay against his arm. Cobby was such a warm and loyal man. Why did she not love him? The heart is a miserable and treacherous thing. It would neither listen to her reasoning nor common sense.

They sat together at the restaurant and ate their evening meal, not saying much. Marie taking time only to comment that she must have moved up in the world to be provided with a date and a menu. She didn't say so, but she was glad to have her old booth back, not to mention the elation that Cobby sat across from her and had no intention of jamming his hand between her legs. No Valant sat at the table across from them, and she wasn't sure she was happy about it or not.

It was as if she needed his influence to function properly. Like she no longer had the ability to manipulate her own behavioral attributes. His watchful eye caught the things she no longer registered about herself. He kept her from shifting. He was a good three quarters her strength. Now that he was gone, she was nothing but mush on the floor.

Cobby took her to the apartment and she rode the elevator to Mickey's private floor without speaking. Even Cobby kept to himself. When the doors opened Marie walked out into the past. She had shifted without her mind going first. She smiled at Cobby who had moved to the bar.

"It's still housekeeping's nightmare."

"It's still mine too," Cobby replied disgustedly.

"Let's run away together, Cobby," Marie stated. He looked up at her and smiled.

"We'd make the street and be gunned down by the men Valant has absolutely everywhere," Cobby returned.

Marie shrugged. "Well, it might be better than living in Eva's personal invention of my hell."

"I doubt they'll say anything if you mark up the carpet."

Marie tilted her head back and laughed ironically. "I should hope not."

Cobby handed her a drink and then took a long gulp of his own. He looked at her for a moment then asked quietly, "Do you want to see him? He'll come."

Marie closed her eyes tightly. "No." She took a long swallow. In a shaking voice she continued, "Oh, Cobby. I hope as a man you are strong, for I intend to drape my miserable self on you when we are alone. I need someone to hold me up. And while I can't make love to you, you will be my everything."

Cobby sighed. "That's why they sent me."

She looked at him, tears in her eyes. "God help you." She finished off her drink then set the glass on the bar. "Well, I think I will retire to my suite where I have every intention of crying myself to sleep. Please do not disturb me." With that she wandered to her room that was still immaculate and cold.

She slipped off her shoes, and turned to her corner to find a pillow and blankets already made into a bed. Someone had thought of her, but she couldn't fathom who. She lay in the darkness, watching the pale lights change on her wall as cars passed, or as other city lights turned off for the night. It was loud. She longed for the solitude of the safe house. She longed to know he was just beyond the door. Longed for the chance to go back to the time before she knew how she felt, to discover him sooner, to know him as a woman knows a man.

At that thought she wondered if after all the time and separation, had he returned to the beautiful and sinful Margo? It caused great unrest in her to think of him somewhere in the night, wrapped tightly in Margo's silky soft skin, moving to a rhythm all his own making. Bitter tears fell silently. After all he had done, why did she care? But, after all he had done, how couldn't she?

*****

February 1943

Vinny inhaled deeply as he looked down at the chess board. He exhaled just as loudly. Vantino sat staring at Vinny, who was across from him. Vantino's head rested on his arms folded atop the back of the chair he sat backward in. The enormous grandfather clock ticked away the time as the stillness of the room went undisturbed. The late afternoon sun reflected off the white marble pieces that sat before the men, and Marie could smell the leather bound books that surrounded them on the shelves.

Marie sat very still as she looked between the two men. She kept her breathing to a minimum. She consciously kept herself from fidgeting. It was excruciatingly boring. Her eyes studied everything within sight that could be seen without turning her head. Vantino looked at her out of the corner of his eye and winked. She tried to stifle a smile.

"It is important, Marie, to always consider your strategy. Think about the moves you want to make long before you ever make them. Consider all consequences to your actions lest you live with a decision that ruins what you have built." His arm reached out across the board and moved a chess piece. "Strategy is everything. Remember that. Strategy is everything."

"And let us hope," Vantino interjected, "That you are a little faster thinker than Old Father Time here." Vinny looked up at him, irritated.

Marie tried again not to smile.

"Know what you are planning to do. Move through your strategy in your mind, so it becomes second nature. So your body moves off muscle memory. Keep it fore front so you don't have to remember what you plan." Vinny didn't look at her as he spoke, just weighed the options and consequences of Vantino's move. "Strategy, Marie. Strategy and courage. The game of life requires both."

*****

1956

Several days past as Marie spent her time once again at the club. She kept quiet and performed her job, looking like a woman bent on putting on the best comeback routine anyone had ever seen. But the truth was, inside she was working on something completely different. She kept it safe inside herself, revealing nothing beyond what looked like a compliant agreement to go along with Mickey's plan. She laughed at jokes and tried to forget about her face. She held tight so her mind wouldn't shift.

She didn't see Valant much anymore. She had decided it would be best to keep to herself and resolved to keep a wall up in case they should happen past each other. She found it would be better to put back the distance between them that had been there before. Besides, he had not sought her out, so it would be easy. The one time they crossed paths he was coming into the club while Cobby was leading her out. She didn't look at him, although Cobby nodded to him. Her heart nearly burst when he came into view.

Mickey and Valant stopped at the apartment one evening, for what she really didn't know. More than likely to see how their bait was holding up, and if she would be able to hold it together. She was polite to Mickey, but avoided Valant. When she handed him a drink and his fingers brushed hers, she merely addressed him as Mr. Valant. Then she returned to the bar where she sat reading a magazine Cobby got for her. Valant never spoke to her.

Marie and Cobby had taken to sitting in the lounge area just outside the apartment and watching the television at night. The first night they had done so, Cobby walked ahead of her to open the door only to turn and see she wasn't there. Marie stood looking down at the television, and Cobby sauntered over to ask what she was looking at.

"Which knob turns it on?" she asked and Cobby laughed.

"Hell if I know."

Marie bent at tried several knobs before she got the right one, then the two of them spent the rest of the evening watching and sharing several bottles of wine. Cobby found the more he drank the funnier Lucille Ball became. Marie laughed nonstop at Lucy's antics.

It became habit after that. Eventually at some point Marie would end up curled up beside Cobby asleep. He would carry her into the bedroom and lay her on the bed. She never made a comment about the fact that she was no longer sleeping on the floor. Cobby would hear her in the night sometimes, crying softly or clearly having a nightmare. So many times she had called out for Valant, but instead of going in to her, he would just light another cigarette and stare into the dark.

His every fiber screamed for him to do something. But he could think of no way out.

In some ways Marie had returned to her old self again. She rose each morning and made coffee, then sarcastically told Cobby she had no use for breakfast. She made no reference to her face, but Cobby noticed that she never looked into the mirror. She avoided them like the plague. He wondered for a while if she had shifted into a past self, but after a time he knew that was impossible. She had come to understand where her strength lay, and it was not in her own reflection. She could avoid the pain of it if she just didn't look.

On the morning of her fourth day, Cobby took her from the restaurant to Imelda's shop. Cobby had been present the morning Mickey himself had come in to give Imelda a talk about how she should and should not act when Marie came back in for the first time. Mickey wanted no possibilities of some remark or action that might make Marie regress into the uninhabitable being she had been.

It hurt Marie. She knew, just as surely as the band had been prepped for her arrival, Imelda had been too. Imelda was tense and looked only into Marie's eyes, never at her scars. It was so blatant that Marie felt worse than if she had just made a fuss over them. Imelda was friendly and cordial, but she spoke of nothing but gowns and what she had planned for the night Marie would return. She was thinking on a grand scheme. She said much, but nothing at all.

That is, until they wandered into the back to take measurements. She had lost much weight since the last gown Imelda had made for her. As soon as Imelda stepped into the dressing room behind Marie, the older woman took her into her arms.

"Oh, Marie," she cried. Marie was unable to hold herself back any more, and she collapsed into Imelda's embrace. Imelda smoothed her hair and cried with the young woman who carried much the world would never see.

For a long while they stood like that, crying, Imelda the only woman that even remotely understood Marie and the situation she now faced. She was the mother Marie should have had. Imelda released her momentarily to bring a handkerchief. Marie blew her nose as Imelda moved her to a sofa. Imelda sat close to Marie and held both of her hands.

"I won't bother to ask how things are."

"Then I won't bother lying to you," Marie replied.

"Things have gotten so bad, Marie. I don't think they would put you through this if they thought there was another way."

Marie was silent as she looked at her hands. When she looked up she said, "How bad?"

Imelda clicked her tongue as she smoothed her skirt. "There has been much violence. Seemed there wasn't a day that went by that there wasn't some kind of bombing or shooting. They even shot up Mickey's house. Killed a guard. Mickey sent Eva away for fear something terrible would happen to her or the child." She sighed deeply. "They are saying that there has been no word of Vinnetti for some time. It is the general feeling that he has been killed. That perhaps is why The Underground has now turned so savagely on the Delano's. Even Mickey's dead wife's family has been targeted.

"Then, about a week ago it all stopped," Imelda said the next part slowly. "About the time Mickey ran the first ad for your return to the stage." Imelda watched Marie carefully for her reaction to this news.

She had none. It was perhaps the ad that helped put a stop to the violence, but, it was also the fact that Marie had again seen Danny G. It was her agreement to go head to head. About that time Mickey must have run his ad, and Danny G had his time and location. Yes, he was planning to kill her in front of everyone. It was a great power play, although she doubted Mickey nor Valant would cower to it. All it would gain was her death and the end of Vinny's line.

As for Vinny, she doubted also that he was dead. If he were, Danny G would just keep striking until he had decimated Mickey's defenses enough to end it. It wouldn't matter to him if she were alive or dead if Vinny was out of the picture. She seriously distrusted the possibility Valant bought into the idea that Vinny was dead. She would no longer be a threat or useful as bait, therefore would have been disposed of long ago. She wondered how he knew that Vinny was still alive.

"Imelda, I need a favor," Imelda looked into Marie's face. "I know that you've been told to make gowns that will cover my chest. And I want you to. All but one."

Imelda looked at her uncertainly. "Are you sure?"

"Yes."

"Which?"

"The black. I need something of great elegance for that final gown. It must be black. Please, you can't tell Mickey or Valant."

Imelda's brows knit together. "What are you planning, Marie?"

"I just want one last chance to be who I was."

*****

Cobby listened outside the fitting room door. Valant had been adamant that he not leave her alone, for a myriad of reasons. He had been concerned she may try to run, but Cobby knew she wouldn't. But, he was concerned about her mental health. She was holding, but he greatly feared she would come apart and Cobby doubted that he could handle it.

Marie took the news that Vinny might be dead well. She remarked nothing. Cobby himself doubted he was dead. He had only a small shred of proof, but it was enough for him. Suddenly, after all the years of plotting his death, it seemed they needed what shield he could provide in this mess. If it came to Mickey and Valant standing alone, it would be very surreal.

His only shred of proof had come about a week ago. Cobby was making rounds alone since Valant was still at the safe house with Marie. Mickey had taken a lot of hits, and they had closely watched the card houses to stop them from being targeted. That put men on the street trying to guess which car had explosive intent. It was impossible. Eva had been sent away, and Mickey rarely left town.

Cobby could hardly bring himself to leave his car anywhere for fear someone would get to it. Then came the problem of getting out onto a dark street alone. He never took the same route twice, and sometimes he avoided the darker more deserted side of Mickey's territory. But, on that particular night he had no choice but to check the venues down there.

He kept a loaded gun on his lap as he drove, then kept it in his hand as he walked. He was losing weight from the stress of it. The only thing to temper his nerves was bourbon. Cobby moved up the alley to the back door which was no longer lit for obvious reasons. He knocked and went in, collecting what money was the house take. That particular house did well, the shadier characters along the docks frequenting the establishment. He inhaled sharply as the guard opened the door to blackness for him. It brought back unpleasant memories.

Cobby moved out and stood still a while waiting for his eyes to adjust, listening. He heard nothing and refused to acknowledge the ice in his veins, pushing one foot in front of the other. He approached his car, and longed to be inside and away.

"Don't shoot me, boy." Cobby jerked in the direction of the voice. A shape stood against the wall, not moving.

"Damn, I dread you. Things never pan out well for me when you show up," Cobby said in a low voice.

"How's the shoulder?"

"Hurts constantly. Thanks for asking."

"You don't show it. Atta boy." He paused a moment. "Let's take a drive."

"What for?" Cobby asked apprehensively.

"Mostly because my car has been around the corner for twenty minutes. Again, I've been with yours the whole time. I know nothing has been done to yours. Come. Let's get away from this alley. Makes me sweat to be in here."

They avoided using names, for that would only serve to verify identity to anyone who might be listening. Cobby moved to the driver's door of his car, then stood waiting for Vantino to get in. He slid into his own seat and turned the engine. He left the alley in a hurry. As they hit the street, Cobby left black marks.

"Where are we going?" Cobby asked.

"Take me to headquarters."

Cobby looked at him in irritation. "Mine or yours?"

Vantino looked at him like he were stupid. "Mine."

"No. No way. I have to drive clear the hell over there with you to watch my back. Then you get out, and I have to drive back across two territories alone. Hell no!" Cobby spat.

"Fair enough. Take me to yours. I'll take your car."
Vantino gave a mock sweep of his hand. "I'll return it of
course." He finished sarcastically.

Cobby glared at him. "Nope. That doesn't work either."

Vantino looked at him squarely. "It's not my fault you get
caught so easily. You're lucky I'm benevolent."

Cobby's voice rose in anger. "What the hell! What choice
do I have but to be out here! Maybe that's the point. They want
me gunned down!"

Vantino looked at him with all the confidence of his
generation. "No. No, boy, you're out here because you're the
only one they know capable of the job. You carry a great
amount of respect and responsibility on your shoulders right
now."

"Thanks for the bolstering talk." Vantino laughed at
Cobby's sarcasm.

"Well, to the meat and potatoes. How's my girl?"

Cobby shrugged.

Vantino looked ahead and said in a hard voice. "I see in
the paper this morning that she will be returning to the stage.
They fully intend to use her as bait."

Cobby said nothing, his face drawn into a resigned pose.

"You don't agree?"

Again Cobby shrugged. "What I agree or don't agree with
holds no weight."

"Do you see her?"

"Sometimes."

"Have they told her the truth? Does she know what they
intend?" Vantino insisted.

"They have told her nothing. But, she knows."

Vantino sighed. "Marie was always so very intelligent.
She had things figured before most of us got out of bed in the
morning. She has weighed her options and the likely outcomes.
She knows that this is the best way. She also obviously decided
that you bunch of shit slime are worth putting her life up for."

"It isn't just us asshole. She knows full well you sit in the
balance, too," Cobby retorted.

"Not me, Vinny, maybe. She knows I will be at her side. I
don't sit in the balance, I'm defending it."

Cobby let out a chuckle. "That's exactly what she said."

Vantino smiled. "That's my girl." Then he turned serious. "Nice cut job." Cobby looked at Vantino. "She got to him, didn't she?"

"Who? Valant?" Cobby asked.

Vantino just smiled. "He did what I always wanted to. Vin wouldn't let me. Said it might make things harder on her. So I tried to satisfy myself with crushing the shit out of him every couple of months. It wasn't enough. And, the longer The Dark Horse knows her, cutting Jerry up won't be enough for him either."

"Perhaps, when this is all over….." Cobby didn't finish.

Vantino grinned. "Her mama really doesn't look any trashier for her lack of teeth, or sons." He looked at Cobby slyly. "You are a sure shot."

Cobby couldn't help but grin in return at the memory. "I'd offer you a drink, but that will have to wait," Vantino stated.

"Where to, old man?"

Vantino pulled out his loaded pistol and put it to Cobby's head. Cobby sighed an aggravated sigh. "I think headquarters will suit me fine." Vantino answered.

*****

Marie put everything she had into readying for her great comeback. With each day she gained more strength, and her performances at rehearsals became a little closer to what she had been before. It was decided the second song of the evening would be would be the popular song written by Les Brown, Bud Green and Ben Homer called, *Sentimental Journey.* It seemed to everyone very appropriate given the fact that no one had thought they would ever see Marie again, except in a sentimental journey. She would debut it alone center stage.

Marie soon realized that she would perform the entire show from the upper stage. They had no intention of letting her get close to the patrons. Especially since they had no idea who they were looking for. But, Marie did. She kept this information to herself. She went along with it, happy that she wouldn't be included in any tricky dance maneuvers. Her concentration could be elsewhere.

Marie did intend to give the performance of her life. That was all part of it, too. If she were going out, she wanted the beautiful sound God gave her to be the last thing that filled the ears of those who would watch her die. The haunting sound wouldn't follow her with finality to the grave. It would live on in the minds and hearts of those who heard her.

As Marie made up her mind, she relaxed some. Vinny had been right. Exploring the possible outcomes only made her more confident in what she was doing. In the end, she worried less about her scars, and in that she found that Valant was also correct. She acted like a beautiful woman, and with time, that was all the ensemble saw. She would never be carefree again, but this was comfortable.

She only saw Valant once from a distance.

She enjoyed her evenings with Cobby, despite the fact that a heavy cloak of doom hung over them. To Cobby, it only radiated throughout his body that they were intertwined. He had no proof that this was true, but he felt it. She was in some way a part of him, and he dreaded the price they would pay together. For like Vantino, Cobby wasn't hanging in the balance, but defending it. That put three against the possibilities of hundreds.

It made him sick.

So, when she curled up next to him and lay her head on his shoulder to watch television until she fell asleep, he let her be. He tried to think of simple things to talk about at dinner. Teased her when he found the heart. Carried her to bed. He would stand over her and watch her sleep, terrified of the things he should say to her, do for her, but the cowardice in him prevented him from doing so.

And so it went, each day one less than the number of days they had the day before.

After rehearsal Marie had gone to the bar to wait for Cobby who was talking with Mickey on the private stage. She had waved to him and pointed to the bar to let him know where she was headed. She didn't fight his presence, knowing it troubled Cobby greatly to be solely responsible for her. So, she always kept in sight and did what she was told. He nodded his consent. It was not as if she were alone, Mickey had men everywhere.

Marie sat and asked the bartender if there was any coffee. Replying there was and he set her up with a cup as well as cream and sugar. She opened a magazine. She read a few articles, then looked back to see if Cobby were coming. He wasn't yet. So she read on, sipping her coffee.

Time drug on and she grew impatient. Rehearsals had ended early for her. The company was covering a new act for the night. Now they played behind her and she looked at them, sorry she couldn't be among them. She turned back to see the bartender refilling her coffee cup. She thanked him and turned another page.

"Bourbon," the deep voice cut through her mind like a shard of glass.

Marie didn't look at him as he sat down several stools away from her. She sipped her coffee, hoping he hadn't noted the trembling of her hand. Had his aura always been so devastating, or had she forgotten in the long days since she had told him goodbye? She turned another page.

"Captivating read?" She felt his eyes burning into her skin.

She smiled as she cast him a glance. "Well, it's not Moby Dick, but then again, what is?" She nodded at him when she finished. "Mr. Valant." She returned to her coffee and magazine as the band became deafening.

He sipped his bourbon, then set it down. "Vinnetti," he said harshly.

She felt her resolve slipping into the mire of deprivation at the sound of his tone. He could play her anyway he wanted to. With one word or touch, she could either be an emotional mess or a woman burning in desire. He could do what he wished or throw her aside. Marie had no defense against what he might do. No way to make the game fair.

"How can a man go from Mr. Valant, to Valant, then to John, and wind up back at Mr. Valant?" he asked in a clipped voice.

She looked at him out of the corner of her eye. Valant looked into his glass as he set it down, then looked directly at her.

"Just tell me what you want me to be," she whispered to him.

"Shouldn't I be saying that to you?" He asked quietly, the anger evident. He took another long drink.

Marie declined another cup of coffee from the bartender when he came round again. She closed her magazine and gathered her sweater. She felt she had best go.

"Excuse me," she whispered as she stood to go.

"Take a drive with me," he said without looking at her. She stopped and looked down at the red carpet.

"I don't think so."

He turned to look at her. "Of all people, you should know best how bad it is to go against me."

She looked away as her lips trembled. She started away from him but he caught her arm. "Take a drive with me." The firmness in his voice made her question her sanity in feeling about him the way she did.

"No." Her voice barely formed the word. He didn't acknowledge her answer, but pulled her away from the bar and across the club to the private hall. He didn't look back at her nor stop, just kept going until the light of day shone bright in her eyes. He looked at the guard who was stood next to his car. The man moved away from the vehicle. Valant took her to the driver's side and opened the door, lowering her in then sliding in himself. His body pressed against hers. Marie closed her eyes and turned her head, afraid of what her eyes would betray.

Valant put his arm around her and pulled her close to him. Marie's head came to rest involuntarily on his shoulder as she whispered, "John." He looked over at her. When her eyes opened to his, his look was dark. She curled her hand against his chest as he turned the ignition with his off hand. They were away.

Marie had no idea what way they were headed. All she knew was the familiar scent that clung to him. How it felt to be close to him, to touch him. She was grateful she wasn't the one in operation of the vehicle, for they would surely die. When he pulled her closer, she buried her face in his neck, feeling his pulse hammering, and the heat of his body radiating through his skin. She clung to him with all her strength.

When the car stopped, there was no sound except that of his breathing. He held her for a long while without moving. He opened the door slowly. "Marie."

The rush of sea air filled Marie's nose. Raising her head she saw a deserted beach. It stretched for a great ways as the sun reflected off the water that rolled relentlessly. "Come on."

He stood and then reached down for her. She grasped his hand like a life line in the rolling wave of the ocean and held it firmly. He pulled her to him, locking her eyes with his. Marie's breathing stopped as she recognized the look that he had given her a number of times that she could now recall and count. This time it did not cause her fear or panic, but merely took her breath away.

"You are the only one who looks at me like that," she said softly.

"Like what?" came his deep reply.

"Without pity or remorse."

"You look the same to me today as you did at nineteen."

She gave him a slight smile. She gazed out to the ocean. "This is beautiful." She walked from him out onto the sand and raised her arms over her head and stretched. She wore the same dark red dress she had on the day Cobby took her away from the safe house. Her heels were black and open toed. Valant watched her closely and moved to the front of the car leaning back against the hood of his black '55 Thunderbird.

She came to sit next to him. "What is this place?"

Valant took in the ocean as he replied. "Mick and I come here sometimes. We started coming here when we were young." He looked at her then said, "Back before life got serious."

She looked down at her dress and smoothed a wrinkle. "I don't think she'll appreciate you bringing me here."

"Margo? The last time she was here was the day she told me she was getting married, and not to me."

Marie closed her eyes. "I hate serious life."

Valant sighed. "Yours has been more serious than mine ever thought about being."

She laughed at that. "What is love, anyway?"

"Beautiful, when it's right in all its forms," he answered softly while observing her.

She didn't reply, merely looked out again into the vast expanse that answered to no one but God.

"Did Alex ever come for me?" she asked.

He was quiet for a long time as he studied her distant gaze. "No."

"I'm glad. I would have felt obligated."

The corner of Valant's mouth twitched as he looked away from her. "I would like to kill every man that ever looked at you. Excepting myself, of course."

Marie laughed and pressed her palms together, then rubbed the bridge of her nose with her index fingers. "What a mess."

"I'll do it, too."

"Can I give you a list to start with?" She looked at him out of the corner of her eyes.

He raised his eyebrows. "I hate to tell you this, but most everyone on the top of that list is already gone." His voice turned deadly serious. "But, I would gladly take care of whoever is left."

Marie raised her eyebrows in return as she nodded her head, allowing that piece of information to soak in. She really wasn't sure what she should feel, or if she should ask for particulars. In the end, she didn't feel it had relevance to what was about to happen to her own self.

"I've never swam in the ocean," she stated.

"What?" He looked at her incredulously.

She shrugged. "Vin had a pool."

Valant snorted. "Snob."

Marie laughed at that. Then she turned very serious. She looked out at the ocean as she reached up with one hand and pulled the pins in her hair loose. It fell softly down her back and shoulders, the light breeze teasing it. "He's my God-Father."

Valant turned to her in surprise. She bowed her head and her hair fell across her face. "My father owed him a debt of gratitude. Since my father and mother thought I would be a boy, they gave him the honor shortly before I was born. Which of course, pissed them off greatly when I came out a girl. That's it. That's the connection you're looking for. My one and final secret."

Valant folded his arms across his chest and pressed a thumb to his lips. "Are you it? Are you the chosen one?"

Marie tucked her hair behind her ear so she could look at him. "Only Vinny can answer that." She paused a moment. "But, I suppose if that was what he had in mind, I wouldn't be here talking with you."

She stood and removed her shoes, then took a few steps out into the sand. "What are you doing?" he asked.

She looked back at him with the left side of her face, a smile on her lips. "I've never swam in the ocean."

"It's colder than you think," he said doubtfully, his arms still folded across his chest.

She said nothing as she lifted her skirt and began rolling down her right stocking. When she finished she tossed it to the side and walked a few feet before rolling down the left leg.

Valant shook his head at her with doubt. Marie stood up straight and turned around to look at him, the wind making her hair shimmer in the late afternoon light. She undid the top button of her dress as she started to walk slowly backward, all the while looking at his doubtful face. She paused for a moment for the dress to slip silently onto the sand.

At that point Valant's hand came away from his chin and he quickly tore off his jacket. He reached down and pulled off his shoes, fumbling in his rush. Marie laughed at him. She raised her shoulders one at a time to slide her slip off her shoulders. It followed the contours of her body down as it made it's descent to the sand. Valant couldn't get the cuffs of his shirt undone and he yanked and pulled to free his arms. In frustration he threw it from him when he was finally free. Marie covered her mouth as she laughed at his comical scene. He uncinched his belt and jerked his pants down, hopping on one foot as he tripped and nearly went down trying to get his trousers off, leaving his undershorts.

Marie's feet were in the water now and she was still going backward, with nothing but her soft underthings left. His lean muscles flexed as he pulled his undershirt over his head and tossed it as well. He was again hopping as he tugged his socks off. Marie looked back up the beach to the car and the scattering of clothing marking the path they took to the water. He finally stood to look at her and locked their gaze. He advanced towards her while she kept moving deeper into the water. The sun reflected off the gold chain that hung about his neck.

Marie laughed gleefully to see him coming, until a large wave hit her, splashing water up to her lower back, soaking her panties and causing a startled cry to escape her throat. He was right. It was colder than she thought. A deep and joyful laugh came from somewhere in Valant's chest as he watched the expression on her face change rapidly. She still stood there in shock as Valant entered the water and came to her, a determined expression on his face. She looked up at him and her breath caught as he took hold of her, pressing stretches of her bare skin to his. He seemed not to notice the cold water as he looked down at Marie. She started to melt against him.

He gave her no warning as he lowered his lips to hers, claiming their awe-struck softness in his warmth and desperation. Every inch of her body molded to his and the kiss was instantly deep, earth shattering, and consuming. Marie wrapped her arms around his neck and kissed him back with all the passion that had burned since the first night they danced together at the safe house.

She no longer feared The Dark Horse or his volatile temper.

He reluctantly broke their contact and pressed his forehead to hers. His arms tightened around her. "Oh, Marie. You make me feel young again," he whispered fiercely.

He swung her up easily into his arms just before a wicked laugh escaped his chest. "I thought we were swimming?" With that he tossed a very surprised Marie into the next wave. She went completely under and when she stood on shaky legs a startled scream erupted from her. Her coal black hair fell down over her face.

"You.." She pointed at him. He again laughed and started to her, but she leapt away and dove under the water.

It was a long and merry game of chase, the cold sting of the water giving way to a feeling of joy and carelessness. It was new for them to see the other in such a way, happy just to be in the presence of the other once again. When at last they did rise from the water, Valant took Marie's hand and led her up the beach, gathering their clothes as he went. He reluctantly helped Marie dress after their bodies dried in the soft sunlight.

"Will you be there? Will you be there for my return?" she asked.

He nodded. Valant reached up to his neck and took hold of the golden chain that hung out of sight beneath his shirt. His fingers fumbled a moment with the clasp before he brought it down to hold before Marie. "Michael the Archangel. My mother gave it to me when I took First Communion. He has battled with me many times. He has served me well. Now I want him to look out for you."

Marie watched out of large brown eyes as he put it around her neck and fastened the clasp. When he finished, he looked down at her with an indecipherable look as he stepped back and slipped his hands into his pockets. With a trembling hand Marie reached up and took hold of it, studying it.

"I can't take this from you."

"Yes, you can," he replied.

"There's something else." Valant said as he looked out to the ocean. Marie looked up at his far off contemplation.

"Mickey has accepted a press engagement tomorrow night at the club." Valant sighed and looked down at the sand. "That means that he needs you there, since this is publicity for your return. Imelda has made you a gown specifically for this." He looked over at her. "Cobby is going to be your escort. I will be there, but I can't be associated with you. It's too dangerous for us to be connected. I have to be where I can look out for you and Mickey."

She was quiet for a long moment. "Why a press engagement?"

"So there's no chance the Underground won't know you're back," he replied honestly.

Marie looked up at him, her hair falling over her face. Valant brushed it aside with a gentle hand. "Let's go." He took hold of her hand again and led her to the driver's side door. She ducked her head as she got in, Valant right behind her. He pulled her to him again, Marie settling in against his shoulder.

It was a short ride back, Marie knowing there was a very real chance she would never be this close to him again. That she would never hear his voice as it formed in his chest and reverberated through her own. Never smell his mixture of bourbon, aftershave, cigar smoke and masculinity. Never feel the touch of his lips on hers. A cold and hard feeling had formed in her. Things were nearly done, and so was she.

*****

It turned out that the press engagement was to take place during the show the following night. For Marie, that meant being thrown into the atmosphere of the club, and being present to hear all the scrutiny her face would create. It had been an easier proposition before knowing she would perform on stage for the last time without having to face it more than once. Now, she would be thrust into the midst of Mickey's people and the press, who would no doubt ask all sorts of horrific questions and make innuendo.

Worst yet, he had closed the club to make it an invitation only affair. It made sense, she supposed, that way only the Underground wouldn't show up before he was good and ready. The actual press portion of the evening was restricted to reporters of merit within LA. Marie was expected to make a few remarks about being glad to return to the stage, how much she had missed it, and such forth. She doubted her previous enthusiasm would be evident as she did this to the cacophony of personal questions.

She dressed in the gown Imelda made specifically for this and spent a painstaking amount of time on her make-up, knowing it would have to be reapplied regularly in order that the scars didn't show through. Her dress was well fitting, following closely to the curves of her body. The skirt allowed ample room for movement while dancing. It was white with black flowered lace over the top, covering her scarring on her chest completely and extending down to her mid-calves. She pulled her hair back with diamond studded combs. A pair of black gloves finished off her attire.

She wished the entire time she could run. When she emerged from the bedroom in the apartment, Cobby sat at the bar waiting for her. He was already dressed in his tuxedo. He stood slowly when he saw her. He pressed his lips together for a moment, as if he knew something he didn't want to tell her. Marie wasn't sure she could take another impact from a surprise, so she didn't ask.

"You look marvelous, Marie," Cobby said in a soft voice.

"Thank you."

He slid his hands in his pockets. "I think that when they see the pictures in the paper tomorrow, the Underground is gonna know they didn't beat you."

Marie looked down at the floor as she replied, "They already know that."

Cobby tilted his head as he looked at her. "What do you mean?"

Marie's head came up and she smiled her actress smile. "Nothing. Let's go."

Cobby looked at her a moment before extending his elbow to her. She took it and they made their way down stairs to his waiting car. It surprised her to see that Frankie was driving them, and that Cobby sat next to her in the back. It now looked as though they were a couple. Marie looked at Cobby with a look that spoke of her realization of something deep was afoot. The corner of Cobby's mouth tugged, but he said nothing.

As they rounded the block the club was on, a line of cars stopped them. Cobby began to look more sheepish. Marie tried to see what was ahead. "Aren't we going in the back?"

"No, not this time." Cobby replied. Frankie looked at her in the mirror.

"What is going on?" Marie demanded. As they got closer
Marie could see the press lined up the steps behind ropes. A
carpet led the way up the stairs to the entrance of the club. She
watched as one of the women who spit on her at the Christmas
party and her husband paraded up the steps to the club. Marie
reached frantically for the door handle. Cobby grabbed ahold
of her hand.

"No. No, Marie."

"This is no press engagement! What the hell is this?"
Marie yelled. Cobby pried her hand off the door handle.

"This is Mickey's way of throwing you back into the
Underground's face. Show them they didn't break you."

"Screw that! Did Valant know about this?" she again
yelled.

Cobby stopped and looked up at her from where he was
stretched out holding her down. His look spoke about how
ridiculous it would be for him not to know. "You knew! You
knew!" she screamed.

"Of course I knew! Why else would I be going along so
easily with it? Hold it together for shitsakes!"

About that time someone recognized Marie and began
yelling out her name. Two cars were ahead of them, but the
photographers abandoned their posts at the rope and swarmed
the car. Panic welled deep in Marie as the flashing and
shouting began. She quit struggling and clasped Cobby's hand
in a death grip. Cobby clasped back with equal force.

"You can do this, Marie. You've got to show them you are
no different tonight than you were that last night." She looked
up into Cobby's face and he gave her a look of confidence.
Frankie pulled to the carpet and stopped. Cobby got out of the
car and pushed his way around to open her door. The flash of
bulbs making the possibility of distinguishing faces impossible.
Cobby reached for her hand and she grasped it tightly as he
helped her out of the car. A great clamoring of voices rose like
thunder as she came to stand full height. Marie just stood there
a moment, contemplating how ironic it all was. She had waited
for this since she was just a child. Dreamed of this exact
moment when the cameras would flash only for her, the press
vying for a position to get a picture of her; the sound of
hundreds of voices all saying her name.

And now she wanted none of it.

Cobby pressed his face close to her ear. "Marie?"

She turned her head and gave him a sad smile. She put her hand in the crook of his arm, then turned a dazzling smile to the awaiting photographers. She tried desperately to remember how to play this role. She raised an elegant hand and waved to everyone, looking for all the world like a woman so thrilled to be where she was. Cobby started them forward as a barrage of questions strung out along ahead of them.

"Don't listen to them, and don't reply," Cobby whispered in her ear. She laughed as if he had said something hilarious, helping to make him look carefree. It occurred to Marie how easy it would be to gun her down at this very moment.

Finally they made it up the stairs to the entrance where a huge group of people stood in the entrance hall waiting to see her come in. As they passed through the doors her name was announced and a great cheer rose among the bystanders. Marie's heart hammered and she longed to run back the way she came. It was a great effort not to cover her face with her hand. Her smile faltered. Cobby covered her hand with his, then pulled her along.

Marie saw Mickey and Eva waiting across the hall by the doors leading into the club. He locked eyes with Marie and a look passed between them, his pressuring, hers accusing. As they made it to them, Mickey reached out with both hands and took hers. He leaned forward and kissed her cheeks.

"So good to have you back, Marie." Lights flashed around them. The sound of murmuring hummed like a power line.

"Thank you, Mickey." Marie repasted her smile. She turned to Eva who also took her hands and welcomed her. Mickey had thought of everything, right down to getting his wife to play along. Hatred burned bright in the eyes of both women. Marie had a suspicion that Eva's may have been for Mickey as well.

"It is so good to see you, Eva. I….." Marie was cut off by the sound of a loud voice.

"Ms. Margo Middleton!"

A piercing went through Marie. Eva looked past her to the entrance doors. Marie looked at Mickey to see that he watched her with a look of genuine regret. Marie turned slowly to see what she already knew she would.

Margo was as beautiful as always, her honey blonde hair swept away from her face to accentuate her heaving cleavage that screamed out of a red bodice. The gown was tight and spoke of the generous curves beneath. In the crooks of her bent arms hung a black lace wrap. Marie's throat felt cut as the threat of crying rose sharp and painful into her esophagus.

He stood next to her, looking more handsome than ever in his tuxedo. Valant looked powerful and enigmatic as he held on to his shattering rose, who looked nothing if not triumphant as she glared straight at Marie. Valant's eyes surveyed the room before coming to rest on Marie, his look hard. Marie's fake smile faded.

"Marie, I would like for you to sit at our table." Mickey's voice cut into Marie. She turned to see his look of understanding, speaking a language different from his words. Acting just became impossible.

"Thank you," she said in a faltering voice, hoping Valant and Margo were sitting somewhere else.

They passed through the doors into the club area where couples were already taking their seats. Mickey led the way down past the bar area to the steps to the stage and dance floor area. Cobby pulled out her chair at a large table that was center front. Marie smoothed her skirt as she sat down, thinking how odd it was to be viewing the stage from this vantage point. It made her feel like a different person.

"Can I get you a drink?" Cobby bent to ask her. She nodded. As he moved away, Marie realized that Cobby needed to leave the pressure. He was feeling the same as she. Mickey and Eva sat to her left around the circular table. Marie tried to keep her fake look of excitement pasted since cameras were still flashing. She pulled out everything she had learned in New York and tried to use it.

"Good evening, Mickey, Eva." Margo's voice lilted through Marie's mind. She glanced up to see Valant taking Margo's wrap from her and pulling out her chair, just across from Marie. Marie ground her teeth and looked back for Cobby. She wondered how easy it would be to go to him. Would Mickey stop her? If he didn't the press would.

"Good evening, Miss Brello." A direct line of cigarette smoke engulfed Marie's face. Her jaw clenched as she slowly turned her head to look at Margo out of narrowed eyes.

"Marlene, how wonderful to see you." Marie's smile came across as more of a snarl when the image of Margo throwing her drink on her came through her mind.

The artery in Marie's neck throbbed as the emotion hit her. She had been played. Valant had manipulated her every step of the way through, finishing out his master piece by luring her into feeling, only to use it to Delano advantage. It was easy to make her do something if she thought she was doing it for the right reasons. Hate reflected in Marie's eyes as she thought again of that first night when she returned to the apartment. She wondered if Valant had flown into Margo's bed once she was gone. Now she knew he clearly had.

Cobby returned and set Marie's drink in front of her. He unbuttoned his jacket and gave Marie a look as he sat down. "Thank you," Marie mumbled.

At that moment Rolly's voice boomed and Marie looked past Margo to see him there, announcing his wishes for everyone to have a great evening. Then she heard him announce her name. A spotlight came on somewhere overhead. A great round of applause sounded at the mention of her name, then at the sight of her. Everyone at the table clapped for her as well, except for Margo, who glared at her, cigarette pinched between her fingers.

Marie inhaled deeply and rose to wave and bow her head in gratitude for their welcome. She looked up at Rolly who smiled. The look in his eyes cut her like a knife. She wanted to run, the panic of the scrutiny welling up within her. The applause went on and her mind flashed intermittently. Her face shuttered and a look passed between Cobby and Valant. Trembling, Marie sat down. The spotlight remained a moment longer, then it shut off, leaving her in the soft light of the table candle. Marie heard the band start up.

Cobby put his arm around the back of her chair and handed her drink to her. She took a long sip and found Cobby had ordered her straight vodka, which as he intended, burned enough to jerk her mind straight.

"Patch job ain't gonna hold," Margo stated as she blew out another stream of smoke. Cobby turned and glared at her.

You're nothing but trash.

Marie's father rose unbidden into her mind. She felt Valant's eyes boring into her. She took another gulp of vodka. Around her lights flashed and her mind flashed with them. She felt the pressure of appearing normal before all the people and press. Margo blew another stream of smoke into her face. Marie shook violently as she tried to force her mind to stay

steady. It refused to clamp down on reality. She watched
Valant as he sat at the table in the safe house cleaning his gun.
Full Fury raced across the finish line, his body reaching and
stretching with each grab of the dirt, sweat flecking the jockey.
Valant violently stabbed Casanov repeatedly. She felt the tip of
the knife dig into her bone. Vodka spilled on Marie's dress as
she could no longer hold her hands steady.

An explosion sounded in Marie's mind with the flash of
another camera and sent her back to Vinny.

They sat alone in the stiff breeze on a hill, the dry grass
around them ruffling and making whispering noises. Marie was
only about eleven, and Vantino leaned against Vinny's car a
long distance away, watching. Vinny looked out at the distant
ocean and sighed. They had been there awhile, Marie patiently
waiting for him to come to his point.

"Nobody has the right to treat you like you are less than
nothing." Vinny spoke with great clarity.

"Nobody has the right to make you into a pawn, a
dependent, a low life. But they are gonna try anyway." He
stopped and looked at her. "The only thing that makes them
successful is if you let them."

Marie had bowed her head then, clutching her hands
together. "You are heir to a far greater God-given empire that
cannot be touched by anyone else's hands but yours. It isn't up
to anyone but you whether or not you touch it." Vinny looked
again to the ocean.

Marie felt confused as he continued. "On earth, do not
allow yourself to be misled, for in the end it is just you and
God. You have already been given much pain in your small
life, but when the time comes, I will stand with you. Always
remember that. I will stand with you, for although you are not
mine, you will be."

Marie couldn't remember what had led him to talk in such
a way, nor could she remember what he meant by these words.
But they made sense now. He had been telling her all along. He
had been reassuring her all along. He had placed her where he
thought less damage would come to her. He knew. He knew his
empire would come down to one sacrifice, and that a woman
would have to make it. She thought she was nothing, when in
reality, she was the center of everything. When he looked at her
again on that hill top, the grown Marie finally read the look in
his eyes.

Love.

Heir to an empire. "For although you are not mine, you will be."

Vinny had given her his blessing when she was eleven. He stood and reached for her hand, and she had taken it. He held it a moment before pulling her up. She looked up at his face and he said, "For this, I shall lay down my life."

Another explosion in her mind sounded as a flash went off near her. She raised her head and looked directly to Valant, who sat tensely with a dark look on his face. Marie tipped her head back and looked down at him. The corner of his mouth twitched. Sadness filled her eyes as she realized what he knew all along. They could not be lovers, for in the end, they were the greatest of enemies. Valant would never be hers, no matter how she tried to convince him. He committed a great sin in the time he spent with her trying to bring her back from the dead at the safe house.

She could give him nothing but her life.

Her mind was steady. Her trembling stopped. She realized what her mind had been trying to straighten out. Her life had always been coming to this.

Marie looked at Mickey with new eyes. She finally saw the fear he held of her and her power, how easily she could start a war. Just one flick of her finger and it was done. She held command over everything that was Vinny's. She looked to Cobby and saw his deep regret at destroying such perfection, how unfair it was to kill something so close to ruling her own world.

Marie became Vinnetti. So she did what came natural to her.

Turning to Eva she said, "You look positively radiant, Eva." Startled, the round bellied woman looked at Marie with eyes that spoke of the self-conscious battle raging within her. For the first time Marie realized that Eva was really just a scared kid, and sitting on top with Mickey was making her old. "I believe motherhood agrees with you." Marie finished as she put an elbow on the table and put her chin in her hand.

Eva dipped her head in an embarrassed smile. "Thank you."

"What a table. I get stuck with a girl without a face and the elephant." Margo's brash voice cut in. Eva's face fell, the power of Marie's compliment dissolving.

The band began to play a version of Frank Sinatra's recent hit, *One For My Baby, and One More For the Road,* as Marie looked at Margo.

"I don't think anything is more becoming than an expectant mother." Marie looked back to Eva. "You glow with such love, very few find that kind of perfect love as that between a mother and child. How lucky you are, to have such love taking root within you." Eva looked again, hopeful, to Marie. Marie looked back to Margo. "To have such beauty take root in the most sacred of ways that a woman can exist." Marie's eyes narrowed. "To be fruitful, as opposed to just being a receptacle for the seed." As Marie finished Mickey's gleeful laughter sounded.

Marie looked at Valant steadily for a moment, his piercing look refracting back. Marie laughed softly as she looked down, then back to Margo. "I'll never know why he chose you over me, but, I do know that you deserve each other through and through." Margo stared in shocked silence as Marie spoke.

Marie looked to Cobby who tried to suppress a triumphant grin. "Well, date and lover for tonight, dance with me." Her eyes were sad although her voice was strong. Cobby nodded happily and rose to take her hand, avoiding the look of hatred from The Dark Horse. Putting his arm around Marie's waist, he moved them to the dance floor, Valant shifting in his chair to watch them go.

"Go easy on him, Marie. He's doing what he thinks is best for all outcomes." Cobby said low into Marie's ear as they began dancing amid the other couples already on the floor. "You aren't gonna be easy to forget."

"Bullshit. He knew, all that time, that he'd go crawling back to that awful woman the moment I wasn't in the way. Why do men think they can fix everything without even asking for a woman's ideas?"

Cobby smiled. "Well, because we're men. We just don't think you capable of rational ideas in a crisis."

She looked up into his face and saw the smile. She gave him a look of misery and said, "Hold me Martin Cobbinelli. I need a man to hold me up right now. How irrational is that?"

"Well, very. Because he's gonna look over here and see me holding you like this and lose his mind."

"He doesn't want me, Cobby," she said in sad desperation, her mouth drooping.

"It's not that. It's just that he can't have you anymore than I can."

Marie buried her face into his neck and cried softly. "Why can't it be you that I love?"

"It would be like making love to your brother, and you know it."

"Not if I loved you."

"You'll see in time that he's right," Cobby said into her ear.

"There's no more time, Cobby. Time is gone. It's just a dreadful way of ending it."

Cobby couldn't speak rationally. He found himself blundering as a man where he had just declared competency. He wanted to tell her there would be time, but nothing sounded as hollow as that. Cobby caught movement out of the corner of his eye and looked up to see Valant shoving to make way to where they danced in the center of the floor.

"He's coming," Cobby stated.

"Don't leave me to him. Please. Let's leave," she pleaded. Valant jerked his head at Cobby with a look that said get lost. The anger radiated out of Valant's eyes and face like the sun.

"Oh, Marie, he is so very angry," Cobby whispered. She clung tighter to him and wouldn't let him go.

"Piss off Cobbinelli." Valant's deep and incensed voice sounded.

"Don't Cobby, don't leave me," Marie again begged.

Valant's body nearly shook with the rage that burned inside him. His right hand clenched into a fist and Cobby knew things would progress poorly here in front of all these people if he were to continue holding Marie. It had been many years since Valant had corrected Cobby with his fists, but he was never above reproach. He was right, too, in that Valant had seen them dancing so close and lost his mind.

"I'll wait at the car for you, just outside the private entrance." With that Cobby moved quickly away from her, taking her confidence and security with him as he wove his way through the dancing couples, not taking the chance of meeting Valant's eyes.

Before the feel of Cobby was gone, it was replaced by the rigid body of The Dark Horse. Cobby had been far more accommodating and warm, but despite the tense and cold feel of Valant, Marie melted against him. With a ragged sigh, he pulled Marie close to him and held her there firmly, not looking into her face. She held him loosely, unable to speak for herself. He put his cheek against hers. The feel and smell of him made her breath shutter and her breasts heave against his chest. She rubbed her cheek against his and Valant's eyes closed.

With sadness, Marie moved her cheek away from his. This was only making things worse.

"That wasn't very nice, Marie."

"Just let me go. I've done what you asked, now let me go. I won't apologize for insulting her."

"You think I care about that?"

"Let me go, Valant."

"Don't call me that," he said flatly. "You want to go?"

"Why wouldn't I? Go back to her. She's waiting for you."

He said nothing, but she felt his jaw clench. He brought her hand against his chest. "I don't care how long she waits."

Marie fought the great urge to kiss him, to lose her mind and deepen the display she knew they were already making. He held her so tight she could hardly breathe, but she allowed him to do so. Her mind told her she should go, that this was only making the inevitable harder. As she opened her eyes again she saw couples staring at them.

"We're not supposed to look like we know each other," Valant whispered into her ear.

"Let me go, John. It's for the best." She shoved him hard and broke from him, weaving through the couples as quickly as possible just as Cobby had done. Valant watched her for a moment, ignoring the whispers from the crowd around him.

Mickey watched Valant abruptly stand and leave the table a few moments before. It surprised him that Valant waited that long. It was few the times Mickey saw that kind of blatant passion in Valant's eyes as he watched Cobby take Marie. Mickey reached under the table and took hold of Eva's hand and put it on his leg, keeping it covered with his own. He looked to Margo.

"Well, that's it then." His voice became razor sharp. "If you ever, ever, say anything like that about my wife again, I will personally cut out your tongue and shove it down your bitch throat. I think you have over stayed your welcome by twenty some years."

Margo gave Mickey a smile that suggested he wouldn't dare speak to her that way. Not The Dark Horses' woman. It faded when she met the fire in his eyes, the trembling in his fist that rested on the table. Mickey waved for a few of his guys that stood close by.

When they came to him and stood silently, he pointed to Margo. "See that the trash gets taken out, boys." He looked to Eva for a moment before squeezing her hand. She smiled shyly at him. He smiled sadly back.

Marie shoved and wove her way past all the people who stared as she went. Shocked whispering went on as she passed; she knew her face was red thus illuminating her scarring. She covered the scars with her hand as a flash went off in her face. She made for the private stage entrance and entreatied Martin to let her out. He did so, so she guessed Cobby had spoken for her on his own way by. The band began Sammy Cahn and Jimmy Van Heusen's *All the Way*.

She hit the private hall to see that two men blocked the side entrance. She made for them at nearly a run when a hand clamped down on her arm. "I can't let you go." She was jerked around to see Valant just before he crushed his mouth onto hers. In desperate desire she placed her hands on his neck then slid them up to the smooth skin of his recently shaven face. His arms again tightened until the air was forced from her lungs. The embrace lasted what seemed an eternity, until finally she broke from him, breathless, but kept their faces pressed together. He shook his head against hers.

"I can't let you go," he whispered.

"You have to," she cried softly.

"No."

Marie shook and a tear trailed her cheek. When she spoke her voice was barely audible. "I'm not like you. I'm not strong enough to have just a piece of you every now and then, make love and part. Watch you go knowing you are going back to her. To live like that will take what there is left of me and burn it. Oh, John. Don't do that to me."

Valant kissed her again. This time with less ferocity and more tenderness, holding her warmly, bringing her to him just as close, but with infinite gentleness. It was a force that enslaved her soul, making it impossible to fight back. She forgot her own words and caved to him, to his power, to his touch. She felt her resolve run through her fingers like sand and blow away in the breeze. She felt his go too, and she knew the battle within himself raged just as violently.

"Give your heart and soul to me," he murmured.

He trailed his lips along the contour of her neck and then back up to her mouth, holding her captivated. "Play fair, damn you," she sighed.

"That won't get me what I want. I don't want to fight rational Marie with words."

"Cobby's waiting for me."

Something close to a growl tore from his chest. The gentleness was gone as his body went stern. "I'm going to kill him. Tear the flesh from his bones and burn the carcass. Put a bullet in his head."

"You don't mean that."

He pressed his face close to hers. "Please don't fall in love with him, please," he begged urgently.

Feeling the upper hand for once in all the time she had known him she said, "You have Margo. Why can't I have Cobby?"

The growl sounded again and he moved them to press her harshly against the wall. "I will kill you both." Then, kissing her deeply, she felt some of his harshness fade. He pressed his forehead to hers. "I'll take your beautiful body in my hands and break it, making it useless, so no man can have you. Don't fall in love with him." The last was spoken forcefully. "You are mine. You have been mine since the first time I heard your voice. I should have taken you to me then, slipped silently away into the dark of night. But I let you go. Let you go knowing you were too young, too scared. Now you are neither."

He brought his lips to hers again with total possession. With their meeting Marie knew she had been his for far longer than that. Her life had paralleled his since she was a child. She had seen him, heard of him, known of him with constant reminders to keep him in her consciousness with the passing of the years. His savagery, his volatility, his ruthlessness, and eventually, his loyalty and determined presence kept him firm in her life.

And after all of that, she wasn't free to belong to him.

"I have to go, John. You know I do." He traced the softness of her cheek with his lips. "You put me here, now let me get myself out."

"No. No, because once you're free, maybe you'll choose Vinnetti over me. Just like you did at the table a few moments ago." His fist bunched taking a hold of her skirt. "You looked down on me. I've never felt so small."

Marie knew this was it. "Don't tell me these things now. Tell them to me day after tomorrow. Tell them to me when I am free to listen. For now, let me go, so I can do what you have rebuilt me for. I can't do that with the fear of dying and being torn from you."

With that he melted into her. Clenching her with all his strength. The feel of the cold brick pressed into her back and the sound of the band spun away. When he finally pulled away from her, he released her but kept his face pressed to hers. He braced against the wall breathing deeply. "Go." His voice trembled.

Marie fled then, knowing she had to. Knowing that to feel his touch, to be held in his arms in the darkness of the night would ruin her resolve and truly render her useless. After making love to him, she would no longer be able to summon the strength she needed to face Danny G. She would bury herself in his arms, and be unable to leave. And in the end, it would get him killed. Danny G would kill him to get to her, just as he would Vinny and Vantino, Cobby and Mickey, as well as Imelda. Anyone that ever had a connection to her. Which might even include Cobby's family.

It was time to set herself free. Time to defend what she loved, for she was all that stood between status quo and destruction.

*****

Cobby leaned against his car smoking a cigarette. When she came out the door, he looked up at her. In his eyes he registered her loyalty to duty. He half expected to be spending the night looking out at the stars from the porch at the safe house while Valant finally made love to Marie through the night. He wondered how she had broken away from him when the two of them were so obviously drowning in each other's current.

He opened the door for her and she slid in without a sound, crumpling onto the seat, lying and covering her face for the ride to the apartment. He had to pull her up and half carry her to the elevator. She wasn't crying, the strength had just gone from her. When they were back in the white carpeted nightmare he sat on the sofa with her for a long time. She just lay there with her head on his shoulder, saying nothing, the two of them staring into the darkness.

After Cobby lit a cigarette she finally spoke in a small voice, "Cobby, do you remember when you said we were intertwined?"

"Yeah."

"Then your fate is woven with mine."

"That's what they say. I don't know how much stock I put into it."

There was a long and silent pause in the dark. "Cobby, I need your help."

"With what?"

Marie sat up and looked at him squarely. "I know who it is."

Cobby slowly lowered his cigarette. His look was mortified. "Who who is?" he fumbled.

"Who you've been looking for all these months," she said, barely above a whisper.

"Bullshit. Nobody including Vinnetti knows who we've been looking for. Have you seen him?"

Marie nodded. "I've spoken to him."

Cobby sat forward. "Who is it?"

Marie's eyes became large at the tone in his voice. She had hoped he would be an ally. Still, she knew she was taking a great risk in asking for him to be. He was still Valant's man, no matter how he felt about her. She shook her head. "I won't tell you. All I am asking for is your help."

"What do you mean you won't tell me? We can have this stopped tonight if you tell us where to find him!" He made as if to stand but Marie put her and on his arm to stop him.

"No," she said firmly. He looked at her. "I said I know who he is. I have no idea where to find him." She looked down at her lap and licked her lips in uncertainty. "He has stopped forcing his way, because I have agreed to go head to head with him." She finished slowly, allowing it to sink in.

"What?" Cobby said almost angrily. This time Cobby did stand. "When did this happen?"

"About the time he quit pushing, quit bombing, shooting...."

"Marie, that was weeks ago."

She stared at him as if waiting for him to catch up with her. He was momentarily struck speechless. "Marie, you can't go head to head with this man." He stood shaking his head.

"Yes, I can." He kept shaking his head. "I have to Cob. If not now than someday, and when someday comes, he will have spent his time systematically chipping away everything I know and love. That includes Valant, who is no doubt top of the list. Don't you understand, Cobby? He's been calling me out!"

"A woman can't play this game!"

"Yes, I can!"

"You can't even keep who you're talking to straight! How are you gonna be sure you've got the right man!"

She stood to look at him, although she was still looking up. "You don't have a choice. This IS going down at the club tomorrow night. He will be there, and he will be ready to draw blood. Ready to make a public example of me. This has nothing to do with gender. It has everything to do with being what he thinks is Vinnetti's heir. It doesn't even matter if he ever kills Vinny, because once I'm eliminated, all he has to do is kill Mickey and Valant. The whole city is his. And if you thought Valant was harsh, this man kills for pettier reasons. He'll kill your family, just because of you. Just to clean the slate."

Cobby was silent. "Cobby, you've suffered hell to keep them living the good life. They won't even see it coming." She knew she'd struck a nerve. Cobby's brows knit together and he pursed his lips.

She stepped to him and met his troubled look. "I understand that I cannot come out of this. I've known this since the night I was cut up." She caught herself before her voice hitched. "Vinnetti knows that too. He is far too intelligent not to have weighed his options. I know he came up with the same outcome I have. As long as either Mickey or Valant remains to raise Mickey's child, then the Delano's hold the power. Still rule supreme. Vinny knows it's better than being ruled by The Underground. That is all that I ask of you. Help me get The Underground away from them. I can handle the rest."

Cobby looked long and hard into Marie's eyes, sought out the answer he was looking for. His face registered such doubt, but she knew that he was running along the same trails she'd been for months. He would come to the same end she had. It all came down to her.

Cobby inhaled deeply. "What do you want me to do?"
*****

Valant stood alone in the dark looking up at the now empty stage. Only a few soft lights reflected off the band stand and microphones. Everything had been cleaned and put back to straights after the night's show. Valant could still hear the music, although it gave a ghostly feeling in his soul. His bow tie lay untied around his neck.

"Eerie feeling, isn't it?" Mickey said as he walked quietly to Valant. Val didn't turn to look at him.

"I want to go back," Valant said in an angry voice.

Mickey gave him a sad and understanding smile. "When?"

"That garden party all those years ago."

Mickey tilted his head back. "Why then?"

"So I could see what she really was. Take that look in Maryanne's eyes as the warning it was. Never held Margo's body against mine in the sand below that overhang. I see now how cheap the whole affair was."

"I think you saw that before now."

"Yes, but I had no reason to care before."

Mickey too looked to the dark stage. "Mickey, no matter what happens, she gets out alive. No matter what."

Mickey nodded silently. "No matter what."
*****

No one slept. Cigarettes burned constant. The dark of the night dragged on, and it seemed as if God had pulled the sun from the sky. Great dread filled with the realization that it would come, it would rise, and eventually descend again. It was an unusual time when fate dangled like horrific nightmare yet to be dreamt. When hope has left, nothing else can remain, either.

When the time for regrets was past, it seemed that regrets were all there was to chew on. Marie spent a great amount of time praying for courage, knowing her strength was minimal. She wanted more than anything for the iconic men who had dominated her life to remain the ones who dominated. She reflected on them and the substance of their existence, realizing how odd it was that she would choose to die for the likes of them. Especially after all the fear that they had caused her.

They were all she knew. If she were a different person, she may have chosen a different path.

Circumstance was merely a stroke of luck. She shouldn't be who she was either. If her little brother hadn't broke away from her and run into the street, Vinny would've never been a part of her life. Nor Vantino. She would never have had a reason to be in the car that day Vantino first introduced Valant to Vinny. Vinny wouldn't have taken Marie to hear that beautiful Italian singer perform, thus igniting Marie's dream. She never would have been there the night Valant came to her father's dive to kill Vinny. Perhaps even, there would never have been a turf fight over it since Vinny wouldn't have cared about it without her there.

Marie knew now, looking back, this had always been the plan. New York was just a lovely stepping stone to here. Now, after all she had been through and seen, after the feeling of real and dedicated love, she never cared to see New York again. She kept thinking of Valant in the early days after she was cut up. How he remained despite the fact that she was so devastatingly marred both physically and emotionally. At the time she could only come up with a few sinister reasons as to why he did so, but now the answer was obvious. Just to think of him wrenched her in a way she had never felt over Alex.

She lit another cigarette.

She looked out the window and scanned the quiet street. She heard a soft noise behind her as the bedroom door opened. She turned in the darkness to see Cobby standing in the doorway. She turned back to look out the window. Cobby moved silently to stand beside her. They said nothing, just looked at each other, the look of dread and fear evident. When Marie dropped her arm at her side Cobby took ahold of her hand.

"You really are something."

Marie smiled at him. "Thanks."

"You know, the first time I walked in here and saw you sitting in that chair, you disturbed me. I really thought you'd be sleeping in that bed, enjoying the creature comforts. When you looked at me, I knew you were gonna rock the foundation. I realized why Valant was so fascinated by you."

She squeezed his hand. "Cobby, you are my only friend in this world I live in."

Cobby looked out the window. "He'll never forgive me, you know. For what I am about to do."

"Who?"

"Any of them," Cobby said.

*****

Marie made rehearsals that morning and the feeling was electric. Some of the performers knew, but mostly everyone else just looked at it as the night Marie returned. They ran through the performance, all the while Marie acting as if she were thrilled to be returning. She had every intention of making her last performance her best.

After rehearsals, Marie caught Steven as he was cleaning and putting his instrument back into the velvet lined case. She walked to him silently and brushed his arm.

"Hello, Miss Marie," Steven smiled a genuine smile that spoke of his affection for her.

"Hello, Steven," Marie replied, smiling warmly at him.

"You ready for tonight then?" he asked as he lowered the clasp on the case, not looking at Marie.

"I need a favor from you, Steven."

He looked up at her in surprise. "Sure. Whatever you need."

She looked at him firmly. "Don't come back here tonight. Stay home with your wife and son."

The smile disappeared from his face. A deep realization came to his eyes. "Miss Marie..."

"No. Don't say anything. Just don't come back here." She looked steadily at him until he nodded slowly. Then she smiled a sad smile. "I am so honored to have worked with you." Marie hugged him tightly. Tears were in Steven's eyes when she released him.

"Goodbye, Steven."

"Goodbye, Miss Marie." She squeezed his shoulder and quickly walked away.

*****

The rest of the day passed with painful speed. It was as if she could step back and watch the passage of time almost like it were a bus passing in the street. She returned to Imelda's for a final fitting, which was more perfunctory anyway as it was too late to change anything. Imelda held Marie for a long time on the sofa while Cobby sat on the adjoining armchair and stared into space.

After a while, Marie squeezed Imelda's hand and stood, offering a strong smile. Imelda wiped her tears and stood to retrieve the gowns for the night's show. They left and returned to the apartment, where Marie spent the remainder of her afternoon closed in the bedroom, looking down at the street below. A great anticipation burned a hole in her stomach. She squelched it by thinking her way through the evening.

When evening came, she held tightly to Cobby's arm and rode the elevator down, then allowed him to hand her into the car. It was different this evening, for she and Cobby found that neither of them had any desire to go to the restaurant for dinner. Marie didn't want the threat of returning food to interrupt her thoughts in her nervous state.

Cobby pulled into the alley and killed the engine on the car. Their eyes met in the mirror and they held for a moment. Marie smiled a soft smile at him in a gesture of confidence. Cobby looked down a moment, then opened his car door and stepped out. He reached for Marie after opening her door. He clasped her hand tightly as he helped her out. He walked her into the club and when they reached the dressing room, Marie looked up at him again and nodded. It took a moment, but he nodded back to her. She moved away from him into the dressing room where chatter and laughing sounded.

Marie took it all in. It was just as it had been before the attack. The girls in the company joked about simple things, talked about the men they were seeing, or would like to see. They helped Marie with her show gown, her hair, her jewelry. Marie worked patiently on her make-up, interjecting comments here and there to lend to the flow of the conversation. The band grew accustomed to Marie's scarring, and now it seemed to them as if she had never changed. That was only because Marie worked so hard to be who she was before, a person now gone. She stepped away from the group to look at herself in the floor length mirror in her private dressing closet.

Marie laughed freely at the funny things said, and gave no indication that this would be the last time she sat where she was. There came a pounding at the door. "Five minutes, ladies!" Marie helped Helen into her costume.

Helen took hold of Marie's hand. "You're gonna be so great! I'm glad you're back." She squeezed Marie's hand and then bent to fix her shoe. As the girls left, they each took the time to give Marie reassurances. Tears came to Marie's eyes as she thanked them, flashing back to a much less pleasant receiving line. It seemed she was a pendulum, swinging violently between two polarities in her life.

When she was the last in the room, Marie turned and looked at the dressing room one last time. She reached up and touched the golden pendant of Michael the Archangel. She recited the prayer to him, then she stepped out.

Rolly stood patiently waiting for her, his head bowed, hands clasped together before him. Marie's breath caught a little when she saw him. When he heard her, his head came up and he smiled weakly. She tried to smile back. At her wavering he came to her and took hold of her hands. His were warm and steady.

"I'm not sure how many times he's going to put you in the 'opening night' scenario, but each time you get lovelier," Rolly said.

"Thanks," Marie whispered. Rolly brushed her cheek with the back of his fingers. He lowered his face to hers and lightly pressed his lips to hers.

"Break a leg," he whispered.

Marie glanced up into his eyes as he offered her an elbow. There was much she wished to tell him, and like Cobby, desperately wished she could love him, but her heart was already gone. As was her life. So, she smiled bravely, and in his eyes she read his understanding. She could never belong to anyone. Rolly was well aware of what was about to happen.

She was grateful for Rolly's strong presence as they walked to the stage door. Already the announcer was speaking over the loud system and her legs threatened not to carry her to her death. She gripped Rolly fiercely as her mind shifted and she struggled to take control again. His warm hand covered hers. She looked up at him and he smiled reassuringly down at her.

"You're alright. It's going to be ok." With that he left her standing behind the band, waiting for her cue to enter.

"Ladies and gentlemen, orchestrator for The Ruby, Mr. Rolly Howard!" A bright beam engulfed Rolly and he stood at his microphone and wished everyone a good evening. The band shuffled last minute placing. Marie glanced at Steven's chair to see it wasn't there, nor was he. She was saddened, but also grateful.

"Oh what a night!" Rolly was stating, Marie's heart hitting overdrive. "I don't know about everybody out there, but when Marie Barelli left us here for a short stint in New York to finish up a contract, I just wanted to crawl under a table and drink myself into oblivion." He stood and shook his head exaggeratedly. The crowd collectively agreed. Marie wanted to run. Marie wanted Valant to show up and give her strength with one of his cold stares. She was always afraid to defy them. She wanted his lips on hers one last time.

"Well, my dream came true here tonight because we finally have our beautiful rose back. And I gotta tell ya, she's prettier to me than she has ever been or ever will be." As he spoke he turned and looked at her. A sob choked out of her chest.

Rolly signaled the band and they started into Carmen Lombardo's *Return to Me.*

"Oh, ladies and gentlemen, join me in telling 'ol New York to go fly a kite," Rolly was yelling now, "and welcome back, Miss Marie Barelli!"

Gathering her courage, Marie pasted on a smile and stepped to the x on the stage floor where the spot light would come on, then follow her to her place. In an instant she was flooded with the blinding light. Her body trembled violently once as she waited for the bullet to rip and her life to end. She was near frozen with the panic that welled in her mind. She knew Mickey had men everywhere. Valant was there as well, lending to her safety as best as he could, but Cobby's words came back to her.

I really think the only thing that scares him, is that when you'll need him most, he won't be able to help you.

The crowd was going insane and the noise of the cheering drown out the band. Since she was right in front of them and their deafening sound, she couldn't image what it was like to be out on the floor. She moved forward woodenly as Rolly began to sing.

Marie's dress was a soft pastel yellow that flowed gently down her body. The chest had fine sheer fabric that covered her scarring. The material moved easily with her. Valant's gold pendant felt like it weighed five pounds the way it hung and reminded her of its presence, protecting her instead of him. She desperately wanted to see him, touch his face, and feel his strong arms as they grounded her.

Valant.

She was now standing before her microphone and realized it would take a miracle to get her voice out. The screaming in the crowd only became louder as she looked out among them for any face she would recognize. She found none. That was in some cases a good thing. Rolly turned and looked at her. She opened her mouth.

Her voice, although trembling at first, could not be heard over the hailing crowd. As her lyrics went on the rioting ebbed, but by then her voice was steady. She prayed constantly for the strength she needed to keep standing and left it at that. She would pray different prayers later when the time came, but for now it was the simple things she felt she could not accomplish.

John...

*****

Mickey looked out over the thriving crowd and felt uncertainty claim his mind. It had been necessary to open the club in this manner, to guarantee that who they sought would be able to get in. It was a perfect cover, nearly impossible to pick out anyone who might be out of place. The whole damn place was out of place. His eyes again drifted to Marie, who, by some miraculous standard, was coping with the situation well. Her voice was unsteady, and she didn't have the stage presence that she once had, but she was still functioning. Which was all they really needed her to do anyway.

Mickey wondered if Vinnetti had men out in that crowd. If so, they were well concealed. When this thing went down, a shit load of innocent people were going to die, but better that than being ruled by a faction such as the Underground. It seemed realistic to sacrifice a few to save many.

What a mess, a genuine shit storm.

Mickey had promised Valant that Marie would live through this night, but, now he realized how impossible it would be to come through with that promise. Mickey desperately wanted to stop everything and return her to hiding, for he knew that now he had exposed her and she couldn't be protected like this. He had been naive to think he could.

Valant moved along the private stage like a caged animal. He looked out over the balcony at every angle and every face, scanning the crowd for any sign of unrest. The anger in him radiated out of every pore. Valant felt helpless, and a helpless Valant was the most dangerous.

Cobby sat and watched Marie from his perch that was concealed by a heavy curtain. His eyes were sad and he made no move, just sat and watched, his eyes burning with intensity. Mickey watched him with interest, for out of them all, Cobby didn't appear to be desperate. No, Cobby just appeared to be waiting, as if what were about to happen was not up to him anyway. He was not so egotistical as to think they could stop it.

*****

It took Marie some time to hit her stride, but after a few songs she was able to gain control over her fears, and look at the purpose of her being there. She had wanted her last performance to be spectacular, and so she began working for that. It was very difficult to see out into the crowd from her vantage point in the bright spotlight. Mickey had written the portion of her performance to be entirely up on the main stage. She wasn't going to get anywhere from so high above the crowd. She needed to get down on the floor.

The floor was packed to the hilt and getting out amongst the throng of people was going to be a disaster. She needed an opening to get onto the floor before it crowded over. The feeling in the room was electrically charged. Had she been there merely in the capacity of performer, she would have reveled in the emotion. But, she was there as something else entirely.

"Ahhhh, Marie," drawled Rolly. The band slowed and now he looked at her from his amplifier. "You know, I recall clear back at our first performance together asking you to marry me."

Marie smiled broadly. "Oh really, Mr. Howard?"

"Uhm hmmm. I do. I remember asking you and you turning me down for a gentleman with something besides cocktail napkins in his wallet."

Marie laughed at the memory. "Yes, I seem to remember something about that."

"Well Marie, sweetheart, I believe I've changed my mind about marrying you."

Marie gave a mock look of disbelief. "Have you?"

"Yes, I have. But, I think it only fair that you know that I have more than just cocktail napkins in my wallet now." After looking out at the audience he gave her a sly look.

Marie couldn't help but grin at him. "Oh yeah?"

His voice turned husky. "Yes ma'am." He winked at the people before them. "So, I think maybe we should just forget about that little time consuming detail better known as the marriage license." At this the male portion of the crowd started to yell and whistle.

Marie raised her eyebrows as Rolly looked at her as if to consider his offer. "Well. That's a mighty tempting offer. But, I'm not too sure." Marie looked out at the roaring crowd. "I don't know ladies. What do you think? He's handsome, he's charming, he's brash. Should I gamble on a wallet full of cocktail napkins with telephone numbers written on them?" At this Rolly laughed hard.

The women of the audience raised out of their chairs and cheered as loud or louder than the men. Rolly shrugged at Marie. "I guess that means you're coming home with me."

The band shifted into Les Brown, Bud Green, and Ben Homer's *Sentimental Journey*. Marie continued to laugh at Rolly as he came to her and took her in his arms, spinning her into a waltz. By now Marie had changed gowns and she was wearing a red number. They danced until Marie's vocal portion of the song came up.

*****

Cobby wasn't sure what was troubling Valant most. Watching the crowd for a killer he didn't know, or watching the lady killer on the stage making a play on Marie. Either way, it didn't really matter, someone was about to die over both reasons. Cobby found it strangely humorous.

Mickey was trying to keep a handle on Valant who was ready to just start killing people in the off chance he hit the right one. What kind of sign they were looking for was anyone's guess. Cobby scanned the crowd again for Vantino whom he was certain would be there somewhere after Marie's comments on dying with The Heart by her side. He really wasn't sure that made him feel better.

Mickey's guys continued to comb the audience. Over two hours into the show, Cobby began to wonder if Marie's hunch had been wrong.

*****

Marie looked to the private stage as she sang. She wondered if he were listening just like he used to, or if he were too busy to pay her any mind. The words she sang hit home for her. For the first time in Marie's life she knew what she wanted. She knew who she wanted. She wasn't entirely certain that it could ever happen, even if she survived the night. That was what cut the deepest. She didn't want to spend her life mourning the loss of a love that couldn't have ever been.

And now she knew. It was time to make her move.

*****

Cobby watched from his perch as Rolly finished out the last of his song. The band quieted and the floor slowly cleared. It seemed to take them forever to continue on with things. His brows knit together as he watched for what seemed like an eternity, but in reality must have only been a few moments. Rolly looked to the left side of the stage where Marie was supposed to be. The floor was empty now, and the lights shut off to focus on the stage once more.

A voice sounded from the darkness on the floor as Marie began to sing. Lighting scrambled to get a beam on her and an amplifier turned on. Her voice was so strong and steady, she really didn't need one. Cobby stood. She was on the floor! She wasn't supposed to be there at any point. He looked to Valant who was watching, an angry look on his face. Rolly on the stage looked panicked as well, and started down the stage stairs to get Marie.

Valant was signaling men to close in on her when he looked up at Cobby. The light came on Marie, and when Cobby looked at her she was dressed in a black gown, a very beautiful black gown. She was moving across the floor as she sang. She wasn't hurried, just made contact with the audience as she moved.

The black dress.

In a moment Cobby looked back again at Valant who caught his look and rage surged from him. Cobby's shoulders slumped and he mouthed something at Valant just before he jumped over the balcony and was gone.

Intertwined.

*****

Marie's voice was as strong and steady as it had ever been. Her heart and soul went into the lyrics she rang out accusatorily, but with a touch of emotion that could never be rivaled. Arthur Hamilton's *I Cried a River Over You,* hit meticulously at every nerve in the room. Marie was an artist, and this was her perfection.

Time slowed drastically. Marie could hear the band behind her clamoring to try to keep up with an unrehearsed song. She moved along steadily looking through the hundreds of people that packed the house. God, she prayed, may she be right. This was her one chance. She hoped Cobby took his cue.

Her knuckles turned white as she gripped the gun tucked neatly hidden in the folds of her skirt. The spotlight made it very hard to see each face, but she moved along knowing if Danny G were watching he might well take her down now before she had a chance to even look at his face. But, she knew everyone could see the scars he'd left behind in his attempt to throw her off her empire in a very nasty coup. She knew they could see from the gasps coming from tables around her. When she changed into the final black low cut gown, she'd washed all her make-up off. She was living proof Danny G had failed. She was throwing it in his face.

Then she saw him. He stood from a table near mid-center. How much he must have paid to sit in that table. A vicious grin spread across his face as he stood and looked at her. She knew she had to be quick, for now Valant would know who they were looking for. And, he would try to stop her.

She raised her gun in an instant to see Danny G answer in kind. Women began to scream as Marie's gun fired loudly, only to have an echo from center front.

Valant bailed over the balcony the same as Cobby had. The crowd was on its feet, shoving and screaming in an attempt to get out of the way of the firefight. Valant grabbed and threw men and women alike as he yelled Marie's name.

Marie prayed that her aim was true as she fired, and knew that Cobby would be firing, far less concerned that his aim was true. He cared not whom he hit as he took aim in the direction of the standing man. The bullet fired from Danny G ripped through Marie and knocked her over backwards. The place was in chaos as deafening screams overtook everything else. No more shots were fired, at least none that she could hear.

Marie rolled over and struggled to her feet, a deep pool of blood already forming underneath her. She tried not to focus on the pain as she started to run for the backstage entrance. She still clutched her gun knowing she would have to use it to get out. Over the crowd she heard the savage bellowing of a man who looked down at the blood spot Marie left behind instead of her lifeless body.

She knew she hit him, for she saw his body jerked just as hers had. It was not her intent to kill him, merely enrage him. It was evident that she had been successful. People shoved to get away from her as she pointed her gun to make way for herself.

Get me out, Cobby.....

More shots sounded behind her, and she knew that Cobby had found his targets. All he had to do was keep Valant from following, and Danny G far enough behind she could get to the alley first. As Marie left the stage and stumbled into the hallway, she left a streak of blood on the wall. As she turned into the hallway, she screamed for everyone to move aside. The band and dance company cluttered the hall.

Cobby fired several times in the air to get a way cleared to the dance floor. He could see several men looking down at the pool of blood. He knew from Marie's description which one was the man Valant and himself had been so tirelessly searching for. He watched in horror as the men moved into the dark beyond the spotlight after Marie. Cobby took an awful chance and fired almost blindly in the direction they had gone. All around him people hit the floor. He fired again only to feel a bullet pierce through his suit jacket and tear through his left shoulder. The burning instantaneous.

Marie yelled into the crowded hallway at her comrades. "Move back behind the stage! Now!"

Unsure of what else to do, they did as they were commanded. Marie started to run the length of the hallway as fast as her legs would carry her. She ran her shoulder into the door jam and left another streak, nearly going down with the pain of it. She heard shouting just before another bullet ricocheted off the wall next to her. She turned slightly to see Danny G coming at her. She shoved through the door.

*****

Valant watched her take the hit and fall. He yelled loudly as he threw a man completely to the ground. Women shrieked. He pulled his gun and pointed it at people to get them to move faster and clear his way. When he again looked at the floor Marie was gone.

As a small opening formed, Valant found Cobby standing there before him with a gun pointed at him, blood running down his limp arm and torso. Cobby's right hand was steady, but his eyes blazed with the knowledge Valant might well gun him down no questions asked. Valant came at him so Cobby cocked the pistol and put it at Valant's head.

"Listen to me. Don't follow her. Don't." Cobby's voice was firm. "We need to get out the private entrance into a car. Now."

"What the hell is going on here?" Mickey yelled.

"Mick, we have got to get to a car. Now," Cobby again stated firmly. "She's gonna make a run for it. If we go now, we can keep up with her." It had not been part of Marie's plan to have them follow her, but Cobby just couldn't give her a gun, get her out of a building, and walk away whistling a tune. He'd shot several of the men who pursued Marie after she hit the man who'd stood to challenge her. Now they had to move. Quickly.

Valant moved away from Cobby and Mickey did, too, but Cobby kept watch behind them as they made their way out into the street where chaos reigned again. People were running and shouting as they tried to get into cars, or simply ran up the street.

"Mickey," Valant didn't have to explain as he got in the passenger side. Mickey took the driver's seat. Mickey was a better tactical driver, and Valant knew they would need that and his own skill with a gun. Cobby got in back. Immediately as Mickey fired up the engine and hit the gas, both Cobby and Valant started looking for anyone that might be dangerous. It was time to kill.

*****

Marie made the short trip across the alley and crawled painfully into Cobby's black Lincoln. She fumbled quickly for the keys knowing it would only be a moment before Danny G appeared in the alley. She was right. Just as she turned the ignition, the door flew open, and he was there firing at her. She slammed it into reverse and accelerated up the alley. Jerking the wheel and straightening the car in the street, she looked ahead. She pulled it into drive just as a bullet took out the back passenger window. She squealed and pressed the accelerator just as a car came up behind her.

That, she figured, was Danny G's ride.

Those waiting for Danny gave Marie a slight head start, which she knew she needed to keep her plan in motion. It was late now, and the streets were dark as she edged on the accelerator. The car was moving along briskly behind her in an attempt to over-take, but Marie kept a steady eighty-five through town. She avoided as much as possible the busier parts.

More headlights appeared way behind Danny G.

Blood slowly trickled down from her left shoulder at a steady rate. She tried not to look at it because it broke her concentration. Instinctively she knew she had to keep herself quiet and her heart rate down to manage what blood she had and needed to carry out her plan. When the blood was gone, so was her consciousness. It stung and burned and her shoulder ached. She so desperately wanted to cry, but forced herself to hold on. Her body demanded unconsciousness.

*****

"Can't you get this bitch to go any faster?" Valant spat at Mickey. Mickey jerked the wheel to get around a car in the street.

"Ah, shit. We got a tail," Mickey said as he looked in the mirror.

Cobby turned to look out the back window. "That'll be Vantino."

Mickey pressed for more speed as Vantino struggled to gain a vantage point. How he was even able to get this close was beyond Mickey. "This is it. It's him or us. If he gets the lead you can kiss your girl goodbye," Mickey stated as Valant turned and demanded Cobby duck.

Valant fired straight behind them to see the car maintain course, not faltering for a moment. Cobby could see in his mind the determined look on Vantino's face. The devil was finally making a play for Delano lives. He also knew that no matter where Valant hit him, Vantino would live long enough to finish the job. Valant fired again.

"We're going out of town? Where the hell is she going?" Mickey yelled. Once this fight was on open road, it would be hard as hell to win.

Valant took time to look way up the highway to the first set of tail lights ahead of them. She was still going like a bat sent straight out of hell. Only now she was swerving violently in an attempt to keep whoever was behind her that way.

"God, may she be as good as I think she is," Valant muttered.

*****

Marie was slouched as far down as she dared in her seat. Shots had taken out her back window as well as one of her rear passenger windows. She looked to the fuel gauge and thanked God Cobby had done as she asked. She was prepared to go head to head with Danny G, but she really didn't want to do it on a road side one gun against four or five after the car she was driving ran short of gasoline. And, she believed Valant was right that they would torture her long before they bothered to kill her.

Every so often her eyes would star over and she would have to move some to get what blood she had left to pump to her brain again. She was shivering from the cold where the wind blew mercilessly through gaping holes. She looked in the mirror to see the car Danny G was driving making another move. She glanced to the seat where her pistol lay. She had fired only one shot. She would need the rest. She jerked violently to block his advance.

Head lights appeared in the oncoming lane. Marie held her ground as long as she could, swerving mere feet from a head on. The shipping truck blared a horn at her, but she barely heard it before she yanked the wheel to resume her post in the middle of the highway. Danny G had attempted a play for first, but failed.

Marie was grateful when the terrain of the land began to climb away from the sea. Her race was nearly run, but the hardest part was yet to come.

*****

"Damn it!" Cobby yelled as another bullet ripped through the door panel and embedded itself somewhere in the dash.

Valant turned with an expression of pure hatred. Turning, he unloaded a magazine out the back window at the car pushing them along. "Let that asshole along beside us!" Valant hollered as he turned to reload from a stash in the glove box.

"No! Then you become an easy target," Mickey returned.

"Just give him a good bashing. Enough to jar his teeth out!" Valant ground out.

"Could it be you have finally found someone as relentless and full of the fury of hell just like yourself?" Mickey asked with an ironic expression on his face. "No wonder you hate each other."

Valant turned amid the return fire to shoot again. "How fast are you going?"

"She's giving all she's got. Much past one-thirty the engine cuts out!" Mickey edged closer to the cut out point.

"Catch her before the cliffs or you'll have to slow and we'll never get her." Valant commanded.

Cobby rose and tried to see through the stars in his eyes. He pulled the trigger completely unsure if he was even shooting in the general direction of Vantino.

*****

The car slammed into Marie with great force. She braced on the steering wheel and kept the tires straight. It was the third or fourth time Danny G had tried to get her off her path. Marie had been mere inches from the sheer drop off to the left hand side of the road once already. It was a game of give and take. She gave Danny G just enough advantage to let him think he was going to gain some ground, then she would creep just out of his reach.

As the road wound and cut back repeatedly, Marie had to force her hand to keep ahead of him. Twice she hit the front end of their car due to lack of space to maneuver. She was so cold now she had stopped shivering. Everything she moved felt like moving a load of bricks. Only a few miles left.

She glanced again at her gun as her tires left the pavement on the left hand side, dangerously close to the edge of the cliff.

*****

"She's drifting again!" Mickey yelled.

Mickey caught up with the car pursuing Marie. All focus left Vantino. It was extremely hard to get a clear shot at them with the switchbacks in the road. Mickey wanted to allow Marie room to move. She had been drifting from one side of the road to the other for some time, but she was able to maintain just enough speed to keep ahead.

Even Mickey had to admire her abilities. He asked several times if Valant had any idea what her plan might be. Valant just pursed his lips, looked ahead at her car, and shook his head.

Vantino struck Mickey from behind.

*****

"Alright, time for the boys in back to go," Marie whispered to herself.

Marie drifted again to the left, just enough for Danny G to make an attempt to pull ahead. Just as his bumper was next to the rear passenger door, Marie jerked the wheel and slammed him against the rock face next to them. She held him there only briefly. When she let them go, the car swerved back into the center of the road, causing Mickey to hit his brakes. Vantino moved to the right to avoid Mickey. His tire sunk into a deep hole. The force of the stop threw Patrick into the dash.

Mickey righted and kept coming.

"Here we are. God, please make my aim be true," Marie prayed.

Marie slowed as stars blinded her and her body was pulled into oblivion. The flow of blood coming from her body a mere trickle now. Danny G lurched forward to come beside her, guns coming from the front and back windows. As the driver came even with Marie and saw the state she was in, Danny G raised his gun from beside him.

Marie sprang to life and raised her gun first, firing rapidly for the driver. Her aim was indeed true, as the first streaks of dawn creased the sky. The driver's head snapped over quickly. Marie hit the brakes. Only a few feet to go. Danny took the wheel over the body of the dead man. The tires made screeching noises as he tried to gain control again.

Marie slowed, and Danny G came to be in the lead. She pulled the wheel hard to the right and moved up the right hand side of Danny G and his struggle for control. Marie hit the accelerator and braced for impact as the engine roared to full capacity. She held the tires firmly to the left and felt the contact between the cars. She pushed with everything her car had.

The hole was in sight now. She forced Danny over even more. Beyond that hole was nothing but endless sky, and stars that had not yet begun to melt with the morning sun. Below was the crashing, relentless waves of the ocean. Danny G's left tires left pavement. Marie pressed her foot harder into the floor.

"Wholly shit!" Mickey yelled. Valant gripped the dash. Cobby watched in silent horror.

Danny G pushed back, but his tires could find no traction in the gravel. The hole was just ahead. It took more power than Marie had anticipated. She knew she wouldn't be able to correct her position in time. She was going over with Danny G. She looked over at him to see him looking at her with a look of utter mortification. She raised her now empty hand and made a gun with it. She fired it at him. Then he was gone.

Marie corrected her position in an attempt to save herself, but she was only able to move to the right slightly before her tire struck a rock. It shot her across the road. She over corrected after she bounced off the cliff on the opposite side of the road and sailed again towards the edge. She was too weak now to hold her wheel steady, thus pulling herself out of it.

"Marie!" Valant yelled as he watched, helpless.

The car fish tailed violently down the road. Mickey had to stop hard to avoid hitting her. He too fish tailed, and struck the rock wall to his right coming to a full stop. Marie kept going as she weakly tried to correct herself. Mickey hit the accelerator to find the car was stuck.

"Get out! We gotta push it free!" Mickey got out to let Valant out the driver's side. He and Cobby pushed as Mickey revved the engine. Cobby had very little to give, but he gave all he had. A spray of dust and rocks flew up as the car broke loose.

"Get in!" Mickey said unnecessarily.

Marie was gone from sight. They moved in pursuit, afraid of what they would find.

*****

Marie's car drifted to a stop on the rim of the turnout. Beyond was a scene of breath taking beauty, the sea void of any wrong doing it had in claiming a car full of lives only a few minutes before. Marie's vehicle idled softly, the tires pressed firmly against the rocks that were the only thing stopping her from crashing into the ocean herself. She had no strength to slide the car out of gear.

Her lips were a dark blue, her breathing shallow and faint. Her head lay back on the seat as her eyes watched the sky start to brighten. A tear slid down her pale cheek as she remembered the afternoon that she and Valant had driven his Jaguar up this very cliff, then stood together to look out at what she was seeing now.

A cold feeling of loneliness crept over her. Marie realized she was going to die alone. She longed to hear another voice, just one last time. Flinging herself forward, she clicked on the radio to hear the beginning notes of a song. Frank Sinatra. A young man she had met in New York several years ago. She liked him instantly. He had a charisma when he sang, an ability to put his own experiences into his voice. Like herself, he'd gone on from New York to win and lose happiness a few times over. Now he reached out of the radio to assist her in the transition from this life to the next. The song felt strangely appropriate. *At Long Last Love.*

She had feared and loathed John for so long. Ignoring and despising him became a past time. It wasn't as if she ever gave him a chance, thinking all along he was merely Asberry Park. Why waste her time on something that was twisted and ugly inside. John seemed almost simple in his deep darkness, his hatred a cloak protecting his soul from any kind of emotion. Having been forced to see the complexities that made up his life, she knew him for what he truly was.

Granada.

She was filled with fear at what was coming. The panic for John was gone. She had set all of them free. Which was what she wanted most of all. Now, they would continue as they had, and despite what God may think, she was grateful. She loved them with all the heart she had, and as a good woman does, wanted life for them more than anything else. But, she knew now the price was dying alone.

Another tear fell.

Our Father, who art in heaven,
Hallowed be Thy name
Thy kingdom come.........

"Marie! Marie look at me," Her eyes rolled to the sound of his voice.

"My darling….." Valant was bent over her, gathering her to him, pulling her from the car.

She could feel something being pressed into the wound in her shoulder and she saw Mickey's fearful face as Valant carried her away from Cobby's car. Without registering the move, she looked up to see Valant looking down at her. She knew they were inside something. It began to move. Her flickering eyesight tried to focus on John's face.

"John…" It wasn't even a whisper, just the movement of her lips.

"I got you." He was arranging Mickey's coat over her.

Mickey was trying to jam a handkerchief into Cobby's own gaping hole while driving back the way they had come. Cobby wasn't much better off than Marie, but he weakly turned to look down at her face. Valant met his look with one of wild desperation.

Valant held her tightly against him trying to pass his own life and warmth to her.

"John……"

"I'm here." He pressed his lips to hers to be met with ice where once vibrancy had dwelled.

"I'm scared." He put his face against hers when she finished whispering. Her fingers reached up to feel his face and left a streak of blood.

"Val…." Mickey said as Vantino's car came into view. It was far down the cliff, but it was broad side, waiting for them. There would be no passing.

"John…" Val looked from the figure he knew was Vantino and looked at Marie. Her lips were blue and her eyes were glassy.

"Valant!" Mickey repeated.

"John……" She shuddered as she tried to continue. He kissed her again. "I love you. Always have." She was able to get out. Valant watched in shock. "Always will." He kissed her again, but when he looked at her, her eyes had closed and she was still.

"Ah… Oh no! No don't go, don't leave me!" He pleaded as he kissed her cold lips repeatedly. "Marie!" He threaded his fingers in her dark hair. "I love you, I love you!" He pressed his face to hers and crushed her as he held her. He raised up to look at her.

"Mickey!" Came his coarse and broken yell. In complete understanding, Mickey turned to look at his shattered brother.

Vantino and his three men raised their guns as the car approached.

"There's only one way….." Mickey said lowly. He slowed the car. "Cobby, put your hands up."

When the car came to a stop, Mickey held up his hands. Patrick yanked Cobby's door open and threw him to the pavement, repeatedly kicking the near dead man. Vantino ordered Mickey out, then put him up against the rock wall of the cliff while another of the four kept a gun on him.

Vantino and Patrick made their way to the back where Valant sat holding the lifeless Marie. Vantino's eyes reflected the devastation Valant felt. He opened the door and Patrick put a gun to Valant's head.

"Give her to me," Vantino demanded. Valant refused.

"Let her go, Val. Don't waste whatever life she may have left in her to save. Let them take her," Mickey reasoned.

Valant looked down and kissed her softly. Vantino took her from. "Take me with you," Valant begged. Vantino moved away with her to his car. "Take me with you, damn it!" Valant yelled.

It took two men to wrestle him to the car and tie his hands behind his back while mashing his face into the trunk. They pulled the keys from the ignition and threw them over the cliff. Valant yelled and roared like something savage. Then they were gone, the sound of the engine fading quickly as they moved as fast as the car would go along the rock face.

Valant jerked and fought wildly to free his arms. He freed himself despite Mickey's efforts to help him. Valant took off at a dead run down the road after Vantino. His heart pounded and his legs burned, but he kept on until Mickey could no longer see him, either.

Mickey made his way around the car to where Cobby lay. He bent over him and squeezed his shoulder. "Hey, Cob. You still alive?"

Cobby groaned slightly. Mickey sighed deeply. "I hope you live. That old bastard Vantino has given you more grief than one man deserves. I hope you get the chance to kill him."

Mickey got Cobby in the backseat and covered him with the jacket that had once covered Marie. Then he hotwired the car. He took is time. He knew well how good it would have been for him to run like Valant was now the day Maryanne died.

Yes, it would be best to let Valant burn some of the fire that would soon melt into agonizing pain. He looked back at Cobby. Come tomorrow, there would be a funeral to arrange.

*****

Cobby drifted in and out of consciousness for some time before he finally dropped into complete blackness. He lay still and silent as death. Only the family doctor could find his faint and erratic heartbeat. He dreamed no dreams and felt the heavy sleep of the dead. It was the first time in a long time that he was at peace.

When he woke several days later, he stared for a while at the pregnant woman who tended to him. She spoke softly to him while changing his dressing, fluffed his pillows, and held him up so he could have some warm liquid spooned into his mouth. He could not think of who she must be. It seemed like he should ask, but even the thought of it took too much strength. So, when she lay him flat again he drifted away. Still he did not dream.

He learned to mark the passage of days by how many different dresses he saw her wearing. For a while he wondered why she changed every time she came to tend him, then with slow dawning he realized she was tending him even when he didn't wake. She spoke in a low tone his brain didn't have the required energy to translate.

When he finally realized it was Eva that cared for him, he was shocked. In the first place that she was stooping to care for him, and secondly that her belly had grown so large. By the looks of it she didn't have long to go. Every so often she would grip her mound and brace it. Her lips would draw into a thin line, then the moment would pass and she would go on about her business.

He had never liked her.

Now he didn't recognize her.

She smiled at him when she caught him watching her, and she would say something he couldn't hear. After a while he finally pieced together "Cobby" and "Still among the living." Her piercing black eyes held no barbs, so he wasn't sure that it was, "Cobby I'm so glad you're still among the living." Or, "Cobby, it's too bad you're still among the living."

He woke to the touch of a different hand. It was larger and firm, but not intrusive. He weakly opened his eyes to see Mickey sitting on the bed next to him, his hand against Cobby's forehead checking the heat that radiated there. After a moment Mickey put his hand down and looked at the younger man. He gave him one of his contemplative stares. Cobby didn't respond.

"You just don't quit, do you?" Mickey asked. "How many times have you been shot now? Four? Five? I know you took a few hits back when you first came to work for Val. That damn Vantino seems to bring plenty of lead when he comes around. Not to mention the hit at the club." Mickey shook his head in disgust.

Mickey looked away from him for a moment, then leveled an intense look at him. "Why? Why the hell did you do what you did?" Mickey's jaws clenched. "You took the one thing he ever loved and sent it to hell and gone. How could you do that to him?" he demanded.

Cobby closed his eyes and thought of Valant.

"You better hope he never finds you. God help you when he does. Right now he thinks you're dead, but that won't last. Remmi's is the safest house I have right now." Mickey stood and looked down at him.

Cobby struggled to mouth something at Mickey. He leaned closer to Cobby to listen. His face registered his understanding. He looked down and again his jaw clenched.

"She's dead. Died right there in Val's arms," Mickey said accusingly.

Cobby swallowed hard and squeezed his eyes shut, and in doing so a tear slid out. He might as well give up now, for he had lost the only two people in his life he cared about, whom he dedicated his life to. One to death, the other to a hatred so hot it rivaled the fires of hell.

Cobby slipped into the black, only this time, he dreamed, and they were of nothing but Marie.

*****

Valant walked up the street and stopped in front of the restaurant Vinny Vinnetti had for decades claimed as his headquarters. The building was lit despite the late hour, and patrons sat at tables scattered around the room. Women laughed and men lay back casually in their chairs as they smoked cigars. No one took notice of him.

Valant very easily reached into his pocket and withdrew his lighter. He brought the gasoline filled bottle up and lit the rag that stuck out the top. Bright orange light reflected off his pale face, the look of hate and determination written clearly. It was obvious Vinnetti had withdrawn from there as no men came forward to stop him from carrying out what he was about to do. He grabbed one of the patio chairs that sat outside the restaurant and flung it with one arm through a large glass window facing the street. Patrons shrieked at the impact, then the small explosion that followed.

Valant stood back and watched it burn for a while, unafraid that he might be gunned down. The flames took little time to engulf the establishment. When he heard the sirens he left the scene. It brought him no relief, for it was not the justice he wanted.

He wanted Marie back.

Somewhere in his mind he registered that where Marie was now, he could not follow. She was a bright and blinding star that spent its fire as it shot one last brilliant time across the sky. Now nothing remained. But, as a self-preservation mechanism, his sub-conscious kept that reality buried. So, he wandered on. He drifted to all the places that Vinnetti had ever owned or run, and he had even made a stop at his home.

It was as if the rumor he died was true. Valant could find nothing of him, or Vantino. He made it repeatedly clear that he wanted Vantino, but regardless of who he killed, maimed, or tortured, Vantino never showed his face.

Vinnetti was just gone, and so was his beautiful Marie.

He loved her so deeply. A dimension of himself he had not known existed until the first time he heard her sing. In one smooth sound she had stilled the beast within him that struggled to gain control. She had mesmerized him. He had sworn to himself he would leave her alone when she was nineteen. She was so young and fearful of him, he knew whatever she gave him would be done out of her own sense of self-preservation.

He had waited so long for her. An entire life time before she appeared, so unassuming, frightened and timid. He had settled for Margo, thinking that was what love was supposed to be. Sacrificing his own happiness to see her get what she wanted, then selling little bits of his soul every time he made love to her as a married woman. Margo was a deep acidic bitterness that now, to think on her, even when they were young, made him spit.

Marie was more than most men he knew. His equal on all playing fields. She was capable of so much more than she had ever been taught to accept as part of herself. Vantino had tried, Vinnetti had coaxed her along, but she refused to see who she really was. Valant had tried the best way he knew to get her past her demons, but that was what made her so lovely. A big heart that was so devastatingly scarred.

He never thought he would ever earn even just her trust, but then she told him she loved him, that she always had, always would. Then she had gone from him.

Not died, surely, for that was too horrific a possibility to even allow himself to consider. Each time he did, something inside his head twitched and it felt like the mass of his brain were moving. So, he avoided it. Contemplating her death meant he had let her down. That literally burned him down.

So he pressed on, alone, for the traitor Cobby lay dead somewhere. And if he weren't, he would be when Valant finished cutting him up. He did not stop to think too much on that one, either. Why Cobby had done what he did, Valant couldn't understand. He was betrayed by one of his own. He cared not to stop and think that she had convinced Cobby in an effort to save Valant's life. The plan was to keep her alive, at all costs. Before his eyes he had watched Cobby help her climb onto the butcher block.

Valant accelerated rapidly down the street to his next destination. If Vinnetti wouldn't respond, then this night his empire would burn.

*****

Mickey could not stop Valant. In truth, he couldn't find him. He spent his time in pursuit, but Valant, was exceptional at his profession. That made it impossible to catch up to him. Mickey always arrived just a minute too late. A deep fear began to form in Mickey's heart that he himself would have to kill his beloved brother. Cut off his own right hand and end the very life that had paralleled his own since he were a mere child.

Valant was all Mickey had left of the golden days of his life. All that remained without him was toil and perseverance. Without him, the comfort and solace of the best years were completely obliterated. And the thought of losing these things made Mickey so full of grief it was as if he were watching Maryanne die all over again. Only this time, Valant nor Julian would be there to drive him to the beach and comfort him in the coming anguish.

It was then Mickey got word. Eva was in labor, and she was struggling greatly.

*****

Valant spent a week tearing through Vinnetti's territory looking for anyone who could tell him anything. Now all he wanted to know was where they had buried her so he could go lie beside her until his own life passed. To run his fingers through the soil that lay on top of her beautiful body. But no one could tell him anything, and Vinnetti's men were getting good at hiding. Almost as if they were told to.

It was still several hours before dawn when Valant had exhausted his path of destruction. He hadn't slept in days. His body demanded he shut down. He had nowhere he wanted to go. He thought of the safe house. But he knew the memories of her there would kill him, and it would be a slow agonizing death. And, he wanted to know where she was.

He drove the darkened and empty streets until he saw lights on.

Like a moth to a flame, he was drawn to them to the point he found himself parked on the street outside the building. He stared for a long while. He recognized it well. He had spent countless hours there as a child. He didn't know how he had ended up there, but he didn't register the last few hours other than the strikes on Vinnetti he'd made. After a while, he slowly exited the vehicle, not even stopping to consider that someone might take him out.

He moved up the stone steps like an old man, relying heavily on the railing. The first handle he pulled revealed a locked door. For some reason this panicked him and he considered tearing it down with both hands. He needed to get in. A voice told him to try the door next to it. It worked.

The soft light from the candles weren't muted by the lights that shone out of the stained glass windows. He moved quietly in, not wanting to be seen. Not for the first time in his life he watched from the shadows. The beauty of the Sacristy called to him as he remembered events from his childhood in this very place. He could see his mother and father plainly on the day he took First Communion.

Valant badly wanted to sit down, to lie down, to drift into some kind of blackness that was void of life. Yet he couldn't. Something wouldn't allow him to. He stepped from the darkness into the sanctuary. As he left the cover of the choir loft above him, he bowed deeply, as if the Presence above in the high rafters of the ceiling pressed down on him. Instinct told him to bow, to fall on his face. To remain upright defied the Presence.

He moved halfway up the aisle, then felt he could intrude no further. He stiffly sat in a pew, covering his face with his hands. They shook uncontrollably as he leaned forward and lay his head against the back of the pew ahead of him. He waited to incinerate.

He sat like that for a long time, just breathing the remnants of incense in the warm air around him. The silence was not the deafening kind, more like it was merely listening to his thoughts, trying to offer comfort. Waiting for him to speak. It knew he had something to say.

"I love it here in the early hours of the morning."

Valant jerked upright to look in the direction of the voice. He had heard no one enter, nor move within such a close range. He considered going for his gun on reflex, but stopped himself.

"It is so quiet in here, and I can feel Him, as if He lit the candles Himself. Very few people see it like this." He was just up a row and about ten feet away. He looked back at Valant with warm brown eyes and a soft smile. He didn't consider him, just waited for Valant to speak. He had short brown hair and a well- trimmed beard. He wore the black clothes and collar of a priest, but he seemed too approachable.

He turned and looked to the Crucifix. "Self-sacrifice." He bowed his head a moment before looking back to Val. "When I was a kid, I used to wonder if He climbed down at night, or if He had to hang there all the time. Even Christmas." He smiled again, then turned to look at Valant. "Rest here is the very best kind. I know you need it."

Valant looked at him with cold eyes. "Have you no idea who I am?"

"I know you. I know you well."

"Then you know they took her from me," Valant said with distress.

"Yes, I know that."

"I don't know if she yet lives, or if she has gone where I cannot ever follow."

"No such place exists."

"You don't understand. My very soul is twisted. I cannot live without her."

He smiled again at Valant. "Then count yourself among the rare and fortunate, because it is few who feel it."

"Feel what?" Valant asked doubtfully.

"Just a fraction of what God felt when you took yourself away from Him." He was quiet a moment before going on. "Sometimes, God has to speak pretty loud before we hear Him."

Valant did not respond. "Rest here, my brother in Christ. Rest."

*****

Mickey had rolled up his sleeves and sweat beaded on his forehead. She struggled on, never making one sound, just slipped into some alter consciousness where questions were ignored. She tried her best to listen to the family doctor. Mickey had never seen a woman in labor. If the doctor had someone else to help, he wouldn't have still. But, as circumstances were, Mickey watched in silent agony as Eva pushed and struggled while the doctor kept up his post. It was a breech baby. By the time Mickey arrived, Eva had been working hard for many long hours. She was tired and weakening, but she still pushed when the doctor ordered for her to.

Mickey's soul cried. To be here again, watching the same thing happen to another wife, in another time. Only now, Eva was conscious and could see her demise coming. He threaded his fingers through hers and smoothed her hair back away from her face. She looked at him in complete devastation and tears burned his eyes. She lay back weakly on her pillows. He kissed her hand and squeezed it.

Her body tensed again and tears came from her eyes. "Come, Mrs. Delano. Push again with all you have. Give it all you have left."

She barely raised her head as she pushed, unable to even raise her legs. She sucked in a ragged breath as the contraction passed and she relaxed. Her eyes were glazed, but she focused on Mickey as he knelt beside her and sponged the sweat off her face. "It's almost over. Nearly over," it was a lie, but he wanted to offer her hope and strength to keep going. She tensed again.

"Alright. Again. All you've got." The doctor said as he wiped the sweat from his own brow.

*****

Cobby leaned heavily on the wall as he slowly made his way down the stairs. The house was still, and he looked up the hallway at the bottom of the steps to see Remmi, Martin, and Frankie at the opposite stairs in stone silence as they waited to hear an infant's cry. He slipped away into the dark and moved feebly out the door.

He made his way in the blackness to the street and slid heavily into Mickey's black Cadillac. He shook the stars from his eyes then turned the ignition. Then he was gone into the night.

*****

Mickey held his son and cried silent tears as he watched the doctor try to save his wife. The bundle wrapped in white towels that rested in his arms was still covered in blood and vernix, his tiny little fingers blurry through Mickey's eyes. He had cried a loud wail when he finally entered the world, ending the pain and long suffering of his mother. But, she had fallen back on her pillows. Although she smiled at her son as the doctor held him up for her to see, she soon closed her eyes and relaxed. The doctor had gone to work.

Mickey felt the crushing weight of loss two fold.

He looked down at his son and kissed his head softly, not caring that the perfect miracle he held in his arms was less than clean. Joy blended with the long carried sorrow and he felt as if he were finally looking at a future. He looked again to Eva.

"She's lost a lot of blood and strength, but she's tough. Toughest Delano woman I've ever worked with." With that the doctor stood and wiped his hands on a towel. Mickey moved beside her and she looked at him out of the corner of her eye. He sat beside her carefully, then bent to kiss her cool lips.

"He's perfect. You did a hell of a job." Mickey whispered fiercely. He held the child where his mother might look upon him. She smiled and held a trembling hand out to touch his soft cheek. It took great effort to do so.

"Well mama, I know you are tired, but the time has come for you to feed your child. Motherhood knows no fatigue nor rest given for," the doctor said.

*****

Mickey's eyes opened with the door. Imelda quietly stepped through. Eva lay next to him, sleeping soundly, and his son was wrapped firmly in receiving blankets in his arms. He had spent the past few hours alternating between running the pad of his thumb across the forehead of his son, and running his fingers through Eva's black hair.

Imelda smiled at him softly, then stepped back out of the bedroom to wait for Mickey. He closed the door behind himself, and glanced down at his sleeping son. "His name?" Imelda asked as she beamed at the red and swollen child.

"I think he will be Georgio Samuel. To honor those whom I never bothered to before."

A look of sadness crossed her features. "I think it suits him."

Mickey's face became very sad. "Thank you for coming. I'd like to stay, but, I have to find him. I hope wherever he is he's still alive." He touched Georgio's face one last time.

"I am happy to come."

"Imelda….." She looked at him after she had taken the baby. Unshed tears reflected in his eyes. She squeezed his hand.

"I know Mickey. I know."

*****

It further saddened Mickey to learn that Cobby was gone. He wanted to take him along, because for some reason he was feeling particularly sentimental. The fact was, he spent the past hours thinking on Cobby's situation and he knew why Cobby had done what he had.

They were two dumb kids saving a man they loved.

He wondered if they would see him again. In the course of just a few days, Mickey had nearly lost an empire fighting an unseen force only to find his salvation lie in the sacrifice of a woman. Now he sat king again with no one to second him. He found that he had cared for Cobby more than he realized, depended on him entirely in the months it had been since Marie's attack and Val's departure.

Now they were gone. All of them.

That's when he got the message. Vinny Vinnetti wanted to meet.

*****

Cobby sat and watched him for a long time. The dawning sun was a vivid pink. The waves rolled continuously against the fine sand and the long beach stretched out before him for a great distance before it met with water. Valant sat on the hood of his car just staring.

Cobby had no strength left, the trip he'd made the night before took all he had. But he refused to quit. It troubled him greatly to know that Valant was alone, grieving, and no one watched his back. It crushed Cobby to see him like that, so obviously broken. The man of strength and stature, filled with a consuming fire was nearly drown out.

After a while, Cobby no longer cared what happened to him. He just wanted to shoulder some of the load. So, he stepped slowly out of the car, stars again covering his vision and pain shooting down his arm. He stumbled down the beach to the man who had been his life, still was. He knew Valant would most likely kill him, but Cobby was a man of great loyalty. He had done what he had to help Marie, all to repay a debt he owed to the man who sat stoically looking out at the ocean. Valant had taken many lives. But to Cobby, the lives he had saved had been lives with great value. The lives he had taken had not been noticed by many.

A round blood spot formed on Cobby's shoulder as he approached Valant. He stopped about six feet away and looked out to the ocean. Cobby swayed greatly with the breeze but remained upright by determination alone. The strong clean smell of the air around him made him close his eyes and inhale deeply.

"You better do something about that blood. You haven't got any more to lose."

Cobby opened his eyes and looked at Valant who still looked out across the water. "It'll quit."

"Yea, 'bout the time you seep dry." Valant sighed. "I won't lie Cobby. I want to jam my finger in that seeping hole and dig around until I find a cluster of nerves, then pull them out the opening. I want to hit you until your face is gone and then watch your bloody carcass sink in that great body of water. I want to pull my knife out and cut you up, not because of what you did to betray me, but because I don't want to admit that I got her killed......." He cut short and balled his fists before him. "I'll never go to hell because I am already there."

Cobby swallowed hard. "Well, then I guess we're in good company."

*****

Mickey softly closed the patio door behind him. Valant lay on a lounger blowing cigarette smoke up at the sky. His body was limp and ragged, and Mickey looked him over for a moment in great distress. He felt the overwhelming urge to do something for Val, something drastic, something lifesaving. His best friend and brother was slipping rapidly from the world of the living, a world Mickey himself would be stuck in alone.

God help me.

Mickey moved slowly to him and sat in a patio chair next to him. Mickey leaned his elbows on his legs and slowly rubbed his hands together. He said nothing yet, so sure his voice wouldn't hold out for even one word. Images rolled through Mickey's mind, the faces of all whom he had loved and had out lived. He realized with great wretchedness as Val's own face passed as well that this was the end.

"How's Eva and the baby?" Val's haggard voice asked.

Mickey nodded his head. "Alright. 'Preciate you bringing Cob." Valant inhaled deeply the stale smoke.

"Just in time to bury him, I'm guessing."

Mickey stopped rubbing his hands together. "That dock trash ended up being pretty useful." Mickey licked his lips. "You know, he did it to save you. Stupid idea or not. That dumb kid loves you."

"For all the good it did him."

There was a long silence before Mickey again spoke. "Remember that time we took my pap's coupe and went up the cliffs? We couldn't have been more than twenty-two. Almost ate shit on that truck?" Mickey spoke slowly.

Val merely grunted.

"I never dreamed back then that I would lose them all. Every one of them. All the players that made me who I am. Every one that made my life good." Mickey paused as he swallowed. "All the passion I had as a kid, the love I made, the mistakes I hardly bothered to notice, all brought me to this. I watched them go one by one. Some I got the chance to say goodbye to, some left so quickly I never saw the open door. And through it all there was you." Tears burned his eyes.

"Through it all, you held me up. You made me an empire, you kept my hand steady. Now, I know, that the time has come for me to say goodbye to you as well. My last thread to my good days, the last person who truly knows Mickey Delano. Now you go, too." Mickey paused to ball his hands into fists.

"You said way back then on those cliffs that I didn't need you. The truth is, Val, it is you who doesn't need me. I have needed you so deeply I'm not sure how to exist without you." Mickey looked out into the late evening sky. "But I know one thing. If this is the life you live now, if this is the pain you have to live with, then brother, I hope Vinnetti catches up with you. I hope he sets your soul free. For its better he do it, than I have to."

Mickey stood and slid his hands into his trouser pockets. "God be with you, Valant, to whatever end He has chosen for you."

*****

"Cobby. Get up boy." Cobby attempted to open his eyes but found they refused to cooperate. "Come on, Cob. Wake up if you are still alive." Cobby twitched. "I need you. Wake up." Cobby began to register it was Mickey's voice.

He shook his head and tried to make his vision work. "Where's Val?"

He heard Mickey sigh. "In the house. Sleeping."

Light flooded Cobby's eyes as he looked up at Mickey. "Where am I?"

"You collapsed at the beach. Val brought you here to my house. I need you. Come on, get up."

"Who's going?"

"Just you and me," Mickey replied.

"No Val?" Cobby tried to remember why such a heavy weight fell at the thought of his great friend.

"No," Mickey stated regretfully. "I have him caught now. Best we keep him that way for his own sake."

Mickey took hold of Cobby and hauled him to his feet and held him steady until Cobby took control of his own body. He rubbed his face for a moment before looking at Mickey with any kind of clarity.

"When did you eat last?" Mickey asked.

Cobby rubbed his face again as he tried to remember. "Eva brought me something last night."

"Bull shit. Eva's been baby bound for going on two days. Clearly you have not fed yourself."

"It just doesn't matter that much." Cobby replied lowly.

"Yeah, it does. I need you."

Mickey took Cobby to the kitchen and was able to get something down his throat. It roused him around enough for him to find a sense of lucidity. Mickey forced meat into him as well as about a quart of milk, Cobby choking back his gag reflex multiple times. Mickey took out some chocolate cake, and for the first time in Cobby's life, he truly didn't want any. That didn't stop Mickey. Cobby ate it a mouthful at a time, trying to end the agony. But, warmth began to flood into his veins and muscles. He felt that he could move without dragging a mountain.

"Let me see that shoulder," Mickey stated.

Cobby undid his shirt buttons and Mickey pulled it off. The bullet wound was red and swollen. A slight hint of blood oozed from it.

"I hate this. Nothing hurts like this," Cobby whispered.

"I used to agree with you," Mickey said as he wiped away blood. "Then I watched my wife deliver a baby that was right side up and backwards. Nothing could ever hurt like that." He chuckled lightly. "You know the damn part of the whole thing is here you are still fevering and living in agony from a lesser

wound, and she's up and moving like nothing happened."
Mickey chuckled again. "Men are the stronger of the genders.
You bet."

Cobby was silent for a while, then asked, "Where are we
going?"

"Vinny Vinnetti has asked to meet."

"Damn."

"Damn what?" Mickey countered.

"Nothing. Just damn. Here Valant's dream of going head
to head with that bastard is a reality and he's off in a coma.
That leaves me, and I have grave doubts having witnessed The
Heart in action multiple times."

Mickey was silent for a moment as he wrapped Cobby's
shoulder with fresh dressing. "You can handle it. If I thought
otherwise I would have put a bullet in you long ago. Although,
judging by the evidence, it wouldn't have killed you."

*****

Vinnetti wanted to meet on the property line. So, it
seemed natural to meet at a place that they both knew; Jerry
Barelli's old dive where the whole thing started. The shooting
at the club had drawn some rather unsavory suspicion from the
police. Although Mickey had done a thorough job of making
sure it was well covered up and no one took any blame, The
Ruby had been closed due to the impending investigation.

He considered himself fortunate.

Both Cobby and Mickey spoke little on the drive to the
now abandoned establishment that was once The Lamplighter
Lounge. Cobby made the drive many times when he followed
Valant on one of his visits to hear Marie sing. He knew the
streets, but when he saw the tumble down old building, he
found it hard to believe something so great as Marie could have
ever existed there.

She was so much more than her humble beginnings.
Cobby missed her deeply. His life was void of whatever it was
she held.

"I won't lie. He asked that I come with you only, so we
could be walking into a trap. It's dark as shit so who would
know anyway," Mickey said with an edge of doubt.

He pulled along next to the front entrance of the building
and looked at Cobby. Cobby shook his head and reached into
his jacket to reassure himself that his gun was ready. "Let's do
this."

Mickey nodded and stepped out of the car and buttoned his suit jacket. The feel of his son's soft head etched along his cheek. He hoped he would see him again. Mickey took note that Cobby stepped from the car without assistance, and despite what he knew must have been great pain, Cobby appeared normal.

Mickey came around to stand next to Cobby as he scanned the street. Mickey took his gun out of his pocket and held it tightly. They stood together as the main entrance to the club slowly opened and the man known as Patrick came out. He looked at Cobby. It flashed in his mind all the times Patrick had beaten him in the months prior, including the day Marie died and he was dying himself. Patrick dragged him from the car and kicked him mercilessly. Cobby wasn't sure what purpose it would serve to kick a dying man. Animosity flared within Cobby.

"You boys put those guns away and come with me."

"Why don't you bring Vinnetti out here to me?" Mickey shot. "He asked to meet me, not the other way around."

"Mr. Vinnetti would like to speak with you inside," Patrick replied firmly.

"Well, that seems stupid since any asshole could gun the both of us down. No. I followed his wishes by just bringing Cobbinelli like he asked. Now he can do me the favor of coming out here."

"There's no need for concern, young Delano." Mickey's head and gun snapped in the direction of the voice, but Cobby's eye's and pistol stayed on Patrick.

"I've honored the truce I made with your father for many years, even when I shouldn't have. I have less reason to break it now." Vinny Vinnetti walked out of the dark from somewhere in the direction of the alley. Behind him the form of The Heart Vantino slowly emerged as well. Cobby moved sideways in an attempt to keep both dangerous men in his peripheral vision.

Vinnetti continued forward. "I simply don't think it wise to speak in the street in these times of unrest."

Mickey raised an eyebrow in surprise. Vinny Vinnetti came to stand before him and they looked at each other for a long moment. It had been many years since Mickey had seen him in the flesh. The last time was probably at Maryanne's funeral. Vinnetti had come to show respect for the dead as well as the Delano family. Mickey had been so distraught he hardly noticed. The memory flickered in Vinnetti's eyes as well.

"It's been many years," Vinnetti's voice was low. "Now we meet this day, and finally, a congratulations is in order. God bless the child."

Mickey nodded his head in recognition, but kept his gun on the older man, distrust shining in his eyes. Vinnetti looked decades older than he had at the funeral. Mickey couldn't fathom what would cause a man to age in such a way. But, to be fair, that was many years and miles ago.

"Please come in, Delano. I have no intent to kill either of you."

Mickey looked at Cobby wryly. Cobby shook his head at Mickey. "This has power play written all over it," Cobby muttered.

Mickey again thinks of the son he has waited so long for.

"Come on Cobbinelli. Be the reasonable young man I know." Vantino spoke with his hands tucked in his trouser pockets. He wore no over coat and his suit jacket was buttoned.

"I'd say the say the same thing about you, but you're an unreasonable asshole," Cobby spat.

The corner of Vantino's mouth twitched. Mickey snorted.

"So, what? We stand out here all night waiting to get killed on a dark street outside some shithole dive?" Vinnetti asks.

Mickey looked at Cobby. "Well, what do you think?"

"I don't give a shit what you do. All I care about is that asshole in the doorway doesn't take boots to me again."

Vinnetti held up both his hands. "Look, all I want to do is talk. Please, trust me." He leveled a look at Mickey.

After a moment Mickey nodded slightly. He held out his arm toward the door. "You first."

Without hesitation, Vinnetti and Vantino moved toward the entrance. Cobby and Mickey exchanged uncertain glances, then moved after them. There were few lights on, just one or two as they walked in. The stage was a gaping black hole, and the building smelled of mold. A damp feel hung heavy in the air.

Cobby scanned the darkness and doubted any of them would be walking away. They moved down by the stage. It gave off an eerie feeling of being close to the dead. The hair on

Mickey's neck stood straight out. Only a soft yellow light lit a few of the tables that had chairs.

Vantino still had his hands in his pockets. He sauntered around one of the tables looking around him. "I like what you've done with the place, Delano. Really kept it up."

Chairs were thrown in piles around the room, tables were over turned. Empty bottles littered the floor. It seemed impossible that less than a year before Marie had been brought home from New York to sing on the very stage that was now a damp blackness. The place had fallen into such disrepair anyone would be certain the place had been abandoned for years instead of months.

"So what's the gig, Vinnetti?" Mickey asked when they had come to a stop below the stage. Vinnetti stood near the steps and looked at him silently.

"I want to renew the truce," Vinnetti said simply.

Mickey shook his head. "What point would that serve?"

Vinnetti held up a hand. "Now listen to me. I have reason to believe that the man Marie so graciously rid us of may just have been part of a much larger problem. I think we might serve ourselves better if instead of bickering between ourselves, we spend resources watching for signs of more trouble."

"She served you well, didn't she? Saved your empire from ruin without you even having to lift a finger." Mickey countered.

"That was not my intention," Vinnetti replied as he shook his head.

"Then what the hell was your intention?"

Vinnetti sighed and reached for a stool not far from him. He moved it to him and sat down on it, his long gray overcoat brushing the grimy floor. He pointed at Cobby.

"I believe the young man would know how this all started. He was there that night. Watched with the same look of disbelief that I'm certain was on my face." He gestured with his hands. "We all stood on the cusp of ending a feud that started with your grandfather and mine. It came down to Delano," he pointed at himself with his right hand. "or, Vinnetti. The Dark Horse held the power to end a turf war. I believe he was going to take his chance, despite the fact that even if he killed me, he would have died. He was ready to die for you and your cause." Now Vinnetti pointed at Mickey.

"He pulled his gun and started for me. How he even got in here without being noticed is still a question." He shook his head. "I stood in this very spot and watched him come. Then Marie started singing. I don't know what happened to him. One second he's gunning for me, the next he is transfixed on her. I should've killed him. I should've fired a bullet through his head and been done with it." Vinnetti ran his thumb across his nose.

"It was her first time on stage. I didn't want anything to spoil her night. I knew you would make a play for this shithole. I knew it would give something away for me to stand so firm in acquiring it. In truth, I owned her father anyway. I wanted to know she was safe. That you wouldn't come sauntering in and her catch your eye. I just wanted to own this outright, no questions asked.

"The very thing I was so concerned about, that you would make a move on her, he did. That miserable asshole. I knew the moment he looked at her. It was so clearly written on his face." Vinnetti shook his head angrily. "So, Vantino kept watch. We kept guys posted and well hidden. We watched him come and go for weeks. Then finally, one night he got bold and spoke to her. That was it. I decided no more. I arranged for her to go to New York."

Vinnetti looked down for a moment then looked back at Cobby. "We knew The Dark Horse was keeping quiet about her because you followed him every time. But you made sure he never knew about it. I think we all watched in horror for a while. Marie was so scared of him we figured it was one sided. It was. Vantino watched him approach her again the night before she left."

Vinnetti shook his head again. "We spent years preparing her. Grooming her. Altering the damage her father had done. From the very moment I pulled her little broken body from that closet, she became my daughter. She was what I had been waiting for. I knew that. I molded her each step, planned her every success, staged everything to make it turn out for her betterment." He paused a moment. "Then in walks some bastard who thinks at nineteen she's fair game." Vinnetti put his hands in his pockets.

"I let her sing because it brought her joy. Something she never had before. I knew when she went to New York we'd have to drag her back here. I knew she'd hate me for it. That what I had built her for was not what she wanted for herself. I thought maybe she'd figure it out on her own, but it took Valant to make her see. In the meantime while she was in New York the guys I have following her start to notice they aren't the only ones following her. Things start happening here. Vantino puts together that maybe somebody has figured out who Marie is to me despite how hard I've worked to keep a distance there.

"Things started to escalate. We could see a hostile take-over, with Marie at the heart of it. So I decide to bring her home and put her where they won't bother to look." Vinnetti pointed to Mickey then. "With you. Doubting he has forgotten her, Vantino goes and asks The Dark Horse to watch out for her, which he does. Until the night she got cut up." He shrugged.

"'For this I shall lay down my life.' An empire, a broken little girl. I would lose my life to protect both. It all went the way I wanted it to. All except the part where Valant took her and disappeared. All except the part where he managed to rebuilt in her in a few months what we had spent her lifetime rebuilding." He spoke the last part slowly. "All except for the part where she found she loved him deeply enough to die for him."

Vantino's shoulders dropped then, his face down cast. "The Dark Horse found in that sweet little girl the desire to fight. Something Vantino and I feared didn't exist. She wouldn't stand up to her family, let alone an entire regimen of men bent on a hostile take-over. We watched that night in horrified shock as she took it on herself and rid the world of Danny G."

"Where is she?" Mickey demanded.

"Please. Let her rest in peace. She's done enough for you," Vinnetti replied.

"All we want is to see her grave. Pay our respects just as you did when my wife died. Allow Valant the closure he needs to survive," Mickey said firmly.

"Closure?" Vinnetti said incredulously. "What will closure do for a mad man? And if you want to talk about respect, it's out of respect for Marie and what she sacrificed that I have allowed him to live. All the while he torches everything I own and murders anyone that may have a slight connection to me. You have no concept of respect!" Vinnetti jabbed his finger in Mickey's direction as his voice raised.

"Allow him to see her grave. That is all he wants. To be able to say goodbye. To lie next to her for the last time," Mickey spoke with certainty.

Vinnetti cocked his head as he looked at the young Delano. "Did that really help you? Or did that prolong the deep hurt? I don't see how disturbing her rest will really heal the mind of a deranged man."

"You don't know what will heal the mind of a deranged man!" Mickey spat.

"Then that brings me to the next problem. If you don't stop him, I will. I've kept my men off him, let him go crazy at my expense. But no more. You either get a handle on him, or I will."

Mickey was silent. He knew it would come to this.

"Perhaps you know of a way to stop the beast without killing him, I don't know. And I don't care. Marie set us free from The Underground. Now we see The Dark Horse is just as bad. But we know him, and eventually I will be able to stop him." Vinnetti finished.

"You can go straight to hell," Valant's voice cut the musty darkness. He materialized out of the black like he always did, only the ember of his cigarette lending to his reality. He walked slowly with his left hand in his pocket, and his right hand holding the cigarette half way to his mouth. "I should have cratered your head one of the hundred times I had the chance. Took her for myself. I never would have led her to such a demise."

Vinnetti arched his brows. "Wouldn't have led her to such a demise? Were you not the one who rebuilt the shattered fine china? Hefted her up for all the world to see? Used her as a lure for The Underground? Were you not the very hand that led her to her demise?"

Valant ground his teeth together. "You son of a bitch, you took her from me. She was mine and you know it," he ground out.

"You said you would look out for her. You failed. Miserably," Vantino shouted as he stepped in front of Vinnetti.

Valant pulled his gun from beneath his jacket and pointed it at Vantino's chest. "Well, she's gone now. It doesn't matter whether you live or die." He cocked it and advanced toward Vantino.

"Valant, don't. You'll regret it." There was no fear in Vantino, only a deep regret of his own.

Cobby looked at Mickey, then left him standing alone to stand beside Valant. "Don't boy. Don't die like this." Vantino spoke softly to Cobby. Vantino held empty hands before him. Cobby's world as he knew it spiraled and he felt the full weight of regret and despair. So much pain flowed though him, he suddenly felt the significance of Valant's choice of death. An intense hatred and wounded confusion radiated out of Valant's eyes as he raised his gun to Vantino's head. Guns trained on both Cobby and Valant. The silence was deafening as Cobby waited to die next to the man he loved as a friend, mentor and father.

"John."

It was a mere whisper, but it crashed through the silence like an avalanche. It hit Valant and emotion rolled across his features.

Vantino held up his hands again but he spoke very softly as he looked at Valant. "You'll regret it, boy."

Valant looked around in the darkness as did Cobby and Mickey. "Marie?" came Valant's ragged voice. "Marie, are you there?"

Nothing but silence met his desperate plea. Valant's breathing also became ragged. "Please be there!" He moved to the edge of the circle of light and looked helplessly into the black.

No sound came. No voice, no reply. Nothing but the echo of his own breathing off molded bricks. Valant looked down and his head bent, shoulders sagged. "My love is my torment."

Valant looked at Mickey who nodded his head in understanding. "Val," Cobby whispered.

"This is why I chose you. No man who loves as you do would harm that which would only cause a deep cut to himself. I knew you would watch over her. I was right." Vantino whispered. "Call for her again."

Valant looked unbelievingly at Vantino who nodded at him. "Marie?" His voice was low.

Silence again, but it was broken by the sound of creaking wood. "Marie?"

Cobby and Mickey exchanged glances. The creaking grew louder.

"I'm here." The voice was barely audible. The sound of the old stage bearing weight brought Valant to the bottom of the stage steps. The sound of shuffling was blending with the groaning of the wood.

"Marie?" Cobby asked in uncertainty.

She slowly emerged into the weak circle of light that surrounded the leaders of two dynasties. She moved awkwardly, her feet heavy. She wore gray slacks and heels, a white shirt was tainted only by the cascading mass of her black hair. Her left arm was bound close to her body. She barely held up her head, her eyes black holes staring out from behind the hair that fell across her face. She had become nothing but sharp points and gray skin.

Her beauty was undeniable even in her state.

Cobby wiped his mouth with his forearm on the hand that held his gun. Sweat had beaded on his upper lip. All Mickey could say was, "God in heaven."

Valant shook as he climbed the stairs to her, still not certain he wasn't dreaming in an alcohol induced stupor. He came to stand before her and she swayed. Valant reached out and brushed the hair away from her scarred cheek, then cupped her face with his hand. Her eyes began to shine some.

"Is it you?"

She attempted a smile. "What's left," she whispered. "John...."

He moved close to her and looked at her shoulder. "Trouble you?"

She nodded at him, feeling his closeness, the white of his shirt reaching out to her. "John."

His arms were around her in an instant and she looked up at him. He ran his hand through her long black hair to smooth it from her face. "I'm sorry my love. It took me so long to get back to you. I was lost in the dark of my mind, looking for you."

The same look he had the night before she left for New York came over his face. He shook his head as he smoothed her hair again. "This time, you leave with me."

Marie put her good arm around his neck. She smiled at him an assured smile, then he pressed his lips to hers. She smelled the wonderful scent of bourbon and aftershave, mixed with cigar smoke. She melted against him and he became all that was holding her up. When she broke the kiss she buried her face in his neck and he held her tightly against him.

Tu, Solamente Tu.

As Marie softly sang Alfredo Clerici, Valant swept her up and against his chest, then disappeared into the darkness with her, the wood of the stage groaning quietly beneath them as they went.

Cobby looked to Mickey with a firm look in his eyes. Mickey gave Cobby a half smile as he nodded. Cobby too, moved up the stage steps and disappeared into the darkness. There was silence as the remaining men watched and listened for a departure they couldn't hear.

"She knows she can never be free," Vinnetti's voice interrupted the stillness. "But, it only seems fair she have the one thing that brings her joy. Without it, she just isn't Marie. Whether she knows it or not, he's held her up for years. She will need his strength now, to head an empire. And the truth is, I don't really think we've seen the last of The Underground. "

Mickey was silent as he thought about this. "You know old man, I think I win." Mickey replied, still looking into the blackness of the stage. "Passion will surely result in the melding of two families into new blood."

"I genuinely hope I am dead by then." Vinny's response evoked a chuckle from Mickey.

"You'll say that until you hold that child. You have your truce, Vinnetti. For now," Mickey's eyes twinkled with mischief.

"Hmmph. You'll be just like your papa. You'll think you're the shit until it comes time to back your son and his ambitions. You'll come begging back for me to go easy on the self-righteous little asshole, just like Georgio did."

Mickey laughed out loud. "We'll see."

*****

Cobby moved heavily as he lowered himself into the car. He watched as Valant left the alley way and turned onto the street next to the club before cranking the engine and sliding it into gear. He hoped he had strength for the drive.

The passenger door opened and Vantino slid into the seat next to Cobby. He smoothed his hair back with both his hands, then grinned. His look was met with one of irritation. "I'm gonna need a ride."

"No. Nope. Not this time you unreasonable asshole." Cobby made a quick grab for his gun and when he turned it on Vantino he found the barrel of a pistol in his face. Vantino's eyes were hard and unyielding.

"How the hell have you lived this long? I must be some kind of incredible asshole to best you time and time again. I've got a good twenty some years on you." His face remained serious only for a moment. Vantino broke into laughter. He pocketed his gun and clapped Cobby on the back. "Oh, the time we're gonna spend together!"

Cobby's face remained irritated as he looked out the windshield and pressed the gas pedal. "Does that prick Vinnetti not allow you a car? Are you too senile to drive?"'

Vantino looked over at him as they accelerated after Valant. "What fun would that be? Driving myself around. Besides, I have you now to take me everywhere I want to go." Vantino followed the comment with and evil chuckle. Cobby glared at him and reached over and switched on the radio. Frank Sinatra rang out loud and clear with *Just in Time*.

*****

Marie lay entangled against Valant, her breathing deep and steady. Every so often she would burrow closer to him, if it were possible. The feel of her bare skin against his sent a deep shock wave of contentment he had never experienced before.

Valant never slept much. Although he knew they weren't alone, and there was no need for him to be laying there listening to the stillness beyond her breathing, he felt no need for rest. He ran his fingertips across her soft hair and smooth skin, convincing himself she was real and in his arms, finally. He brought her back to the safe house and she had cried as he carried her in. She had clung to him on the ride home just like she had to the beach that day, following the contours of his neck and chest with her hand, unbuttoning his shirt to feel his skin. It was like a narcotic.

He owed Vinnetti. His very life. He knew it was Marie's desire that she be here with him, and like himself, Vinnetti loved her deeply and would give anything he had to make her happy. Even give her to the man he hated most of all. He suspected Vantino had much to do with it as well.

The beast within him was silent and still. He had found his purpose, and he intended to fulfill it with all he had. He had lived to further Mickey before, but now he lived to further

Marie. Everything she wanted, everything she needed, all that she would become. He was hers. He traced the contour of her back down to her buttocks and she arched her back in response.

"You don't sleep do you?" she whispered in the darkness.

"No," he whispered back

She moved her head slightly so she could look at him, her eyes heavy with the need to sleep. "I love you, John Valant, always have, and always will."

His fingertips traced the pendant of Michael the Archangel where it rested nestled comfortably between her breasts. How many times Michael had battled on his behalf, Valant couldn't know.

"Just say it Valant. I don't want to have to look at a sketch book to figure it out."

Valant raised his head to look at her shocked. "What?"

"You are damn talented," her eyes held his. "Cobby is always looking out for you. He's the one who gently kept prompting to see what was before me."

"I used to clean my gun in the endless hours of the night thinking of how I would kill him if he was making love to you at the apartment."

Marie laughed and tucked her head against the soft hair of his chest. "What?" he demanded.

She again looked at him. "I think Cobby would have turned the world over to find a way to make me love you if I didn't."

"You said you kissed him once."

"Yes," Marie's voice full of amusement. "Even his mother didn't buy the sincerity of it."

Marie ran her hand down his neck and across the expanse of his chest. He exhaled deeply. "Are you ever gonna say it to me?"

Valant's voice was deep when he replied. "I've waited a long time for you. Spent a lot of time hoping you'd come around."

He kissed her and in a very low voice whispered, "Don't ever go from me again. I can't be me without you."

"Oh, John." Marie's voice shook. "You've been my courage since the first time you spoke to me that night all those years ago. When my brother took me from you."

"You've haunted my dreams every night since I first heard you sing. I deeply feared you'd never get over your scars.

Never be what I knew Vinnetti would force you to be." Valant plunged his hand into the mass of her hair. He looked down into her eyes and for a moment the granite disappeared and Marie could see the emotion that ran just below the surface. "I love you, even though you are a damn Vinnetti." He quickly kissed her again muffling any response she was trying to make.

"Thank you John, for always being there, even before I knew I wanted you to be."

"I told you. I'm not sure he exists anymore."

Marie smiled. "Then I guess we're even. The beautiful singer doesn't exist anymore, either. You were the one who told me to become whatever was next. I am what came next."

His thumb traced her scars. "You were always this. It wasn't the singer that I wanted. It was fire and intelligence you didn't know you had. You are my equal."

Tears filled Marie's eyes. "Not your equal. Surely I'm not strong enough to be that."

"Marie, my love, you are my only weakness. May the world never know that truth."

"Then you really do understand me better than I give you credit for. Please don't leave me. Don't send me away. I love you so. It will kill me the second time we part."

Valant moved against Marie, the length of his body claiming hers. He kissed her deeply, the intensity of the feeling blocking out all but the sensation he brought to her.

"Then I better keep us together." Valant whispered in the dark as he moved over her.

*****

Vantino blew a long smoke string into the dark towards the stars twinkling overhead. Cobby sat next to him on the hood of his own car and smoked silently. He was tired and weak, but he felt the last of the fever go. He knew things were going the other way now. He suspected it had something to do with Marie who lay inside in happiness.

Intertwined.

He felt the deep connection when she walked out on that ruin of a stage. Something in him made his heart beat again. He lowered his cigarette.

"Where was she? All that time?"

Vantino looked at him. "Mexico. She recently acquired a safe house down there."

"Is that where Vinnetti was hiding out?"

"Yeah."

Cobby thought a moment. "This is rather awkward. Us out here, them in there."

"Get used to it, boy."

"Sometimes I think about that night after the explosion. How you crawled into that car outta mine. I have to laugh." Cobby started to chuckle as he spoke.

Vantino grinned. "Yeah. That was fun."

Cobby took another drag and exhaled it slowly. "She didn't finish them, did she?"

Vantino looked over at him, his look dark and hard. It was this look that earned him a reputation. "No, but she will."

*****

Mickey entered the house through the kitchen door. He moved silently as to not wake the sleeping house. He had Patrick drop him at the restaurant. Then Mickey found his own car and drove to Remmi's. A single soft light was on in the kitchen above the bar. Remmi sat beneath it. He was folding what looked like baby diapers.

He looked up when Mickey entered the room, surprise and relief in his face. "Hey, Mick. I was beginning to wonder about you."

"Uncle Rem." Mickey nodded at the pile of folded cloths. "Imelda put you to work, eh?"

Remmi glanced down. "Oh, no. I need something to do. This was quiet. That little bundle makes a man size mess."

Mickey smiled, then he reached out and squeezed Remmi's shoulder. "Thanks, Uncle Rem. I appreciate you helping me out like this. Means a lot to me."

Remmi shrugged. "Ah, I get kinda lonesome rattling around in this big house by myself. Been a long time since this house smelled like women."

Mickey smiled softly. "If I know Imelda, she's got it reeking by now."

Remmi sighed. "Damn nice built woman. The right age, too. But I'll be damned if I'm not just a little scared of her."

Mickey laughed and patted his shoulder. "I only ever knew one man that could harness that one down."

"You like some coffee?" Remmi asked.

"Yeah, that'd be good." Mickey said as he walked out of the kitchen.

He looked down the hall and waved at Martin who sat by the door reading the sports section. He quietly climbed the stairs and walked to the apartment where Eva was resting. Mickey bent to kiss her and lightly touched her hair. She didn't wake, so he moved out into the adjoining room where a small table lamp shone.

Next to it Imelda sat rocking Georgio, smiling down at him. She hummed an old Italian lullaby. The baby made small fussing sounds from within his tightly swaddled blankets.

"Hush, let mama sleep. She needs her strength. You took much from her coming into this world."

Mickey leaned in the doorway and smiled. "I think he might be one you can't manipulate."

Imelda looked up sharply at him. "Well? Where is Valant?"

"I suspect lying somewhere in the dark making love to a beautiful young singer."

Imelda smiled broadly and tears glistened in her eyes as she looked again at the little pink Georgio. "Finally, happiness to the Delano men. After all these years."

Mickey sauntered over to an armchair opposite Imelda and sat. He leaned forward to get a look at his infant son.

"Well, what now Mickey? Where do we go from here?" Imelda asked as she looked at Mickey from the corner of her eyes.

Mickey shrugged as he looked at her. "Time will tell, Imelda. Time will tell."

*****

ABOUT THE AUTHOR

Being a native of the American West, Lyn Miller has lived out her life among the people and traditions that make this great country the envy of the world. With her husband and three children, Lyn spends her time immersed in the true grit and determination of the cowboy spirit and among horses. It is this grit and determination that drove her to write a novel, to tell a story the world hasn't yet heard. May you enjoy reading it as much as she enjoyed writing it.

53396251R10293

Made in the USA
Lexington, KY
04 July 2016